Beyond the Forest

A Novel by Ann D. Stearns

Beyond the Forest

By Ann D. Stearns

ISBN: 978-1-934582-55-8

Library of Congress Control Number: 2014941349

Back Channel Press
Salem, N.H.

Text layout and design by
Zynt Author Services

Cover photograph by Jessica Stearns

Printed in the United States of America

Dedicated to

my devoted and patient husband, George,

and our loving family

A Note from the Author

I was a town girl from Massachusetts and George was a dairy farmer from New Hampshire when we were married more than fifty-four years ago.

We were blessed with three wonderful children who learned the wholesome values of farm life, drank rich, creamy milk from the cows and ate fresh vegetables from the garden and healthy meat from the farm.

In my youth I had a fondness for animals, especially horses and horseback riding, and later on the farm my love extended to the cows and calves and a very special pig.

My love of animals, passion for knitting and especially my Swedish ancestry compelled me to write this book, an imaginary tale of what it might have been like to live in Sweden, come to America and fulfill a dream.

So, pour yourself a cup of coffee, snuggle into a comfy chair and enjoy what lies *Beyond the Forest*.

Ann D. Stearns
June 2014

Contents

Norrland

1902–1933

Preface

Thousands of years ago the northern part of Sweden, now called Norrland, was covered by a thick ice sheet which when melted left in its wake a rugged landscape of high mountains and large river valleys. Trees sprung up, multiplying across the vast northern land into thick forests of spruce and pine.

Winters here are cold and dark, the languid sun causing long nights and shortened days of only partial light. In mid-winter there is almost total darkness. But in summer the sleeping sun awakens to flood the land with glorious light and warmth. As the forest comes to life again, wolves, lynx and bear appear in abundance as do deer, foxes, badgers, rabbits and other small animals – and of course the majestic moose. It is a land of hardy folk as well.

These deep evergreen forests have been home to generations of Gunderson men, strong, rough woodcutters who barely earned enough to feed their families; hardworking thrifty men, frugal with their money as well as sparing in conversation and sympathetic feelings toward their wives and children. Why bother to speak when a nod, a shrug or some other knowing gesture would do just as well?

Wives often compared their insensitive husbands to the unbending, impenetrable trees of the forest. Indeed, these rugged men who had lumbered in the woods every daylight hour as long as they could remember were greatly influenced by their domination of the massive, defenseless trees that fell so easily to their swinging axes.

Many women of the northern forests were jealous of the attention and admiration given to the well-cared-for horses who accompanied their husbands every day into the forest. At the end of a busy day they would overhear the men uttering words of praise to their faithful four-legged companions, gently caressing their necks, kissing their velvety noses and rubbing down their tired, muscular bodies until the horses' coats shined brighter than a noble woman's finest satin gown.

Often the virtues of being a horse were discussed by lonely, neglected wives as they gathered in church or walked together along the winding country roads. Dressed in their drab homespun woolens, they sympathized with each other, comparing their inferior status to these rival, sleek creatures that appeared to receive attention deserving of a new bride.

A son's first toy was an axe and he soon learned how to use it. Great expectations were put upon young boys who indisputably followed their fathers, uncles and older brothers into the forest depths to join the tough army of woodcutters. Fortified with axes and saws, weapons of warfare in defeating the enemy of stately trees, their reward was the final blow that severed these colossal giants from their lifelines and the proud satisfaction of watching the trees fall to the ground with a loud ricocheting thud that was somewhat akin to the last whooshing gasp of a wounded enemy soldier. The eager horses were then cinched to the dead and dying logs, their taut muscles straining to pull the heavy load to the mounting piles of casualties in the wood yard.

Not much had changed from those long-ago years.

Gustav Gunderson

During the summer of 1902 three young boys followed a group of burly Gunderson men into the forest. These rookie woodcutters were all about fourteen years of age, although one of the boys seemed nearly twice the size of the other two and already possessed the muscular body of a full-grown man.

His given name was Vidar, a moody stranger who had recently claimed land to the northwest where he intended to plant potatoes. He was ill tempered, crude and kept mostly to himself, rarely speaking one word from his firmly clenched mouth that had somehow forgotten how to smile. He was darker skinned than the others and his face was pockmarked and spotted with brown moles. Small beady eyes peered out beneath his thick bushy eyebrows that scowled under a high, broad forehead.

The old loggers thought growing potatoes here in Norrland's vast forest a ridiculous idea and they snickered among themselves about Vidar's odd notions and appearance. His face reminded them of a large speckled potato and they nicknamed him Potatohead, but none dared say it loud enough for him to hear. They tolerated his menacing looks and stubbornness because of his great strength and the fact that he could do more work than any two of them.

The second boy was Otto Kronberg, tall, fair-haired and handsome, whose cheerful disposition and joke telling were a happy contrast to the surly, brooding and ugly giant. Otto was a likable kid with a natural gift of conversation who lived in the village and had come to work in the forest during summer vacation from school.

Gustav Gunderson, son of Old Ivar, the rough overseer and owner of this great parcel of land, was the third boy, a gentle soul who seemed out of place in this rugged environment. Unlike most Gunderson boys who for hundreds of years had naturally followed in their fathers' footsteps, Gustav Gunderson was not a murderer of trees. He had been transplanted from a different time and place; a foreign tree, frail and sensitive, overshadowed by the sturdy rough spruce and pines of Sweden's northern forest; a dreamer whose creative talent forced him down a different path from his ancestors.

Gustav's mother had died giving birth to the scrawny babe, but fortunately his understanding and sympathetic older sister, Anna, was there to care for him, spoiling and protecting the frail child from the harsh outside world. Only ten years old at the time, she was big for her age, strong, independent and familiar with household chores.

Ivar lamented the fact that somehow the genes of his two children had been mysteriously switched; that his rugged tomboyish daughter was more adept at cutting down trees in the forest than the skinny weakling he had for a son. Gustav's thin frame barely allowed him the strength to carry his burdensome axe, let alone wield the heavy blade to fell a tree. But since a woman's place was in the home, Ivar had no choice but to try to make a man out of his son. For years Gustav tried to live up to his father's expectations, but he failed miserably.

Even though the Kronberg and Gunderson families lived more than ten miles apart, they considered themselves neighbors. Mrs. Kronberg had befriended Anna after her mother died and treated her as one of her own, advising and visiting whenever needed and usually bringing along her son Otto to play with Gustav. The boys were complete opposites in stature and personality, but because Otto was talkative and outgoing, he was a good influence on the shy Gustav.

From an early age Gustav sketched everything he saw, from a coffee pot on the stove or a bouquet of fresh flowers in a vase to his sister as she busied herself with everyday chores about the cottage. Anna secretly encouraged his artistic talent by providing scarce scraps of paper and bits of charcoal to occupy the long lonely days he spent with her in the forest cottage. Ivar, thinking this was a passing fancy, overlooked the idle time his son spent drawing foolish pictures, but after a while he took things into his own hands. When Gustav was almost fourteen years old Ivar sent him to work in the forest along with Otto and the one called Vidar, under the supervision of the old woodcutters.

Poor Gustav usually lagged behind all the rest wishing he was home with Anna. He didn't look at the forest as a place of destruction. Instead he saw the wondrous beauty of the various plants and animals that lived there. He hid scraps of paper under his shirt and a charcoal stub in his pocket. Often as they went into the forest, it wasn't very long before Gustav was nowhere in sight.

The men knew he had been sickly as a child and that Old Ivar was ashamed of his puny son, so they ignored his frequent absences thinking he was resting somewhere behind a tree. They found him one day sitting on a log sketching two squirrels scampering around an old pine stump, the likenesses of which amazed them. After that, the men looked forward each day to seeing Gustav's latest artistic portrayals of forest life, lavishing praise on his fine sketches of woodland flora and fauna.

So when they told Old Ivar about his son's fine work in the woods, it was no lie. After all, Gustav was doing very fine work, albeit they were referring to his fine artwork and not to his woodcutting ability. Because of this the men felt justified that all was fit and proper, especially since Vidar did twice his share of work. Gustav had a small place in his heart for the ugly giant because he knew if it weren't for Vidar, he would be in deep trouble.

When summer was over the three boys went their own ways. Otto returned to school in the village and Vidar went back to harvest his own trees in preparation for cultivating his land for growing potatoes. Gustav spent the fall and winter doing menial chores at home, practicing his reading and writing with Anna and sketching when his father was away from the cottage...until one fateful day in in February.

Anna was kneading dough for the weekly bread baking when suddenly Ivar burst through the kitchen door. Rage and determination flared on his crimson face as he stomped across the room, holding a large wad of crumpled papers in one hand and dragging poor Gustav along behind him with the other. She wanted to intervene in Gustav's defense, but was afraid of increasing their father's anger.

Gustav stood in front of the black iron stove as their father held up a precious drawing, slowly tearing it in pieces before ceremoniously tossing the treasured remnants into the ravenous fire. Gustav's belly ached with each loud rip. He would have preferred a good whipping than to watch the destruction of the cherished images he had so painstakingly created on paper. Holding back tears, he watched in mute disbelief as the exquisitely detailed picture of his beloved cottage went up in flames, a colorful meadow of wild flowers turned to gray ash and a meticulously drawn sketch of a massive bull moose shriveled up in a fiery death. But when the flames touched the sweet portrait of his sister, Gustav screamed Anna's name and she rushed to his side. Her sudden appearance disoriented their father and he stomped furiously out of the room shouting words not fit for girl nor boy to hear.

Anna put her arms around the stricken boy. Only then did he allow himself to cry.

"He can burn your pictures, but you must not let him destroy your talent and creativeness," she whispered in her brother's ear. "After the snow is gone and the weather is good for traveling, you must go to Stockholm and live the life of your dreams."

She did not forget her words and neither did Gustav. It was not until after the Midsummer celebration, when the men were lazy from too much food and drink, that Anna packed a large bundle of leftovers for Gustav to carry on his back. She gave him a pouch of coins she'd been saving – Christmas and birthday gifts from her father. Then she walked down the dirt path to watch her brother run to the bend of the gravel road. He stopped briefly to put his hand up and she waved back. And then he was gone.

She missed him already, this brother who was like a son to her, but she had no choice but to help him find his own way in the world. She stepped into the woods, sobbing until there were no more tears, then walked back to the cottage. Today would soon be tomorrow and she must make the best of it, even if it meant playing dumb as to the whereabouts of Gustav.

Each year Gustav sent her a Christmas card. Otto Kronberg delivered the mail in his sleigh whenever the snow was agreeable for traveling on the cottage path. They'd have coffee together while Anna read the news from Stockholm. Although living in the old city was exciting and beautiful, Gustav at first had found the transition from his isolated forest cottage to the bustling city difficult and confusing; he was just fourteen years old with only menial jobs to support his art. Although he missed the company of Anna and her fine cooking, he could not bring himself to face their father again.

After settling down in a rooming house with other young artists, he felt more comfortable and slowly found his way around the city. He apprenticed under an old retired art teacher for several years and eventually sold a few noteworthy paintings. Moneywise he had little to show for his efforts, but his heart was content knowing he had the freedom to do as he pleased.

Return to Norrland

Anna had faithfully cared for their father during the eight years Gustav was in Stockholm and now she'd written that he had died suddenly. She needed her brother to come home to help settle the family affairs.

Except for his sister, the old cottage held no happy memories for Gustav. If it hadn't been for her, he wouldn't be traveling back to Norrland today. As he walked along the winding country roads he had time to observe the northland with a fresh new perspective. Within him stirred the deep yearning to capture the likeness and spirit of this wild country on canvas.

Most shocking of all was the revelation that his birthplace was no longer the dreaded home of an unhappy childhood. The old remembrances had been replaced by Anna's womanly touch, the cottage bringing forth the wonderful scents of freshly baked bread, fruit pies and roasting meats that had been so long absent in Stockholm.

That summer Gustav painted in effortless creativity. It was as if someone else was thinking and acting for him, magically blending the colors on his palette in perfect harmony, moving his hand swiftly and effortlessly across the canvas in flawless strokes, flowing as a river in springtime. He was happier than he'd ever been before; that is, until one late August day when he and his sister rode to the village in the oxcart to purchase supplies.

Anna insisted on going to the post office first to pick up the mail.

Gustav sat patiently in the oxcart for over fifteen minutes before his sister finally returned. A pleasant aura of smugness about her face suggested that something amusing or satisfying had occurred inside the building. She said nothing, avoiding his eyes as she settled herself on the seat beside him and looking down the row of stores.

"I'd like to go to that little dress shop on the corner, the one with the bright blue sign," she said, pointing to a place at the end of a row of attached buildings. She still had not explained to him what kept her for so long in the post office, and now he must wait even longer. Regardless, he slapped the reins lightly on the back of the ox, which looked up drowsily from its dozing and didn't move a step. Because the ox was such a slowpoke, Anna had aptly named him Slofock. Gustav clicked his tongue loudly and pulled sharply on the left rein to move the cart in the general direction of the shop.

Anna looked in her bag and pulled out a slip of paper.

"I'll be awhile," she said, giving him a list of penciled words. "Perhaps you can buy the groceries and then come back and pick me up." He sat with the list in his hand, watching her walk briskly across the street. She was taller than he and had always had more stamina. Dressed plainly in her worn blue cotton skirt and white blouse, she had a buoyancy in her step today, touched by a smidgen of arrogance. Before reaching the door she glanced at the window, untied her white kerchief and stuffed it in her bag. For an instant her red hair glowed like a beacon against the gray doorway before being extinguished as she disappeared into the shadows...just as her beauty had always been hidden from view in the remote forest cottage. It was as if today Gustav had observed his sister as a very attractive woman.

He saw dresses hanging behind large panes of glass as well as flowered hats, umbrellas and fancy satin bags. His curiosity intensified then because Anna had always made her own clothes and had never worn anything on her head but a kerchief or an old straw hat that once belonged to their mother. Her handbags were made of homespun cloth, and the first and only place he'd ever seen an umbrella was during his years in Stockholm.

When he returned from shopping, Anna was standing on the sidewalk looking a bit ruffled. Little wisps of hair from her braid formed tight ringlets around her flushed face. He had never seen his sister looking so radiant. When he told her this, she hastily rummaged in her bag and covered her hair with the now wrinkled kerchief.

"It wasn't my intention to embarrass you," he told her.

"You didn't embarrass me. I've always been self-conscious about my red hair, but...today, especially... I'm grateful for your compliment."

"Why today?" he asked himself, urging Slofock along the village street. Even when they reached the privacy of the forest road, Anna remained silent, still wrapped up in her own thoughts. Gustav was a patient man; he would wait until she was ready to confide in him.

After supper, when the dishes were washed and dried, Anna brought her sewing to the chair by the window facing west. The evening summer sun still provided enough light for her to sew...something that was relaxing and allowed her to think more clearly. Gustav smoked his pipe and watched her for a while as he mulled over the events of the day. His curiosity intensified upon seeing the empty boxes near the stove.

"I see you've opened your purchases from the dress shop."

Anna's face suddenly went blank, her hands falling to her lap. She fumbled in her pocket and pulled out a letter, reading it again as if for the first time, the reassuring words both comforting and exciting her.

"I've been wanting to tell you all day, but I didn't know where to begin."

Gustav slowly exhaled a long stream of smoke while anticipating her long-awaited explanation.

"In less than a month I'll be going to a small village by the Baltic Sea," Anna began, glancing at her brother for his reaction to this news. Gustav rested his pipe on the table, then gave her his full attention. He was thinking that his sister did indeed deserve a vacation and encouraged her to go. After all, she'd never been more than ten miles from their isolated cottage all these years, first taking care of him and then their father.

"And how long do you plan to be away?"

"I didn't say that correctly after all," she said apologetically. "What I meant to say is that I will be moving away…for good…to be with Lars Kronberg." Gustav leaned forward in his chair so quickly that he hit the table and knocked his pipe on the floor.

"So…you will be married soon?"

A slight blush colored Anna's cheeks. "Yes. Probably within a few weeks."

Contemplating her forthcoming marriage was embarrassing and left her mind empty of words. She looked down at her sewing, brushed some invisible flecks from her skirt, and picked up her needle.

It wasn't that she hadn't thought of marrying before. In fact she'd often had visions of how married life might be, but her remembrances were mostly of the strained and loveless marriage of her mother and father. Later she had observed the curiously romantic and amusing relationship of her neighbors, Ingeborg and Otto Kronberg, who always seemed to have a private joke between them and showed a brighter light on the subject of marriage. It was Otto's brother, Lars, who had given her the flutters the first time she saw him sitting in Otto's buggy and now she felt that way every time she thought of him.

Today the reality of Lars' impending visit gave her both joy and pangs of trepidation…especially when thinking too seriously about how it might be in bed with a man. Anna looked up to see Gustav grinning at her and her face reddened. It was as if he could read her mind.

"Ah…now I know why you've been so busy sewing lately," he said with that same silly grin. "And how did all this come about?"

Remembering the first day she met Lars dissolved those intimate thoughts. Anna took a deep breath and then the words flowed endlessly.

"Lars came to visit his brother two years ago on some family business. They stopped here one day. Otto went into the woods to find father, but Lars, who was down with the gout at the time preferred not to walk that far and sat in the parlor to wait until Otto returned. I prepared the coffee tray and we had a nice friendly chat. I liked him immediately and it appeared he felt the same towards me." Then Anna gazed dreamily out the window, leaving Gustav anxious to hear more.

"So...tell me about Lars," he said. "I vaguely remember him, but if he's anything like Otto, then I needn't worry about you."

"Lars is much like his brother, though several years older, more heavy-set and quieter than Otto. He's been a fisherman most of his life, but his joy is working with wood, especially now with boat building. While confined to the house in winter, he makes lovely wood carvings." At that point Anna rose from the chair and went to her bedroom, returning with a delicate wooden sculpture cradled gently in her hands, her face beaming and looking as young as he remembered so many years ago.

"When Lars returned the next spring he gave me this gift," she said, gently placing the delicate carving of a majestic bull moose with a cow at its flank in her brother's hands.

"You know how I've always been fond of moose," said Anna.

"Ah yes," exclaimed Gustav. "And so are moose fond of you. How well I remember that day when that orphan calf followed the old loggers out of the forest...walked right up to you and drank the whole pail of milk you'd just taken from the cow."

Gustav inspected the delicate carving. He had seen beautiful sculptures in the store windows of Stockholm before and this intricate wood carving was far superior to many of those artistic masterpieces.

"This carving is an exceptionally fine piece of work," he said. "It tells me more about the man you are going to marry than words can say. I can see he is a lover of animals and that he is a caring, thoughtful and gentle man." He looked up and met Anna's eyes. "I wish you both much happiness."

"I am already a happy woman, but...it worries me that no one will be here to care for you, especially when winter comes and that old sadness returns. You remember how it used to be when you tried to avoid the winter darkness by hiding under the bedcovers until noontime."

Gustav had forgotten about the cold and darkness of this place. He told her then about the artificial lights of Stockholm that sparkled all night long...the banquets, dancing and parties, and the women who made him forget about the darkness.

"Women?" she asked emphatically. "Why didn't you bring one home with you?"

"Most were not the marrying kind. I can think of maybe one who made as good coffee as you and none who ever served me a good homemade pie."

"I didn't think I would ever marry either," admitted Anna, "but this house was so empty without you. No one to love and play with...no one to tell stories or laugh with. I think the winter will be lonely for you, too, if you don't find someone to share your life with."

"My painting fulfills my life, Anna. Please don't concern yourself about me."

"Well, maybe so...but there are a few household chores I should probably teach you."

Since Lars would be arriving very soon, Anna showed Gustav how to brew good coffee and made him watch carefully how she kneaded the bread dough and churned the cream for butter. She reminded him that the hens would be giving fewer eggs when it grew cooler and stated emphatically that he not forget to bring Bruna to the potato farm for breeding before the winter snows or he wouldn't have any milk next spring.

After a brief ten o'clock ceremony and small family dinner at the Kronberg farm, Lars and Anna drove Gustav to the crossroads where they took the road east. He stood in the middle of the road watching the horse and buggy grow smaller. Just before they disappeared around the bend he saw Anna turn and wave. He gave a hearty wave back and then walked north up the gravel road toward the cottage. It was a sunny cool autumn day and his stride was swift and confident. Anna had left him a week's supply of food, a fine crock of cheese and large baked ham. He guessed it was about three o'clock, but already the sun was low in the sky and the tall pines cast long shadows across the road. Winter wasn't far off.

It wasn't until he opened the front door to unfamiliar silence and an all-encompassing emptiness that he realized Anna would not be coming back. That thought hit him like a punch in the stomach. He grabbed his sketchbook and pencils and headed for the barn, where he stayed much too long in the comforting warmth and company of the ox and cow, until the last vestige of light faded into the gray cob-webbed timbers above him.

Gustav awoke the next morning with a cold nose. Adorning the windows of his bedroom were frost pictures resembling feathery trees and shooting stars, reminding him that he'd forgotten to bank the stove with wood the night before, one of the many chores his sister had always taken care of that now belonged to him.

A week later Otto Kronberg stopped in to see how things were going with his friend. He smiled knowingly as Gustav related the misadventures of living alone.

"There's still time before winter sets in to find a wife, Gustav. My eldest son's teacher might be a good fit for you. We can stop in at the school next time we go to the village."

Gustav thought about Otto and his wife with a touch of envy. His old friend had finished school, married Ingeborg Nilsdotter and fulfilled his dream of working for the Swedish government. Already they had two fine young sons and were living comfortably on the old family farm with Otto's parents.

"Anna thinks I should marry, too," Gustav said, "but I've got to have some money coming in before I think of marriage."

Otto looked around the room, now in disarray, overcrowded with paints and brushes, finished paintings and several easels holding partially completed canvasses.

"You have a great talent, Gustav. I know of a few wealthy

families in the south of Sweden who might be interested in some of these landscapes of the Norrland wilderness."

Gustav grew uneasy, his eyes darting from one painting to another almost in a state of panic. He cherished each painting and was reluctant to part with any of them. Like children, each was an extension of himself and he enjoyed having them around to look at and remind him of pleasant things. Otto understood his friend's predicament and didn't press him. He knew from years ago that it always took Gustav a long time to make up his mind about most anything, but especially about letting go of any of his beloved paintings.

Otto had other visits to make today, but knowing his friend needed money for supplies before winter, he decided on a different tactic that he hoped might work to his advantage. He rose from his chair as if to leave and put on his hat.

"There's no hurry on my part," he said. "When you decide, just let me know."

"Must you leave so soon?" asked Gustav.

Less than an hour later, Otto walked out to his buggy, a fine painting under each arm and a wide grin on his face.

By late November three feet of snow blocked the long path to the dirt road, isolating Gustav from the outside world. So much snow would be too difficult for the old ox to walk through; his only transportation now was an assortment of old skis he'd seen laying across the rafters in the barn.

The gray twilight days of winter made the forest appear frozen in time, and Gustav's free-flowing artistic river slowed to a trickle and eventually froze, too. He missed being outside in the sun's warmth and walking the endless forest paths where interesting surprises awaited him at every turn. Suddenly, he felt again the old pangs of sadness that plagued him during his childhood when the days became night and the tired sun slept on the horizon for most of the day. The northern sun was a seasonal friend who went on vacation in late autumn and didn't return until spring. He should have done the same, but it was too late for that now.

The Kronbergs had invited him for their holiday celebrations and he was counting the days until Christmas Eve day, a smorgasborg of food, drink and good family fun. He had painted individual portraits of the two Kronberg boys, whose likenesses were quite similar, but being more than four years apart had different interests. Erik, almost a year old, stood joyfully clutching a brown stuffed bear to his chest, and Johan, five, sat proudly in a small cart holding the reins of his favorite pet goat. Gustav wrapped the paintings carefully in old newspapers.

Gustav cleaned and polished the best looking pair of skis, then started out on a trial run on an old trail he remembered as a boy when he used to ski to Otto's house. Skiing through the woods was much shorter than using the road, cutting the distance almost by half, but the skis dragged heavily beneath his feet in the deep snow and in less than a quarter mile he had to sit down and rest. Then he continued on with renewed vigor. Despite the extreme cold he began to feel very hot beneath his clothes; sweat trickled down his chest and back and his leg muscles quivered like jelly. Suddenly the trees danced slowly around him and the glittering snow flashed into blackness.

He awoke flat on his back looking up at a small patch of blue sky blinking at him between the swaying tall pines. It was time to turn around and go back home. He remembered how Otto had offered to pick him up in the sleigh and he had refused. Such an idea sounded very good to him now, but it was too late for that. Besides, there was no guarantee that Otto's horses would be able to get through the deep snow, which might be deeper still by Christmas.

Gustav now had second thoughts about his pig-headed reasoning, but that same stubbornness prevented him from changing his mind. Sheer mental determination pushed him further each day until at last he had the endurance to ski three miles, then turn around to ski the three miles back to the cottage. This approximated the six miles or more to the Kronberg farm. Much of the trail was an overgrown logging path and easy to follow, although heavy snow sometimes caused his head to bump into low hanging evergreen branches. The cold air was exhilarating. He was able to breathe deeper, accomplish the outside chores quicker each day and sleep much better at night. He even sharpened an old axe, chopped down some large trees growing too close to the house and split the logs into small lengths for firewood. His father would have been proud.

Gray clouds hung low above the trees on Christmas Eve morning, but Gustav felt undaunted. He gave the animals double portions and hoped the full water buckets wouldn't freeze before he returned tomorrow. With the paintings carefully placed in a leather bag on his back, he struck out on the path at high speed, the skis having a mind of their own as they propelled him swiftly through the forest. His practice sessions had laid a solid base for the first half of the journey and he was making excellent time. However, the snow had to be broken fresh for the remaining portion and it took much longer than he expected. He was encouraged to press on with delicious images of Ingeborg's warm kitchen and the mouth-watering Christmas Eve dinner awaiting his arrival.

Gustav was not disappointed. The aroma of fresh bread and roast pork met him as he broke free of the forest and glided into the Kronbergs' yard. Otto greeted him at the door with a warm mug of mulled wine laced with a good amount of brandy and vodka. A bright red tablecloth covered the long kitchen table set with white candles, fragrant evergreens and Ingeborg's finest china. In a corner sat Otto's parents, dressed in black, sternly observing their overly excited grandsons chasing each other around the room. Gustav bowed respectfully to his elders and tried to make small talk with the disapproving old man, who spoke Swedish with a heavy German accent, causing the befuddled Gustav to nervously nod and smile until rescued by Otto.

Gustav could have made a meal on just the tender pork, homemade applesauce and frosted sweet rolls, but politely tried a spoonful of each vegetable, in addition to a large baked potato. Otto then turned the conversation to Vidar and all he had accomplished on his piece of land while Gustav was away in Stockholm.

"Remember that summer when we worked in the woods?" said Otto. "How Vidar, the one they called Potatohead, would cut down two or three trees to our one?"

The sheepish look on Gustav's face told him that he had not forgotten how Vidar, with his great strength and speed, had made it possible for him to idle away his time sketching in the woods.

"Vidar surely has made a name for himself here in Norrland these past eight years," continued Otto, as he slathered his potato with thick brown gravy. "He cut down all that forest land northwest of here and found the best ground for planting potatoes. You should buy a cartload next fall."

Gustav stopped mid-chew, his jaw dropping about an inch as he stared wide-eyed at Otto.

"What's the matter, Gustav? Do you feel ill?"

"I just remembered something!" Gustav answered with alarm. "Anna specifically told me not to forget to bring Bruna to the potato farm before the first snowfall...I never thought to have her bred and now it's too late."

"Well, don't worry," interrupted Ingeborg, knowing of Gustav's ever-present absentmindedness. "I always have too much milk in the springtime and you can borrow one of my goats to see you through."

Gustav thanked her, not saying what he was thinking. There was something about her goat's milk that he never liked. It tasted like the smell of an old ram, which was why he always drank his coffee black at the Kronberg house. Not only that, but unlike cow's milk, the milk from a goat was already homogenized, so there was no rich, thick cream to rise to the top for pouring over berries in summertime.

Throughout the meal, Johan and Erik had merely picked at their food, furtively glancing toward the platters of cookies, pies and puddings that waited on the dessert table. The five adults, too stuffed with dinner to eat dessert, took their coffee into the parlor, while the boys each grabbed two handfuls of frosted cookies and followed them. Johan and Erik sat amongst the presents looking up in wonder as their father lit the many candles decorating the massive Christmas tree.

Gustav watched Johan and Erik anxiously opening their many toys, remembering only too well how meager the Christmases of his youth had been. For a moment he was full of misgivings, thinking he should have given the boys something other than each a simple painting. To his great surprise they were both delighted and enthusiastic with the exact likenesses of themselves. Little Erik toddled around the room kissing the little bear in his picture, while Johan politely bowed and thanked Gustav, proudly showing it to his parents and grandparents.

Gustav didn't sleep well in the Kronberg's cold attic. It seemed he had just gotten to sleep when Eric and Johan burst into his room announcing it was time to rise for the morning church services. The Kronberg farm was less than a mile from the village and it was their custom to always walk to church very early on Christmas morning. They set out in the chilly darkness, each holding a lighted taper and so bundled up with warm clothing that they could barely move in a straight line.

Otto led the procession, followed by his parents, the two boys and then Ingeborg, with Gustav in the rear. Other neighbors joined in, forming an irregular line of bobbing light spheres. The procession of worshipers continued into the church where everyone placed their candle in special holders in front of the altar, giving the interior a warm, comforting glow. The dreamy atmosphere, aided by the extreme heat radiating from the church stove, set Gustav up for a long overdue nap, his eyelids growing heavy and his head nodding to the monotonous drone of the minister's sermon.

The skinny school teacher Otto had introduced him to last month sat in the choir to his left, turning stiffly now and then with a frown on her pinched face, as if Gustav was one of her naughty students. He hadn't really liked her anyway and quickly looked away each time. She had come briefly to mind last night when he'd found the coveted almond in his bowl of rice pudding, a prize that promised marriage within the year. Somehow he got through the sitting and standing, the long sermon and the hymn singing to finally enjoy the coffee and fancy breads served afterwards.

Christmas dinner was a delicious reprise of the meal on Christmas Eve. Ingeborg had prepared double batches of everything, including the rice pudding. The elder Kronbergs seemed more jovial today, perhaps due to Otto's generous refills of holiday Glogg, laced with lavish amounts of brandy. Robust laughter ensued when once again Gustav found the prized almond. Otto and his father exclaimed that receiving two almonds was a special omen, offering the likelihood of him having to choose between two women. That was good news to Gustav because he'd already eliminated the school teacher as a wifely prospect. Now he still had a chance of finding another.

Skiing the winding path through the never-ending forest seemed much longer on the way home, especially when accompanied by thoughts of the empty cottage awaiting him. Most of his merry Christmas feelings sadly had been left behind at the Kronbergs'doorstep. He knew he was almost home when he heard the ox and cow bellowing from the barn, the sound echoing from tree to tree, reprimanding him for staying away for too long. He felt guilty seeing their empty pails and feed troughs and the cow's full udder leaking in the overnight manure.

The hens had fared better, but the eggs in their nests were frozen solid. He boiled them for supper anyway and by eight o'clock had slipped into his cold bed, pulling the covers over his head, wishing he had a woman to snuggle with. He dreamed that night of milk pails overflowing with creamy rice pudding and plump almonds, and of being surrounded by voluptuous women dressed in ribbons and bows.

January was a dark and snowy month, forcing Gustav to stay

mostly indoors where he painted sundry still life pictures...of rifles leaning against a pair of old boots, food and dishes arranged artfully on a table, or empty vases setting on the windowsill against the wintry background of snow-covered trees.

He went to bed early, sometimes falling asleep in his old leather chair, sleeping until the late rising sun awakened him, the cattle bellowed loudly from the barn or his stomach cried out for something to eat. His thick beard and head itched and he needed a fresh change of underwear. A heap of dirty laundry already lay piled on the kitchen floor and he was in dire need of a hot, soaking bath. But why bother? There was no one else within ten miles of here, except for the ox and cow, which smelled much worse than he did. Living this way was the only benefit of not having a woman in the house, although he sorely missed Anna. It was only when he thought of her that he felt guilty about his slovenly appearance.

In February the sun stayed long enough in the sky to touch the tips of the tallest trees and he looked out to see five hens tiptoeing gingerly across the barn roof. Carefully the bravest one picked her way toward a patch of sunlight at the further end of the ridgepole while the others followed, wriggling and pushing against each other to catch the last rays of the warming sun. He grabbed his sketch book and quickly captured the amusing scene that he later painted on canvas, his favorite scene of that winter.

Eventually snow on the path melted into thick mud, buds appeared on the birch trees and Gustav felt signs of life within himself. He took a bath and while shaving his thick beard he heard a knock on the door along with Otto's familiar voice.

"Got stuck in that mud of yours and had to walk around through the woods, but here is the money from those two paintings I sold," he said as he tossed a heavy leather pouch on the table. After Gustav counted the money Otto gave him a letter he'd picked up in the village. It was a Christmas greeting from Anna with a short note saying she hoped spring would bring him cross country for a visit, and that she had a surprise for him. Gustav thought maybe Anna was expecting a baby, but Otto suggested that she might have found a special someone for him to marry.

"I would be happy either way," Gustav replied, remembering the long winter alone in the cottage.

"Surely you won't be travelling such a long distance in that old ox cart of yours, will you?"

"Better than walking all the way," said Gustav.

"I think your chances of finding a good woman would be much better if you borrowed my two driving horses and covered buggy...not to mention the time you'll be saving."

"You are a good friend, Otto. I don't think Slofock would make the trip. He and I thank you very much for your kind offer."

And so it was that when the grass was tall enough in the pasture, Gustav let the cow out to graze and the hens to scatter into the fields and forest to forage on their own. He drove Slofock down to the Kronbergs where Otto would pasture him with the goats until Gustav returned from Anna's.

"Good luck to you, my friend," said Otto. "We'll be expecting to see a lovely young lady sitting beside you when you come back."

Gustav hoped that would be true and slapped the reins gently on the horses' backs. Instantly they fell into a fast trot, a speed he was not used to with Slofock. Gustav's head jerked back and he held on for dear life until they slowed down at the end of the drive. He looked back to see Ingeborg and Otto rollicking in gales of laughter. Gustav waved and quickly held the reins with both hands. Once on the straight road he had more control over the horses and before long there was no need to guide them, so he took out his harmonica. He was feeling more optimistic than he had in months.

Village by the Sea

Gustav had been traveling for many days when the horses began to act strangely, sniffing the air and tossing their heads as if bothered by flying insects, but he could see nothing nor hear anything out of the ordinary. Stiff and sore from riding in the buggy all morning, he decided to walk along beside the horses, guiding the way toward a wide-open, grassy knoll where the horses might feed for a while. He removed the bits from their mouths, hung the bridles from their necks and set them free to graze while he stretched out on the ground in the shade of the trees.

He awakened to the sun shining bright and warm on his face. The horses had roamed to the top of the knoll and the buggy was tipping low on one side. He sprinted toward them, but half-way up the hill an awful stench took his breath away. Perhaps some animal died close by and that is what the horses had smelled earlier, so he gathered the reins and led them back down the hill.

Hoping to leave the stench behind, he continued on the road, driving the horses at a fast trot. However, the smell grew stronger again as they climbed to the top of a steep incline. Below was a small village and the culprit causing the stench: the rotting remains outside of a fish cannery.

The village circled a small harbor overlooking a large expanse of deep blue water with no land visible on the broad horizon. "This is the Baltic Sea," Gustav said to himself and the impatient horses. He knew from the high bluffs to the left and the stone lighthouse at the end of a long, curving peninsula to the right that this was the village Anna described in her letter, although she never mentioned the foul smell of the fish cannery. Hoping the air would be better on higher ground, he turned the horses toward the bluffs where he might do a quick sketch of the quaint stone lighthouse across the bay.

He hitched the horses beneath the shelter of a clump of white birches, grabbed his sketchbook and easel, and ran up the narrow, winding path to the bluffs. With each breath came the cool, fresh air blowing in from the sea. With his eye on the lighthouse, he began setting up his easel. Suddenly a woman walked to the edge of the cliff looking far out across the water, the wind blowing her kerchief and revealing the pleasing outline of her body as the woman's skirts billowed out around her slender ankles. He envisioned her being swept off the steep bluff, either by accident or on purpose, and attempted to intervene, but in so doing knocked over his easel, causing the sketch pad to be caught in the strong wind, propelling it far above their heads.

For a moment they both stood transfixed, watching the pad of paper open up and hover briefly in the air, flapping its white pages as if to save itself, before fluttering down slowly like a wounded bird to the rocky shoreline far below the cliff. Their eyes met briefly and it was then that he noticed she was wearing spectacles. They only magnified her beautiful blue eyes. She turned away and ran in the opposite direction. He followed, but she was soon a fleeting blur running amongst the rocks, finally disappearing behind a thicket of scraggly bushes.

Gustav's artistic eye gathered much visual information about the woman in just those few moments. He saw her clearly in his mind as if she was still standing there: the wind against her white blouse and dark skirt, playing with the tight brown curls about her pale, oval face, and then her startled look, first expressing surprise, then concern, with almost a glimmer of a smile before shyness caused her to run away.

He rummaged in his jacket pocket and found a folded sheet of paper with directions to the Baltic Sea that Otto had hastily scribbled. On the blank side Gustav drew a detailed sketch of the woman's face and a quick outline of her blouse and skirt, with the stone lighthouse in the background. Then he drove the horses toward the village, holding his breath while passing the fish cannery, all the while hoping for another glimpse of the woman he could not forget. He wasn't overly worried though. The village was small and surely Anna would know from his drawing who the woman was.

About ten minutes later he approached a small farm with the carved wooden sign in the shape of a fishing boat that Anna had told him about. It was hard to miss: an almost life-sized carving painted bright yellow with KRONBERG written in blue letters on the bow. The back yard was aflame with tulips, daffodils and other brightly colored spring flowers. From their midst Gustav saw Anna walking briskly toward him.

"What a lovely surprise!" she cried, her great belly preventing the close embrace he'd anticipated. "I've had your room ready for weeks now, hoping you'd drop in."

"And I can see your big surprise, as well," he said.

Anna blushed as she looked down, caressing her protruding abdomen. Then she took his arm. "Lars is in the barn. He'll be anxious to show you some of his work."

She continued to talk about her husband as they walked along the garden path.

"As you know, Lars has been a fisherman all his life, as well as a builder of boats.

This winter he has been fashioning lighter, more refined pleasure boats called canoes for use in the lakes and river waters of Sweden."

The wide barn door was open, the bright sun illuminating Lars busy at work sanding a curved piece of wood. Upon hearing his wife's voice, he glanced up, recognized Gustav and brushed off the sawdust from his clothes. They shook hands, these two rather shy men smiling at each other with the formalities of 'hello' and 'how are you?' Their conversation temporarily ended there and Anna filled in the empty space that lingered expectantly between them.

"Lars has an eye for fine wood," she told Gustav. "See how he brings out the beautiful grain on the side of this slender canoe?" She was definitely proud of her husband. As an artist, Gustav was much impressed with the darker inlaid pieces of wood around the top edge of the canoe depicting various lake fish. He was familiar with many of the species, especially trout, carp, pike, perch and of course, the eel.

Then Anna took both of the men's arms and led them to a long shelf on one wall that held an array of carved sea creatures with their unique markings. Lars, an expert on aquatic life, became more talkative now.

"Of course, you probably recognize these," he said to Gustav, pointing to the trout, perch and pike, common lake fish in all of Sweden. Then he continued to walk along explaining about salt-water fish: herring, salmon, halibut, bass and mackerel, as well as seals, walrus and numerous species of whales. Then he chuckled. "This is one of my favorites. An angler called the sea devil." He winked at his wife, who now lagged behind them. "These sea devils scare Anna. When I catch one I must cut off his big ugly head before she will cook it." Anna wrinkled her nose and shook her head at the two grinning men.

"I'm going to the kitchen to make some coffee," she announced. "Come in when you finish looking around." She took a few steps and hollered back, "Oh Lars, don't forget to show Gustav your ocean liner."

The men walked further to the back of the barn. In the corner was the carving of a very, very long, wide ship.

"I've seen many freighters tied up in Gothenburg," explained Lars, brushing dust from the black hull. "And I envisioned a passenger ship of similar size. Something as luxurious as a grand hotel for people traveling to America," he added, speaking with much pride. "Such a ship could easily carry hundreds of people plus much cargo. Probably would weigh over 15,000 tons."

Gustav's eyes grew wide with wonder and much anxiety. "What would keep such a ship from tipping over on the choppy sea?" he asked, knowing he could neither swim nor keep his own small body afloat. Lars' technical explanation was much too complicated for Gustav to understand and he was not convinced that a ship of such magnitude would make it across the Atlantic Ocean to America.

Gustav now began to think Anna's husband might have a peculiar, foolish streak in him. Some artists he'd seen in Stockholm had odd and unusual ideas, too, but many of their paintings sold for good prices, so he nodded judiciously and complimented Lars on what an extraordinary ship he'd built.

After dinner Anna surprised her brother even more by revealing that she and Lars would surely be two of the first people to travel to America on such a ship. Poor Gustav wished to think no more about these eccentric ideas and changed the subject to what was foremost on his mind.

"Before I came here today I went up to look out over the bluffs and saw the woman I want to marry," he said.

Both Anna and Lars looked at him in amazement, thinking at first that perhaps he was joking. His description of the girl who ran to the edge of the cliff could have been any one of many women in the village, but then he showed them his drawing.

"Wouldn't this be Karin Halensdotter, the girl who lives near the canning factory?" Anna asked, giving the sketch to her husband. Then she looked almost disapprovingly at Gustav. "She's older than you...more my age than yours...and..."

Gustav interrupted. "Not a word more, dear sister. I've made up my mind and nothing you say will change it!"

Anna knew how obstinate her brother could be. "Forgive me, Gustav. It was only that I'd already considered two younger girls. You took me much by surprise. I've seen Karin in church many times and I shall be very happy to introduce you to her on Sunday." Her face softened then and she smiled warmly. "Unless you can't wait that long." Chuckles spread around the room and Anna poured another round of coffee.

Anna thought to herself about the situation. It isn't every girl who might wish to live in an isolated cottage deep in the forest of Norrland. By way of the church gossips, she had heard about Karin's miserable situation at home. Quite possibly the poor girl might be agreeable to such an arrangement.

Karin Halensdotter lived with her mean-spirited and pompous father who worked in the cannery. Every night he dropped his slimy, fish-smelling clothes in a heap on the kitchen floor for her to wash, hastily devoured his supper and either fell asleep or walked the short block to the tavern. Years ago, after her mother had passed away, her father began spending more time and money in the village drinking and gambling; most recently taking up with a woman whom Karin believed wanted their house for her own.

Karin spoke once to her father about this, but he took offense at her accusation, making her life miserable by criticizing her cooking and housekeeping, never taking into account the money she earned from doing washing and ironing for the wealthy village families. If it wasn't for her hard work, they would surely have lost the house by now.

Being on the bluffs was a happy diversion from the long hours of work at home and the ever-present foul odor of decomposing fish from the cannery across the street. She found peace there, high above the dreariness below, and the freedom to dream of living in some faraway place where the air always smelled sweet and fresh and where there were servants to do all the cooking and cleaning.

It grieved Karin to think of yesterday, a day when her dreams might possibly have come true. How foolish she had been, a grown woman, running off like a frightened young child when confronted by that concerned young man on the bluffs. His handsome face had accompanied her on the walk home, causing her to glance back several times in hopes of seeing him again. She had lain awake last night thinking about him and early this morning she had returned to the bluffs hoping he might be there. But instead she had found only disappointment and emptiness.

It wasn't until after Sunday services when the congregation gathered downstairs for refreshments that she noticed his blond head among a wash of other yellow-haired men. He looked in her direction as if his gaze might draw them together, but her feet were heavy and would move neither forward nor backward. A great warmth spread from her chest to her cheeks as he zigzagged his way through the crowd. She hadn't felt this way since being a schoolgirl, the first time she had been invited to dance with a boy.

After being properly introduced by his sister, Gustav and Karin went to the food table, taking their plates and coffee outside to enjoy on the front steps. After a casual walk through the village Karin had a bold moment: she asked Gustav to come for dinner the next evening, an invitation he eagerly accepted.

Karin spent most of Monday morning cleaning the house and preparing a meal of roast chicken, vegetables and custard pie. Then she bathed, put on her best dress and sat by the parlor window facing the road. As Gustav turned into their yard her father went outside. For a short time the men talked, unharnessed the horses and led them to the barn. She was struck by the tenderness Gustav showed toward the glossy black horses; how handsome he looked in his fine brown suit in contrast to her father's baggy pants and worn shirt.

She went into the kitchen to settle her fluttery heart and made last minute dinner preparations. In the background she heard the robust laughter and gravelly voice of her father, whose rough, garrulous manner overpowered Gustav's futile attempts at conversation as they took their places at the table. She was grateful that her father was in a good mood tonight and would hopefully treat her with more respect than usual. He had seemed overly pleased, although suspiciously curious that she had invited a man to dinner.

She had a lot on her mind to say to Gustav, but with her father present could only ask questions of a general nature, about his artwork and how it is living in northern Sweden. Gustav was comfortable telling them about the beauty of Norrland, but did not mention the isolation or long dark winters. He commented favorably on the fine meal she prepared and was not shy about helping himself to second portions.

She was flattered by this. He had fine manners and his warm smile revealed even, white teeth. It gave her pleasure to watch him eat, thoughtfully enjoying every morsel of food and relishing the taste. Such a contrast to her father, who normally sat hunched over his plate, elbows on the table, gulping spoonfuls of food into his mouth, swallowing too fast for the tongue to be satisfied...although tonight he was on his best behavior.

After coffee and custard pie, her father pushed back in his chair and asked Gustav to go to the saloon with him for a drink, but Gustav said he had other plans and politely refused. Karin was saddened to hear this. As they stood by the horses watching her father walk toward the village, she could not help but reveal her feelings.

"I'm sorry you have other plans tonight..."

Then he took her hand. "My plans are to take you for a buggy ride."

Karin was thrilled to be seen riding through the village with the handsome Gustav Gunderson. She felt a bit giddy as she waved to acquaintances along the way and to anyone else who curiously looked up as they drove by. They stopped near the bluffs and he helped her down from the buggy, continuing to hold her hand as they climbed along the narrow, stony path. Their connected hands sent thrilling quivers through her body. Perhaps it was the same for him, too, because he stopped midway to timidly embrace her, so fleetingly that afterwards she wondered if it actually had happened, or if she had only dreamed of it.

He positioned her on a large rock with the stone lighthouse in the background and began sketching her in profile. Occasionally she turned to look at him and they exchanged warm smiles.

"Shall I remove my hat?"

"If you wish," he replied, stopping to stare as she unbraided her hair, the golden highlights glittering amongst the wavy brown strands in the gentle breeze. For a while he pretended to draw, gazing longingly at the enticing scene before him. She turned to him again.

"Is everything all right, Gustav?" she asked. "Perhaps I'd look more attractive without these spectacles on my nose." Her voice brought him back to his drawing again.

"No, leave them on," he said abruptly, then explaining in a softer tone, "I'm more used to you with them on." The truth behind this was that the spectacles made her look special, more knowledgeable and refined than most ordinary girls. He was reminded of the genteel wife of a middle-aged artist he apprenticed with in Stockholm. While visiting their home she had entertained them by eloquently reading from the old classics. Gustav had been impressed by her expressively articulate way of speaking, and by the fact that she wore spectacles. Such was his first impression of Karin, but also there was the way the glass magnified the size and color of her eyes. In them he observed at least three beautiful shades of blue and he could not wait to begin painting her image on canvas with his lavish assortment of oil paints.

Every afternoon they returned to the bluffs and with each sweep of his brush, he fell more in love with Karin. As the painting neared completion his emotions toward her swelled to the point that he could sit no more. Shyness melted into heated passion as he took her face in his hands. Losing himself in those sea-blue eyes he unabashedly kissed her tempting, full, sweet lips and he felt her go limp in his arms.

"Are you all right?" he asked.

"I've never felt better than I do right now," she replied with an inviting smile.

"Will you marry me?" he asked all of a sudden.

Gustav had rehearsed this same scene in his mind for days, but for Karin his words were a surprise. He heard no answer, but felt her concern as she pulled away from him.

"I'm sorry," he said apologetically. "I shouldn't have asked you without your father's permission."

"I don't care what my father thinks," she stated firmly. "I'm sure you've noticed that we barely speak to each other."

Gustav nodded, his face creased with worry.

"What is it then?" he asked.

And when she still did not answer he began to doubt himself.

She touched his cheek gently. "Oh, Gustav, you must know that I love you, but...well, you are only twenty-three years old, and I was thirty-one last November." She looked away and leaned her head on his chest.

Gustav took her face in his hands again and looked into her eyes. "Age means nothing to me, Karin. If it makes you feel better, I've always been told I look and act older than my years, and you certainly look much younger than thirty-one, so we are actually the same age."

"I like your reasoning, Gustav," she said with a playful laugh. "I can think of no reason why we can't be married."

Sometimes love takes a long time to grow, but instantaneous love filled the hearts of Gustav and Karin. They were married on the bluffs with Anna and Lars in attendance. Karin's father was not there; he had not been invited to the wedding. Karin had packed her few belongings and put a note on the kitchen table after her father went to the cannery. She wrote that she would be marrying Gustav Gunderson later that morning and would be leaving afterwards for Norrland. She had baked three loaves of bread and put enough cooked food in the icebox for several days, surely long enough before his woman friend arrived to take over the affairs of his house.

It was late spring and they were anxious to get back to the cottage in time for planting the garden. Karin was excited about living in the forest where the air smelled of pine and spruce, and Gustav already had images of Karin in his head that he wished to paint on canvass.

When the warm summer turned into the cool days of autumn, Karin reminded her husband to bring the cow to the potato farm to be bred.

The Potato Farm

A dark cloud hovered over the potato farm, but not of the type that would empty its burden of rain to eventually reveal the sunshine. This ominous cloud was felt rather than seen, even on the sunniest of days. An atmosphere of melancholy and fear shrouded this place. The inhabitants, humans and animals alike, were influenced by the authority it held over them. No stray dog, fox or other woodland creature dare step out of the shadows; one sniff sent them scampering back into the forest.

Infrequent visitors might have done the same, but from a distance they noticed nothing out of the ordinary. However, as they drove closer to the farmyard, like the stray dog, they also sensed a dark presence, but by then it was too late to turn back. They had driven here for one purpose, to buy the finest potatoes in northern Sweden, and they weren't about to go home empty handed. Fear kept them huddled together in their wagons, until suddenly out of nowhere loomed the monstrous figure of Vidar, filthy from work in the fields, his large, hairy hand beckoning them toward the potato shed. This brooding, ugly giant was the dark cloud.

Vidar's origins were questionable. Neither folk of Norway or Sweden would claim him, nor was he certain of his ancestry, but somewhere in the corners of his mind he recalled a remote mountain cave very near the invisible line dividing these two countries...and he remembered the delicious taste of potatoes.

There was no father in his life, nor could he now envision his mother's face, although he remembered being called Vidar. His childhood had been spent moving from place to place with this person or that. He was someone who never belonged anywhere or to anyone. He learned to work in the soil and forest, dreaming of a place to call his own and one day he struck out to find it.

Searching for fertile ground was his mission. With a sharp axe in his hand and a great sack of seed potatoes on his back, he spent the early summer days and nights walking through forest and field examining what lay beneath his feet, every so often scooping up a handful of earth to examine. Then, after smelling, squeezing and even tasting the dark loam, he would analytically watch the fine particles fall from his hand to the ground until, at last, he found the perfect soil for planting potatoes.

This portion of the forest was owned by Ivar Gunderson and Vidar made arrangements to work for him that summer and as long as it took to pay for the large parcel of land. Then the hard work of cutting trees began, followed by digging out stumps and picking rocks in preparation for the plowing and planting of his first crop. With just the right amount of rain and long summer days of sunshine, the plants grew thick and green. Often he put his hand into the soft dark soil to feel the small round fruits and when they reached a proper size he dug enough to fill two large sacks, hoisted them on his back and set out through the forest. A gravel road led him past other hovels and small farms, but he rarely saw any people. When they spied him coming down the road they kept their distance, hiding in the trees or behind closed doors.

In the village women pulled their children into the stores and men moved close together, blocking the doors while gaping at this ugly giant who smelled of old sweat and the animal hides he wore for clothing. A few of the old men remembered talk of such a one who had worked in the woods for Ivar Gunderson many years before; they whispered among themselves that indeed this was the one called Potatohead.

Vidar was apprehensive as well, for never had he seen so many people in one place nor such large buildings clustered together. When he spoke, they didn't answer and when he opened the sacks they shook their heads and backed further away. A mongrel dog followed too closely, sniffing his rank leather garments, and watchful eyes saw the swift kick that sent the scruffy hound running for safety under the nearest porch.

Dropping his bags in the middle of the road, he raised his fists and hollered obscenities that reached the ears of every villager. The commotion aroused a sleeping drunk, a skinny little weasel of a man, who in his stupor had no fear and offered Vidar a bottle of whiskey in exchange for a sack of potatoes. Vidar roared with laughter at the one-sided bargain, but then a powerful thirst persuaded him to give the man a fair share and he drank the contents down as if it were cool spring water. Soon the buildings began to move, swirling in the air around him and he took a few stumbling steps before falling lifelessly to the ground in a great heap.

He awoke later to a crowd of people circling around him shouting and hollering as if celebrating a special event. Their outstretched hands held shiny coins as they clamored about desiring to buy his potatoes. Grinning in the background was the skinny drunkard eating a raw potato as if it was an apple, and Vidar realized the man was responsible for spreading news of the fine tasting potatoes. When both sacks were empty, he tossed the man a coin and the villagers made room for him to enter the stores and spend his money. He bought himself a hat, some new clothes and enough supplies to fill his empty sacks.

After that he was welcomed in the village to sell his potatoes, although most women still backed into the shadows and children hid behind their mothers' skirts. Vidar drank his liquor slower now, enjoying the company of the village men, who clustered around him for rounds of free drinks, listening to his simple talk and laughing at his crude jokes. But when Vidar suggested buying a horse, the men all shook their heads. None had forgotten that first day when he kicked the village dog. Nevertheless, word spread far and wide that Vidar had the best potatoes in all of Norrland, even though many had second thoughts about buying them when they saw the bleakness of that place.

Gustav led the cow with confidence along the narrow path with its many twists and turns. Around each bend there was something different to see, things an ordinary person might not notice. To most, one grouping of trees looked very much like another, but to his trained artist's eye each separate scene was unique in color, form and the way one tree interacted with another. It was the same with flowers. Even among the same species he noticed variances of shade, posture and delicate shape. Each animal, too, was a distinct individual, revealing its special beauty, outline, interesting behavior and often humor. He captured these unique moments in his mind for future reference.

After stopping at the lake to drink and rest, he followed a less-traveled path, an uneven trail of mostly moose tracks that Anna said would eventually bring him to a swampy area and then an open field. She had walked that far once, but turned back upon seeing the grim sight of the gray, ramshackle buildings that lay across the fields of potatoes.

Gustav wasn't concerned until he walked around the weathered gray barn and saw Vidar taking long strides toward him. The surrounding trees, cabin and barn, everything shrank in comparison to the one he remembered as Potatohead. Otto had told Gustav how it was at the potato farm, and even though he remembered how Vidar looked as a boy, he was still much taken back upon seeing the farmer's great size and intimidating stare. Yet the grim farmer's sneer seemed almost to broaden into a smile as he grunted and took the cow into the barn, saying not a word to Gustav.

Gustav watched from a distance as the bull's neck stretched through the thick boards to touch the timid cow's nose, snorting and pawing the ground as Vidar opened the stall door. The bull was aggressive and not too accurate. Gustav observed that Vidar took great pleasure in watching the breeding process, but his peculiar curiosity made Gustav uncomfortable and he went outside to smoke his pipe.

After purchasing two sacks of potatoes, Gustav tied them across the cow's back and led her swiftly around the barn toward the first field, glad to put this place behind him until next year.

Karin settled happily into the little forest cottage and was the bright spot in Gustav's life that next winter. He had no more sad thoughts about the darkness for she kept the rooms well lit with candles and lamps. Karin also took it upon herself to go through many of her husband's paintings, choosing those she liked best to decorate the walls, especially the one of her on the bluffs overlooking the sea and lighthouse, which she hung in their bedroom. Another found its place in the sitting room; a graceful waterfall tumbling down a mountain ravine into a wide blue river that meandered through a lush valley of purple and pink lupine blossoms.

In winter when Gustav ran out of artistic ideas, she arranged household objects on a table: an old copper coffeepot, porcelain sugar and creamer and a flowered cup and saucer; a white candle burning in a pewter candlestick beside an opened book with a blue-tasseled marker and a pair of her old spectacles in the foreground; a loaf of partially sliced bread on a chipped plate with a slab of yellow cheese, a knife, goblet and the bottle of red wine Anna had given them after the wedding.

There were the times, too, when she caught him watching intently as she went about her household duties, only to find he was sketching her with disheveled hair and wearing an everyday old skirt and blouse.

"I'll pose for you tomorrow," she would say, "when my apron is fresh and my hair newly pinned up." But he preferred catching her unawares. He told her spontaneity gave his sketches more character, so to please him she often carried on with her work as if he weren't there.

In June their joy was multiplied by the birth of a daughter they named Ingrid. She arrived screaming and kicking, a fussy, demanding baby who wanted constant attention from her mother and who frustrated her father in his attempts to pose her for a sketch or portrait.

She was a bright spot in their lives, a precocious, mischievous child with a will of her own. After making the necessary adjustments that all new parents must do, they finally adapted to her aggressive manner, out-going personality and often erratic schedule.

Five Years Later

On a cold and snowy Christmas Eve in 1917 Karin felt a dull pain in her stomach. She took to her bed and a few hours later gave birth to a second daughter, who slipped out quietly and painlessly. The baby slept through her very first night and every night after that, never causing her parents a moment of concern or worry. Such was the difference between the lively, capricious

Ingrid and this quiet, blasé little girl they called Eva. She was cheerful, obedient and helpful from an early age, the perfect model for Gustav's sketching and painting. There was one other noticeable difference between the two sisters: Ingrid had straight blonde hair, while Eva's was curly and bright red.

At first Ingrid loved playing with her baby sister. She was like a living doll that wiggled, laughed and cried. But as with any new toy that one outgrows, Ingrid soon tired of little Eva. As they grew older Karin was hard-pressed to keep them harmoniously occupied. Ingrid, devious and full of mischief, was a born troublemaker, while Eva was quiet and unpretentious, always eager to please.

Even though the girls didn't get along a lot of the time, as a family they had plenty of wonderful experiences together, especially the days spent at the lake. They called it 'Our Lake.' That large body of water situated in the middle of the forest didn't really belong to them, but they'd never seen anyone else there and since it was Gustav's favorite place to fish, he had long ago claimed it as his own.

In the cool of the morning, on the hottest days of summer, they'd tramp single file along the narrow, winding, sun-dappled path through the sweet fragrance of the spruce and pine forest, Karin with her knitting and blanket, Ingrid and Eva carrying baskets of food and drink, and Gustav leading the way with fishing poles, worms, sketchbook and pencils.

Once at the lake Gustav had only fishing on his mind, while Karin settled herself on the blanket to knit and relax...without feeling the usual guilt she had at home when ignoring the dirty clothes waiting to be washed or some other household chore clamoring for attention. Eva would have preferred to stay on the beach knitting, too, but her father expected his girls to help harvest fish for the family dinner.

Eva didn't like fishing, but never let on to her father how she detested hooking the defenseless worm. She felt sorry for the struggling creature that always tried to wiggle out of her fingers, and if no one was watching she would often drop the line into the water with an empty hook, setting the worm free behind her in the bushes. Then she could gaze out across the green-blue water toward the panorama of mountains, their summits showing traces of snow even on the warmest of summer days. For a long time she thought those rugged mountains marked the place where the earth stopped.

She was always on the lookout for moose foraging on the perimeters of the lake. Sometimes only the dark line of their back was visible. Then a large head would emerge, shiny and dripping with water, leisurely chewing the succulent green plants, oblivious to its surroundings. Moose were the largest mammals in the forest and there was no finer sight to see than a mature bull moose wearing his magnificent crown of antlers. Those kings of the forest were usually docile and curious, but during the autumn rut they could not be trusted.

One day in October, as the Gunderson family made its way to the lake for the last picnic of the year, a massive bull moose stood crosswise in the logging road, daring the people to pass. It was clear that today the road belonged to him, so Gustav led everyone into the woods to go safely around him. Returning again to the road he told Karin and the girls to walk briskly and keep together while he kept watch in the rear.

Gustav heard the big bull snorting, trotting loudly behind him, and he told Karin and the girls to quicken their pace. Then a terrifying growling sound caused them to turn around, only to see Gustav standing in the middle of the road waving his arms furiously and making that awful growling sound again as the moose came closer. Karin ran toward her husband hollering and waving the large, unfolded blanket to help scare away the moose. When Ingrid and Eva joined in screaming, the bull abruptly stopped in its tracks and looked down his nose at each one of them. The King of the Forest grunted, raised its massive, antlered head to sniff the air, and trotted with great purpose into the forest.

They all felt a bit foolish upon seeing a patient cow moose standing just inside the woods, no doubt wondering what all the commotion was about. The bull walked up behind her, sniffing the air again, his half-smiling lips revealing the cow's desirable scent. Then she quickly turned on her heels and coyly trotted further into the forest, her noisy suitor crashing through the brush in pursuit of his trophy. By then all the Gundersons were laughing at how foolish they all must have looked and were grateful that their only audience had been a couple of suspiciously amused moose.

Whenever Gustav worked around the farm Eva was close behind him, beside him or right under his feet. He called her his little shadow. So when the old cow had trouble calving one day, Eva was there to see it all. At first there wasn't much going on, but she could tell her father was concerned about the cow's slow progress as she struggled to push out the calf. He finally admitted it was going to be a difficult birth as only one little hoof was visible in the balloon-like sack protruding from under the mother's tail. How shocked Eva was to see her father's hand disappear inside the back of the cow! Realizing this, Gustav informed his daughter about the birth canal that led to where the calf was and explained that he was trying to find the calf's head and other front leg in order to position them for birthing.

How elated they both were to finally see two little black hooves and a soft pink nose emerge. Before long a wet, reddish brown calf dropped into the soft hay.

"Ah, it's a heifer!" exclaimed her father enthusiastically, as the old cow lapped the calf's sticky hair, mooing softly to encourage the little one to take some milk. Finally the calf stood on wobbly legs to hungrily nurse until her belly was round and full. Then she looked around and suddenly walked over to rest her head in Eva's lap. Gustav, seeing the loving bond between the two, told his daughter that from now on she would be responsible for taking care of the calf. Eva named her Stella because of a white star-like marking on her forehead.

Stella was allowed to run free with her mother, but she often wriggled under the fence when she saw Eva. There was no danger of Stella running away; she was always close to Eva's heels and once followed her up the back steps into the kitchen, slipping and sliding on Karin's polished floor like a child's first attempt at ice skating.

The two of them became inseparable, the attachment between them even stronger than Eva's relationship with her own sister. Sometimes when Eva had enough of Ingrid, she'd escape to the barn and talk to Stella, who always listened and never talked back. The heifer was a sympathetic listener whose strong shoulder and gentle ways soothed and comforted her. But even though Stella was a reassuring and calming presence, she was still just a cow. As Eva grew older there were times when she needed a real person to confide in, someone besides her own mother or father. That person was Otto Kronberg.

Otto was Gustav's oldest friend. He always arrived immaculately dressed in a fine suit and tie, driving his two magnificent black horses pulling a fine black buggy. The first time Eva saw him she thought he was the King of Sweden, so tall, dignified and handsome he was. He held a glass over his right eye when reading fine print. Her father said it was called a monocle, something that distinguished him from any man Eva had ever known.

He worked for the Swedish government, a job that involved visiting farmers and other landowners, so it was Otto who usually came to visit Gustav, rather than Gustav making the long trip by oxcart to his friend's house. He often brought bags of grain, flour, sugar or other items the family might need from the village, plus books of learning from his own extensive library.

Because of the long, snowy winters and the isolated area where they lived, Karin began teaching the girls at home. Ingrid was a dreamer like her father, always gazing out the window and dilly-dallying when told to practice her numbers and letters. Eva, on the other hand, was eager to learn from the time she was two years old, and could read whole sentences before the age of three.

Her shyness and thirst for learning endeared her to Otto, who went out of his way to please and encourage her. Once he confessed that she was the daughter he never had, so it seemed very natural for her to consider him more as an uncle than a friend. There was nothing too silly for his ears to hear, but there were two things Eva was too embarrassed to mention, Ingrid's constant teasing, and the jokes about the map of Scandinavia.

One day Otto walked into the parlor carrying the largest book Eva had ever seen.

"This book is called an atlas," he told her. "The pages are filled with maps of countries all over the world." Then he thumbed through the many colorful pages until he found the one he was looking for.

"Ah, here is the map of Scandinavia...and this is our homeland." he said, tracing his finger along the black irregular boundary of Sweden. Finally, he pointed to a tiny, round blue spot in the middle of a huge expanse of green.

"This patch of blue is your father's favorite fishing spot."

Eva didn't believe him. She'd been to that lake before and knew how large it was. Not even she could fit on that small page, so she knew he was joking. This was just another of Mr. Kronberg's fairy tales. That was the end of Eva's first geography lesson. She was about three years old at the time.

Several years later the map made more sense to her. Eva knew now that the outline of Sweden was merely a miniature illustration, but she was still too young to understand the eye-winking jokes between her father and Mr. Kronberg, especially the one regarding the long, narrow shape of this appendage which they referred to as 'hanging limply' between Norway and Finland. Karin's face always turned a bright red then, immediately causing her to leave the room with both girls in tow. While her mother splashed cold water on her face, Eva sat innocently at the kitchen table watching Ingrid snicker behind her apron as if she knew something that her sister didn't.

Later in the afternoon, Eva hid behind her father's big chair while inspecting the map of Scandinavia, puzzling over what had made her mother's face turn beet red. However, she found nothing funny or unusual about the picture of Norway, Sweden and Finland. After she and Ingrid went to bed, when the bold darkness of night makes words come easier, Eva found the courage to ask her sister what the joke had been all about. Ingrid burst into giggles, which made Eva even more curious.

"Tell me, Ingrid. I want to know. I want to know right now!"

Ingrid, enjoying her sister's frustration, didn't answer right away. Finally Eva gave up and pretended to be asleep.

"Eva?" whispered Ingrid after several moments of silence.

"What do you want?" murmured Eva in her sleepiest voice.

"Remember that night when we woke up thirsty and heard Mama and Papa in the kitchen... and what we saw when we peeked around the corner?"

"How could I ever forget seeing Papa's naked backside stepping out of the washtub!" whispered Eva.

"And when he turned around, what did you see?"

"Ingrid, how dare you ask!" said Eva, too embarrassed to put what she'd seen into words. "What I remember most is you grabbing me and then pulling me back to bed, and how you tried to explain about the difference between boys and girls."

Nothing that Ingrid said that night made much sense to Eva. It wasn't until she was older that she understood the association between seeing her father naked and the map of Scandinavia.

It was about this time that the teasing started. Ingrid had always been one to make mean and nasty remarks about anyone or anything she didn't agree with. Now her spiteful comments seemed mostly directed toward Eva.

Ingrid's obsessive teasing worsened every time the man they called The Finn came around. The Finn was a peddler who traveled all over Norrland each spring and autumn selling flour, sugar, spices, kitchen utensils, pretty bolts of cotton cloth and colorful skeins of yarn, almost anything that a farmwife might need. In his wagon were boxes of toys and books for children, as well as all kinds of tools and implements for men. He also had boxes of second-hand clothes and shoes to sell or swap, as well as new and used items for the barn and the caring of farm animals.

The Finn was a stocky, middle-aged man with an ever-present smile etched on his ruddy face, a teller of jokes and funny stories. He always told the girls how pretty they were and made them giggle when he placed his hand behind their ear and magically pulled forth a piece of candy. Word had spread around the countryside that he was a wandering gypsy from Finland, which made him all that much more mysterious. However, the most obvious feature was the wild red hair that stuck out around his cap like a frizzy halo – a persistent reminder for Ingrid to tease Eva.

"What nice frizzy hair you have," she'd say pulling Eva's long braids, or "Why is it that you are the only one in our family with red hair?" But it didn't stop there and Ingrid continued the needling. "All gypsies have red hair, you know," she'd say in her authoritative big-sister voice, "and they sell their babies, too."

Ingrid's words bit like a snake, the spiteful insinuations about The Finn and selling babies causing Eva's face to turn crimson, often forcing her to run crying to the barn in embarrassment.

Was Ingrid inferring that The Finn also sold babies? Worse than that was the possibility that he had sold ***her*** to Mama and Papa! And since she and The Finn were the only ones with red, frizzy hair, did that imply that The Finn might be her real father? These puzzling notions buzzed in her head like aggravated bees, especially in the days after the peddler's semi-annual visits.

This was an extremely touchy subject, one about which Eva had never dared asked her parents. She did muster up enough courage one day to mention The Finn to Mr. Kronberg, but her tongue could not get around the embarrassing words about selling babies, which stayed forever locked up in her head after that. These worrisome notions intensified in the dark hours of night as she lay wide awake while Ingrid slept peacefully beside her, knowing that Eva's shyness would prevent her from telling anyone.

Dag and Suvi

Vidar was on his way home from the village one day when a horse and rider approached from the north. He appraised the strong young horse and in his mind saw a tireless worker that might pull fallen trees and stumps from the forest, plow and cultivate more virgin fields and haul wagonloads of potatoes into the village. When he noticed it was a woman astride the sturdy black horse, his mind concocted a plan...a way to get this fine steed for free, and a woman in the bargain. He stepped out into the middle of the gravel road, causing the horse to stop suddenly. A small child shyly peeked out from behind the woman's woolen cape, but he knew not if it was a girl or boy. His plan did not include a child and he almost changed his mind. However, the horse's deliberate eye, broad chest and muscular legs caused him to reconsider. This beast was more powerful than any he'd seen in the village; how envious the locals would be the next time he came to deliver a load of potatoes.

The travelers were tired and dirty, carried few belongings and seemed desperately in need of food and drink. The woman was not overly attractive, but, of course, neither was he. At least his new hat covered most of his grimy hair and shadowed his narrow, dark eyes. He put his best foot forward, trying to assume a concerned and caring demeanor. It seemed greatly to his advantage to offer the young one a drink from the metal can of milk he had brought from the village.

The child gulped down several swallows and then the mother drank...a small price to pay for his selfish intentions. Then he opened one of his sacks and broke off a chunk of bread for each of them, which they devoured ravenously like hungry wolves at a fresh kill. To entice them even further, he opened the sack wide enough to reveal more bread, cheese and various tempting foodstuffs, causing the woman and child to stare with a deep yearning. After giving them more bread, he stepped back to contemplate his next move. With three mouths to feed, five loaves of bread wouldn't last very long. He looked up to re-appraise the gaunt woman.

"You bake bread?" he asked gruffly. The woman nodded. Knowing he might have fresh bread every day brought him pleasure and enough daring to ask about buying the horse. The woman registered shock at his question and held tightly to the reins.

"No!" she declared. "Blix not for sale!" Of course, he hadn't intended on buying the horse anyway and tried to get on the woman's good side by admiring the handsome steed.

"Fine strong horse," he stated, raising his hand to stroke the gelding's muscular shoulder. The horse looked down at him nervously, sidestepping a few paces, but the woman did not see the anxious look in Blix's eyes as she rubbed his neck to soothe him.

Vidar chose not to tell the woman about the village that laid but a few miles to the east. Instead, he continued negotiating his plan to purchase the horse, which in the end should cost him nothing but a promise to give the two weary travelers a place to live.

"Have big farm...sturdy cabin for you and child," he said in his most convincing manner. She remained silent, her face softening somewhat as she considered his offer.

"Chickens, eggs...moose meat... fields of potatoes," he added, glancing up to her with a less grimacing smile this time.

Dwelling places were few and far apart in the great forest, she thought to herself, and much uncertainty lay ahead. She looked away from him, her eyes following the tall pines skyward as she pondered what her duties might be on this man's farm. She felt a chill, but attributed that to the cool afternoon breeze and thought again of her child. With winter only a month or two away, they would desperately need food to eat and a warm place to live. Suvi had grave concerns about her daughter living in the same house with this man and immediately concocted a plan. She would pretend Dagny was a boy, dress her in boy's clothes and call her Dag.

"My name is Suvi," she revealed suddenly, gripping tightly on the leather reins. "My child is called Dag. We will go with you."

"Me...Vidar,"he mumbled, hoisting the two large sacks to his back and leading the way back along the gravel road. No one saw the menacing grin that creased his face, nor could he remember the last time he'd ever smiled. It grew a little wider as he turned left onto a wide dirt path toward the northwest, his pace increasing as he thought more about the woman.

Dag had been too young to remember her own father and much of their life in the north, but her recent memories were more vivid: the long bumpy ride through the forest with her mother, cold nights sleeping under the spruce and pines or in some farmer's barn and the empty ache of hunger in the pit of her stomach. Her first good remembrance was the cold sweet milk that ran smooth and sweet down her throat filling the hole in her belly. She dreamed of drinking that milk for the rest of her life and at first was only a little afraid of the big, dark stranger called Vidar who led them through the narrow tree-lined path.

Their first view of Vidar's farm was a small gray hut next to a large potato field, where on the second day Suvi was put to work. At first Dag was allowed to sit near her mother in the fields playing with the tiniest potatoes, those that were barely worth scrubbing for the cook pot. She made little trenches in the ground, planted them in rows and covered them with soft dirt, then dug them up again and started over, copying what she saw her mother do in the field.

Sometimes Vidar grabbed a handful of these tiny potatoes and ate them as if fresh peas from the pod. Dag tried doing that once, too, but found them gritty in her mouth and spat them out when no one was watching. But many times after that, hunger forced her to eat her fair share of newly dug raw potatoes and some that were not so fresh. Except for the morning porridge, they ate potatoes with every meal and usually meat from moose or some other wild creature Vidar snared or shot in the woods.

When Dag was about three or four, she was given an empty sack to fill with the small potatoes left behind in the rows. It was fun following behind her mother, but the pleasure lessened as she fell behind, alone and tired from dragging the heavy sack behind her. It was hot backbreaking work and she had to stop often to rest. When Suvi returned on the next row Dag jumped in behind her and started picking again.

Vidar never called her Dag, only by the chore he demanded her to do, using words like "Come," "Get," "Hold," "Dig," "Push" or "Pull." And so it was she learned to work in the potato fields, hoeing and planting, digging and picking, holding, pulling and pushing this and that until finally only the raising of his fist would get the job done. Dag learned early to be obedient and quick, anticipating his wishes and foreseeing the chore at hand. That was her self-defense from his meanness and cruel ways.

Suvi was convinced their life was better now with a roof over their heads and food on the table, but Dag knew her mother had seen happier times. Her mother often told Dag stories about her simple, carefree life in the far north.

Suvi's people had owned no permanent huts or houses on the frozen tundra in the north of Sweden. Their dwelling places were tent-like structures called "lavvus" made of poles and skins which they carried from place to place as they followed the migrating herds of reindeer. The reindeer provided meat to eat and skins for their clothes and homes. Although mostly wild and nervous creatures by nature, some had gentle temperaments and became easily trained to pull sleds. Britta was one of them and Dag never tired of hearing the story of the little reindeer.

"I was about four or five years old," Suvi told her. "I remember waking in the night and not being able to get back to sleep, then wandering outside to watch the colored lights flickering across the endless sky. The reindeer herd was bedded down for the night, but one lay off to the side groaning and thrashing about.

"I watched as the silhouette of a young cow stood up and

began sniffing and pawing the ground. Suddenly she jumped back, snorted and circled to the other side of the herd. When I looked back to where she had been, there was a lump on the ground. It moved slightly and I walked closer to discover a tiny calf struggling to get up in the slippery birth leavings. It was very cold, too early in the year for a calf to be born, so I wrapped it in my apron and carried the little one back to the warmth of my bed where it slept until morning.

"Everyone was surprised that the newborn had survived, but the mother would still have nothing to do with her calf. Grandmother milked the cow several times each day and it was my job to feed the baby. I named her Britta, which means 'strong.' She was my special pet, following me everywhere as if I were her real mother.

"Later when we moved to a different place, Britta and I headed out across the tundra to investigate the vast new land, but I accidentally fell into an ice crevice and my screaming went unheard by anyone except for my Britta, who stood far above me looking down with wide, questioning eyes. I searched for a way to get out, but the crevice only grew narrower and the sound of cracking ice frightened me. When I looked up again, Britta was gone.

"I was cold and sat shivering in the darkness watching the sun creep up the side of the crevice and then disappear over the edge. I must have fallen asleep, for the next thing I knew my brother was behind me and I was being lifted out of my icy prison. When I was safely resting on the tundra, my Britta began licking my face.

"It had been Grandmother who heard Britta bawling outside her lavvu and saw her standing alone in the twilight. She told the men to go looking for me and it was Britta who led them directly to the crevice where they discovered me sleeping on the bottom. From then on my little reindeer could do no wrong and everyone looked to her as a symbol of good luck."

Thinking of the reindeer always caused Suvi's face to brighten, with the hard lines around her mouth softening with a rare smile, and her gray eyes becoming soft and dreamlike as she thought of that special place in her heart. It was the same when she recalled the wonderful days at the miner's house.

Suvi was in her thirteenth summer when she and her father went to live with an older, married brother who worked in the iron mines. The brother's wife resented this intrusion of her privacy. After a year Suvi's father said the cabin was full of bad air and arranged for his daughter to work in the kitchen of the mine owner's house.

The massive stone edifice stood in the middle of a grassy open space in the middle of the forest. It was both beautiful and foreboding to young Suvi, especially when the thick wooden door closed behind her with a thunderous bang of finality. A maid led the way through a dim hall, past winding stairs and darkened rooms to the kitchen and finally down a narrow passageway with many closed doors on either side. The maid opened one of the doors, gave Suvi a lighted candle and without a word marched back toward the kitchen. It was a small cold room, but many thick blankets were folded at the end of the bed. Suvi sat on the soft mattress, wrapped herself in a blanket and instantly fell asleep.

The owner's wife was a kind and patient woman, explaining carefully about the duties expected of a kitchen maid. Suvi had her hands in water most every day washing anything that needed to be cleaned...floors, tables, vegetables, cooking vessels, common dishes. Finally she was trusted to handle the delicate china and beautiful crystal goblets.

Eventually she was allowed to walk up those winding stairs in daylight bringing breakfast to her mistress. She learned how to attend to her mistress's wishes, changing her wide bed with luxuriously soft silk sheets, and thick satin quilts piled high with large, plump pillows.

"How I wished to slip between those silky sheets and feel the softness against my skin," Dag's mother told her, "but all I dared do was hold a silken pillow against my face for a second or two when she wasn't looking.

"My mistress believed every woman should know how to read and write and since I was quick to learn, she began teaching me about numbers and letters. I read quite well, but always had difficulty writing. She showed me much affection and made me feel special, an ability that was also inherited by her son when he came home from school on holidays.

"Occasionally I observed him watching me and when he smiled I felt strangely important, for we were both of an age where boys and girls begin noticing each other. My mistress had a large mirror in her bedroom and I'd stand before it wondering what attracted him to me. My reflection didn't show the beauty of other girls in the village, but I was neat and clean and often made him laugh. He had a way with words and I was a good listener.

"One night he came into my room and when he held me I felt loved and comforted and his kiss was soft and sweet. As we lay on the bed he kissed me again and I felt the wonder of his touch on my bare skin. I felt love for him and after that he was always welcome in my room.

"When my belly grew large, the mistress asked who did this to me and when I told her it was her son, she grew alarmed because of what her husband might do. However, she was with me when you were born and made certain we were taken care of until I gained my strength back. She enjoyed holding the child of her son, but when her husband came home from his stay at the mines, he demanded to know how this had all happened and he wouldn't have us in his house after that.

"Your father hid us for a year in a small cabin in the forest, but he was kept busy in the mines and we saw each other only when he was able to get away to bring us food and supplies. He promised a better life for us and knowing my love of animals he gave me one of his finest horses, the one you know as Blix. Your father died in a mining accident. I knew I wasn't welcome in the village and it was difficult staying on in the cabin when food was hard to get. I had to sell a broach and necklace he'd given me so we could survive that winter, but I could never part with Blix, the only living thing besides you that he had given me. I knew he would be the means of us getting to a better place."

Her mother always broke into tears then. Dag would console her and they would cry together.

"So, you loved my father very much?" Dag would always ask.

"Yes, I loved him with all my heart."

"Did he love you?"

"He loved us both," her mother would reply, hugging her daughter with comforting reassurance.

The Kronbergs

Eva was almost five years old the first time she visited the Kronberg farm. Riding in the ox cart with her father down the winding gravel road was a great adventure, made even longer by the unhurried pace of Slofock.

Eva sat impatiently scanning the forested landscape for a view of the Kronbergs' bright red house that her father had described to her.

"Are we almost there?" she asked at every bend of the road. The first time, Gustav informed her they had barely gone a mile...and still had at least nine miles to go. Finally she grew tired of looking around all the twists and turns in the road and found other questions to ask.

"Why does the road curve every which-away? Wouldn't we get there faster if we just drove in a straight line?" Gustav laughed and agreed that would be a good idea. He told her the road followed the path of the winding stream, which was here long before the road was built. Eva thought the stream would run faster in a straight line, too, but her father guessed the water was too much like Slofock, and not in any great hurry to get where it's going.

"Where did all this water come from?"

"You are full of questions today, Eva," he said, turning to smile at her, "but that is how children learn, eh?" Then he explained how snow melts on the mountains and trickles down the ravines in waterfalls and tributaries; how the little streams grow wider and stronger as they make their way through the valleys, forming rivers that may run quickly or slowly meander.

"Are we meandering, too?" she asked, watching the blue water moving slowly and peacefully through the forest.

"Yes, I'd say we are definitely meandering now," replied her father, prodding Slofock to a faster pace.

As they approached the sprawling farm Eva was struck by the enormity of the house, the bright red color and long wrap-around porch. The roof sat high above the ground and beneath it were two rows of windows outlined in white, a dozen shiny eyes looking back at her in the bright morning sun; such a contrast to their small gray cottage hidden in the shadows of the tall trees, with only a few dull blank windows sleeping in the shade.

Five kid goats frolicked in front of a large white barn. Back and forth they ran, in and out of the wide open door; white as snow in the bright sunshine, turning gray in the long shadow cast by the tall barn. Eva longed to touch one of them and ran across the dooryard, but a dark figure suddenly emerged from the shadows. One glance at the high, black, manure-splashed boots caused her to run back to the safety of her father. Then the outline of a woman lumbered toward them. She carried two large pails that slopped milk on the ground as she shouted across the yard.

"Otto's in the house. Go in and make yourselves at home!"

"That's Mrs. Kronberg," whispered Gustav. Eva was shocked by her undignified appearance, compared to her husband, who she had always seen dressed in a fine suit. The woman looked untidy, almost shamefully sloppy, with the hem of her dress hitched up around her waist and bare legs showing above dirty, black boots. Such a contrast, too, from Eva's mother who was exceptionally neat, clean and modest, rarely showing a trace of ankle beneath her long skirts. Gustav read his daughter's mind.

"Don't be too quick to judge Mrs. Kronberg. She is

hardworking, honest, and a fine cook and mother." Then he explained how young Ingeborg had brought to the farm a dowry of three pet goats, halters, work clothes and a well-stocked bridal chest filled with cooking pans, dinnerware, linens and other kitchen supplies, and how those three original goats had now multiplied into a herd of more than thirty bountiful milkers. The Kronberg family had grown also. In addition to Johan and Eric, Otto and Ingeborg now had two more handsome sons, Torsten and Mats.

Otto Kronberg met them at the kitchen door wearing a dark blue suit and striped blue and white tie. He had planned to visit some farmers on his way to Stockholm that afternoon and was glad they stopped by early in the morning. After Otto invited them inside, they sat around a long, highly polished pine table surrounded by eight matching high-back chairs. As the men talked, Eva looked around the surprisingly neat and clean kitchen. The walls and cabinets were painted the same brilliant yellow as the cross on the Swedish flag that waved outside. Even though the sky was overcast, the kitchen seemed as bright and sunny as a fair summer's day.

Tall cabinets covered almost the whole of two walls. Eva sat quietly speculating what interesting items might be stored behind all those closed doors. Then Mrs. Kronberg burst through the door accompanied by two young boys. Her eyes locked on to Eva.

"My goodness! Haven't you grown up to be the prettiest girl!" she said. The boys stood near the door smirking and nudging each other. Then their mother grabbed the tallest one by the arm and the other boy followed.

"Boys, this is Eva Gunderson. Eva I'd like you to meet Torsten and Mats." Eva, embarrassed by their silly grins, smiled back shyly. They bowed respectfully and took their seats at the table. "Wash your hands!" ordered their mother, and the boys ran over to the sink fighting for the bar of soap.

Mrs. Kronberg placed a large milk jug on the counter and opened one of the cabinets, disclosing many shelves of dishes, mugs and glassware, enough to serve dozens of people. The two boys, sitting across from Eva, began kicking each other under the table until their father's stern glance made them sit quietly.

"Your boys have grown since I last saw them," commented Gustav

"Ah, they grow like weeds," said Otto. "Torsten is eight now and Mats is seven."

"And the two older boys? Are they still in school?" asked Gustav.

"Johan, my eldest, is seventeen now. Taller than I and more rugged, but not much of a scholar. He takes great interest in Ingeborg's goats."

"So, you will have someone to take over the farm in your old age," commented Gustav.

"Thank goodness," said Otto with a great sigh. "Erik, on the other hand, is not much help in the barn. He's upstairs studying. Can't seem to get his nose out of his books, but I can't complain about that, can I?"

"Not at all," said Gustav. "He'll be after your job in a few years."

"That may be, but he dreams of being a geologist." From the empty look in Gustav's face, Otto explained further. "He wants to be a scientist and study the origins of the Earth."

"Oh, I see," said Gustav. "Sort of like a scientific gardener." Otto, not wishing to go into more detail, nodded and began talking about his two younger sons.

"Torsten is a bit of a daydreamer and a sometime whittler, always dressing up like a pirate and running around with a long sword he's fashioned out of wood. He's pretty good at carving animal figures, too."

"Like your brother, Lars?" said Gustav.

"Well, Torsten could do a lot worse. I know of no better wood carver than my brother."

"I can certainly agree with that," replied Gustav. "Years ago when I visited Anna and Lars, he showed me all his beautiful works of art."

When Otto gazed thoughtfully out the window, Gustav heard

Mats giggling. "And what about that little blond rascal kicking his brother?"

"Ah, Mats...his mother's baby...and spoiled rotten, too. But don't tell Ingeborg I said that," he whispered.

"What are children for then, if not to be spoiled a little," said Gustav regarding his own two daughters.

By now a second cabinet door had been opened revealing shelves laden with loaves of golden bread, small jars of red jam and larger glass containers filled with cookies and other delicious looking baked goods. Mrs. Kronberg took down one of the cookie jars and placed it between Eva and the two restless boys, who each thrust a hand into the jar at the same time, chewing and swallowing broken cookie pieces so quickly that Eva doubted they had time to taste their sweetness.

Eva had never been around boys much, and their antics reminded her of Ingrid...selfish and annoying, always in too much of a hurry. Mrs. Kronberg shook her head and placed a lovely tray of pastries between Eva and her father, then poured the men's coffee and three large glasses of milk for the children.

The boys gulped down their milk and wanted more. Eva took a sip but found it had an odd taste and smell, much different from the cow's milk at home. When Mrs. Kronberg walked behind her, that same odor drifted by and it dawned on Eva that it was goat's milk in her glass.

She ate the delicious pastry, savoring each mouthful of lingonberry jam and sweet frosting while the boys finished their second glass of milk. Then they grabbed another handful of cookies and raced each other to the door, jumped off the top porch step and disappeared.

Eva was brought up to finish everything on her plate and to drink all the precious milk that the cow provided, so she sat looking out the kitchen windows pondering what to do with the remainder of her milk. Every once in a while she saw the boys running around the door yard yelling and hitting each other with long pointed sticks, but the hollering soon turned into crying and their mother rushed outside.

The men, engrossed in sharing news and jokes, weren't paying much attention to Eva, who took this opportunity to quietly sneak her glass to the sink, guiltily dumping the remaining milk down the drain just before Mrs. Kronberg returned with Torsten.

Eva was surprised to see the older of the two boys with a bump on his head and bleeding from a scratch on his arm, while Mats stood in the doorway smirking as if he'd won a great battle. Again she was reminded of Ingrid as he grinned with a proud look of superiority. After Mrs. Kronberg smoothed everything over between the boys, she made them promise to be nice to Eva and told them all to go outside and play. The boys darted out the door and Eva reluctantly followed them to the grassy yard, but when they picked up their sticks, she returned to the safety of the porch and sat in a big rocker near the door.

It wasn't long before she heard whispers and tapping noises beneath her chair. A stick inched its way toward her through a wide space between the planks of the porch floor. As the stick came closer, she forced it back down until it hit something...or someone. She heard a shriek and a commotion under the porch, then caught a glimpse of the two boys running toward the barn. Eva felt justified that she'd taught one of the boys a lesson. Hopefully it was Mats.

Her father appeared on the porch soon after and went to the barn to get Slofock. Eva followed until the boys came running out the barn door. When they saw her they ran into the woods, neither seeming to have had any bad effect from her assault with the stick.

Mr. and Mrs. Kronberg stood on the porch waving goodbye. Eva always thought of them as she had seen them that day: he in his fine blue suit and tie and she in her kerchief, too-high skirt and farm boots. They were an odd couple, but both nice in their own way. She had grown to love Mr. Kronberg, and when his wife gave her some pastries wrapped in a towel to take home, Mrs. Kronberg had a place in Eva's heart, too.

Since much of Otto Kronberg's work involved being on the road visiting farmers and other landowners, it was easier and quicker for him to stop in to visit the Gundersons than for Otto to fuss with Slofock and make the long trip by oxcart to the Kronberg farm. Otto often brought with him bags of grain, flour, sugar or other items he thought his friends might be running out of. So it was two summers later when Eva accompanied her father to the village and they stopped in to visit the Kronbergs again.

This time Mr. Kronberg took Eva beyond the spacious kitchen to a special place he called the library. High wooden shelves surrounded the walls from floor to ceiling on all four sides of the room, towering far above her head. Each shelf held a section of books separated by beautiful porcelain figurines of finely dressed men and women, horses, birds and flowers, plus elaborate wooden inlaid boxes small enough to hold in her hand.

Mr. Kronberg asked Eva to lift the cover of one of these magical boxes and when beautiful music filled the room, she looked around for the orchestra. When he told her it was inside the box she knew he was joking; there was not even enough room in the little box to hold her father's tiny harmonica. Otto and Gustav laughed so hard that the room shook and the figurines nearly walked off the shelves. Eva didn't see the humor of it until years later.

Past the library was a long curving stairway. Of course, she had never seen a flight of stairs in the middle of a house before, and when Mr. Kronberg noticed her puzzled face he suggested she go up to the second floor and look around. Eva's first thought was fear, but curiosity and her complete trust in Mr. Kronberg forced her to take a few steps. Halfway up she stopped to look back, but both Mr. Kronberg and her father had vanished. The anticipation of what lay ahead was strong enough to push her forward, so she held tightly to the hand rail and walked up the wide, polished wooden stairs. When her feet were firmly planted on the top step, she looked to her left down a long narrow hallway and saw a bright blue window.

She tiptoed by an open doorway revealing an unmade bed and clothes strewn over the floor. She stopped, thinking someone was in the room, but heard no sounds and continued walking past several closed doors until she stood in front of the blue window, which wasn't really blue after all. The blue she had seen was the sky showing through it. At home in the cottage there was no second floor, so she could not see any sky through the small windows, only the tall pines and spruce at the edge of the forest.

The window was open so she poked her head out to see the beautiful landscape spread out below. It was as if she were a bird flying high above the ground and looking down on the tops of bushes and small trees, the white backs of goats grazing in the pasture, and the gray shingles on the porch roof where a black cat crept slowly toward an unsuspecting robin. While clapping her hands to warn the bird, her head bumped against the window and a voice spoke behind her.

"Don't fall out the window" said a skinny blond boy with a mischievous smirk spreading across his face. Even though Mats had grown nearly a foot taller, Eva remembered that grin from two years before and quickly darted down the hall and stairway, hiding her embarrassment behind a potted fern. In an instant Mats slid backwards down the wide stair banister, gaining more and more speed until finally he was propelled across the hall, eventually somersaulting into the parlor to the astonishment and amusement of the coffee-drinking adults.

He sheepishly rubbed his head and struggled awkwardly to his feet. Before he'd taken one step, his father grabbed his arm insisting on an apology to Gustav for his foolish actions. Then he noticed Eva standing in the doorway.

"Eva, you remember Mats, don't you?"

It was her turn now to smirk knowingly at Mats, who glanced foolishly in her direction with a very red face, no doubt wishing he was anywhere else but there after his blundering exit from the banister.

The next time Mr. Kronberg came to visit he brought Mats with him. Gustav, Karin, Ingrid and Eva sat politely in the front room listening as Mr. Kronberg told them the latest local gossip and news of Stockholm and Gothenberg. Mats sat quietly at first, but after a while he grew uneasy in his chair, fiddling with his thumbs and looking in Eva's direction. Soon he was making funny faces, which she tried to avoid, but his silly actions usually caught her eye. He seemed to enjoy making her blush.

Mats was still a tall, gawky kid, his pale blond hair dangling thickly over his forehead so that he had the odd habit of tossing his head back suddenly as if he had a hitch in his neck. Then for a while Eva could see his blue eyes...until the hair slipped over his forehead again. His eyes would be covered then, but she knew he was still watching her.

It wasn't long before Mats was feeling quite at home at the Gunderson house. He ate as if he'd gone for days without food, but Eva knew better; his mother was a fine cook. Karin said he was just a growing boy and probably had a sweet tooth. Ingrid took all this in and thought he was sweet on Eva, too, and began teasing her about Mats Kronberg.

There was no way Eva could avoid being in the parlor when Mats came with his father because she and Ingrid were expected to politely sit and listen to any company that came to visit. From that day on, after Karin served coffee and everyone had eaten a small lunch, Eva would be the first to take the dirty dishes to the kitchen. After washing and drying them it was easy to sneak out the back door and make a beeline to the barn. This strategy worked for a little while, but Mats was not one to give up easily. His inquisitive nature soon discovered Eva's hiding place. Away from the scrutiny of his father, he became a different boy, pulling her braids, telling jokes, and trying to make her blush. Finally it became easier to remain in the parlor and try to ignore him.

Eva enjoyed listening to Mr. Kronberg talk about the weather, the crops, who was sick, who had died and all the local village gossip. He told about traveling around Sweden and how he listened to everyone's problems in order to report back their concerns to the government. Mostly though she loved to hear funny stories about the farmers, shopkeepers and rich landowners who lived in other areas of the country. Mr. Kronberg was friendly with everyone, rich or poor, and was equally at home in the great houses of the nobility as he was in a peasant's cottage.

He said once that being rich didn't make a man smarter than one who was poor, nor was a rich man happier than a poor man, but he did admit that having enough money to buy the necessities of life made one's life a lot easier.

Eva had never thought much about money before that, but she'd seen pictures of ladies in satin dresses and decided it might be fun to be rich just for a day. She was fascinated by his tales of the arrogant nobility who strutted around their great manors entertaining guests with elegant parties, exotic foods and dancing, but he had many interesting stories involving the lower class, too.

Eva's favorite story was about a poor widow named Ulla who had many children, and her rich neighbor, Torborg Hendrikson. Torborg had the best of everything...the fattest pigs, strongest horses, and hens that laid the largest eggs. However, his cows were all quite mediocre until the day he bought Matilda. On that day he bragged to all his neighbors how this new cow could give more milk than any other cow in Norrland.

"Matilda's udder is so large she must wear a brassiere to keep from stepping on her teats when lying down or getting up!" he told each one of his neighbors. Many of the farmers were not as knowledgeable as Torborg and had never heard the word 'brassiere' before, but when he described in great detail about this newest of woman's apparel, they were all very eager to come that night to see Torborg milk his famous cow for the first time. Word also got around to Ulla. So, when all the farmers gathered in Torborg Hendrikson's barn that night, Ulla stood quietly watching in the background.

The men snickered among themselves, making jokes regarding the fastening and unfastening of brassieres, as Torborg adjusted the straps around Matilda's back. When her udder was raised high enough to accommodate the milk pail, he proudly sat down on his stool to milk his magnificent new cow for the first time.

Within seconds Matilda's swift kick sent poor Torborg onto the floor and into the soft manure. He brushed himself off and tried again, but every time Matilda felt his rough cold hands on her udder she kicked him to the floor again. His arrogance quickly turned to humiliation as the men chuckled and murmured among themselves.

"Try it yourself!" he shouted to them all. "Any one of you who can fill a pint container of milk from Matilda can take her home; I want no part of her now." The men were eager to try, but like Torborg, every one of them failed to get a drop of milk in the pail.

All the while, Ulla stood by the door thinking that surely it wasn't that difficult to milk a cow. She'd worked as a dairymaid in her youth and was told she had the magic touch. Not knowing this, the men urged Ulla to try her luck; surely it would be much fun to see a woman kicked into Matilda's fresh manure.

Ulla thought only of her hungry children as she sat down on the stool talking soothingly to the cow and gently massaging her udder. The milk began to flow, even before Ulla's hands touched Matilda's teats. When the pail was filled, Torborg fetched a second one, hoping that this time Ulla would surely be kicked by the cow and he wouldn't be shown up by a lowly woman. Everyone looked in amazement as Ulla filled three pails with milk and they all applauded as she took the rope and led Matilda out of the barn.

Torborg was not one to go back on his word, so he could do nothing more than join the others and watch his magnificent Matilda walk down the dirt path behind the victorious Ulla.

Mats giggled every time the word 'brassiere' was mentioned, especially when his father tried to describe what the contraption looked like and its purpose. Eva, on the other hand was mostly interested in Ulla outsmarting the pompous Torborg and the fact that in later years she became rich and famous for her magnificent cow and all the fine milk she sold.

Mats was visiting the Gundersons one day when The Finn drove his wagon into the yard. Ingrid took him aside and whispered in his ear, his eyes darting back and forth between Eva and The

Finn. Eva feared Ingrid was telling him tales about their similar red hair and all the suspicions she had about The Finn, gypsies and the selling of babies. She moved closer to her mother to look through a pile of old books, which solved the problem for that day, but after that Mats took great pleasure in pulling her braids and teasing her about her red hair and making snide remarks about The Finn. She'd glare at him, but the merry twinkle in his eyes conveyed the fact that his teasing was only a way to make her blush and was not mean-spirited like Ingrid's. Thankfully summer was almost over and Mats would soon be back in school.

That autumn the family made plans to take its final trip to the lake that year, but at the last minute Ingrid came down sick and Karin had to stay home to look after her. Eva was overjoyed that Ingrid wasn't going because now she'd have her father all to herself.

They walked single file along the narrow path enjoying the tranquility of the forest, the many butterflies and bees making last visits to late-blooming flowers, chirping birds fluttering from tree to tree on their way to warmer climates, and squirrels busy gathering food for winter. Every once in a while the sun shown down on a clump of poplars, their green leaves already turned a bright yellow, quivering and rustling in the breeze like sparkling pieces of gold.

After a small lunch under the birches, Gustav led the way through the woods toward his favorite sheltered cove, but before Eva had time to step onto the little beach her father suddenly pulled her back into the bushes. It was too late; she had already had a glimpse of what he hadn't wanted her to see: a girl wearing a pink dress dancing on the shore. Without a word, he quickly steered Eva toward the path that led to home. Several times she asked who the girl was, but received no response, her father hastening his pace even more.

When they arrived home Karin looked into the empty basket wondering where all the fish were, until Gustav whispered something about the 'strange one.' After a quiet supper Karin and Eva went out to the front steps with their knitting. For a long while Eva's two needles lay idle in her hands. Who was this girl in the pink dress? Why had she not seen or heard of her before? Surely she couldn't live very far from the lake, but where? Jumbled thoughts played hide and seek in Eva's head as she tried to muster up courage enough to ask a simple question that seemed too difficult to put into words.

The evening shadows crept toward the cottage as Karin knit white snowflakes onto a background of medium blue.

"Do you need help with your knitting?" she asked.

Shaking her head, Eva picked up her knitting, but two stitches slid off the needle and became lost in the previous row.

"Tell me about 'the strange one,'" the words tumbling out of her mouth so rapidly that even she was surprised to hear them. Her mother's fingers stiffened and she put down her knitting, then took a deep breath and gazed somewhere over the treetops.

"I know only what is talked about in the village, but everyone has a different story and I don't know what to believe."

"What kind of stories?"

Karin shrugged her shoulders. "Perhaps when you are older you will understand," she said.

"What is there to understand?"

"Well...nothing really. It's only hearsay, needless gossip passed on by word of mouth. Probably no truth to it at all." Then Karin went back into the house to check on Ingrid.

Eva sat for a while in the dimming light remembering something Mats told her about a boy who lived at the potato farm. Mats had been hunting rabbits one day and saw the boy in the woods twirling around in a dress.

"So, you know him?" Eva had asked.

"Not very well," he had said with shrug, "but I've seen him every year when we buy potatoes. Anyway, who else would it be? No one else lives around here but us."

Then he had pulled her braids and laughed. "Unless it was you out there dancing in the middle of the forest."

She had blushed and thought he was joking, so she hadn't

thought about the incident again.

"I guess Mats wasn't lying to me after all," she now said to herself.

Ingrid was asleep when Eva went to bed. She wanted desperately to talk to someone and began tickling Ingrid's cheek with the end of her braid until she rolled over and opened her eyes.

"Have you ever seen 'the strange one?'"

"What are you talking about?" groaned Ingrid as she turned to face the wall.

"The boy at the potato farm...the one they call 'the strange one.'"

"You must be dreaming, Eva," she said, and fell back to sleep.

For a long time Eva lay thinking about the events of the day. Surely there must be some truth to what Mats had said, but was it really a boy she had seen today dancing in the pink dress? For the first time Eva could remember she was wishing that Mats would come to visit so she could ask him again about 'the strange one.'

Dag

Dag was in her tenth spring when early one morning she and her mother found a fresh moose trail while walking through the forest. They followed the large split-hoof tracks, hoping to come to a stream or swamp where the moose came to drink. Surprisingly, the trail opened up to more water than Dag had ever seen in one place.

"Is this an ocean?" she exclaimed, running toward the water's edge. Suvi followed her and scooped some water into her hand to taste it.

"No, this is a lake. The water is sweet, not salty as in the oceans." Suvi didn't know why oceans were filled with salty water, but Dag was glad this wasn't an ocean because she was very thirsty.

They sat on very soft ground that wasn't dirty at all. Suvi told her the clean dirt was called sand, probably dirt washed by the lake. They laid down and gazed up to the tall trees waving against the sky. Suvi drifted off to sleep and Dag watched feathery clouds lift from the high points of land across the lake where a faint white half moon hung low in the sky.

"Is that where the moon lives?" asked Dag when her mother woke up.

"Perhaps it is where the moon sleeps when the sun rises," Suvi answered.

"Where did the mountains come from?"

"They didn't come from anywhere," replied Suvi, standing up to stretch. "I think they've been there from the beginning of time."

"When was the beginning of time?"

"When the earth was born," Suvi said, wading slowly into the lake, then splashing her face with water. Dag followed, cupping her hands to drink.

"Was the water here when the earth was born?" she asked.

"You are full of questions today," said her mother. "I don't know all the answers, but I'd say the earth came from the sky in a rush of water just like babies are born from their mothers' bellies."

Then she had to explain to Dag the way it was with babies before they are born and how they live in a sack full of warm water. Dag drank again. The water was cool and fresh and sweet. Then she waded deeper into the lake.

"I want to go under the water and know how it feels to be a baby again."

"Maybe in a month or two when the water warms up," said her mother, rubbing her arms. "It is much too cold today."

On the way home they collected spruce pitch and chewed its tangy sweetness while gathering fresh pine needles to bring home for tea. Approaching the farm, all was quiet except for Bull moving about in his stall and the ravens calling to each other in the tall pines behind the potato shed. There was no sign of either

Vidar or Blix. Suvi and Dag had stolen another secret time together, a precious memory known only to them.

Dag loved Blix, just as Suvi had loved her pet reindeer. But she saw his spirit breaking as he was forced to work long hours in the fields and forest. Never before had he been hitched to stubborn trees that were too heavy to pull; never had he worked all day in the blazing sun or winter cold or felt the sting of the whip when he fell to his knees from exhaustion. Wishing only to please, his patient and obedient nature was easily dominated. When Dag heard the snap of the whip and loud swearing echoed across the fields, she felt sorry for Blix, who strained at the traces and was whipped when the harness broke, as if that was any fault of his.

On rainy days and often in winter when there was no work to do outside, Dag found comfort being in the barn with Blix and making certain he had fresh bedding and feed. Sometimes after a good brushing she'd kick off her boots and climb into his crib, covering herself with fresh hay. It wouldn't be long before she smelled his sweet grainy breath as he nuzzled her cheek and hair. She'd stroke his velvety soft nose until he closed his eyes, his head drooping to rest on her chest. She wondered what horses think about, what he would say if he could talk. They were best friends and sometimes as he munched slowly on the hay she'd tell him things that were too private for her mother to hear, knowing that her mother had problems of her own and didn't want to bother her with more. She often felt sorry for her mother, sorry for Blix and sorry for herself.

Dag would hear Old Bull rattling his chain in the next stall. Her mother had said never to go near him, but he looked docile enough so she did try to pat him once. His ears went back, both eyes narrowed with meanness and his head rammed into the boards just inches from her face. She never touched him again, although she often threw him a few handfuls of hay because she didn't think he meant to be mean. Vidar had made him that way.

Even though Vidar was stronger than any man, he was not nearly as strong as Bull. They were two of a kind; a bull-headed man trying to dominate an even more stubborn beast.

One day when Blix was so lame he couldn't walk out of his stall, Vidar got the idea of putting the bull to harness. Minutes later he was flat on the ground and Bull was galloping across the field with pieces of leather trailing in the wind behind him. Vidar finally got to his feet and staggered into the kitchen, wailing and moaning from a huge bump on his head. He was bleeding heavily from a deep gash in his arm, which her mother plastered with grease and wrapped in clean cloths.

Dag pictured Old Bull dead in his stall, but when she went out to check on him, he was standing in the potato field contently chomping the lush green plant tops. A smile of satisfaction spread uncontrollably across her face thinking about Vidar's bloody arm and how he'd finally gotten a taste of how it felt to be the beaten one.

Old Bull did have a gentle side, but only when someone brought a cow to the farm for breeding. A mellowness came over him as the receptive cow's special scent transformed him into a curious state of temporary affection. Approaching the cow from the back, his ears slightly laid back, lips quivering and nose sniffing deliciously into the air, he was as docile as a kitten. Usually about this time Suvi came along and pulled her daughter out of the barn. But once Dag had been there long enough to see the bull lunging roughly against the cow, forcing her to fall on her knees.

From their first day at the potato farm, Suvi had insisted that Dag dress like a boy. She fashioned Vidar's old clothes into shirts and pants for her daughter, although even then they were much too big for her. "You'll be safer this way," was all she had said. "Safer from what?" Dag wondered. At the time she could only think that the long shirts and pants would keep her body cleaner from the dusty potato fields and that was a good enough reason.

Dag had never told her mother how Vidar had grabbed her one day in the potato shed, pulled her trousers down around her ankles and put his rough hand between her legs, forcing her to the floor, and then rubbing himself against her and poking her until she was left hurting, bleeding and feeling filthy. She wondered if that poor defenseless cow had felt the same way.

Dag imagined everyone else in the world lived exactly as they did, that Vidar and her mother were just like all fathers and mothers and her growing-up years were similar to the lives of children everywhere. She didn't know any differently, but something about Vidar's behavior never seemed right to her.

Ever since that first day at the lake with her mother, Dag dreamed of going back to feel how it might seem to be surrounded by water, to wash her body of uncleanness and to feel what it was like to be born. It wasn't until she went to the lake alone the first time that she realized how other people related to one another.

Nestled away from the main beach in a secluded cove, Dag removed her dirty work clothes and slipped into the cool water, submerging her head and feeling the purifying smoothness caressing her skin as she glided through an endless place of newness. The cleansing water enveloped her body like a silky cocoon. Then, suddenly, like a butterfly emerging from its darkened pupa into the light of a higher place, she rose toward the surface as if escaping from her old self and all the bad memories. A supreme happiness settled over her. She felt pure, peaceful and safe.

While floating for a while on her back, luxuriating in the warm rays of the sun, she heard children's voices. Two girls ran across an adjacent beach and into the water, squealing at the coldness and lifting their skirts high above their knees. Dag ducked under water and swam toward the little cove to hide in the junipers.

When a man's voice called the girls in to shore, Dag saw a woman knitting on the beach, her fingers causing the stitches to move swiftly from one end of the needle to the other...all without taking her eyes off the view across the lake. Dag had tried to knit once, but the stitches kept slipping off the needle. She was ashamed to give her mother the holey scarf on Christmas, but she had no other gift to give. Her mother had held the scarf to her cheek saying how soft it was as tears welled in the corners of her eyes. She wore it every day until summer.

The father and two daughters stood on the shore fishing. The older girl was having all the luck catching fish while the little red-haired one paid no attention to her line and thoughtfully gazed across the water toward the mountains. She eventually slipped away to join her mother and began to knit. Dag immediately felt a connection to this quiet girl, who seemed about her own age and was nothing like the loud and bossy older girl.

Every so often the man turned his head to catch the woman's eye and Dag saw the exchange of love between them in their smiles. For the first time she was seeing a real family. Eventually the father and older sister came in from fishing and the mother spread a blanket with bread, cheese and sliced apples. Dag hadn't eaten an apple since her mother shared one on the road before they'd met Vidar so many years ago. Her mouth watered remembering its sweet juiciness.

This father hugged his children, spoke in a soft voice, yet seemed no less of a man. He showed a quiet strength, but he was playful, too, and Dag almost laughed out loud when he tickled the two girls and they dragged him into the lake while he pretended to be afraid, and then all three fell splashing into the water and got soaked from head to toe.

Later he carefully helped his wife rise from the blanket and with a hearty laugh picked her up, running toward the lake as if he were about to throw her in, too, but at the last minute he set her down on the sand and kissed her for a long time. As they laughed and kissed again, Dag was reminded of how it might have been between her mother and the miner's son.

Vidar went to the village with a load of potatoes one warm September day, so Dag ventured out alone on the moose trail again. She carried a small lunch and an old pink dress that belonged to her mother. It was another day of discovery.

Completely exhilarated from a cold swim, she glided toward

shore and ran onto the beach to dry off. She felt much as she had the first time she'd come here alone to swim in the purifying water...set free, at least for a little while, from her former insignificant self that was always hidden under over-sized dirty work clothes. Eagerly she put on the pink dress and began to dance on the small patch of silky sand.

There was a rustling in the brush, then the glimpse of a man's face. In an instant he was gone, but he wasn't alone. The sound of a girl's voice came from the woods and Dag silently followed them, staying off the path and struggling in the uneven undergrowth so as not to be seen.

This was the same man and his youngest daughter that she'd seen before. The father hurried along the path and the girl struggled to keep up, but fell further and further behind. However, Dag had no trouble keeping an eye on her because she had hair as red as The Finn's. At times she thought it was none of her business to be following them, but an intense curiosity pushed her forward. A thrill surged through her body, as if she were reading a forbidden book and could not stop until the story ended. Then the path opened up to a beautiful scene and both father and daughter disappeared behind a pretty cottage.

The farmstead was neat and clean, almost lost among the tall pines and spruce, with only a small pasture behind the barn. A velvet green lawn surrounded the cottage with red, pink, yellow and white flowers growing abundantly on either side of the front porch. After a long while, the red-haired girl came out of the house with a book under her arm and walked toward the small barn where a cow lay dozing under a clump of birches. She sat down on the grass, leaned her head back against the cow's shoulder and opened her book. The cow methodically chewed her cud for a while, then reached over to lap the girl's long, plump braid which eventually became undone. The girl laughed and ran her fingers through the wavy red mass, kissed the cow's brown cheek and settled herself comfortably against the cow again.

This girl, whose red curls fell almost to her waist, was more beautiful than any Dag had ever seen, much like the picture of a goddess in one of her picture books. Dag's hand spontaneously fondled her own thin, dark hair that had been cut short like a boy's for so long. She'd been born with black fuzz all over her head, which finally grew in straight and very thin. Her mother had dark hair, too, but it wasn't until the yellow-haired strangers came to the farm to buy potatoes that her mother told her about the differences between the people of the far north and those who lived in the south.

Dag wanted to stay longer, but the walk home was too long and her mother would be worried if she was late. She was also anxious to tell her mother about their neighbors, the neat cottage and all the beautiful flowers.

When she arrived back at the potato farm, Vidar sat on the front stoop of the gray hut. Dag hesitated, thinking to avoid him by sneaking into the barn, but it was too late. He had already seen her. With her mother nowhere in sight she could do nothing but walk toward him. He stood up to his full height with his disapprovingly hateful look and ordered her never to leave the farm again. He roughly grabbed her arm, forcing her to the ground shouting there was always work to do and that wandering in the woods was a waste of time. There was liquor on his breath and she had visions of him dragging her to the barn, but her mother appeared in the doorway and he let go of her.

Visitors

Suvi and Dag had enjoyed much freedom when they first arrived at the potato farm and were able to spend time investigating the surrounding countryside: following moose tracks to a new river, a secluded waterfall, or new mountain top. Sometimes they discovered just a pretty flower, bird, squirrel or fox. Vidar, noticing their frequent absences, soon put an end to all that by keeping them busy...and worn out with farm work.

When Vidar delivered wagonloads of potatoes to the village he usually drank heavily with the profits, arriving home in a drunken stupor with an empty money bag.

"The village men are always on the lookout for a sucker," Suvi had once said to Dag with a smirk. "When they notice his roll of bills, they cluster around him at the bar or slide their chairs around his table like old friends, full of compliments and praise for his wonderful potatoes and applauding his humor and foul stories."

Suvi had seen with her own eyes how it was in the saloon when strangers see an opportunity to have a free drink. Dag was too young to remember, so her mother told her about their first visit to the village.

"After the potatoes were delivered, he drove us to the edge of town and stopped near a brook under some trees. He told me to stay there until he returned, but after too many hours had passed and the sun slipped behind the trees, I was uneasy and worried because you were still very young and we were far from home.

"I gathered up the reigns and slowly walked Blix into town, but something startled him and he reared up causing me to drop the reins. A clean, well-dressed man grabbed the bridle and recognized the horse, saying that Vidar was in the saloon across the street with a bad case of intoxication. Two other men stood just outside the blacksmith shop grinning, but I didn't think it was funny at all. Intoxication sounded like a serious disease to me.

"I went inside the darkened saloon and asked the many faces that turned to look at me where I might find the man with a bad case of intoxication. They pointed to a heap on the floor and more snickering traveled around the room. Finally two men took pity on me and offered to carry him to the wagon. But he needs a doctor, I told them in all seriousness, not knowing then that intoxication was a fancy name for plain old drunkenness. They informed me that it was nothing that a good night's sleep wouldn't cure, so I drove Blix back to the farm and left Vidar in the wagon to sober up. His bag of money was limp, so I knew he'd spent most of the potato money. I felt ashamed that day, but was not humiliated as I was on the next visit, which was about a year later.

"Again he told us to stay in the wagon until he returned, but after we had sat too long in the cold wagon, I walked into the saloon and stood just inside the doorway. Vidar had his back to me as his thirsty cronies buttered him up for more free drinks. He ordered another round and held up a fistful of bills which the serving girl stuffed between her breasts as she cleared the empties away. Our hard-earned money was being wasted on gluttonous leeches and I stupidly confronted him, but I don't remember any words passing between us; only a shattering blow to my head.

"My head ached and my arm felt as if it had been pulled out of its socket. You were crying, saying how he'd dragged me out by my arm and tied me to the wagon seat. I felt worse than a disobedient dog and shunned by all the staring villagers who sneered and talked behind their hands as they walked by. That was the last time we went to the village and I never meddled in his affairs again.

"Remember, Dag," said her mother sternly, "your past is your best teacher and it is best to learn from your mistakes the first time because the next time will be worse." Dag thought there was more to the story, bad things that her mother didn't want to speak of, so Dag said nothing and tried to remember her mother's good advice.

Dag learned early to be obedient, anticipating Vidar's wishes and foreseeing the chore at hand. Because of Vidar's great physical strength, Dag's mind and quick thinking were her only defense from his evil spells of meanness, rage and repulsive desires. However, he wasn't as stupid as he looked and she wasn't always prepared for his surprisingly cunning ways. Suvi told her once that they were merely puppets on his manipulating strings, but Dag hoped she'd have more power over Vidar's authority than a toy dummy at the mercy of someone's controlling hands.

Much of the time now Dag lived in the memories of the family she'd seen at the lake, often pretending the red-haired girl's kind and gentle father was her own. She'd seen other men come to buy potatoes, but usually saw them at a distance. One other man that influenced her was The Finn.

Dag and Suvi were not allowed to go outside when The Finn's wagon was there, but that didn't prevent them from peeking through the windows when no one was watching. One time the men had their backs toward the kitchen as they squatted down to inspect a wheel on the peddler's wagon. The Finn had parked very close to the front door that day so that Dag and her mother had a very good view of items piled in the rear of the wagon. Suvi pointed out to her daughter various kitchen items, bolts of colorful cloth, a pile of books and a box of children's toys. When The Finn suddenly stood up and looked toward the window, he saw their faces pressed against the glass. When Suvi saw his fleeting smile she quickly pulled her daughter back into the shadows.

They all wore a sorry array of cast-off clothes, mostly old shirts and pants that The Finn had received in trade from some poor farmer on his route. He in turn exchanged a quantity of these hand-me-downs along with other necessities for an equal amount of potatoes. On that particular day, after The Finn had driven away, Vidar came in for a drink of water and threw an armful of old clothes and rags on the kitchen table before returning to the fields. Hidden beneath a worn homespun table cloth Dag found several used story books, a pencil and several sheets of yellowed paper.

From then on The Finn always remembered Dag in some small way and every time she watched his little covered wagon bumping back along the dirt path she'd think how things might be different if she and her mother could someday hide in his wagon and ride far away from there.

For years they labored in the potato fields from morning until night. When the plowing and planting was done in one field, they moved on to begin all over again in the next one. Weeds grew quickly in the long daylight hours of summer. Pulling them was a backbreaking and endless job. Vidar, believing that potatoes did better in new ground, spent the days cutting down more trees and preparing additional fields for cultivation.

When he heard about a novel idea of crop rotation, he planted last year's potato fields to grass, which was sometimes harvested and other times turned under to fertilize the soil for next year's potato crop. At first this was good news to the ears of Dag and her mother, but harvesting large fields of hay proved difficult. They were given sickles and scythes, but weren't strong enough to wield the heavy blades to mow the tall hay in one fast sweep as Vidar showed them. His rows were cut short and neat. Theirs were uneven and choppy, to say the least. They did their best, but it was never good enough and they heard about their failures every night.

Although most of the potato crop was sold in the village, an occasional wagon sometimes appeared in the farmyard. Vidar was working deep in the forest one day when a man drove in with his wife and children asking to buy potatoes. Dag helped Suvi fill two large sacks, which they carried back to the wagon. At first Dag was excited to see another family, but these folks were different from those at the lake.

The mother sat stiffly beside her husband, looking down with a stern face as if Dag were some wild animal that might go away if she didn't speak or move. Then two yellow-haired boys peeked around the back of the wagon giggling, pointing to Dag and calling her 'the strange one.' It was obvious they were making fun of her and she ran back to the kitchen.

"What is strange?" Dag asked her mother later.

"What do you mean?"

"Those boys in the wagon...they laughed at me, saying 'the strange one.'"

Suvi considered this for a while, probing her mind for the

right answer before responding.

"To me, the word strange means unknown," she told Dag at last. "Those boys have never seen you before, so you are unknown to them...just as they are unknown to us."

"So, they are strange, too?"

"Yes," replied Suvi. "Because we don't know each other we are all strangers."

Dag was young enough at the time to completely accept her mother's explanation.

Ingrid

Autumn passed, as did the long winter, and there was no mention again about 'the strange one,' except in the back of Eva's mind when she thought about the boy at the potato farm. Spring arrived and the Gunderson cottage slowly came to life again.

From the barn window early one morning Eva caught a glimpse of her sister darting into the forest. After at least three hours Ingrid returned, sitting on the porch as if she'd been there the whole time. Eva knew better and curiosity got the best of her.

"Where did you go today?"

"Oh, just for a walk in the woods," replied Ingrid, trying to subdue a widening smirk that wouldn't go away.

"For three hours?"

Ingrid looked around, not knowing what to say, and Eva didn't press her to answer. But when her sister was gone even longer the next morning, she did.

"Did you get lost in the woods again?"

"Mind your own business and leave me alone," warned Ingrid, stomping out of the room.

Eva was suspicious and told her mother, who at first thought nothing of it. Remembering her times on the bluffs, Karin told Eva that sometimes girls just need to be by themselves for a while. However, it wasn't long before the few hours lengthened to half days, and there were many times when Ingrid didn't return home until suppertime.

Eva followed Ingrid one day, staying just inside the woods and watching her walk down the gravel road when a wagon approached. A man helped her in and they rode in the direction of the village.

When Eva told her parents about this, they were very concerned. But it was more than that. What Eva witnessed that day was the closest thing to an argument she had ever heard between them. Her father blamed her mother for Ingrid's bad behavior. Her mother said the fault belonged to him.

"She's just like you were when you were a boy and ran off in the woods to draw...and then to make matters worse, you went away to Stockholm for eight years, so don't be telling me it's my fault that Ingrid has the wanderlust."

Gustav sat across from her, bewildered, silently gazing out the window.

"But we haven't done anything to cause her to run away," he said sadly after a while. Karin, regretting what she had said, came over to him and put her hand lovingly on his shoulder. "I shouldn't have said that, Gustav. I know how things were between you and your father. You are the gentlest and kindest man in the world and Ingrid's running away has nothing to do with your past or mine."

She kissed him on the cheek, disappeared into the kitchen and came back with coffee and a lunch tray. Eva nibbled on an apple as her father sat glumly holding his cup until the coffee turned cold. Gustav did blame himself, obsessed with the inadequacy he felt in not being able to control his elder daughter, and his wife saw his dismay.

"Everyone has problems in their lives," she stated abstractly as she stared out the window. "Life is like a garden. Troubles are like weeds. Though small at first, they can eventually shade and overpower the delicate flowers." Karin wasn't speaking to anyone in particular, more for her own benefit perhaps, to soothe her own mind. "It is best to work a little every day cultivating harmony, weeding out obstacles when they are small enough to be eliminated quickly and easily." Then she sighed thoughtfully. "Ingrid's running away is partially my fault. I should have stopped her before things got this far."

Eva listened attentively, feeling the pain of both her parents, the room suddenly crowded with everyone's unspoken thoughts. Perhaps she was at fault, too. In her mind she saw a garden. Ingrid was an overpowering weed while Eva and her parents were wilting flowers huddled beneath her.

Later that afternoon Otto Kronberg drove into the yard with a sullen Ingrid sitting in the buggy beside him. He took her arm and led the way to the sitting room.

"While driving through the village an unfamiliar wagon passed me and I noticed Ingrid hiding among the many boxes of strawberries."

That would account for her overly red lips, Eva thought, waiting eagerly for what might come next.

"I scolded her for riding with a stranger and put her in my buggy. She finally admitted to me that she would rather live in the village."

Otto saw his friend's shoulders droop, dejection written over his face as he stared at the woven rag rug at his feet. Karin glared at Ingrid, who stood tight-lipped, looking aimlessly about the room, avoiding her mother's eyes. The silent air grew heavy around them until Otto loudly cleared his throat.

"I was thinking," he said, scratching his head, "that Ingrid might stay with us for a while. There are many opportunities in the village and only a short walk to the school. We would be happy to have her and we could, well, keep a better eye on things."

Karin spun around and scowled indignantly at Otto.

"So, you think we cannot look after our Ingrid?" she shouted, her face turning crimson.

"No, Karin, I don't think that at all," said Otto apologetically. "I thought if she were closer to the school she wouldn't feel so...isolated."

"Isolated?" she repeated loudly, turning now to face Ingrid. "Did you tell Mr. Kronberg that you feel isolated living here with your Papa and Mama?"

Ingrid glanced at her mother and then back to Mr. Kronberg's stern face, then slowly nodded in agreement. Karin took a deep breath and addressed her husband directly. "Come with me and help with refreshments."

Gustav thought it odd that she should ask him to help with woman's work and looked at each of his daughters, neither of whom was moving an inch. Karin, he noticed, was standing, hands on hips, glaring at him. "Are you coming, Gustav?"

Then he got up and followed his wife obediently into the kitchen.

Otto listened to the clatter of metal and china and the sound of muffled voices from the next room. It was clear to him that Karin and Gustav were discussing his proposal and he sat nervously with his head in his hands, having second thoughts about the wisdom of suggesting such an outlandish idea. Eva picked up her knitting, but Ingrid stood by the window gazing toward the path to the gravel road.

Finally Karin returned with the coffee tray and informed Otto that they had agreed to accept his offer. Ingrid never moved a muscle and continued to stare out the window. Eva couldn't tell if she was pleased or not, but she was thinking that if Ingrid lived with the Kronbergs there would be no more arguments or teasing and that she would have a bedroom all to herself. She thought again about Ingrid as a stubborn weed. At that moment Eva made the decision to be the tallest, strongest and most beautiful flower in the Gunderson garden.

It was arranged that Ingrid would stay with the Kronbergs during the week and return home on weekends. Since traveling was much faster in Otto's horse-drawn buggy, he usually brought Ingrid home on Friday and picked her up on Sunday afternoon, but there were times when Otto was detained in Stockholm on Fridays and Gustav was more than happy to make the long trip by oxcart to pick up his first-born daughter, who he dearly missed and felt the guilt of her absence. Eva and Karin often went along, too, but it was a slow, bumpy ride in the oxcart.

Village life appeared to mature Ingrid, but not in a good way. She often arrived home on Fridays with an air of stubbornness and indifference. She was bossier than before, constantly blaming Eva when things didn't go her way. Karin and Gustav tried to make the weekend visits happy occasions, but Ingrid was still expected to help around the house. Mostly she neglected her chores and was downright disagreeable to everyone, pouting and saying naughty words under her breath.

Eva remembered years ago when Ingrid talked back to her mother and the loud screaming moments later when her mouth was washed clean with lye soap. Eva had never been punished that way, but she found great satisfaction knowing that Ingrid had. One time she put her tongue on a piece of that bitter cake and could only imagine how awful it was to have a whole mouthful of soapy suds. When Ingrid grew taller than her mother that type of punishment was promptly ignored. Instead, Ingrid was sent to her room until she was ready to apologize.

Very little snow fell the following December so Ingrid was able to come home every weekend, including the Christmas holidays. Much to the surprise of everyone, she cheerfully took part in the cookie baking, trimming of the tree and other family traditions. Karin prepared an abundant smorgasbord of various meats, vegetable dishes and a delicious assortment of holiday desserts. There were more gifts under the tree that year than ever before, including Karin's knitted sweaters and hats as well as colorful knit scarves that Eva had made. There were also fancy wrapped presents Gustav had splurged on during his trips to the village that previous fall. For the Gundersons it was the most lavish and merry Christmas any could remember.

Two days after Christmas Gustav brought Ingrid back to the Kronbergs. The New Year brought a wild blizzard that dropped five feet of snow in three cold, blustery days. They didn't see Ingrid again until springtime, after the snow melted and the mud had dried on the path to the road.

One beautiful Friday in late May Mr. Kronberg brought Ingrid home to spend another weekend at the cottage. Ingrid informed her parents she must read a book for school, so she was left alone much of the time to finish it. But whenever Eva peeked into their bedroom, her sister sat with the open book in her hands staring out the window as if she were in some far-away place. Other than that, Ingrid quietly did whatever was asked of her and treated everyone with respect.

Karin and Gustav marveled at the great change in their eldest daughter. The ride back to the Kronbergs was pleasant and uneventful. Ingrid's goodbye hugs were much tighter and longer than usual that day, which seemed a good sign to her parents that their decision to let her go to the village school had been a good one. They looked forward to having her home for summer vacation in about two weeks.

Ingeborg found a note on Ingrid's bed one morning. In it, Ingrid thanked the Kronbergs for their kindness during the year. She knew they were busy and said that a friend would bring her home. Ingrid's bed was neatly made and all her belongings were gone.

Early summer was a busy time on the Kronberg farm, and if Otto hadn't been stuck in the field with a broken plow, he might have been more suspicious about Ingrid going home with someone else. Instead, he was thankful for the opportunity to repair his machinery and get on with the spring plowing.

So the Kronbergs were surprised when Gustav stopped by on his way to the village inquiring about Ingrid. Otto showed him the note she had written and then he and Gustav drove to the village to look for her.

Events could have been worse, but they were bad enough. Gustav learned that Ingrid and her boyfriend, Olle, had gone to Gothenburg a week earlier to board a ship to America. Gustav was grief-stricken. There was little he could do but send a message to the ship and hope for an answer. Ingrid and Olle were indeed on the ship, which was then more than half way across the Atlantic Ocean. There was nothing more Gustav could do.

Karin and Gustav were crestfallen. Sadness followed their every step that long summer, holding them hostage as with a ball and chain. Karin wandered from room to room, eventually finding solace in her knitting while Gustav was a prisoner in his chair, useless and devoid of creativity.

No longer did Eva have to live in the shadow of her sister's demeaning influence and criticism. Ingrid had been the obnoxious weed that overpowered the flowering Eva. The sudden removal of that weed caused Eva to blossom, hoping to spread joy throughout this saddened house. But trying to be that cheerful, inspiring flower wasn't an easy job.

She spent her time trying to encourage her father and helping her mother with cooking and housework, learning quickly how to brew good coffee, bake bread and make nutritious meals. She mastered the family's favorite almond cake, a dessert that none of them could resist eating, even in these sad times.

Eva understood her parent's sorrow, although hers was of a different sort. She sometimes suffered from the guilt of not feeling any sadness at all that her sister had run away. It wasn't as if Ingrid had died; all she had done was run away with a boy from the village. Ingrid was fifteen now...old enough to take care of herself...and she was going to America, the most exciting place in all the world. Eva was both happy and a little envious of her sister.

Karin now viewed the village as an evil place, and even though Eva was ten years old, Karin did not allow her to attend the village school. When Otto stopped in to visit, which he often did now, he brought educational books from his extensive home library for Eva to read. She enjoyed geography, especially the parts pertaining to America, but her favorite book was one titled

Learning English in Six Weeks.

As time passed Karin and Gustav became frustrated with Otto spending much time talking to Eva in English, a language that neither of them understood. Eva delighted in Mr. Kronberg's undivided attention, while her mother took up her knitting and her father often fell asleep from boredom.

Four Years Later

Karin hadn't been sick. She just went to sleep one August night and didn't wake up. Since Ingrid ran away she had lost weight and much of her effervescent cheerfulness, but so had Gustav. Karin's sudden death was a grievous shock to both Gustav and Eva. Gustav, especially, could not accept the fact that his wife had died. Even though Karin was eight years older than her husband, she had been too young to leave him. It wasn't fair, he thought…not for him, nor for Eva.

For weeks Gustav would not allow Eva to put clean sheets on his bed, as if scouring the old ones would wash away every last vestige of his wife. He clung to every last piece of evidence of her. Karin's brush and comb remained on the bureau just as she'd left them, and an unfinished sweater still set on the table next to her favorite chair, as if she might suddenly appear and wish to take up her knitting again. He stayed in bed late in the morning gazing longingly at his memorable painting of her on the bluffs, picked at his food at mealtimes and sat in his chair afternoons napping or staring blankly out of the window.

Eva encouraged her father to paint or go for a walk, but his contentment came only from living in the past and talking about the old times. She was glad she'd learned how to cook and bake and had paid attention to how her mother carried out the household chores. Keeping house gave her an incentive for getting up in the morning and doing outside work gave her solace, especially spending time in the barn with Stella.

Eva was milking Stella one morning when her father appeared in the open doorway saying he must bring the cow to be bred before cold weather. He asked if she would accompany him. Eva was surprised because never before had she been allowed to go to the potato farm. She supposed her father didn't wish to leave her alone, although she felt quite grown up at the age of fourteen.

Although apprehensive about seeing Vidar, she was curious to see this ugly giant they sometimes called Potatohead, and she was excited about walking through the forest and seeing the lake again. Most of all she hoped to get a glimpse of the boy who lived there and possibly learning the truth about 'the strange one.'"

Eva carried a basket of bread, cheese and two apples in one hand and a small birch branch in the other, occasionally tapping Stella gently on the rump to make her walk faster. Stella tended to dawdle, looking around now and then as if to make certain Eva was still behind her. A raven circled overhead and fluttered to the top of a tall pine, jumping down from bough to bough to study them.

"Look, Papa. It's the old raven."

Her father already knew he was there. "He's been following us ever since we left the cottage. Didn't you hear him?"

"Yes, I hear ravens all the time. Do you think he is keeping an eye on us?" Eva asked, and Gustav responded the way a father should.

"Of course. He will warn us of any trouble."

They stopped at the lake and ate half of the bread and cheese. Eva cast an eye around for the girl in the pink dress, but saw only a few fish jumping out of the water. She wanted to ask her father about 'the strange one,' but bringing that up might spoil a perfectly nice day, so she put the thought aside and threw out a crust for the raven. He fluttered down from the tree, cocked his head, and walked in a circle around the bread. Thinking the crust might be a trap, he carefully scrutinized his prize; then quickly ran in to grab it and jumped back a few paces before flying to safety to enjoy his feast. He returned within minutes and did the same thing.

"He seems to like you, Papa."

"Ya, he's a good boy," said Gustav, talking to the raven more than to his daughter while holding out a small piece of cheese in his hand. The raven cautiously walked up to him, slowly reached forward and took the cheese as if they were old friends, which they were.

He was the offspring of a young raven Gustav had found many years ago on the woodland path, flopping on the ground with an injured wing. His mother had defiantly protected her baby by standing tall and ruffled, fluttering her broad wings and flying up into Gustav's face to scare him off. He left the two in the path, not wishing to further enrage the parent, returning later to find the young one alone and lying very still. Gustav carefully picked him up and brought him home.

He encouraged the raven to drink and left tiny scraps of moose meat in the special cage he made. In the morning not a morsel was left and the raven was standing with his beak through the chicken wire looking for more. One day Gustav opened the cage door and soon the raven was strutting around the room pecking noisily against the windows until finally Gustav let him go outside. His injured wing kept him from flying away and Gustav continued feeding him leftover food every day. The raven's eyes were always on his rescuer. He followed Gustav about the farm and often perched on his shoulder.

Eva had never heard a raven talk, but her father said he taught that old raven to say "good morning," "please," and "thank you," and there were other words the raven picked up on his own that sounded much like "come down here," "where the devil are you?" and "what a mess you make."

That was long ago, before Eva was born. Her father said that one spring after his wing was healed the raven flew off into the forest and later returned with his mate and two young ones. It wasn't long before all four of them would eat out of Gustav's hand. Each year members of the family came back to visit the place where the kind man made sure they had something to eat, but through the years their numbers had dwindled. This year only this one dared to eat out of Gustav's hand, his timid mate staying at a safe distance away, watching.

Gustav stood up, put his hand in his pocket and searched through his coins while the raven tipped his head back and forth waiting. Finally he tossed a piece of shiny metal on the sand and the raven was on top of it in a second, pecking at it, jumping back and forth excitedly, curiously eying the bright object. Finally he grabbed it and flew away.

"He won't eat that, will he?" Eva asked.

"Many birds like shiny objects, especially crows and ravens," he said. "No doubt he'll bring the glittering jewel back to his nest, a special gift to please his mate."

He told her that many animal species bring trophies home to their mates, just as people like to buy pretty things for their loved ones. He was smiling. She was pleased to see him acting more like his old self today. Gustav rubbed Stella's ears affectionately and started up the path to the potato farm.

Eva followed behind thinking about what her father said and how she'd also grown to love the ravens. At first she thought they were a nuisance... pesky, large black birds that weren't especially pretty from a distance. But when they came closer and the sun caught their dull black feathers in just the right light, they become a rainbow of shimmering highlights, as if wearing a festive sequined coat of many colors.

She learned that they were the smartest of all birds, crafty and full of tricks, especially when showing off with their comical upside-down flights and somersaults. Their clever mimicking calls were often a warning to other ravens, and to humans as well, that a stray animal might be lurking in the woods.

Eva remembered her father telling about the great god, Odin, and his two beloved ravens, Hugin, the thinker, and Munin, the one who remembers. Early each morning, Odin, the mythical god of prophecy and war, sent his two feathered companions out into the world to observe the great happenings of the day. It was the ravens' keen perception and wise counsel that made the old Norse god such a powerful force.

Eva remembered that day at the Kronberg house when she looked down at objects below from the upstairs window. Sometimes she envisioned herself as a raven and how it might feel to soar at panoramic heights; to journey on a bright summer's day across the deep blue Swedish sky looking down at the great expanse of green forest and vast tundra; to follow the migrating reindeer and the swift-flowing rivers. Would America look the same as Sweden from those heights? She thought about all this while following Stella along the narrow, winding path.

As they walked along the forest floor, the air, scented with sweet moss mixed with pine and spruce, felt cool on her arms and legs and her nose was icy cold. It seemed darker here, too, north of the lake; the tall pines towered high above her, letting through little light. Tiny specks of blue sky peeked through the tops like stars in the night. Every so often, her father's reassuring voice trailed back asking if she was still there, and she would answer a bit breathlessly that she was.

Finally the big trees thinned out to groves of birches and poplar, the bright sun warm against her skin. Before they reached the edge of the forest her father stopped, telling her to be quiet and stay hidden in the safety of the trees until he returned. From there Eva observed a barren field, in the middle of which a man and a boy were prying out a good-sized, stubborn rock. When a metal bar slipped from the boy's grasp, the rock rolled back into the hole. Eva heard the man swearing. Then he hit the boy on the side of the head, knocking him to the ground.

The man looked up to see Gustav and Stella crossing the field. He raised his hand briefly in acknowledgment, before leading the way toward a group of small gray buildings. He was much taller and more broad-shouldered than her father and he walked with a slouch. From where Eva stood in the shadow of the birches, the man's facial features blurred into a large brown mass shadowed by his wide-brimmed leather hat. She stiffened at the thought that this was indeed the one called Potatohead, and little by little, slid her back down the big birch until she was sitting on the ground.

Vidar plodded across the uneven ground, his long strides widening the gap between Gustav and Stella, whose pace had slowed without Eva's prodding. She watched Stella stop to look at the boy, who was now making his way toward the woods. Afraid to move, Eva pretended to be asleep, although she could still see him through almost-closed eyes.

The boy stopped about thirty feet away near a stone wall, staring in her direction. He wore a cap, dirty brown trousers and a stained shirt that hung loosely on his slight frame. The cap was much too large, shadowing part of his face, but something about him reminded Eva of the girl in the pink dress. She was too bashful to speak and shyness finally caused him to walk away, his bare feet kicking up little puffs of loose dirt as he shuffled across the field. For a while she watched him pick up small rocks and stones, adding them to other piles scattered about the field. After a while dark clouds moved in from the north and thunder rumbled in the distance.

Finally she spotted her father making his way back with Stella. He walked swiftly over the uneven ground with Stella having to trot behind him, her udder swinging from side to side and two heavy sacks of potatoes bouncing from her shoulders. Eva's mouth watered for the taste of a freshly baked potato smothered with butter.

Gustav glanced at Eva, beckoning her to follow and she hurried to take her place behind the cow. This wasn't a good time to ask about the boy she had seen in the field, so she decided to wait until they stopped at the lake.

Once there, her father walked to the water's edge to let Stella drink. The sky was overcast and a fine mist blew in from the lake. Eva briskly rubbed her arms as her father squatted down to scoop up water in his hands to drink. She was thirsty, too, but today the water looked uninviting; it was dark and gray, not the usual beautiful deep blue. Eva smiled to herself remembering the first time she'd seen the lake this same gray color.

"Where did the blue water go?" she had asked her mother.

"It didn't go anywhere, her mother had told her. "This is the same water as always." Then she realized that her daughter had probably never been here on a cloudy day before.

"You see, Eva, the water mirrors the sky. When the sky is blue, the water reflects its blue color, but now it is cloudy causing the water to look dull and steely gray."

Even so, the water tasted different, and she drank only enough to quench her thirst before joining her father to finish the bread and cheese. She gave him an apple and he leaned back against a tall pine tree, slowly relishing its sweet juicy taste while Stella grazed on some weeds. Questions simmered in Eva's mind and finally words came bubbling out of her mouth.

"That boy in the field... is he the son of Potatohead?"

"I would guess he might be," said her father.

"Does he have a sister?"

Gustav paused, looking across the lake as if the mountains might give him an answer, but he did not reply.

"That girl...the one in the pink dress..." Eva stopped talking because her father immediately threw half his apple into the bushes and grabbed Stella's halter.

"It's getting late. We must go home now," he mumbled, not looking at Eva as he led Stella into the woods. Eva knew her father was upset. Food was too precious to waste and it was not like him to throw away half of a good apple, especially one from his favorite tree. She ran to catch up, tripping on roots and uneven ground in the darkened path. It was a long, silent walk home.

Tomtes in the Kitchen

When Dag first saw the man with the cow, she'd noticed something red in the woods behind them...a fox maybe. When she looked again, the metal bar slipped out of her hands and the big rock fell back into the hole.

Afterwards she felt stunned by Vidar's blow and hoped the man with the cow hadn't noticed. Even so, she felt humiliated watching them walk across the field. Then the fox caught her eye again, but it wasn't a fox after all. Sitting against a big birch was that same red-haired girl she had seen at the lake many years ago!

Excitedly she walked toward the woods, but stopped because the girl was asleep. Observing the girl's clean white blouse and skirt, Dag looked down at her own filthy, boyish clothes, then slowly turned around and went back to pick up more rocks. At the time she was glad the girl had been sleeping and hadn't seen her standing there like some outlandish idiot, too timid to say a word.

Later, after thinking about words she might have said, she wished that the girl had seen her, that they had spoken and gotten to know each other. Why was it always easier to look back and see what might have been? That was a question she asked herself much too often.

One September morning Dag was late getting up, her back and arms aching from the many bushels of potatoes she'd dug and helped load on the wagon the day before. She heard Blix snorting in the yard. By the time she got dressed and looked out the kitchen window, there was only a thick cloud of dust rising where the path turned toward the main road.

"He's in a hurry to get somewhere," Dag reported to her mother, who was standing by the stove stirring the morning porridge.

"To the village again," replied Suvi with a slight smile. Vidar would be gone at least until suppertime and Dag knew what her mother was thinking; they would have the farm all to themselves today.

Three days earlier Vidar had brought potatoes to the village, returning home near dusk with a wagonload of lumber. All the next day Dag and Suvi had heard sounds of the saw and hammer from behind the potato shed. He told them nothing and they did not ask, so they could only guess what he was up to. "Arguments come from asking foolish questions. Patience will reveal what we need to know," Suvi had told her daughter that day.

"Perhaps after breakfast we can go down to the shed and see what he's been doing," Suvi suggested to her daughter. However, Dag's curiosity was now elevated to a point where she could barely stand it.

"Can't we look now and eat later?"

Like two excited children, they dashed out the door and crossed the dooryard, avoiding piles of sawdust and scattered pieces of scrap lumber before looking up to see two long sides of a fine new addition to the old potato shed. Standing at the wide-open end they felt dwarfed by its large size. Already Suvi had seen enough.

"I'm afraid this means more work for us in the fields next year," she said dejectedly and Dag agreed it would take a lot of potatoes to fill the huge space. They carried their heavy thoughts back to the kitchen and ate their porridge in silence.

By afternoon they had both done a lot of thinking and each came up with the idea of leaving the place. They would have to plan carefully to make their escape, but with winter approaching, Suvi decided to wait until spring.

When the sun dropped behind the forest and Vidar still had not returned, Suvi left a cold plate of sliced moose meat, bread and cheese on the table and went to bed. In the dark of night she heard noises and saw the flickering light of a candle in the kitchen. Thinking that Vidar was probably eating the food she left out for him, Suvi rolled over to face the wall, still continuing to hear strange noises coming from the kitchen. Finally the outside door slammed shut and the hut was quiet again.

The next morning Dag heard a commotion in the kitchen and heard her mother's frustrated voice. It wasn't unusual for Vidar to be angry in the morning, so Dag remained in her room. When she didn't hear Vidar's voice, she peeked into the kitchen. Her mother was alone, searching frantically through the old wooden cabinets.

"Are you talking to yourself again?" asked Dag. The stove wasn't lit and the room felt cold, yet her mother's face was moist with sweat.

"I can't find the cheese, nor the bread I baked yesterday." Then she pointed to the stove. "And where's the coffee pot? Even the coffee beans are gone."

Dag tried to calm her mother and helped search through every cabinet, shelf, nook and cranny, but still they came up with nothing. "Where is Vidar?" asked Dag.

"I haven't seen him since yesterday morning," said her mother in a state of anguish. "What if he comes in and there is no hot coffee waiting on the stove?"

Dag couldn't bear to think of that happening, but neither could she listen to the panic in her mother's voice. Her mind naturally went to a different place and she tried to think of something amusing to say.

"Well, maybe we had a visit from the tomte," she suggested playfully. This was enough to bring her mother back to her senses and she sat down at the table. Dag had always believed in tomtes and hoped they watched over their farm, but she'd never seen one. Tomtes were usually kind and helpful, but they were also known to do mischief in barns and houses, especially when they didn't approve of the way things were being done.

"I would think they'd be playing tricks out in the shed on Vidar and not be bothering us in the kitchen," said Dag.

"That's why I try to stay on the good side of them and put a bowl of sweetened porridge on the front step every Christmas Eve," said her mother.

Dag knew it was a good sign when the porridge was gone, but on most Christmas mornings it had not been touched, except for the very cold air that had frozen it solid. Even so, the porridge never went to waste. Usually the frozen mess was warmed on the stove and given to Blix for a special treat.

"Have you ever seen a tomte?" Dag asked.

"They can't be seen," her mother replied, "but you can tell if they have been around. Something will be out of place or perhaps missing altogether." Thinking about the missing coffee pot and food made Dag hopeful that perhaps a tomte did come to visit, but if tomtes couldn't be seen, how was it known that they were dwarfish old men dressed like farmers? Someone must have seen one once because in a picture she had seen, the tomte wore a pointed red hat, green jacket, boots and had a long white beard, so it would seem they'd be easy to spot.

"There's smoke rising from the shed chimney," shouted Suvi. Dag saw her mother's face relax into a smile of revelation.

"It was Vidar who took them!" she said. Then she began to laugh hysterically.

"What's so funny?" asked Dag.

"I was just imagining Vidar trying to prepare his own breakfast."

"So, you think he took the food and the coffee pot?"

"I'm sure of it," said Suvi with a sigh of relief. "I remember hearing him in the kitchen last night and the outside door slamming shut afterwards. Vidar never came back to bed."

"But why would he do that when he can be waited on here?"

"I have no idea why he does what he does," said Suvi, giving her daughter a hug. All of a sudden they were both very hungry.

New Ideas

Mr. Kronberg came to visit more often now and his visits were a cheerful diversion for both Eva and her father. One day the conversation turned to new inventions, and Mr. Kronberg showed them photographs and brochures about automobiles being mass-produced in America.

"The Swedish nobility in the south have been buying automobiles as fast as they can be unloaded off the ships," he told them enthusiastically. "I'm actually thinking of buying one myself, perhaps next summer."

Gustav's head snapped around, his eyes grew big and his jaw dropped in astonishment. Eva had seen that expression once before… a look that said, 'and what would you want a crazy thing like that for?' Her thoughts went back to a day years ago when they all went to the village.

It was Ingrid's birthday and she'd wanted to pick out something special in one of the clothing stores. As usual she was very insistent, eventually making her father feel so guilty that he had to give in to her.

With Slofock in the lead and Gustav sitting high on the wooden seat prodding him along, Karin, Ingrid and Eva sat in the cart, made more comfortable by a thick layer of fresh hay. It was a long, hot ride and they stopped half way to eat a small lunch and give the tired ox a rest. Ingrid wolfed her bread and cheese down instantly, then complained all the while the others were eating that they'd never get to the village in time to buy her present.

"Slofock needs time to rest and eat, too," Gustav reminded his eldest daughter as she sat impatiently with a long brooding face. When he finally stood up, Ingrid ran to the cart and hopped in, but Gustav had other plans. Eva went with him as he led the ox through the woods to a little stream. Slofock sniffed the air enjoyably, arching his neck and moving his head back and forth as if acquainting himself with these new surroundings. Then he stepped gingerly into the cold water. After several moments of pleasurable deliberation he finally proceeded to drink.

"It will take a while for him to get filled up," said her father, as he sat on a rock nearby and filled his pipe. Eva smiled to herself thinking how those two completely understood each other.

"You love Slofock just as much as I love Stella, don't you, Papa?"

"That I do. We've plowed many gardens and lugged countless logs out of the forest to keep the cottage warm in winter, besides taking us wherever we wanted to go."

The old ox was a thoughtful dawdler, just like her father, and it was a while before he finished drinking and started nibbling on some grass. Needless to say, Ingrid was in an extremely sour mood when they finally returned. She pouted all the way to the village.

One sight of the old church steeple and Ingrid was a different girl. She stood up excitedly looking first to the right, then to the left and finally pointed to the dressmaker's shop. Eva could see the anticipation sparking through her sister's body, from her tippy-toes to her bobbing head as she yelled for her father to stop.

"I want that red bathing suit in the window!" she shouted. The skimpy red piece of material hung next to a beach display with several more subdued and modest suits. That's when her astonished father's head swiveled around in shock, with the same look on his face as when Otto Kronberg said he might buy an automobile.

Parental opinion concerning that particular red bathing suit was a unanimous 'no,' and Karin recommended a more modest blue one hanging beside it. Ingrid grudgingly agreed and they went into the store, but once inside she would consider no other suit but the red one.

"That's enough!" said her mother. "There's no reason why you can't wear the same bathing suit you had last year." Ingrid was furious. So as not to create a scene, her mother took firm hold of her ear and marched her protesting daughter back out to the cart.

No one sympathized with Ingrid's obstinence, and not one of her big tears was enough to prevent her father from urging Slofock to a more appropriate store. Once there, she would not budge from the cart. In order that the trip wasn't a total loss, Karin and Eva went into the store and picked out a lovely doll with a red outfit and had it wrapped in brown paper.

Karin placed the bundle in Ingrid's lap and Gustav waited for her to open it, but she just sat there with a long face and wouldn't look at her present. Ingrid never spoke a word all the way home, went directly to bed and never came to the supper table.

Eva was very hungry and knew Ingrid must have been, too,

but she knew how pigheaded her sister was when she didn't get her way. It wasn't until after Ingrid ran away to America that Eva discovered the same doll hidden in the closet behind a box of their outgrown clothes. The doll was more beautiful than Eva had remembered. She placed it on top of the pillow on Ingrid's empty side of the bed.

It had been Karin's suggestion years ago that Gustav build a special room with a southern exposure; a place to better capture the sun's light on those early spring and late fall days when it was too cold for him to paint outside. A window from the kitchen looked out on this spacious, sunny room. Three walls were mostly of glass, so it was almost like being outdoors. Karin had taken much pleasure observing her husband as he painted, watching his brush deftly dance across the canvas, leaving splashes of color here and there until a familiar form took shape.

She'd be working in the kitchen sometimes with one eye out the window and see him straighten his back, inspect his work, then turn to see if she was there and they'd exchange a loving smile. Eva remembered hearing their voices flowing through the open window as her mother prepared meals or washed dishes.

It had also been a fun place to play on rainy days or to watch the first large snowflakes fall in early winter before the weather turned too cold. Eva remembered very clearly her father sitting out there, seeing his breath in the frosty air as he worked in two pairs of pants, an extra sweater and his favorite blue woolen cap pulled down over his ears as he tried to finish a painting during the few hours of sunlight peeking through the trees.

After his wife's death, Gustav avoided going into the sunroom for a long time. It wasn't the same without Karin's smiling face in the window. Many things were overlooked or put off that autumn, including the paying of important bills. When Otto dropped in and told Gustav that the taxes on the cottage were overdue, Gustav confessed that he was short of money and had no idea how he might pay the bill. For a while the two men sat quietly in the front room enjoying their pipes, but Otto was busy formulating a plan.

"In my travels lately, I've been spending much time in the art galleries of Stockholm and Gothenburg. Some say I have a fine, critical eye and many of my wealthy contacts have asked me to purchase paintings for them." Gustav looked at Otto skeptically, suspicious about his friend's motives.

"So, are you saying you think I should sell some of my paintings to pay the taxes?"

"And why not?" asked Otto, grinning. "Do you intend to forever hide your masterpieces here where no one else will ever see them?"

Eventually they went into the sunroom. Eva watched through the kitchen window as Mr. Kronberg sorted through some of the finished canvasses while her father stood aimlessly looking around the room. The thought that someone else might enjoy her father's paintings pleased her and the possibility of having money to pay the taxes was even better. However, knowing the paintings were like children to him, parting with any one of them would be difficult.

Finally there were only two paintings that her father would agree to sell, but Mr. Kronberg was very insistent on a third one, a sweet country scene of Eva and Stella under the white birches. In the painting she appeared in profile, a daisy headpiece encircling her braided red hair, reading a book as she leaned against a dozing Stella.

This was Eva's favorite, too, and she remembered so well that very day; picking daisies along the edge of the forest when Stella, following too closely as usual, suddenly grabbed her bouquet for an easy lunch. Eva continued to pick another large handful, then sat in the shade of the birches to weave the stems together. Stella nibbled on some clumps of grass and then with a great sigh, lay down behind her, watching as she finished the circle of daisies.

When she placed the flowered coronet on her head and leaned back against Stella's soft shoulder she saw her father sketching them from the porch. He held up his hand, signaling for her to remain there. Then he brought out a book for her to read while he finished the sketch.

After a while she felt Stella's nose poking her head, and upon hearing her father's laughter, turned to see the lovely daisy headpiece dangling from Stella's mouth. Her father was finished sketching by then and Eva went into the house, allowing Stella to enjoy her prize.

The two men discussed the fate of this painting for a long time. Her father stood with his hands on his hips in a stubborn stance, his feet apart and firmly planted on the floor, while Mr. Kronberg persistently tried to change his friend's mind. Curiosity finally prompted Eva to serve the men a small lunch...a good excuse to join them in the sun room, find out exactly what was happening and perhaps add a few convincing words of her own. Mr. Kronberg was pleased and asked her to sit down and join them.

"I was just telling your father that I've become close friends with a family who I think will pay a fine price for this painting of you and Stella, but he is undecided about selling it."

Eva glanced at her father, who pathetically looked back at her. She spoke directly to Mr. Kronberg.

"I think paintings should be enjoyed, rather than hidden away accumulating dust, but perhaps Papa needs more time to think this over," she said, pouring a round of coffee.

Her father nodded thoughtfully and helped himself to a piece of almond cake. Mr. Kronberg did the same, complimenting on what a fine baker she had turned out to be. His mind, though, was still on the business of the day.

"By selling just this one painting," he told them, "there should be enough money to pay the taxes, buy your winter supplies, and still have money left over."

Eva was stunned to hear how much the painting might be worth, as was her father, but he still wasn't ready to part with it just yet.

After three cups of coffee and as many pieces of almond cake, Mr. Kronberg gave his final pitch. "I look at things this way, when someone wants what you have, and offers more than twice as much as you think it is worth, that's the time to sell."

In the end Otto Kronberg prevailed and what he'd told them proved true; the taxes were paid, winter supplies purchased and there was still money to spare.

Vidar's Experiment

The next spring grass seed was planted in one field, but all others were left barren, except for the two small fields closest to the new shed, which were planted in potatoes. Why Vidar had worked so hard to cut trees and cultivate new fields each year, only to now leave them grown to weeds was a mystery to Suvi, as was the reason he spent most days hidden away in the new addition, often sleeping there nights as well.

Sounds of a hammer hitting metal resounded from the shed every day and their curiosity mounted with each passing hour. The door of the new addition was kept locked and the windows were too high to look through. One day when Vidar went to the village they poked a few knots out of the wooden boards and peeked inside. The room was dim except where the sun shone through and cast light on some metal scraps that reminded Suvi of the copper pots she'd used at the miners house. Since they wouldn't be harvesting so many potatoes this year, it was unlikely he'd be making more potato bins, and surely not out of copper. Everything now was very mysterious. However both mother and daughter were satisfied about these favorable changes that gave them much free time to do as they pleased.

Except for hauling potatoes to the village and bringing supplies home, Blix's days were mostly spent resting in the barn or grazing in the nearby pasture. No more was he the sad, tired nag waiting fearfully in his stall each morning, his head hanging down to his knees, dejected, bracing himself for the heavy harness and tedious days plowing and cultivating.

Blix thrived with Dag's good care, welcoming her each morning with a friendly nicker, his hooves dancing in the stall, eager for a canter down the lane. Under her mother's teaching, Dag learned how ride, always staying within the confining stone walls of the farm, though often she stopped to look down the forbidden path to the lake.

One day toward the end of summer, Vidar returned from the village with sugar and flour and other necessities, but there were many more bags of sugar piled in the wagon than was needed in the house. There were other items, too, hidden in wooden boxes. Dag watched through the kitchen window as Vidar backed the wagon to the shed door.

"If I circle around, I can hide behind the bushes near the old pine," she told her mother. "Perhaps I can find out what's hidden in the boxes."

Suvi wasn't sure this was a good idea, but curiosity changed her mind.

"Well, all right, but be careful he doesn't see you," she advised. "And don't do anything foolish, like climbing that tree!"

Climb the tree? That was all Dag could think of doing now. The old pine tree had several lower limbs spaced fairly close together, with thick boughs to conceal her from the eyes of both Vidar in the shed and her mother in the house.

It turned out to be a difficult climb to where she could look down on the potato shed roof, but in order to get a clear view of the wagon, she had to climb higher, and then crawl out on a good sized limb to see beyond the thick boughs below.

When a dead branch snapped, she grabbed the one above her with both hands and hung, suspended in the air, until finally swinging to a nearby limb. The noise made Blix look up. He side-stepped, forcing the wagon against the barn, exposing a box of clinking bottles. Dag heard Vidar's gruff voice from inside the shed swearing at Blix to keep still and she slowly inched back toward the trunk of the tree, climbed down and ran back to the kitchen to tell her mother.

"Unloading bottles of what?" exclaimed Suvi. When Dag told her the bottles were empty, memories came back to Suvi's mind of copper kettles, bags of sugar, potatoes, and empty bottles. All these blended together and Dag saw a knowing look come over her mother's face.

"You know what he's doing, don't you?" said Dag.

"I have a good idea, but I'm not certain yet. Perhaps tomorrow we will learn more if we go down to the old shed and pretend to be sorting out potatoes."

The strong odors of raw potatoes and wood smoke met them as they approached the shed. They heard loud thumping and grinding sounds coming from the other side of the wall as they sorted the potatoes.

"That smell reminds me of when they made potato liquor at the miner's house," Suvi told Dag.

"Liquor is made from potatoes?"

"Oh, yes," her mother said. "If you carefully prepare the potatoes and distill it correctly, you will have some of the best vodka in the world."

The odor of sour potatoes was much stronger the next day when they went back to the shed.

"Yes, he is definitely making potato liquor. I remember well that pungent odor," said Suvi, wrinkling up her nose.

"Pungent? What is that?" asked Dag.

"Pungent is a very sharp, overpowering smell that tickles your nostrils and makes you do this." She pinched her nose and made a funny face and Dag couldn't help but giggle. It had been a summer of many laughs.

About two weeks later they heard the clinking of glass again as Blix walked slowly by the kitchen with Vidar holding a very tight rein. A gray tarp covered the back of the wagon as they watched it move at a snail's pace along the uneven dirt path toward the village.

The next day he returned, passed out and slouched in the

wagon seat. The wagon, partially covered by the tarp, revealed many full bottles and several broken ones. Dag unhitched Blix and walked him to the barn while Suvi grabbed a full bottle of liquid to bring back to the kitchen. She was sitting at the table with a black-striped woven sack in front of her when Dag returned.

"My mistress gave me this as a parting gift," she said. Dag watched anxiously as her mother gently removed a bundle from the sack and unfolded a gray cotton cloth that revealed a luxurious satiny material of green and gold stripes with tiny pink flowers. Not even The Finn had cloth as beautiful as this, thought Dag.

"The miner's wife had her clothes specially made," explained Suvi. "I remember one of her ball gowns was made out of this very same cloth." She carefully unwrapped the satin covering, only to find a third layer of soft white cotton. The shape beneath it felt very familiar to Suvi and her eyes grew brighter with remembrance.

"Until now I'd forgotten what the miner's wife told me that last day. 'Go in peace and may you always drink from clear pure streams.' Those were her very words."

Concealed in the soft cotton was a sparkling long-stemmed goblet.

"Is this thin glass for drinking?" asked Dag, for she always drank from an old tin cup.

"This is fine crystal, Dag, not ordinary glass. Listen." Then she held up the goblet, flicking the rim with her fingernail to make the sweetest ringing sound.

"Can I do it?" said Dag eagerly.

"Be very careful," warned her mother. Dag was afraid then that the thin goblet would break and did not touch it, but she admired the etched leafy pattern encircling the rim, wishing the goblet might ring all by itself.

"Go ahead and tap it gently," encouraged her mother.

Finally she did, but the sound was dull and nothing like the beautiful sound her mother made.

"Sometimes late at night I kept the miner's wife company

and we drank together from goblets just like this one. Drinks taste better from a fancy crystal goblet…try this and you'll see what I mean."

Suvi poured fresh water in the goblet for her daughter to drink.

The water was cold and sweet and Dag had to admit it did taste much better than water from her old tin cup. She watched her mother open the bottle of potato liquor, filling the goblet half way, and then holding it up against the sunny window.

"This vodka is not as clear as it should be," she said, and then took a little sip. Then she ran to the sink and spat it out.

"Not even a crystal goblet will make this liquor drinkable!" she said, wiping the last traces of liquor from her lips and shaking her head. "Now I understand why he came home with the bottles…no one in the village would buy his liquor."

The next morning they were awakened by loud swearing and the sound of breaking glass. Glistening pieces of broken bottles were scattered on the wet ground behind the barn as Vidar, in a mad rage, hurled one after another against the stone wall. Dag was shocked when her mother intervened.

"Wait now, Vidar! Those bottles can be washed and used again." He turned as if he might throw one at her, but his rage was nearly spent and he sat down heavily on a stump. Dag did not want to be there, but her feet were glued to the ground as Vidar picked up a full bottle and removed the cap.

"No good," he said, thrusting the bottle toward her mother. Suvi pretended to take a sip, contemplating what to say that would not offend him further.

"It's…not so bad. Perhaps if you distill the liquor a second time, it will taste better."

Dag could tell that her mother was picking her words, and for once Vidar was listening. Her explanation made sense to him and he carried a crate of bottles back to the shed.

"You took a chance by speaking to him like that," Dag said later.

"Yes I did, but it was a gamble worth taking. Good vodka should bring in a lot of money and that will mean a better life for us."

Dag agreed. This had been one of their best summers yet. It was much better for Vidar to be busy in the shed and not bothering them in the house.

Twice after that Vidar came to the kitchen with a bottle for Suvi to taste and each time it was sweeter and clearer than the one before. She took other chances, too, such as suggesting he wash the potatoes and cut rotten parts away before mashing. The final run brought a smile to Suvi's lips.

"They won't refuse to buy this batch," she told him, after she'd taken a few sips and rolled the liquid in her mouth. Dag knew her mother was being truthful because after he left she didn't dump this bottle out by the steps like she had the others.

The wagon passed slowly by the kitchen the next morning. Vidar was slouched in the wooden seat, looking neither to the right nor left, the leather brim of his hat shading most of his brown face except for a slightly satisfied look about his mouth. He kept Blix walking at a snail's pace so the bottles wouldn't clink and break.

"I see the touch of a smile on his lips," said Suvi. "At that speed he won't arrive at the village until tomorrow!"

"He might be gone for days!" Dag laughed excitedly, and they both had the same idea. Suvi made a picnic lunch and mother and daughter spent a glorious day relaxing at the lake.

The Bridal Chest

For months Eva had walked past her mother's old wooden bridal chest, emotionally unable to lift its cover, the personal contents being too sacred for her eyes. Curiosity had prompted her to open it many times, but trepidation always pulled her hands away, postponing the decision for another day.

She awakened early one dark morning to a howling wind and a penetrating coldness so real that she imagined herself lying outside in the snow beneath the wavering, tall pines. When her hands felt the soft mattress and the blankets which now held little warmth, she knew she was in her own bed and that the fire in the stove had long burned down.

She immediately thought of her father and ran to his room, but he was peacefully snoring and felt warm to her touch. She nursed the faintly glowing coals with dry kindling, filled the stove with chunks of wood and curled up on the floor in front of the stove wrapped in an old quilt. Then she dreamed that her mother was sitting in the chest, beckoning her to look inside. There were no material objects in the chest, only the wonderful feelings of love, harmony, and the joy of being with her mother again. She took this dream as a sign, a good omen that today was the right time to open the chest.

She knelt before the worn pine box, her hand caressing the delicate flowers adorning its lid, lovely bell-shaped linnea blossoms that grew wild in the woodlands of Sweden. Lifting the lid released the clean, fresh scent of cedar and revealed a top layer of undergarments, an assortment of white kerchiefs and everyday aprons in colorful stripes of white, yellow, red, blue and gray. Beneath those were two, crisply ironed white aprons and head caps, and a never-worn native costume of Norrland.

Beneath the costume was a beautiful knitted afghan in soft shades of pink, green and white. Pinned to the corner was a small, folded piece of paper with the words, 'for Eva on her wedding day.' While Eva held the afghan against her face, all the suppressed memories of her mother released themselves in a wellspring of tears.

On a second, more brilliant afghan of blue, purple and yellow was a handwritten note that had been crumpled and smoothed out again.

Dear Ingrid,
Your birth opened up an exciting new world for your Papa and me and your insatiable curiosity made every day a new adventure, an instant cure for Papa's winter sadness as you rekindled his joy of sketching and painting. I knitted this afghan for you to put in your bridal chest.

Eva wondered if her mother intended to throw this note away and then thought better of it, but that was something she would never know.

Underneath several old children's books was her favorite book of all, ***Learning English in Six Weeks,*** a book she had thought was lost. She sat on the floor for a while, picking out the many words and phrases she still remembered from those special times with Mr. Kronberg when they spoke only in English.

Then a pile of envelopes tied with a red ribbon caught her eye, mostly old Christmas cards from Anna and Lars. Eva recalled sitting around the candlelit table on Christmas Eve when her father read aloud Anna's messages about their life on the Baltic Sea, where the sky came down to meet the great expanse of water and there were no mountains on the horizon.

Anna was a good storyteller and wrote in a large flowery script.

In one card she wrote of their only son, Jonas, born the same year as Ingrid, a quiet, serious boy who amused himself by playing his father's old accordion. Eva remembered how she used to think about the Bible story of Jonah being swallowed by the great whale and always pictured Jonas sitting in the belly of a whale playing the accordion.

Another card told of their move to Stockholm, where Lars had so many requests for his boats that he hired laborers to keep up with the demand. Now he was too busy designing, instructing and selling those boats and had little time to work on them himself. Anna wrote, "Lars misses the time working alone crafting something beautiful with his own two hands out of wood from specially selected trees he has cut down himself."

Eva could understand how Lars enjoyed creating beauty from wood. She felt the same way about knitting strands of colorful yarn into beautiful scarves and sweaters. In her heart she formed a close bond with her only uncle, whom she knew only through Anna's words. When Lars eventually bought a violin for Jonas, Anna couldn't write enough about her talented son, creating in Eva a similar attachment to Jonas, who created beautiful music with his hands through the bow and strings of a violin. But that was after they had moved to America.

The return address on the last envelope was torn off and Eva could make out only the letters *USA*, but inside there was mention of a place called Minnesota.

Dear Gustav and Karin,

We love it here in Minnesota, the land of 10,000 lakes, which reminds us so very much of Sweden. We are so proud of our Jonas, who excels more each year with his violin playing and performs in the great halls of Minneapolis. He plans to study music in either New York or Boston next year.

Although Lars has a great amount of money in the American banks, he is content to have only a small farm by the lake and to work leisurely on his fine hand-crafted boats and carved figures of Sweden, especially tomtes and woodland creatures that sell well in America. There is no rush here, no competition and it doesn't matter if it takes a year to complete a vessel. Lars is happy doing what he loves and because of that I am happy, too. I still appreciate the money you always sent to me at Christmas when you were away in Stockholm, so again I return the favor. Please buy something special for you, Karin and the girls.

Love,

Anna and Lars

Eva could not imagine a place with so many lakes. With so much water, must they travel everywhere by boat? Hopefully a card would arrive this Christmas, so she could write back and tell of her mother's passing...and learn more about this place of 10,000 lakes.

Effects of Vodka

When Vidar returned from the village later the next day, Dag and her mother watched the wagon pass by the house, the gray tarp flapping in the wind, exposing bags of grain and kitchen supplies. When Blix stopped in front of the barn door and Vidar remained sitting on the wagon seat for a long time, they took the long way through trees and hid behind some bushes. They could hear Vidar muttering to himself and thumbing through small pieces of paper in his hands.

"He seems to be in a good mood," said Dag.

"That he is. And probably a little drunk, too," said her mother.

Then Vidar stood up suddenly, looked around and stumbled to the ground, a snowfall of paper flying from his hands, scattering across the dooryard in the stiff breeze.

Suvi excitedly picked up some pieces that skipped around her feet and showed her daughter. "This is real paper money!" she exclaimed. "More than I've ever seen before." They both gathered as many bills as they dared until Vidar pulled himself up to his knees and began picking up the bills that had fallen around him. Suvi and Dag then ran back through the woods to the cabin to count their windfall.

"This is more than enough to keep us fed for years," exclaimed Suvi.

"Hurry, mother, he's coming!"

Suvi hid all the bills in the flour bin for safekeeping and brushed the flour from her hands. "I hope he doesn't miss what we've taken."

Vidar surged through the door, holding up a large wad of bills in each fist. The smirk on his face told Suvi he was pleased with the liquor sales and probably didn't suspect anything.

He threw the money on the table, pulled three bottles of vodka from his pockets and sat down heavily in his chair. He took a long drink and slid another bottle across the table toward Suvi. Considering this a time of celebration, she sat down and nervously took a sip as he proceeded to count the money, stacking the bills in little piles on the table. His drunken concentration did not allow an accurate tally and he started counting the bills over again...and again...until he gave up altogether.

"Selling vodka much better than potatoes," he mumbled, finishing off his bottle. He seemed more cheerful than Suvi had seen him in a long time; free of anger, relaxed, eyelids drooping from want of sleep. Quickly he stuffed the money into his pocket, pushed his chair back and clomped across the kitchen floor to the bedroom. They heard the creaking of the bed and within minutes a barrage of loud snoring.

"So, I will be seeing his ugly face when the sun rises tomorrow," said Suvi, dispiritedly. She had grown accustomed to him sleeping in the barn and having the bed all to herself, not having to submit to his crude maleness. Dag glanced at her mother in a knowing way, but Suvi was thinking only of herself.

"Go put Blix in the barn, Dag, and rub him down good. Then we will eat."

When Dag returned, the cabin was dark. She lit a candle and saw her mother still sitting at the table, her eyes glassy and unfocused. Her bottle was empty and she was unsuccessfully trying to fill the crystal goblet from the third bottle. She looked up dreamily toward Dag and giggled. Never had Dag seen her mother acting so giddy and foolish.

"Ah, this is how I remember it...so smooth and sweet on my tongue." Suvi held up the goblet and gazed into the transparent liquid as if it might tell her fortune. She looked at the girl across the table and saw her as a friend, a drinking partner and not her daughter.

"Have a drink," she said, thrusting the goblet towards Dag,

who grabbed it before it fell from her mother's hand. Dag, curious about this liquid that caused her mother to be so deliriously happy, took a sip. The vodka was tangy and sharp on her tongue. She made a face and Suvi laughed, saying the next sip would taste better...and the one after that would taste even better. Then Suvi's eyes closed and her body slumped back in the chair.

"Mother? Are you alright?"

Suvi opened one eye, grinned stupidly at her daughter and passed out. Although fearful of seeing her mother this way, Dag was consoled. Her mother's face had never looked more beautiful and peaceful, as if the liquor had put youth back into her face.

She carefully dragged her mother across the kitchen floor. Vidar's immense form was spread across the width of the bed, so Dag brought Suvi to her own little room, lifted her onto the bed and tucked a blanket neatly around her.

Dag sat alone at the table. Aside from Vidar's snoring, the kitchen was ghostly quiet. She picked up the crystal goblet, wanting to feel the same pleasure that had transformed her mother into such a joyful state of bliss. She took a sip...then another...and then a longer drink. The cool liquid felt soothing and delicious in her mouth and throat. When the goblet was empty she filled it again from the remaining bottle.

Soon the room went in and out of focus, everything swirled around her, and she felt herself falling. Knowing faces flashed before her eyes: Vidar's lecherous stare, her laughing mother, the red-haired girl and her family at the lake. The next thing she remembered was awakening in her own bed. Her mother's face was solemn again and she was gently rubbing Dag's cheek. "I found you on the floor in the kitchen."

"The goblet..." said Dag anxiously. "Is it broken?"

"The goblet is still on the table, but the vodka is all gone."

"I took a sip," Dag confessed. "You looked so happy. I wanted to feel that same happiness, and so I drank more."

Suvi could not scold her daughter. All this happened because of her own reckless behavior.

"I'm so sorry...I was not a very good example for you last

night." Then Suvi went to the kitchen, poured some strong hot coffee in a cup and returned.

"You'll feel better after you drink this," she told Dag.

Letters from America

Eva almost missed seeing another small packet of letters hidden beneath a scrap of brown woolen cloth. There were no envelopes and no return addresses on any of the letters. Her hands shook at the sight of her sister's signature at the bottom of the first letter.

September 1928

Dear Mama, Papa, and Eva:

I hesitate to write thinking how you must feel about me leaving so abruptly and without telling you beforehand, but it was something I had to do.

I met Olle one day in the village and we fell in love. He had often thought about going to America and when we found out that I was pregnant, we thought it best to leave immediately. He knew how ashamed I was and that I could not go home in that condition and shame you as well.

Sailing across the Atlantic Ocean was very exciting. The very best part of the trip was the bathroom we shared with another family. How very large the bathing tub was, and there was no need to pump any water. With only the turn of a metal faucet the tub filled instantly with hot water…and lots of sweet-smelling soaps, too. What luxury!

New York City was dirty and crowded. When others suggested going further north, we boarded a train to Boston. At first we lost our way on the narrow crowded streets, but now we have settled into our little apartment…and even have our own faucet tub! The first month we took a lot of baths, thinking that the water was free as it was back home and on the ship, but when the water bill came we had no money, so now we are back to taking one bath each week. I take mine first and Olle uses the same water for his, but I also wash up every morning in a small basin as we always did in Norrland. Almost everyone in this apartment house speaks Italian and I am already missing my Swedish shipmates, but I don't complain. Olle has found carpenter work and we are happy in our three little rooms and that is all that matters. I hope I'm worthy of your forgiveness and that you will write soon.

Love,

Ingrid

"Why hadn't Mama told me about these letters?" Eva said aloud to herself, glancing toward her dozing father. She wondered if he had seen them, but did not wish to open new wounds by asking now and risk making him feel bad all over again.

Learning of her sister's pregnancy was a huge surprise. Ingrid had never been one to play with dolls much and Eva could not picture her sister being a mother and having to take care of a real baby. Neither could she visualize a faucet tub filling itself with hot water. Ingrid was probably stretching the truth like she always had in the past.

A note was written on a Christmas card three months later.

December 1928

Dear Mama, Papa and Eva

I have not heard from you. Did you receive my letter of last September? I pray all is well in Norrland and that you are in good health. Olle and I plan to have a tree just like the one pictured on this card, but ours will have only a few gifts underneath. I am knitting a sweater for Olle, but wish you were here, Mama, to help me make the buttonholes.

Mr. Johnson, the man Olle works for, invited us to join his family for the Thanksgiving Holiday this past November. On that day every house in America is roasting a turkey (which tastes much like chicken) with bread stuffing. We also had fresh apple cider, riced potatoes with rich gravy, squash, onions, cranberry sauce and frosted cinnamon rolls. On the dessert table were a variety of pies: apple, blueberry, cherry, custard and pumpkin, plus a sweet Indian pudding made from molasses and cornmeal. All the men had a small slice of each pie, so Olle had to sample each one, too. I had room for only a small dish of delicious warm pudding with ice cream melting over it.

Thanksgiving is a time for being grateful, remembering when the early pilgrims arrived in Massachusetts and celebrated their first bountiful harvest with the Indian natives. We felt we had a lot in common with those brave souls who came to this strange land so many years ago and settled in this very same state. We feel so blessed.

Merry Christmas!

Love,

Ingrid

People in America must be very wealthy to have so much food on the table at one meal, thought Eva, her stomach rumbling at the thought of roasted turkey and all those different kinds of pies, especially now when she and her father were trying to get by with mostly porridge, bread and cheese.

April 1929

Dear Mama and Papa and Eva,

I am writing now to tell you that we had a son on March 21, your birthday, Papa. His name is Gustav Olle; we call him Gus. He arrived hungry as a bear at ten and one-half pounds and already sleeps through the night.

Having a baby of my own has given me a new view of life. Being a parent now, I realize even more how upset you must have been when I left so suddenly for America. It was selfish and thoughtless of me not to confide in you, but at the time I could not bring myself to tell you of my pregnancy. I was scared and couldn't bear to be away from Olle. I am begging for your forgiveness.

I pray that you will write soon.

Love,

Ingrid

"I'm an Auntie!" Eva said aloud. "Oh, yes, Ingrid, I do forgive you. It's time to forget the past and move on." How desperately she wanted to hold little Gus in her arms.

As she opened the next letter a photograph fell from the paper and into her lap. She knew at once that the faces in the picture were of Ingrid, Olle and little Gus. Even though her father had told her about cameras and the photographs they made, Eva still felt puzzled by how the likeness of a person could be revealed on a piece of paper.

August l929

Dear Mama, Papa and Eva,

I wonder if you have received my letters. Little Gus is almost five months old now and such a happy baby with eyes the color of our lake on a sunny day. Soft blond fuzz has grown on his bald head like a golden halo and he is so serious when he looks at me, scowling sometimes when he tastes a new food. He makes us laugh when he opens and closes his mouth like a fish out of water. I'm sure he will be talking, as I did, by the time he is a year old.

Automobiles are very popular here in America, as well as service vehicles. Mr. Johnson has several Ford trucks for his business and is teaching Olle how to drive. That way Olle can use one of them to get back and forth to work each day and also be able to transport materials to the many building sites in the area.

Mr. Johnson took this photograph of the three of us on Thanksgiving. Many people in America have cameras and Olle is hoping to buy one in time for next Christmas. .

I wish I had a photograph of you all to look at every day. You must be quite grown-up now, Eva. I wonder if Mr. Kronberg knows about cameras. Perhaps he could take a picture of you all.

I pray that I will hear from you soon.

Love,

Ingrid

Eva sat for a long time staring at the three smiling faces looking back at her and thought about the America she had read about in Mr. Kronberg's geography and history books. From Ingrid's letters, this vast country seemed an even more wondrous place of fine food and grand inventions.

When she opened the last letter there was another photograph of Ingrid and Olle sitting stiffly in two chairs with little Gus standing between them looking at a baby in Ingrid's arms.

September 1930

Dear Mama, Papa, and Eva,

Over a year has gone by and I still have not heard from you. I am worried that something terrible has happened and pray that you will write me a few lines so I know all is well.

I am writing this letter to tell you of the birth of our beautiful daughter, Nina Irene, born on August 6. Little Gus is exactly what a big brother should be; always making certain she is all right, touching her face and talking to her as if she understood, and perhaps she does, because she always gives him the sweetest smile. Gus is almost one and one-half years old, very smart and preoccupied with taking things apart. He doesn't always get them put together right, but what concentration and persistence he has!

Do you recognize me with my short hair and plumpness around my middle? That's the price of two babies and eating too much of my own cooking. It bothers me that Olle can eat twice as much as I do, but continues looking thin and trim as ever. He has recently been promoted to assistant foreman and that means more money and a chance to hopefully move to the country in a year or two. I long for the sight of green grass and open spaces, although from my kitchen window I can see a beautiful yellow maple tree glittering in the autumn breeze about two blocks from here.

A professional photographer took this picture. He told us to look serious, but little Gus kept smiling and couldn't take his eyes off of Nina.

Please write soon.

Love,

Ingrid

Eva could not understand why these letters had never been shown to her. Both her parents were such private people. How much better things would have been if her mother had shared these letters and her sad feelings. By keeping the letters secretly hidden she was only hiding her grief, a heartache that possibly made her die too soon. It wasn't good to keep everything bagged up inside like a sack of wet grain ready to burst its seams.

Then suddenly an idea popped into Eva's head. Perhaps her mother had been afraid that she, too, might leave if she knew of all the good things Ingrid described in her letters about America.

"Oh, Mama, don't you know that I would never have left you and Papa?" Eva cried for her mother and sister and for all the unspoken words that might have made a difference. Then she sat down and wrote all the jumbled thoughts swirling in her head as if she was writing an actual letter to Ingrid.

Afterward she felt some peace and more connected with her sister. Perhaps in this way a path would open up between them and Ingrid would be prompted to write another letter.

December

The crisp, clear October days and bright autumn colors slowly turned cold and gray as the November sun continued its downward path toward the horizon. In the afternoons Eva and her father sat in the sunroom moving their chairs to follow the fleeting rays of light and warmth until one day the light suddenly vanished behind the forest and the cottage lay in the shadows of the great trees.

The ever-present cold and stillness of mid December was broken only by the north wind thundering through the trees, the howling of wolves and yipping of foxes, as the impotent sun struggled to pull itself above the horizon each morning, only to lay helpless and weak in the endless twilight.

Eva was reminded of when she was a little girl and first noticed the winter sun disappearing behind the trees. The next morning it did not rise, nor did she see it the next day, although the sky was a cloudless deep blue. She thought the sun had died.

Her mother reassured her that the sun would return with the spring and it did. She thought about the wandering reindeer, woodland moose and other animals of the forest. When the cold and darkness came and they didn't feel the warmth of the sun on their backs anymore, were they afraid, too? And did they rejoice, as people did, when the sun returned to fill the summer days and nights with ever-present light? Did animals think? Did they worry about the unknown? So many questions had been asked that day and she had never forgotten the answers.

"Animals live in the present moment," her mother had told her. "They don't worry about what happened yesterday, nor about tomorrow. They have keener senses than we do and a supreme awareness of their surroundings. Their natural instincts make them more accepting to nature's ways. It is wise for us to learn the meaning of acceptance."

After that Eva tried to accept everything that came her way, living each day at its fullest and not looking back nor too far ahead, but it was obvious her mother didn't live the life she preached. She never accepted Ingrid's leaving. Eva understood her mother better now. She saw how situations changed a person and how unforeseen events happen that one is not ready or willing to accept. Surely her mother never thought Ingrid would unexpectedly run away to America, nor did Eva ever think that someday she might be burdened with the daunting chore of taking care of her father.

The winter sadness that had plagued Gustav in his youth returned; those long dark months of winter when he stayed in bed too long in the mornings and moped around the house during the day waiting for spring to return.

This gloomy atmosphere now pervaded the cottage, invading Eva's space as well. She began to understand the meaning of the word isolation and why Ingrid had escaped to the village so often. Isolation, she discovered, was an emptiness that couldn't be filled up, a place of forced confinement smothering the emotions and frustrating the will.

For a short while she had been able to cheer her father with happy remembrances, but those stories soon grew old. She took to reading aloud to him, but his absent gaze told her he wasn't listening. He could not see beyond the darkness and his brief, incoherent mumblings were of a different time and place, as if the past were holding him hostage.

As the drowsy bear hibernates from the outside world by sleeping away the winter in his solitary den, so was her father, in muddled obscurity, imprisoned in his chair, detached and mostly unaware of his surroundings, hibernating in his own way from sorrow and loneliness.

It became a daily struggle to get her father out of bed and she then had to coax him to eat at every meal. If he pushed the food away, she fed him with a spoon, and when he clamped lips together tightly, she became frustrated, irritated by his stubbornness and her own inadequacies. She could not count how many times she'd run to the kitchen crying in desperation. What if he became sick or died? Would she be held at fault? Feelings of guilt plagued her during the night, depriving her of much needed sleep, and she awakened each morning tired and discouraged, dreading the uncertainty of facing another day.

The tiny mirror in the hall looked back at her with a face she didn't recognize. The natural optimism and rosy outlook of her youth was now overshadowed by the unexpected burdens and overwhelming responsibilities of caring for her father, a situation over which she had little control. Acceptance was now an unrelenting challenge. No longer was her father the strong, understanding and wise man she once knew. Her former protector was now the weak one and she his guardian. Adjusting to her new role of mothering her father and the great burden of being completely responsible for another's life was challenging and very demanding.

A three-day blizzard filled the path to the road with heavy wet snow, insulating them even further from any connection with the outside world. Grateful for the winter supplies Mr. Kronberg brought in November, she knew he probably wouldn't be coming back until spring. Since he also brought their mail, that meant there would be no Christmas cards from Ingrid or Anna until the snow melted from the path, which might very well not be until April.

Eva awakened one morning to a sparkling meadow of ferns and flowers, a picture the frost etched on her bedroom window during the night. That was a positive sign that turned her thoughts to Christmas, which was only five days away. Why she was suddenly feeling happy was a mystery, for this Christmas would be far different from any other she had known.

She had made a knitted hat and scarf for her father, but there would be no gifts for her his year. She constantly reminded herself that Christmas was for giving, not receiving. However, happy childhood memories would not let her forget that she needed a present to open on Christmas Eve. It was also her birthday.

After the breakfast dishes were washed and dried Eva opened the door to gusty winds that whipped her cape, blowing the hood from her head and causing the icy air to sting her face and neck. Happy to be out of the house and invigorated by the boisterous weather, she ran hoodless down the snow-trodden path to the barn.

Stella and Slofock welcomed her with turned heads and expectant eyes. They were glad to see her, and unlike her father, always ate whatever she put in front of them with delight and great enthusiasm. Cleaning manure from their stalls had never been a distasteful chore for Eva; she rather enjoyed making dirty things clean again, whether in the house or barn. As she milked Stella, the only sounds were the melodic ping of milk hitting the metal pail and the faint rhythmic grinding as the two animals methodically chewed their cuds. She also heard the occasional tinkle of bells, but attributed the sound to the sweet tones of the wind singing through the timbers.

That merry sound reminded her of the Christmas Eve when Mr.

Kronberg invited her family to midnight service at the village church. She had been about eight years old at the time. December was free of heavy snowstorms that year and Mr. Kronberg had been able to drive the horses and sleigh easily through the long path from the road.

She remembered standing outside on that starlit night in the freezing cold. Shivers of excitement ran up and down her spine as the first jingling bells penetrated the evening stillness. The delightful sound became louder until finally through the darkness she saw four burning torches on the corners of the sleigh. Two spirited black horses stopped abruptly by the porch steps, tossing their heads as clouds of frozen breath rose above their frost-fringed nostrils. Mr. and Mrs. Kronberg sat in the sleigh behind them in their furry capes, shouting out in unison, "Merry Christmas!"

Everyone settled into the sleigh bundled in heavy blankets which Mrs. Kronberg proudly announced she'd made from the skins of her beloved, departed pet goats. Eva remembered Ingrid making a disgusted face and refusing to touch the fur blanket, but it wasn't long before her sister disappeared beneath the skins, either to get warm or to join the noisy Kronberg boys who were already playing by her feet, and sometimes tickling her legs.

Even though Eva's cheeks were nearly frozen stiff and her lips numb from the chilling wind, she wasn't about to hide her head under a blanket and miss one second of this great adventure. The bright moon illuminated the snowy landscape, transforming it into a mystical fairyland. Every now and then another sleigh suddenly emerged from the dark forest, their glowing lights and tinkling bells joining the festive parade of sleighs and horses.

She tried to avoid the hand that sometimes tried to grab her foot, but one swift kick finally put an end to that. Mats kept a good distance from her all during church, so she felt justified in knowing he'd been the culprit under the blanket trying to get her attention.

The church was cold and drafty even though a red-hot stove fought desperately to throw its heat toward the congregation.

Everyone kept their outside clothes on, huddling together on the wooden pews until it was time to rise and sing hymns. The sermon dragged on, as white flickering candles cast a soothing gentle glow over the drowsy congregation.

Eva had leaned against her mother's shoulder, eyes heavy with sleep, and dreamed she was riding a black horse through the candlelit forest where jingling bells adorned every tree. Suddenly she felt a tugging at her ankle and saw Mats laughing up at her. The jingling bells grew louder and she awakened to see Mrs. Kronberg standing before her holding a tray of coffee and sandwiches. She wore a red knitted hat with over a dozen little silver bells that tinkled whenever she moved her head.

Eva had slept all the way home, but she vividly remembered hearing bells jingling. She was probably dreaming of Mrs. Kronberg's most unusual musical hat.

Suddenly Stella stopped chewing and looked toward the barn door. The sound of bells was much louder now and Eva peeked out the small window to see two brown and white goats emerging from the trees, their leather harnesses decorated with tinkling brass bells, and Mrs. Kronberg sitting in the sled behind them wearing the same red hat.

Usually it was Mr. Kronberg who came to visit, so at first Eva feared something dreadful had happened. However, the smile on Mrs. Kronberg's face told a different story. Eva was so emotionally starved that at the sight of another woman she instinctively reached out to give her a hug; a momentary gesture that seemed embarrassing to the older woman, who seemed always determined and full of business. Mrs. Kronberg was a woman of few words. Today she was no different as she quickly hoisted a bag of grain on her back and carried it into the barn.

Ignoring Eva's offer to help, she ran back for a second bag; then looked approvingly at the ox and cow. "Use scant measure...grain should last through mud time," she said before hurrying back to the sleigh. Then she loaded Eva's arms with small bundles, slung a sack of potatoes over her own shoulder, a large ham over the other and headed for the cottage.

Eva followed behind. She could almost smell the ham roasting in the oven. They hadn't had much more than porridge since she boiled the last tough old hen on Sunday. She was surprised to find her father standing by the parlor window, although he looked puzzled seeing two females enter the room.

"Papa, you remember Mrs. Kronberg, don't you?" The Kronberg name rang a bell.

"Where's Otto?" he asked, looking about the room.

"Stockholm," said Mrs. Kronberg. "He asked me to stop by. T'was tough going. Snow so deep I almost turned back."

"It has been a long winter," said Gustav, dejectedly.

"Ya," she replied. "And it's only just begun."

Gustav scratched his head. "Just begun? Isn't this February, Eva?"

"No, Papa. It's only December. We haven't had Christmas yet."

There was a look of concern in Mrs. Kronberg's eyes. "Is he unwell?"

The question caught Eva quite by surprise.

"Well...he...he's been a little confused since Mama died, and..."

Not wanting to delve into their private problems, she asked her guest to sit down and escorted her father to the table.

"Mrs. Kronberg brought us grain for the animals, potatoes and a ham. Wasn't that kind of her?"

Gustav studied the woman sitting across from him. "Ah, yes, very kind indeed. You and Otto have always looked out for us."

Pleased that her father was now acting close to normal, Eva went to the kitchen to brew coffee, ashamed to have only stale bread and a little cheese for lunch. She heard Mrs. Kronberg's voice and saw her open one of the cloth bags.

"For you, Gustav," she said. "I know how you love mince tarts."

Eva breathed a sigh of relief as he took a big bite out of one of the tarts, his face relaxed and happy. "Nothing like good company and delicious food to bring cheer and normalcy into a home," she thought.

Before Eva had a chance to pour the coffee, her father reached for another tart.

"Made from neck meat...Mats killed a big bull moose last year," said Mrs. Kronberg with great pride in her son. Eva couldn't remember how long it had been since she last saw Mats.

"Is Mats still going to school in the village?" she asked.

"Heavens no! He's in Stockholm... at University," she said, sitting up very straight in her chair.

This surprised Eva. Mats had never seemed like the studious type, but things can change in a few years. They certainly had for her.

"My Mats...he some different now...go to America soon." She said no more, her smile quickly dissolving into somberness. Like all Swedish parents, she wished the best for her children, but didn't want them to go to America to find it.

Eva poured another round of coffee and tasted one of the frosted lingonberry pastries. It must have been ten years since Eva was first in Mrs. Kronberg's kitchen, but the older woman still remembered Eva's favorite sweet.

"Delicious! Where did you learn to make such flaky pastry?"

"My Mormor. She taught me everything."

Eva had never known her Mormor, her mother's mother. In fact she had never known any of her grandparents and was curious to know more about Mrs. Kronberg: where she was born and raised, about her precious goats, why she learned from a grandmother and not a mother. There was a sadness about Mrs. Kronberg's face, so Eva turned the conversation back to Mats.

"I think it's been almost four years ago that Mats came here with his father. Wouldn't you say, Papa?" He smiled at her, but showed no sign of hearing her question. Mrs. Kronberg picked right up on his inattentiveness.

"Is your father deaf?" she whispered to Eva.

"I don't think he hears as well as he used to," she replied. "Or sometimes I think he just prefers not to answer."

"Same with Otto...only hears what he wants to hear!"

Mrs. Kronberg reached again into a bag, took out four little packages wrapped in blue and white paper and placed them on the table. She glanced around the room. "You don't have your tree up yet?"

Eva was embarrassed that she had made no preparations for Christmas.

"Well...I guess I'm not in the mood for Christmas this year."

Mrs. Kronberg looked Eva in the eye. "How can you not be in the mood for Christmas?" Then she spun around and peered out the window. "I get tree," she said, marching toward the door, the bells on her hat ringing noisily with each heavy, booted step.

It wasn't long before she returned carrying a freshly cut little spruce tree.

"Do you have a stand for the tree? Some decorations?" Mrs. Kronberg's demanding tone of voice made Eva scurry into her father's room to get the special box labeled *Christmas* that was stored under his bed.

Soon the little tree stood in the corner between two windows, decorated with many old porcelain ornaments, strings of little paper Swedish flags and small, thin, white candles in their holders fastened to the sturdiest branches.

Mrs. Kronberg then placed four bundles beneath the tree and stood back with her hands on her hips. "Now you are ready for Christmas!"

Christmas at the Cottage

The front room, smelling of spruce and the lingering scents of baked ham and fresh bread, felt almost like every other Christmas Eve, except only two chairs were occupied tonight. Eva lit the tiny white candles on the tree, illuminating the room with a fairyland atmosphere. She missed her mother, who had always filled the cottage with evergreen boughs, transformed night into day by lighting white tapers in her favorite red wooden candelabras and baked a lavish dinner with cookies, cakes and pies for dessert. She missed Ingrid, too. Christmas was for children and she longed to see Gus and Nina.

Her father had eaten a good dinner and for that she was well pleased, although his traditional child-like spirit of past Christmases now was absent. He watched contentedly as she stood admiring the beautiful tree. Besides the usual woodsy smell of spruce, other wonderful aromas filled the space around her; a strange but fragrant mixture of coffee, tobacco, and roses.

Eva looked over Mrs. Kronberg's gifts. A little sniff told her one was tobacco and she gave it to her father. He enthusiastically asked for his pipe, which he hadn't used in months. Then she selected a gift for herself, smelling the scent of roses as she unwrapped two fragrant cakes of pure white soap that Mrs. Kronberg surely had made herself.

Gustav opened another package. Holding it to his face, he breathed in deeply and smiled at the little sack of roasted coffee beans.

"Would you like a fresh cup of coffee?" she asked.

"You bet I do!" he responded immediately.

"Just enjoy your pipe now, I won't be long."

When she returned from the kitchen there were two packages left under the tree; one that she made for her father and the other for her from Mrs. Kronberg, which jingled when she picked it up.

Eva ripped open the package, thinking of only one thing it could possibly be, and she wasn't disappointed when she saw a red hat with silver bells. Mrs. Kronberg had not forgotten that special night many years ago at the village church when Eva had admired her musical hat. Eva put on the hat, shaking her head to make the bells jingle as she twirled around the room.

Gustav watched his jubilant daughter dance in front of the tree and when she excitedly gave him the gift she had made for him, he was caught up in the gaiety of the moment. Eagerly unwrapping the package, he put the scarf around his neck and placed the knitted hat jauntily on his head. Eva reached up to a shelf above her father's chair and took down his old harmonica. He fondled the small instrument in his hands, the silver metal reflecting the brightness of the candles still burning on the tree. She reticently suggested he play a tune, though she had little hope of that happening.

Methodically he raised the instrument to his mouth, surprising her by playing several familiar hymns. His foot unconsciously began to tap on the wooden floor and soon he was playing all the old traditional Christmas melodies. Eva sang along, the glorious sounds echoing from the walls of the suddenly enchanted room.

The candles on the tree burned low, so Eva carefully extinguished them. Gustav watched, sipping his second cup coffee, and for a moment he saw his beloved Karin standing there. When she turned, he saw his daughter's face, and suddenly realized he had no gift for her this year.

Immediately he rose from his chair, took the single candle burning on the table and walked with speed and purpose toward his bedroom. Eva followed, stopping in the doorway as he rummaged through a bureau drawer. His voice sounded small and weak as he stood before her attempting to say words that were difficult to say.

"I bought this...this Bible for your mother's birthday before she...when I was in Stockholm the last time," he said thoughtfully, caressing the soft, luxurious velvet box. "I want you to have it." His voice was soft as a whisper, his eyes filling with tears.

When Eva saw the beautiful leather Bible with onionskin pages edged with gold, she hugged her father tenderly and for a while they were comforted in each other's arms.

They sat down at the table and Eva opened the Bible, carefully turning the delicate translucent pages, showing him some of the beautifully engraved pictures of familiar Bible stories her mother had read to her. When she came to the Book of Luke, she read aloud passages about Mary and Joseph and the birth of Jesus.

The blessed story breathed new life into the two of them.

Afterward they were both uncommonly hungry. She watched her father's absolute pleasure as he enjoyed Mrs. Kronberg's mouth-watering mince tarts and she slowly relished the sweetness of a frosted lingonberry pastry. They had only each other tonight, but it was more than enough. What she'd feared would be the worst Christmas ever turned out to be one of the best.

Christmas at the Potato Farm

A month before Christmas Vidar moved back into the cabin for winter, hogging the best space near the stove, the heat releasing his foul smell and permeating the room. With him came the remaining supply of potato liquor, which he consumed daily because of his boredom from not being able to work in the potato shed. Combined with the warmth of the stove, the liquor often induced a pacifying stupor that would leave him snoring in the big chair all night long.

Because the stove's heat was limited to a small area in the kitchen, Suvi usually came to her daughter's bedroom on these evenings, the two huddling together in warm blankets while Dag listened again to stories of her mother's life at the miner's house and especially about the extravagant Christmas celebrations.

Living there had opened Suvi's eyes to a world of lavish living and sumptuous days of feasting, dancing and generous gifts under a candlelit tree decorated with brightly-colored glass balls and strings of tiny Swedish flags with their yellow crosses on a bright blue background. She assisted her mistress in setting the lace tablecloths with sparkling silverware, fine china decorated with hand-painted pink roses and gold leaves, and those thin crystal goblets that sang like bells when tapped swiftly and gently with a silver spoon or with a flick of fingernail.

A festive red cloth covered a separate table which was laid with roast beef, smoked ham, pickled herring, sausages and tiny meatballs in onion gravy, while another table groaned under the weight of potatoes baked in rich cream and dishes of colorful root vegetables like beets, carrots and turnips, plus many breads, cheeses, fruits and relishes.

Suvi also helped bake braided yeast breads adorned with white frosting, cherries and nuts, and rich buttery cakes, sweet fruit pies and fancy cutout cookies of gingerbread sprinkled with cinnamon sugar. In the center of the dessert table was the centerpiece: a special rice pudding in which an almond was hidden. Whoever found the almond received a special prize. Dag never tired of hearing these stories and her mouth always watered thinking about all the delicious food. She dreamed every Christmas of eating sweet rice pudding, finding an almond and receiving a special prize.

Suvi had hoped to make rice pudding every Christmas since they first arrived at the farm, but Vidar never remembered to bring home any rice until this past spring. However, he had forgotten about the spices. When The Finn drove into the yard last September Vidar was occupied in the potato shed making liquor and Suvi had run out to speak secretly to the peddler.

"I need some cinnamon and nutmeg," she told him. Then, looking around to make certain Dag would not hear, she whispered, "and would you have any whole almond nuts?"

"I have only some mixed nuts, but surely you can have a few almonds," he said in a low voice, picking out a handful from the container of assorted nuts.

She paid with bills taken from her money stash in the flour bin and was feeling quite rich that day, so she and Dag rummaged through boxes of old material, sewing supplies and ribbons. Suvi picked out some warm flannel cloth to make them both new nightgowns and while Dag finished looking through another box, her mother spied a pretty rag doll beneath a pile of old clothes. She hid the doll under the flannel cloth, so Dag would not see, and went to the front of the wagon to pay for her purchases.

Dag picked out a length of yellow silk ribbon and showed it

to her mother, who thought the purchase a bit frivolous.

"And where would you wear such a fine ribbon?" she asked disapprovingly.

"I'm not going to wear it. I just want to look at the beautiful color and feel the softness." The Finn noticed Dag's downcast face.

"No charge for the ribbon," he said to her mother.

Suvi smiled down at her daughter approvingly. "You may have the ribbon and do with it whatever you wish."

Dag thought a lot about Christmas at the miner's house and a week before Christmas she asked her mother if they could have a tree in the cabin. After searching for the perfect little tree, they propped it up in the corner by the front door and tied pine cones on the branches for decoration. When Vidar came in from evening chores, he thought it a foolish idea to have a tree inside the house. He picked up the little spruce, broke it in half with his bare hands and threw it outside in the snow. Dag was glad he hadn't burned it in the stove and later retrieved the broken tree, tied it together with old rags and placed it beside her bed.

Although Christmas was just like any other day to Vidar, he never objected to the good tasting holiday food that Suvi prepared. He had extra money in his pockets this year from the liquor sales and had purchased more winter supplies than usual. Because of an early blizzard, Suvi had been able to freeze a can of fresh milk under the snow for holiday baking.

Two days before Christmas Suvi showed Dag how to mix sweet cookie dough and roll it very thin on the table. Then they carefully cut the dough into delicate star shapes and sprinkled them with sugar before baking.

When the first pan of cookies came from the oven and their wonderful aroma reached Vidar's ample, bulbous nose, he immediately grabbed two large handfuls of the delicate cookies. Cramming them into his mouth he ravenously devoured the fragile cookies like a starving dog afraid that another might steal them away, scooping up the remainder of the cookies to eat by the stove.

Suvi and Dag were shocked that their hours of painstakingly artistic work had been unappreciatively wasted by Vidar's inconsiderate greediness. Anger surged through Suvi's body. She felt like throwing the rest of the dough in his face, but knew at once that was not an option. Instead she defiantly snatched gobs of the remaining dough, pounded the lumps with her fist and baked two pans of man-sized cookies. By then she had released most of her anger.

"There," she said. "He can eat those and we'll make more cookies later."

After supper, when Vidar had fallen asleep in his chair, Suvi mixed up a new batch of dough and she and Dag cut out dozens of delicate star shapes. There were a few mistakes, odd shaped cookies that could be eaten right away, but there were plenty more perfect ones to hide in the cupboard for Christmas Eve. After Dag was asleep Suvi wrapped the precious little rag doll in a piece of flannel left over from the nightgowns she'd made for the two of them.

After a hearty Christmas Eve dinner of moose steaks, turnip, potatoes and gravy, Vidar took a bottle of vodka and relaxed in his chair by the stove.

By the time the dishes were washed and dried and the kitchen cleaned up, Vidar was asleep. It wasn't long before Dag came out of her bedroom, her face aglow with mischievous anticipation, wearing a yellow silk bow in her hair.

"What have you been up to now?" asked her mother.

"Just getting things ready for our celebration. Can we eat in my room?"

"That's a good idea," replied Suvi glancing at the snoring Vidar. "You bring the cookies while I get something from under my bed." Dag lit a candle and sat on the floor by the little tree where she could see her mother's expression as she entered the room.

"How beautiful!" exclaimed Suvi, kneeling down to inspect

the squares of yellow silk glittering on the branches of the little tree.

Dag took a yellow bow from under the tree and gave it to her mother, who tucked it in her braid.

"I'll be right back," said Suvi.

She returned wearing a clean new nightgown and carrying a small tray with two cups of milk. She set the tray down and gave her daughter a package to open, a matching nightgown that Dag immediately put on.

The wind whistled through cracks in the walls and very little heat found its way into the bedroom from the big stove in the kitchen; however, neither Suvi nor Dag were aware of the cold this evening as they sat in front of the little tree feeling very queenly in their new gowns and golden silk bows sparkling like crowns on their heads. Daintily they sipped their milk and slowly ate too many delicious sugar star cookies.

"I'm glad you picked out the yellow silk ribbon," said Suvi as they lay together in Dag's bed under warm quilts. "It surely brightened up our Christmas Eve."

"Dag? Are you awake?" whispered her mother, but she heard only her daughter's deep breaths of sleep. "Merry Christmas, my dear girl," she whispered.

Suvi rose early on Christmas morning to make the rice pudding. As it baked in the oven she cooked the breakfast porridge and prepared a tender moose loin saved for this special day.

Vidar yawned, scratched his chest and sat down at the table. Suvi, ever watchful and attentive, immediately filled his mug with hot, strong coffee and placed a full bowl of steaming porridge before him. Not wishing to spoil the beginning of a wonderful day, Dag stayed in bed under warm covers until the door slammed and Vidar had gone to do morning chores.

As they ate their porridge, Suvi found it difficult not to say anything about the surprise rice pudding, but she could think of nothing else. "I made something special this morning."

"Rice pudding?" Dag said hopefully as she breathed in the

sweet aroma of something different baking in the oven.

"How did you know?"

"Well, I went to sleep dreaming about finding the almond and getting a wonderful prize," replied Dag.

"Tell me about your dream."

"I was walking in the forest where bright yellow ribbons hung from every tree. The path led me to a lake and I dove into the water. Soon I was swimming in thick cream that tasted sweet and smooth. Rising to the top I found myself sitting on a lake of rice pudding, scooping up handfuls until I could eat no more."

"So, I suppose now you are sick of rice pudding and you won't eat any of mine," sighed Suvi.

"It was only a dream, Mother. I didn't really eat any pudding."

"Well, sometimes dreams can seem very real." Suvi could only think of her own dreams which were often worse than real life.

"Do you want to hear the end of my dream?"

"Of course...I want to know if you found the almond."

"Oh yes! It opened up in front of me, big as a shiny gold mountain. Inside were flowers of every color, glittering Christmas trees, beautifully wrapped presents of all sizes and more food than I could eat in my whole life. A woman walked toward me. She was wearing a satiny gown of green and gold stripes with tiny flowers just like that beautiful cloth that was wrapped around the goblet."

"So, you saw the mistress at the miner's house?" Suvi asked eagerly.

"I didn't remember her, but she knew my name. 'Come with me Dagny,' she said, taking my hand. All of a sudden I was sitting in a very soft chair, wearing a red dress with lace and frills and there was a silver box in my lap. When I lifted the cover there was a beautiful doll dressed in white with a golden crown on her head."

Dag looked so happy, but Suvi could not help but think of the lowly prize she had for her daughter and how it would compare to the queen-like doll in Dag's dream. Suvi quickly put aside her rag doll thoughts and considered only her jubilant daughter.

"You must have felt very special in your dream."

"I did. Whenever I think of it I feel good all over again."

"A beautiful dream is like a happy memory," said Suvi, who often lived in her past remembrances. "Keep it tucked in a drawer of your mind...where you can pull it out any time to make you feel better."

Like a bad dream, Vidar came back from morning chores, but it didn't matter. Dag and Suvi could only think about the wonderful rice pudding baking in the oven.

The three of them sat at the kitchen table. This being the darkest time of the year, Suvi had rationed her candles in order to have extra light for this festive Christmas dinner. Although she and Dag owned no best clothes, they felt quite dressed up wearing the yellow satin ribbons in their hair, each able to see the other's glittering bow in the bright candlelight

They ate mostly in silence with only their private thoughts for company. If Vidar noticed the special red cloth beneath his plate, the extra candles on the table or the festive ribbons in the girls' hair, he did not comment, being too busy gorging himself on potatoes, turnip and moose loin.

As Suvi ladled out the pudding, Vidar grabbed the bowl intended for Dag, the one with the almond hidden inside. She watched in horror as he slurped it down like he always did with his morning porridge.

Suddenly he emitted a horrendous growl, spat out a mouthful of pudding, and on the table Suvi saw a bloodied tooth and the broken almond. He picked up his rotten tooth for them to see and threw his bowl of pudding against the opposite wall, tipped over the table and stomped out of the cabin. His blind rage allowed Dag to save her bowl of pudding, which she hid under her shirt and put in her room for safekeeping. Suvi glanced out the window to see Vidar filling his mouth with snow as he made his way to the barn.

After the table was righted, the broken bowls picked up, the spattered walls and floor cleaned, Suvi sat down at the bare wooden table and put her head in her hands. "All that wonderful pudding gone to waste and you probably never even had a taste," she said, her eyes filling up with tears.

"Remember my dream and you'll feel better," said Dag. Then she disappeared into her room. Suvi was glad that her daughter didn't seem too disappointed and brushed away her tears. When Dag returned there was a secret glow on her daughter's face.

"See what I have!" said Dag revealing the almost full bowl of rice pudding that she'd salvaged from Vidar's explosive outburst. Suvi's eyes filled with happy tears. Quickly she went to the cupboard where the almonds were hidden and slipped one into the bowl of pudding while Dag found two clean spoons.

How much more enjoyable it was eating their pudding without Vidar there, especially when Dag found the hidden almond and Suvi presented her with the long-awaited prize. Many fourteen-year-old girls would probably have considered themselves too old for a doll, but Dag had never had a real doll before. In prior years, a Christmas like this one had never been celebrated at the potato farm. This year, with Vidar busy making vodka in the shed, Suvi had more time to think and plan. She also had money of her own and this had given her a new confidence.

Another Neighborly Visit

The joy of Christmas soon faded with each stormy day. More snow filled the path to the road as bone-chilling cold continued through January. The influence of darkness was contagious, affecting Eva as well as her father, as it spread like an unwanted intruder through the forest and into the little house. Their separate worlds suddenly stopped turning as if frozen in time, a reflection of the frigid landscape that did not bend nor yield, unforgiving and immobilized by the ruthless impact of cold and darkness. Suddenly father and daughter were like strangers.

Gustav had succumbed to its effect soon after the New Year.

He had lost all interest in eating and was more withdrawn than before, sitting idly in his chair gazing out the window as if looking for the sun to rise above the trees again. Eva went about her duties with oblivious detachment, akin to living in a dream where everything was slow moving and out of reach. She found no satisfaction in the mundane keeping of a house and was physically and mentally drained from the pressing responsibility of caring for her father.

The simple everyday task of preparing nourishing meals became more difficult. If her father did not eat, she would have to feed him slowly with a spoon, something she found degrading, but it had to be done. How frustrating it was when he stubbornly refused to open his mouth. It would be her fault if he starved to death and thinking of this plagued her with guilt.

Yesterday he hadn't eaten a single bite all day and she'd run into her room, picked up her hairbrush and thrown it against the wall, then fell on the bed screaming into her pillow. And one day last week she found herself in the forest standing barefoot in the deep snow unable to remember how she got there. Snow fell from an overhead branch as a large bird fluttered out of the tree. She'd probably been screaming then, too, and scared him off.

Knitting became Eva's only real pleasure. Like her mother she found solace in creating something beautiful and useful from two needles and whatever yarn was available. The challenge of seeing a difficult and complicated pattern take shape into a lovely afghan or sweater kept her mind busy. Knitting gave her a feeling of accomplishment when every other aspect of her life seemed to be falling apart.

"Knitting is a good way to relax and sort out worrisome thoughts, solve daily problems and to escape from the drudgery of everyday life," her mother had told her years ago.

Eva had always thought of knitting as a passion; not as an escape or a reason for not doing some unpleasant thing. Now she understood better her mother's words. In fact, she could see herself growing more like her mother each day as her so-called passion turned into an escape...a way of forgetting what needed to be done and replacing it with something more pleasurable.

Time passed quickly as her needles clicked away and colorful patterns evolved before her eyes. It was only when the twilight faded from the sky and the window darkened that guilt washed over her again. Once more she had given into selfishness. She had knit away another day that might have been better spent cleaning the cottage, washing dirty clothes or just holding her father's hand. Now she must go to the barn in the dark, wasting precious oil in the lantern to take care of the animals.

When she returned from the barn her father was slumped in his chair and she was unable to rouse him. After shaking him gently, his eyes opened, but they did not meet hers.

"Are you feeling all right?" she asked.

"Karin...you came back," he said smiling.

She thought better of correcting him and played along with the game.

"I'm here," she said, holding his hand. Then he relaxed and fell into a peaceful, easy sleep.

For two days he would not eat, although he did allow her to give him water from a spoon, and after that he swallowed a little porridge each day. Her old frustrations returned, bringing along with them feelings of anger and resentment, unwanted visitors, burglars who attempted to steal her patience and sanity. Again she was overwhelmed by unanswered questions about her father, why he seemed to be drifting away from her and the inadequacy she felt in trying to make things right again.

February arrived with noticeably longer days and Gustav began to be more aware of his surroundings. The bear had come out of hibernation. On occasion he smiled at her across from the room and on good days he sat at the table eating his meals and exchanging a few words. Her father looked thin. Over the winter he had become an old man.

On sunny days after lunch they bundled up in hats and heavy sweaters and sat in the sunroom. Being there was like sitting in the middle of the forest, but it was much warmer because the three glassed-in walls let in welcoming heat from the midday sun.

One day while the sun was still shining, giant lacy snowflakes slowly floated down against the dark pines. They were twice the size and fluffier than Eva had ever seen before. Suddenly a slight breeze changed their course, transporting them across the windows like tiny ballerinas dancing on a stage. They reminded her of pictures in a book that Mr. Kronberg had showed her of the Stockholm Ballet. Before she had time to speak to her father a gunshot echoed through the forest.

"Who could that be?" she asked springing from her chair.

"Probably some hunter shooting crows," said Gustav disapprovingly. In a few moments Eva saw a man emerge from the woods. He was bent over, skiing quickly toward the house. Running into the front room she saw the snowy back of a man removing his skis. He seemed very tall and wore a blue knitted cap pulled down over his ears and forehead, but the dark scarf covering his nose and mouth frightened her and she didn't answer his first knock. He knocked a second time.

"Hello. Is anyone in there?" said a voice sounding much like that of Mr. Kronberg. Then she opened the door a crack to examine this scary man with only his eyes showing above the frosted scarf.

"Aren't you going to invite me in, Eva?" he asked, removing his hat and scarf. Now she was embarrassed to see Mats Kronberg standing before her. His face was much thinner, but the twinkling blue eyes and lopsided grin were much the same as she remembered.

Perhaps she looked different too, because he was speechless for a long moment and she felt heat rising to her face as he appraised her. To take attention off herself, she opened the door wide and invited him to come in.

He swiftly slid the large pack from his shoulders and gave her two rabbits. "Probably the freshest meat you will ever eat," he said with a wink. "Nice and fat, too, for this time of year." He brushed the snow from his clothes, stomped his feet and stepped inside. Gustav came in from the sunroom as Eva went to the kitchen with the still-warm rabbits. He scowled at the tall intruder.

"You didn't shoot my crows, did you?" he asked, as his eyes slowly adjusted to the dimness of the room.

"No, sir. Just a couple rabbits." Mats walked closer to shake Gustav's hand. "And how are you today Mr. Gunderson?" Gustav was relieved that no crows had been killed and glad to hear a familiar voice.

"Is that you, Otto?" he asked hopefully.

"No, sir, I'm his son, Mats." Eva could tell her father was still confused and showed them both to the table.

"Papa has been hoping your father would come to visit," she said to Mats. "But I keep reminding him the snow is much too deep in the path for any horse to travel through. And now more snow is falling."

"My father is looking forward to visiting as well," said Mats. "He doesn't ski anymore and asked me to stop in today."

Eva watched Mats open his pack. He placed small bags of coffee beans, sugar, and flour on the table as well as some goat cheese and sausages. Lastly he opened a white linen cloth revealing freshly baked mince tarts and frosted lingonberry pastries. Eva thought to herself, "Mats' mother might be a bit odd at times, but she surely was good hearted and had a fine memory for what people loved to eat."

"Thank you so much, Mats," she said aloud. "Excuse me while I brew some fresh coffee."

In the background Mats' voice was loud and clear as he told her father of his plans to sail to America next year. Mats had the same gift of gab as his father and it was comforting to hear lively conversation in the house again.

The coffee was almost ready when Mats entered the kitchen. He placed a bag of rye flour on the counter beside her.

"Be careful when you open this. Mother packed a dozen eggs in with the flour so they wouldn't get broken."

"How clever of her to think of doing that," replied Eva. "Please thank her for everything, and thank you, Mats, for coming all this way in the snow." Her smile of appreciation showed him how beautiful she had become.

"My pleasure," he replied, stepping behind her, tugging at her braid like he used to years ago when he teased her in the barn. Too old for pigtails now, she wore only one long braid wound around her head as her mother had.

"And how is my little Eva?" he whispered. She felt his warm breath on her ear; his hand playing with the wispy curls on her neck, sending tingles up and down her spine. She was at a loss for words, attributing her feelings to being starved for affection for too long a time.

"You must be almost sixteen now," he said to fill up the empty space.

"Fifteen last Christmas," she replied as nonchalantly as possible, even though she felt him pressing firmly against her backside. His arms crept slowly around her waist, his rough cheek rubbing gently against hers. She closed her eyes for a moment to enjoy the security of his embrace, his nearness releasing the spicy aroma reminiscent of his father. She might have let him kiss her then, but thinking about Mr. Kronberg and the old times brought back a flood of emotions that resulted in a sudden outburst of tears. She covered her face and cried uncontrollably.

At that point Mats didn't know what to think. He turned her around and held her for a long time. She inadvertently put her arms around his waist and leaned against his chest, his hand gently caressing her head as if to stop the tears.

"How silly of me to cry," she said finally, pulling away from him. "It's just that I've felt so alone all winter, taking care of Papa...and here you are being so kind to me." Her sweetly enticing smile almost brought them together again, but her father stood in the doorway asking about the coffee.

"It's all ready, Papa. I'm sorry I took so long."

That was a lie; she wasn't sorry at all. What she wanted was for Mats to hold her again, to feel cared for and protected, and to know how it feels to be kissed by a boy...to be kissed by Mats Kronberg.

The Worst Days

The January cold sneaked between the pine logs, an uninvited visitor that sometimes crept in quietly and other times blew through strongly enough to set the kitchen curtains in motion.

During the day Suvi and Dag wore their outside clothes while preparing meals and doing household chores. When it wasn't snowing Vidar found work to do outside, usually chopping logs for firewood and sometimes in the forest cutting down more trees. There was a lot of shoveling to do after it snowed and old paths that were filled in by blowing snow needed to be cleared again. Yes, Vidar spent a lot of time shoveling and much time repairing broken shovels, for he was not careful and was easily angered. Winter snow and ice took its toll on his patience and on his implements. Coming in from the cold, eating a hearty supper and drinking too much potato liquor made him fall asleep in his chair by the stove. On the coldest nights Suvi and Dag wrapped themselves in blankets and slept on the other side of the fire.

By the first of February the last bottle of potato liquor was empty and Vidar's offensiveness returned. Idle time exposed latent cravings and the lustful look returned to his eyes. Many afternoons Dag stayed in her room, away from his embarrassing stares.

She heard them in their bedroom, even in the middle of the day. No matter if Suvi had her hands in the bread dough or was washing the floor, she never refused him. She told Dag once that it was less hurtful to give in than put up a fuss, that rejection angered a man and only made matters worse. What's going to happen will happen and one might just as well be done with it quickly and get on to better things.

She was speaking about herself, of course, and didn't know that Dag had already tried to refuse him and had figured out for herself that it was better to give in. He'd threatened her afterward, too. "Don't tell your mother," he warned. "Or you'll see Blix dead in his stall," so she'd kept everything to herself.

She and her mother were both good at pretending, but deep snow and frigid weather kept them all inside, too close to each other to pretend everything was all right. Suvi became lethargic and moody, spending endless hours gazing toward the north and remembering better times, while Dag was bored and always aware of Vidar's evil eye. They both envisioned ways of leaving this place and talked in hushed tones at night about how this might happen.

Vidar accepted winter better than they did, but sitting by the kitchen stove for prolonged periods of time made way for lustful fantasizing about the noticeable blossoming of Dag and it wasn't long before his evil urges were put into action.

The winter darkness caused everyone to go to bed early. One night while Vidar slept by the fire, Suvi had a dizzy spell and went to her bedroom. Dag washed the dishes and was scrubbing the kitchen floor when she heard Vidar's chair creak. He wasn't snoring and she suspected he was awake and watching her. Without looking his way she quickly blew out the candle and went to her room, lying in her bed listening for Vidar's snoring to begin again. Instead she heard his heavy footsteps walking across the kitchen floor. Aware that he was standing in her doorway, she made no sound and pretended to be fast asleep.

Suddenly the covers were stripped from her bed and the rough bulk of him straddled her hips, his hands on her firm little breasts. She could barely breathe, but one loud scream awakened Suvi, who quickly lit a candle before rushing to her daughter's room. Dag saw the flame and the horror in her mother's face. Suddenly the room was very bright. Vidar's shirt and hair were on fire as he jumped from the bed and ran out of the room.

"Put on your warmest clothes. We must leave now!" said her mother. "Hurry, I can see him outside rolling in the snow." Suvi pulled on her boots, grabbed her cloak and a loaf of bread, but as they ran toward the door, they saw Vidar's silhouette blocking their way.

"Stay behind me," she whispered to Dag, as she grabbed an iron fry pan. They were not in total darkness. A ray of moonlight flooded through the east window and they saw Vidar's gigantic silhouette lurching toward them. Suvi raised her arm, attempting to hit him over the head, but he grabbed her arm with great force and she dropped the pan. In the time it clanked unseen in the darkness, Dag grabbed a chair and gave Vidar a good blow to the head, which did nothing but enrage his fury. He picked her up and threw her across the room. When she didn't get up he spent his rage on Suvi.

Dag regained consciousness and heard her mother moaning beside her. She could make out Vidar's form sitting in a chair just outside her room, but the pain in her head caused her to lie back on the pillow. When she tried to lift her arm, it wouldn't move. Dag and Suvi were both tied to the bed with very thick rope.

"It's my fault that you are hurting so," whispered Suvi. "I was foolish to think we could ever run away, especially in winter."

"Perhaps we can in the spring when he is busy in the fields," suggested Dag.

"Yes," sighed her mother, "We will try again in the spring."

For the remainder of winter, Vidar kept a very close eye on Suvi and Dag. When he had to go outside they were chained to the stove and at night they were chained to their beds. Later when he began making the liquor again, they were chained to an iron post in the shed like a pair of disobedient dogs.

Even though the potatoes left over from last year had been put into the cellar of the shed and covered with a deep layer of straw, the top layers and those on the outer edges had frozen during the exceptionally cold winter. These had now begun to soften and become rotten, the foul stench taking their breath away as they separated the bad potatoes from the good. The spoiled ones were put into an old wagon that Blix was forced to pull through the frozen fields to be dumped at the edge of the forest.

They often plotted their escape, but the brass key that could set them free hung high on the shed wall not twenty feet away and just out of reach.

Spring Joy and Sorrow

Spring emerged from its winter sleep as a curious child; the sun crawling slowly across forgotten territory, cautious and hesitant at first, and then wildly inquisitive as it discovered new areas to explore. The Norrland sun will not be rushed and winter's grip remained tight and firm until late March. Animals and humans had no choice but to accept her ways and patiently wait for spring's warmth to thaw the frozen land.

Finally the sun peeked over the trees, searching every mountain and valley, every hidden rock and sheltered plant, overspreading the vast land with energizing brightness. Light danced across the rooftops, creeping down the side of the barn to meet the still-frozen ground. Snow melted in front of the cottage and the crocus poked their yellow and purple heads through the muddy earth.

Gustav was drawn to his favorite old chair on the porch and Eva brought her knitting to sit with him on warm afternoons. They breathed in the fresh sweet fragrance of spruce and pine and listened to the varied songs of birds returning to their spring nesting places. They often saw foxes dart across the lawn in pursuit of adventuresome mice and sometimes heard lumbering moose moving toward open waters and summer feeding areas. All this activity plus the sun's warmth and light triggered the latent hopes stirring within the heart of Gustav.

"We should hitch up Slofock and go visit Otto," her father suggested one day, and she'd tried to explain that the ground was still thawing, that they'd have to wait until the mud firmed up in the path.

"Has the path dried out yet?" he asked every day until finally he got up to see for himself. She ran after him to guide his faltering footsteps across the soft and spongy lawn stopping on the last bit of dead grass to observe the slick and muddy path to the road.

"It looks fine and smooth to me," he told her, but she knew better and attempted to show him that driving through it would not be possible.

"Watch me," she said, taking two big steps from the edge and sinking in over her ankles. Then the frost let go beneath her feet and she fell on her hands and knees, thrashing about in the foot-thick muck like a drowning swimmer. She was not in the best humor when she finally stood again on firm ground with mud-caked clothes and a dirt-splattered face. Gustav, regarding her as some ghoulish apparition rising from the bowels of the earth, was startled and started walking back to the cottage.

"It's me, Papa!" she shouted, slogging her way toward him and wiping the mud from her face. Then he turned, roaring with laughter, upon seeing her familiar smile and red hair. It felt good to see him in a jovial mood and she forgot about her embarrassment for getting into such an unladylike predicament.

He didn't ask her again about riding in the oxcart, but he did take pleasure in reminding her over and over about that unforgettable day.

After a few weeks of mild weather, the ground firmed up and dried sufficiently for Mr. Kronberg's buggy to easily make it up the path. Eva ran down to the barn to meet him, anticipating his bear-hugging embrace, and she was not disappointed. In his arms all her worries and concerns evaporated into nothingness like the fog on a sunny morning.

"How thin you are, Eva!" he said smiling down at her. "I was just telling Mrs. Kronberg we should have insisted that you and your father spend the past winter with us."

That idea had never occurred to her, even on the darkest days. Yes, her father probably would have done better at the Kronbergs, but who can know what might have been.

Gustav showed great interest as his old friend placed small bags of rye meal, sugar and coffee on the table, along with a ham shank and a round of goat cheese, but something was missing and his face lengthened into sadness. Eva fondled the bundle hidden in her lap that Mr. Kronberg had given her. Then she opened the linen napkin in front of her father. It did her heart good to see his happy smile as he picked up one of the mince tarts, closing his eyes peacefully as the sweet fruity delicacy touched his tongue.

They sat around the table like in the old times. Mr. Kronberg kept up his usual line of chatter causing Gustav to nod in agreement now and then, although for the most part he remained quiet and thoughtful. He seemed satisfied just to look at his old friend and quietly enjoy the delicious tarts and slowly sip his coffee. Otto noticed how Gustav had failed during the winter, but he never spoke of it nor would he take any money for all the food he and his family had so generously given to them the past winter. He promised to return within a week or two with a surprise.

Gustav went downhill after his friend's visit. Eva tried to keep his spirits up with talk about the big surprise, but her father didn't like surprises and he paid little heed. A few mornings later she found him lying in bed, incoherent and looking around in bewilderment. He would not eat, so she sat holding his hand and read favorite verses and stories from the Bible. He was comforted by her voice although his pale blank eyes gazed unknowingly toward the ceiling.

Eva awakened to a gloomy stillness, instantly knowing all was not well. Through her window the sky was a steely gray, the trees of the forest dark and unmoving; the atmosphere inside the cottage, cold and still as if in mourning. She struggled to rise and knew even before she entered her father's room there was no life in him.

Panic and indecision tightened her stomach into an unyielding, taut rope. She ran to the porch for a breath of fresh air, shouting Mr. Kronberg's name, pleading for him to please come quickly. She knew he couldn't hear through the thick forest so many miles away, but the ultimate release was felt throughout her body and she ran in her bare feet and nightgown down the path to the road.

After that everything was a blur. She remembered the coarse pebbles pricking her feet and seeing something big and shiny and black coming toward her. It was hours afterward that she realized Mr. Kronberg had come to show them his new automobile and she'd spoiled his surprise with the news of her father's death. It was the first time she'd ever seen Mr. Kronberg cry.

After the funeral, she stayed the night with the Kronbergs and they discussed her future. She needed money and would have to find a job, but there wasn't much employment in the north, especially for a young girl.

"I know of a nice family near Gothenburg," Mr. Kronberg said. "I'll put in a good word for you."

"Gothenburg?" Eva remembered such a city in the south of Sweden from her geography lessons. "That's so far away!" she thought to herself. She also understood that changes must be made and she trusted Mr. Kronberg's judgment. He offered to sell the cottage and the animals, but Eva was distressed about selling her beloved cow. Stella was all she had left of her past. She needed time to think things over.

About a week later, Eva was awakened by a knock on the door. She peeked through the window in the gray morning light and saw Mr. and Mrs. Kronberg standing solemnly on the front porch. After splashing cold water on her face and patting down her hair, she dressed, tied a clean apron around her waist and opened the door.

Mrs. Kronberg nodded as she followed her husband into the front room, the wonderful aroma of freshly baked bread drifting from the covered loaf she gave to Eva. The bread was still warm and Eva wondered what time Mrs. Kronberg got up this morning to prepare and bake bread by this early hour.

"Please sit down. I'll get you both some coffee," she said as Mrs. Kronberg's eyes swept from wall to wall, finally settling on the disarray of clothes and household items scattered at one end of the room where Eva had been sorting through her parents' belongings. Too late to worry about the clutter now, she thought, and headed for the kitchen.

If she took time to grind fresh coffee, they would know for sure she was a late riser, so she quickly reheated the pot from yesterday. There was no sound coming from the next room as she hastily sliced the bread and arranged the coffee tray, wishing she had some jam or just a little butter.

Finally the three of them sat looking at one another, drinking yesterday's coffee, and eating the fresh bread, each contemplating the appropriate words to say in the hushed, nearly empty room that had somehow forgotten the good times. If only she hadn't overslept and been better prepared for company, thought Eva, supposing that Mrs. Kronberg had already cleaned her barn, fed the goats and done all the milking, besides baking bread and fixing a huge breakfast for her own family. Considering the reason for this early morning visit, Eva had an empty feeling that life as she'd known it had finally come to an end. Finally Mr. Kronberg put his cup down and cleared his throat.

"The Lindholms will be expecting you to begin work on Monday, so we should plan to leave very early on Sunday morning."

"So soon?" she asked, glancing anxiously out the window toward the barn. Mr. Kronberg knew she was thinking about the animals.

"We've decided to buy Stella and Slofock. That way you will know they have a good home and won't be worried."

All week long Eva had battled with the question of selling Stella and now, in an instant, the problem was resolved. She quickly wiped a tear from one eye and then the other, not knowing if the cause was joy or sadness. Mr. Kronberg's solution was so simple that she wondered why she hadn't thought of it herself, but then realized she had been side-stepping the whole idea and not seriously considering selling her beloved cow at all. Now that the decision had been made, she was well prepared when Mr. Kronberg suggested going to the barn to see the animals.

The strong scent of fresh manure met them at the door. Eva knew it was no secret to the Kronbergs that she had not yet been to the barn this morning to do the chores, but they said nothing. Her feelings of inadequacy evaporated as she rushed to give Stella and Slofock fresh water and forked hay into their cribs while Mr. Kronberg quickly moved in to hoe back the manure and his wife gathered fresh straw to spread in their stalls.

"Looks like she'll be dropping a calf next month," he said, gently punching Stella's right side and feeling her udder. Mrs. Kronberg seemed overjoyed at the prospect of having a newborn calf to add to her collection of baby goats.

"I do the milking, you know," she said, smiling at Eva. "I will take good care of Stella and her baby."

Eva was comforted by her words, reinforcing even more her decision to let go of the past and face the future with optimism and courage.

Mr. Kronberg fished into his pockets and counted out several large bills, but Eva held up her hand in protest.

"I owe you more than that for all the food you've given us," she told him, but he wouldn't hear of it and tucked the bills in her apron pocket, telling her he would be back tomorrow to pick up the cattle.

The sound of light rain tapping against the window awakened Eva early the next morning and she found both Stella and Slofock still laying in their stalls. Stella rose quickly for her grain, but Slofock, thinking the grain would still be there until he's good and ready, lowered his head for another nap.

"You'd better get up, Slofock, or you won't have time to eat."

She rubbed his forehead and he lapped her arm with his rough tongue before slowly rising to his knees.

She was milking Stella when a wagon pulled into the dooryard. Mr. Kronberg had surprised her again by arriving early, but today she was almost ready. The barn door opened and a voice called out, "Good morning," but it wasn't Mr. Kronberg.

It was Mats who leaned against the stall looking down at her with his lopsided grin. She smiled up at him, noticing the gray, rain-soaked shirt he wore, revealing bulging muscles and large veins in his arms. The sight of him made her stomach quiver and she felt heat rising into her neck and face.

"Where's your father?" she asked, hoping to divert attention away from herself.

"He's fixing the harness on one of the horses," he said, hunkering down beside her, so close that his knee touched hers. "How can anyone look so beautiful this early in the morning?" he thought to himself.

She felt his gaze and milked faster, but Stella had nearly dried up and Eva's efforts came to nothing.

"Looks like she's given out already," he said, taking the pail and hanging it on a nail behind him. Eva attempted to walk past, but his arm blocked her way.

"I'll let you go by, but it'll cost ya." He stood looking down at her again with that silly grin on his face. She knew the price, but just shrugged her shoulders and smiled as if she had nothing to give him, her thoughts on that kiss she'd been dreaming about since last winter.

Her reaction teased his emotions. He had thought she might dash by him and run out of the barn, but here she was only inches away looking up at him almost expectantly. His fingers traced the outline of her cheek, sending shivers down her spine, the twinkle in his eyes now replaced by a more serious look of intent.

He took her face in his hands and the softness of his lips pressed gently on hers...slow and sweet at first, but then she felt the cool, rough boards against her back and the hardness of him against her belly. His kiss became more forceful and insistent, his moist lips parting hers. When his searching tongue met hers, she pushed him away.

Mats' arms hung limply by his sides as he backed slowly out of the stall. All tenderness had vanished from his face. In its place was a look of surprise and bewilderment, or maybe rejection. It hadn't been her intent to hurt his feelings, but the intensity of his kiss had more than surprised her and she'd acted in haste.

"I'm sorry, Mats. I shouldn't have pushed you away like that."

Either he didn't hear what she said or it was too late for an apology. Mats had already gone into Slofock's stall and was leading him out of the barn.

Eva was glad when Mr. Kronberg came in to get Stella, but seeing her beloved cow go out the door for the last time made her cry and she remained in the barn until she heard Mats hollering.

Stella was giving the men a hard time. Mr. Kronberg pulled on her halter, enticing her with a dipper of grain, while Mats pushed from the rear. Eva could tell that Stella had no intention of going up those steep planks and into the wagon. She walked closer, knowing very well that Stella would follow her up the ramp easily with no halter on at all, but it wasn't her place to interfere with the men.

Eva observed Mats' impatience as he grabbed Stella's tail roughly in his hand, twisting it up over her back as he leaned his shoulder against her hind end. Stella balked, then side-stepped off the ramp, causing Mats to slip and fall to the ground. With a very red face, he grabbed a hefty stick and hit the cow with a hard blow on the rump. Such rough treatment didn't set well with Stella and she broke free and ran back to the barn.

"I'll get her," Eva shouted to the men, guessing at this point they might be willing to let her help.

When she and Stella returned, Mr. Kronberg was waiting by the wagon, but Mats sat in front with his back toward them. Eva took Stella's head in her arms, stroked her nose gently and rubbed her behind the ears, all the while soothing her with soft, kind words. Eva saw Mr. Kronberg wink at her, nodding approvingly as she led the obedient cow into the wagon and tied her beside Slofock.

Mats never said a word, nor did he glance Eva's way all the while Mr. Kronberg discussed plans for their trip to Gothenburg on Sunday. She had two strikes against her; one for pushing Mats away in the barn and now another for showing him up by proving she could do something better than he could. She liked Mats but today she learned something new; he still had a few child-like traits he should have already grown out of.

It was decided that Mr. Kronberg would pick her up the day

after tomorrow at the early hour of three in the morning. As she watched the wagon lumbering down the narrow path, neither Stella nor Slofock looked back. They were going to their new home and had already accepted their fate, and so should she. Taking a deep breath, strength rushed through her veins and she walked back to the cottage a little taller, remembering her mother's words regarding acceptance.

The next day was warm and spring-like. After everything was packed and the cottage thoroughly cleaned, Eva found herself standing in the yard with absolutely nothing to do. The scent of spruce permeated the air and the woodland path beckoned for one last visit to the lake. There was a need deep within her to walk through the forest just one more time to revive all her happy memories, see the flowers and bushes in bloom, remember the sight and sounds of every bird, animal and tree, to smell the earthy aroma of the forest floor and to sit on the little sandy beach for one last look at the mountains rising above the clear blue lake.

Walking to the lake seemed much shorter than before. Sitting in the shade of a birch grove reflecting on her mother, father and Ingrid, she carefully placed each sweet remembrance on a shelf in her mind where in the future she could open the pages of her memories to relive again the happy events of her life in Norrland.

Eva thought about 'the strange one,' too, her gaze turning northward toward a dark line of tall pines whose tops were lost in a fog of threatening gray clouds. Remembering the potato farm and the ugly giant sent a chill through her body. However, today would be her last and only chance to see the boy again, to maybe ask him about the girl in the pink dress and hopefully find out more about 'the strange one.' At the very same time, Eva had a most unusual craving for a freshly baked potato that prompted her feet to start out on the uneven path to the north.

The way seemed longer here and darker, too, under the tall trees that grew thick along the narrow, crooked path. Finally she came to the familiar birch grove overlooking the small group of gray, ramshackle buildings across the field. The uninviting scene was more desolate and bleak than she recalled and the stony field was now overgrown with dry brown weeds. A rotten stench wafted across the field and took her breath away.

Deep wheel ruts cut across an adjacent field and in the distance a horse strained to pull a heavy wagon. Shouts of a man echoed across the field, making her cringe as he slapped the reins across the stumbling horse's back. The poor creature fell to its knees only to feel again the stinging reins, and she vividly remembered Potatohead hitting the boy that day when she and her father brought Stella to be bred. Thoughts of Potatohead almost made her turn back, but the desire for a baked potato and the hope of learning more about 'the strange one' was too strong.

The rough uphill climb to the stone wall was difficult, but then she saw a second field to be crossed. This field was much smoother, newly planted to rye and much easier for walking. She heard the man shouting again, fainter now as he neared a stone wall at the edge of the forest, a warning for her to hasten her pace.

Approaching a small lean-to, Eva heard a chain rattling. Inside was a mean-looking bull, glaring at her from one of the stalls. At the end of the farm yard, almost hidden by tall pine trees was a small cabin made of logs, and across from that stood the largest building of the three, an older barn with a new addition at the rear.

Slowly she made her way to the corner of the old barn. Between wide cracks in the shrunken gray boards came the soft murmur of women's voices and she saw two people sitting in the middle of several piles of potatoes. The wide front door was open and Eva peeked in. As her eyes adjusted to the dim interior of the barn she recognized the round-faced boy, who immediately stood up, pointing to the wall next to her.

"The key! The key!" he shouted impatiently. Then a woman rose from behind a pile of potatoes. It was then Eva heard the chains and saw that these two were tied like dogs to a pipe driven into the ground.

The woman spoke slowly in a firm, unwavering voice as if to

calm the excited boy.

"There's a key just above your head on the wall. Please give it to me."

The key hung from a nail that was bent backwards toward the wall and Eva was unable to slip the key off. The woman looked around the large enclosure and gestured to a further corner.

"Quickly, get that iron bar. Then you can reach the key," she said with more urgency in her voice.

Eva tried several times to dislodge the key but the nail was more like a spike with a large head, making it difficult to lift the key over it, plus the bar was heavy and unwieldy.

"Hurry, before he gets back!" screamed the boy in a high-pitched voice that sounded more like that of a girl. The air was charged with fearful anxiety, but finally the key fell to the floor. Eva picked up the key and gave it to the woman, who, with fumbling fingers, tried in vain to unlock the chain from the boy's ankle. Finally they all heard a loud snap and the boy was free, but his expression suddenly turned to horror as he stared toward the open door.

Eva felt an ominous presence behind her, but she didn't need to turn around. From the burly shadow looming across the dirt floor beside her, she knew at once it was the ugly giant called Potatohead.

The woman whispered to Eva, "Get out of here! Now!"

Eva's legs felt heavy as lead, her body refusing to move as the doorway darkened and Vidar moved closer.

"Well, what have we here?" he bellowed, gaping at her like some predatory animal greedily anticipating a tasty meal. Words numbed on Eva's lips and the woman spoke for her.

"Perhaps she's come for a few potatoes. Is that right, child?" Eva nodded and the woman stooped to gather several large, firm potatoes from one of the good piles.

"Only two, please," Eva managed to say.

"No charge for just two," said the woman, loud enough so Vidar could hear. Then she whispered in Eva's ear again, warning her to run away while she still had a chance.

Eva spun around quickly, but Vidar's firm grip on her arm stopped her, causing the potatoes to fall to the floor.

"Leave those," he said gruffly, pulling her away from the doorway. "Better ones out back."

Vidar covered a lot of ground with only a few steps, almost dragging Eva behind him, the stench of rotting potatoes growing stronger as the room grew dim. Large wooden bins blocked her view of the woman and her son and she heard only Vidar's heavy breathing as he pressed her firmly against one of the bins. She struggled to get free, but he grabbed both of her wrists and held them with his left hand in a painful grip behind her back. He groaned with a satisfied sneer that revealed a mouthful of rotting blackened teeth.

Cool air swept across her chest as he ripped open her bodice with his right hand, crudely groping her soft breast. Eva screamed as his rough beard scratched her tender skin and she kicked against his shins as hard as she could. She might as well have been kicking a thick pine trunk; for now he was angered even more and she had a very sore foot.

He forced her to the ground and she grew faint from the smell of his foul breath and the potent stench of old sweat, suffocating her in a sea of putridness. A cool hand touched her warm thigh and she struggled unsuccessfully to get away. Her screams were muffled by his smothering heaviness that was slowly squeezing the breath out of her. She had morbid thoughts of dying and being found in this unwomanly manner.

Suddenly there was a loud thud and Vidar's head dropped heavily on the ground beside her. "Get up!" shouted the woman. Eva rolled to the side and scrambled to her feet.

Vidar moaned, slowly rising to his knees. Eva realized then that the woman had probably struck him with the iron bar, which she raised again with a furious grimace, striking him on the head. Each time Vidar moved, she hit him until he finally collapsed on the floor, blood oozing from his head and running down his cheek. For such a small woman, she had great strength and determination. Or was this an act of vengeance, the result of many years of pent-up anger that she was finally able to release? The woman raised the bar again, but Vidar wasn't moving and Eva shouted for her to stop.

"You don't want murder on your hands, do you? If he dies, you will go to prison. Your son needs you." With glazed eyes, as if in a trance, the woman turned to look at Eva. She had spent her rage. Her shoulders relaxed and the bar fell from her hands with a loud clang. Then the boy came forward to comfort her, causing Eva to draw the ripped parts of her blouse together, tucking them securely into the waistband of her skirt. They all stared in disbelief at the motionless heap on the floor. Feeling very apologetic and humble toward this beautiful young girl, the woman curtsied.

"My name is Suvi and this is my daughter, Dagny. We are so sorry..."

Eva also curtsied, always being respectful toward an older person, and introduced herself.

"I am Eva Gunderson. My father used to buy potatoes here when he brought our cow to be bred." She was unconsciously looking at Dagny and thinking back to that one time she accompanied her father and saw the boy in the field. Dagny, aware of Eva's confusion, was remembering that day, too. She removed her cap, rumpling her thin dark hair with her fingers, and looked down at Vidar.

"Because of him, Mother always made me dress like a boy," she explained to Eva. "Except when I went to the lake alone and could wear mother's pink dress."

For a moment Dagny and her mother exchanged sympathetic looks. Eva didn't know what to think at first, but then everything came together. 'The strange one' wasn't strange or peculiar at all; just a girl who had been forced to wear boy's clothes because of this terrible man she lived with. Now that Eva understood about the girl in the pink dress, she felt sorry for Dagny.

Vidar's labored breathing sounded magnified in the stillness of the big barn. Suvi, as if now suddenly reminded of his presence, grabbed one of his legs and ordered Dagny to take the other one.

"We must drag him to the post and chain him there before he wakes up."

Eva immediately saw the irony of all this and found it oddly amusing that he was to be chained, as he had chained them. Perhaps Suvi had thought of this scenario before, because she knew exactly what she was doing as she attached a chain to each of his wrists and snapped the locks shut. They all breathed a sigh of relief that Vidar didn't wake up in the process.

"Let's get out of here," said Suvi.

After the big door was closed and locked the three of them stood in the middle of the dirt path with little to say. The sun was hidden now behind clouds that threatened rain and thunder rolled in the distant hills. So much had occurred in such a short time that none of them could understand the full significance of it all. Blix whinnied softly as he walked toward them pulling the empty cart. Dagny went over to remove his harness and led him to the well to drink.

Suvi took this time to explain to Eva how Blix brought them to this place so many years before, when Vidar had been more considerate and easier to get along with, and afterward when he made the liquor and started drinking heavily.

"What will happen to him now?" asked Eva.

Suvi thought for a moment and replied. "I will have a doctor from the village come to look at him, but Vidar will never see our faces again."

By admitting that, the idea became a reality, and her tired, care-worn face brightened with joyful anticipation as she ran toward her daughter.

"We're free, Dagny…free from him and this awful place!"

Eva watched them embrace, giddy with happiness and wild, exuberant dancing. Blix looked up questioningly from drinking to watch them skipping playfully around the well.

Eva was happy for Suvi and Dagny, but she also felt dirty, wishing only for a good hot bath to wash away all memories of Vidar, so she began walking toward the gap. Stopping by the stone wall she turned to see Suvi leading Blix toward the cabin, but Dagny still lingered by the well looking toward the gap. Eva waved; then Dagny slowly raised her hand. There was so much they wanted to know about each other, but both had more pressing matters on their minds now. Dagny waved one more time before disappearing behind the lean-to. Then Eva hurried back across the fields.

Only when she came to the forest did Eva slow down long enough to gather her thoughts. Although today was one she'd rather forget, two good things happened. One was that she arrived in time to give her two neighbors the key to their freedom, and secondly, she understood more now about 'the strange one.'

Thunder rumbled again from the north and a cooling breeze pushed Eva to a faster pace. She thought of Vidar, who must be the strongest person in the whole world and might easily break his chains. Did he know where she lived? Would he try to track her down? Every sound in the forest caused her to turn around in fear and the path to the lake seemed very long.

Dark clouds covered the mountain tops and a thick mist hovered eerily over the pewter-colored water. When large drops of cold rain splattered on her clothes and skin, she took one last, lingering look across the murky lake and then ran back to the path that would take her home.

Once inside the cottage, Vidar's image flashed before her eyes sending waves of anxiety throughout her body. Realizing she would be alone tonight, she slid a heavy bureau in front of the back door and pushed the dining table against the front door, then closed the windows and curtains before building a fire to heat water for a bath.

She took off her shoes and stockings, removed the ripped blouse and shift and threw them into the stove. Watching the fabric shrivel, smolder and finally be consumed by hungry flames, she hoped those horrific moments in the potato barn would be as quickly extinguished from her thoughts.

A hot bath helped soak away the day's bad memories, but the fear of Vidar remained. Sitting in her father's big chair, she understood what was missing now: that solid sense of security, of knowing and believing that no matter what terrible thing ever came along, her father would protect her from all harm.

Her eye caught sight of his rifle hanging on the wall. She knew how to load the gun; her father had shown her one day after a fox stole her favorite laying hen and she'd been mad enough to want to shoot the furry little thief. She had sat on the porch steps with the gun in her hands for several evenings watching the coop. One night about dusk, the robber came back. The rifle was heavy and she'd missed, but the bullet pinged loudly on a metal bucket, scaring the fox away and he never bothered the chickens again.

Remembering that evening made Eva smile and for the first time since morning she felt hungry enough to eat the last scraps of bread and cheese. There was milk in the spring house, but at this point she was not brave enough to go outside, so she heated up the morning coffee and drank it with a good dose of sugar.

Eva wrapped her father's afghan around her shoulders and sat in the darkened room with the gun across her lap watching the front door and listening to the creaking sounds a house makes when the wind blows. Rain tapped melodiously against the window next to her and eventually lulled her into a fitful sleep.

She dreamed about a huge dragon with dark, blotchy skin chasing her through the forest, his mouth spewing smoke that smelled like rotten potatoes. She tried in vain to run on legs that barely moved, while each step of the dragon made the earth tremble beneath her feet.

Eva awakened hearing the rumble of thunder. With her heart pounding and a throbbing in her head she peeked through the curtain, but the pelting rain blurred her vision and she saw what looked to be a moose rounding the corner of the house. For some reason this gave her a measure of comfort and for a while she listened to the storm move away.

When the old clock in the corner chimed three times, she rose from the chair and lit a candle. Then she dressed, slid the table away from the front door and walked slowly from room to room, remembering the highs and lows of her fifteen years of living here in the great forests of Norrland.

A New Beginning

Suvi and Dagny were trotting down the same gravel road as they had those many years ago when they first met Vidar. This time, as a wagon approached in the distance, Suvi avoided any confrontation and turned the horse into the woods.

"We had bad luck on this road once before," she told her daughter. "We'll let Blix have his way through the forest for a while."

Dagny leaned against Suvi's back remembering how her mother always told her things happen for a reason, and good or bad they must be accepted and dealt with; the good being enjoyed, the bad endured and made better. Perhaps they should have waited to see what the wagon might have brought, she thought to herself. It might have been something surprisingly wonderful. Now, by avoiding the situation she would never know.

Dagny also thought about Eva arriving unexpectedly at the farm today. She had come for a good reason...to buy potatoes. Things hadn't turned out well for Eva, nor had they for Vidar, but for Dagny and her mother, this had been a day of extraordinary good luck. Still, there seemed no fairness that Eva had to suffer for their good fortune.

When the first drops of rain began to fall they found a sheltered place near a fast-running stream so that Blix could rest. He drank his fill and grazed by the water's edge, then stood thoughtfully looking into the water, his head drooping slightly and then a little more until he was asleep on his feet. Suvi and Dagny relaxed on the forest floor and ate some bread and cheese, the quietness interrupted only by the fast flowing bubbling stream. They, too, dozed off, until Dagny was awakened by Blix nuzzling her cheek and her giggles roused Suvi.

For a long time they continued riding through the forest, although neither could tell which direction Blix was going until the passing clouds thinned over the rising moon. Instantly Suvi knew they had traveled too far to the west when an open space appeared in front of them. It was as large as one of their potato fields.

"Poor Blix must have been going around in circles trying to get back to the farm," she exclaimed. Dagny shuddered as Blix persisted on walking toward the great expanse of gray. Then his feet sloshed into wetness and he lowered his head to drink. Across the way moonlight revealed the familiar outline of mountains.

"Look!" cried Dagny, "The mountains! He's brought us to the lake!"

They rested a short while on the sandy beach listening to thunder rumbling from the north as raindrops pattered lightly on the birch leaves above them. Lightning flashed behind the mountains, illuminating the sky and Blix jumped back to face the bushes. Suvi talked softly to him and rubbed his neck.

"Blix will be more comfortable in the forest," she said. "We should keep moving. It is better we have more space between us and the farm."

All of a sudden Dagny didn't feel so safe here. Neither had mentioned Vidar's name, nor the possibility of him getting free and following them, but now fear materialized in her mind and she was eager to leave.

"If we go this way, we will come to the cottage where Eva lives," she told her mother. "Perhaps they will let us stay there for the night."

"Perhaps," replied Suvi, jumping quickly on Blix's back. "You can lead for a while so he stays on the right trail." Dagny was pleased to have something to do, but soon Blix was pushing her along with his nose.

"So you are as anxious as I am to be far away from here," she whispered to him, and he walked faster.

Dagny thought about Vidar's untimely arrival at the potato shed today, and the familiar craving in his eyes. To him Eva was a great prize, a beautifully wrapped package he was compelled to unwrap.

How she wished Eva could have gotten away before Vidar showed up. Her mother said everything happens for a reason, so who knows what might have been. Dagny knew one thing; it had been a good feeling to see him chained to the iron post and the smile of satisfaction on her mother's face.

After they had packed their few belongings and settled themselves on Blix's back they had heard the rattling of chains and Vidar swearing in the potato shed.

"Should we give him some food before we go?" Dagny had asked, thinking that even a chained animal needs water and something to eat. They had looked at each other disdainfully as if deciding which of them might open the shed door, but neither wished to see his ugly face again.

"I have a plan," was all her mother had said, reining Blix away from the farm. Dagny was satisfied with the answer, but as they passed the lean-to she slid to the ground with a plan of her own.

"I'm going to give Old Bull some hay and water."

"Hurry. It looks like rain," replied Suvi. "Just like my Dagny to think of everything," she thought to herself. Then Suvi saw the bull prance around the dooryard before trotting eagerly into the woods.

"I must have left the latch unhooked," Dagny said with a smirk. Her mother just smiled and urged Blix along. They were both thinking of their own freedom and how Old Bull should have a chance to go to a better place, too.

Flickers of light shooting down through the trees reminded Dagny about lightning striking a tree in a farmer's field one night, killing two cows that stood beneath it, and she hastened her pace.

The thunder was directly overhead now, the cold rain falling so hard and fast that the canopy of trees could not hold the wetness. The path narrowed and her feet slipped on the wet ground.

"Are we on the right path?" hollered Suvi.

"I think so," replied Dagny, although she wasn't certain.

"Come sit behind me. Blix can pick his way for a while."

A brisk wind caused low hanging branches to swing back and forth slapping against their heads and backs, soaking through their clothes. They crouched low, hoping Blix would guide them in the right direction.

Suddenly he stopped abruptly. Sheets of rain blocked their view, but through the blur there appeared a small opening and the outline of a building.

"That's it, Mother. That's the cottage!"

"They've gone to bed already," sighed Suvi, noticing that no light showed through any of the windows. They were both disappointed, but Dagny was still optimistic.

"I remember a barn," she said. "Perhaps we can bed down there."

Dagny was surprised to see no animals inside the barn; not even the red and white cow was there. Blix made his way into one of the stalls and began rummaging in the feed trough.

"They're probably out to pasture now," said Suvi, wasting no time in arranging a bed of hay for the two of them. It was dry and snug inside and they stretched out on the soft hay listening to the gentle rain on the tin roof.

Almost immediately Suvi fell asleep, but Dagny was wide awake thinking what an extraordinary day this had been...a day filled with extreme mixtures of every kind of sadness and joy imaginable ...all because this girl named Eva happened to stop in to buy some potatoes. She should have thanked her at the time for setting them free, but tomorrow would soon be here and she could barely wait until morning to see Eva again.

The night had many sounds. Rain tapped gently on the roof, an owl hooted from a nearby tree and some animal howled in the distance. Her mother's breathing was deep and louder now and

Blix stood contentedly munching hay.

Light flickered through a small window. She watched it slide across the timbers and then vanish into a far corner. Suvi stirred beside her.

"Was that lightning?" she whispered.

"I don't think so," replied Dagny, observing a steady brightness through the window.

"Those are the brightest lanterns I've ever seen," exclaimed Suvi as two narrow beams of light illuminated the cottage. Suddenly two figures appeared out of the darkness and disappeared inside the house. Then they were back, carrying a long box toward the two bright lanterns.

"Do you think they are robbers?" exclaimed Dagny.

"Maybe someone died and they're taking out the body," suggested her mother, "But it seems odd to be doing such a thing in the middle of the night."

They watched the two figures moving about. One of them ran toward the barn.

"Quick, hide in the hay," ordered Suvi.

Dagny was scared, afraid she might sneeze and give them away.

"Hold your nose and breathe through your mouth," whispered her mother.

The door opened, and a moment later slammed shut, alerting Blix, who stepped nervously in the stall. Then all was deathly quiet again.

"I don't think they are thieves," said Suvi. "Someone grabbed the coil of rope hanging on the door as if they knew it would be there."

The two figures worked behind the lights, then a third walked out of the house carrying two heavy sacks, pausing briefly to look back at the cottage.

"That's her!" said Dagny, a little too loudly.

"Hush up," warned her mother as they listened to three people talking and laughing.

"Well, they all appear to know each other and seem very

happy, so I doubt there's a body in that box," whispered Suvi, very much relieved.

Doors slammed, then a rumbling noise caused the beams of light to circle around the dooryard, lighting the bushes and trees. Following behind was a large, square object silhouetted against the moving lights that appeared to glide down the path all by itself.

"What kind of a contraption is that?" exclaimed Dagny, poking her head far out the window. "It's moving, but I see no horse or ox pulling it."

Suvi strained to see, too, as the lights bounced along the path. "This is a peculiar place, Dagny. I think we should get out of here before they come back."

Exiting the Past

The oddest thing was that Eva didn't feel sad about leaving Norrland. Of course there was nothing left now but memories, and after yesterday she didn't feel safe living there all by herself.

She knew Mr. Kronberg was coming in his new automobile. He had given her a ride home in it the day of the funeral. Shiny and black it was, with soft, plushy seats, and the ride was as smooth as floating on a cloud. In front were two glass lamps that he said made it possible to drive in total darkness. She hadn't believed him, just as she hadn't years ago in the library when he said the orchestra was inside that magical little box.

"I would never lie to you, Eva," he had assured her. "I'll be picking you up on Sunday a little after three in the morning. You will see the lights then and know I am telling you the truth."

She believed him now. Two bright lights had come bouncing up the dirt path making the dooryard like daytime. Then she'd seen two men walking toward the cottage. She was surprised to see Mats and wondered if he would also be driving to the Lindholms.

Mats was talkative and making jokes as they entered the room, acting as if nothing out of the ordinary had happened two days before. Eva certainly hadn't forgotten his kiss in the barn and how he'd mistreated Stella, but she was too much relieved upon seeing these two friendly faces to let anything of the past bother her. It had also occurred to her that after this trip, she might never see either of them again, so she'd put on a jolly face, choosing to make the best of this very important day in her life.

They carried her mother's wooden bridal chest out to the car and while she took a last look around the house, Mats came running into the kitchen asking for a piece of rope. She told him there was one coiled up on the inside of the barn door, but for someone in such a hurry, he lingered long enough for them both to remember last winter when they'd been in the kitchen together.

She saw that same yearning in his eyes when she smiled, but he must have remembered the time in the barn and that feeling of rejection because he suddenly spun around and ran toward the door. She left her foolish, romantic thoughts in the kitchen and went back to the parlor.

The stove was cold, the house was neat and clean and no candles were burning, except for the one she held in her hand. Sometime in the future Mr. Kronberg would return. She'd left a note by the door telling him to sell the furniture and keep the money in payment for everything his family had done for her and her father during the past winter.

Then she blew out the candle, picked up her bags and shut the door for the last time.

Suvi and Dagny

At first light Dagny opened the barn door to gaze upon the cottage. For years now she'd held its beautiful image in her head and each time the picture had been magnified, the buildings becoming larger and more ornate, the flowers growing abundantly more vivid and colorful.

Everything today looked smaller and a bit dreary, though it

was still far nicer than the rough, drafty log hut back at the potato farm. The white paint had turned grayish on the thin boards under the roof and windows, the flowers fewer and less brilliant and the grass sparse and long in the front yard. Lacy curtains showed through several windows and she was curious to know what the rooms behind them looked like.

"You look a little dreamy-eyed," commented Suvi. "What are you thinking?" Dagny took her time to answer, not daring to reveal how much she wanted to go inside the cottage, walk around the rooms and see how this family lived.

"Nothing much," she said, "Except this place doesn't look quite how I imagined it from before."

"Our minds can play tricks on us," replied her mother, thinking back to her time at the miner's house and wondering how much of it was true. "We sometimes imagine things to be better than they actually were."

"I haven't seen anyone about, but there's a creek in the pasture. Perhaps I'll take Blix down for a drink."

When her mother made no objection, Dagny led the horse along the stone wall where a small shelter straddled the creek. It was made of river stones with a low tile roof and a small wooden door. The smell of sweet moss enticed her to open the door and to her surprise she saw a small metal jug setting on a low, flat rock.

The jug was half full of very cold milk, old enough to have a thick layer of cream on top. She wanted to stick her finger into the creamy thickness, but did not. To eat another's food without asking was something she could not do. Suddenly she found herself running to the cottage and knocking on the door.

When no one answered, she opened the door just wide enough to peek in. It was disappointing to see only a few filled sacks and furniture pushed to one end of the room partially covered with quilts. She hollered into the dim room, and when no one answered, she called again. It was obvious that the people who live here had gone away and forgotten about the milk in the springhouse, so she ran back to the creek, grabbed the jug and hurried Blix back to the barn.

Suvi listened intently to everything Dagny said about her early morning adventure. Then Dagny set the little jug on the floor between them.

"It would be a shame for this nice fresh milk to sour and spoil now, wouldn't it?" said Suvi in a teasing way as she broke some of their bread into little chunks. Then they both made pigs of themselves dipping pieces of bread into the thick, rich cream until it was all gone and then drinking their fill of the milk. They hadn't had fresh milk since Christmas.

Before long they both had terrible bellyaches and Dagny ran outside to throw up. She felt better after that, but what her mother ate stayed down and now she felt much worse.

"Go up to the cottage and see if there's any mustard," she told Dagny. "If not, then a handful of salt will do." Dagny was happy and sad at the same time, and although worried about her mother, she jumped at the chance to have a good reason for snooping around inside the cottage.

The door swung wide open, allowing the sun to shine on the highly polished wooden floor, illuminating the golden hue of the pine boards covering the walls of the large room. To her right was a door. She tiptoed across the glossy floor and saw a large black stove. It shined like Blix's back after she had washed and brushed him really well, and she couldn't resist sliding her hand across the smooth, polished surface. Looking about the kitchen she thought of all the tasty meals that must have been prepared in this room full of interesting cupboards and drawers.

There was no mustard, but she did find enough salt to fill a small cup. Her intention was to hurry back to her mother. However, another interesting room caught her attention. A fine, carved wooden bed covered with a soft green blanket invited her to sit down. Sewn on the corner of the pillowcase were the letters EVA. She laid her head on the pillow and closed her eyes, feeling as if she were floating on soft, billowy clouds on a fine summer's day.

"I'm lying on Eva's bed!" she said out loud to herself. Then she opened her eyes to take in every inch of the room. She stood up and opened the drawers of a small bureau. They were all empty except for the bottom one. In the back corner was a fine bristle brush with a broken handle. She held the soft brush in her hand for a very long time, then put it in her pocket for a keepsake, her only remembrance of the girl who saved her from a life of misery.

She fondled the delicate lace curtains, gazed through the window overlooking the barn and remembered her mother. Snatching the cup of salt, she ran out of the room. As she approached the front door she noticed a handwritten paper on one of the sacks. The writing was merely lines to her, but hopefully her mother could make some sense out of it.

Suvi put some salt in a dipper of water and walked behind the barn. Dagny heard her gagging and heaving on the other side of the wall and covered her ears. When it was quiet again, Dagny took the brush from her pocket and began brushing her hair. After a while her mother returned.

"I had to go to the creek to wash up," she said, laying her head against the hay, "but I feel much better now."

Dagny felt guilty about taking something that didn't belong to her and stuffed the brush back in her pocket. If her mother knew, she would probably make her return it, but she desperately wanted something that belonged to Eva, something to remember her by. Probably Eva didn't want the broken brush anyway and left it behind on purpose, otherwise she would have taken it with her. As her mother rested, Dagny's head was full of these thoughts that kept going round and round in her mind. The brush was soon forgotten when she put her hand back into her pocket and felt the paper note.

"I found this inside. Perhaps you will understand some of the words."

Suvi studied the paper carefully and finally her brows lifted when she recognized the name Eva.

"This is written by Eva."

"What else does the paper say?"

"The words are not quite the same as what I know," Suvi finally told her. "But it seems to say something about giving clothes to the poor and selling furniture, and about moving south."

"Are we going south, too?" Dagny asked hopefully.

"All I know is that we won't be traveling north again, but first we must go to the village so I can tell someone to go back and check on Vidar."

"Are you going to tell them what happened?" asked Dagny.

"Not exactly. I was thinking we could just say he had an accident and that a doctor should look in on him."

Dagny mulled this over for a moment.

"If he'd had an accident would he chain himself to a post?" she asked.

"Not likely," chuckled her mother, "but by the time they get there it won't matter. We will be long gone and it will be up to Vidar to explain how he got into that predicament."

Dagny was amused, too, wondering what he might say and they both had a good laugh.

"Put the note back where you found it. We must be on our way."

Dagny ran back to the cottage debating whether or not to return the brush. She was in deep thought when Suvi and Blix stopped by the porch.

"Are you staying here or coming with us?"

Dagny saw her mother was still in a good mood and showed her the brush, confessing that she'd taken it and the reason why.

"My mistress had a brush like this. It is made of tortoise shell...from the shell of a turtle."

Dagny looked closer at the lovely shades of brown, yellow and gray. "It is probably expensive. I should probably return it."

Suvi saw dejection written on her daughter's face.

"It appears to me that the family has moved. I'd say Eva probably didn't want the broken brush, especially since everything else was removed from the drawers. I'm sure if anyone else found it, they would probably throw it away."

"So, I can keep it?"

"For now it will be safe in your hands. Perhaps we will all meet someday and you can return it to her then. If she really wants the brush, she will be glad you saved it for her."

With a clear conscience, Dagny placed the brush in her pocket and closed the door.

The village was quiet today, the only noise being Blix's hooves clomping along the dirt road. All the shop doors were shut tight and Suvi noticed that not even the old saloon was open for business. She was disappointed to see not one person to ask about going to the potato farm and looking after Vidar.

"Look down there!" shouted Dagny, pointing to a crowd of people exiting a large white building. "Why is there a bell hanging on the roof?"

"It's a church, Dagny. Today must be Sunday and that's why all the stores are closed." Suvi reined Blix to the side of the road and dismounted.

"Wait here. I'll only be a little while."

Dagny watched her mother talk to a man in a dark robe and soon they both disappeared behind two large doors of the church. The noontime sun bore down on the tranquil village with no breeze to cool the air. Beads of sweat rolled down Dagny's face, neck and beneath her dirty old work clothes. A family walked by, staring at her, and she was reminded of the scowling woman and taunting children back at the potato farm that day when they called her 'strange one.' She laid her head against Blix's neck and closed her eyes.

"Wake up! See what I have!" said her mother excitedly. She held up an armful of clothes, showing Dagny a variety of skirts and blouses that were not faded and worn, as well as some colorful striped aprons. "The church man gave these to me."

Dagny took the clothes and Suvi led Blix out of the village and into the woods.

"Why aren't we going by the road. Wouldn't it be faster?"

asked Dagny.

"The church man told me there's a lake about a mile into the forest." Then she looked up and smiled at her daughter. "Wouldn't it be nice to go bathing and pretty us up for traveling in style?" Dagny thought that was a fine idea.

The lake was small, no bigger than a pond, with a rocky shore, clear water and very secluded. After bathing they sat on a large, flat rock to dry off.

"How did it go in the church?" asked Dagny, stretching out to get the full benefit of the sun.

"Better than I ever expected. The church man promised to go to the farm tomorrow. And to make certain he did, I told him he could have all the free potatoes that would fit in his buggy." Then Suvi chuckled. "You should have seen his eyes light up as soon as I mentioned free potatoes. That's when he showed me the box of used clothes and said I could take anything I needed. A kindly doctor was there who heard me talking about Vidar and the free potatoes, so it was decided they would both drive up this afternoon after dinner."

"What if Vidar doesn't want to give away his potatoes?" asked Dagny, knowing how he never gave away anything of value.

"Well, that will be up to him. He will be angry at first, but I feel certain he will see the benefit of doing so, even just to save face when he goes to the village next time."

While they were putting on their new, clean clothes, Suvi found the folded piece of paper that the church man had given her.

"This is called a map," she told Dagny. "It's a drawing of the whole of Sweden." Then she pointed to a place all covered in green. "We are here now, in the middle of this forest." Then her finger traveled almost to the bottom of the page. "This is a place called Gothenburg...a fine place to visit and one of Sweden's largest cities."

"Will we be there tomorrow?" Dagny asked hopefully.

"Oh, no. The church man said it may take weeks to get there

on horseback."

"But it doesn't look very far on the map," Dagny said.

Suvi saw her daughter's confusion. Suvi didn't understand much about the map either. She pointed to each city, explaining what the man had said about how many days it might take to get from one to the next. "It will be good, Dagny, to have such a great distance between us and the potato farm."

"You are right," said Dagny. "Vidar will never be able to find us that far away."

They were both wearing white blouses and dark blue skirts with striped aprons of different colors and clean white kerchiefs on their heads. Suvi jumped up on Blix's back, but Dagny ran ahead, twirling around in the road, her skirt flaring out as if she might take flight. She stopped and shouted back to her mother.

"I feel like dancing all the way to Gothenburg!"

The Lindholm Manor

1933 – 1934

The Ride

As the automobile bounced along the uneven path to the gravel road, Eva leaned her head back on the seat, watching the headlamps flicker on the passing trees, comforted by the familiar, spicy scent of Mr. Kronberg's smoldering pipe tobacco.

Under different circumstances she might have been more talkative on this exciting adventure, but even on an ordinary day conversation did not come easily to Eva first thing in the morning. Her brain needed an hour or so to prepare for a new day with the help of at least one strong cup of coffee.

Mats sat beside her, his arm occasionally touching hers. She welcomed his nearness, knowing she was safely in the company of two strong men. Fatigued after her traumatic experience at the potato farm and subsequent night of anxiety, she was lulled into a deep, sound sleep by the soft, cushiony seat and gentle motion of the automobile.

If Eva had looked his way, Mats would have spoken to her, but not especially to apologize, although the idea had consumed his mind for two days. He'd had time to reflect on his childlike behavior in attempting to load Stella on the wagon and wished to explain why he acted so impulsively, but so far no excuse had proved very convincing. How thoughtless and stupid of him to strike the cow, a precious pet she had raised from a calf. His anger had only pushed Eva further away from him; not only that, but she had shown him up by easily walking Stella up the ramp.

Afterwards he had made matters even worse by sitting in the wagon and sulking like some three-year-old who didn't get his own way. Apparently Eva wasn't one to hold a grudge; she had greeted him with a big smile this morning, so he decided to put the Stella episode behind him in the hope that she might have forgotten about it, too.

As the heavily forested landscape slowly changed to a mixture of woods and open fields, intermittent glimpses of the rising sun became visible, randomly penetrating the automobile's dim interior so that Mr. Kronberg now had a clear view of the back seat. He turned to look at his son.

"Looks like Eva is all tired out."

"Ya, that she is," replied Mats, yawning.

"Your mother packed some coffee and sweets. When Eva wakes up we'll stop for a lunch." Mats didn't respond. He wasn't in the mood for talking, at least not to his father.

"Did you hear what I said, Mats?"

"Ya," he replied, glancing at Eva, "we'll eat when she comes around." He studied her profile in the soft morning light, leaning so close he could hear her deep breaths of sleep and smell a sweet soapy fragrance of roses. For the first time he noticed the sprinkling of tiny freckles across her slightly up-turned nose, her pink lips parted as if waiting for a kiss. If his father had not been in the front seat he might have kissed her right then.

A few reddish-blonde ringlets escaped from her neat braid and he envisioned how she might look with her hair brushed out and flowing about her shoulders. He turned away, hoping to focus on something outside the window, but she was there, too, in his imagination, as he recalled her sweet first kiss and how she didn't like it when he kissed her the second time. He hadn't meant to kiss her that way, but he couldn't help it, and he felt that same desire now.

Leaning against the seat, his eyes rested on the back of his father's head, noticing as if for the first time the whiteness of his hair. He remembered what his father had told him about respect and having control over his emotions and desires, something about "impulsiveness can dig a deep dark trench, but patience will keep your head above ground." He had always thought there was no fun in being patient, but now he realized that patience would have probably prevented his aggressiveness in dealing with the cow as well as forcing his kiss on Eva.

Mats lit a cigarette, opened the window a few inches and slowly exhaled. He watched the white cloud linger for a moment as if deciding which way to go. Then the smoke thinned to a narrow line, was swept through the open window and disappeared. He rolled up the window. When he exhaled the second time he saw the smoke disperse and spread out around him, but the haze didn't go away until he opened the window again.

There was probably a lesson there but he couldn't figure out what it was at first. He knew it was the draft, or force of air, that had caused the smoke to escape through the open window. Perhaps the lesson had something to do with patience versus force; if he wished to keep something or someone, then he shouldn't use force, or else they would flee, like the smoke being swept out the window...or forcing that damn cow to get into the trailer or his sensuous kiss on Eva. It was a silly scenario, but he made a conscious decision: from now on he would go easy with Eva.

The gravel road was much smoother. When the car rounded a sharp curve Eva's head touched his shoulder and he put his arm around her. The corners of her mouth turned up into a slight smile as she nestled herself against him and he wondered if girls and boys dream about the same things. He dreamed things that he'd never tell anyone, not even his brothers, but Eva's dreams were probably about knitting, baking cakes or taking care of her cow. If she did dream of him it would be of that gawky kid who pulled her braids and teased her until her face turned bright red. He had acted foolishly with Eva. It was about time he grew up.

After about three hours of traveling, Otto stopped the car at a roadside turnoff. He spoke to Eva, who was in such a deep sleep that he didn't ask her again if she wanted anything to eat. He and Mats were both hungry for coffee and sweets, so they ate silently by the woods while she slept in the car.

Eva awakened hours later to see a bustling village through the car window. Her dry mouth brought up an image of herself snoring with a gaping mouth and she hoped she hadn't drooled. The sun was already high in the sky and she guessed it must be close to noontime.

"You must be hungry, Eva," he said, noticing that she was

stirring. "I was just telling Mats that I have an appointment in town and that you both should eat at the restaurant across the street. Excellent food. Mats and I stop there every time we go to Gothenburg."

The sidewalk was busy with farmers, businessmen, women and children going this way and that. As they crossed the street three young girls about Eva's age approached them wearing bright red lipstick and too-short skirts. Their mouths opened and closed in unison, reminding Eva of Stella and Slofock chewing their cuds after lying down in the pasture. When she mentioned this to Mats, he laughed, saying they were actually chewing gum.

"Hi, Matsie! Haven't seen you in a while," shouted one of the girls as she continued chewing and smiling at the same time. Mats tipped his cap politely and steered Eva around the little group toward the restaurant door.

Once inside, Eva elbowed his arm. "Matsie?" she said, raising her eyebrows and grinning. A slight look of guilt came over Mats' face, but he was saved from explaining when a woman showed them to a table against the wall. Eva had gotten her point across and let it pass. A good-looking guy like Mats probably had lots of girlfriends and what he did wasn't really any of her business.

"You can order anything on the menu," he said, showing her a folded paper with a jumbled list of words and numbers that made no sense to her. A waitress set two cups of coffee on the table and looked at him.

"The usual, Mats?"

He nodded and she scribbled on her pad, then looked at Eva, who flushed with embarrassment at the thought of having to make a selection. She was hungry enough to eat just about anything and finally put the menu down.

"I'll have the usual also."

The waitress eyed Mats to make sure she had heard correctly.

"We'll have two usuals," he stated firmly, leaning back in his seat to observe Eva. He was amused by her reaction to everything going on in the restaurant.

"You remind me of a six-year-old's first visit to a candy store" he said.

"I remind you of a six year old?" she repeated. "And I've never been to a candy store." She didn't understand his joke, but no matter; he loved her plain innocence that somehow always surprised him.

She looked around the room, engrossed with the many paintings hanging on the walls, especially one directly above their table. She spoke of the delicate brush strokes and how smoothly the colors flowed across the paper, a sharp contrast to the thick oil-based paints that her father always used when painting on canvass.

And as if he could read her mind he said, "That painting is called 'Breakfast Under the Big Birch,' by Carl Larsson. He paints mostly in pen and ink with watercolors and often his subjects are of his wife and children; that's his family eating outside under the birch tree. I suppose the empty chair at the end of the table is his."

Eva was impressed with Mats' artistic knowledge.

"I never knew you were interested in art."

"It isn't that I'm all that interested," he admitted. "Being the youngest at home I got to tag along to the galleries and museums with my father and picked up a lot of information along the way."

"And I'm learning more about you every day, too, Mats."

All the paintings in the dining room were homey farm scenes by the same artist. One was of the red farm house where Carl Larsson and his family lived. Others were of various rooms in the house, showing his wife or children doing household chores such as watering window plants, churning butter, weaving or just reading or writing letters. A few were of men working in the fields plowing and mowing hay or women harvesting potatoes and milking the cows.

"I love this one the best," she said, admiring the painting above them of the artist's family eating under the birch tree.

"I thought so," he said. "I'm thinking it has something to do with the dog."

Before Eva could respond, Mats stood up. "There's something I've got to take care of. I'll be right back."

It wasn't long before the waitress arrived with their dinners. Eva barely noticed the thick beef steak smothered with onions. It was the two huge baked potatoes on either side that startled her, bringing back vivid scenes of yesterday, their mottled brown skins reminding her too much of Vidar. Her stomach twisted into a hard knot and a sour taste rose in her throat so that she had to look away for fear of throwing up right there.

She glanced around the crowded dining room at everyone talking and eating. One woman was sternly telling a young boy to finish his plate, but it was plain to see he didn't want to eat his carrots. When she turned to talk with the man beside her, the boy quickly hid the three carrots in his napkin and placed them under his chair. When the woman saw his empty plate, she patted the smug-faced youngster on the head and gave him a few cookies from the dessert tray. Eva smiled as she wrapped one of the potatoes in a napkin and placed it on the floor between her chair and the wall. Throwing away good food was something she would never think to do, but in this case it seemed her only option. She had carefully removed the ugly skin from the remaining potato and was mashing it up with lots of butter when Mats returned.

He immediately began attacking his piece of steak, and to her relief never noticed what was missing from her plate. He was unusually quiet, but neither did she have anything important to say, although her thoughts were on where he might have gone and why. Perhaps it had something to do with the gum-chewing girl. Curiosity finally broke the silence.

"Is everything all right, Mats?"

"Couldn't be any better," he said, glancing across the table and smiling. "Good steak, don't you think?"

"The best I've had in years," she said in all truthfulness, stabbing a large chunk and cutting it into smaller pieces.

A well-dressed man came over to their table and walked behind her chair. Eva's heart sank thinking he would see the napkin on the floor and pick it up. Instead, he reached up and removed the painting from the wall. Couldn't he have waited until they left the table to do that? she thought to herself. Of greater importance was that he didn't discover the baked potato hidden by her feet. How embarrassed she would have been if he'd picked up and opened the napkin for everyone to see! Knowing Mats as she did, she knew he would never let her forget about that.

Mats sat in the car with a bulge under his jacket. He wanted to surprise Eva, make his gift a special occasion, but the little kid inside him couldn't wait and he immediately placed the brown-wrapped bundle on her lap. She felt the wooden frame beneath her fingers and everything fell into place; Mats' sudden departure from the table and the man taking down the painting made perfect sense to her now. He was anxious for her to open the package, but his father was full of talk, so he waited.

"How was dinner?"

"Fine, as always" replied Mats, hoping to end this conversation.

"I supposed you had steak and baked potatoes, as usual."

"Yes, Pa, we both did."

"I had a good meeting and fine meal, as well," said his father, puffing deeply on his pipe. Then he went into great detail about what was said at the meeting and what everyone had to eat.

Eva listened politely with her hands folded on the package, smiling inwardly at Mats' disinterest and agitation. Finally his father ran out of things to say and concentrated on his driving.

"Aren't you going to open it?" whispered Mats.

Of course she knew what it was by now, but she slowly lifted the paper from one corner, just enough to see the little girl with a doll in her lap and the wonderful dog sitting across from her. Mats had been right about the dog, which surely must have been a special pet to be sitting in a chair at the family table. Anxious to see the rest of the painting, Eva ripped off the remaining paper. A woman sat next to the dog as he gazed longingly at her plate as if he were expecting a taste of sausage or slice of bacon. A girl sat beside her, across from two boys, whose backs were toward the artist. Another young girl sat beside the one holding a doll. The two women wore hats and fine dresses, as did the three young girls. Eva surmised the family might be of noble status, since neither she nor her mother had ever worn hats while eating breakfast. Carl Larsson was an exceptional artist, and he must have had a great sense of humor as well, to have painted the dog and each member of his family with such love and thoughtful detail.

Eva brushed away small tears of joy, then briefly touched Mats' face. "Thank you so much," she said, and then without thinking, she kissed him quickly on the cheek. For Eva, her tender response was no different than a kiss she might have given in gratitude to her mother or father, but to Mats it was different; her kiss stirred up old emotions and he was barely able to keep himself from kissing her back.

Looking at her and smiling, he said, "Well, perhaps the painting will make you think of me once in a while."

"I don't need a painting to be reminded of you," she said, bashfully. This brought to Mat's mind all the foolish things he had done in the past that had made him look like a fool.

For a long while they silently looked at the painting, both thinking their own special thoughts, and when her hand absent-mindedly slipped from the frame and touched his thigh, he took her hand in his and she did not withdraw it.

Mrs. Lindholm

It was late evening when they approached the entrance to the Lindholm manor. In the headlights Eva watched Mats open the wide metal gate with its delicate patterns of vines intertwined with leaves and flowers. She looked around for a house, but saw only large fields on either side of a winding dirt driveway edged with tall trees and bushes. Because of the summer twilight everything was colored in muted shades of gray, except for a large white barn that came into view at the top of a hill.

Then the driveway suddenly turned sharply to the right, and standing on a grassy knoll was the house: a long, three-story mansion of yellowish hue looking down on them with the golden glow of more than a dozen lighted windows. How many rooms would be in such a house, Eva wondered, noticing many upstairs windows that had no light behind them. She had seen many other mansions today, but none as colossal and grand as this one.

Mr. Kronberg stopped in front of a graceful stone archway to let Mats and Eva out of the car and then drove to another building at the end of the house. They went up a few steps to a landing where two long narrow windows framed a heavy wooden door. Eva peeked through one of the windows and saw a brilliant crystal chandelier illuminating two life-sized portraits hanging on the wall. Suddenly chimes echoed throughout the entranceway.

"How beautiful," she exclaimed, grabbing Mats' arm. "This must be how it feels to stand in the belfry of the old stone church in Norrland."

"Press here and you can hear them again," he said, pointing to a button beside the door. Cautiously she put one finger on the button. The chimes rang loudly and at the same time the door opened. A maid immediately recognized Mats and invited them into the foyer, but Eva felt out of place and hung back.

"Shouldn't I enter through a back door?"

"Don't be silly, Eva. You are my guest tonight," said Mats.

The brass chandelier was much larger than she had thought. Dangling from its graceful brass arms were hundreds of round and pointed crystals, the many facets brightly reflecting light and illuminating the two larger-than-life-sized paintings hanging on the wall.

"May I present Mr. and Mrs. Lindholm, also known as Anders and Augusta," he announced, stretching his arm out to include the two paintings. Mrs. Lindholm, lavishly dressed in a crimson satin gown, sat stiffly in an elegantly scrolled mahogany chair holding a black lace fan. Light blonde hair curled in long tight ringlets framed her stern face, while a white bird crouched in the corner of a gilded cage behind her.

Mr. Lindholm's handsome face revealed kind blue eyes and a warm smile in which Eva saw a fine mixture of both her father and Mr. Kronberg. He was wearing a brown tweed jacket, tan riding breeches and high black shiny boots, and sat comfortably in a reddish-brown leather chair. His right hand rested gently on the head of a sleepy brown-and-white dog and in his left hand was an intricately carved pipe. The picture suggested to Eva that both man and dog might have just returned from hunting or a walk in the woods and she was instantly drawn to this gentle man who seemed more of a humble farmer than a wealthy shipping magnate. In comparing the two portraits Eva found it difficult to imagine these two being married to each other.

By now Mats had wandered across the room. "There's a more beautiful girl over here," he said, pointing to an adjacent wall.

"All I see is a large mirror," she said.

"Come over here and I'll show you."

Looking in the mirror, she was embarrassed to see her reflection standing awkwardly in the middle of the lavish hall and hid her flushed face in her hands. She heard him laughing, and suddenly he grabbed her by the waist and lifted her high in the air, swinging her around as a father might play with his young child.

Now Eva was laughing, too, and for a time she was that young child, but then she caught a glimpse of her heavy brown shoes and bare legs in the mirror, and in the background descending a long stairway was the real Mrs. Lindholm dressed in an elegant satin gown of royal blue. Eva gasped, stiffened, and with a beet-red face told Mats to put her down.

"Oh, Mats, how good it is to see you again," exclaimed Augusta Lindholm in a loud gushing voice. He bowed and took her hand, but she brushed formality aside and embraced him in a too-long hug that released an overpowering scent of lilacs.

"My dear, you are taller and more handsome than ever," she said, still avoiding the fact that Eva stood less than a foot away.

Eva's embarrassment lessened as she watched the redness creep up the back of Mats' neck. Never having seen a man blush before brought a smile to her face.

"Mrs. Lindholm, this is my neighbor, Eva Gunderson," he said immediately, as if to draw attention away from himself. Eva curtsied politely as Mrs. Lindholm's sweetness quickly turned to scrutiny, those same penetrating green eyes in the portrait appraising every feature, from Eva's red hair to the worn shoes on her feet and back to her hair again. Had those annoying frizzy wisps escaped from her braid as they so often did? Was her dress wrinkled? Or was she just not up to this woman's expectations?

Augusta was not displeased; she was merely trying to hide her astonishment upon seeing this absolutely beautiful young woman, something her friend, Otto, had neglected to mention when describing his poor neighbor.

"Welcome to our home, Eva. Mats' father has spoken very highly of you," she said, her forced smile melting into softness as she took Mats' arm.

"Well, you both must be hungry. Let's have a bite to eat in the breakfast room."

With a grand sweep of elegant blue satin, she ushered Mats past the wide stairway and down a long narrow hall. Eva followed, noticing the high, floor-to-ceiling windows draped in golden brocade on one side and on the opposite walls, portraits of people with vacant, dark stares dressed from an earlier time. Every so often an open doorway to the right revealed large, carpeted rooms with heavy furniture and gold-framed landscape paintings hanging on the walls. Eva's shoes sank into the plush maroon and gold rug, which felt like thick, spongy moss. She had to dismiss the strong desire to kick off her shoes and run barefoot through the hall.

It was Mrs. Lindholm's bare back that made Eva blink twice, the fine white skin extending beyond the tiniest waist she had ever seen. How did such a dress stay up with only two thin straps no wider than fine strings across her shoulders. She thought the gown was most indecent.

All this occupied Eva's thoughts until they came to a wide archway. Mrs. Lindholm flicked a switch on the wall revealing a much brighter and less formal room than any of the others. A lace tablecloth covered a long oval table set with a bouquet of yellow spring flowers and a large bowl of fresh fruit. Three walls of the room were painted white and the fourth was mostly taken up by a very wide window that Eva thought must surely have a beautiful daytime view. Light blue curtains drawn across the window matched the upholstered seats of eight white high-back chairs that were evenly lined up along an adjacent wall like well-dressed soldiers standing at attention.

A maid entered and placed five of the chairs around the table. Mrs. Lindholm instructed her about refreshments and then turned her attention to Mats again.

"Sit down and have some fruit. Gerta will be back soon with the coffee tray; meanwhile, I'll hunt up your father and Anders so they can join us." Eva felt as if she wasn't really there, that the invitation to sit at the table didn't include her, but then Mats pulled out the chair next to him and told her to sit down.

"Of all the rooms in this house, this one is my favorite," he said, giving her a small cluster of grapes. "From the window there's a grand view of the gardens, dairy barn and surrounding fields."

"It's so bright and cheerful here," she said looking around the room. She ate a few grapes, wondering what her own room would look like and then Mats began talking again.

"Everyone comes to the breakfast room in the morning, but not always at the same time. Anders...I mean Mr. Lindholm...is usually here very early, as is their son, Karl, who is about the same age as me. Mrs. Lindholm usually arrives later or sometimes has breakfast in her room and Gunnar, their oldest son, straggles in whenever the spirit moves him. Karl and his father are very much alike, intelligent and serious...real down-to-earth guys that don't talk down to anyone. Gunnar is a lot of fun, always the life of the party, but not much of a farm worker or interested in getting his hands dirty."

The maid returned and poured coffee into thin porcelain cups. Mats immediately took the one decorated with purple violets and began to drink. Eva was glad because she wanted the other cup, the one with a bouquet of daisies on it with a saucer that had smaller blossoms painted around the rim like the daisy chains she used to make at home.

"Good coffee," she said, after taking a long, delicious sip. "Seems to taste better in these fine china cups than the thick plain mugs I'm used to drinking from."

"Coffee is coffee to me," Mats replied. "I don't care much what I drink from as long as I have enough of it."

"Well then, you'll probably need a dozen of these small cups to satisfy you," said Eva, smiling. He chuckled. "You're right about that, Eva, I'm ready for the second one already."

The maid brought in a tray of bread and a platter of cold meats and cheese. She was not the same pleasant maid who greeted them at the door. This one was plain, unsmiling and painfully thin, her sleepy eyes too tired to look anyone in the eye, but she did refill their cups before going back to the kitchen.

"That's Gerta," said Mats with a raised eyebrow and a shrug of the shoulders. "Glum Gerta...never have seen that girl smile."

Eva, keeping any negative impressions about the maid to herself, commented instead on the two beautiful seascapes hanging on the wall. One showed a cozy harbor with many small boats and a lighthouse at the tip of rocky jut of land curving out to sea. She was reminded of the one her father had painted of her mother sitting on the bluff overlooking the sea with the stone lighthouse behind her, the place where her parents first saw each other.

A large white ship with black smoke stacks sailed across the second painting and in the foreground huge blue-green waves seemed to be crashing into the picture frame.

"Is that ship sailing on the Atlantic Ocean?" she asked.

"Ya, probably it is...and the ship is one that once belonged to the Lindholm fleet. They don't own any ships now; sold out to Augusta's brothers and retired here to the farm."

They heard Mrs. Lindholm's shrill laugh long before she came into the breakfast room. She had her husband on one arm and Mr. Kronberg on the other. Except for a crown, she looked radiant as a queen. Mr. Lindholm, on the other hand, was more casually dressed as if he had just walked out of the painting in the grand hall, although Eva thought he was better looking in person. He walked directly over to shake hands with Mats and then, without waiting to be introduced, took Eva's hand.

"Welcome to our home, Eva," he said, his warm blue eyes looking kindly into hers. "Otto has told me so many nice things about you." She attempted to rise and curtsy, but was shocked when he reached out and kissed the back of her hand, much to the surprise of his wife.

The room soon overflowed with cheerful conversation as they sat around the table enjoying their coffee and late evening lunch. Anders Lindholm was thoughtful and soft-spoken, but still commanded the attention of everyone with his brilliant use of words. He told about writing his memoirs, which included a brief history of Sweden during his lifetime and how it impacted farming and the shipping industry.

Eva felt more comfortable now that Mr. Kronberg was here, but she was keenly aware that tomorrow everything would change and she would be a mere servant. In the meantime, she sat a little straighter and made up her mind to enjoy the fine food, company and funny stories of the old days.

Finally Anders and Otto retired to the study for smoking and a nightcap. Mats might have gone with them had Augusta not asked him to stay. She rang a little silver bell, but Gerta never appeared, so she reluctantly poured another round of coffee and offered Mats and Eva a plate of sweets. The room was quiet for a moment, except for Augusta's fingernails tapping on the table. A suspiciously determined look came over her face, as if she was considering something of great importance.

"Well, now," she said at last. "You remember the Almgrens don't you, Mats?" Not giving him a chance to answer, she continued, "They're arriving first thing in the morning and this has created an awkward predicament for me. Unfortunately, Gunnar and Karl are in Gothenburg for a few days so their daughter will have no young man to keep her company. I was wondering if you might help me out by staying over for a day or so to entertain her."

"Almgren?" asked Mats, trying to jog his memory.

"I'm certain you remember Jenny Almgren from Stockholm. I think she was here when you visited four or five years ago for Midsummer." Mats nodded disapprovingly.

"Ya, she really stood out in a crowd." How well he remembered that chubby twelve-year-old with thick blond braids who followed him around like his shadow and kept all the other girls away.

"And what a tease you were that year, grabbing her long braids as if they were reigns of a horse," admonished Augusta.

"Well, she was rather horsey, if you know what I mean," he snickered. Augusta didn't share Mats' humor and glared at him.

"Perhaps you can redeem yourself now, Mats. I really need you to help guarantee her visit is a happy one."

Eva listened with amusement as Mats tried to wiggle out of this sticky situation, the skin reddening slightly above his collar again. It was apparent he didn't want to spend any time with Jenny, but neither could he bring himself to refuse Mrs. Lindholm.

He finally put on a sad face. "I'm sorry, Augusta, but Father is counting on me to assist him at the art gallery tomorrow. Perhaps I could help you out another time."

Augusta sat back in her chair with a distasteful frown, playing with a brilliant blue-green gem hanging from her gold necklace. Eva could not help but notice her long shiny red nails and the sparkling rings on her fingers, but no amount of expensive jewelry would be able to make her attractive at this moment. All softness had melted from her face, her lips pursed and silent as she contemplated a different strategy.

Mats glanced at Eva and smiled, but this scenario wasn't over yet. Suddenly, as if revitalized, Augusta sat up straight in her chair.

"That is unfortunate," she stated, looking directly into Mats' eyes. "You'll be missing out on a lot of fun." Then she leaned forward against the table, her breasts rounding above the top of her bodice and her red-painted lips stretching into a forced smile.

"Did you know that Jenny works as a model for a fine agency in New York? She promised to show us photographs of her trip across the United States last year."

Augusta had Mats' full attention now, but she wanted to be assured he would agree and delivered her last punch. "On second thought, after losing all that weight and having her hair cut short in the American way, I think Jenny will probably consider herself too sophisticated for a country boy like you, especially after spending so much time with all those citified American boys."

Upon hearing of Jenny's impressive metamorphosis, it didn't take long for Mats to reconsider.

"Probably Father can get along without me," he said. "I'll be glad to help you out."

"So kind of you, Mats." Then, as if dismissing him, she said, "Why don't you go to the study and tell your father about the change in plans." Eva saw the satisfaction in Mrs. Lindholm's face. Mats was smiling, too, as he rose from the table.

"Good night, ladies," he said enthusiastically. "Looks like I'll be seeing you both tomorrow then." Mrs. Lindholm wasted no time in ringing the little silver bell by her plate. This time Gerta appeared instantaneously, as if she had been listening by the kitchen door.

"Gerta, please show Eva to her room."

Eva learned one thing about her mistress tonight: Mrs. Lindholm was a cunning, manipulative woman who got what she wanted, one way or another.

Augusta and Anders Lindholm

Augusta was thankful that Mats had come today. It was a great relief to know that Jenny would have the company of someone her own age. Now Augusta wouldn't have to waste precious time trying to please the only daughter of the over-indulgent Almgrens. Jenny might be pretty and smart, but she was obsessed with herself, a spoiled brat, just like her mother. If it wasn't for Mr. Almgren and Anders being such good friends, Augusta would have discouraged the visit altogether.

Anders and Otto were still downstairs when Augusta went to her bedroom. She struggled with her gown, cursing that she had given her maid the night off and that now she must do everything for herself. She always looked forward to this time of night when she and Johanna discussed the events of the day. At this moment there was so much she wanted to say and no one here to listen. Taking the pins out of her hair, she thought about Mats and Eva, deliberating whether there was, or ever had been, anything serious between them. Such a handsome couple; of course they'd had intimate moments, she fantasized, remembering their laughter and merriment as he spun her around in the hall tonight.

Augusta grew up and played with the boy across the street and they'd been like brother and sister even after they were grown, but she couldn't imagine a sibling-like relationship between the alluring Eva and virile Mats. She liked Mats. He had always gotten along well with her own two sons; his personality and character were somewhere between her serious Karl and fun-loving Gunnar. Probably Mats was more like Gunnar, she thought, their heads both easily turned by a pretty face.

She lay alone and wide awake in the big bed with only the company of a vision: the intimidating and unsettling picture of Eva's perfect young face and body that wouldn't go away. For a fifteen-year-old, she was amply developed. In fact, Augusta had noticed right away that Eva's breasts were much fuller than her own. She could not admit to herself that she was actually jealous of Eva Gunderson.

Otto's description of Eva had been accurate, but not completely thorough. He'd said Eva was well-mannered, respectful, clean and had fine teeth, but he had neglected to mention the girl's incredible beauty and refined bearing; she was such a contrast to other peasant girls Augusta had employed from

Norrland in the past, large-nosed farm girls, crude and often careless in their work who were either painstakingly shy or extremely wild.

Augusta would say she had nothing against peasants. They had their place in society and some had become quite famous. The Kronbergs had peasant roots, but through hard work and self-improvement Otto had risen above his lowly beginnings and was considered equal to many of the Lindholm's upper-class friends, although Otto's wife was certainly from a different tree.

Augusta was still awake an hour later. She'd been thinking of her husband, who, like Otto, was born a peasant, but with determination and hard work had made something of himself. Anders was now a rich man, the son of a humble farmer whose land harvested little more than stones and large rocks. From the time he could hold a shovel and hoe, Anders was sent to the fields to work, and for years he had tried to make a living on his parent's unproductive land.

There was one good thing about the farm; it was only a ten minute walk to the village school. Also, it had been his good fortune to have had an intuitive teacher who recognized his academic abilities, teaching Anders everything the teacher knew and exposing the boy to books in his private library. Anders, a fast reader, absorbed knowledge like a sponge and possessed a mind that could remember in great detail every book he ever read. A scholarship enabled him to attend a school of higher learning.

Being an enterprising young man, he worked at various part-time jobs during his university years. Through his friendly nature and dedication to work, he came to the attention of the owner of several cargo and cruise ships, a man named Josef Borg. Anders quickly climbed the ladder of success, and on the top wrung stood the shipping magnate's lovely daughter, Augusta Borg.

It had been his rugged handsomeness that turned Augusta's head. He'd made her feel alive, kindling the tiny flame that smoldered from the first time she saw him working on her father's ship, his tanned, rugged shoulders gleaming with sweat in the hot sun as he swabbed down the decks.

Her mother had demeaned him and tried her best to discourage her daughter from this man of menial means. As a distraction she allowed Augusta to have the horse she had always wanted. At that time the Borgs lived in Gothenburg, but on weekends and summers Augusta and her mother drove north to an old estate that they owned where the horse was stabled. An old man lived in the barn in exchange for taking care of the horse and doing odd jobs on the farm. The manor house was in need of new paint and the roof leaked in the old barn, but her father was too busy to take on the responsibility of making necessary repairs. Augusta didn't mind about the neglected buildings as long as she could ride her horse through the fields and forest paths and swim in the small lake across the swamp. One day she brought Anders to see her horse, but it was the farm that caught his interest.

Anders was a visionary. He saw beyond the massive ramshackle house, the barns in need of paint, overgrown fields and the neglected lawns and gardens. He imagined this dream farm in brilliant color and refinement; a golden-colored mansion adorned with white columns and trim with velvety green lawns, colorful gardens and beautiful fountains. He saw large white barns, fenced-in pastures full of fat cattle, fields cleared of small trees and bushes and planted in hay and grains.

Augusta's father gave him full rein to make the changes he had proposed and later surprised Anders and Augusta by giving them the farm as a wedding gift.

Sleep evaded Augusta and she wished Anders would come to bed. All her fears seemed magnified in the darkness and tonight she worried about her two sons, alone in the big city of Gothenburg. Karl was her youngest, but he seemed more responsible than his older brother, and probably spent much of his day in the library researching new farming methods. But what about the evenings? Would Gunnar coax Karl into the dance halls, where drinking and promiscuous women lured men and boys into their rooms?

Gunnar surely was the more adventuresome of the two, impulsive and temperamental. But for a twenty-one year old, he had good business sense and Anders trusted him completely with running the farm. When company came on weekends, his fine conversation and joke telling entertained everyone at the dinner table, and later in the ballroom he always had a pretty girl on his arm as he showed off his dancing skills.

She thought Karl the better looking of the two, fair and ruggedly handsome, intelligent and thoughtful like his father. But not once had she ever seen Karl on the dance floor. Usually after dinner he disappeared, either to his room or back to the barn to check on baby pigs or a pregnant cow or some other farm-related problem. He spent much time reading and putting into practice new techniques in raising leaner pigs, breeding cows to give more milk and researching new grains to plant for larger yields. Nor was Karl afraid of hard work. Often he was in the barn doing common farm chores or working long hours in the fields alongside the farm hands at planting and harvest time.

Until recently Augusta had no concerns about Karl. He had been and still was his mother's joy, but he was definitely lacking in social skills. How would he find an acceptable young lady if all he could talk about was the care and improvement of animals and field crops? She blamed herself for his disinterest in girls. After he was born, the doctor said she probably would have no more children. She had kept Karl a baby for too long, breast-fed him for five years and made him too much of a mama's boy. Now she was paying the price for her selfishness.

Augusta heard the clock downstairs striking twelve times and Anders had still not come to bed.

Cook

Eva followed the maid's silhouette down the long, dim hall. Neatly stacked beside a dark wooden door were her few belongings. Gerta unlocked the door, walked across the room and turned on a lamp that set on a small table by a single bed. A quick glance about the room also revealed an open window, an old chair and a wooden bureau against the opposite wall. Gerta gave her the key.

"Best to keep the door locked...never know who might be wandering about," she muttered.

Still wondering who might be walking in the hall this time of night, Eva brought in her bags and dragged the wooden chest by the bed. She was relieved to see Carl Larsson's painting lying on top of the chest and immediately picked it up to look closer at the dog and the seven people eating breakfast under the birch tree. She placed the painting on the old bureau where she would see it first thing in the morning, then put on her night dress, pulled down the bedspread and sat gazing at the little lamp whose soft glow was like a comforting friend. Not wishing to be in the dark, she left the light on and laid between the clean white sheets. The mattress was surprisingly comfortable and she lay there breathing in the familiar scent of pine and spruce that drifted through the open window.

She dreamed of a fragrant forest and the bright cheerful breakfast room. At first Mrs. Lindholm was sitting across the table from her, but when she looked again a dog sat there. This was not the sweet brown dog in Carl Larsson's painting, but a mean, tooth-baring yellow beast glaring at her plate of bread and cheese. When the dog barked, Eva awakened to someone knocking on her door.

She sat up quickly in the early gray light of dawn and heard the knocking again, and then a voice saying, "Good morn, Eva. Cook here."

Eva unlocked the door to see a short, stout, round-faced woman whose wide smile crinkled her nose and eyes upward in such a jolly way that Eva did not immediately notice her missing front tooth.

"You can call me Cook," she said extending her plump hand in a firm grip.

"Good morning, Cook," said Eva, curtsying to the older woman.

"No need to curtsy to me," replied Cook with a hearty laugh, but Eva could tell the older woman was pleased by Eva's respectfulness and there was a moment of instant bonding between the two servants.

"It will be a welcome change to see a pretty face every morning," said Cook with that same merry smile. "As soon as you're dressed, come to the kitchen." Then she winked. "But this is the only time you'll be getting a personal invitation for breakfast."

Eva watched Cook waddle down the hall, her broad hips silhouetted in the dim light, so wide they appeared to bounce against the walls. Then she hurried to the washroom.

Her room faced east and in the few minutes she'd been washing up, the morning sun had risen enough to illuminate the opposite wall. She gasped when seeing an ugly woman dressed in black staring down at her with piercing green eyes and a stern face. It was only a painting, but the figure was life-size and scary to look at. The woman's hair was pulled back severely, accentuating her frowning eyes and large ears, whose lobes stretched downward from the heavy gold earrings she wore. A long string of pearls hung around her high-collared neck and she held an open book in her bony hands. Not wishing to see that dreadful face again, Eva took down the painting and put it in the corner facing the wall. In its place, she hung the charming Carl Larsson painting.

As she walked down the hall, mouth-watering breakfast aromas grew more intense, making her feel quite at home and her belly crying for something to eat. When entering the kitchen she first noticed the two huge cooking stoves. Cook stood in front of the larger one, her bulky frame dwarfed by its monstrous size. Bacon sizzled in a metal fry pan, porridge simmered in a shiny covered pot and eggs were waiting to be cracked and fried.

Without turning around, Cook acknowledged her presence. Eva knew at once this room was Cook's domain and she suspected nothing happened here that went unnoticed by this wise older woman. She felt somewhat intimidated as she looked about the room.

Long wooden cabinets lined every wall from floor to ceiling and even around the many windows, so that not an inch of space was wasted. She guessed there were more than twice as many cabinets as in the Kronberg kitchen, but not the same cheerful yellow.

On closer inspection she found them attractive. The fine wood was stained in a light shade that made the beautiful grain show through and many cabinets had panes of glass, so that what was inside was easily seen. That alone made the kitchen interesting, especially when Cook opened the doors and showed her the fine china, crystal glasses and goblets, as well as the lavishly engraved coffee trays of silver and pewter.

"Now sit yourself down," said Cook. "I'll wait on you this morning, but after that you're on your own." Then she placed two big mugs of coffee on a long wooden table that set in the center of the room and went back to the stove. Eva took a seat by one of the mugs and looked at the floor, which was desperately in need of a good washing. Soon Cook was back with two platters filled with porridge, bacon, eggs, cheese and fruit.

"I'm sorry for the filthy floor," she said apologetically, as if she could read Eva's mind. Cook took a sip of coffee and continued. "We've been short of help and, as you can see, the floor needs a good scrubbing. If I could get down on my knees, I'd never be able to get up again."

Eva smiled briefly at the picture in her mind of Cook's backside scrubbing the floor; then she looked closer, at the many dark grease spots and ground-in dirt between the wooden boards, knowing full well this would be one of her daily chores. No matter how long she scrubbed, this floor would never look like the spotless ones back home where her mother insisted they always be clean enough to eat on.

Suddenly the breakfast room door flew open and Gerta rushed in, grabbed the coffee pot and disappeared back through the same door. She looked frazzled and most likely had forgotten to comb her hair.

"That's Gerta," said Cook. "Not the finest sight to see first thing in the morning, eh?" Eva smiled, remembering having had similar thoughts about the maid last night.

After breakfast the atmosphere changed to a more hectic pace. Guests had arrived and Gerta was busy setting up the main dining room for the noon meal, stomping in and out of the kitchen with large trays of fine china, silverware, goblets and small vases of spring flowers that Eva had just picked for the occasion.

The kitchen floor would have to wait until evening as there were vegetables to prepare and apples to peel and cut up for pies. Already the aroma of roasting chicken filled the kitchen. Mr. Kronberg stopped in briefly to say goodbye before driving on to Gothenburg. He told Eva that he would be coming back in a few days to pick up Mats before returning to Norrland.

She didn't see Mats at all the whole day. After the dirty dishes, silver, glassware, pots and pans were washed from supper, she began scrubbing the floor. By that time Cook had retired for the night, and although Eva's arms and legs were aching, she was determined to make the floor look as good as new. She was relieved that Cook had shown her how to turn the lights on and off, although now her fingers hesitated to touch the little switches on the wall. Mustering up her courage, she quickly flipped one switch and then another. Tired and relieved that all the work was done, she sat down at the bare long table, laying her head on her arms to enjoy the cool spring breeze wafting from the open kitchen windows.

She awakened to a shuffling noise and saw Cook's face illuminated by a lighted candle. Eva quietly backed into a dark alcove leading to the storage room and watched Cook walk toward the ice box. To her amazement, Cook pulled out a pan of rice pudding, dipped in a serving spoon and began eating tomorrow's dessert straight from the pan. Soon the ice box door closed and Cook scuffed back across the kitchen floor into the dark hall.

Eva wondered if this midnight trip was a nightly event for Cook. She, too, felt hungry for a taste of rice pudding, but instead had a drink of water and went to her room. She removed the pins from her heavy braid and stretched full length on the bed, thinking about tomorrow when she hoped to get a glimpse of Jenny Almgren and her American haircut.

Suvi and Dagny

It was a long dirty ride through the middle of Sweden and each day seemed a repetition of the one before. At first they bedded down at night in the forest, but as the landscape gradually changed from tall, thick trees and raging rivers to humble farmlands they slept in the corner of a farmer's field or in a vacated shed.

The sun god had been on their side, blessing them with mostly fair weather and hopefully the waxing moon would last until they reach Gothenburg.

More prosperous farms began to appear, neat red cottages and barns painted with white trim, fenced in pastures, each with its own cow or two, a few pigs, chickens and a horse. Since their meager supply of food had run out, Suvi had been forced to buy bread and milk to supplement the berries and greens gathered along the way.

The secret cache of bills from the flour bin was still hidden beneath her shift and so far untouched. Certainly this windfall of money should be used for something more enduring and significant than squandering it away on food that was here today and gone tomorrow. Suvi had grander plans for that money, although she had not yet decided what that purpose might be; so they were always on the lookout for work to exchange for a hot meal or a few coins.

As larger farms became more prevalent they helped with rock

picking and planting, often being allowed to sleep inside the farmers' barns until the work was completed. They were usually given food and drink and when Blix worked alongside them he received a portion of grain and hay.

Many of these estates had elegant homes of wood or stone set on velvety green grass with flower gardens, and some had water spouting out of metal fountains of various shapes and sizes. One day the mid-day sun was so hot that Dagny had the outlandish idea of taking off her clothes and cooling off under the glistening drops of water, but of course she was too embarrassed to do such a childish thing and kept these thoughts to herself.

Enormous barns were surrounded by fenced-in pastures where sleek horses and large herds of fat cows with bulging udders swished their tails and grazed contentedly on the green grass. In between these large estates were more moderately-sized houses and barns with orchards and large fields of vegetables and small fruits. One day they smelled a wonderful aroma and saw on either side of the road rows of low green plants with plump red berries.

"They look good enough to eat, can I pick one?" asked Dagny, but Suvi was looking around and noticed a man sitting on the porch of a neat white house.

"No. You stay here with Blix," she told Dagny. "I'll go ask if they need any help with the harvesting."

The man's chair seemed to move by itself and Dagny was thinking what fun it must be to ride in a chair with big wheels such as that, when her mother returned.

"They are expecting harvesters tomorrow and won't need any help until the end of the week. He can't pay much and said we'd do better in the city."

Then Suvi took Blix's halter and began leading him down the road. When she saw Dagny looking sadly from one field to the other, she remembered something else.

"Oh, I forgot to tell you. The man said we could pick some strawberries to eat along the way."

Dagny lost no time in filling her apron and sampling many of the largest berries before catching up with her mother, who had already picked her share and was almost out of sight on the gravel road.

"Strawberries are the most wonderful things I've ever tasted," said Dagny, her chin dripping with strawberry juice. "Can we come back in a few days?"

"Perhaps. The man's horse has gone lame and he offered to buy Blix. He said Gothenburg is no place for horses and boarding him in the city would be very expensive."

Dagny nearly dropped the berries in her apron. "Sell Blix? You told me you'd never sell him," she replied, wide-eyed, and holding a half-eaten strawberry in her hand.

"Of course I won't sell Blix," she said tenderly, stroking his soft nose. "The man is considering hiring the three of us to plow some fields and plant new strawberry beds for next year." Then Dagny finished her strawberry and ate another.

"We're still going to Gothenburg, though, aren't we?"

"Not until we find some water to rinse out that apron of yours."

Dagny was dismayed to see the bright red blotches on her new striped apron.

"Don't worry about the stain," said her mother, "Those strawberries are worth more than any bothersome stains that a little cold water will quickly wash out." Her mother always had a way of making her feel better. They finished the berries and soon found a small stream where Blix could drink and in no time all traces of strawberries were rubbed out of Dagny's apron.

"That man must be rich to have a fine chair on wheels," said Dagny, spreading her apron on a sunny rock to dry.

"He might be, but I'd rather be poor and have my legs to get me around, wouldn't you?"

"The man has no legs?" asked Dagny.

"He has legs, but they don't work very well. He's a cripple," replied her mother, with a touch of sadness.

A bend in the road revealed many tall buildings where black smoke belched from stone chimneys and menacing structures rose to great heights on either side.

"I don't like this place," hissed Suvi, urging Blix into a trot. Dagny put her arms around her mother's waist and leaned against her back, squinting up at the gray buildings and smelling the soot-filled air. She felt small and closed in by the very high buildings that soared into the blue sky higher than the tallest trees in the forests of Norrland. After a while they rode by smaller, more hospitable buildings with large windows that displayed all kinds of fascinating things and foods they had never seen before.

"Slow down, Mother," she said, pointing to a butcher shop with large roasts of meat, neatly sliced steaks and feather-less chickens hanging from strings. Next was a smelly fish market where an enormous ugly fish stared blankly through the glass, its mouth open wide as if it might swallow them up in one gulp. They passed another place with large wooden boxes filled with fresh vegetables and fruits of all shapes and colors that even Suvi had never seen before.

The delicious aroma of freshly baked bread met their noses long before they came to the bakery where men and women sat at small round tables drinking coffee and eating fancy pieces of cooked dough.

"Can we stop for coffee and bread?"

"Of course not," stated her mother. "We are not dressed suitably for such a place, and even if we were, we have no money to spend being waited on."

Dagny watched the proud ladies in their fancy dresses and wide hats that shadowed their faces, but she knew some of them were watching her, too…looking down their noses disapprovingly like the snobby woman who came with her husband and children to the farm that day to buy potatoes.

"Some day I'm going to have a beautiful dress," Dagny said to herself. She had barely taken another breath when they passed a dress shop.

"Stop Mother! Look at that beautiful yellow dress in the window!"

"Such foolishness," exclaimed Suvi. "Money spent on things

like that could be better spent elsewhere." Dagny didn't agree, but she didn't say anything. Her eyes had been opened and her mind was busy envisioning herself wearing a dress as bright as the summer sunshine.

Her mother turned Blix down a narrow alley where brick walls rose up on either side, then turned left again. In the distance Suvi saw the butcher shop. Urging Blix to a fast trot, they passed the shop and went back toward the tall buildings and smoking chimneys. They were headed north again.

"Where are we going?" asked Dagny. She felt her mother stiffen.

"We're going back to the strawberry farm."

A Visit from Mr. Kronberg

Overburdened with preparing meats and vegetables for cooking and the dirty work of washing heavy pans, cleaning up sinks and washing down tables, not to mention scrubbing the kitchen floor, Eva looked forward to washing and drying the fine china and crystal, work that brought a little beauty into her days. Other than that, one day passed very much like the next until the first week of June when Mr. Kronberg made a surprise visit.

She hadn't seen him since the day she'd caught sight of the snooty Jenny Almgren hanging on Mats' arm, gazing up at him as if he were some mythological god. They were rounding a corner of the house, but Eva had a good look at the back of Jenny's head. Her hair was short as a boy's. In fact from the rear Eva couldn't tell the difference between the two of them, except that Jenny wore a very short skirt and high-heeled shoes.

"Jenny has Mats living high on the mountain tops with his head in the clouds," Mr. Kronberg had commented that day. "Eventually he will stumble down a rocky ravine and she won't be there to pick him up." He had put his arm around Eva as if to comfort her, but perhaps he was trying to ease himself from worrying about his son. He had told Eva many times that she was the daughter he was never able to have; he'd also said once that she was the one he favored as a daughter-in-law.

Eva was washing dishes when someone came up quietly behind her, put their hands over her eyes and said, "Guess who?"

Of course, she knew it was Mr. Kronberg's voice right away, and even though elbow deep in soapy water, she wrapped her arms around his neck for a big hug. They sat long enough at the wooden table so that Cook brought them coffee and cinnamon rolls.

Eva's questions did not have the answers she hoped for. The cottage hadn't been sold, although a few people had looked at it. One of her father's paintings was hanging in a buyer's house, but no money had been exchanged yet. Nothing of any great importance had happened in Norrland.

"How are Stella and Slofock?" she asked.

"Oh, just fine. They seem to be adapting very well. By the way, Mrs. Kronberg sends her good wishes."

"Say 'hello' to Mrs. Kronberg for me, too," said Eva, adding, "and how is Mats?"

"Fine, last I knew. He's living in Stockholm, studying architecture at the university there."

"Architecture?" Eva thought the word sounded very important, but Mr. Kronberg could tell she had no idea what it meant.

"Let me try to explain," he said, leaning back in his chair and taking a big puff on his pipe. His face took on the serious expression of teacher that she remembered from years ago.

"The origin of the word architecture is from the Latin word meaning builder or carpenter...more commonly known now as the art of designing buildings."

It was easy for Eva to picture Mats making wooden furniture, but building something as large as a house was a different matter. She expressed her thoughts to Mr. Kronberg.

"Oh, Mats doesn't actually build houses." Then he went on to explain. "He draws the outline or design of a building on paper with specific measurements as to length, width and so on...sort of like a picture with instructions that a carpenter would use when building a house."

Eva nodded, but she couldn't visualize the energetic and impulsive Mats that she knew sitting all day drawing pictures of houses. Such a sedentary way of life didn't suit his active lifestyle. Perhaps Jenny Almgren had been a good influence on him after all.

"Well," said Mr. Kronberg, rising from his chair. "I should be getting along. I still have a few stops to make before going home." When he picked up his suit coat, he saw the white paper sticking out of his inside pocket, the main reason for his visit today.

"And to think I almost forgot to give you this," he said, dangling the white envelope in front of her face. "The postmark is from last November," he added. "Must have gotten misplaced or else it takes a heck of a long time for a letter to arrive from America."

When Eva heard the word *America* she wanted to open the letter right away, but Mr. Kronberg was holding his arms out for a goodbye hug.

"I'll be back for Midsummer. You can tell me about the letter then," he said. She walked him to the door and stood on the steps, waving as he drove down the driveway.

Eva heard Cook rattling pans in the background. She put Ingrid's letter in her apron pocket and returned to the sink. Washing the remaining dishes, she thought about her mother on Christmas Eve. She liked to wait until everyone had opened their gifts before she opened hers. 'Anticipating is half the fun of Christmas,' she always said as she sat with a wrapped gift in her lap wondering what might be inside. But it wasn't just about Christmas, although her mother always anticipated Christmas from the first snowy day of winter. It was the feeling of expectancy she had about everyday things, looking forward to what little surprises might be in store for her or anyone else.

Now was a good time to test her mother's idea of anticipation,

Eva thought to herself, so she left the letter in her apron pocket. As she peeled the potatoes, cut up the turnips and hulled the strawberries she thought about Ingrid and what might be written in the letter. The hours passed so quickly that she wondered why she hadn't tried out this anticipation theory before, although lately there hadn't been much good to look forward to.

Finally the supper meal was over. She left the sparkling kitchen and went directly to the washroom. She was as excited as if she was going to a party, her own party, and the letter was her gift. In her clean nightgown, resting comfortably against the soft pillow, she opened Ingrid's letter.

November 1932

Dear Mama, Papa and Eva,

It is nearly four years since I wrote my first letter to you and still I have not received a response, so all I can do is to try again and pray that you will find it in your hearts to forgive me and hopefully write back so I know you are all well.

People in America send beautiful Christmas cards to all their friends and relatives each year, so I'm sending this one to you showing the American Santa Claus and his eight reindeer. The story goes that Santa and his reindeer ride across the United States on Christmas Eve bringing gifts to every child. Each reindeer has a name, but I can only remember the one called Cupid. If Gus were here he could recite all eight to me very quickly, but he is playing at a friend's house this afternoon.

Supposedly the sleigh lands on each family's roof and Santa slides down the chimney to put gifts in children's stockings which are usually hung over the fireplace. Since we don't have a chimney or fireplace, Gus and Nina hang their stockings on the bedpost by their heads, hoping they will get a good look at this American Santa Claus in his bright red suit. In order that Santa could easily come into the house, they made sure I didn't lock the front door. With children, Christmas is such a wonderful time. They think of everything!

I enclose a recent photograph of the four of us. A neighbor took this picture with his camera, but he took such a long time to get everything just right that the children got tired of smiling and none of us look very happy. I'm hoping to have a better one taken on Christmas.

Did you ever ask Mr. Kronberg if he had a camera? Perhaps he knows someone who does and could borrow it the next time he comes to visit. I would love to have a photograph of the three of you, so I can show the children their grandparents and auntie.

Do you recognize me with my extra pounds? I am looking more like you, Mama, every day. The food is so abundant here and it is a pleasure to prepare delicious meals, but I love my own cooking too much!

The seasons here are much like Sweden, but the autumn daylight hours seem longer. Olle says this is because the angle of the sun is shorter here than it is in Norrland. Winter days have more sunlight, too, which is good. I never did like those long dark winters.

It is cloudy and cold today and there is talk of snow already, but we don't worry about being snowed in all winter. The city has plow trucks that push the snow out of the roads making it possible to travel every day of the year all winter long.

I am getting better at knitting sweaters. Knitting must be a motherly thing because I never enjoyed knitting when I was younger, as you know quite well Mama.

We wish you all a very Merry Christmas.

Love,

Ingrid

Eva sat on her bed holding the photograph. It wasn't a very good picture, but it made her laugh. Olle was looking down at a squirming Gus while Nina rubbed her eyes and Ingrid looked straight ahead with wide eyes and a forced smile.

That night Eva had a strange, but happy dream that she was riding in the American Santa's sleigh. It was as cold as that night when she had ridden in Mr. Kronberg's sleigh to church on Christmas Eve when she was a little girl. The funny thing was that Santa had the face of Mr. Kronberg and his two black horses were pulling the sleigh through the night skies.

Below were the lights of villages and cities sparkling in the blackness. Soon the horses stood on one of the roofs. Eva looked down the chimney and saw a golden glow at the bottom. She was seeing the flames of the old stove in the cottage back in Norrland and was afraid, but Mr. Kronberg took her hand and they slid down a very long tunnel.

It wasn't the least bit hot when they reached the bottom and tumbled out into a large room filled with white candles. They were in the old church. Eva saw Ingrid, Olle and the children sitting in a pew just as they were in the photograph. Mrs. Kronberg was walking toward them with the coffee tray wearing her jingling red hat.

She awakened with the photograph in one hand and the Christmas card in the other, the sun shining brightly through her window. She dressed and hurried to the kitchen, relieved to see Cook still eating her breakfast.

More Letters

All day long Eva thought of the many things she wanted to tell Ingrid and how she would write about all the sad news of their parents. Sitting on her bed that night she stared at the blank piece of paper for a long time gathering her thoughts. Starting a letter, she thought, must be similar to an artist just before he brushes the first colors across a bare canvass, afraid he might make a mistake that he would have to correct. She couldn't remember her father sitting idly at his easel wondering where to begin; he seemed to have the picture already drawn in his head and went right to it. So, she got her thoughts in order and began.

June 8, 1933

Dear Ingrid,

Mr. Kronberg visited yesterday and gave me the letter you wrote last

November. For some reason it was delayed, misplaced or lost in either your post office or here in Sweden. I sit here not knowing how to write about bad news.

First I must tell you that we buried Mama two autumns ago and last spring Papa went to join her. It was a very difficult and lonely time and I often wished you had been there with me. In looking back I see mistakes I made and ways I could have made things better, but sometimes when you are going through a bad time everything seems to be falling around you and it is hard to rise above it.

In looking through Mama's bride's chest last winter I was surprised and confused to find three letters from you that Mama never told me about. I have no idea why she kept them a secret, neither do I know if Papa ever saw them. If he had, he never mentioned it to me. Unfortunately there were no envelopes with your letters, so it was only yesterday that I knew of your address in America.

Mr. Kronberg has been so kind to me, almost like a father, offering to keep an eye on the cottage and trying to find a buyer. He also took most of Papa's paintings to sell in Stockholm, but I did keep several small ones; the one Papa painted of Mama on the bluff before they were married and some of you and me as children. When I have enough money, I will mail one of them to you.

I have moved from Norrland to a beautiful farm in the south near Gothenburg. I work for the Lindholm family as a lowly scullery maid washing dishes and pans as well as cleaning every inch of the kitchen and preparing vegetables for cooking. Some days I don't know if it is sunny or raining and frequently am so tired from the long hard hours that I kick off my shoes and fall into bed, often waking in the morning still in my dirty clothes.

Cook is my only friend and looks after me like a mother hen. Other girls work in the house and dairy, but so far they haven't been very friendly. Cook says the gossipy maids are probably jealous of me, but I don't understand why; they all have better jobs than I do.

There is one other maid I see every day when she comes to the kitchen to bring trays of food to the dining rooms. Her name is Gerta. She also brings back all the dirty dishes for me to wash, but she keeps mostly to herself. Never have I seen her sit down to eat a meal, preferring to grab a bite of leftovers now and then, somewhat like a hungry bird pecking here and there for scraps of food. I feel sorry for her. She is painfully thin with sloping shoulders that seem to carry the sorrows of the world wherever she goes. I have never seen her smile and wonder if she keeps her long face all the while she serves meals to the Lindholm family.

Gunnar and Karl are the two Lindholm sons. Gunnar came into the kitchen just this morning. He sat with one buttock on the table where I was working and helped himself to a piece of just frosted coffee cake, first plucking a cherry and taking his time relishing its texture in his mouth and then winking at me. While finishing the piece of cake, he joked with Cook, asking about my red hair and if I had a temper to match. Then he took a handful of nuts I just prepared for cookies, so that I had to crack and cut up more. Needless to say, he didn't make much of a good impression on me. Cook said he came to the kitchen to check me out, whatever that means. What I do know is that he makes me feel uncomfortable.

She told me that Karl is nothing like his brother. He keeps to himself and is more interested in farm animals, especially the cows. So he can't be all that bad, can he?

Midsummer preparations are already underway. I understand the Lindholms have all their friends here for Midsummer Eve and the following day, so many will be staying overnight. More work for the upstairs maids and lots of food for us to prepare in the kitchen. I will sleep with your letter under my pillow in the hope it will bring me good dreams. This letter is growing very long and sleep is overtaking me. Till next time.

Love,

Eva

July 1933

Dear Eva,

I am so thankful for your letter. When I saw the Swedish postmark and return address I nearly fainted. The washing can wait for I can think of nothing but you and all that has happened since I left. I broke down and cried thinking about Mama and Papa, and it saddens me to think of you caring for Papa alone last winter. Winter was always lonely for me in Sweden, even in the best of times. When you are young you don't think that your parents will ever die and now I have a lot of regrets, but I never could have done what you did. You are such a brave and caring girl.

It puzzles me that Mama never mentioned my letters to you. You must have thought I was a terrible sister to run off and you not know where I was. I am sorry that my leaving brought them such pain.

I am a different person now. Being a mother has given me a new perspective on what life is all about. The past cannot be changed, but I can make the present a better place, and that is what I try to do. Remember, Eva, everyone makes mistakes. We must learn from our errors and move on to improve ourselves. If we go back and repeat them, we are not growing toward our perfect self.

You can see by the enclosed photograph that Gus has very light-colored hair. I wish it was in color so you could see Nina's hair. She was born with bright red hair, but when that fell out she was blonde with light reddish highlights. My friends say she is a strawberry blonde. Not as curly as yours, but it definitely has a natural wave. Every time I brush her hair I think of how you must have felt when we were little and I teased you about The Finn and your red hair. How unkind and thoughtless I was. I am so sorry and ask that you please forgive me. Oh the naughty things children do, although I don't remember you ever being naughty.

It doesn't seem like we have been in America for almost five years already. Gus is four years old now and Nina almost two and I feel another one stirring in my belly. Olle is busy with carpenter work and the foreman is very nice. He lets Olle bring home scraps of wood which he makes into toys for the children and some of the pieces were even large enough to make a cradle and a chest for clothes. Even though America is going through some hard times now, we are doing very well.

Olle bought a second-hand camera as a Christmas gift for all of us and took these pictures, except for the one of him and Gus, which I took. Olle, of course, is the one with no head! As you can see I need more practice using a camera.

Write soon.

Love,

Ingrid

August 18, 1933

Dear Ingrid,

So far this summer has been very hot and dry, almost unbearable most days working in the kitchen because of the busy stoves. Today there was cooler air blowing in from the northwest and I did my sit-down tasks in front of a little window near the pantry trying to catch every little breeze.

It was interesting what you said in regard to learning from our past mistakes. I should have done some things differently, too, like being more cheerful and less selfish in taking care of Papa, but sometimes I let frustration and resentment get in the way, and I regret that now that he is gone.

It was difficult to watch a strong happy father turn into a weak sad stranger. Toward the end he often refused to eat and had to be fed like a baby. One day I could take no more and threw a dishful of food against the wall. As you can imagine that only made matters worse because then I had to clean the wall and floor and I had one less bowl in the cupboard.

There have been so many wonderful times in my life. Why do we forget what is good and the bad comes back to haunt us?

Well, enough of this looking back! I must tell you more about this beautiful place. Here there is electricity that brightens a room with the flick of a switch, making kitchen and household chores easier, quicker and cleaner. Cook says that electrical current improperly used can be deadly, so I always say a prayer before I push a button or flip a switch. Mr. Kronberg told me there is electricity in America. Do you have it where you live?

I sit here looking at the three new photographs you sent. I love the one where Gus is holding Nina and also the one of you and the children on the front porch. The one with Olle and Gus is interesting, and very good of Gus. By the way, I like Olle's nice shiny boots! Good luck next time!

Love,

Eva

A Pitcher of Cream

After noontime chores, Cook asked Eva to go down to the spring house to get extra cream for the evening dessert.

"You need a change," she said. "Take your time and enjoy the fresh air."

It was mid September and a perfect day to go outside for a walk. Eva was familiar with the spring house and knew exactly where the cream pans were left to cool after morning milking. She had only to skim a quart of cream from the top, rinse the ladle and then hopefully have enough time to take the long way back around the pasture to see the cows before returning to the kitchen.

First, though, she had to pass through the milk room where the milking machines were washed and hung to air dry. This morning the door was open and a man sat on the floor surrounded by small metal parts and a peculiar looking contraption. She looked down on his thick crop of honey-colored hair and blue shirtsleeves that were rolled to his elbows as he diligently worked on the machine.

Not wanting to confront him, Eva decided to walk around the barn to the spring house, but while stepping backwards she slipped off the step and fell against the open door. The man looked up just as her pewter pitcher clattered across the milk room floor and in an instant he was on his feet helping her to get up. He was a young man about her own age.

"Are you all right?" he asked, but she was embarrassed by his concern and could only nod before hastily retrieving the jug.

"Ah, so you've come for cream. Well, you're just in time," he said, picking up the few remaining metal pieces and fitting them into the machine. Just in time for what, thought Eva, watching him set a large jug under one spigot and a smaller one under another spigot of the contraption. The muscles of his forearms flexed as he lifted a forty-quart milk jug from the floor with less effort than if he'd picked up a feather. She was briefly reminded of the morning Mats came to the barn to pick up Stella. He had muscular arms, too, and now she wondered why she associated the manliness of a man by the sight of his strong arms. Already she felt that same uncontrollable excitement tingling through her body.

"Come closer," he said, slowly pouring milk into the machine.

The sun, shining through a small window, highlighted the golden hairs on his deeply tanned forearm and she noticed for the first time the fine-quality material of his shirt. He was not just an ordinary farm worker.

"Watch these two spigots," he said, but she was looking at the handsome features of his face that were so much like those of Anders Lindholm.

Suddenly milk began pouring out of the two spigots and he was talking again.

"Skim milk is coming out here, and over there is your thick heavy cream." He seemed as excited as a young child who had just received a new toy.

"This cream separator arrived yesterday," he told her. "It's a new invention I saw in a magazine, supposed to be quicker and more sanitary than leaving milk pans out overnight for the cream to rise. Not only that, as soon as the cows are milked nearly all the milk will already be separated and ready to be cooled for delivery to the creamery."

He was smiling at her now, expecting some kind of response, and she saw in his eyes the same blue-green color of the lake back in Norrland.

"It is...it's just magical," she said, but then she wasn't certain if it was the machine, the lake or his eyes that enchanted her.

"By the way, I'm Karl Lindholm."

"Pleased to make your acquaintance, Mr. Lindholm." she said

with a slight curtsy, although she had already figured out who he might be.

"You can call me Karl. I'm not much more than a common farmhand around here."

She felt heat rising in her neck as he looked down at her with thoughtful, caring, very blue eyes tinged with emerald green.

"My name is Eva Gunderson," she said, turning a deeper shade of red.

"Gunnar was right about you," he said as he filled the pitcher with cream.

"Right about what?" she asked.

"He said you were the pretty one."

Karl noticed her flushed face as she turned away. He picked up the pitcher and followed her to the open door.

"Eva..." he said in a soft, low voice, "don't forget your cream."

He was grinning down at her. She felt a little foolish, thinking she had forgotten all about the cream, but instead of showing embarrassment, she smiled and thanked him. It was like a little private joke or subtle feeling of camaraderie that passed between them, a special emotional bond that she couldn't explain.

Gunnar had been curious about the new cream separator and was closing the pasture gate when he first saw Eva's red hair. As he made his way toward the milk room, he noticed Karl standing beside her, so he stopped to light a cigarette, then leaned against the fence post to watch her taking long strides up the grassy hill, swinging the pitcher of cream in her right hand.

Eva stopped midway to catch her breath and looked back toward Karl. He raised his hand slightly and she waved back. When he saw Gunnar walking toward the milk room, Karl went back inside.

"There's a wench I'd like to bed sometime," he said in his crude way. Usually Karl didn't oppose his brother; it was easier just to agree with him, but today he could not hold his tongue.

"Leave her alone, Gunnar. She's a nice girl."

"Oh, she is, is she? Has she tickled your fancy now?"

Karl ignored his brother and poured more milk into the separator. His flame of excitement about the new machine had diminished and now he had no interest in explaining its operation to his brother.

"You like her, don't you?" said Gunnar, breaking an awkward silence. He was teasing and was surprised by his brother's hostile reaction when Karl turned around, a bit red in the face, and looked him straight in the eye.

"I told you, she's a nice girl. Leave...her...alone. That's the end of it!"

"Okay, Karl, I was just kidding."

Gunnar hadn't seen Karl this angry since the time he had dared his brother, then only eleven, to go skinny dipping in the river. As soon as Karl went in the water, Gunnar grabbed his brother's clothes and ran back to the barn to tell the farm hands. Karl could hear their loud chuckles and snickering as he ran up the driveway scantily covered with a couple of small spruce boughs, hoping that none of the maids were there watching, too.

Cook was sitting on the kitchen stoop when Eva returned.

"Sorry I'm late," said Eva breathlessly.

"I told you to take your time and enjoy yourself," she said with a wink as she followed Eva into the kitchen. "Sit down and catch your breath while I get us some coffee."

They sat quietly for a while, although Eva could tell Cook's mind was buzzing for information and wondered if she'd seen her in the doorway with Karl.

"So you've met the second son, I see," Cook said all of a sudden. Eva took a long sip of coffee and swallowed it slowly as she arranged her thoughts.

"Karl was in the milk room putting together the new cream separator...and..."

"Oh, so it's Karl now," said Cook with another mischievous wink.

Trying to be as nonchalant as possible, Eva described how the cream separator worked, but she knew her red face was telling a different story.

"I've always liked Karl," Cook said. "He's a very caring person, with both animals and people...and he's quite good looking, too. Wouldn't you say?"

A Juicy Red Apple

Cook didn't think of herself as a matchmaker, but she knew of Eva's shyness and thought to help things along a bit. The farm hands had picked most of the apples in the orchard and put them into the cold cellar, but Cook knew of a special tree that ripened late. Just the other day she had eaten one and knew the apples were ready for picking.

When she saw Karl walking toward the orchard a few days later carrying a pair of long pruning shears over his shoulder, she told Eva to run down to the tree at the far end of the orchard and pick a couple dozen apples.

Eva walked across the lawn and down the hill past the cow barn. She had just come to the first row of trees when she saw two men on ladders trimming branches. She hastened her pace, keeping her eyes focused where the apples hung heavily on the branches like bright red ornaments on a Christmas tree.

Her basket was almost full when someone came up from behind and grasped her around the waist. Two strong arms held her so tightly that she screamed and dropped the basket, spilling most of the apples on the ground.

"I've got you now," said a voice she recognized immediately.

Hearing a woman's scream, the two farm workers jumped from their ladders and came to Eva's rescue.

"I caught a thief stealing our apples," shouted Karl to the men. "What shall we do with her?" He was in a jovial mood and the men played along with him.

"Well, I know what I'd do with her," said one of the grinning men, "but I guess she's yours now," and they returned to the middle of the orchard.

Karl helped her gather the dropped apples, then picked one high up on the tree and polished it on his sleeve. "Sit down and share an apple with me," he said taking her hand.

"I'd like to," she said looking back to the house, "but Cook is waiting and I'm late already."

He knelt in the grass and gently pulled her down beside him. "I think Cook can wait a few minutes longer. Anyway, it was my fault that you spilled the apples, so she will have to deal with me."

Eva relaxed then and watched him cut the apple in two equal halves with his pocket knife.

With the precise skill of a surgeon he neatly cut one of the halves into four identical slices, cutting out the seedy cores. Then he touched her lower lip with the apple's juicy white edge, teasing her to take a bite, which she did. It was cool, crisp and incredibly sweet. When he offered her another she was reminded of Adam and Eve and giggled in amusement at the picture in her mind of her and Karl in the Garden of Eden.

"What's so funny?" he asked.

She had not intended to reveal anything, but her mood was especially light and she forgot about her shyness.

"Wasn't Eve the one who tempted Adam with the apple?" she asked, feeling a bit giddy as she took a slice and held it to his lips. Then they took turns feeding each other until the apple was finished.

"I do feel a bit like I'm in the Garden of Eden," he joked, lying back on the grass and observing her face in the soft shady light. She was not only the most beautiful girl he had ever seen, but there was a sweetness and grace about her that he found irresistible. He had never wanted to kiss a girl before, but that had all changed now.

Eva, too, was smitten with Karl's wholesome good looks, his commanding presence, yet calm and patient manner. She might have let him kiss her, if she hadn't glanced back at the big house with its imposing windows that appeared to see everything. "I must get back to the kitchen," she replied, even though she wished she could stay in the orchard all day.

"Let's go, then," he said, helping her up. She reached for the basket, but he picked it up.

"It's a bit full," he said. "I'll carry it back for you."

Cook was all smiles when she saw them walk through the door. She had another pleasant surprise for Eva. "The postman just brought the mail. Looks like another letter from America."

Memory of a Yellow Dress

Dagny thought surely they would leave the strawberry farm when the late fields had been harvested, but Bertil, the man in the chair with wheels, convinced Suvi to stay on for the final plowing, planting and mulching of new strawberry beds for next year. After that, there was always another reason to stay a little longer. Her mother loved the little farm and Bertil was kind to both of them.

Bertil's wife was a poor cook and an even worse housekeeper. She did make tasty porridge, but after breakfast she would sit on the wide porch drinking coffee, reading a book or sewing until almost noontime; then she'd have to rush around the kitchen trying to put a quick meal together. Frequently she was gone for a whole day shopping in Gothenburg and sometimes vanishing for a week or more to visit family and friends.

It was during one of her long absences when Bertil suggested to Suvi and Dagny that they tidy up the kitchen and prepare dinner. He always kept the larder well stocked with fine meats, vegetables and condiments, but much food spoiled because his wife neglected to use it in time.

The delicious odor of roast pork brought him into the kitchen and what he saw amazed him. The dull copper pots sparkled, the greasy wooden floor shined and the dusty furniture was polished to its original beauty. Bertil had told Suvi that his wife came from money and she had brought an extensive dowry when they were married, but that was ten years ago...before the accident.

He then gave them free rein to clean the entire house, something Suvi had learned to do quite efficiently at the miner's house. This relatively humble home was much smaller, but most of the furniture was from a finer time and needed to have only a good amount of elbow grease to make the pieces look like new. She uncovered many beautiful treasures hidden away in the corners, and when the curtains were washed and the windows sparkling clean, Bertil was well pleased, if not astonished, at the wonderful transformation.

The farm was a fine home for Blix, too. He had more than enough to eat, was never overworked and had the friendly company of the old lame mare. Although Dagny was a big help, she did not share her mother's love of cooking or housekeeping. With idle time on her hands she grew restless. It didn't set well with Dagny when she learned they might spend the winter here. The city beckoned her, especially those beautiful shops whose contents grew more spectacular in her mind as each day passed. She could not get out of her thoughts the dress shop with the lovely yellow satin gown hanging in the middle of the dressmaker's window.

Bertil was a kind man and Dagny enjoyed pushing him around in his chair, plus he'd always give her a piece of candy from a little sack he carried in his pocket. He wasn't at all threatening and she felt comfortable being with him. On the porch, where they often sat after dinner, he would tell her stories and sometimes she confided to him her innermost thoughts; mostly her dreams of going back to Gothenburg. One day in late September he asked her to harness Blix to the wagon.

"Your mother doesn't care about going to the city," he said. "I have a doctor's appointment and wondered if you might like to drive me to Gothenburg." Dagny was ecstatic and ran to the bedroom to find her best blouse and skirt. Passing by the long mirror, she stopped and smiled to her reflection, twirling around as she had that memorable day when the church man had given her mother an armful of clothes and later when she had felt like dancing all the way to Gothenburg.

At the time, Dagny hadn't realized how long it would take to get here, but Gothenburg had proven to be much more than she had ever imagined. Feeling that same giddiness now, she skipped through the house and out to the barn to help Bertil into the wagon.

The yellow dress was often in her mind while laboring in the dusty strawberry fields, but today when they passed by the dress shop there was only a purple one hanging in the window.

They left Blix at the stable and she pushed Bertil up the sidewalk into to a large brick building. When safely in the doctor's office, he said she would be free to do whatever she wished for about an hour's time. Dagny had dismissed all thoughts about the yellow dress. It had been a foolish notion to think she would ever own such a fine gown, but now her imagination set her to dreaming again and she walked back to the dress shop.

The door was open and she heard a woman's voice.

"May I help you?"

The woman sat under a bright lamp sewing. She squinted over her spectacles at the young girl, regarding her kerchief, peasant clothing and heavy farm shoes.

"We don't have any work, if that's what you're looking for."

"Last summer...in the window...there was a yellow dress," said Dagny, shyly looking around the room.

"Oh, yes, the gold satin gown. It's over there," said the woman, pointing with her needle to a row of dresses hanging in a closet. "I show gowns in the window for just a short time. If they are out in the sun too long they will fade." Dagny found the yellow dress and was about to take it off the hanger when the woman suddenly stood up and shouted.

"You mustn't touch the gowns! I can't sell them if they are soiled." Dagny looked down at her hands, darkened from holding the leather reins, and backed away. The woman felt sorry for her and spoke in a kinder tone.

"Did someone send you here to ask about the dress?"

"No...I just thought it was beautiful."

It had been a slow day. The woman was tired of sewing and needed a change of pace. Plus she liked this young girl.

"Well, you have good taste. In fact it is a perfect color for you, but the dress would need a few alterations."

"Alterations?" said Dagny.

"The bodice would have to be taken in a little and the waist let out. Come with me," said the woman walking to the rear of the room. "You can remove your blouse and skirt in here," she said, opening the curtain to a small dressing closet.

"Take off my clothes?" Dagny exclaimed.

"My dear," said the woman, "I can't take accurate body measurements over your bulky garments now, can I?" But Dagny wanted no part of this measurement business. She ran out of the shop and didn't stop until she came to the bakery. Bertil had given her a few coins, so she used one to buy a frosted bun, eating it slowly as she made her way toward the butcher shop.

When she stopped to look at a paper in the shop window, a stout man in a bloodied apron opened the door.

"Looking for work?" he asked. "I saw you reading the help wanted sign." She thought of running away from here, too, but his jolly round face made her pause and consider the possibility.

"What sort of work?"

"Come inside and I'll show you," he said, stepping back so she might pass through the door.

The room was cool and smelled strongly of aged meat. A slight woman stood behind the counter trimming fat off steaks, her white hair tinged with yellow and pulled back severely from her pale, wrinkled face. When she looked up, Dagny saw a serene pleasantness about the woman's eyes, her welcoming smile making Dagny immediately more comfortable.

"This is my wife," said the butcher affectionately. "Our meat cutter moved away and she's been filling in until we can find a replacement." Then he folded his chubby arms across his chest. "So, young lady, have you had experience in cutting meat?"

"I've helped carve up a moose or two," she replied, feeling suddenly confident and grownup.

"Ah...yes. I thought you must have come down from the north." He saw her as honest and hardworking and hopefully as a female friend for his wife. "I think you will make a fine meat cutter. How about giving it a try?"

So many things whirred through her mind, but it was the yellow dress that made her tell him that she would take the job. She wanted that dress more than anything in the world and the sooner she began earning money, the better. But how would she tell all this to her mother and Bertil?

The long ride proved a favorable interval for Dagny to explain everything to Bertil and by the time they arrived at the farm she had won his approval. Now she had to convince her mother.

"You can't work alone in the city! No, I won't allow it."

Bertil heard Suvi's outburst and wheeled himself into the kitchen. Suvi was peeling potatoes and had her back toward him, while Dagny sat at the table wiping away her tears. The room was eerily silent, except for Bertil drumming his fingers incessantly on the arm of his chair.

Sometimes when Bertil was overtired or worried he absent-mindedly did this, his face turning serious as in deep thought. The first time Dagny saw him tapping his fingers was when she had asked him a question about the farm. She couldn't remember now what the question was because the constant tapping had made her nervous and she'd walked out of the room to tell her mother.

"It's just a habit," Suvi had told her, "something brought on when he's anxious or undecided about something."

"But his face went all blank and he kept staring at his fingers."

"Well, not everyone copes with worry in the same way. Some people withdraw from fear and others must express it physically. It was the same with your father when he had concerns about the miners. He would pace back and forth staring at the floor with that same serious look until finally he came up with a solution." Dagny still didn't understand, so Suvi added her own explanation. "Of course Bertil cannot walk, so I'm guessing he must let out his frustrations through his fingers." By that time Dagny had grown more sympathetic.

"I'm sure Bertil's problems are much more bothersome than most men," admitted Dagny, "him being tied down to that chair all day long and not being able to do things a man should do."

Dagny thought back to that as she sat with her head in her hands, but she was more concerned that her mother was not in favor of her working in Gothenburg. Suvi continued with dinner preparations, her mind on Bertil and what was bothering him.

Finally the tapping stopped and Bertil spoke as if nothing unusual had happened.

"I've never heard you two quarrel before and I don't see any reason for it," he said.

"The butcher is a kind man and so is his wife. They have the best meat in the city and only the finest people trade there. I think it would be a suitable and respectable job for Dagny."

Her mother's response came after a few moments. "Well, where would she live? It's much too far to travel to Gothenburg every day and I don't want her living in one of those run down boarding houses on the edge of town." The tone of her mother's voice had changed from outright denial to thoughtful consideration, so Dagny told her more of what she learned at the butcher shop.

"The butcher and his wife live above the shop. They said I could sleep in the spare room...and they have a little brown dog, too." She watched her mother kneading the biscuits, which Suvi did much faster and for a longer time than was necessary. Bertil continued talking.

"The old couple had only one daughter. She died very young and I know they would take very good care of Dagny. I think it would be a good experience for her to be away for a while and see how it is to be on her own, don't you agree, Suvi?"

A faint smile passed between Suvi and Bertil, but Dagny thought nothing about it, except that they had come to some positive conclusion. Finally her mother leaned her tired, floured hands on the counter and looked back at Bertil and her daughter's expectant face.

"I'll think on it," she said finally, patting the mound of dough and then cutting out little circles with the round biscuit cutter. Dagny placed them on a large metal tray and while they baked she set the table for dinner. Bertil watched the two of them working harmoniously together. He was thinking affectionately of Suvi and anticipating their own future here alone at the farm and wondered if her thoughts were the same.

Reading a Letter to Cook

Eva put Ingrid's letter in her apron pocket, picked up a knife and began peeling an apple. Then Cook sat down across from her with a damp towel in her hand.

"These are too good to waste on pies. You can eat the one you're peeling," she told Eva. "I think we'll just put the rest of these apples in a bowl for the family to eat in the breakfast room." Then she pulled the basket to her side of the table and began polishing them one by one. The kitchen was quiet except for the ticking clock and the crunch of Eva's crispy apple.

Cook grinned at Eva with an expectant look, as if waiting to hear about her visit to the orchard. She had been curious since Karl had accompanied her back to the kitchen and was carrying the basket of apples. She had also seen that twinkle in Karl's eye when he'd apologized for Eva's late return. When Eva still said nothing, Cook remembered the letter from America.

"It's early yet," said Cook. "You can read your letter now if you want to."

Did Cook intend for her to read the letter aloud? thought

Eva. She had told Cook interesting snippets of previous letters, but had never read one to her before. Eva opened the envelope, deciding she would read the letter very slowly and leave out anything that Cook should not hear.

August 1933

Dear Eva,

The summers here are hotter than I remember in Sweden. This morning I've already done two washes in the old washing machine, another wonderful invention that saves much hand scrubbing time and is also kinder to my hands. It has a little roller that squeezes out most of the water, although it does cause creases and deep wrinkles sometimes.

I've also cleaned up the breakfast dishes and made all the beds. Don't feel like doing another thing today but sitting in a chair with a good book and fanning myself, but, of course I cannot waste time doing such a frivolous thing. I don't remember having such sticky hot days in Sweden. People here say it is the humidity that makes one feel so depressingly hot. Humidity is when the air is full of steamy water. You can't see it in the air, but there is an uncomfortable dampness that hangs heavily inside and outside of the house, especially in July and August.

Eva scanned the next paragraph and decided not to read it to Cook.

My poor sister! I'm sorry to hear of your difficult times, first taking care of Papa and now having to work in that hot, dirty kitchen. And to think that you must scrub filthy, greasy floors and wash all those dishes and pans! You are an angel and someday you will be rewarded for your kindness and hard work.

Eva began reading the next paragraph aloud.

I laughed reading about…

then Eva gasped and read the next few sentences to herself.

...Cook eating pudding out of the pan and drinking lemonade from the pitcher. No, I wouldn't do that either, but perhaps she doesn't even know she is doing it. She may be sleepwalking.

"What was so funny that made Ingrid laugh?" asked Cook, expectantly, when Eva suddenly became embarrassingly silent. Of course, Eva could not relate any of what Ingrid had written about Cook, but she was able to compose herself and read on about the next funny story.

Do you remember Mr. Kronberg telling of a farmer who got out of bed at two o'clock every morning, milked his cow and then went back to bed? When his wife got up to make breakfast the full milk pail was always setting on the kitchen floor. For a long time they thought a helpful tomte was milking their cow, but actually her husband did it when he was sleepwalking.

Cook laughed so hard that tears came to her eyes and Eva was able to finish the letter.

I think you should come to America. We could make room for you here. Winter isn't a good time to travel, I suppose, but you should think about coming next summer. Perhaps by then we will have a place in the country and you could have a room of your own.

Does Mr. Kronberg have a buyer for the cottage yet? You could use some of the money to pay for your voyage.

Enclosed is a photograph of me and the children sitting on our front porch.

Love,

Ingrid

Eva showed Cook the photograph and asked if she had ever seen a camera.

"Mr. Lindholm bought one of those picture making machines

two Christmas's ago," said Cook. "He walked around all day clicking that box; even came here and pointed it at me. Came back a couple weeks later and gave me a photograph of a fat lady with a face that looked familiar. 'Where did you get a picture of my mother,' I asked. And he laughed and said it was a picture of me. I didn't think that box was very flattering and I told him so."

Cook suddenly became quite serious. "I've been thinking about you and Karl and...well, I don't quite know how to say this."

"What about Karl? Is it something bad?" asked Eva.

"Oh no. I've never heard anything bad about Karl. This has to do with letters you write to your sister. Do you ever discuss the Lindholm family?

"A little, perhaps," she replied. "Why do you ask?"

"I know how young girls are," she said. "How they like to talk about boys and things."

Cook was stammering and unsure of how to put into words what she wanted to say. "Well, you should know that Mrs. Lindholm has charge of the incoming and outgoing mail, but most importantly, she is not above reading other people's letters. I think she is just plain nosy and this is her way of keeping track of everyone, especially the servants."

Eva was shocked that someone would open another's mail. What if Mrs. Lindholm had already read Ingrid's letter. The knot in her stomach tightened as she thought about what might happen to Cook if Mrs. Lindholm knew about her nighttime adventures in the kitchen. And what had she told Ingrid in previous letters about Mrs. Lindholm or Karl?

"I don't think I've said anything unkind about the Lindholm family." she said. "Not that I can remember, anyway."

"Too late to worry about that now," said Cook. "The postman and I have a little understanding. He always brings my mail directly to the kitchen and if I have a letter to be mailed I give it directly to him. He is good about doing things like that, especially when I offer him coffee and treats. Mrs. Lindholm, of course, is none the wiser."

"So did the postman deliver my letter here today?" asked Eva.

"Yes," said Cook. "As luck would have it, he also had a letter for me and when he didn't recognize your name, he asked about you and gave the envelope to me."

Eva was so relieved that she wanted to jump up and down with joy. "So, there is no chance that Mrs. Lindholm read this letter from my sister?"

"No chance at all," said Cook. "The postman said that from now on he would deliver all your letters to the kitchen."

Eva should have felt like she was floating on a cloud, but during the day little worries crept into her mind; things she might have told Ingrid in past letters that Mrs. Lindholm might have already read. That night she wrote to Ingrid.

September 1933

Dear Ingrid

Cook told me today there is a good possibility Mrs. Lindholm might have read the letters we have written to each other. I can't sleep for worrying that I might have said something not very nice about Mrs. Lindholm. And what about Karl? Did I mention to you about the day we met in the milk room?

Well, what's done is done and there's nothing I can do about it now. In the future I'll be giving my letters directly to the postman and he will deliver your letters to the kitchen just as he does with Cook's mail.

Gerta has been sickly of late and guess what? I have a lovely new uniform, white cap, blouse and apron that I wear over a black skirt. I have been helping out in the breakfast room since Gerta took to her bed, and also serving on weekends in the banquet hall.

Karl is thoughtful and polite, always thanking me with a smile when I refill his coffee cup. Well, I know how men love their coffee. Some love their liquor too. On weekend parties I sometimes bring drinks to the men's smoking room which can be a challenge; especially when they empty too many glasses and liquor does the talking for them. I must watch myself and keep on my toes to side-step a pinch or wandering hand, especially from Gunnar.

Olga, a neighbor girl, began working in the kitchen this week. She is round and short like Cook, but quiet as a mouse, a bit slow and clumsy, not very particular in preparing fruits and vegetables or scrubbing the floor. With Cook's guidance she is doing better and we hope she will at least stay through the busy Christmas season.

As far as I know the cottage has not been sold. Thanks for your invitation to stay with you if I ever decide to come to America. I have dreamed of going there for a long time but, of course, I must first fulfill my service here and then hopefully I will have saved up enough money for the voyage.

Love,

Eva

The Butcher Shop

Dagny's first day at the Butcher Shop was both exciting and tiring. Breakfast was served promptly at five thirty in the little kitchen and when the clock struck six times the shop opened for business.

Dagny was impressed by the elaborate brass clock that had the privilege of setting alone atop a large chest of drawers and rested majestically on a white woven cloth, surely a place of honor in this humble dwelling. The kitchen-dining room was brightened by this sparkling sunny face that no doubt was the most expensive item the couple owned. However, it had been the glorious song it sang that had stopped Dagny in her tracks that first morning. After breakfast, the butcher went out to open up the shop.

The old woman grinned. "He likes to get out there early to talk with the other shopkeepers. Sometimes I think men enjoy gossiping more than women do."

"I saw you looking at my clock," she said proudly, pouring them both another cup of coffee. "It is a replica of one that stood in the tower of my great-grandfather's village in Russia."

"Russia must be the most beautiful place in the world," said Dagny, admiring the clock with all its bright metal filigree.

"I've never been to Russia, but my grandfather was born there. He told me Russia is the largest country in the world."

"Larger than Sweden?" asked Dagny, remembering the long journey from Norrland. The woman chuckled saying Russia was almost forty times as large as Sweden. The puzzled look on Dagny's face caused the woman to take down a jar of raisins. She counted out forty and placed them in a group on the table, spreading them out carefully so they were all touching each other.

"Let's assume these forty raisins is the area of Russia." Then she picked out one of the raisins. "This one is the size of Sweden." Dagny knew better, but just sat and looked at the raisins, which weren't very big at all.

"Do you see how it takes forty Swedish raisins to fit into the size of Russia?

Dagny didn't understand, but nodded her head slowly as if she did.

"I know how difficult it is to make this comparison, but some day you will understand," she said, picking up the raisins and putting them back in the jar.

Dagny looked up at the clock again, fascinated by its Russian origin, wondering if everything in Russia was so magnificently beautiful.

"So you are Russian and not Swedish then?" asked Dagny, scrutinizing the old woman.

"Well, let's see now. My Russian grandfather married a woman from Finland. They had a son, my father, who married a girl from Gothenburg, who became my mother. She was from a long line of Swedes, so that makes me half Swedish. The other half of my ancestry, from my father, is part Finish and part Russian."

Dagny was puzzled by this string of events and looked the woman over from head to toe. Under all those wrinkles she thought the old woman had once been very beautiful and thought surely it was her face that was Russian, but she wasn't certain of that.

"So, what part of you is Russian?" she asked. The old woman

laughed so hard that tears dropped from her sparkling blue eyes.

"Well I look just like my Swedish mother, but everyone tells me I must have gotten my artistic talents from my grandfather, so maybe it is my brains that are mostly Russian. Someday when we are not so busy, I will show you my quilt paintings, but for now we must go to the shop."

Dagny first learned about preparing chickens. They were alive in a pen behind the shop, but when the butcher brought them into the shop they had their heads cut off, dripping with blood and some of them still wiggling. They were scalded in a tub of hot water and laid on the table for Dagny to pluck. It was boring work and the feathers kept sticking to her hands and making a mess on the floor. She would much rather have been cutting up big pieces of meat or grinding beef and pork to make meatballs. She thought about Russia, Sweden and the raisins. By eleven o'clock her feet ached from standing on the hard stone floor.

Dagny looked forward to dinner where she might sit and listen to the chiming clock again, but instead the butcher's wife brought a tray of cold meats, cheese and bread into the shop where they could eat and still wait on customers. Then she disappeared into the kitchen with the dirty dishes. The door between the shop and kitchen banged heavily. It was a large, thick door that kept the coldness of the shop from entering the main house in winter, but it also kept out the sound of the beautiful chimes.

Supper that night was a simple beef stew and biscuits, reminiscent of the moose meat and potatoes her mother had simmered on the stove in Norrland, but here the company was more jolly and the beef stew tasty and full of cooked meat scraps, enough for all to have second helpings. The butcher cleaned out the pot for a third helping and finished the delicate buttery biscuits. Unlike Vidar, he was good company, telling funny stories and behaving much more dignified while eating at the table.

"I'm in the mood for a raisin cookie, aren't you, Dagny?" said the butcher, patting his round belly. "My dear wife thinks I'm too fat and hides my favorite cookies, rationing them out as she sees fit, but tonight we must celebrate your first day with us." He smiled at his wife and there was nothing she could do but fetch three cookies for this special occasion.

"This is a delicious cookie," said Dagny politely, but in reality it was stale and she wasn't especially fond of raisins. Already she was missing the luscious sweet pies her mother had made from the fresh fruits in Bertil's abundant storeroom. The three of them lingered at the table drinking coffee until bedtime, when the clock chimed eight times. This was her favorite time of the whole day.

Dagny's bedroom was hot and stuffy, and she struggled to open the only window, which overlooked the back yard. A faint breeze brought in a putrid smell that quickly overpowered the small attic room. Looking down, she saw many large round containers of animal bones and scraps of fat with hundreds of flies buzzing around them. She shut the window to about an inch and opened the door a crack in hopes of catching a bit of draft from the hall, then she draped her clothes over the back of a wooden chair and brushed her hair. After she laid down on the hard straw mattress, she stroked the soft bristles of the brush. It gave her some measure of comfort.

Not much air found its way into the little attic room, but through the cracked door she clearly heard the clock strike nine times. She rolled over on her stomach remembering the soft feather bed she and her mother had shared at the strawberry farm and the four large windows where fresh, cool, country air blew through their room every night, and where sleep always came quickly.

She was nearly asleep when something pressed against her arm and lapped her face. It was the same little brown dog that had sat in the old woman's lap after supper as they drank their coffee. Dagny picked him up, cuddling him against her chest and didn't hear a sound until morning when he jumped off the bed to go downstairs.

Dagny worked slowly and deliberately at first, but once shown how to sharpen her knives, the trimming became easier and soon there were rows of neat steaks and roasts laid out on trays ready to be put in the showcase. Every weekday night they had stew which routinely changed from beef to chicken to pork and back to beef again, with fish chowder thrown in now and then. Sometimes on Sunday there was a roast chicken with potatoes and gravy, but usually it was a meatloaf made out of ground scraps of leftover meats from the week before. Dagny never went away from the table hungry and was always treated fairly and compassionately by the butcher and his wife.

One cold November day an icy rain fell, making the roads and sidewalks too treacherous for riding and walking. The butcher fell asleep in his chair waiting for customers and his wife told Dagny to put down her knife and wash her hands.

Afterwards she was led to a back room where a brightly-colored quilt covered a large bed and beautiful pictures hung on all four walls. The old woman smoothed her hand over the center portion of the old quilt. "I started making this middle part when I was about ten or eleven; then just before I was married I added on more rows to cover a double bed." she said.

"My mother was a seamstress and she showed me at a very early age how to make the needle take very small stitches. I practiced on little scraps of cloth, sewing them together to make coverlets for my doll's bed and later for my own bed. There was much material left on the cutting room floor; large and small pieces of cotton, wool, silk, satin, and fancy brocades that were mine just for picking them up and taking them away. I saved them all, folding each one carefully and putting them in a box in my room." She laughed then. "It wasn't long before I had more boxes than would fit under my bed...and I still have boxes of material under this one."

All the while she talked, Dagny gazed at the beautiful quilt and the many pieces of cloth that were sewn together to make colorful designs.

"Those pictures on the walls...did you paint them?"

"Look close," said the woman, "and you will see they aren't painted, but are indeed small pieces of cloth sewn together to look like a painting." Dagny couldn't believe what her eyes saw: a farm scene with animals and men working in fields, a landscape of mountains, valleys and a river made of patches of every color blue she could think of, a busy market scene with people dressed in bits of colorful cloth and a vase in shades of white, gray and pale yellow holding pink and lavender flowers on a dark green background.

"They are beautiful," exclaimed Dagny, looking so close her nose almost touched the cloth. "But your stitches are so small I can't even see them."

"The stitches are all hidden in the back. Let me show you," said the woman picking up a pile of stitched cloths that had no backing on them yet. She turned the top one over so Dagny could see where each little piece of cloth was sewn to the other and then ironed flat and neat.

"Here's one you might like," she said, pulling a cloth from the middle of the pack. Dagny saw tall trees with thick brown trunks and green tops like the spruce trees back in Norrland, and clumps of white birches with their small, light green leaves bordering the forest. Rows of flowered pieces of all colors decorated the foreground, surrounding a tiny white cottage with blue shutters. Dagny's eyes blurred with tears. "I was hoping it looked like the cottage you described to me."

"Oh it does!" said Dagny, as she smoothed her hand over the green lawn and flower gardens.

The woman was touched by Dagny's reaction. It was one of her first attempts at quilt painting and not one of her best works. "I want you to have this," she said, rolling up the cloth carefully and placing it in Dagny's hands.

As they were leaving the room, Dagny noticed something else: a small table covered with a lace cloth with a small framed picture. What struck her was the little bouquet of pale purple flowers lying in front of the picture.

"Where did you get such flowers this time of year?" she asked.

"They are dried flowers," said the old woman sadly, "from the funeral flowers for our little girl." Tears formed in the corner of her eyes as she picked up the picture and showed Dagny the round angelic face of a child with curls all over her head. The child's eyes were closed as if sleeping.

"T'was taken in her casket the day she died...thirty-six years ago." She began to sniffle and placed the picture back on the table. Then she walked hastily back to the kitchen.

Dagny had never seen a dead person before, but she was rather glad now that she had. It was comforting to know that in death a person looked very much like they had in real life. She wished she had a picture of her father.

Dagny went out of her way to be kinder to the old woman, who in turn became more generous in doling out her stash of cookies, always remembering to slip one into Dagny's hand before she went upstairs to bed at night. The old stale cookies had long been eaten up and these freshly baked ones tasted much better, but Dagny still ate around the raisins, hiding each one under her pillow until she had forty of them. She intended to solve the puzzle of how much larger Russia was than Sweden, but the little dog kept eating the raisins before the mystery could be solved.

Dagny was helping to stock shelves in the front showcase when the woman from the dress shop came in.

"Hello there. I'm sorry if I scared you away that day last summer," she said with a warm smile. "No one has purchased the gold dress. If you still want it, you could pay me a little bit each week and perhaps by Christmas you might be wearing it." Her voice was soothing, almost motherly, but Dagny was undecided now about spending her hard-earned money on such an extravagance. She told the woman she'd have to think about it.

The shop was closed on Sundays and sometimes Bertil and Suvi picked her up and they'd go to the park and eat the picnic lunch Suvi had prepared. Dagny liked to stand outside the shop watching for Blix to appear at the far end of the road, his pace quickening when he saw her. Then he'd come to an abrupt halt, nickering as he nuzzled her arm. She always drank her morning coffee black on Sunday, saving the precious lump of sugar to give him before climbing into the buggy.

When the weather grew too cold for picnics in the park, Bertil took them to a small café at the edge of the city where there was a barn for Blix to have some hay and get warmed up. Dagny loved the café with all the delicious aromas of coffee, cocoa and breadstuffs of all kinds baking in the ovens. She liked to watch the ladies in their fine dresses, imagining how she might feel sitting there wearing the yellow dress.

One day she told them about the woman in the dress shop, but her mother thought buying such a fancy dress was nonsense and would not discuss it. Bertil, on the other hand, was more understanding and even gave her a few coins to put towards the first payment.

"When you have paid for the dress, we can all go to the theater to see a play," he told her.

Every day she dreamed of the day she would wear the golden dress and during the first week of December, with Bertil's help, she made the final payment. True to his word, Bertil bought tickets to the theater for the next Saturday evening.

"But how can I go to the theater in my fine satin dress knowing that mother must wear one of her everyday cotton ones?" said Dagny.

"I must let you know, Dagny, that my wife is in Stockholm seeking a divorce. Your mother can choose from a number of fine gowns hanging in my wife's closet. I'm sure she will not miss one little dress, and if she does, so be it. I shall not worry about that, and neither should you."

The woman at the dress shop combed Dagny's hair back into a roll and fastened it with little clips of rosebuds made out of the same satin as her dress, and then she curled the side strands into black ringlets that danced from her head as she walked.

Dagny was more interested in what all the other women were wearing to the theater than the production itself and could remember little of the first act. During intermission she could not remain seated and walked out to the reception room to be noticed by the other guests, but mingling with the upper class wasn't something she knew much about. They promptly ignored her and she tried her best to walk graciously toward the nearest wall where she felt more secure. Someone had left a lace fan on the table beside her and as she fanned herself in the grandest manner, a man approached her.

"You look familiar to me. Have we met before?" he asked, but she knew him immediately. He was no doubt the most handsome man she had seen come into the butcher shop, always immaculately well-dressed and usually buying the best tenderloins of beef.

Feeling a bit over-confident in her new hairdo and gown, she replied in her most fashionable voice. "You might have seen me in the butcher shop trimming your fine tenderloins." Her response amused him and she noticed his straight white teeth.

"Ah...you are a clever girl, aren't you? By the way, I think you are wasting your time in a butcher shop. I can give you work where you can wear beautiful dresses every day."

She saw her mother wheeling Bertil toward them and was immediately thrown back to her natural roots where shyness overcame her tongue, and she had nothing more to say. The man tucked his card beneath the bodice of her dress, kissed the back of her hand and disappeared into the crowd.

"Who was that man?" asked her mother.

"Oh, just someone who buys meat from the butcher."

Later as Dagny undressed in her little room, the card fell to the floor. There was nothing on it but some letters and a series of numbers that meant nothing to her, but she was certain the man would be in the shop again and she would ask him then about the card. For now she was ecstatic thinking about a place where she could wear beautiful dresses every day.

The next Wednesday she cut her hand severely with a sharp knife and was not able to work in the shop.

"This is very unfortunate indeed," said the butcher. "It is so close to Christmas and I need your help now more than ever. If you aren't better in a day or two, I'm afraid I'll have to find someone else to take your place."

When Bertil and her mother came on Sunday, she was worse. Her hand was swollen and the pain made tears come to her eyes. Suvi gathered her daughter's things and they brought her back to the strawberry farm.

Two Letters

November 1933

Dear Eva,

Your letter arrived much later than usual, but I was so happy to hear how well things are going for you. In fact your life sounds a lot more exciting than mine, although I am very contented here. My family is my inspiration and joy.

No, I don't remember you saying anything negative about the Lindholms.

So, what about Karl? You did mention how he loves animals and that you saw him in the milk room, but you never elaborated on what happened there and now I'm very curious!

How nice that you are out of that horrid kitchen and doing something clean and enjoyable. I'm sure you look beautiful in your black and white outfit. I wish I had a picture of you. Better yet would be one of you and Karl!

We celebrated the American Thanksgiving holiday at the home of Olle's boss. Thanksgiving is a day of fun and feasting. On that day most every house in America is roasting a turkey and having bread stuffing, potatoes, squash, onions and cranberry sauce. Dessert is a meal in itself with various fruit pies, such as apple, blueberry and cherry, as well as custard and pumpkin. We also had Indian pudding which is made with molasses and cornmeal, somewhat like porridge, but sweeter and served with vanilla ice cream.

Vanilla ice cream makes any dessert taste better and is especially good with pies and very common for children's birthday parties served with a piece of fancy decorated cake. Ice cream is made from rich cow's cream mixed with eggs and sugar to make a custard. Before the custard is frozen, vanilla or chocolate flavoring can be added and sometimes ripe fruits like peaches and strawberries.

This card illustrates how an American home looks at Christmastime. I am hoping that we will have a tree just like the one pictured here, but ours will have only a few gifts beneath it. I am finishing a blue sweater with white snowflakes for Olle similar to one Mama made for Papa. Do you remember the pattern? In the evenings I knit sweaters for the children while Olle is busy making toys, and a special surprise for me. We wish you a Merry Christmas.

Love,

Ingrid

January 3, 1934

Dear Ingrid,

I think my last letter arrived late because I had to hold on to it longer than usual. The postman comes to the kitchen only when he has mail to deliver to either Cook or me, so I had it in my apron pocket for nearly a month before he came. But that is a small price to pay to know that no one else will be reading my letters.

Happy New Year! This house has been a place of beauty and light practically the whole of December and through the twelve days of Christmas as well. Electricity gives us summertime all year long. Unless you look out the windows or go outside you wouldn't even know it is winter.

First I must tell you about Christmas at the Lindholms. Evergreen boughs, wreaths and garlands adorned the mantles, staircases and windows and a massive spruce tree decorated with sparkling glass balls, tiny porcelain figurines and strands of beads and Swedish flags welcomed all who entered through the great front hall. Smaller trees were sprinkled throughout the house with a special family tree in the parlor where on Christmas Eve and Christmas day the many white candles adorning its branches were lit for the singing and dancing 'round the tree' celebration.

Everyday menus were transformed to much more elaborate dishes and Christmas Eve topped them all with many guests attending in their holiday finery. I've never seen such an abundance and variety of food at one time; a smorgasbord of tables with stuffed pork loin, meatballs, roast ham and chicken, oysters in mustard sauce, salmon with dill, creamed and pickled herring, fruit salads, breads and cheeses, baked creamed potatoes and vegetables of all kinds. Another table was spread with an array of lavish desserts: fruitcakes, almond and spice cakes, varieties of pies and decorated cookies, puddings and custards, sweet dumplings, cheesecakes, chocolate candies, nuts and other tempting sweets. And to think that I had a part in creating some of those delicious dishes!

My Bible is stuffed with paper scraps of recipes and little tricks that Cook has taught me. Yesterday I helped make a braided sweet bread wreath filled with cut up fruit and nuts with white frosting, cherries and nuts on top.

We were all surprised to learn that Gerta was seen sneaking out of the house very early on Christmas morning carrying two large satchels and running toward the woods. Word has it that she is pregnant and will not be returning. I'm sorry for her and happy for myself. Unless someone else is hired I will probably continue serving in the dining rooms.

Fortunately for me Olga is still performing my old chores. She arrives very early each morning, often before Cook and I get to the kitchen. Cook takes pity and gives her a plate of cold leftovers until the coffee and porridge are ready. I don't know if this is true, but Cook thinks the girl's grandmother sends her off through the forest without anything at all to eat, one less mouth to feed at home. Her clothes are ragged and the buttons on the man's coat she wears do not fasten across her ample chest.

The poor girl is pitifully bashful and if asked a simple question her chin drops and any words remain hidden in a downcast pout. There is nothing quick nor thorough in her nature and her work needs constant inspection. More often than not, the dishes need rewashing. I'm still delegated to wash and rinse Mrs. Lindholm's fine crystal and china, wiping them dry of any water spots.

Christmas morning there was crumpled brown paper and a pile of hand-me-down clothes on the table where Olga eats; no doubt a gift from Cook. A package was waiting for me from Cook also, many skeins of yarn in beautiful shades of blue that I plan to knit into a shawl. I knitted a green and white hat for Cook and a similar one in red and white for Olga, who immediately put it and wore it for the rest of Christmas Day.

So now on snowy Sundays I spend my spare time knitting and putting to good use the yarn Cook gave to me. I'm trying to remember the striped ripple pattern Mama used to make for wraps and afghans. Using these varied shades of blue reminds me of the undulating waves of a seascape in the breakfast room. Knitting always makes my mind wander to beautiful places.

Love,

Eva

Recuperating

Dagny soaked her hand each morning for the next week, resting in a chair for several days with smelly black salve slathered over the wound. By Christmas her hand wasn't swollen anymore and the soreness was almost gone, but she was still not allowed to do much around the house. She sat by a window that looked out toward the paddock and it gave her some joy to watch Blix and the mare frolicking in the snow. He looked free and happy. She wanted the same for herself. Pictures of Gothenburg crept into her mind as she fantasized about a place where she might wear beautiful dresses every day…a distant dream now that snow was on the ground and Bertil had said they wouldn't be going back to the city until springtime.

While her hand was healing, he had often wheeled his chair into the parlor to keep her company. He talked about the recent storms that had dumped over a foot of snow, and how he always stockpiled enough food for winter use. He never rode to Gothenburg after the first snow unless the weather turned warm enough to melt the icy roads.

"I didn't always feel that way. When I was younger I used to love riding through the city in my sleigh listening to the harness bells tinkling in the crisp cold air."

"I would think it great fun to ride in a sleigh," she said, excitedly. "Do you still have one?"

Bertil's face grew solemn, his hands rubbing nervously together before gripping the arms of his chair. When the persistent tapping began, part of her wanted to leave the room, but the rest of her was curious about why the mention of a sleigh caused Bertil to react this way. Finally he spoke in a weak, hesitant voice.

"My sleigh was painted bright red with gold trim and had very fast runners," he said with sad eyes looking out the window toward the barn. "It's in several smaller pieces under the hay mow." Then he cleared his throat and began telling her about the accident that had happened over ten years ago. She could see that thinking about that day still pained him.

"The road was icy, and it had begun to snow when the runners skidded around a turn. The sleigh tipped and careened over an embankment, pinning me underneath. I thought surely someone going by would have seen tracks in the snow or at least my mare would be standing nearby," he said, "but much snow fell that day and no one found me until the next morning. Fortunately I was dressed warmly and had a fur blanket, but I never had feelings in my legs after that."

Dagny, of course, was concerned about what had happened to the horse.

"She ran back through the forest, until her harness became tangled up in a fence. A farmer saw her the next morning calmly foraging on a pile of hay, the leather straps wrapped tightly around a fence rail by her back legs. The accident was no fault of hers. I like to think she was trying to find her way home so my wife would know something bad had happened and I'd be found." He nodded toward the barn. "That's her out in the paddock with Blix."

Dagny was sorry for Bertil, and sorry for herself, too. She'd hoped to be working in Gothenburg soon after Christmas, and now she was stuck here for the winter. She never told her mother or Bertil that the butcher was going to hire someone else, or that the man at the theater had offered her work, but she did show Bertil the card with the numbers on it.

"What do you suppose they mean?" she asked.

"It appears to be a telephone number," he said, pulling out his doctor's appointment card and showing her a similar series of numbers arranged in the same manner. "Where did you get this?"

"That man at the theater gave it to me."

"I don't recognize his name, but Gothenburg is a very large city." Bertil was suspicious and warned her about calling a strange man.

"He isn't strange," she said with some authority. "I've seen him many times before at the butcher shop and he's always polite and well dressed."

"Dagny!" he said emphatically. "Some men can't be trusted. You must be careful who you talk to."

"I will," she agreed, but his words had rushed past, their meaning lost because her mind was thinking about the place where she could wear beautiful gowns every day of the year.

The farm had been good for all three of them. Bertil seemed much happier, more talkative and not so moody, but since returning from the butcher shop Dagny had noticed a change in her mother. They still slept in the same bed, but now a wide invisible gap divided them. Dagny asked her mother one night if she had done something to offend her.

"Of course not. Why do you ask?" Dagny couldn't put her feelings into words and just said that things didn't seem the same between them now.

"Life is change, and the way we look at life and love changes, too. We must adjust and adapt to our new surroundings."

Dagny had also observed a closer relationship between her

mother and Bertil; longer conversations, secret smiles and sometimes a loving touch. Does a mother's love for her child lessen as they grow older? Had Bertil replaced her in her mother's heart? Something her mother told her one day answered these unasked questions.

"As we outgrow people, we find new ones. You are growing up, and soon you will leave me forever and go your own way; I must prepare myself for that, don't you see?"

Dagny saw some sense to this. She wasn't the same girl she'd been last year and next year she would be different still. She had outgrown this place and was ready to leave it behind and seek her own future.

Sometimes she woke in the night and reached over to her mother, only to find she wasn't there. She often fell asleep waiting for her to return, but one night she lay awake watching the moon rays slide across the ceiling and knew it had been over an hour before her mother slipped quietly back under the covers.

"Are you not feeling well?" asked Dagny.

Not knowing how to explain her absence, Suvi said she was feeling much better now. When this happened over and over, Dagny grew concerned about her mother's health and asked again. Finally Suvi admitted she had gone to Bertil's room.

"Often he gets up in the night. I fear he might fall trying to get in or out of his chair, so if a noise awakens me or I wake up unexpectedly, I go and check on him."

This satisfied Dagny until she began thinking about what her mother had said about love changing. What her mother had been trying to say was that she loved Bertil. Dagny had grown fond of him to.

During the last week of January the weather turned very warm. Every trace of snow melted from the yard and soon the roads were bare and dry. An aura of spring filled the air, filtering through the house and bringing warmth into every corner, invigorating its occupants, especially Dagny, who had been moping around, bored and uneasy since New Year's Day. As the three of them went out to the barn, Blix whinnied, prancing around the paddock like a young colt.

"So you'd like to go out for a drive, too," said Bertil, revealing his own inward thoughts to the horse.

This idea took Dagny quite by surprise. "Can we drive to Gothenburg today?"

"I was thinking we might," he said with a wink. "Your mother and I were discussing how you missed living in the city and are anxious to go back to work."

"Get your things ready," said her mother as she led Blix into the barn. Dagny looked at them in amazement, not believing what her ears were hearing. Both Bertil and her mother were smiling, as if this had been some prearranged surprise for her, or perhaps the fulfillment of a personal plan of their own. It didn't matter either way; she was happier at that moment than she'd been in a long time and wasted no time in running back to the house to pack her bags.

When Dagny returned to the barn, her mother had harnessed Blix and was helping Bertil to his seat. "I have much work to do in the house, so I won't be accompanying you today."

Then Dagny felt guilty about leaving. "I'll help you with the work and we can all go tomorrow," she suggested.

"You know I don't like the city. My joy is working here on the farm. She took her daughter's hand and looked into her eyes. "You remember what we were discussing the other night…about life and love?"

"Yes, I remember," said Dagny, realizing that now everything had changed and they were going their separate ways. They reached out and hugged each other tightly, both remembering their troubled past, but expectant of a happier future.

What her mother said allowed Dagny to have no regrets about leaving the farm, though she would miss the delicious strawberries. Missing her mother wasn't something she had thought about until she and Bertil had ridden a few miles down the gravel road.

"It is less than ten miles to Gothenburg," he reassured her.

"Winter will soon be over and springtime will bring us all together again."

The Boarding House

Dagny did some errands for Bertil in Gothenburg and then he let her off at the butcher shop. She waved confidently as he drove away. She wasn't at all surprised to see a new man working at her old table, cutting off chunks of meat from a side of beef. The butcher's wife invited her in for coffee and inquired about her hand. Everything looked the same in the kitchen. She was especially glad to see the clock again and decided to stay until eleven o'clock.

Although Dagny was happy to see the old woman, her mind was on the little card in her apron pocket. She sat drinking coffee and eating raisin cookies until the beautiful brass clock chimed eleven times. Then she showed the old woman the card.

"We don't have a telephone, but there is a public one down the street." She gave Dagny instructions on how to use the phone and gave her a coin to use for the call.

A woman answered and told Dagny a man would meet her at the café across the street from the Square in about an hour.

Two plainly dressed men sat at a table drinking coffee. Dagny felt comfortable enough to sit in a corner of the café next to the storefront window where rows of breads and sweets set her mouth to watering, but she was much too excited to eat anything. One of the men stared in her direction and she looked out toward the Square, which wasn't square at all. Two wide roads crossed near a patch of green grass that allowed people to sit on black iron benches where a half-naked statue spouted out streams of water.

Walking brusquely by the shop were men in dark suits and a few stylish ladies with overly large hats carrying various sized packages. One held a child's hand, who Dagny thought would much rather be free of his mother's grip to run freely down the sidewalk. Everyone appeared to be in a great hurry, including a man walking directly toward her table.

She didn't recognize him at first with his head down and loosened tie hanging askew on a wrinkled shirt, but his voice was familiar. Dagny stood up and gathered her bags as he mumbled something under his breath, grabbing her arm so forcefully that she felt like apologizing for interrupting his day. They, too, hustled along the busy sidewalk until a long, windowed contraption stopped in the road nearby. He pulled her toward the door and up a couple stairs to an empty row of seats. He noticed her discomfort as the vehicle maneuvered through the busy street and his face relaxed into a faint smile.

"Never been on a tram before?" he asked. But just then the trolley car came to a screeching halt, forcing her to lean heavily against him, embarrassing her into silence. As people around her began standing up, she, too, attempted to rise, but he pulled her back. "We don't get off here," he told her sternly. The door squeaked open and everyone standing in the aisle got off, and then those waiting outside came aboard. After a while Dagny became used to the stopping and starting, noticing out the window that most of the interesting little shops had been replaced by tall brick buildings and and a few ramshackle wooden houses.

"We get off here," said the man, picking up one of her bags and pushing her down the aisle. The door flew open and she stepped out into the shadows. The sky above looked very small and there were no trees or green grass. Not a soul was in sight but the man, leading her into a narrow alley that twisted and turned through the brick and wooden maze. Finally they came to a street, turned left and stopped in front of a large wooden building with a faded, weather-beaten sign that she could not read.

They walked up a flight of rickety stairs to a long, darkened hall; a single light at the very end faintly revealed two rows of worn, wooden doors that stood like sleeping sentries on both sides of the hall. He stopped at number nine, but he said it was actually room six; the top nail was missing so the nine hung upside down. It didn't matter to her; she always got the two numbers mixed up anyway.

He opened the door and walked in. "This room needs a good airing," he said, opening a small window that looked out to a brick wall. She stood in the doorway looking around the tiny room. There was a bed in one corner with a large slanted crack across the headboard and a small wooden bureau against the adjoining wall. In front of the narrow window stood a small table and chair.

"Don't stand there all day. Come in and shut the door!" he said loudly. He was annoyed and Dagny thought it was because of her.

"Perhaps I should come back another time," she suggested, backing up further into the hallway. He grabbed her arm and pulled her into the room, slamming the door shut behind them.

"You do as I say, do you hear?" he ordered, still gripping tightly to her arm. She obediently nodded her head and dared not move an inch. He saw this wasn't going well and changed his tone.

"Put on that yellow dress of yours and we'll have a bite to eat later," he said lightly pinching her cheek. And fix up your hair, like it was at the theater that night. Then he reached in his pocket and gave her a key. "Always keep the door locked when you're inside or if you leave the room...and don't lose it."

"Is this your house?" she asked shyly.

He laughed. "No, I just own what's inside."

She locked the door and sat on the lumpy mattress. It was stained and smelled slightly of old urine. Clean sheets and blankets were piled up on the table, so she made up the bed and laid down on the yellowed coverlet. What had she gotten herself into? This was worse than her old room at the potato farm. At least back there the air was fresh and she had a fine view of the green forest and the rising summer sun.

She unpacked her things and put on the golden dress, her

stomach growling as she remembered the tender steaks he sometimes bought at the butcher shop. She tried to arrange her hair as the woman in the dress shop had done, but she had no pins to keep it piled on her head and left it hanging down in little waves left from her tight braid.

After a while she stood looking out the window. In the alley below a black and white cat chased after a crumpled piece of paper. She watched it bounce lightly along the narrow passageway with the cat catching it and then letting it go until they both skipped out of sight. Slowly the shadows moved up the brick wall to a balcony above, where a glass door sparkled with the last rays of the sun. She watched the darkness travel across the railing, sneaking slowly up the door and leaving everything below in muted shades of gray. Leaning close against the milky glass, she could just make out a thin strip of bright blue sky and the thought occurred to her that if she moved her bed by the window she might catch a glimpse of the moon as it rode across the sky at night.

The door knob rattled, followed by loud pounding. "Unlock the damn door!" said a familiar voice. She obeyed and he walked past her. "I've already eaten," he said, placing a loaf of bread and a chunk of yellow cheese on the table. Then he opened a bottle and gave it to her.

"Sit down and have a swig," he said, loosening his tie and sitting on the edge of the bed watching her. She tried to hide her disappointment and took a sip from the bottle…and then another, its sweet fruity taste slipping smoothly down her throat and soothing her anxious belly. The bread was soft with a crisp brown crust and the cheese deliciously sharp, making her even more thirsty.

He placed another bottle on the table and walked behind her, touching her hair and neck on his way to the window. He told her about other rooms downstairs where food was served and men came to drink and amuse themselves. His voice was softer now, more jovial and he seemed in a much better mood than before.

She smiled up to him and took a long sip from the new bottle, but this one caught in her throat as if it were on fire, making her eyes water, and she quickly ate some bread to compose herself. He chuckled saying the next swallow would taste better, so she obliged by taking a small slow sip that indeed was better tasting and pleasantly warming.

He spoke of a woman named Victoria, and mentioned other things that didn't make much sense to her clouded mind, which wandered back to the strawberry farm and then to the forest lake and the calm peaceful cottage with its many flowery beds in colors of pink, yellow, white and shades of red.

He was behind her again, his hand slipping under her bodice. When she turned suddenly to stand, the room began spinning. Then she was lying on the bed, his face distorted and blurry looking down at her as the ceiling circled dizzily above her head. She felt herself slipping back to those times in the potato shed, but this man was different. He smelled of flowers and spice, had gentle hands and took his time with her. When he was finished he slid off the bed and buttoned his trousers.

"So you weren't a virgin after all," he said rather disappointingly. What was a virgin? Had he expected her to be something else than what she was? She was naked down to her rumpled stockings and she pulled up the sheet to cover herself. He tossed a few coins on the bed. Then the door slammed, jarring her head and she didn't bother to lock the door.

She fell into a deep sleep and woke with a piercing headache. Loneliness enveloped her like a smothering blanket. The thought came to grab her things and run, but the sharp pain in her head made her lie down again. Where would she go? To the butchers? Back to the strawberry farm? And how would she explain to them her mistake...her foolishness in taking up with this man? Like her mother, she would see this through, take what life gave her and try to make it better.

Victoria

The room was surprisingly bright when she awakened the second time, but her head was still pounding. It must have been almost noon for the sun to be so high in the sky. The light hurt her eyes and she ducked her head under the covers, her mouth dry as she lay there yearning for a cup of hot coffee. Eventually she had to relieve herself and looked under the bed for a night pot. It hadn't been emptied for a long time; a brownish-yellow crust had formed on the bottom, but she used it anyway and put on her shift. Vaguely remembering something about a bathing room at the end of the hall, she peeked out the door and saw a woman carrying a large towel on one arm and a basket on the other.

When Dagny knocked on the door of the bathing room, a voice said to come in. The same woman sat at the end of a long bench, looked up and smiled.

"Have a seat. You're next after me."

Dagny sat down facing a large, foggy mirror, beside which hung the painting of a young girl sitting on a cushiony pink chair brushing her long brown hair. Dagny's hand absentmindedly went up to her own head trying to smooth out the snarls from last night.

"You must be the new arrival," said the woman, whose blonde hair was piled haphazardly on her head, her bright blue eyes looking out from beneath dark lashes.

"I came yesterday," Dagny said shyly, appraising the woman, who appeared younger than her mother, but it was hard to tell under her colorful face.

"My name is Victoria. I'll be happy to answer any questions you might have," she said, rubbing something red from her fingernails. If Dagny hadn't been so bashful, her first question might have been how the woman's fingernails had gotten so red, but she sat and quietly listened as Victoria continued.

"It was a busy night. Probably my makeup is all smudged," she said, dipping her long fingers into a small jar. She smoothed white cream over her face and wiped it off with something that looked like soft paper. Then she rummaged through a small pouch. "Probably you've never worn lipstick, have you?"

Dagny eyed the small metal tube with a red tip and shook her head.

"Come here and sit by me," said Victoria, patting the space beside her.

She steadied Dagny's chin with her hand and told her to smile. Dagny felt a cool smoothness tickling her lower lip and her smile grew wider.

"That's good," she said, tracing the upper lip to make it appear fuller. Finally Victoria sat back and held up a small mirror. "Look here."

Dagny watched two red lips moving as she opened and closed her mouth. She thought it humorous and laughed at herself. Victoria pulled the mirror back so Dagny might see her whole face. "See how pretty you look?" Then Victoria gave her the little tube of lipstick and a piece of sweet smelling soap.

Later that afternoon Victoria came to Dagny's room with an armful of dresses.

"I've outgrown some of these and others have been left behind when girls moved on. Some are your size and others we can make fit," she said, placing each gown side by side across the bed, a satiny rainbow of bright, shiny colors that immediately spread a cheerful atmosphere in the drab little room, as well as in Dagny's heart.

She liked the red one and tried it on first, but the black lace ruffle around the bodice hung limply on her meager chest and kept slipping off her shoulders.

Victoria could see that Dagny was disappointed. She grasped the excess material under Dagny's arms and raised the neckline a few inches. "I'm pretty handy with the needle. Perhaps I can take it in here and there so it will fit better."

Dagny tried on a light purple dress with a darker sash and large bow in the back. It fit quite well, but had a very narrow skirt that tripped her up as she walked.

"Watch my feet," said Victoria, as she took a few very tiny steps. But Dagny's heavy shoes got in the way and she stumbled again. "With different shoes and a little practice, you'll soon get the hang of it," said Victoria.

Some of the gowns needed to be shortened, but the last two fit perfectly. One was dark green with tiny white roses cascading down the bodice, making her waist appear quite slim. The last one was shorter than the others, a bright blue with a wide, full skirt that spread outward in silky waves as Dagny twirled around the room. Victoria watched her and smiled. "I always liked to dance in that one, too."

She picked up the broken brush and gathered Dagny's hair together at the back of her head, securing all loose ends with little clips, while Dagny watched attentively in the mirror. "A few curls around your face and you'll be in business."

"Business?" asked Dagny. Victoria smiled. "I'll stop by around six and bring some shoes. We can eat supper together in the dining hall and discuss your duties."

Coffee with Mr. Lindholm

It was late April now and Eva had not heard from Ingrid since December. The old postman had not been seen since the blizzard of January fourth and she worried that her mail had been intercepted by Mrs. Lindholm. Cook was worried, too, but didn't let on her concerns to Eva, saying only that it wasn't unusual for mail to be late in winter, especially this year because of the unusually heavy snows.

Mr. Lindholm sat alone in the breakfast room, the morning sun filling every nook and cranny with a warm, friendly glow. After reading the newspaper, he became more talkative and tried to engage Eva in conversation. His fatherly manner, similar to that of Mr. Kronberg, gradually melted her self-consciousness, but it was difficult for her to find the appropriate words to discuss the mail situation. She would leave the kitchen with words on the tip of her tongue, but when she saw his face those words vanished like a scampering mouse in the storeroom.

The boys were helping a neighbor and Mrs. Lindholm wasn't feeling well and wouldn't need a tray until ten o'clock, so he asked her to sit down and join him for a cup of coffee. This unusual invitation shocked Eva. What did he want to talk about? Was her work not satisfactory? Perhaps he'd seen her and Karl together. Nervously she filled two cups and sat down near the kitchen door. He slid his chair around to face her.

"I want to tell you what joy it is to have you serving here...such a refreshing change. If you have any questions or concerns, please feel free to ask me." His sympathetic and relaxed manner let her know he had only good things to say, washing away her worries. Finally he went over to the window and looked out as if contemplating the weather. To Eva's surprise, she heard her own stammering voice asking the dreaded question.

"Sir...there...I mean...is there a problem with the mail? I've been expecting a letter and the postman...well, we haven't seen him for months."

"Ah, yes. The old man came down with a bad cold and then had a turn for the worse, but he's doing better now and should be back on his route soon. Meanwhile I've been picking up the mail."

"Have you noticed a letter addressed to me?" she asked.

"Mrs. Lindholm usually sorts out the mail and delivers it, so I see only the business correspondence she puts on my desk. I'll speak to her about it and let you know."

"Oh, please don't bother Mrs. Lindholm. It's not that important, really...it's...well, I haven't heard from my sister since before Christmas."

"I didn't know you had a sister. Is she back in Norrland?"

When she told him that Ingrid lived in America, he was full of questions. How old was Ingrid? Was she married? Where does she live? Had Ingrid learned the English language before going to America?

Eva answered each question, and then told him how Ingrid had always been more interested in boys than books.

"Mr. Kronberg and I spent a lot of time speaking English together," she said. Then she laughed. "Mama would be bored and leave, busying herself in the kitchen while Papa usually fell asleep in his chair. I'd have no idea where Ingrid disappeared to."

"So your parents had no use for English…I can understand why they might think that way. We old folks find it difficult to change our ways. I don't know much English myself."

"My favorite book is ***Learning English in Ten Weeks.*** Would you like to read it?" she asked eagerly.

"You are a clever girl, Eva, and yes I would enjoy looking through your favorite book sometime." Then he leaned forward, rested his arms on the table and looked into her eyes. "Now, say something to me in English."

Taken by surprise, her mind went completely blank.

"I can't think…I mean, so much has happened over the past few years..." He could tell she was flustered and tried to put her at ease.

"I understand," he said, pouring them both another cup of coffee. "I didn't mean to upset you. So…what other kinds of books do you enjoy reading?"

"I like history, and stories about animals and people of other lands, especially life in America."

"We have an extensive library upstairs. Mrs. Lindholm spends a lot of time there and I'm sure she would be happy to help you pick out some books to your liking."

"I'd like that," she said respectfully, but at the same time she was uncomfortable with the idea of being alone with Mrs. Lindholm in the library.

A week later she still hadn't heard from Ingrid, so she eased her mind by writing her thoughts on paper just in case the postman did show up.

April 15, 1934

Dear Ingrid

I haven't received a letter from you since December and hope that you and your family are in good health. Did you receive the letter I wrote in January telling you about the lavish Christmas celebrations? The holiday season was fun and exciting, but I was glad when things slowed down and got back to normal. The first week in January I moved into Gerta's room and Olga now occupies the one that was mine. She works full time and is more particular in washing the fine china and crystal, taking great pride in polishing the silver.

I finished the variegated blue shawl and had enough yarn left over to make a scarf and matching hat, but now my needles lay idle and my fingers are itching to begin knitting again.

Spring has forced the trees and bushes to bud and the little green shoots of crocus, tulips and daffodils are poking through the still cold earth. With the longer days and abundance of sun, the ground is thawing in the fields and the farm hands have emerged from their winter isolation. I see them every day now dragging fallen spruce limbs, dead trees and other burnable materials to the field behind the barn. At first I thought those scraps were intended for the wood stoves, but one afternoon Cook invited me to walk down to see how the brush pile was progressing.

I'd forgotten about how you and I used to gather dead sticks and branches to celebrate the end of winter on Valborg Night, but I couldn't believe the size of this brush pile. It is already wider than our little cottage in Norrland and taller than the chimney, and the men are still adding to it! The more brush, the bigger the fire and the better it is for chasing away evil spirits. That's what Cook told me. She thinks there is no better way to spend an evening than to watch a good fire.

Sounds a bit scary to me, although I always did enjoy sitting in front of the stove at home watching the flames leap across the dry wood, crackling and hissing and feeling the warmth on my face.

The cows went outside for the first time this week and it was hilarious to watch them run excitedly around the pasture, their large udders swinging back and forth as they pranced and bucked like horses with burrs under their saddles. I'd be doing the same thing, too, if I'd been shut up in the barn all winter in a stall where I could take only a few steps forward and back.

I did feel somewhat like that at first, being cooped up in the kitchen most of the day, but now that I'm allowed to serve in the breakfast room and other rooms I don't feel so confined. I sometimes serve breakfast to Mrs. Lindholm in her bedroom or bring a coffee tray to her husband's study in the afternoon. I find it most enjoyable serving the Lindholm family and always do my best to be neat, obedient and to always be cheerful. Oh, the power of a simple smile that turns a grumpy morning face into a happy one!

Last Sunday when Cook was deciding what dessert to make I suggested having an almond cake like Mama used to make. Since it was my idea, she thought I might as well be the one to make it, so I did. The almond extract was strong and pure, smelling so wonderful that I wanted to perfume my hair with it! I must confess that I added a few extra drops to the cake. There is no need to scrimp on ingredients like we did back home, so I threw an extra handful of slivered almonds on top, too.

After dinner, Karl came into the kitchen looking for another piece of cake. Cook told him that I was the one who made it and he would have to talk me. There was one large piece left, so I put it on a plate and gave it to him. He told me it would taste better if he had someone to share it with, so I cut it in half and gave the plate back to him.

You will never guess what he did. He sat down, took one piece and slid the plate over to me. "It's you I want to share it with," he said. Then Cook brought coffee over for the two of us. I must say it pleased me to watch him enjoying my cake.

Seeing his face each morning brightens my whole day. I think of him all the time and sometimes talk to him in my mind, probably because I'm at a loss for words when we come face to face. Did you ever talk to yourself about Olle? I suppose it is rather foolish to daydream like that, but thinking about him brings me much joy.

Please write soon.

Love,

Eva

Visitors

Victoria paid for Dagny's supper that first night, although the meal did not include a tender steak. She met a few other girls, but they all looked very much alike with their curly blonde hair, bright red lips and darkly painted eyes that made them look like scared wild animals. Dagny's black hair and darker skin made her feel conspicuous, uncomfortable with her plainness, wishing she'd thought to brighten her own lips with the little tube Victoria had given her.

At first, self-consciousness prevented her from enjoying the evening and she hadn't understood much of what Victoria told her, although some bits and pieces flashed through her mind later that night. She enjoyed the music and gaiety of the big darkened room downstairs and after being encouraged by a few drinks, she remembered dancing, and later being in her room with a man.

There were many just like him after that, men of all ages, but mostly younger boys, some not much older than she, who wore dark blue uniforms and odd-looking caps on their heads. They were sailors, she found out, lonely boys in a strange city who had been out to sea for too long a time. Some were quiet and shy like herself and others full of talk and big egos, but all had only one thing on their mind. She felt sorry for all of them because they were away from their families.

She loved wearing a different gown every evening and although socializing didn't come easy, the whiskey eased her shyness and made it easier to get through those first challenging weeks. Sometimes she'd waken during the night, reach under her pillow and fondle Eva's brush in her hands, caressing the fine bristles that reminded her of Blix's mane and the times she crawled into his crib to find comfort. Then she would find peace and fall back to sleep.

More than once she'd packed her bags and walked down the hall to go back to the strawberry farm. Once Victoria met her on the stairs asking questions and she'd made up an excuse and returned to her room. Another time she made it to the main entrance, but a freezing wind hit her face and forced her back. She had looked around the strange and uninviting place lurking outside the boardinghouse, slammed the door and went back upstairs to the safety and warmth of her little room.

Even if she did find her way back to the farm, what would she tell her mother and Bertil? What happened at the boardinghouse was too embarrassing to talk about and how else could she explain her absence without lying...something her conscience would not allow. Sometimes it was just easier to drink away the loneliness and shame.

Sometimes men came for other reasons. One art student asked to draw a sketch of her sitting in front of the window holding a wine glass. Afterwards he wanted only to share the wine he had brought with him.

He came several more evenings with brushes and paints until the painting was finished.

"You made me look so pretty," she remembered saying when he put a few coins in her hand. Then he asked if he could come back some time and draw her lying on the bed with no clothes on. "Why me when there are so many other girls here that...that are more womanly than I?"

"You are different from the others," he told her.

"Different?" she asked.

"Unique might be a better word. I've drawn many fair blonde girls, but when I saw your darker skin and raven-colored hair...well, I guess I was curious." Then he asked her again if she would pose nude for him.

"Perhaps from the backside," she told him. He made a few sketches and then sat on the edge of the bed, but he only wanted to talk. She was surprised when he told her he was more attracted to boys than girls. This boy was sweet, kind and interested in what she had to say. She thought of Blix, who had been gelded and wasn't attracted to mares, except to be friends. Up until then Dagny had enjoyed his company, but after his peculiar revelation, her mind was stuck on a picture of this boy being gelded like a horse.

Another time a man from the neighborhood church dropped in. He tried to convince her to leave this place and find proper work. He talked of sinners, repentance and other words she knew nothing about, and he talked of God and Jesus.

"I pray to the sun and the moon," she told him.

"Well the sun isn't God, but you might picture God as a great light full of goodness and that we humans are the individual rays of that sun."

"So that means that we are all good like God?" she asked.

"Yes, in spirit we are all reflections of God."

"I can see the moon and the sun with my own eyes. Where is your God?"

"My God is everywhere."

"What does He look like?"

"God isn't a material object you can see, but his reflection can be seen wherever there is beauty and kindness and love."

"God must have walked right by this place," said Dagny sadly.

"God is right here. I can see him in your beautiful smile and in your lovely dress."

"God is in my dress?"

"The person who sewed your dress had great talent. See the fine embroidery in those little flowers? Talent and intelligence come from God."

This was all mighty confusing to Dagny. This dress had been worn on many occasions here at the boarding house and she was embarrassed to think of what his God might have seen.

She liked what he said about God's special love and that she was a perfect child of God. He gave her a little prayer about God's ever-presence, saying if she trusted in God with her whole heart she would always be encircled in his loving arms and guided by his wisdom.

Her favorite visitor was Captain, an old retired seaman with grayish white hair and a full length beard. His weathered face was lined with deep furrows and happy creases around his bright blue eyes and generous, talkative mouth. She'd seen him chatting with other men downstairs and was curious about a paper he had spread out on the table.

"I've traveled all over the world," he told her. "Just put your finger anywhere on this map and I can tell you something about any country or body of water. She put her hand out slowly and touched a white spot near the bottom of the paper.

"Ah, yes. Antarctica...the fifth largest continent in the world. Roald Admundsen was the first explorer to put his country's flag on the South Pole," he told her. "For a Norwegian, he was a smart man, but not as smart as us Swedes." He chuckled then and poked her arm gently as if they were old Swedish friends and she laughed, too. "Can you imagine a place that has high mountains, but you can't see them?"

"What good is a mountain if you can't see it?"

"That is quite true," he acknowledged. "But in Antarctica the mountains are covered by a huge ice sheet that is as thick as the mountains are tall."

She asked him where all the animals live.

"There are only penguins, seals and a few species of birds that can live in that harsh land, plus some mites and ticks and a kind of worm that freezes up in winter and thaws out in the few months of warm weather."

"Would I freeze and thaw out, too?"

"Humans are not made to survive freezing and thawing like that little worm," he told her. "The climate is too harsh and people must be always bundled up with layers of warm clothing, but even so, many have perished in that inhospitable land."

"My mother lived in the far north of Sweden. She thought it must be the coldest place on earth. Is Sweden on your map?"

He showed her the cluster of Scandinavian countries, tracing the outline of Sweden with his bony, gnarled index finger. Immediately she recalled the butcher's wife describing how much larger Russia was than Sweden.

"Russia...show me where Russia is!" Dagny said excitedly.

Captain's hand swept over a very large area of land that went from Finland all the way to the Pacific Ocean. She looked back to Sweden and then to Russia again. All of a sudden the raisin concept made sense to her.

"Russia is a very big place; almost forty times the size of Sweden," she said proudly.

"A very intelligent observation, young lady," he said with much admiration. He was pleased to have such an interested audience and became a frequent visitor.

May Miracle

One warm sunny morning in May, Eva found a note on the kitchen table from Cook informing her that the Lindholms had departed early for a day at the lake. Cook was visiting friends in the village and planned to be back by four o'clock to prepare a light supper for the family. She left a plate of food in the icebox for Eva and wished her a happy day.

Eva relaxed on the still-shaded kitchen steps nibbling on a thick slice of cheese, a warm breeze informing her that fresh manure had recently been spread on the old garden spot near the pasture, an odor she was familiar with and found not at all distasteful. One could not expect a garden to thrive without a good dose of cow dung.

The farmhands had already finished their morning chores and, being Sunday, they would be free to do what they wished until the evening milking. She watched the slow, scraggly parade of young men plodding along the snake-like path through the field between the barn and woods, followed by a cluster of maids. She guessed they were off to an afternoon by the river.

She'd been there once before...last summer when the maids invited her to join them for a picnic. The day dawned hot and sultry and relaxing by the river had seemed like a good idea. After a long, hot walk through fields and woods, the trees suddenly thinned out to small bushes, then to grass tufts and muck. The boys splashed through the swamp, but the girls waded in slowly, following closely in single file, their wet feet slipping on the undergrowth. Eva trailed behind them wondering what might be lurking beneath the murky water. Armies of insects descended upon them all and they hurried to the further edge of the swamp where white birches and willows shaded the riverbed.

Two of the girls immediately kicked off their shoes and tiptoed into the gently flowing water, their skirts hoisted to their hips. In a few minutes they ran back to shore giggling as they unbuttoned their blouses. Eva sat on the mossy bank watching their skirts drop to the ground and then to her surprise off came their shifts and stockings.

"They're only going to wash themselves," said a rather plump maid still dressed in her shift. When Eva remained on the bank the maid stopped at the river's edge and called back, "Aren't you coming in?" Eva looked around for signs of the men.

"The coast is clear. I can see the men downstream swimming in the rapids," shouted the maid standing knee deep in the river rubbing her arms vigorously with soap. Bathing in the river did look very inviting, so Eva joined the girls, although even in her shift, she felt quite naked.

She was giving her hair a final rinse when blood-curdling screams came from the woods and then three naked boys exploded from the trees bouncing and prancing on the riverbank like wild animals, all extremities flapping unabashedly in the sunlight. They scooped up the girls' clothes and threw them in the water. Eva watched the squealing girls swim down river trying to retrieve their fast-floating pieces of clothing...the boys in close pursuit. Fortunately she had undressed behind the bushes where her clothes remained safely dry and ready to put on again.

Eva could laugh at all this now as she pondered what to do this morning. The barn would be cooler than anywhere else and since the farm hands would not return until later in the day, she would have the place all to herself. Cattle grazed on the hillside and she remembered how Stella used to love eating a slice of old bread. She put some stale crusts in her apron pocket and walked down the pasture path hoping to entice a cow or calf to come over to the fence for a treat.

The grass in the pasture was lush and green. Several cows had already laid down in the shade of a birch row methodically chewing their cuds and paying little attention to three young calves that darted in and out amongst them. Eva noted the similarity between this bucolic scene and the families who sometimes visited the Lindholms on weekends. She had witnessed their energetic young children running through the mansion halls and gardens while their mothers ignored them, preferring to sit on the porch enjoying the company of other women. Animals and humans were alike in so many ways, especially in respect to mothers and their offspring.

The calves were standing knee deep in a water hole as she approached the gate. When she called to them, the inquisitive youngsters turned their dripping noses to look at her, but they remained stiff-legged and uncertain, sniffing the air, their large round eyes cautiously watching as she walked closer.

Eva leaned against the wooden gate with her back toward them, a trick she often used to arouse Stella's curiosity. It wasn't long before she heard them sloshing around in the water and out of the corner of her eye saw the largest calf advancing toward her. Not wanting to get left behind, the other two followed and soon all three stopped abruptly in a cloud of dust not far from the gate. Now it was just a matter of patience. She offered them a crust of bread through the fence and the bravest one ventured forward to nibble at it. As she rubbed the first calf's neck, the other two crowded closer for her attention, poking her apron with their noses for some bread.

After lapping up the last crumb they trotted back across the pasture. It was then Eva noticed a bank of clouds advancing over the hill and the silhouettes of two cows moving slowly along the ridge. Just before they disappeared over the rise she got a glimpse of a man walking behind them. She blinked and the figure was gone. Was this just a figment of her imagination? She looked up at the thick billowing clouds and hurried to the barn.

After morning milking all the cows were driven to the pasture for the day, so the two huge sliding doors at either end of the barn were open, creating a fresh draft of cool air. Wisps of hay scurried around her feet in pirouetting whirlwinds, picking up more chaff as they skipped across the floor before collapsing against the empty cow stalls. Eva felt like dancing and skipped through the empty stalls, swinging around the wooden stanchions to the music in her head...until she heard a thump in one of the box stalls at the further end of the barn. She was surprised to see a very pregnant cow thrashing about in the straw, moaning and straining in hard labor.

Unlatching the stall door she spoke soothingly to the cow, trying to comfort the distraught animal, but her wild eyes and flailing legs made Eva back up against the wall. When she saw the calf's head and only one pale hoof inside the protruding sac, she remembered the day her father helped deliver Stella. Stella's mother had been quiet and calm, but this high-strung creature wouldn't allow Eva to get close enough to touch her.

Perhaps it had been a man she'd seen on the ridge after all...probably one of the hands who had stayed home to keep watch on the pregnant cow. She ran out and yelled across the pasture but only a faint rumble of thunder answered her call for help. She ran toward the fence and shouted again, but saw only the dreamy-eyed cows lying on the hillside, the nearest ones looking up mid-chew to see what the noise was all about. She hollered again as the wind whipped up sand around her feet and large drops of rain sprinkled her face. Then lightning struck behind the hill forcing her back to the barn.

The cow was lying flat on her side now. She seemed quieter, raising her head toward Eva with sorrowful eyes as if pleading for help. Then, with a great sigh, her head fell back to the floor with a loud thump. The poor cow was all worn out. Fearing for the mother's life as well as the calf, Eva knew she must act quickly and rolled up her sleeves. Kneeling behind the cow, she gently slid her arm into the birth canal as she had seen her father do so many years before. The passageway felt strangely soft and warm at first and quite slimy, but then her arm felt a great pressure as if it was being squeezed and released. She probed deeper, wishing her arm was just a few inches longer when the stall door squeaked open and she heard a man's voice.

"Ah, so it was you I heard shouting over the hill." At first she was happy and relieved that someone was here to help, but when she saw it was Karl Lindholm, she was too embarrassed to say anything. Humiliated that he had witnessed her in the midst of such an unladylike act, she carefully withdrew her arm, hiding it quickly beneath her apron.

Karl had been surprised at first, too, seeing a woman attempting to deliver a calf in the only way that a human possibly could in a difficult birth, but what he felt for Eva was pure admiration. Here was one so sympathetic and caring that she risked getting hurt herself by trying to help with the birthing.

Karl was soaked through, his trousers plastered to his thighs, tan shirt clinging to his chest and arms as he stood briefly with his hands on his hips looking down admirably at her. She was feeling a dizzying combination of awe and excitement. She had felt the same way when Mats came into the barn that rainy morning when she was milking Stella. What was it about a man's muscularity that made her knees go weak and her stomach do flip-flops? Did every girl feel this way about a man?

She thought about all this in the few seconds he smiled down at her and self-consciously said the first thing that came to her mind. "I saw my father do this when our cow had trouble calving years ago," she said, knowing her face was turning beet red. Then Karl hunkered down beside her to examine the cow and his nearness made her feel faint and limp like soft bread dough.

"I think you are a very brave girl to try doing this all by yourself," he said, probing deeply into the cow, the firm muscles of his arms tensing and relaxing as he gently worked on the suffering animal. Suddenly a contraction stiffened the cow's legs, causing Eva to immediately forget about herself. She grabbed the cow's wet, floppy tail so it wouldn't hit them in the face and rubbed her soft flank.

"There now...easy girl," Karl whispered to the cow. She responded to his voice and relaxed. Then without warning she let out a mournful groan, straining to push out the watery sac. Suddenly with a big gush of liquid, the calf slipped out onto the straw and the mother rose to clean her little one, lapping clean its wet face and body as the calf struggled to stand, slipped and fell back to the floor. Karl rushed over to set the calf on its feet again.

"A heifer!" he exclaimed to Eva, excited as a little boy opening his favorite present on Christmas Eve. "Five bulls in a row and today you have brought me good luck." Karl was ecstatic as he rubbed his hands on the straw and awkwardly put his arm around Eva's shoulders. Like two proud parents, they stood looking down at the calf who now stood solidly on her four black hooves seeking her mother's udder, while the cow mooed softly encouraging the baby to nurse.

"How about we name her Eva, in honor of you," he said proudly as she blushed and looked away. "You probably saved the calf's life, and perhaps the mother's as well. How can I thank you?"

"I didn't do all that much," she said, looking away. The storm had passed by now and the sun streamed through the small window, illuminating the room with a soft, warm glow. It was then she noticed her soiled blouse and skirt, embarrassed because her arm was coated with dried slime and dirt. Probably her face was dirty as well. "I must hurry back to the kitchen and get cleaned up."

There was more Karl wanted to say. Instead he watched her run up the grassy hill. How charming she was in the breakfast room, and now so serious and concerned about the cow and calf and not afraid to do what had to be done. She was a mixture of all the qualities he admired; not like other girls who came to his mother's parties who were vain, artificial and self-centered. He was still smiling as he went to the pump to fill two buckets of water for the thirsty cow.

Eva took a leisurely bath, washed her clothes and hung them outside to dry. All of a sudden she was starving and went to the kitchen for some leftovers. She thought about Karl and what he might be doing that very moment. Was he thinking of her? She even thought about going back to the barn but that seemed a brazen idea. She fought the reckless impulse to see him again. She took a plate of food outside and sat on the kitchen steps to eat. There was a good view of the barn from there and if he were looking toward the house he would surely notice her. Someone did wave, but it was only Cook with an armload of bundles trudging up the drive on her way home from the village.

The Sickness

Like scattering rodents fleeing from their dark winter hiding places to enjoy the warmth of the summer sun, springtime also drove many men to seek entertainment elsewhere in the city. Dagny, too, wished to leave her dreary room for a better place, but for now she felt safe here. Happiness would have to wait until courage and opportunity showed her a way out.

Dagny opened her lone window to a fresh warm breeze. It was the middle of May and on the balcony above was the black and white cat she'd seen in the alley that first day. He lived there with a gray-haired old woman and was usually curled up in a chair sleeping in the noonday sun. He looked as comfortable as she had been last night after the delicious dinner Victoria had brought to her room.

Every morning for the past few weeks Dagny had been sick, gagging and throwing up bile in her night pot. When Victoria heard of this, she came to her room with a cup of dark tea made of bitter herbs.

"This tastes awful," said Dagny, screwing up her face and

refusing to take another sip.

"It's my grandmother's special recipe and worked every time for me...now drink!" she ordered, standing with hands firmly on her hips with glaring eyes that made Dagny swallow the vile liquid in two large gulps.

"You may have cramps tonight. Just go to the bathing room and sit on the toilet until the sickness passes from you. There will be some blood, but don't be afraid...that's only a natural effect of the tea."

There was no blood that night, nor cramps, so Victoria made her drink more tea the next morning. Around four that afternoon, after two more cups of tea, Dagny felt better. She had left her sickness in the toilet bowl.

That evening Victoria brought a dinner tray to Dagny's room.

"You won't be working tonight, so stay in bed and get your rest. The meat and eggs will give you strength."

Acting more compassionately now, Victoria plumped up Dagny's pillow and gently kissed her on the forehead before leaving the room.

Dagny pulled the tray closer and picked up a glass of milk, drinking it all down before lifting the silvery metal cover from the plate of food. What she saw caused the cover to slip from her hand and go clattering across the room. Was she dreaming again of her days cutting the tender little loins of beef in the butcher shop? She cut a small piece from the little browned circle of meat and chewed it slowly. Truly it was more flavorful than she had ever imagined, nearly melting in her mouth. She took another piece and leaned back on the pillow savoring its delicate flavor, doing this after each small bite until the meat was all gone. She fell asleep thinking that if there were only two foods she could have in this life, this would certainly be one, the second being a big bowl of fresh strawberries.

In the morning, the tray still set on her lap with the remaining unappealing mound of cold scrambled eggs still on her plate. Awakening with a great hunger, she took a small bite, found it tastily well-seasoned and had cleaned the plate by the time

Victoria came to pick up the tray.

"You are looking quite well this morning," said Victoria. "I brought you a bowl of porridge and a pot of coffee in case you didn't feel like walking down to the dining room."

"I'm feeling much better, but I'm passing a lot of clotted blood."

"That's to be expected," said Victoria, placing more clean cloths on the table and taking away the soiled ones. Since Dagny viewed her condition merely as a case of a heavy monthly bleeding, Victoria let her think that was the case and did not elaborate about 'the sickness.'

While Dagny was recuperating, Captain stopped in several times to show her pictures of places he had traveled. She learned about the British Isles, Germany, France, Italy and the Mediterranean Sea as well as the faraway places of Africa, India, China, and Japan. The people of Europe looked pretty much like those of Sweden, but others were uncommon looking individuals with curly black hair and dark brown skin, while others were of smaller stature with yellowish skin and slanty eyes. What caused people to look so different? The Captain hadn't an answer for that question, but he guessed it might be because of the climate in the areas in which they lived.

"So, if I went to China my skin would turn yellow? And if I went to Africa I would be black?"

Captain wanted to laugh, but he kept a straight face because this young girl was a curious one and eager to learn. "That is a good question," he said. "I have been to both places and my skin never changed color. There are basically four different races of people in the world and they have varying shades of white, red, yellow and black. Sometimes they intermarry and more subtle colors evolve in their offspring." Dagny seemed satisfied with the Captain's answer and he showed her more photographs taken in North and South America, including a place in the United States called New York.

"So you think the buildings are tall in Gothenburg, eh? Well, you should see the sky-scrappers in New York City." At that point

Captain unfolded the map even further across the bed. "Did you know it is possible to board a ship right here in Gothenburg, cross the Atlantic Ocean and about a week later arrive in New York City?" he said, sliding his finger from one place to the other across the wide expanse of blue. The map was confusing to Dagny, just like her mother's little map of Sweden that didn't show how very long the trip would be to Gothenburg or the butcher's wife and her raisins showing how large Russia was in comparison to Sweden.

"The ocean must be much larger than the lake back in Norrland, especially if it takes a week to sail across," she said.

The Captain chuckled. "Aye, that's the truth, my girl. He showed her a photograph of a ship setting in a large expanse of water.

"When you feel better I'll take you down to the pier so you can see big ships like this one and you will get an idea how huge the ocean really is."

From the Library Window

Augusta's favorite, plush pink brocade chair was strategically placed by a large library window overlooking the panoramic view of barns, cow pastures and distant fields fading into the rolling hills to the north. From here there was a clear view of the long, winding driveway, the first glimpse of the mailman and the arrival of expected guests, as well as the departures of servants and family members. She was also able see anything unusual along the well trodden path from the farmhands' quarters to the woods. If someone wasn't where he or she was supposed to be, or a cow had escaped from the pasture or a beggar was headed for the kitchen, Augusta could see it all...and she usually did.

This all-encompassing view was the main reason why she had demanded the library be moved upstairs. In this room that was originally a corner bedroom with windows looking out from each wall, she needed only to turn her head from one window to the other to see the old carriage house that was now a garage for the family automobiles. Apart from the many windows, every other conceivable place on the high walls of the room was taken over by beautiful oak shelves that held her favorite novels, volumes of encyclopedias and other reference books, as well as thick texts on history, economics and business that had belonged to her father. One shelf was devoted to all the old classics, an extensive collection that had once belonged to her grandmother, an invalid for most of her life whose only enjoyment was reading.

Augusta's morning ritual included stopping into the library before breakfast to plan her day. Surveying the scene below and beyond always gave her a measure of comfort, somewhat akin to prayer, and a feeling of authority knowing everything was just as it should be and that everyone was in their rightful and proper place. A pair of Ander's old binoculars rested behind the curtain on the windowsill within easy reach. They were good for bird watching, she told her husband, but understanding her inquisitive nature, he knew she was just plain nosy.

Between the house and barns several oval flower gardens dotted the well-manicured lawn. In the center of this expanse of lush green, a circle of deep pink rose bushes and three wooden benches surrounded her favorite fountain, an ancient metal structure of two young boys looking into a pool with frogs and birds sitting around its rim; a nostalgic reminder of simpler times, when her two sons were little, when she knew where they were and didn't need to worry what they were up to.

Johanna has been Augusta's personal maid for over thirteen years, waking her in the morning, drawing her bath, helping her dress as well as brushing and arranging her blonde curls, thus allowing plenty of opportunity for idle gossip.

She rather looked forward to dusting the library shelves and the many porcelain and metal figurines of refined ladies and gentlemen, prancing horses and other farm animals, various short and tall vases and countless other family trinkets that decorated the wide spaces between groupings of books. When her mistress was away the pink chair stood tall and lonely by the window inviting her to relax in its plush softness and read a tantalizing love story.

She called this special spot with the bird's eye view 'Augusta's Lookout,' but it was Johanna who first saw Gerta returning from the forest with a young farmhand last August...not once, but several times. There had been other shenanigans in the past involving maids and farmhands, and times when she'd observed Gunnar bringing ladies to his room.

When the Lindholms went to the lake that first hot day in May, Johanna started out to the river with the other maids but the soaring heat caused her to turn back. It seemed the perfect time to sit in the library and read. She had just settled into the pink chair when a bright lightning strike caused her to look out the window. What surprised her even more was to see the red-haired maid hurrying toward the dairy barn from the cow pasture. Thinking she was probably going after some milk, Johanna went back to reading her book.

Drops of rain tapped against the windowpane and she looked up at the thick clouds rolling across the sky. It was then she noticed a man walking along the pasture fence. By now there was a steady rain, but through the binoculars she clearly saw Karl Lindholm and he was on his way to the barn also.

If it hadn't been raining so hard Johanna might have gone down to the barn to look around, but she wasn't sure that the girl was still there. Not wishing to get soaked for no good reason, she continued reading, which seemed a lot more exciting at the time.

She had been reading for an hour or more when the redhead ran across the lawn toward the kitchen. Johanna almost fell out of the chair when she saw Karl's face looking out the open barn window. He stayed there long enough for her to grab the binoculars and get a good look at his happy, thoughtful face, making her wonder what he was smiling about. Oh, to have been a fly on the barn wall she thought, reproaching herself for not going down to the barn to spy on them

Johanna told all this to her mistress that evening, implying a few suggestions of her own that the incident was more serious than it actually was. She had a way of glamorizing reality with the romantic stories she read. All this replayed in Augusta's mind that night and when Anders came to bed she told him what Johanna said.

"Don't make things into more than what they are," he said rolling on his back and closing his eyes, but Augusta was wound like a top and wouldn't stop talking.

"With all the attractive and well-dressed young ladies I've invited to parties lately, never did I dream that a peasant girl might turn Karl's head."

"For goodness sakes, Augusta. For a year now you've been worrying about Karl not being interested in girls. I would think you'd be overjoyed to know that he's finally found someone of interest."

"But not that girl!" she shouted. "You wouldn't want him getting serious with a kitchen maid, would you?"

"You know Karl. He was probably giving Eva an agricultural tour of the barn, showing her his latest breeding charts or perhaps just discussing the weather and what crops he intends to plant."

"As if any normal girl would be interested in hearing about such things!" she said.

Anders rose up on his elbow. "Eva is a lovely girl and quite charming. If you ask me, Karl could do a lot worse." Then he kissed his wife and rolled over to face the wall.

Augusta laid there a while, thinking about what her husband had said. "So...you think Eva is charming?"

Anders pretended to be asleep. Sometimes the best answer was no answer at all.

The Gift

Eva returned to her room after washing her hair one evening when there was a knock on the door. Thinking it might be Cook, she opened the door and was surprised to see Karl standing there...and she clad only in a thin shift!

He stood silent for a moment, feeling as self-conscious as she, his eyes lingering on her tousled, wet hair dangling in tight ringlets down to her chest. For a moment he forgot why he was there.

"I'm sorry," he said. "I've come at an inconvenient time."

She shook her head wondering whether she should apologize for her appearance or invite him in.

He held a large brown package in his hands and offered it to her. "This is for you...for your help in the barn last week."

"You don't need to give me anything. I was happy to be of service," she replied, but he insisted she take it.

"I should go now," he said, nervously glancing down the hall.

She watched him walk away, breathing the invisible aroma of spicy lavender that still lingered in the doorway. If only she could capture his lovely scent in a bottle to enjoy whenever she wished.

Beneath the brown wrapper was a box wrapped in white paper decorated with little pink roses and tied with a lacy white ribbon. The box was so beautifully wrapped that she was content just to sit and look at it for a while. She finished towel drying her hair, then brushed it out while anticipating what might be in this very large and mysterious package. She could not remember ever receiving such a large gift, except for a wooden sled her father had made when she was five years old.

Finally she undid the lacy ribbon and carefully removed the delicate paper, folding it neatly for safekeeping. She lifted the cover to see a fluff of white tissue paper, beneath which was what she thought might be a blanket, but instead it was a dress made in a lovely bluish-gray color...something that she could picture Mrs. Lindholm wearing to receive guests in the afternoon. She put on the dress, amazed that Karl could have picked out something that fit her so well. Walking sedately around the room, she had a very strong urge to run down to the entry hall and look at herself in the big mirror. Of course she couldn't do that...or could she?

Eva walked down the hall and into the kitchen, tip-toeing through the breakfast room and past Mr. Lindholm's study, where a faint light glowed beneath the door. Then she hastened down the long hall past all the staring eyes that watched her from the old paintings hanging on the wall. A dim light revealed the upstairs hall above the wide staircase, but all was quiet except for her pounding heart.

The crystal chandelier glowed softly in the hallway and she bravely walked toward the mirror, gathering up her long red hair and piling it on top of her head. She smiled at the refined lady reflected in the mirror and turned around slowly to see how she looked from the back. Then she took a few quick steps and twirled around, watching her reflection dance around the small room and acting a bit foolishly. Faster and faster she spun around, her skirt flaring out above her ankles like rippling blue waves...and in the blur of spinning she saw Mr. Lindholm standing in the doorway grinning back at her. She stopped in the middle of the hall and covered her blushing face with her hands, her feet now too heavy to move.

"It's alright, Eva. I heard the floor creak outside my door and came by to investigate. I didn't realize who it was until you walked under the chandelier."

Eva was speechless, patting down her disheveled hair, while thinking how to explain why she was dancing all by herself in this part of the house.

"You look incredibly lovely tonight," he said walking toward her. "I'd be honored if you'd dance with me."

Mr. Lindholm had a way of making her feel at ease. Shyly she allowed him to take her hand and gracefully followed his lead around the hall. There was no music, except for Mr. Lindholm's humming. She was unfamiliar with the tune, but the melodious pitch kept her feet dancing in step with his as he swept her around the room. She felt very much a lady and quite dignified in her new dress as she caught glimpses of their stylish reflection in the mirror, both unaware they were being watched on the stairway by the maid, Johanna.

A Day in Gothenbury

The next Sunday Eva put on her new dress with the intention of going to the lake. The fine material draped softly about her hips, light and cool against her skin as she walked confidently down the drive to the main road, not caring one little bit if anyone was observing her.

As she unlatched the metal gate a slow-moving automobile stopped behind her. When she saw it was Karl, she opened the gate wide enough for him to drive through. Then she closed the gate and secured the latch. The car stopped and Karl rolled down the window.

"Ah, my little veterinary assistant! How lovely you look today."

Still in a positive, slightly reckless mood, she curtsied low, lifting her skirt wide on either side to show it off.

"Thanks to you, kind sir, for this beautiful dress."

"I'm driving to Gothenburg today. Would you like to join me?" And without thinking twice she agreed.

"And where were you going before I changed your mind?" he asked her.

"Just to the lake. It reminds me of our lake back home."

"So, you had your very own lake in Norrland?" he asked with a grin.

"Papa always called it our lake, but it didn't belong to us...only in our hearts."

Karl noticed a trace of nostalgia in Eva's voice. "I'll take you there first. We have plenty of time before I'm due in Gothenburg."

Less than five minutes later, Karl stopped at the edge of the beach where numerous families had already spread their blankets and were either sunbathing or playing with children at the water's edge. Fine crafts with huge, billowing sails sped across the blue waters, while smaller fishing boats puttered here and there in search of a good catch.

"So, do you like swimming or fishing best?" he asked. Then

he held up his hand. "Don't answer yet. Let me guess." She tipped her head slightly to look at him, waiting for his response.

"Perhaps neither of those," he reconsidered. "I suppose you'd rather lie on the beach soaking up the sun like those girls over there."

Eva shook her head and smiled. "I did that once and came home with a face full of freckles. After that Mama made certain I wore a wide-brimmed straw hat. But as you can see I've grown neglectful about doing that."

Until then he hadn't noticed the sprinkling of tiny freckles on her nose. Even though they added to her wholesome beauty, he did not tell her so and continued to answer his own question.

"Well, being a country girl, you probably prefer fishing."

"Actually, if you want to know the truth, I always favored sitting on the beach to knit with Mama," she said. "Never did like sticking my hook into those defenseless little worms."

Karl nodded sympathetically. "Down here we go fly fishing."

"You're joking with me," she said, smiling up at him. "People don't fish for flies?"

"No, we use flies to catch the fish."

"Well, I wouldn't like putting a fly on the hook either," she said, wrinkling up her nose.

Karl burst out laughing, but Eva didn't see the humor of it.

"I'm not talking about those pesky black flies that hang around the barn," he replied. "I make special artificial flies, called lures. You put them on a hook and they attract the fish." Karl reached over to the back seat. "Here, let me show you."

Inside a small metal box were dozens of brightly colored feathers and beads tied on to tiny hooks.

"They're so beautiful," she said, "but I wouldn't think a fish would want to eat one."

"Well, fish don't actually eat them. Different species of fish are attracted to certain shapes and colors and before long they're hooked on the line. Usually I can reuse the same lure over and over again."

"You must have a lot of patience to make such fine works of

art as these," she said, picking out one and running her fingers along the yellow-beaded body. "This reminds me somewhat of a dragonfly and I love the beautiful blue-colored feathers of his wings."

"You may keep that one if you like," he told her.

She didn't know where to put it, so he reached over and hooked it through her braid. "Don't forget it's there or you might prick yourself on the barb." Their eyes made contact when his hand brushed her cheek and she smiled up to him, the intoxicating scent of spicy lavender putting her in the mood for a kiss. He smiled back and winked. "I think we should move along if we're to get to Gothenburg today," he said, starting up the car.

Karl was very relaxed at the wheel, but drove much faster than Mr. Kronberg. Even so, many cars passed them on the wide, smooth-coated tar road. Large farms dotted the landscape and after a while she didn't feel like they were moving very fast at all. Karl kept up a line of chatter describing the different field crops and various breeds of cattle.

"Those light red and white ones over there are Ayshires. Sweden imported them from Scotland. The black and white ones on the hill are Holsteins from Germany." Eva had never seen so many cows before, nor had she known Karl to be so talkative.

He continued with a long discourse on the best and worse breeds, how good conformation led to better health, which cows gave the most milk, had the highest butter fat and how it was now possible to breed a cow with bulls from countries as far away as France and Germany.

Eva remembered how her father walked Stella through the forest to the potato farm and back. It seemed a long way to travel and took the better part of a day. She couldn't imagine how long it might take to bring a cow all the way to France to be bred. He attempted to explain how the breeding was done, but a sudden awkwardness prevented him from saying the words *artificial insemination*. Instead he talked about improving a herd of cows by studying their bloodlines.

"Bloodlines?" she asked.

"By that I mean ancestry," he said. "Similar to the genealogy of a person...like a family history. If your parents are strong and healthy and live to a ripe old age, then chances are you will also have those same traits. With cows it is the same. Cows should have a straight topline, well attached udder and sturdy legs as well as an amiable temperament." Then he laughed. "Of course, they should give a lot of milk, too." Eva understood that and smiled.

"I generally look through the breeding catalog and research a number of different bull prospects, studying the physical attributes of his sire and dam, as well as their grandparents and even their great-grandparents to find the right bull to breed to a specific cow."

Eva looked at him with a mixture of awe and bewilderment. She had never thought much about cows having grandparents or keeping a family history of Stella.

"My father always bred our cow to a true Swedish Mountain bull. He told me he wanted to keep the breed pure," she said.

"That's a fine idea. They are a sturdy old breed. In fact, I've been thinking seriously of starting up a small herd of Swedish Mountain cattle...just as a hobby. Gunnar thinks it's a foolish idea. Compared to Holsteins, they don't give nearly as much milk...and my brother is all about making a profit. Plus they are hard to find these days."

"I know where you can find one," she announced proudly. And then she told him about the day Mr. Kronberg and Mats came to pick up Stella.

Karl laughed picturing Mats trying to load Stella onto the truck. "Cattle can be pretty ornery if they make up their mind not to do something, but it doesn't do any good to get angry with them. I like Mats. He's good company, but I don't think he's cut out to be a farmer."

"I don't think he is either," said Eva. Her mind was back in Norrland thinking of how things used to be.

They were both quiet for a while watching the landscape roll by. The farms grew smaller, replaced by houses with fenced-in yards, most with a barn and some livestock. In the distance tall chimneys spouted blackish smoke that hung in low, cloud-like streaks above the city of Gothenburg. Eva hadn't expected the place to be so dismal and dirty.

"This is the old part of town...older buildings, mills, factories and such," said Karl, as if knowing her thoughts.

After a while newer structures appeared, neat brick and stone buildings with trees and beautiful flowering shrubs and finally a large grassy park. Well-dressed men, women and children sat on benches and blankets listening to a small band. Karl drove slowly, the lively music escorting them by the park, then fading as they continued down a narrow, cobblestone side street. Being Sunday, most of the shops were closed and they quickly found a parking space in front of a millinery shop. Karl took her arm, but she paused for a moment to look at the lovely broad-brimmed hats decorated with veils, flowers and large plumes.

"These hats are beautiful, but much too big. How do you suppose women keep them from falling off their heads?" Eva said.

Karl had no answer for that, but he did point out a smaller straw hat with a pretty blue bow.

"Oh, yes! That would be my favorite one,"Eva responded.

They stopped at an outdoor café where Karl ordered wine and open-faced ham sandwiches. He seemed to know exactly what to do and Eva was relieved that she didn't have to make any choices. Two couples sat at a table nearby. Eva was fascinated by one of the women. She wore a dark purple satin dress with a matching wide-brimmed purple hat decorated with very long feathery plumes in gorgeous shades of pink and lavender that waved and fluttered in the air like a rare tropical bird Eva had seen in picture books.

"Are those real feathers on that woman's hat?" she whispered.

"I think so," he said, "but probably they've been dyed, wouldn't you say?"

Eva agreed. "I wonder how many birds gave their lives to decorate hats just like that one." She was merely vocalizing her feelings. It wasn't really a question she expected to be answered, but Karl did anyway. "Hundreds, maybe thousands, given all the women in the world today who can afford to buy such fancy hats. Unlike you, most of them give barely a thought about where the feathers come from. They just want the most beautiful hat in town." Eva watched other women parading by with feathery hats and shook her head in dismay.

"That's what I like about you, Eva. You look at things differently than most girls." He reached for her hand, but the waiter came with a wine bottle and two goblets, putting what might have been a tender exchange aside for another time.

After lunch Karl had to leave for a short business appointment. He asked the waiter to bring extra coffee and to keep an eye on Eva.

"I shouldn't be long," he told her. "If someone bothers you, go inside and wait for me there."

In a few minutes the waiter filled her cup, looked up and down the street and disappeared behind the two glass doors. Later he came back and asked if she needed anything else. She didn't see him again.

Suddenly the shrill voice of a woman made everyone in the café look up. A young girl and a sailor were walking on the sidewalk toward the café. He had a bottle of liquor in one hand and his other arm was around the girl's waist, which was a good thing because she stumbled and nearly fell down. The girl wore a too-tight, green satin dress with an indecently low neckline and her dark hair was piled on her head in an untidy bun.

Eva sipped her coffee hoping they would walk by, but the green dress stopped suddenly. "You with the red hair!" shouted the girl, "I know you!"

Everyone turned to look at Eva, the only one with red hair. Embarrassed, she nearly ran into the restaurant, but there was something behind the painted face that looked vaguely familiar. The sailor took hold of the girl's arm, but she pulled away.

"Come on...don't make a scene," Eva heard him say, but the girl paid no mind and leaned forward against the table, so close that Eva could smell the strong scent of whiskey mixed with cheap perfume.

"I'm Dagny…from the potato farm," she whispered with that same sad expression that Eva so well remembered.

"Oh Dagny! I'm sorry I didn't recognize you at first."

The sailor looked up the street and swore. "Let's get out of here," he grumbled, pulling Dagny away from the table. At that moment Eva saw Karl running toward the café. The sailor must have seen him, too, because he hustled across the street almost dragging Dagny along behind him. She glanced back toward Eva, stumbled, and the two of them disappeared down an alley.

"You look a bit flushed, are you all right?" said Karl. He was out of breath and sat down beside her. Then he took her hands in his. "I'm sorry…I never should have left you alone."

"Don't be sorry, Karl. In fact I'm rather glad this all happened. He was gently rubbing the back of her hand and she felt amazingly relaxed now. "You won't believe this, but I know that girl."

He didn't know whether to laugh or be serious. "Now that beats all. My sweet innocent girl is friends with a prostitute?"

"Prostitute? What is that?" she asked. Then he got a little red around the collar thinking about how he would answer.

"It's not good, is it?" she said, thinking about the mean sailor and Dagny's disheveled appearance.

"That's a good way of putting it," he said. "Let's get back to the car."

For the most part they rode home in a comfortable silence. When they were about halfway home he asked how she came to know Dagny. She thought a while and told him just enough to satisfy his curiosity.

The endless twilight cast its soft glow in the evening sky as they approached the metal gates. Karl drove under some trees and turned off the ignition.

"I bought you something today," he said, reaching into the back seat and placing a large white box in her lap.

"You shouldn't be spending money on me," she said.

"Well, I don't have anyone else to buy things for. Anyway, my piggy bank was full and I had to empty it."

She laughed and proceeded to untie the bows on either side of the box. Lifting the cover she was astonished to see the very same straw hat she'd admired just hours before in the millinery store window. The finely woven straw was soft and flexible and the blue ribbon matched perfectly with her dress. "I've never had a hat as fine as this. Thank you so much." After she put it on, he remembered what the shop owner had said about the ribbon streamers.

"On a windy day, you can tie these under your chin like this." He fumbled with the ribbons until finally there was some semblance of a bow.

How strikingly beautiful she looked at that moment. The lacy straw encircled her face as a golden frame enhanced a fine painting, a masterpiece that he was almost afraid to touch. He had never kissed a girl before, but realized that things like that come naturally when the feeling was deep and true. After he touched her warm lips gently with his, she smiled up at him. Then he kissed her longer the second time. If it wasn't for the wide-brimmed hat, he might have kissed her again, so they sat holding hands for a while.

"It would be better if you went on ahead," he said finally. He knew how the maids gossiped and exaggerated every little thing, distorting the truth to tell a better story. "I'll drive up the back way so no one will be talking about us in the morning." Then he opened the gate and watched her walk up the drive. She felt his gaze, which made her even more self-conscious. Even though she tried her best to be as ladylike and dignified as possible, her legs felt like jelly and the distance seemed unending. Finally, at the bend of the road she turned to see him still leaning against the car. His hand went up and she waved back.

Behind the cover of bushes, when she could see him no longer, her suppressed happiness was released in a joyful shriek. She ran unabashedly up the driveway, skipping and twirling, dancing to the polka music playing in her head. She looked toward the large yellow manor house, its many gleaming windows reflecting the evening twilight, and her hat slid back on her neck. Quickly she placed the hat securely on top of her head, tightening the blue ribbons around her chin. Walking more sedately now, she bowed her head, hoping the wide brim might hide her hair and face from any nosy observers.

Eva did not know that Augusta sat in the library keeping an eye out for Karl, who should have been home two hours before, and noticed someone walking directly beneath the window. The woman's face was hidden by a large straw hat, but her dress was much finer than any maid might wear. Curiosity caused Augusta to dash out of the library and run down the hall for a better look, but by then the girl had vanished.

Later she asked Johanna if she had seen a girl in a blue dress walking on the drive.

"Not this afternoon, but 'that redhead' was wearing a fine blue dress that night when I saw her dancing in the hall with Mr. Lindholm."

Augusta didn't like being reminded of that episode in the hall. She had been so angry with Anders the next day, but in his thoughtful and persuasive way he had explained everything just as it happened, reassuring and asserting his complete and everlasting love for her. She surprised herself when she believed his every word and was able to forgive him. Eva, on the other hand, still presented a problem in regard to her son. A day never passed without her wondering what went on in the barn that day when she and Anders were at the lake.

Augusta saw a light in the study and walked in.

"Oh there you are, Karl, when did you get home?" He ignored her question with the news of his meeting in Gothenburg. "Dr. Franzen has finalized our itinerary. Father and I will be leaving for Denmark on the eleventh of July and after a week of conferences and farm visits we'll proceed to France, Germany and Switzerland. We should be back around the third week in

August." By then Karl had his hand on the doorknob.

"I have more work to do in my room, so I'll say goodnight."

The Transformation

How surprised Dagny had been to see the girl at the café, the same angel who had delivered her from the chains of bondage that fateful day when she and her mother rode away from the potato farm for good.

One glimpse of that red hair had riveted her feet to the sidewalk, but the whiskey soon bolstered an inner urge to proceed toward the café. The liquor had numbed her senses, making her act too boldly and unladylike. Now she wished their meeting had been under different circumstances, at a more proper time when she was sober and more properly dressed.

Eva had blended right in with the other fine ladies at the cafe. Had it not been for the red hair, Dagny might have passed by without noticing her. It appeared that Eva had risen far above her humble beginnings and had made something of herself, but that impression came from more than the fine dress she wore. Her graceful manner and the calm reassuring way she spoke revealed a maturity that Dagny saw lacking in herself. Eva had been kind and sympathetic, treating her as if they were old friends.

Dagny had wanted to stay at the café and talk longer and now she regretted not standing her ground and confronting the sailor. His grip had been so strong that she had black marks on her arm a week later. She'd had no choice but to leave, having been dragged behind him like a stubborn dog. When they reached the tavern he steered her toward a back table. She was glad to sit down and get off her feet, but she didn't want any more liquor.

When he poured out two glasses of whiskey something magical happened. Sitting across from her was not the sailor. A golden hue passed between them and what she saw was Eva's compassionate face and calming influence. Immediately she pushed her glass away and ordered a cup of strong hot coffee. Then the sailor was there again, but now she ignored him. Her mind was working in a different direction. When the coffee was gone, she ordered more.

"Hey, I don't have all the time in the world today," he said, impatiently.

"Neither do I," she replied, as her mind grew clearer with each sip.

"What are you trying to do, sober up on me?" He knew how she needed a good amount of drink to do things his way.

Dagny was aware of other men gawking at them, all rather amused at the little scene being played out. Well, she would give them a bit of entertainment. Standing at her full length and holding up her cup, she saluted them, drinking down the coffee in one long draught. Applauded by her boisterous audience, she slowly poured the bottle of whiskey over the sailor's head and marched out the door.

"Where are you going?" shouted the outraged sailor as he took off after her, but she already had a hefty lead on him. When she stopped to look back, he was standing in the middle of the road flailing his arms and shouting obscenities.

"And good riddance to you, too," she said to herself. She stood with her hands on her hips watching him walk back toward the alley. From the rear he was quite bow-legged and walked like a monkey. What had she ever seen in him? Liquor had been distorting her vision, but now her perspective was clear and she was ready to move forward.

Seeing Eva had been the catalyst that generated her latent yearning for something better, causing an extraordinary transformation in her thinking and giving her the strength to change.

Working at the boarding house seemed like a bad dream from which she had now awakened. The sun suddenly looked brighter, the sky bluer and her view clearer. In the distance she saw the ocean and realized she had been here before; Captain had brought her down this very road last week.

She ran to the beach, pulled off her shoes and stood where the sand meets the sea. The waves rolled in, cresting, breaking and splashing toward her. The foamy mass of bubbling water frolicked around her ankles, cool and soothing on her tired feet. She could not resist tasting the sparkling bubbles, but the water was salty on her tongue, just as her mother had told her many years before.

Then she walked along the beach where the receding waves had moistened the sand, her footprints following behind, until the next wave rolled in and washed them away. She took a dozen more steps and looked back and the same thing happened, reminding her of something the pastor had told her about God washing away all sins. At the time she hadn't understood what the word 'sin' meant, but it was clear to her now that sin was something bad. She visualized all the bad things she had experience in her life being washed away just like her footprints vanished into the sea. It was another transforming moment.

Continuing to walk along the beach she came to an outcropping of large smooth rocks that formed a secluded area into which only the sea might look. She removed her green satin dress and sat on a rock in her light cotton shift. After a while she removed that, too, and waded out waist-deep in the water. The water was very cold, but she dived in and paddled around until her legs felt numb, then floated back to her private cove and sat in the warm sun.

The only sounds were the tiny ripples of water creeping slowly across the sand and an occasional wailing squawk from a circling white bird. Feeling uncommonly calm and relaxed, she laid down on the soft sand, stretching her arms and legs out to absorb each warm ray of the sun. Surely the sun god was looking down on her today.

She awakened to the loud squawking of three large, gray and white birds. They looked down from a protruding rock, regarding her suspiciously as if the cove might belong to them, and she hastened to put on her clothes and shoes. The water was only a foot away from where she lay in the cove, suggesting that the ocean had moved closer to her.

Looking out upon the undulating blue-green sea jogged her memory about what Captain had told her about ocean waves and the tides. He said the moon circled the earth once each month. When the moon was close to the earth the tides were high and when the moon was farther away the tides were lower. She had been impressed that her moon god was strong enough to move such a great amount of water and today she had seen it happen before her very own eyes.

After she left the cove Dagny saw that no one else on the beach seemed concerned about the water inching toward them. Most adults lay on colorful blankets that dotted the sand, reminding her of the beautiful quilt the butcher's wife had made. She walked by children playing at the water's edge. They were filling little pails with wet sand and said they were making a castle. She wanted to stay and play with them, but a man called out her name. It was Captain. He was sitting on a blanket facing the ocean.

"So, young lady, what brings you to the beach today?"

"It's a long story," she said, looking down at him.

"Well, I've nothing better to do today than listen to a nice long story," he said, patting the blanket and inviting her to sit down. He poured her a cup of fresh water and waited while she drank. She took her time thinking about what to tell him and finally the words came out.

"I saw a friend of mine from Norrland today."

"How nice," he said. "Was it that red-headed girl you told me about?"

"Yes...she was sitting at a café drinking coffee just like a proper lady." Then Dagny gazed across the water toward the horizon as if not knowing what to say next.

"Well, it's always nice to see old friends," said Captain. Then he poured himself a drink and waited for her to continue. Sadness touched her face for a moment, but then she smiled.

"I'm not going to work at the boarding house anymore," she

blurted out suddenly, with a radiance he hadn't seen before.

"Well now...I'm glad to hear that," he said. "Do you have other plans?"

"Didn't you tell me last week that passenger ships sometimes hire local girls for room cleaning and waiting on tables?"

"I probably did. That's what I usually tell all the young girls at the boarding house."

He gestured toward a row of buildings on the road behind the docks. "Tomorrow, we'll go to that white building, the one with the big Swedish flag on the roof, and see if they are hiring."

"Can we go now?" she asked.

He appraised her rumpled green dress and straggly, windblown hair. "I'll pick you up tomorrow morning and we can have a little breakfast on the way. You might wear something else...a simple cotton dress perhaps?"

"Oh, yes," she said. "I'll wear my best blouse and skirt." Then they both enjoyed sitting in the sun and breathing in the fresh salt air. Dagny thought about the tides and how Captain had said that if she put a note in a bottle, the outgoing tides would carry the bottle far out to sea. Eventually the bottle would wash up on some distant shore...probably in North or South America or maybe in some isolated island in the Atlantic.

"Will the tide be going out tomorrow morning?" she asked.

"Yes, I think it will." He thought it odd she would want to watch the tide go out, but he silently did some calculations in his head and came up with the proper time.

"I'll be at the boarding house at exactly seven o'clock," he said. "That will give us plenty of time to eat breakfast."

Dagny hadn't been able to sleep that night and was the first one in the bathing room the next morning. She was glad no one was there, especially Victoria, who was always asking questions about where she had been or where she was going. It was best that her leaving would be a surprise. She had plenty of time to brush her hair, braid it neatly around her head and put on the fine blue skirt and white blouse that the minister had given to her mother almost a year ago.

After making up her bed, she laid out all the colorful gowns neatly in a row on top of the spread. Only the yellow dress belonged to her. Except for that one lovely evening at the theater, it was now a reminder of bad memories. But she had a plan for that dress and was taking it with her today.

Several times she'd poked her head out the door to look at the clock at the end of the hall. When it was almost seven, she left the door open and sat down to wait. She knew it wouldn't be very long because Captain was a man who was never late for anything.

"Well, don't we look fresh as an ocean breeze this morning!" he said, grinning from ear to ear in the doorway. Slightly embarrassed, she walked out into the hall, fumbled with the key in the lock and dropped the yellow dress. He picked it up and gave it back to her.

"Of all your gowns I always liked this one the best."

"The others were borrowed," she said. "I bought this one when I worked at the butcher shop, but for me it was bad luck."

"How so?" he asked.

"It brought me here."

"Aye…so are you going to bring this bad luck along with us today?

"Only as far as the beach. I want to throw it in the ocean and watch my bad luck float away."

"Brilliant idea! I like your symbolism, Dagny," said Captain. "By the time we have a little breakfast, the tide will have turned and your dress should drift quickly out to sea."

Later, as the two of them stood at the water's edge, Dagny once again slipped off her shoes and stockings and waded into the water. After a large wave tumbled in around her ankles and the water began to recede, she ceremoniously threw the yellow dress as far as she could, then watched impatiently as it floated too leisurely out into the ocean. As the tide ebbed and flowed, the golden fleck was carried further and further away until finally it disappeared from view. She ran back to Captain, a wide smile brightening her usually plain face.

"So...do you feel better now?" he asked.

"Yes," she said. "I feel like a new person."

"You do look different," he said. "I can already see fresh beauty in your face and manner."

If it hadn't been for Captain she probably wouldn't have gotten the job. He knew the man at the front desk and also the personnel director down the hall.

"You're a lucky girl," said the man. "Come back tomorrow. Be here by eight in the morning and I'll give you a letter to get you on board the ship."

Dagny walked back to the strawberry farm that afternoon worrying the whole way if her mother and Bertil would scold her for not writing or visiting before now. The two of them were sitting on the porch holding hands when she walked up the driveway. Suvi apologized for not coming to see her at the butcher shop and said that Bertil had been sick, but was feeling better now. Since they both assumed she had been working at the butcher shop, she didn't tell them anything different.

Surprisingly they were in favor of her decision to work on the big ship and were pleased to have her stay overnight. The next morning at a very early hour the three of them got in the buggy and drove to Gothenburg so she wouldn't be late for her first day at work. She hugged them both and said goodbye to Blix. They had been through a lot together, but he had a good life now and the mare to keep him company. Her mother and Bertil appeared to have moved on, too. Now it was her turn.

Midsummer Eve

It was late June, almost Midsummer, time of the summer solstice, the longest day of the year. There was as much preparation for

Midsummer as there had been for Christmas and except for a multitude of cold dishes, the menu was very similar. Raising the tall birch pole had been a celebration in itself and Eva had helped decorate the maypole with green-leaved birch branches, wreaths, flowers and the many colorful streamers hanging from the crosspiece. Why it was called a maypole was a mystery to her, because Midsummer was always in late June. Nevertheless, dancing around the maypole was a wonderful tradition no matter what one wanted to call it.

Rather than the more formal celebration of Christmas, Midsummer had a country-like atmosphere. Long tables and chairs were set up for invited guests in the newly harvested hay field near the apple orchard. Beyond those were additional tables for the farm workers and maids, including any personal servants of the guests. The maypole was placed between these two dining areas. Servants would have their turn around the maypole after the family and guests had finished with their celebration.

Every time Eva looked out the window, more people had gathered on the lawn and now the fiddlers were setting up to play. She brought a tray of cold tea and lemonade to the front porch, where many older women were sitting in rocking chairs, chatting and watching the festivities below while their husbands were gathered on the lawn near the punch bowl. She could hear their riotous laughter and glanced around for Mr. Kronberg. She wondered if Mats and Jenny would be coming, too.

Older guests were dressed in their best finery and most of the younger couples wore their native Swedish costumes: the women in white blouses, dark vests and fine printed shawls, colorful skirts and a variety of white caps on their heads; the men in yellow knickers, black vests over loose, white, long-sleeved shirts, white or tan stockings and buckled shoes.

The weather couldn't have been more perfect. The sun shone down from a bright, blue sky and a gentle, cooling breeze flowed down from the north. It wasn't until after dinner that Eva saw Karl. She had just arranged the dessert table and was filling an empty tray with dirty plates to take back to the kitchen when he came up behind her. He looked dashing in his yellow knickers and white shirt, explaining how he'd been detained in the barn by a guest who wanted to look at the new milk separator.

"But enough about that," he said, glancing around the dessert table. "I was looking for a piece of your delicious almond cake," he said with a wink.

Eva held up an empty plate of crumbs. "It's a good thing I made two cakes. I'll bring the other one down when I come back."

She returned to the kitchen, sliced the loaf of almond cake and put it on a tray with about two dozen crystal goblets. She had just stepped off the kitchen steps when she collided with a group of rowdy boys who had run around the corner of the house. After that, everything seemed to move in slow motion. The shimmering crystal goblets slid slowly off the tray as Eva tried to save the almond cake. As she fell to the ground, a woman gasped and took the cake from her hand as the shattering stemware tumbled around her in a melodious mass of broken pieces.

Eva scrambled to gather up the broken shards and heard Mrs. Lindholm's chastising voice.

"See what you've done!" she shouted. "These are precious heirlooms and cannot be replaced!"

"I'm sorry," said Eva with tear-filled eyes that blurred her vision, making it almost impossible to pick up the sharp pieces.

Karl had witnessed the whole incident. Noticing her bloody hand he bent down and lifted her up. He spoke to her in barely a whisper. "Go to the kitchen and soak your hand. Wait there for me." Then he addressed his mother.

"It wasn't her fault," he said in Eva's defense.

"Don't contradict me, Karl! It is plain to see who dropped this tray."

"I don't want to argue with you, Mother, but I saw exactly how this happened. A group of boys came racing around the corner of the house and two of them bumped into her. If anyone needs to be reprimanded, it is the Sanderson boys and their friends."

"Well...the girl should have been more observant," said Augusta, gazing despondently at the pile of broken crystal.

"I'll have someone come down to clean this up," said Karl, thinking this would be his opportunity to go to the kitchen and care for Eva's hand.

Cook was hovering over Eva like a mother hen when Karl arrived at the kitchen. Eva was soaking her hand in a bowl of warm water tinged a deep pink. She looked up and he could see she was still upset. "I'm so sorry to have caused such a...commotion," she said.

"Accidents happen, and it wasn't your fault" he said, guiding her toward a sunlit window where he could inspect her wound more closely. He saw a sliver of glass protruding from the cut.

"Keep soaking your hand," he told her. "I'm going to get my tweezers."

Cook saw Eva twinge. "He knows what he's doing," Cook said reassuringly. "Karl would make a fine doctor. He treats the cows all the time; and sometimes they come into the barn with very serious injuries." Cook declined to go into detail for fear of frightening Eva even more, but she remembered very well seeing the poor cow that had been gored by an angry bull. Karl had slept in her stall for over a week, tending to her wounds and rolling her over from one side to the other until she was able to stand on her own. Cows were always coming in from the pasture with scrapes, sore feet and wounds of all kinds.

Karl returned with a box of clean gauze and bandages, iodine, salves and the tweezers. Eva felt only a little prick as he carefully removed the sliver of glass. Then he gently wrapped her hand with gauze. "Keep your hand dry and you'll be fine."

"Yes, doctor," she replied in jest, and he knew she was feeling better.

"And no more tray carrying today!" This was an order, but his firm lips softened into a smile. She could not agree to that. There were still guests to serve and dirty dishes to remove from the tables, both of which involved carrying heavy trays. Cook suggested she go to her room and lie down for a while, but Eva preferred to sit on the stoop and watch the festivities below.

From the orchard came the familiar traditional melodies of the fiddlers and accordion players as the procession of guests made its way to the maypole. Soon everyone was holding hands and singing as they danced in a ring around the beautifully decorated pole. Most beautiful was when they held the colorful streamers forming a wheel of undulating waves as the dancers circled the pole. She laughed when they sang the frog song, hopping like frogs and acting foolishly, but that was the fun of it all, especially with the help of beer, vodka or cider that had been in the barrel too long. Finally they dispersed into pairs to dance the favorite Swedish hop, the hambo, waltzes and country polkas. In her mind Eva was dancing, too, her right foot tapping abstractedly to the lively rhythmic beat of the music.

When she saw the guests returning to the banquet tables she went back into the kitchen.

"Remember what Karl told you about not carrying trays," said Cook.

"I don't see any tray, do you?" joked Eva, holding up a cold pitcher of fruit punch in her good hand. "Anyway I'm feeling just fine now."

She was down by the orchard pouring beverages when Karl and a young boy came to the table.

"Eva, Frederic has something to say to you."

The shy boy looked up at her, his straight blond hair covering one eye, and she thought of young Mats sitting in the parlor so many years ago. She smiled and he looked down to the ground, red-faced and bashful. Karl put his hand on the boy's shoulder, whispering words of encouragement. Then Frederick stood a little taller and told her he was sorry he knocked her down.

Eva reached out to Frederic and pulled him close to her. "That's all right," she said. "I think we both should have been paying more attention to where we were going, don't you think?"

Frederic nodded in agreement.

"You will try to be more careful from now on, won't you, Frederic?" asked Karl.

"Oh, yes, sir," he replied. Then Frederic looked up at Eva and saw that blood had soaked through the gauze. "Does it hurt?" he asked.

"Right now it doesn't hurt one little bit."

"I'm really sorry," he said.

"I know you are," she said. "Now go along and play with your friends."

Augusta and Anders joined the remaining guests sitting on the long front porch. After a busy day of entertaining, plus that disastrous episode involving her precious crystal goblets, Augusta wanted only to lean back against the chair and enjoy the cool evening breeze. Twilight had settled in and the view across the lawn was somewhat obscured, the bright colors of daytime now having dulled into varying shades of gray so that Augusta was unable to distinguish one person from another. Most couples had now gathered into little groups near the banquet tables and every so often a man's robust laughter or a woman's shriek pierced the peaceful surroundings.

"I think everyone had a good time, don't you?" commented Anders after a while.

Augusta agreed, but her attention was now focused on Gunnar and another young man, who were talking rather loudly by the porch steps. They both appeared quite inebriated.

"It certainly looks as if Gunnar is having a good time," she said leaning in the direction of her son to better hear what he was saying.

"It's an old pagan custom, a sign of fertility actually, symbolizing the impregnation of the earth." Gunnar was pointing to the maypole where a few servants were still dancing and celebrating. "Those circular wreaths on top represent the female element and the long pole is the man's...ah...the male..."

"That's enough, Gunnar!" shouted Augusta. "Can't you see

we have guests here? Take your discussion elsewhere." Gunnar put his hands up as if surrendering and stumbled awkwardly down the stairs with his companion.

She watched them disappear around the corner of the house. At the same time she noticed Karl carrying a large tray of dishes up the hill toward the kitchen. Following a few steps behind him was a girl. Even in the dim light Augusta could make out her red hair and knew it was Eva. Her anger over the crystal incident returned, but it was not only because most of her fine goblets were broken; she was bothered now by Karl's confrontational attitude. It wasn't like him to be so.... so...testy. He had humiliated her by speaking up in defense of a servant, and this behavior was inexcusable. This wasn't the first day she had noticed a difference in her younger son. There were other, less important circumstances that had come up lately, sharp answers to her questions, or no response at all, walking off with a shrug of his shoulders or just avoiding her completely. She had voiced her concerns to Anders, but he'd brushed them away as nothing.

"Karl's probably going through a rebellious stage like Gunnar did when he was sixteen."

"But Karl is different. I don't recognize him now," she said with a pout. "He's not my sweet little boy anymore."

"The fact is, Augusta, that your little boy has now become a man."

Karl would always be her baby. Her boys had grown up too fast and Augusta didn't like to think that she, too, was growing older.

Augusta went into the house to find Johanna. She needed a stiff drink, but Johanna talked her into lemonade and said she'd bring it out to the porch. Ander's chair was empty when Augusta returned. There was no one else there, except for two elderly men at the far end of the porch enjoying their pipes.

She was in a sour mood and couldn't get Eva out of her mind. That girl was trouble. She had guessed as much that first night when she saw Mats swinging her around in the hall. Augusta had hoped to keep the new maid hidden in the kitchen until she could find someone else, but that plan had blown apart when Gerta ran away, leaving them short-handed just before Christmas.

It was Anders who suggested Eva take Gerta's place. How the men had stared and gawked at her in the banquet room; even the women commented how lucky she was to have such an efficient and attentive serving girl. But she knew those same women were secretly glad not to have such an attractive maid around their husbands and sons. A fire still smoldered within Augusta when she thought of her husband dancing with Eva that night under the chandelier.

"It was nothing," he had told her. "When I heard footsteps outside my study I went out to investigate, and there she was in the grand hall twirling around in front of the mirror without anyone to dance with." She'd thought Anders was different from other men, but they were all the same…always on the lookout to get their arms around a pretty girl or…she couldn't bear to think of everything else some men did. At least Anders was faithful to her in that way. Well, she thought he was…she felt as sure as any woman could be.

Johanna set a tray on the table with two glasses of lemonade. "Where is Mr. Lindholm?" she asked. "I brought him a glass, too."

"I don't know where he is…and I don't care," said Augusta. "You may have the lemonade. Sit with me for a while and rest yourself."

They sat quietly listening to the fiddlers. This was Augusta's favorite holiday and she loved the endless twilight of Midsummer. The musicians would play as long as the guests wished to dance. Three couples had been waltzing, but now there were only two. They moved slowly like birch trees bending back and forth in the wind.

"Can you make out who the dancers are?"

Johanna didn't answer. She was asleep. Every so often a muffled snort escaped from her gaping mouth. She wasn't a pretty girl to begin with, and sleeping did nothing to improve her appearance. Except for her chubby, round-faced children, Augusta thought that most people weren't attractive when their faces relaxed in sleep, their open mouths hanging loosely in dopey sadness. She didn't like to think of how she might look while sleeping.

Karl saw Eva loading a large tray with dirty dishes and came over to the table. "You're not intending to carry that heavy tray up the hill are you?" he jested. Truth be told, she was planning on doing just that, but did not want to admit her intentions to Karl.

"I'm feeling much better now."

"Well, I can't let you do that," he said, looking back toward the maypole. He saw other maids and farm hands lying on the grass having a good time. Not wishing to intrude on their fun, he picked up the tray.

"That's my job!" she shouted, but he ignored her and continued taking long strides up the hill. A few heads turned to look at them, so in order to make less of a scene she grabbed the pail and rag she had been using to wash the tables and followed him to the kitchen.

When Cook saw Karl, she was quick to grab the tray. "You shouldn't be doing that!" she exclaimed. "Olga, go down and get the rest of the dirty dishes." As Olga rushed out, Eva walked in with her pail and rag. Cook knew right away what Eva had been doing and shook her head.

"Didn't I tell you that Olga would scrub down those tables?" she whispered, so Karl would not hear.

"I just wanted to help," said Eva. Feeling she had been scolded, Eva slowly put away the pail and hung the rag to dry. Karl was gone when she came back, but Cook was in a better mood then and spoke in a softer tone. "You've done enough, young lady. Now go along and enjoy yourself."

"I was enjoying myself. Cleaning tables seemed like a good excuse to be down near the fiddlers."

"I love fiddle music, too," said Cook. "The crowds are thinning out now. If you go the back way you can sit in the orchard. No one should bother you there."

"Will you come with me?" asked Eva.

"I'm too old to be sitting in the grass listening to music...and I wouldn't be able to get up afterwards."

"Well, I'd be there to help you up," replied Eva.

Cook winked at Eva. "Now, go on with ya...find someone else to have a good time with," Cook said. Then she literally pushed Eva out the door.

Eva stood on the stoop smiling to herself. Then she ran down the pasture path and around the dairy barn to the orchard. The summer twilight was bright enough for her to pick her way, but not to be seen. She found a big tree and sat beneath it. Then she leaned back against the broad trunk, closed her eyes and listened to the music, imagining that she was dancing with Karl.

Something tickled the side of her neck. Thinking some hair was caught in the tree bark, she reached behind and felt a hand that wasn't her own.

"I was hoping you'd come back," said Karl, sitting down next to her. Eva didn't know what to say, except for telling the truth.

"I was thinking of you...and here you are," she said. He grinned and picked up her bandaged hand.

"Does it hurt?" he asked, pressing ever so gently on the wound.

She felt nothing but her heart beating double time. "Sometimes it smarts a little when I accidentally bump it against something," she said.

He carefully unwrapped the bandage and inspected the wound. "Seems to be healing well," he said. Try to keep the bandage dry." She smiled, nodding in agreement.

He slipped a bottle of wine from beneath his vest. "In the meantime this should make you feel better," he said, offering her a taste. She took a sip and then drank more.

"I don't know what made me so thirsty."

"I know why," he said, "you've been working too hard." He took a few swigs and offered her more.

"It tastes very nice." she said, relishing the smooth, fruity taste.

"I'm glad you like it. Making apple wine is a hobby of mine."

She looked at him with admiration. "Is there anything you can't do, Karl?"

"Well," he said, looking toward the fiddlers, "I don't dance very well. Perhaps you could teach me."

The two couples looked as if they were asleep on their feet. Eva laughed. "I wouldn't call that dancing. They're just holding each other up."

"We could probably do that," he said. Then he took her good hand and helped her up.

Augusta watched the pair of dancers swaying slowly back and forth as another couple joined them. She sat up straight and poked Johanna with her elbow.

"Look at the dancers...is that Karl?" she asked impatiently. Johanna sat up and rubbed her eyes. "I don't know," she replied, yawning, "Can't see well enough from here."

"Run down and find out who they are...and hurry back."

Johanna sneaked around to the left behind a gathering of servants and hid behind a tree where she had a clear view of the three couples. Seeing clearly Eva's red hair and Karl's handsome profile, she ran back to report the news to her mistress.

Augusta was fit to be tied. Not able to sit still, she paced back and forth incessantly across the porch.

"The dancers are leaving!" yelled Johanna.

Augusta stopped in her tracks and shouted back. "Well, don't just sit there. Go back and follow them. I want to know every little detail."

Johanna passed by the weary line of fiddlers as they walked up across the lawn, but Karl and Eva were nowhere to be seen. She picked her way through the small groups of servants asking if they'd seen Karl. One of the men grabbed her ankle and offered her a drink. Johanna was torn as to what to do. If this had been anyone else, she would have brushed him off, but it was Einar, her favorite of all the farm workers. After taking one long good look around for Karl and Eva, she plunked herself down on the grass and began making small talk as they shared his drink. When that was gone, he opened another bottle and she began looking around for Karl and Eva.

"You aren't thinking of leaving, are you?" he asked.

"I'd like to stay, but I should find out where Karl is."

"I saw him dancing with that redhead. He's a lucky one, eh?"

"The mistress is looking for them. Do you know where they went?"

Einar was more than a little drunk and had trouble fixing his glazed eyes on Johanna. "I could tell you where I think they are," he said, touching her thigh, his wandering eyes looking past her toward the apple trees.

"They're in the orchard, aren't they?" she said.

"That's where they were headed last I knew," he said. "Let's go behind those bushes over there."

Johanna was torn between obeying her mistress and having the one man she'd had her sights on for over a year now. The minute she began wondering when she might ever have another chance with Einar, he sat up, pitched forward and passed out in her lap. Just my luck, she thought. Then she grabbed the bottle of whiskey, took one long gulp and cautiously made her way to the back of the orchard.

After the other two couples had wandered off, Karl told the tired musicians to go to the kitchen for some refreshments. Then he and Eva went back to the tree where he'd left the bottle of wine.

"We might as well finish the wine before it spoils," he said with a wink.

"I don't know much about wine, but Mama and Papa had wine on occasion," she said. "I've never known wine to spoil, even though they usually made a bottle last for almost a week or more." It was like a little joke and her charming giggle made him love her even more. Then they sat in the cool grass and took turns drinking until the wine was gone. She rested her head on his shoulder and they spoke briefly about the events of the day.

Eva was feeling unusually playful and a bit giddy. She put her arm behind him, picked up a little twig and tickled his ear. As his hand went up to his head he heard her giggling again.

"A pretty big mosquito just bit me and I think I know where she is." Then he grabbed her around the waist and laid her down on the grass. They were both laughing now and she pretended to wiggle out of his grip, but he pinned her down, gently steadied her head in his hands and kissed her smiling lips.

"Do you want to stay here for a while?" he whispered, nuzzling her neck. Eva certainly wasn't ready to go back to the kitchen. Besides all the wine she had drank, the slow dancing had put her in a dreamy mood. She could not forget how they'd swayed back and forth to the slow strains of the violins. He'd held her closer then and she'd leaned her head against his chest. She remembered him kissing her temple, her cheek and then brushing his lips teasingly against hers, and how he held her tighter after that, as if afraid she might run away. She wished the dancing had never ended.

"I could stay right here all night long," she replied to his question. She lay quietly now in his embrace, but her body was alive with new sensations and she could feel it was the same with him. He looked down upon her with such tenderness that she became lost in his eyes. Her sweet smile was irresistible to him and he couldn't get enough of her. It was the same with Eva. Then he kissed her again, like Mats had done before. This time she didn't pull away. Instead she held him tightly and passionately kissed him back.

She was startled when he suddenly rolled over on his back. He put his arms under his head and stared into the branches above. He knew how the bulls were at breeding time, but now his own body was making him feel self-conscious. He drew his knees up to hide the cause of his embarrassment. For someone who was always in control of things, he'd now let his emotions get the best of him. All day long, he had waited for the time when they could be alone, but now he had second thoughts. He cared for her too much and things were getting out of hand.

His rational mind had kicked in, pressuring him to distance himself from the possibility of a regrettable situation, yet his body failed to respond and was telling a different story. He sat up and looked toward the house. People were still milling about the lawn and there was movement on the porch. Nearby the farm hands and maids were laughing and talking noisily. It was possible they could see him, too.

Eva lay on her back watching him, wondering why he had drawn away from her. Had he not liked her kiss? Finally she could stand the silence no longer and rose up on one elbow to look at him. He seemed in deep thought. "What are you thinking?" she asked.

Her voice brought him back to the present and he turned to her.

"I've been thinking of you all day," he said, turning to face her, "and now…" He struggled with his words; they were mixed up too much with his emotions.

Eva reached out and put her hand on his arm. "I've been thinking of you all day, too," she said. Then he took her hand in his and kissed the back of it, played gently with her fingers and kissed the softness of her palm.

Karl could stand it no longer. He helped her up and led her through the orchard to the secluded path behind the cow barn. He walked with a purpose. She was glad to see him smiling and acting in his normal, carefree manner. All the cattle were out to pasture and the barn door was open, beckoning them to come inside. Karl put his arm around her waist as they walked past the empty stanchions and box stalls toward a stairway at the end of the barn. The sweet aroma of yesterday's fresh cut hay met them in the dark, narrow stairwell to the second-floor haymow, where soft moonlight shining through an open window welcomed them. Karl scooped her up in his arms and lowered her down on the soft fresh hay. She reached up and put her arms around his neck and stroked his blond hair. How soft and fine it was.

His kisses grew longer and harder, his hands stroking her neck and arms, brushing against her chest and finally fondling her firm breasts. When she felt his lips touch the softness of her chest, all shyness and caution vanished in a whirlwind of emotion. She held him close, caressing his head, stroking his hair and feeling unusual and wonderful sensations pulsating within her body. Unable to hold back her overflowing love and deep yearning, she unabashedly gave herself up to him.

Afterwards, he lay back on the hay beside her. In the quietness, he reached for her hand, which reminded him of his plans for the next day.

"I won't be able to rebandage your hand in the morning," he told her. "Father and I are leaving very early for Gothenburg to meet with the adviser for our trip to Europe, but I expect we will be home in time for dinner."

Eva was about to reply when a noise made them both sit up. "What was that?" she whispered. He pulled up his knickers and ran to the head of the stairs to listen. "Probably just a mouse," he told her, but he had seen enough to know it was a rat, a very big rat named Johanna.

There had been no passionate interlude for Johanna. Just as well, she thought to herself. She'd read enough romantic novels to know that men have their way with women for a few brief moments and then the woman is left alone to take care of some wretched bastard child. She wanted none of that. Straightening out her apron she cautiously made her way to the orchard in hopes of finding something interesting to tell her mistress, but saw nothing but an empty wine bottle. Thinking back to the day she'd seen Karl and Eva by the dairy barn, she ran down the very same path they had taken less than twenty minutes before.

She quietly made her way through the empty cow barn, looking into the box stalls, until she came to the stairs. She had been to the haymow before when she was young and foolish. Slowly she tip-toed up the wooden stairs, stopping now and then to listen, but it wasn't until she reached the top step that a soft moan and the rustling of hay got her attention.

Anyone could be in the loft. Now she had to find out exactly who it was. Half-naked men looked very much alike to Johanna; she'd seen their bare behinds and more when swimming down by the river. What she now observed was different than the romantic episodes she'd read about in books. The reality of it was almost too embarrassing, but she could not help herself from watching and listening as Karl's familiar voice spoke Eva's name. Feeling suddenly weak and light-headed, she proceeded down the stairs, slipping halfway and bumping into the wall. She listened for a moment and heard footsteps from above. Quickly she ran down the rest of the way, back through the barn and across the lawn toward the house.

The porch was empty of guests except for the late arriving Otto Kronberg, He was the first one to spot Johanna racing up the grassy hill from the barn, her skirt and petticoat flying above her knees, billowing out like some gigantic black and white winged bird that was unsure where to land, her cap askew and hair sticking out every which-a-way.

"Looks like something scared the wits out of your maid, Augusta," he said.

Johanna scrambled up the porch steps two at a time, her wild eyes informing Augusta that the news wasn't good. Words spilled from Johanna's mouth, senseless mismatched phrases punctuated by loud gasps as she tried to catch her breath.

"Calm down," hissed Augusta as she directed Johanna to a seat further away from where Anders and Otto were sitting.

"I found 'em in the hay loft," said Johanna, glancing at the men and covering her mouth. "They were...well, I didn't actually see them doing it, but I heard sounds...and I saw them laying in the hay together." Johanna stifled a nervous giggle, but Augusta had heard enough. Not only was she agitated with this recent development, she was equally displeased that her husband had ignored her previous concerns about Karl and Eva. Augusta didn't care if Otto was here or not, she was going to confront her husband and she was going to do it now.

She stood brazenly in front of him with her hands on her hips, looking to Anders like some angry peasant woman watching a fox run off with her favorite hen. He grinned at the thought.

"It's no laughing matter, Anders. Did you hear what Johanna said?"

"I heard a sufficient amount." he said.

"Well, I hope you're satisfied! Perhaps now you'll speak to Karl and put an end to this...this unacceptable dalliance." Anders glanced over to Otto who was discretely looking the other way, pretending not to hear.

"We'll talk about this later, Augusta," he stated firmly.

"That's what you always say," she said, stomping back into the house. With a long sigh, Anders leaned back in his chair and closed his eyes. He wanted to forget about the whole unpleasant incident and especially the little talk Augusta wanted him to have with Karl. Otto, on the other hand, being somewhat curious and wanting to know more, tried to make light of the situation. "I'm guessing that Augusta isn't pleased with Karl's taste in women," he said.

Anders shook his head. "For years she's been worrying that Karl wasn't interested in girls, and when he finally does find someone, all she can do is complain because the girl isn't 'good enough' for him.'"

"So, who is the lucky girl?"

"I think you might know her," said Anders in jest. "She's a charming red-head from Norrland."

Otto laughed. Then, while smoking his pipe, blew out two perfect smoke rings. "It's none of my business, Anders, but I can think of no finer girl for Karl than Eva Gunderson."

Anders watched the two rings rise above them, growing larger and coming closer to each other against the darker landscape. "Aye, I can't agree with you more."

Then a strange thing happened: the rings merged together and became one just before dispersing into the gray sky.

"Did you see that?"

"I did," said Otto

"What do you make of it?"

"I'd say it's a sign, hopefully a good omen."

The Next Day

Sleep evaded Eva. She lay awake with disturbing thoughts, her stomach churning with worry and a touch of regret about their recklessness in the hayloft. What if something came of their love making? She knew about cows and breeding, and the calf that came nine months later, but she was uncertain about the mystery of a man and a woman. Ingrid had told her once there was only one day in a month when a baby could be made. She said other things that had not made sense at the time, but Eva had only been eleven then.

"When you become a woman you will understand," Ingrid had said in an authoritative tone of voice. However, if her sister had known so much, how was it she became pregnant? Hadn't Gerta quit working because she was expecting a baby? Eva had her doubts about this once-a-month theory. If she got pregnant, she would have no home to go back to.

She remembered the snowy Sunday afternoon when Mrs. Lindholm showed her the family library. Eva had picked out a book called ***Small Business and Family Farming in America***, which Mrs. Lindholm said would be boring and much too difficult for her to comprehend. She then had directed Eva to another section and showed her a novel that Johanna told her about.

Eva took both books to her room, but only read half of the novel. It was a troubling story of the difficult life of a pregnant girl who eventually gave birth alone in an abandoned barn. She raised the child by scavenging food from fields and woods, resorting sometimes to stealing from farmer's barns, always looking back for fear that someone was watching or following her. The girl in the story blamed herself for smiling at a boy in a way that made him want to kiss her. She had paid no heed to her mother's strict warnings about being alone with a boy.

At the time Eva viewed the story as someone else's problems that had nothing to do with her, but now she understood how the girl felt and it scared her. Had she enticed Karl by smiling up at him in the orchard? Like the girl in the story, Eva blamed herself.

She should have kept her head and been strong enough to heed the little voice inside that told her 'no,' but that utterance was too hushed, a faint whisper that slowly faded, lost in the fervor and excitement of being with Karl. There were too many 'ifs.' If she had not gone to the orchard, if she had not drunk so much wine, if she had not smiled at Karl and kissed him back, if she had kept her legs together...she wouldn't be worrying now.

Finally Eva fell into a fitful sleep, dreaming that she was the very girl in that dreadful story and awakening in a sweat with a pounding headache. She was almost half an hour late arriving in the kitchen but no one was there. She poured herself a cup of coffee and sat down at the long table.

The morning sun cast rays of soft light across the rich, mellowed, golden-brown pine boards, giving the bare table an imposing presence with nothing on it but her small earthenware cup. The rest of the kitchen was dim and foreboding. Instead of the usual hustle and bustle of daily meal preparations, the room was an empty cavity of stillness, an ominous void that threatened to swallow her up. Had she already missed Karl and his father, who she now remembered were leaving early for Gothenburg this morning? Hoping to see him, she peeked into the breakfast room, but the table was set exactly as she had left it. Where were Cook and Olga? Had she misjudged the time and arrived too early? If so, who had fired up the stove and brewed the coffee?

A door squeaked and Cook emerged from the storeroom. "Well, look who's here...the all-night gadabout!" she said, shuffling over to the coffee pot. She poured herself a cup, grabbed a plate of leftovers from the counter and sat down beside Eva. Eva's face turned beet red. "I'm sorry to be so late," she said staring into her cup, wondering how much Cook had seen or heard about last night.

"Never you mind now," said Cook, pulling over the platter of food so it set between them. "Midsummer's a time for merriment; for staying up late and not accomplishing much the next day." She sat with an expectant grin waiting for Eva's response. Enough time elapsed so that Cook had a question of her own.

"So, did you find a good spot to hear the fiddlers?"

"Oh yes, the orchard was a perfect place," said Eva, but what was she to say after that? Another long silence hovered around the two.

"I sat on the stoop and listened to them for a while," said Cook. "Then I walked down by the porch. Mrs. Lindholm seemed very upset. Afterwards I saw Johanna run down the hill toward the orchard."

"I saw no sign of Johanna last night," said Eva.

"She might have seen you…or Karl." When Eva made no comment, Cook continued. "You weren't in the orchard with Karl, were you?"

Eva drank her coffee slowly and blushed a bright crimson. Cook took this as a positive answer and said, "I thought as much." Then she went to the stove to get the coffee pot and refilled their cups. "You must be very careful, Eva. Mrs. Lindholm is very possessive about her boys, and Johanna is her convenient and willing spy. Between the two them, not much around here goes unnoticed."

Eva's face burned with embarrassment thinking that Johanna might have been the noise they heard on the stairs. How long had she been there and what had she seen? Eva tried to calm herself by thinking about something else.

"Did Karl and his father leave for Gothenburg already?"

"Ya. They didn't have time to have a proper breakfast," said Cook. "Came directly into the kitchen for coffee and a little bread and cheese. Then hurried back out again. Neither one looked very wide awake to me."

"Is Olga sick today?"

"No, she's fine," said Cook. "Gone to see her grandmother. Hasn't been home since day after Christmas." Eva was happy for Olga, but she was not looking forward to serving breakfast to Mrs. Lindholm, especially after hearing what Cook said, not to mention her breaking the heirloom crystal goblets. She had missed seeing Karl. Already the day after midsummer was a big disappointment.

"Don't look so glum," said Cook with a twinkle in her eye. "There may be a surprise in store for you yet."

When the dreaded bell sounded from the breakfast room, Eva straightened her apron and put on a brave face. She nearly dropped the coffee pot when she saw Mr. Kronberg sitting across from Mrs. Lindholm. She wanted to fly into his arms, but restrained herself. He read her face and rose quickly to give her a warm embrace.

"Perhaps we can go for a little walk after breakfast," he suggested, "If that's all right with you, Augusta?"

"Of course, Otto. Take all the time you need," she replied smugly as she slowly unfolded her napkin, smoothing out the ironed creases and dabbing the corners of her pursed, crimson lips.

Otto and Eva walked to the pasture, passing by a small enclosure that Eva had never noticed before. Clustered around the gate and clamoring for attention were eight white goats.

"I brought them down yesterday," he said. "Karl has this notion of making goat cheese, and because my wife had difficulty with her knees last winter, we decided it was time to cut back on our livestock."

"I'm sorry to hear about Mrs. Kronberg. Is she better now?"

"She seems to be, especially with this warm summer weather, but she's not one to complain," he said, watching Eva pat each white nose sticking through the gate. She laughed when they nibbled at her fingers, but when one grabbed her apron she backed away.

"Those critters got out one day and snatched everything from the clothes line. My wife didn't bat an eye…just picked up all the clothes and washed them over like nothing had ever happened. She said they were just having a little fun. Never have seen her get mad at one of them."

Not wanting to concern Eva, Otto did not mention that because Johan, Erik and Torsten were not living with them anymore, he was considering selling the farm. He did tell her that

Mats would be going to America sometime in July.

"Jenny Almgren lives in New York City," he said. "Mats is planning to attend architectural school there and eventually they intend to be married. Of course, I'd rather he was marrying you."

Eva smiled up to him.

"More than anything else, I would love to have you as my father-in-law," she said, smiling again and squeezing his arm. "I like Mats. We've known each other for such a long time that he seems more like an older brother to me." She hadn't forgotten the little crush they'd had, but that seemed a long time ago. She could only think of being with Karl now.

They came to the stone wall separating the pasture from the big barn and sat down on two flat rocks in the shade of a large maple tree. Otto filled his pipe and smoked for a minute or two while Eva sat quietly enjoying the lovely warm breeze that sometimes smelled of spicy tobacco. Otto glanced toward the house and was reminded of the purpose for this morning's walk with Eva.

All through breakfast he had been distracted by Augusta's one-sided conversation. She had vehemently stated her concerns about Karl and Eva. If Anders didn't do something about the situation soon, she was going to make some changes herself.

"What kind of changes?" he had wanted to know.

"Eva might find herself back in the kitchen scrubbing floors and helping in the kitchen," she replied.

"And Olga would be your serving maid?" Otto chuckled at the thought. "Good luck with that one!"

"Well, at least then I wouldn't have to worry so much about Karl and Eva seeing each other in the dining room every day," she said.

"Listen, Augusta. If Karl and Eva want to see each other bad enough, they'll find a way. Have you forgotten how it was when you were young and in love?"

"In love?" she said with an uneasy snicker. "Fornicating in the hay sounds more like 'in lust' to me." He had taken a long puff from his pipe and looked at her with raised eyebrows. "Call it what you may, Augusta, but I wouldn't make too much of it if I were you. Karl will be going away soon and perhaps that will end it all."

"Ah yes, Otto, you have just given me an idea."

"Are you going to share your idea with me?" he had asked, noticing a sinister look in her eye.

"I'll need time to plan everything out," she said. Then her voice took on a sweeter tone. "However, I would still like you to talk with Eva. You know how I feel about the classes mixing together. Eva would be more receptive to the idea if she hears it from you." When Otto didn't respond, Augusta continued. "Karl has a fine future ahead of him and I wouldn't want him dragged down by some low class peasant."

Otto had taken offense at this remark and was not keen on doing Augusta's dirty work. He did not contradict her; she was, of course, his good friend's wife. He also knew Eva better than anyone else. "I'll see what I can do," he had told her.

This situation had put him on unfamiliar ground. Instructing his sons on farm work and teaching them good morals had come easy, but he'd never had a daughter of his own. How was he to approach her on this delicately personal subject? He would have to start with generalities.

Otto thought about all this as he sat on the uncomfortable stone wall smoking his pipe.

"So, how are things going for you here, Eva?" he said for a starter.

"Everything was going very well until yesterday when I accidentally dropped a tray...and Mrs. Lindholm's favorite heirloom crystal goblets went crashing to the ground." Eva sighed, unconsciously adjusting the gauze on her hand.

"Did you cut yourself," he asked. She nodded. Dropping the tray had faded in her memory since being with Karl last night, but now the whole incident was playing back in her mind.

"I started picking up the broken glass, but Mrs. Lindholm

was very upset. I tried to explain, but she wouldn't listen and sent me back to the kitchen." This was the opening Otto had been looking for.

"Material things are very important to Mrs. Lindholm and she can be very demanding. She is very much like her mother, an aristocrat in the strictest sense and a very selfish and bigoted woman who believes strongly in the total separation of the nobility and peasant classes. This notion of not mixing with the lower classes was ingrained in Mrs. Lindholm at an early age and that's why she draws a firm line between her family and the servants."

"But Mr. Lindholm was just a common farmer, wasn't he?" asked Eva.

"Yes he was. Mrs. Lindholm's mother was against them seeing each other, too, and did everything she could to prevent the marriage, but her daughter was just as demanding and conniving as her mother. A hostile standstill prevailed for a long time...but you can see who won the battle."

"I noticed how determined she could be about getting her own way the first night I was here," said Eva, remembering how she manipulated Mats into changing his mind about Jenny.

"She is good at doing that, for sure," Otto said. "And that's why I must caution you to be very careful and discrete in your associations with Karl. Don't get me wrong, Karl is a wonderful boy, but just be aware of whoever else might be watching or listening when you are with him."

Eva was dumbfounded to hear him say Karl's name. Were her feelings about Karl so obvious that even Mr. Kronberg could tell? If Cook knew about last night, perhaps by now everyone had gotten wind of their dalliance in the barn. Just thinking that Mr. Kronberg might know what she had done was shameful. She felt heat rising to her neck and tried to think of something else.

"That house has many curious eyes," he said, as if he were reading her mind. Eva's face was burning now and she turned her red face to look away from him.

"I'm sorry. I didn't mean to embarrass you," he said.

Then all of her bottled up emotions exploded into tears and

she sobbed into her apron. He put his arms around her and she buried her face into his chest. This wasn't the way he had expected things to turn out.

"There, there my sweet girl. Everything will turn out fine. You wait and see." Her tears subsided, but her face looked blotchy and sad.

"I love you like a daughter, Eva. And I want you to know that I think you and Karl would make a fine match, but you must take things slowly. Remember what I've said and be careful. Time always finds a way for a right idea to unfold."

They sat a while until she came to grips with herself.

"I do have some good news," he said. "The cottage has been sold, as well as all your father's paintings." He gave her an envelope of paper bills. "A bank is the best place for such a large amount of money. Until then I suggest you sew a pocket in your shift to keep the money safe."

"After your mother died, your father, God rest his soul, instructed me to put your name as sole beneficiary to the cottage and his paintings, so all this money is now yours."

She held the envelope as if it were a wounded bird and did not open it. She was thinking of her sister.

"I had planned to give Ingrid half of everything. Would I be betraying Papa's wishes by doing that?"

"The money is yours to do with as you see fit," he advised, "but, keep in mind, that you were the one left behind to care for your mother and father, so you deserve to keep most of it."

"I'm worried about Ingrid," said Eva. "I received a letter from Olle saying that she had been sick, lost her memory and was unable to write. He said she was getting better, but since then I've written two letters with no response."

"I'm sorry to hear that," said Mr. Kronberg. "I wouldn't worry too much. Most men aren't very good at letter writing. I'm sure he's been busy trying to keep the family together."

That night in the dining room Karl's eyes met hers briefly once or twice while she served the simple supper meal. The absence of his usually engaging smile made him look tired and preoccupied with his own thoughts, almost as if he was avoiding her. Perhaps someone had given him a warning, too, and this was his way of being careful. After the meal was finished, she cleared away the dirty dishes and went back to the kitchen. When she returned with the coffee, there were maps, papers and various brochures strewn across the table.

She heard Mr. Lindholm tell his wife the trip would be extended two weeks longer to include seminars on making cheese and visits to goat farms in Italy and Switzerland.

"You always wanted to see the Alps. Perhaps you might meet us there." Anders was excited at the prospect, but Augusta turned her nose up at the idea.

"No thanks. Climbing up some steep mountain to see a herd of stupid goats isn't my idea of having a good time."

"I was thinking you might meet us in Zurich for a trip to the museum, take in a play or go to a concert," he replied, deflated by her flippant reaction. Seeing a play or attending a concert was very appealing, but Augusta had more pressing matters to take care of while the men were away and disregarded his invitation.

Eva refreshed everyone's coffee and brought in dessert. She couldn't get out of her head a picture of Mrs. Lindholm climbing a rocky ledge in her satin gown and high-heeled shoes, surrounded by a herd of curious mountain goats. This caused her to slop a few drops of Karl's coffee into his saucer. When she attempted to replace it with a clean one, his hand brushed hers and she saw the familiar tenderness in his eyes again.

"I don't need a new saucer, Eva." His voice was so calm and caring as he looked up at her; he might just as well have said, "I love you."

Augusta picked up on this tender exchange and told Eva she was dismissed for the evening. Karl, not wishing to make an issue of what happened, began discussing the proposed cheese factory. His mother, then, turned her negative comments toward him.

"Where do you get all these newfangled ideas, Karl? First it was those mechanical milking machines and then that crazy idea of breeding cows with tubes of semen. What do they call that disgusting procedure?"

Karl, who was already perturbed with his mother, answered slowly, enunciating each syllable of the two words.

"Ar..ti..fi..cial in..sem..in..a..tion."

She glared at his insolence, but then ignored it.

"So much simpler to use the bull and I'm certain that he would agree with me. Not very exciting for him, and frustrating, too, to see all those attractive cows in the next pasture and never having a chance with them."

Anders smiled at his wife's off-color joke, but Karl thought it crude and was glad Eva was not there to hear it.

Augusta wasn't finished yet. "How much is this cheese factory going to cost?" She didn't give anyone else a chance to answer. "Don't get me wrong. I love cheese, but isn't it easier and cheaper just to drive to Gothenburg and buy it like we've always done before?"

In desperation Mr. Lindholm looked at his wife, then carefully folded up the maps, collected the papers and brochures and put them in his briefcase. He excused himself from the table, picked up his coffee cup and asked Karl to join him in the study.

Augusta didn't look so imposing now.

"Good night, mother." said Karl politely, observing how insignificantly small she seemed, sitting alone in the big dining room, somewhat like a naughty child left in the corner as punishment for some wrongdoing.

Karl had much to tell Eva about the forthcoming trip, so after leaving his father's study he stopped by the kitchen. He was surprised to see the light still on and thought it odd that Johanna was sitting at the long table reading. She looked up, as if caught in a wrongful act, her cheeks, puffed out like a gorging chipmunk, as she tried to hide a piece of cake behind her book. Proceeding to Eva's room was now out of the question, so Karl looked under a covered container in the middle of the table, grabbed a large slice of chocolate cake and went to his room.

That night Augusta was already in bed writing in her diary

when Anders came to bed. She had finished her entry long ago, the diary being merely a prop, an excuse to be awake so she might have a serious discussion with her husband. She'd sat for an hour or more thinking about her son and Eva, so when Anders slipped under the covers, she was ready to talk.

"Did you see how they looked at each other?" she asked.

"Who are you talking about?"

"Karl...didn't you notice how he looked at Eva tonight at the dinner table?"

"Not really. I guess I was too busy eating," he said

"Karl's future depends on the woman he marries," she stated. "He must keep his sights high and marry an intelligent, fashionable girl of his own class who will be an asset to him, and not a simple peasant girl whose innocence and inexperience will cause him unhappiness and debt."

"Who said anything about marriage? Karl can look at anyone he wants to as far as I'm concerned."

"Well, he should be looking at girls of his own status. I was thinking we should have a party this weekend for the young folks."

"You can't force love on anyone, Augusta."

"I'm not forcing anything. It's sort of like going to the dress shop and picking out the gown you like best."

"I wouldn't know about that," he said.

"All we need do is to invite all our friends who have young girls his age and let Karl choose for himself."

"You know how Karl is. He rarely shows up for parties. Anyway, I think Karl has already made his choice," replied Anders.

"Well, that has got to change. I want you to have that little talk with him tomorrow before things really get out of hand." Anders sighed and rolled over to face the wall. "Did you hear me, Anders?"

"Yes, dear. I heard you."

Augusta put her diary on the table and turned off the lamp. She wasn't a bit sleepy. Anders hadn't thought much about the party idea, so she lay for a long time thinking of other ways to keep Eva and Karl away from each other.

Augusta's Evil Scheme

Years ago Anders had spoken to both of his sons about not getting physically involved with a girl, an embarrassing little talk that he felt must be voiced to young boys. Gunnar had rolled his eyes as if abstinence was a thing of the past, but Karl had readily agreed with him. He was four years younger at the time and his red face had shown his embarrassment. Up until then, breeding was something he thought was done only between bulls and cows.

In order to satisfy his wife and spend a few harmonious days at home before sailing for Copenhagen, Anders decided to have the man-to-man talk with Karl that he knew his wife expected of him. Augusta knew immediately this had transpired. She had passed Karl in the hall and he had completely ignored her good-morning greeting, walking by quickly with his head down as if in deep thought. In the following days she observed much restraint between Eva and her son. In fact they quite ignored each other in the breakfast and dining rooms, and she saw no sign of them being together anywhere else, and neither had Johanna.

Anders couldn't remember now the exact words he'd said to Karl, but it was mostly about using restraint. At the end he had put his hand firmly on his son's shoulder. "It is good that we will be away from here for a while," he said, "You'll be able to concentrate on other things and come back with a clear head."

Karl hadn't responded, except for a polite nod, and then walked slowly across the room as if he had just been beaten. Anders had wanted to run after his son, hold and comfort him as he had done when Karl was a young boy and had fallen and severely cut his leg. The wound had taken a long time to mend and he still had a long scar on his shin. Hopefully Karl would get through all this without it leaving a permanent mark in his life. Anders wanted to tell his son to forget what they had talked about and just to follow his heart and let the future take care of itself, but Augusta had come through the door at that moment and broken his train of thought.

Concern creased her husband's face. She attempted to cheer him up by wrapping her arms around his neck, giving him a peck on the cheek and making promises for later that night. Anders had stood stiff and unresponsive, his hands to his side leaning against his desk.

"I need a drink," he said, brushing her off. He poured himself a shot of whiskey and stood silently by the window. He was ignoring her, she thought, but he would get over it. He always did. She smiled triumphantly to herself and said she was going to the breakfast room.

Haying season was in full swing and several days of warm, dry weather kept Karl busy in the fields supervising the mowing, raking and gathering of hay. He often arrived at suppertime so tired that once he dozed off with his fork in hand. No amount of hard work could erase the picture in his mind of Eva's lovely smiling face. It didn't matter if he was laboring all day in the hayfield or lying in bed at night so fatigued that every muscle in his body ached, the excitement and passion of that Midsummer evening constantly flashed through his mind. It wasn't easy to deny himself the pleasure of holding Eva in his arms and making love to her again, but he would not break his promise to his father. For now he could only wait until the end of August.

Eva often saw him leaving on the empty wagon and returning with a full load of hay, his silhouette high on the stack moving slowly against the landscape of sky and hills until disappearing into the barn. She, too, plunged herself into doing extra chores about the kitchen, often rewashing the glassware and fine china that Olga had done unsatisfactorily, or sometimes scrubbing the kitchen floor over again. Keeping her hands busy lessened the heavy pain in her heart.

Eva had been the one who ran out to the field with cold water and a noontime lunch for the men, but no more. Cook explained that after Midsummer, Mrs. Lindholm had drawn up a new set of kitchen rules. That job had now fallen to Olga

"Looks as though Olga will be doing most of the outside chores," she said. Eva looked through the list. From now on she wouldn't be bringing up the milk and cream, gathering vegetables or picking berries. However, she would be allowed to pick flowers from the gardens on the lawn and arrange them for the dining room tables. There was a note on the bottom of the page for Cook that said, 'Eva's spare time can be spent learning how to prepare basic meals and doing other kitchen work."

"I get the message," said Eva. "That's her way of preventing me from accidentally coming in contact with Karl."

"Looks like that to me, too," said Cook. She winked at Eva. "Don't worry. If Karl wants to see you, he'll find a way."

"He's too busy now with the haying to think about anything else," said Eva. "Sometimes he can barely hold his eyes open at suppertime."

"Karl's a good worker, no doubt about that," said Cook. She looked up at the clock. "And if I don't get to work there won't be anything to eat tonight."

Karl never wandered into the kitchen anymore and rarely made eye contact with her at mealtimes. Sometimes she could not help but glance at him now and then sitting at the table, his shirtsleeves rolled carefully up to his elbows revealing his strong muscular arms, tanned from the summer sun, his handsome face a rich bronze against the whiteness of his shirt. She loved the casual look of the farmer in him and her stomach knotted up with the pain of wanting him so much.

It was uncanny how Mrs. Lindholm could time her arrivals to the breakfast and dining rooms to coincide precisely with the exact moment that Karl walked in from the fields. Eva realized this was not merely happenstance; it was clearly an intentional act to prevent any private conversation between the two of them.

Augusta had been spending a lot of time in her pink chair lately.

She was there one day when Johanna came in to dust. They discussed books for a while and then the subject of Karl and Eva came up.

"Men are so impractical when it comes to women...always motivated by a pretty face and that bit of plumpness under their blouse," said Augusta.

"When you say ***men***, are you referring only to Karl or to men in general."

"Don't mince words with me, Johanna. What difference does it make?" Johanna continued with her dusting and didn't answer.

"Well?" said Augusta impatiently, "Tell me what you're thinking. I know there's something on your mind." Johanna had worked for Mrs. Lindholm for a very long time and Augusta usually knew what Johanna was thinking even before Johanna did herself.

"I was thinking that it might not only be Karl you should be worrying about."

"Don't keep me waiting. I know there's something you want to say, so tell me now!"

Johanna leaned on the wall for support, holding two armfuls of books as if they might protect her, all the while trying to find words that would not upset her mistress.

"You haven't forgotten about the time Mr. Lindholm and Eva were dancing in the hall, have you?"

"No, I haven't forgotten that. Is there something more I should know?"

"Well...I...I've seen them talking...Mr. Lindholm and Eva. They were sitting in the breakfast room, drinking coffee together just like old friends."

Augusta stood up quickly and turned around to face Johanna. "And when was that?" she asked in a loud voice.

"Sometime last spring...um...when you had those sick headaches and I had to go down to the kitchen to get your breakfast tray."

"So it was more than just one time?"

"...Maybe a few times," said Johanna.

"Maybe more than just a few times?"

"Maybe."

First it was Karl...and now her husband! Augusta was enraged, and more determined now than before to find a way to be rid of Eva.

"We've got to do something!"

"We?" replied Johanna backing into a shelf and knocking over several books.

"Yes, you are the only one I have to turn to now. My husband must be shown a more unfavorable side of Eva, some disgraceful attribute or incident that he would find not so...charming." Augusta waited impatiently while Johanna straightened up the books.

"Are you thinking?" she asked.

"Yes, ma'am, but I don't think Eva has any disgraceful attributes...except for that time in the barn."

"Don't remind me of that, Johanna. We've got to plan some kind of scheme, some unfortunate situation where Eva will feel pressured to leave of her own accord."

Johanna saw the sinister look on Augusta's face. "I'll try to come up with something," she said, and went back to dusting the shelves.

Augusta came upon the solution to her dilemma quite accidentally the next morning when her emerald earrings were missing. After Augusta feverishly hunted for over half an hour, Johanna arrived to help her dress, but she couldn't find them either.

"Do you think someone stole them?"

"That is quite possible," said Augusta. Stealing was something she hadn't thought of until now.

It was while brushing Augusta's hair that Johanna snickered.

"What on earth is so funny, Johanna."

"I found your earrings, ma'am."

"You did? Where are they?" Johanna didn't answer right away. She was thinking how best to tell her mistress.

"Well? I'm waiting!" said Augusta, sternly.

"They're…they're hanging on your ears, ma'am."

Augusta had a moment of feeling very foolish, but already an idea had developed in her head, a plan in which she would accuse Eva of stealing.

"You, Johanna, will hide my diamond brooch in Eva's bureau, perhaps under some clothes in the bottom drawer. But we will have to wait until after Karl and his father leave on their trip. That way there won't be so many questions. They won't learn about her departure until they come home, and Eva will be long gone by then."

"But where will she go?" asked Johanna.

"I haven't decided on that yet, but I think Mats is leaving for America this summer. I'm sure my old contacts with the shipping company could arrange for Eva to sail on the very same ship as he is."

"Will he agree to that?" asked Johanna.

"Mats will have no choice in the matter. I can handle him." Johanna should have known that, but there was still one question that bothered her.

"And what will Karl think when he returns and finds Eva has gone to America with her old friend?"

"She's a thief, Johanna. Knowing that, Karl wouldn't be interested in finding her. However, if he is curious I'll just suggest that something serious might have happened between them. Eva and Mats are old friends…maybe even more than just friends, if you know what I mean."

"I see," replied Johanna. "But the whole idea sounds very complicated to me."

"Don't be so pessimistic, Johanna. Just think of this as an exciting game of intrigue and mystery, like one of those romantic novels you like to read. Only this will be so much better because you will actually be one of the characters in my little plot." Augusta was excited, but Johanna was nervous, troubled by doubt and anxiety, worrying how this would all turn out and if she could safely do her part in this evil scheme.

The Ring

Karl and his father left early after a hurried breakfast on the eighth of July. Eva stood in the breakfast room that overlooked the lush green lawns and gravel driveway. The morning sun glanced on the rear window as the car slowly moved away, but she could see no one inside. Mrs. Lindholm stood on the cobblestone walk fervently waving a white handkerchief.

Karl had looked tired at breakfast, quiet and subdued, sipping his hot coffee and then gazing into its blackness as if hoping to see a glimpse of the future. His father had done most of the talking, interrupted occasionally by his mother, but he'd heard little of it. He was preoccupied by his own thoughts.

When it was time to leave, he let his parents pass through the door before him. He watched them walk down the hall and turned to Eva, who had already begun to clear the dirty dishes from the table. He looked incredibly handsome walking toward her in his trim black trousers, the collar of his white shirt still unbuttoned and a striped tie hanging askew around his neck. How blond his hair was, bleached sandy white by the sun, but his tanned face was serious and determined, as if he had something on his mind.

"Did you forget something?" she asked.

"Not really," he said, placing his jacket on the table. "It was my intention to see you alone." He took her hand and put a ring on her finger. The ring was too loose, so he placed it on her middle finger. "This ring belonged to my grandmother...my father's mother. She gave it to me before she died and told me to give it to someone who appreciated beautiful things, so I want you to have it...something to remember me by until we see each other again." The center stone was an oval of rich, deep pink encircled with brilliant white gems.

"Are these diamonds?" she asked, thinking the ring too expensive for her to wear.

"They are," he said. "The large stone is called Alexandrite in honor of Alexander the second, Czar of Russia. It is unique in that it changes color depending on the light." When he brought her to the window the stone turned a beautiful shade of emerald green.

"It is beautiful," she exclaimed, "but I can't accept such an expensive ring."

From down the hall came Mrs. Lundberg's shrill voice. "Hurry up, Karl, or you're going to miss the ship."

"It would please me to know you are wearing my ring. It is said the stone inspires love." Then he smiled down at Eva, that familiar, charming grin that had been absent these past long weeks. "I love you," he said. Then he gave her a brief, tender kiss, releasing her for one last look, as if committing to memory every inch of her beautiful face.

"Thank you, Karl. I love you, too. I won't take it off until I see you again."

"Promise?"

"I promise."

"Are you coming Karl?" came that same shrill voice down the hall.

Eva was aware of the ring for the rest of the day, always careful not to bump it against the sink, counters, table or anything else that might mar its beauty. Looking at the ring eased her mind and helped fill the gnawing pain in her stomach, but the night was long and empty knowing she would not see Karl until the middle of August.

Augusta's Scheme Unfolds

Cook noticed the ring immediately, but didn't ask any questions. When she put the events of the day together, she guessed what probably had happened and knew that, given the right amount of time, Eva would eventually tell her all about it.

Three days later Augusta ordered a gathering of all the servants in the breakfast room, told them to sit down and proceeded to deliver some startling news.

"My diamond brooch is missing. Has anyone seen it?"

Everyone looked at one another in grim silence as Mrs. Lindholm walked around the table shaking her closed fan over each cowering head. All maids were present, except for Johanna, who was mysteriously absent.

"Whoever is responsible for its disappearance should confess immediately or there will be trouble for all of you." They sat in disbelief, young boys and girls, and even Cook, each one growing more suspicious of the others as the minutes ticked away.

"Well, now, my diamond brooch just didn't get up and walk away by itself, did it?" she said flamboyantly, tapping her fingernails on the table. They all shook their heads in agreement.

Augusta continued walking around the room enjoying her theatrical moment, waving her fan more aggressively and feeling a great sense of power. "I'm waiting," she said, looking with stern eyes at each fear-filled face, threatening them as a lawyer might cross-examine a criminal.

"One of you is a thief! And you are making this very difficult and stressful for both me and the others, so speak up right now!" Augusta felt perspiration on her upper lip, between her breasts and the small of her back, and fanned herself vigorously. Of course, no one stood up to confess because each thought another was the guilty one. The minutes seemed like hours and at some point Johanna had sneaked into the room and taken a seat by the door.

Finally Augusta brought her interrogation to a close. "It's much too hot to stand here all day. If the guilty one doesn't confess, then I will have to search all of your rooms."

If a vote was taken, bashful Olga would have been chosen as the guilty one, she being the newest employee and an odd one at that. She felt their stares and looked down nervously at her twiddling thumbs, then sobbed uncontrollably into her apron.

Cook glared at Augusta and put her arm around the girl's shoulders. In all her years working at the Lindholm's, this was the first time anyone had been accused of stealing. There was something amiss here and she was hard-pressed to keep from speaking her mind, but she would have been a fool to speak up to Mrs. Lindholm.

"Well, you leave me no alternative than to begin the search right now," said Augusta, closing her fan with a quick flick of her wrist. "Since Eva's room is closest, we'll begin looking there." Eva was relieved to be first. Perhaps she'd be allowed to remain in her room afterwards.

Johanna took her time looking here and there, under the mattress, in back of the mirror, and behind a picture on the bureau, just as her mistress had instructed her to do. Then Johanna opened the top drawer and then the next until she reached the bottom one. No one was more surprised than Eva to see Johanna turn around with the diamond brooch in her hand.

Astonished faces whirled around her, a dizzying array of surprise, condemnation and disbelief. Feeling faint, Eva stumbled to her bed and sat on the old, worn quilt. Augusta held the diamond brooch for all to see, her little scheme ending even better than she'd expected. "You may all go back to work now," she ordered, waving her hand in a grand flourish. She, too, was in a hurry to get out of the little hot and stuffy bedroom.

"I'll deal with you later, Eva." Then she turned on her heels and left the room with Johanna trailing close behind. Cook had lagged behind the rest and sat down beside Eva, putting her arms around the trembling girl.

"I didn't take that brooch. I would never steal…never…never."

"Now, now…" said Cook, stroking Eva's hair. "I know you wouldn't steal a crumb from a fly. You're a good girl." Eva leaned her head against the softness of Cook's ample chest and wept. Cook tried to sooth her with comforting words, but Eva was thinking of Karl, who was hundreds of miles away. He would believe her innocence. If he was here he would get to the bottom of this mess and find the true culprit.

"The best thing to do now is to get back to work. No sense sitting around making yourself feel worse," said Cook.

"I can't face Mrs. Lindholm...not after she accused me of being a thief!" sobbed Eva.

"Well, you aren't a thief. I know that, you know that and I'm sure Olga agrees."

"Do you think she will send me away?

"Where can you go that Karl won't be able to find you?" said Cook. "Probably all this will be forgotten by the time Karl and his father return, so I wouldn't waste time worrying about it." Cook didn't believe her own words, but Eva did, and they went back to the kitchen.

"We'll make something extra special for dessert tonight. Nothing like a bit of sweet to take away the sour. Chocolate cake always makes me feel better. How about you?"

"Yes, I like chocolate, too," said Eva. She wasn't the least bit hungry, nor did she have any desire for making a cake.

Meanwhile, Augusta sat in the parlor sharing a triumphant moment with Johanna. "I think my little plan was a great success, don't you?"

Johanna just nodded. In the excitement of playing her part in this devious scheme, she hadn't foreseen how this deception would affect everyone, especially Eva. In retrospect she felt weighed down with twinges of guilt.

Noticing Johanna's reluctance to join in her little celebration, Augusta attempted to make her feel better.

"I want to congratulate you for doing an exceptional job hiding the brooch and pretending to look for it. You are quite the little actress." Praise will lift anyone's spirits and soon Johanna was feeling better about herself. After all, she rationalized, it was her duty to obey and please her mistress, which was exactly what she had done.

"What's to become of Eva?" she asked after a while.

"Don't be concerning yourself with that. I'll take care of everything." Then she cautioned Johanna. "Just remember, this is our little secret. Give me your word that you will never tell anyone."

"I'm guilty of hiding the brooch. Why would I tell anyone?" said Johanna.

"Give me your word!" shouted Augusta.

Out of excuses, Johanna slipped her hands under her apron and crossed her fingers. "I will never tell anyone."

Augusta was never so glad to see anyone then when Mats showed up at the door two days later.

"You don't know how timely your arrival is," she told him as she reached up to give him a fond hug. "I've been trying to ring up your father to see when you were leaving, but no one answered the phone."

"He probably isn't home and mother is afraid of all these newfangled inventions, especially the annoying telephone that rings all by itself." Augusta remembered meeting his mother once and was not impressed. "Personally I love the telephone. Couldn't live without it."

"My ship leaves this afternoon, so I can't stay for more than two or three hours," Mats said. Augusta wrote down the name of the ship, time of departure and expected destination.

"I've only come to say goodbye. Is Mr. Lindholm here?" Mats was disappointed to learn that he and Karl had left for an extensive trip.

"I have a few things to take care of," said Augusta. Why don't you go into the study, help yourself to a drink and relax until lunchtime." Mats looked at his watch. It was a little after ten o'clock. "Sounds good to me," he said.

Augusta would have preferred a few days notice, but it was still morning and she had plenty of time to call the shipping office and reserve a ticket for Eva.

She said nothing about this to Mats. Neither he nor Eva were to know about her plan until the very last minute. Only Johanna knew, of course; it was she who would inform Eva to put on her best dress and be in the dining room by eleven o'clock. Then, while Eva was having dinner, Johanna would go to her room, pack all her belongings and put them in Mats' automobile.

When Augusta told Cook that Mats would be having lunch and that Eva would be joining them, Cook had her doubts about Olga serving in the dining room. Hopefully, all the girl would need was a cleanly washed face, a freshly ironed apron and a little guidance.

Nothing could have come together more smoothly. Eva looked beautiful in her blue dress, and Mats' good humor put everyone at ease. Augusta was jubilant watching Mats and Eva chatting about old times and thinking she was actually doing both of them a favor by bringing them together again. So what if Mats intended to marry that Jenny Almgren. He'd be better off without her. She was happy-go-lucky and always keeping her eye out for a better catch. Eva and Mats had a lot more in common, living in the same northern village and being childhood friends...and probably more than 'just friends.' Eva would settle him down and make a good wife and mother. Many a romance had been rekindled on a sail across the Atlantic.

At first Eva was uncomfortable sitting beside Mrs. Lindholm and being served by inattentive and clumsy Olga. Her mistress hadn't shown any signs of displeasure when Olga slopped soup on the tablecloth, filled the coffee cups to overflowing, and knocked over Mats' water glass. In fact, Mrs. Lindholm seemed a bit too cheery and obnoxiously friendly to both Mats and Eva, who was finally able to relax and enjoy Mats' jokes and conversation...until Mrs. Lindholm looked suspiciously at Eva.

"That ring looks vaguely familiar. Where did you get it?" Mrs. Lindholm had the same accusing look as when Johanna had found the lost brooch in Eva's bedroom.

"It was a gift," said Eva nervously.

"Let me see," she said, taking Eva's hand and inspecting the stones. "Oh, it's the wrong color. My mother-in-law had a ring with the same setting, only the center stone was green.

Apparently Augusta had seen Ander's mother wearing the

ring only in sunlight and wasn't aware of the color change. Eva was very much relieved.

After dessert was served, Mrs. Lindholm cleared her throat and stood up as if she was about to make a speech. She looked at Mats and then at Eva.

"I have a wonderful surprise for you Eva. I've made arrangements for you to go to America with Mats." Eva's fork slipped from her hand and clinked loudly against the fine china plate. Mats stopped chewing and swallowed his mouthful of pie in one gulp. Instantly, everything came together for Eva. Her intuitions had been correct. This special occasion was merely a facade, an easy way for Mrs. Lindholm to discretely banish her, not only from this house, but from Sweden as well. In the vast country of America Karl would never find her.

With her hands in her lap Eva fondled Karl's ring and remembered the promise she'd made. How could she leave him without saying goodbye? What would he think when he came home and she was gone? Cook was the only one she could trust. She had to get back to the kitchen and tell her of this absurd plan and give her Ingrid's address so that Karl would know where to find her. She had to act quickly, while there was still time.

"Well, I should probably go pack my things," she said, rising from her chair. Eva had taken only one step toward the kitchen when she felt Mrs. Lindholm's firm grasp on her arm.

"Everything has been taken care of, my dear," she said. "Your belongings are all packed and waiting for you in Mats' car." Right away she whispered in Eva's ear. "Under the circumstances...and I'm sure you know what I'm referring to...this is the perfect opportunity for you to leave here with no questions asked. If you do as I say, nothing will be said about the real reason for your sudden departure. Do you understand?"

"Yes ma'am," said Eva, looking down at the rug.

Then in a kinder voice that Mats could hear, Mrs. Lindholm addressed her again. "This will be a lovely chance for you to see your sister again and make a new life for yourself."

Eva tried to smile, but everything was moving too fast and

the room seemed to be crumbling around her. Surely no letter she wrote to Karl would ever reach him. His mother would undoubtedly be inspecting all incoming mail very carefully after this...and what excuse would she give Karl? That she had willingly gone to America with her old friend Mats? Would he believe her? Her eyes welled up with tears and she blinked to hold them back.

"My dear, I know how unhappy you've been lately. Surely this is the chance of a lifetime, don't you agree, Mats?" Mats didn't know Eva had been unhappy, but he agreed and pushed his chair back.

"Well, it's getting late," he said. "We should be on our way."

Mats accepted Eva's company without controversy. In fact, he thought it would be fun to have an attractive woman on his arm while aboard ship. She felt as if she were in a dream, everything moving in slow motion as Mats guided her out of the breakfast room. She couldn't feel her legs, as she drifted back down the same hall where she had come almost a year ago, those same bleak portraits glaring down at her in condemnation, like judges pronouncing her guilt and sentencing her to a lifetime of misery.

At the end of the hall they passed by the large mirror and she saw their reflection. Gone was the shy country girl and carefree Mats who had swung her round and round and made her laugh. Then the wide front door opened and they walked down the stairs to the car.

The last thing Eva heard was Mrs. Lindholm's sharp voice. "Have a wonderful trip, you two." Eva didn't look back.

Through the open window came a soft, cool breeze. Eva had the strange feeling of being uncontrollably swept away from everything she knew and loved, an unsuspecting leaf suddenly torn away from its branch, tossing aimlessly in the wind...to be suddenly dropped in an unfamiliar place. It was summertime, but there was neither light nor warmth in her heart. She felt only the gloom and cold of winter.

America

1934 – 1935

Farewell to Sweden

Eva remembered little of the ride to Gothenburg. She'd seen it all before and the voice in her head was Karl's, even though it was Mats doing all the talking. Closing her eyes, she pretended Karl was sitting at the wheel.

After a while Mats stopped asking questions, amusing himself by repetitive humming that caused Eva to doze on and off. His plan had been to sail to America alone, attend architectural school there and marry Jenny Almgren. Today, he had merely stopped in to say goodbye to the Lindholms and had been stunned to see Eva sitting beside her employer, Augusta Lindholm, as if they were old friends and not maid and mistress. Eva's pale face and the gleam in Augusta's eye immediately told him that something was amiss, but it wasn't until this most unusual meal was over that he learned of Augusta's plan.

Mats found it odd that Eva seemed more surprised than he upon hearing she would be accompanying him on the voyage to America. After a stern warning from Mrs. Lindholm, Eva had reluctantly agreed, although she seemed distraught and very confused. Something serious had happened between these two, but so far Eva had not yet disclosed anything. In fact, she had barely spoken to him since that rather bizarre noon meal.

He turned to look at her. She was facing the window and possibly asleep, her reddish hair neatly braided round her head. He could see the curve of her cheek and neck, peachy cream against the bluish neckline of her dress, and he could see the rounded curve of her bodice. She had become a woman since last summer. So shy she was then, always blushing at the least provocation. He had forgotten how beautiful she was, this backwoods daughter of his father's best friend whom he'd liked even as a child...and desired more than any other girl. But that was before he'd met Jenny, who had turned his head with her aristocratic upbringing, American education and modern lifestyle.

As vehicles passed him on the tarred road, he drove faster to keep up with the traffic, trying to replace thoughts of Eva with images of Jenny and what she might be doing in America at that very moment.

Eva opened her eyes. Mats was still humming as she gazed out the window, the sun flickering between the passing trees, showing briefly the hillsides, green with flecks of white, red and black: grazing cows and horses she remembered during her first ride to Gothenburg with Karl.

She had worn the same dress that she had on today, the dress Karl had given her as a thank you for helping deliver a calf back at the Lindholm farm. "I fell in love with Karl that day," she thought to herself, remembering his muscles bulging from beneath a rain-soaked shirt as he worked on the cow; seeing also the gentleness he showed toward mother and calf. Afterwards Karl had looked admirably into Eva's eyes, impressed with her help in such a difficult birth. He had put his hand around her shoulders and she'd felt their bodies touch. Then, like proud parents, they'd watched the little heifer nurse hungrily from her mother. It was then she had looked down at her soiled blouse and skirt, feeling such embarrassment, and had run back to the kitchen.

She smiled, remembering the night he had shyly knocked on her door with a large box in his arms; she with her hair down around her shoulders and dressed in a scanty little shift. He'd seemed nervous as he thanked her again, then hastily gave her the beautifully wrapped package and hurried back down the dark hall.

Her thoughts drifted back to Midsummer night... dancing with Karl to the fiddlers, drinking wine with him in the orchard and those unforgettable moments when she gave herself up to him in the haymow.

It struck her now that she might never again see her beloved Karl. She sat up straight in the seat and looked straight at Mats.

"Are you all right?" he asked. "Looks like you've just seen a ghost."

"I don't understand what happened today," she said. "I was

hoping all this was just a dream."

"Aye...I can hardly believe it myself, but I have a paper in my pocket to prove that a room on the ship is reserved in your name."

Eva rested her head back on the seat, closing her eyes to help stop the tears.

"So, it wasn't your idea to go to America?" he asked.

"I had no idea...no idea at all...and to think that someone else packed all my things. I hope they didn't forget anything"

"Very suspicious, if you ask me," he replied, hoping that she might explain more, but she was thinking again of Karl and what he would think upon arriving home from his trip to find her gone. Mrs. Lindholm had promised not to say anything to anyone about the stolen brooch if Eva did as she was told, but certainly Karl would ask why she went to America so suddenly without saying goodbye to him. What would Mrs. Lindholm tell her son? That Eva had had willingly gone to America with her old friend Mats Kronberg? She could not bear to think of Karl's reaction.

Eva wished she'd had time to speak with Cook...to inform her of the situation so Karl might know the truth. But Mrs. Lindholm had made certain that she talked with no one. At first her tears fell like a gentle spring rain, then the dark clouds exploded into a torrential deluge that wouldn't go away. "Where do all these tears come from? Is there no end?" she thought to herself.

Mats realized something bad had happened, but he didn't know what to do. He was always baffled when a woman cried, so he drove at a faster pace and concentrated on the thickening traffic.

A flutter of seagulls announced their arrival with friendly, high-pitched calls. Eva rubbed her eyes and watched the noisy gray birds settle single file along the top of a long sign that read GOTHENBURG PIER.

Mats eagerly jumped out of the car and removed several bags from the back seat, but Eva sat looking toward the busy dock.

Men, women and children walked toward the massive ship like a slow moving millipede crawling across a branch. The insightful insect would no doubt be guaranteed a leafy lunch, but would these humans be as certain of their safe voyage across the wide Atlantic? Eva shuddered at the thought and opened the car door, quickly covering her nose with her hand. Mats grinned at her.

"Don't like that good salt air blowing in from the ocean, Eva?"

"Smells like old rotting fish to me," she replied. Then she peered through the back seat window.

"Mama's wooden bridal chest...did you see it?" she asked hopefully.

"No chest...only these three bags and my two leather cases."

Eva leaned against the car and her hand impulsively went to her chest. She felt the familiar bulge under her bodice and breathed a sigh of relief. How thankful that she had done as Mr. Kronberg suggested and sewn a pocket in her shift to safely hold the money from her father's paintings and sale of their cottage. Pangs of longing returned when she looked down at the ring, now a beautiful sea green, her only tangible reminder of Karl.

"I've already sold the automobile," said Mats, putting the keys under the front seat. "My friend is coming to pick it up later." Excitedly, he put one of her bags under his arm and picked up his two leather cases. "Let's get in line. I'm anxious to go aboard, aren't you?"

Eva robotically followed him, dragging one bag that was too heavy to carry. She had a measure of hope that it contained everything that had been in the wooden chest.

She walked gingerly on the rickety wooden ramp. There were gaps between the worn rough boards, wide enough to reveal the dark abyss of murky water beneath her feet. It swayed gently, causing her to lose her balance.

"Don't look down," said Mats, grabbing her arm. "Keep your eyes focused on the ship."

She looked up at the immensity of the vessel, larger than the Lindholm's manor house, the black smokestacks looming wide and tall above the deck. What kept such a large ship afloat? Would it topple over during rough stormy seas? The ramp swayed again, bumping loudly against the ship, and the overwhelming fear of falling into the water returned. She knew how it was to get water up her nose. Ingrid had held her sister's head under water at the lake one time...long enough for Eva to lose her breath in a flood of water. The frightening memory came back to her now and she saw Ingrid's laughing face. Fortunately, her father had seen it all. He'd promptly held Ingrid under water just long enough for her to flail her arms. Ingrid hadn't thought it was so funny then and never held Eva under water again. The memory put Eva in a better humor.

"What are you smiling about?" asked Mats. Then she lost her balance again.

"I'll tell you later," she said, looking toward the deck at a yellow-skinned couple talking to a man in uniform.

Many passengers were aboard and had already congregated in little groups along the railing. Some appeared lost and afraid, while others waved happily to friends or family standing on the dock, all with their own reasons for going to America. Laughing children raced back and forth along the promenade and their confidence gave Eva some comfort, but it wasn't until she felt the solidity of the highly polished deck beneath her feet that she felt more secure. Looking over the railing made her woozy, so she started to walk across the deck.

"Hold on young lady, I have to check your credentials." A uniformed man motioned for her to stand in line. After he checked Mats' ticket and gave him directions to his cabin, his manner grew more heated. The man occasionally dropped his head, looking over his eyeglasses toward Eva and studying a paper in his hand.

"Gunderson? There's no Eva Gunderson listed here."

"Augusta Lindholm called today to reserve a room," said Mats. "Perhaps I should go to the Captain's quarters."

"Oh...a late arrival?" The man squinted at the stylish woman who now stood before him. "Let me see now," he said, fishing in his pocket to examine a small piece of paper. "Ah, yes...Gunderson, Eva, Room 8 bottom deck." He looked up again. "You don't look like a chambermaid to me."

"She's not a chambermaid, sir," said Mats bluntly. "She's traveling with me."

"Well, late arrivals have to take what they can get." He gestured to his left. "Go down those stairs and someone can direct you to the servants' quarters."

Mats was about to object when Eva put her hand on his arm. "Let's go," she said. "As long as there is a bed to lie down on, I don't care where my room is."

Mats unlocked the door of a dark, windowless room, a ghostly white lampshade the only visible object. He turned on the lamp and placed her bags by the small bed. He thought the furnishings too simple and meager, with only a small table sitting between the bed and a threadbare upholstered chair...a worn hand-me-down from one of the upstairs cabins, no doubt. Eva wasn't used to luxury, at least not for herself, and wished only to unpack her things and lie down to let loose her bottled-up tears.

"I think I'll stay here while you find your room," she told him.

"Come with me," he said eagerly. "We need to find a good place to stand when the ship leaves. It will be our last view of Sweden." She could not say no to his pleading eyes.

They joined other passengers on deck and watched the waterfront activities. A few patient Swedes were still waiting to board as busy workmen shouldered bundles, bags and heavy trunks up the ramp. Rambunctious children darted back and forth playing tag or hide and seek.

Eva noticed a plump young boy leaning against a wooden post, stuffing himself with cookies from a paper bag. A curious, scrawny yellow dog sniffed by his feet picking up crumbs, occasionally looking up to the boy for a more substantial treat. Eva felt a twinge as he kicked the dog away, but in so doing, the boy lost his balance and slipped off the dock, falling head over heels into the dark waters. Urgent cries for help sent two men into the water to save the thrashing boy. She didn't feel one bit sorry for him; he got what he deserved for kicking the little dog. The boy had dropped his bag of goodies and the watchful dog found them. She smiled as he proudly carried his bounty away from the dock, his head held high and tail wagging victoriously.

Once again she thought of Karl and was filled with an overwhelming emptiness. Even though Mats was by her side and hundreds of people milled around her on the deck, she had never felt so alone. Her hands gripped tightly on the railing. If she let go, she might find herself running back down the ramp to find Karl...to say all the words left unspoken. She, of course, knew this was a preposterous idea; Karl was in some far-off country by now and quite impossible to find. Eva's tears splashed on the wide wooden railing, trickling into the Swedish sea, a few drops of herself that would eventually wash up on Sweden's shore to remain there forever.

"Why so sad, Eva? You aren't missing Mrs. Lindholm already, are you?" joked Mats, putting his arm around her shoulders and hoping to learn more of her sudden departure. Eva wanted to tell him about Karl and about Mrs. Lindholm's accusations regarding the stolen brooch, but she was too embarrassed and said nothing. When the great engines fired up, the ship suddenly lurched sideways away from the dock, forcing her against Mats so that he held her more tightly. She laid her head against his chest and was comforted.

Across from the dock, rows of small souvenir shops, fish markets and food stalls were strung along the shore as far as she could see, dwarfed by much taller, weather-beaten warehouses behind them. Rising in the distance was the outline of Gothenburg's municipal buildings and the tall steeple of a cathedral. No mountains rose in the distance...no trace of fields or farm or the great forests beyond. Eva's stomach tightened with the realization that never again would she see the old familiar faces and places. Only the memories remained, tucked safely away in her heart like precious hidden jewels.

The buildings on the waterfront receded slowly as the ship

pulled away from the shore. Soon the whole of Gothenburg was a city in miniature, a toy city such as what a child might build with wooden blocks. Everyone remained on deck watching their Swedish homeland grow smaller and smaller until only a faint gray line separated the sea and the sky. And then in a blink it was gone. The sky, like a huge curtain, had suddenly dropped down to meet the sea, shutting them off from the old country, their relatives and friends. Some stood silently, as if mired in their past lives, while others smiled at each other hopefully. Children, unknowing what the future might hold, ran around shouting, their faces exuberant with expectation and the promise of adventure.

Eva was anxious for the privacy of her room, where she could lay down, close her eyes and bring all her memories into focus; she wanted to imprint a clear picture of Karl in her mind to preserve it forever before it, too, faded and slipped from view.

"Don't open your door to anyone, Eva," she heard Mats say as he put the key in her hand. "I noticed a bathing room down the hall. Other than that, don't go anywhere until we know our way around. I'll be back in an hour or so." Mats spoke as if she were but a little child. She locked the door and curled up on the little bed feeling more like a helpless newborn babe.

The dining room was much nicer than she had expected, bright and cheerful with a blue rug and yellow tapestry drapes framing large windows overlooking the sea, these blue and yellow Swedish colors predominated the room. Various sized tables were covered with white linen and set with plates of the same blue and yellow colors of the Swedish flag, while crystal goblets waited to be filled with pitchers of ice water. Eva and Mats sat at one of the smaller tables by a window overlooking the wide expanse of ocean. Small groups of watchful gulls circled around the ship. An old lady stood on the deck throwing crusts of bread over the rail and an occasional gull swooped down to grab a treat. Only one brave one landed on the deck, its dark eyes darting around suspiciously as he scrambled from one morsel to another, always keeping a safe distance from the woman.

"Seagulls don't seem as smart or sociable as the ravens back home," said Eva, remembering her father's pet raven.

"Birds are all the same to me," replied Mats. "I've shot a lot of ravens. They never seemed very smart to me."

"You killed ravens?" Eva glared at Mats, who immediately knew he'd spoken too quickly. Not having any brothers, Eva had no idea that shooting ravens was a young boy's sport, so Mats smoothed things over by explaining how flocks of ravens could ravish crops and he'd shoot into the air to scare them off. "Oh," she said softly, not entirely believing him, but wanting to think what he said was true.

Hot coffee was served with plenty of cream and sugar and a tempting basket of sticky nut buns was set between them. Mats ate three before the salads were brought. He ordered the meat entré, a thick slice of roast of beef, and Eva had a seafood casserole. Both were served with mashed potatoes and fresh green beans. Eva was surprised at herself...how very much at ease she was wearing the dress that Karl had given her. She felt confident and comfortable, her manners more than equal to any other woman there. Eva's keen observations of the Lindholm family and its many guests had paid off. How she wished it was Karl sitting across from her.

The same dark-haired man with yellow skin she'd seen earlier caught her eye from across the room and smiled. She quickly looked away and giggled.

"What's so funny?" asked Mats.

"That man...he has a long thin braid trailing down his back."

"Japanese men wear their hair like that. I've seen paintings of them in Stockholm."

"That woman sitting with him...she seems much younger than the man," observed Eva. "Do you suppose they are father and daughter?"

"Could be," said Mats. "But those Orientals all look the same to me."

"And I suppose us Swedes all look the same to them, too."

"Probably we do," said Mats, who, for the moment, could not take his eyes off the young Japanese girl whose shiny, long black hair hung beyond her waist.

The room grew loud with the chatter of guests and scraping of chairs as everyone found a place to sit. An atmosphere of festivity filled the room and for a while Eva was able to lose all feelings of confusion and sadness.

She and Mats walked around the promenade deck after dinner until the sun fell below the horizon, the ocean now an ominous sea of blackness. Eva looked around in fear as the ship appeared to move aimlessly across the smooth, dark water.

"How does a ship find the right way with no roads or signs to direct it?" she asked.

"I don't know, but I mean to ask the Captain and find out," he said.

"Perhaps the Captain uses the sun and moon to guide it," she surmised, glancing up at the almost full moon.

"I doubt that," said Mats. "How would he steer the ship on a cloudy day?"

Eva shuddered thinking about the ship drifting off in the wrong direction and possibly becoming lost during a bad storm. "I'm tired, Mats. I'd like to go back to my room."

Eva emptied the three bags onto the bed and began sorting out the clothes. They were badly wrinkled from being haphazardly jammed together with all her other belongings. She was very relieved to find most of the contents that had been stored in the wooden chest, the afghans her mother had made and the Norrland folk costume, plus all of the letters and photographs that Ingrid had sent. Wrapped in an old, blue wool skirt was the Carl Larsson painting that had hung on the wall of her old room, but those her father had painted were missing.

She smiled discovering her two favorite books in the bottom of the bag: *How to Learn English in Six Weeks,* and the book about farming and starting your own business in America that she'd borrowed from the Lindholm library. The second bag held everything that had been in the bureau, but the third bag was full of clothes she had never seen before. Were they some sort of peace offering from Mrs. Lindholm? There were two old-fashioned, dark-colored dresses, one black and one green, that would be wearable with a few alterations, a couple of blue skirts that would have to be taken in at the waist and several white blouses. Two pairs of ladies shoes had tumbled out and fallen on the floor. They were both loose on her feet, but with a little stuffing in the toe or heavy wool stockings they would do quite well.

Eva fell asleep with the English book in her hands, dreaming about crowds of white-, black- and yellow-skinned people boarding a large ship. They were pushing and shoving her toward the deck, shouting familiar English phrases she had been reciting out loud that very night. She saw Karl's face behind her on the shore and tried in vain to go back, but a great human wave swept her toward the ship. When she finally stood by the rail, Karl was gone. There was only the thin gray line of Sweden disappearing before her eyes. The crowds were gone, except for the oriental couple, who ushered her toward a long stairway. Down and down she went, faster and faster until she saw a door marked with a large ***Number 8.*** She awakened breathlessly, her heart pounding wildly in her chest.

The Oriental Couple

Mats and Eva fell into a comfortable routine, their more or less brother-sister relationship giving each a strong sense of confidence and safety. Mats made friends easily and on the second day the Japanese man, who introduced himself as Yoshi Kaneko, invited them to his table for dinner.

His companion's name was Sayuri, whose air of arrogance reminded Eva of a younger Mrs. Lindholm. Sayuri seemed to enjoy being the center of attention and had a much too high opinion of herself. Any further resemblance stopped there, for this girl was painfully thin, had yellowish skin and very long black hair. Eva mistrusted Sayuri's small, slanty eyes and the pouty, red lips that appeared to hold much of Mats' attention as he listened carefully to her every word.

Sayuri was on summer vacation from Uppsala University where she was studying the culture and language of Sweden. Eva found it very strange to hear Swedish words coming out of a Japanese mouth, but Mats was intrigued by this foreign woman's attention and charm. He sat in awe of her intelligence and wit, relishing the subtle compliments she made about his rugged Swedish handsomeness. Eva soon tired of her sugary comments in the same way that too much candy might make one sick.

Eva preferred the company of Mr. Kaneko. He seemed kind, was soft-spoken, and spoke very good Swedish and English. The long, thin braid that she had found amusing at first now made him look very distinguished and scholarly. He taught her common American phrases and tidbits of everyday life that Mr. Kronberg would not have known since he'd never been to America. However, both men had easy smiles and were good story tellers.

At first Eva was of the impression that they might be a student and teacher traveling together, but later she thought their relationship was closer than that, given the way Sayuri flirted with him just as she did with Mats and the many other men aboard ship. Or perhaps it was just her way.

Sayuri and Mr. Kaneko usually dined together, but they associated with separate friends between meals. Eva had observed Mats and Sayuri on occasion talking to each other on the deck and once she saw them upstairs disappearing around the corner of the hall that led to Mats' room. There were times, too, when Eva found herself exclusively in the company of Mr. Kaneko. He loved to talk and she was a good listener, eager to learn about his adventures in America and other countries.

He noticed her ring in the dining room one evening and thought it was a ruby, but the next day was surprised to see it was like an emerald, the most beautiful shade of green he'd ever seen.

"I've been admiring your Alexandrite ring. Do you know its origin?"

"By origin, do you mean who gave it to me?" she asked.

He inspected the ring carefully. "I'm sure whoever gave this ring to you must think you are very special because this particular stone is of superb quality." Eva nodded in agreement, but said nothing of Karl. Just thinking about him brought forth pangs of loneliness and she didn't want to cry in front of Mr. Kaneko.

"The first Alexandrite gems were found in the emerald mines of the Ural Mountains in Russia on Prince Alexander II's birthday," he told her. "When a miner later brought some 'so-called emeralds' back to the light of the campfire he was puzzled because the green stones were now red as rubies. The next day in the bright sunlight, the stones had mysteriously turned back to green again."

"It surely is magical how the colors can change so dramatically," she said.

"The gem is known to bring its wearer strength, good luck and love," he told her. "I would say you should find an even greater amount of strength, much good fortune and a deeper, more satisfying love because of the very intense color changes of this particular stone." She hoped what he said was true and she was comforted to think that perhaps someday she and Karl would be reunited.

Mr. Kaneko was an avid card player and after dinner one evening he invited Eva and Mats for a game of rummy. Swiftly the game changed to poker, which Mats was eager to learn. Eva was reluctant to part with any of her money and just watched. When Mats unfolded a wad of bills from his pocket Eva was shocked. She thought he should have been more careful about showing his bankroll in public, but it was obviously too late to say anything now. Mats lost a lot of his money the first hour, but later he had a winning streak and won back all of it and more besides. Mr. Kaneko was quite impressed.

"Perhaps you shouldn't bring all your money to the table," Eva suggested later on the promenade.

"What if I need it? Then I'd have to go all the way back to my room to get more."

"I just don't think it's a good idea to reveal to strangers how much money you have."

"Actually the money is safer with me. I wouldn't trust keeping it in my room," he replied. "Anyway money gives me power…and power makes a man play well and win at cards."

Mats was a bit of a show-off. Eva hoped he wouldn't have to pay later for his arrogance. "Well, if you change your mind, I'd be happy to keep it for you."

After breakfast Eva sometimes sat on one of the many lounge chairs with her sewing. The light was perfect for making alterations on the two dark-colored dresses. First, though, she would lean back and close her eyes, enjoying the warm sun on her face and arms. She'd think of Karl as she remembered him in the dining rooms and working in the fields. She saw them together in the orchard, in the milk room and in the hayloft on Midsummer Eve.

Her thoughts sometimes went to her sister. She hoped by now Ingrid had gotten her memory back. Did she remember Mama and Papa and her life back in Sweden? Did she have to learn all over again how to write, to cook and care for the children? Lastly, but most important of all, she hoped to be able to find her sister in the vast country of America.

Once she fell asleep in the chair, awakening to the sound of Mr. Kaneko's voice. Mats was sitting next to her and Mr. Kaneko was studying the palm of his hand.

"This is how I see your life played out in my mind. But remember, you have the power to change the future by making positive choices," he was telling Mats. "I suggest you be cautious and not give in to detrimental impulses or be swayed by conflicting forces." The seriousness in Mats' face concerned Eva at first, but then he shrugged it off as nothing.

"So you're awake at last," said Mats. "Want your fortune told?"

No, she didn't believe in fortune tellers. Mr. Kaneko was content to let it rest there, but Mats persisted.

"Come on, Eva, it's only a game." And when she returned to her sewing, he tempted her. "If you do, I have a surprise for you."

"What a tease you are, Mats. You know I can't resist surprises," she replied, holding her hands out toward Mr. Kaneko. He looked at one hand and then the other.

"I see struggles in your past and future. You will meet new obstacles along the way, but that is life. Problems come to us so that we may learn and grow stronger...stepping stones to perfection in this life or the next. Beyond these I see a long life of personal fulfillment and ultimate happiness."

Mr. Kaneko continued to hold her hand, comparing it with Mats'. Then he removed a small note pad from his vest pocket and began to draw lines and curves. "I see two rivers flowing side by side and they are a beautiful blue color. See here how straight and strong they are. You both must have grown up in good and proper families with happy childhoods. The rivers are close to each other, so I assume you might have lived in the same neighborhood." Mats was skeptical about all this and shrugged his shoulders. "That could be true of a lot of people."

"I'm just setting the scene...please let me continue," said the serious Mr. Kaneko.

"The river on the left represents your life, Mats, and this one on the right is yours, Eva. Notice how both rivers flow fairly straight and narrow until each widens into what appears to be a circle or pond. Both rivers have become sluggish and muddied, indicating confusion or indecision."

Eva nodded in agreement, but Mats still wasn't taking any of this to heart. He'd done mostly as he pleased and saw only good in his future.

"From here, Eva, your river runs fairly straight with only these few gentle curves. That is quite normal. Mats' river, on the other hand, appears to wallow in a pond of uncertainty before becoming a wide, straight river again. It seems you have both made positive decisions and moved on with your life. Further along the rivers almost touch each other, the sign of a chance meeting between the two of you, or perhaps that you are thinking about each other in a serious way." Mr. Kaneko looked up at Eva and Mats and couldn't resist smiling. Then his thin black eyebrows came together in a scowl and he cleared his throat.

"The rest is a mystery to me," he said, stalling for time. "See, Mats, how your river becomes narrow and turbulent, veering off sharply to the left?" Eva gasped as the pencil ran off the paper and she saw Mats' expression turn grim. Realizing he has been taken in by this silly game, Mats recovered immediately and made a joke of it.

"So, I drop off the face of the earth in a waterfall?"

"Not necessarily," replied Mr. Kaneko. "If you continue with your current mode of thinking you might encounter a waterfall," he said calmly. "As I said, you have the power to change and put things on a straight course again before any serious situation arises. It is all about your attitude and the choices you make."

Meanwhile Eva continued to follow her river in the drawing. Except for a few bends, her river flowed straight and wide in a northerly course to the top of the page.

Mats took all this in and Mr. Kaneko saw the concern in his face.

"You are a strong, healthy boy, Mats, so I'm sure all will turn out just fine. As I said before, you must control your negative impulses and focus on positive and realistic goals. Remember, you have the power to change the course of your life."

Mats shrugged his shoulders. He didn't believe that one's life could be told by lines on one's hand or rivers drawn on a piece of paper. His future looked very bright now; he had inheritance money from his father, architectural school waiting for him in America and a beautiful girl he intended to marry. Life couldn't be better.

"I say to you both: stretch your imaginations and discover what is really important to you. Nothing is impossible. Ask yourself: what do I feel passionate about? Then work diligently to bring this passion to fruition...and your lives will express fulfillment and joy."

"Thank you, Mr. Kaneko, for your wise words. I'll keep them in mind," said Mats, rising from his chair. Then he followed behind a group of giggling young women who had walked by seconds before.

"He's off to find his passion," said Eva with a chuckle.

"And what is your passion, young lady?" Mr. Kaneko asked curiously. "A smart girl like you must have a talent hidden away somewhere."

"I don't have a talent, really, although I do love to knit," she said after a moment. Then she remembered what she had decided while reading Chapter 5 in the Lindholm's library book about starting your own business by doing what you love most.

"I do have a dream in the back of my head," she admitted timidly.

"And what is your dream?"

"Someday. I'd like to have my very own yarn shop."

The oriental couple joined them for dinner that evening. It was then Eva remembered to ask Mats about the surprise he had promised her.

"I'd forgotten all about that," he replied. "There's a Masquerade Ball on Saturday night and I was hoping you'd go with me."

"I'd love to go, but I don't have a costume."

"You could wear one of my kimonos," suggested Sayuri, smiling sweetly from across the table. "Why don't you and Mats come to my room after dinner and pick one out?"

"What is a kimono?" asked Eva.

"It is difficult to describe," replied Sayuri. "Simply put, a kimono is a beautiful silk gown that Japanese women wear for special occasions."

Sayuri's room was on the upper deck and very elaborately furnished. Large seascapes hung on two of the cream colored walls. A large bed covered with a satin spread of pink and purple flowers, and matching pillows, took up the third wall. Above the bed hung a huge rectangular mirror that showed Eva's tentative reflection as she followed Mats across the room. Two pink, upholstered chairs stood on either side of a wide window overlooking the ocean. Mats immediately sat in one of them, looking very much at home. Eva wondered if he'd been here before.

Sayuri opened the door to a closet and laid several gowns neatly across the bed. They looked more like wide strips of embroidered satin to Eva; nothing like the gowns worn by guests at the Lindholm parties. There was one long strip of dark blue accompanied by a second strip of lighter blue. Another was pink with maroon.

Sayuri noticed the frown on Eva's face. "Perhaps you'd rather wear this white one with green stitchery depicting a dragon with matching panels of white and green." Then she wrapped the pieces around Eva's shoulders and waist. Eva was not impressed; she felt like a huge package that might come undone as soon as she took a step.

"This one suits you very well," said Sayuri. "Don't you think so, Mats?"

"Turn around so I can see the back," said Mats. When Eva attempted to take her normal stride, she nearly fell over.

"Just take tiny baby steps," said Sayuri, demonstrating with quick short steps across the room.

"We should probably cover your hair with a black scarf, don't you think?"

"You don't like my hair?" asked Eva.

"Your hair is very pretty, but I've never seen a geisha with red hair." Sayuri showed Eva a photograph of herself in a dark blue gown with a band of light purple around her waist, her black hair piled smoothly on the top of her head. "This was when I was in training as a geisha."

"Why is your face so white?" asked Eva.

"That is the geisha way." Then she wrapped Eva's head in

the black scarf and fastened it with a white silk flower. "There. Now all you need is some white powder and very red lipstick." When Sayuri was finished, she led Eva to the mirror. "What do you think?"

"That is me?" said Eva, her bright red lips forming the words in the mirror. She wrinkled her nose and blinked her eyes. She thought she looked like a clown, but didn't say so. She heard Mats snickering in the background. When Eva turned to scowl at him, he hid his face behind a magazine. "I'll have to think it over, Sayuri, and let you know tomorrow." Already Eva had made up her mind not to go to the masquerade ball.

Halfway down the hall she informed Mats of her decision. He stopped short and glared down at her. "You aren't going to the ball?" he shouted.

"Do you know how foolish I'd feel with a white face and a black scarf wrapped around my head? Not only that, I'd be tripping all over myself in that tight skirt. I'd rather just stay in my room and read or knit."

The stern look on Mats' face reminded Eva of the time he tried to load her pet cow on the truck. Stella had balked and would not walk up the ramp and Mats was 'fit to be tied.' She saw this same anger now as he stomped down the hall in front of her, spouting out words for her to be a good sport and that he couldn't go to the ball unless she did.

His extreme disappointment caused her to think seriously about the situation as they walked in silence to her room. Like the sun coming out on a cloudy day, she looked expectantly into his eyes. "Listen, I have an idea. If Sayuri is wearing a costume native to Japan, why couldn't I wear my native costume of Norrland? It isn't fancy, but I'd feel right at home wearing it. What do you think?"

Mats' face relaxed into his lopsided grin. "Sounds like a good idea to me," he replied. "Tomorrow, we can ask Sayuri what she thinks."

Eva was late arriving for breakfast the next morning. It surprised her that Mats hadn't knocked on her door earlier, but now she knew why; he was sitting with Sayuri in the far corner of the dining room. Eva recognized the back of his blond head. She knew Sayuri had seen her walk in, because their eyes had met briefly, but the girl had quickly looked away, put her hand on Mats' arm and engaged him in deep conversation. She had claimed him for her own this morning.

Eva headed for the breakfast buffet, poured herself a cup of coffee and buttered a bran muffin to take back to the deck. She was relaxing in the sun when Mats finally came along. He told her Sayuri said it would be fine for her to wear the Swedish dress; in years before she had observed many girls dressed in their native Swedish costumes. Then he reclined in the deck chair, placed his cap over his eyes and promptly fell asleep. Hearing him snore and watching his open mouth quiver with each long breath, she discovered that sleeping was a detriment to his handsomeness. He must have had a long night to fall sleep so quickly in such bright sunlight.

Revelations

At first Eva felt too quaint and insignificant following Sayuri into the banquet hall. All eyes turned to watch the elegant geisha dressed in a white and maroon kimono shuffling along with tiny, quick steps, bowing her head demurely to each person as she passed by. As it turned out, there were many other women who wore their Swedish folk costumes and Eva easily blended right in with the crowd. There were also clowns, barmaids, witches and devils, queens with crowns and glittery eye masks, and even a black cat.

Mr. Kaneko explained to her about two other costumes that she didn't recognize: an American Indian squaw and a western cowgirl. She thought the Indian quite beautiful in her fringed leather dress and many feathers and beads, but she wasn't sure about the pretty young cowgirl in leather breeches wearing high heeled boots, a pistol on her hip and throwing a rope around men she wanted to dance with.

Mr. Kaneko preferred to sit and talk, so Eva and Sayuri took turns dancing with Mats. Toward the middle of the evening a girl in a clown mask with thickly braided hair made out of yellow yarn tapped Eva on the shoulder.

"Meet me on the bottom deck at nine o'clock tomorrow evening," whispered the expressionless mask. "I'll be wearing a black hooded cape." Before Eva could reply, the girl ran back toward the banquet tables and disappeared behind one of the blue curtains.

"Who's your friend?" inquired Mr. Kaneko.

"I have no idea. She wants to meet me on the deck tomorrow evening."

"Well, be sure to bring Mats along when you go. Some people here can't be trusted."

"I hadn't planned on going at all," she replied.

After that three young men asked Eva to dance. One was a glass blower from Orrefors who was going to a convention in Chicago to learn how to engrave glass, another was a student hoping to study forestry in Minnesota, and the third planned to visit his family in northern Maine. Finally Mats returned to dance a fast stepping polka. Then the music slowed and the lights darkened for the last dance. She leaned her head against his chest, pretending he was Karl.

"You're awfully quiet, Eva."

"It's been a long day," she said, brushing away a tear in the semi-darkness.

The next morning, gray clouds hung low above the black ocean. Eva looked down on angry waves crashing against the ship in a mass of bubbly foam and hoped the rain would come by evening. Then, she would have good reason for not meeting the masked one, even though she was curious to find out who it was. Sudden changes in weather usually excited her, and she would have stayed on deck to be a part of nature's fury, but today the violent pitching back and forth made her dizzy. Suddenly she felt queasy and lost her breakfast into the churning sea below. Her stomach felt much better in the afternoon and she was delighted that evening to hear that guests were advised not to go out on deck after dinner because of strong winds and heavy rains.

The next morning she was nauseous again, but today the weather was clear and no white caps troubled the calm water. Mats told her many people had been sick and that some had gotten pills from the ship's doctor. When she felt no better she went to the infirmary.

Eva sat alone in a small room of total whiteness. There was not even a picture on the wall to look at, so she watched through a narrow door as a woman dressed in white shuffled through a folder of papers. She was rounder than Cook, her fat jowls pulling her face unpleasantly downward in a dour, uncompromising way that made Eva wish she hadn't come. Then a man in a white shirt poked his head around the corner and asked her to come into the next room. They sat on either side of large, highly polished wooden desk, so mirror-like that she could see his reflection on its surface. She had never been to a doctor before and sat anxiously on the edge of her chair. Noticing her nervousness, he leaned back comfortably with his arms folded across his broad chest and began talking about the weather and making little jokes to put her at ease.

He was Swedish, too, and appeared to have all the time in the world just to sit and idly talk about everything from the customs in America to being especially careful with her money. There were swindlers and other unseemly folk in America interested in taking advantage of newcomers, especially young women.

He showed her five different bills and explained how much each was worth. Then he took some change from his pocket and described four common coins. Eva found all this very interesting and was just beginning to relax when the nurse announced the arrival of another patient. The doctor stood up then and looked into Eva's eyes with a tiny flashlight, felt her neck and listened to the beating of her heart. Then he sat down again. "You must be about sixteen years old?" he asked.

"I turned fifteen last Christmas Eve."

"So, have you been with a boy recently?" he asked.

"I am with Mats. He told me to come and get pills for seasickness.

"I doubt it's the rolling of the sea that is making you sick," he told her. "I rather think you might have had a sweet roll in the hay before you left the old country, ya?" He gave her a little wink, but now all she could think of was Mama's delicious sweet rolls and the last time she'd eaten one.

"Yes, I do remember having a sweet roll in the barn once, but that was a long time ago. I was probably eight then. I might have had two rolls."

"Only eight years old, you say? And two rolls in the hay?" Eva thought he would fall out of his chair laughing and when he called for the nurse and told her about the sweet rolls, the downward curve of the nurse's mouth rose slightly, but never quite made it to a smile.

"Another pregnant one?" she mumbled to herself, but loud enough so Eva heard. "Are these Swedes out to populate the world?"

Eva's heart sank. "Pregnant?" she thought to herself.

"Come with me," beckoned the nurse, steering her into an adjoining room. "Take off your clothes and lie down on the table," she ordered, giving Eva a small white sheet to cover herself with.

No man was going to see her naked, so Eva laid on the table fully dressed with the sheet over her. When heavy shuffling steps approached the bed, Eva saw the nurse scowling as she whipped off the white sheet with a flick of her hand. "The doctor can't examine you with your clothes on. Now do as I say and get undressed!"

Eva sat up abruptly and jumped off the examining table, marched out of the room and ran out to the hall. In no time she was back on the deck leaning against the railing, pondering her newfound dilemma. She recalled what Ingrid said about there being only one day each month a woman could get pregnant. It seemed a rare coincidence that something should come from being with Karl for just one brief time. She gazed at her ring. It was a rich greenish-blue, the color of a translucent wave about ready to crest and fall back into the sea. Now she missed Karl even more than before. She wanted to feel his arms around her, hearing his reassuring voice saying that everything would be alright.

Then Mats came up from behind and grabbed her around the waist. "Don't fall overboard!" he said, pulling her away from the railing and tickling her ribs. His cheerful intervention had broken her melancholy thoughts and she was able to put on a happy face.

"I'm glad you're feeling better. Did you see the doctor?"

"Oh, yes...he was very nice." Then, not wanting to discuss the matter further, she said, "I feel like walking around the promenade," and she coyly took his arm.

"We've got a half an hour to waste before dinner," he replied. Then he told her how he'd spent the morning talking with some of the sailors and the crew. "I wouldn't mind being a sailor," he told her. "Being on a big ship in the middle of the ocean would be like a working vacation all year long, not to mention all the fun waiting in the next port." Eva listened with half an ear. She was thinking about the doctor. How could he tell she was pregnant just by looking at her? Was it that obvious?

"Do I look different to you, Mats?" she said all of a sudden.

"You look good to me. You always have."

"Seriously, Mats, have I changed in any way?"

"Hmm...you certainly seem more cheerful today."

Eva stepped back a few steps. "Look at me, Mats...from my head to my feet. Do I look the same as I did last year?" She did a little pirouette and then stood with her hands on her hips, her head cocked to the side with a grin waiting for an answer. Mats made a big deal of looking her up and down, squinting and raising his eyebrows.

"Now that you mention it, you do look different," he said at last.

"I do?" Her hands fell to her sides and she walked back to him. "In what way?"

"Well...you aren't that bashful little girl I used to know anymore. You look...well, you look like a woman now." She took his arm and they began to walk again. So Mats thought she looked like a woman...like a pregnant woman? She stopped and looked him in the eye.

"So, last year I was just a girl and now I'm...what...fat?"

"You might have gained a pound or two, but in all the right places," he said sarcastically with his lop-sided grin. Then he slipped his arm around her waist and pulled her toward him, his face touching hers. "Oh, Eva, how am I ever going to live without you?"

"Mats, don't talk like that. What would Jenny think?"

"It's just that we've been friends for so long. I'm really going to miss you."

"I know," she said softly. "I'll miss seeing you, too."

After supper Eva excused herself from the game room and walked alone on the promenade. The setting sun lay in a mass of bright golden clouds surrounded by a reddish sky, the promise of a fair day tomorrow. "Red sky at night, sailor's delight" she'd heard a sailor say one evening such as this. When she reached the stern, a long wake of churning water trailing behind the ship reflected the last remnants of light, its turbulence both frightening and beautiful at the same time.

"I was hoping you'd be here tonight," said a voice behind her. Eva grasped the rail. Her visit to the doctor and ultimate concern about being pregnant had consumed her thoughts all day and she had completely forgotten about seeing the masked one again. "Do you remember me now?" said the girl, removing the concealing hood from her head. Eva turned and gasped.

"Dagny! I can't believe it is you!"

"Ya, it is me," said Dagny in a faint whisper. She had tears in her eyes and Eva was crying, too, as they hugged each other silently, the sound of rushing water filling the emotional void.

Then suddenly each spoke at once, causing them both to giggle and from then on, endless Swedish words flowed as free and fast as the churning wake below them.

"It's a bit frightening looking down at that powerful surge of white water," said Eva holding tightly to the protective rail. "Somewhat like being at the top of a high waterfall and looking straight down."

"Ya, it is," agreed Dagny. "At first I couldn't walk close to the railing. Just the sound of rushing water scared me. Now I come here early every morning before anyone else is up to let my doubts and fears flow away in the rough sea." Dagny's eyes closed. She took a deep breath of fresh air and blew it out slowly from her mouth. A peaceful serenity touched her face. "There...I feel all clean inside now! Try it, Eva. You'll see what I mean."

Eva inhaled deeply, letting her breath out slowly over the turbulence. Yes, she could almost see her worries fall into the bubbling mass below. "You are right, Dagny, I do feel much better now."

Soon the flaming sun dropped into the sea and the pinkish clouds turned misty gray. The long trailing wake behind the ship turned dark and foreboding, the sound of churning water louder than before. Eva stared at the menacing water below, its force seeming to pull her over the edge, and she quickly backed away. Shivering in the chill air, she took Dagny's arm. "Let's go to my room where we can talk."

"You're going the wrong way!" shouted Dagny, as Eva led her down the stairs toward the chambermaid's quarters. Eva was smiling to herself in the dim light as she unlocked the door to room number eight. Dagny was flabbergasted. "I don't understand...if you are a guest on the ship, why is your room down here?"

"I should feel lucky that I'm not sleeping in the broom closet!" said Eva, plunking herself down on the little bed. For reasons she could not explain, Eva felt a sister-like closeness to Dagny, a relationship that seemed stronger and more familiar than she had ever had with Ingrid. They exchanged notes on growing up in Norrland. Eva spoke of the times with Karl in the milkhouse, the birthing stall and Midsummer Eve, also touching briefly on the awful circumstances forcing her to be banished to America. It felt good to unload all the thoughts and worries she'd been keeping to herself for so long…things she was too embarrassed to tell Mats.

"Sailing to America was not your idea?" asked Dagny

"No, it was a complete surprise." Eva told her about the bizarre dinner with Mrs. Lindholm and Mats and how quickly her life had changed in a very short time. Eva looked down at her hand. "Karl gave me this ring the day he left on a trip with his father. He told me to wear it until we saw each other again and I promised that I would. Now I don't know if I will ever see him again."

"So, you will never take off the ring?"

"Not until I see him again."

Dagny didn't know what to say after that because Eva looked so sad. She got up and sat beside her on the bed and shyly put her hand on Eva's arm. Dagny felt more comfortable now about telling Eva about the strawberry farm, the yellow dress and how she'd been fooled into getting a job at the boarding house. Then she talked about the men and what she was expected to do and how drinking strong liquor made everything easier. "I'm ashamed about what I've done and how I acted that day at the café."

Eva was shocked at first to hear all this, but she also understood that Dagny had somehow been trapped into a situation that was difficult to get out of. Now it was her turn to comfort Dagny.

"You see…we are not so different after all. We've both become stronger because of those challenging times," said Eva, taking her friend's hand in her own. She thought to ease Dagny's mind, but this simple gesture gave Eva new courage to say what she could tell no one else. "I've done things I'm ashamed of, too. At least you didn't get pregnant like I did!"

The whites of Dagny's eyes grew large as she looked expectantly about the room. "Where is your baby?"

"It is too soon for that," responded Eva. "In fact, I'm not positive I am pregnant, but the doctor on board said I might be. I only confided this so you would know that I, too, have made mistakes."

"Babies aren't mistakes. They're miracles," said Dagny.

"That would be true if I was married," said Eva. "I should have thought about the consequences beforehand."

"That reminds me of why I wanted to meet you on the deck." Dagny spoke in a whisper, as if someone else might be listening, and Eva leaned closer to hear every word.

"I was working the buffet the night of the Masquerade Ball and saw your red hair...and the tall boy dancing with you. I'd seen you both before walking around the ship and there was something I needed to tell you." Dagny looked down at her hands, nervously rubbing her fingers together. "Well, since I'm not allowed to mingle with the guests, I had to think of some way to speak with you without being noticed. That's when I saw the clown mask in a box of old costumes in a corner of the kitchen."

"I've been wondering what that was all about," said Eva. "You were very mysterious that night...but tell me more."

"That girl with the yellow skin and long black hair...the one who also danced with your friend?"

"Sayuri?" asked Eva.

"I don't know her name, but I've heard things about her from the other maids."

Dagny looked down at her hands again and Eva covered them with her own, saying, "What kind of things?"

"Well...she brings men back to her room, the rich ones, and gives them a special drink. It makes them drowsy...just long enough for her to take their money and gold, and then somehow they wake up in a strange place and can't remember anything. I know it's true because I've seen empty glasses on the table...and other maids have noticed potions and pills in the bathroom."

"I have not trusted Sayuri from the beginning," said Eva. "I suspected Mats was seeing her."

"Ya, he has been to her room. I saw him leaving early one

morning. You must warn him about that girl."

"Thank you for telling me, Dagny. I'll speak to Mats in the morning."

After Dagny went to her room, Eva decided not to wait until morning. She must warn Mats as soon as possible. Just before entering the game room she heard Sayuri talking loudly about being dealt poor hands and losing a lot of money. Eva hid behind a clothes rack until Sayuri stormed out of the room with Mats running after her.

"Wait up, Mats," Eva called.

"What are you doing here? I thought you went back to your room," he said rather abruptly.

"I have something important to tell you," she whispered.

"Can't it wait until morning? I'm in a bit of a hurry right now."

"I need to talk with you... now!" she said firmly. Mats listened impatiently as she disclosed what Dagny had told her.

"That's a lot of hogwash, Eva. Don't believe everything you hear, especially from a lowly chambermaid." Eva wanted to explain who Dagny was, but by then Mats had turned away, his long strides widening the distance between them.

"Well, don't say I didn't warn you," she shouted.

Mats raised his hand, then turned toward her briefly. "No need to worry, Eva, I can take care of myself." Then he turned the corner and was gone.

The Painting

Sometimes between meals when the guests were busy enjoying themselves on the deck or in the game rooms, Dagny sat on one of the wooden benches placed on either side of the entrance to the main dining room. From here she had a good view of a large painting where two young girls sat across from one another at a table set with wine bottles, goblets and a plate of fruit. The pretty girl in a blue dress reminded Dagny of Eva. Her face was upturned, looking at a man standing behind her as if they were in conversation.

Dagny, imagining herself to be the other girl, wore a black dress and held a small dog up to her face, so close that it appeared she might be about to kiss the dog's nose. It always gave her pleasure to think that she and Eva were spending a lovely afternoon together, a comforting scene that helped fill some of the empty places in her heart. She mentioned this to Eva one evening.

Eva remembered having seen the painting, but hadn't paid much attention to it. While Mats was busy playing cards, she and Dagny went back to the dining room to look at the painting together.

"How beautiful!" said Eva. Then she looked closer at a little brass plaque beside the painting. "The painting is called 'Luncheon of the Boating Party,' by Auguste Renoir."

"Oh..." said Dagny, hesitant to reveal that she was unable to read English.

For a while they sat looking at the painting.

"You probably think I'm foolish to pretend it is you and me in the painting," said Dagny.

"I don't think it is silly at all," said Eva. "Part of the fun of looking at a painting is putting yourself in the picture...somewhat like reading a book and pretending you are one of the characters, wouldn't you say?"

"I'd much rather look at paintings. I'm not so good at reading," said Dagny.

"Well, I agree with you that those two girls could very well be you and me, and it pleases me to know that you've been thinking of us together, because I've thought a lot about you, too."

Dagny turned to look at Eva. "I have you to thank for changing my life. When I saw you in Gothenburg that day I knew how far I'd fallen. You looked so fine...such a lady sitting there in your pretty dress."

"You changed yourself," said Eva. "I just happened to be there when you realized that your life was going nowhere, although I did pray for you when that man pulled you across the street."

"How do you pray for someone?"

Eva thought a moment. "Well, I sort of talk to God...in my mind. I asked him to take care of you and show you the right way."

Dagny smiled. "Your God did take care of me. All of a sudden I had the strength to say no to that man and almost immediately I was free of my past."

Eva took both of Dagny's hands. "I'm so happy that we found each other again."

That evening Dagny stopped by to visit Eva. She was much more relaxed now, trusting enough to tell Eva about the pink dress, how she would put it on after a swim in the lake. "Wearing that pink dress and dancing around the secluded beach was the only time I felt like a real girl." Eva listened quietly as Dagny talked about Vidar.

"Mother didn't want me looking girly in front of him, so she always made me wear those old baggy hand-me-downs from the Finn so I'd look like a boy. I never told her that it didn't matter to Vidar what I wore." Then Dagny shared the heavy secrets she had carried inside for so long.

Now everything came together to Eva about 'the strange one,' but because of Dagny's sadness, she tried to think of more pleasant things to say.

"Did I ever tell you I have a sister in America?" said Eva, in an attempt to elevate the gloomy atmosphere of the darkened room.

"So you will be living with your sister?"

"I'm not sure. She invited me to come last year, but then something happened. She lost her memory and I haven't heard from her since before Christmas."

"I don't intend to be a chambermaid much longer. I've saved my money and have been thinking of paying my fare to America."

"That's wonderful," exclaimed Eva. "Facing the new land would be a lot easier if we stayed together."

"Well...that's sort of what I was thinking, too," admitted Dagny.

Eva showed her the book, *Learning English in Six Weeks.* "I can help you with what little English I know and we can learn new words together."

"No need to bother with that," said Dagny with great authority. "Where I plan to live everyone speaks Swedish."

"I didn't know there was such a place in America," replied Eva.

"It's in Aroostook, Maine...a town called New Sweden," said Dagny excitedly. "On the last voyage a man was giving out maps and talking to groups of people about how they could get land in New Sweden. I found one of those maps crumpled up in the hallway, but I could make no sense of it. I'll bring it tomorrow night so you can look at it."

Eva watched Dagny walk down the hall in her black cape and cumbersome shoes, her long, deliberate strides reminding her of Mrs. Kronberg lugging milk from the goat barn. That day seemed like such a long time ago.

Then Eva locked the door and began taking her hair down. How bizarre it was that she and Dagny happened to be on the same ship at this particular time. Was fate bringing them together for some unknown reason? She didn't know why, but she believed that people were here on earth to help each other. Why Mrs. Lindholm and Sayuri had come into her life was yet to be discovered.

It was a relief to loosen her braid, the weight of which had left her with a slight headache. She brushed out her hair with long, slow, soothing strokes until a loud knock sounded on the door. Thinking it might be Dagny returning with the map, she unlocked it, and was shocked to see Mats leaning against the door frame and looking down at her with glassy, unfocused eyes.

"What happened? You look awful!" she exclaimed as he

staggered across the floor and fell lifelessly onto her bed with a loud groan. She felt his forehead and then the slight roughness of his unshaven cheek. "Mats...can you hear me?"

Slowly his face relaxed, his tongue moved slowly across his dry lips, but his eyes remained closed.

"Sayuri...is that you?"

"No, Mats, I'm Eva. Somehow you found your way to my room...and I'm glad you did. Were you with Sayuri tonight?" He shivered and she covered him with a blanket.

"You were right, Eva," he sighed after a while. "As always...you were right." His eyes fluttered open, trying to focus on her face, then closed again.

It was apparent now that she wouldn't be sleeping in her bed tonight. She slid the old stuffed chair across the room to where she could keep an eye on Mats and wrapped herself in a blue knitted shawl. Sayuri's drink was potent stuff. Eva hoped that Mats still had all his money.

The small table lamp cast eerie shadows on the ceiling. Mats blinked, his eyes following the wall down to the floor. Rising on one elbow he saw Eva in the chair beside him and then his head dropped to the pillow again. Was he dreaming? Often he had imagined what she looked like with her hair down and now she was only a touch away. Turning toward her again, his finger traced the curly waves of red hair softly framing her peaceful, sleeping face. The shawl had fallen slightly to reveal the plumpness of her breast above her cotton shift and he resisted the temptation to feel the softness of it. His body longed for her, but he looked away, staring blankly at the ceiling.

Finally she stirred and looked over to him. "How are you feeling?"

"I'm not sure. Last night is still a big blur."

She drew the shawl across her chest and walked over to get a good look at his face.

"You do look much better this morning," she said, touching his forehead.

"Aye, and you look better than ever," he said, grabbing her arm. The look in his eyes was intense. "Lie down with me, Eva...please..."

He pulled her down and she fell against him, knowing in an instant how much he needed her. She might have given in if it hadn't been for Karl. Part of her wanted to say yes, but a greater part, her everlasting love for Karl and deep concern for the baby, made her push him away.

"I can't, Mats...I'm sorry... I just can't," she said, rising from the bed and backing into the shadows. He stood up immediately, agitation flooding his face like the mean bull at the potato farm.

"Who in God's name are you saving yourself for?" he shouted. The room shuddered from his explosive words and then became uncomfortably silent. She had to tell him the truth.

"I like you, Mats," she said finally. "I like you a lot, but I'm in love with someone else."

Mats was speechless, stunned by this new revelation as Eva continued.

"And have you forgotten that soon you will be marrying Jenny Almgren?"

"Aye, that is true," he said, seeming to wilt like an uprooted tree drained from its source. Then he slowly made his way to the chair and sat down with his head in his hands. Eva took this opportunity to put on her dress and began braiding her hair.

"So, who is this lucky guy you are so much in love with?" he said finally. "Someone in America?" He laughed sarcastically at the ironic thought that each might be going to America for the same reason, to marry someone else. Eva didn't know why he was laughing, but was glad to see him in a better mood.

"What time is it?" she asked. His watch was not in its special pocket and the chain was missing, too. He stood up and frantically checked every pocket in his trousers and came up with nothing but a handful of small change and a wrinkled handkerchief. Eva gave him his jacket, but there was no chain or watch there. In addition to that, all his inheritance money was gone, as well as his father's gold money clip. He sat down and swore under his breath.

"That Sayuri...she's made a fool of me...I'm gonna wring her skinny little neck!" This wasn't the time to say ***I told you so.*** Instead, Eva was too busy formulating a plan of her own.

"Listen to me!" she said, with an authority that surprised even herself. "If you run upstairs now and accuse Sayuri of stealing your money, she will only deny it and you will have gained nothing."

Mats hands were gripping the arms of the chair as if they might propel him across the room, but she leaned down to keep him seated, her face a few inches from his. "It does no good to act in anger." Her expression reminded him of the day he tried unsuccessfully to load Stella onto the truck and how foolish he'd felt afterward. Slowly and more than a bit unwillingly, he leaned back in the chair and listened.

"We must find Dagny," stated Eva. "I'm hoping she can unlock the door to Sayuri's room, so we can search for your watch and money."

For a moment Mats remained sitting in the chair pondering Eva's strategy, surprised at her good sense and logic.

"We don't have much time," she said, impatiently. "Isn't the ship supposed to dock in New York around eleven?"

Then, as if awakening from a puzzling dream, Mats followed her out of the room to the upper hall. Eva was praying that they would see Dagny and that Sayuri and Mr. Kaneko were already in the dining room eating breakfast. Luck was on their side when Dagny emerged from a room with an armload of dirty towels. From the anxious look on Mats' face she knew something bad had happened.

"Have you seen Sayuri this morning?" asked Eva.

"Ya, she went down the hall with that man friend of hers about ten minutes ago...probably gone to breakfast."

As they all rushed to Sayuri's room, Eva quickly explained everything to Dagny.

The room looked exactly as Eva remembered it, except for the large open trunk on the floor and two smaller cases lying on the flowered bedspread. Her heart thumped wildly in her chest as Mats stood looking around the room.

"What if Sayuri returns before we're done searching, Mats? Perhaps you should stand lookout at the end of the hall."

"Good idea. I'll think of some excuse to detain them so you'll have more time."

Meanwhile, Dagny was already rummaging through the big trunk. "Look at all these beautiful gowns!" she exclaimed.

"Be very careful," advised Eva. "We must leave everything just the way we found it, or else Sayuri will notice something is amiss." Eva found nothing but brushes and combs, cosmetics, several pairs of shoes, and an umbrella in the first case. The second one contained mostly an array of undergarments which Eva embarrassingly looked through until she uncovered a collection of brightly colored silk bags.

"Sayuri must have a different purse for each gown she wears," exclaimed Eva, holding several up for Dagny to see. It was then Eva noticed a pink padded box at the very bottom of the case. Lifting the cover she saw the watch and chain and the gold money clip with Mr. Kronberg's initials still holding a large wad of paper bills.

As Eva and Dagny quietly tip-toed down the hall to surprise Mats, he suddenly turned around and ran toward them.

"Sayuri's coming. Let's get out of here," he said, taking an arm of each girl and steering them around the closest corner. Now safely out of sight, they slowed down and were able to catch their breath and talk.

"Did you find anything?" asked Mats. Eva winked at Dagny, who couldn't keep a straight face and began to giggle. Eva coquettishly looked up to Mats with both hands behind her back.

"Which hand do you want?" she asked.

Relief swept over Mats' face as he played along with the game. "Let's see now. I'll take the left hand."

"Oh, too bad, Mats, you picked the wrong one...but I'll give them to you anyway," she said with a glint in her eye, holding out the watch and chain and gold clip full of bills. How thrilling it was to see his face light up as he counted the money and found it all there! He put his arms around the two girls. “I can’t thank you both enough for what you’ve done for me today.”

Mats and Eva were enjoying their coffee on deck when Mr. Kaneko came strolling along.

“Are you packed already?” he asked.

“What little I have won’t take more than five minutes to put together,” said Mats.

“I travel lightly, too, but not Sayuri. She’s been in her room for over an hour now.”

“We were hoping to get a glimpse of land before the crowds gathered,” said Mats, trying to avoid any talk about Sayuri. Mr. Kaneko looked at his watch.

“It’s only thirty minutes after nine, so we’ve got a good hour yet. By the way, I want to say what charming company you both have been on this voyage, especially you, Eva...such a ray of sunshine on a cloudy day.”

“And I’ve enjoyed your company as well,” she replied graciously. “I loved listening to all your interesting stories and good advice.”

“And you, Mats, have grown into a marvelous poker player. It’s not often I get beaten in cards.” They shook hands.

“It’s been a pleasure, sir. I’ve learned a lot from you.”

Mr. Kaneko put his hand on Mats’ shoulder and took Eva’s hand.

“You two should stick together,” he said. “I feel confident that Eva would keep your river running smoothly on a straight and even path.” Eva didn’t know what to say and glanced up at Mats.

“We’re just friends,” he said. “In a few hours we’ll be going our separate ways.”

At that moment Mr. Kaneko saw love pass between them...a friendly love, perhaps, although in Mats’ eyes there seemed to be more than that. Mr. Kaneko wasn’t surprised. Eva was a beautiful woman. He'd seen many heads turn to look at her.

"I've left my camera in my room," he said. "Maybe we can meet later so I can snap a few photos of the two of you."

"That's a great idea," said Mats, and Eva agreed. Mr. Kaneko tipped his hat and Mats and Eva decided to go to their rooms to get their bags.

First Views of America

Commotion prevailed above them on the promenade as Eva and Dagny struggled up the stairs with their belongings. Upon reaching the top step they were met by a rush of enthusiastic passengers shouting that land had been seen. Immediately the two girls were caught up in the crowd moving toward the bow of the ship. The throng abruptly halted as everyone strained to have their first view of America. Eva looked around for Mats and saw him, red-faced and out-of-breath, zigzagging his way toward them. It was only ten o'clock, but word from the captain was that friendly winds had brought the ship in ahead of schedule.

"I'm so glad we got your papers in order yesterday," said Eva.

"Ya," said Dagny. "I was afraid things wouldn't work out. That man in uniform was very scary, especially when he said I didn't have enough money to pay for the voyage."

"Yes, he was. I'm glad I was there to make things right."

"I'd still be stuck here working on the ship if it wasn't for you, Eva. I'll pay you back as soon as I can." Then Dagny began to cry.

"Now, don't you worry about the money now," said Eva, putting her arm around her friend. "We're together and that's what matters most."

Eva kept her eye on the long strip of gray that very much resembled her final view of Sweden's coastline. Perhaps her expectations had been too high. Mr. Kaneko's elaborate descriptions of America had painted a striking masterpiece of luxury and prosperity in her mind, but from here it seemed that America was no different than Sweden.

Then the smoky haze lifted somewhat, disclosing a skyline of extremely tall structures. On closer observation Eva noticed many buildings poking up through the grayish cloud, their numerous windows sparkling like precious jewels in the late morning sun. Mr. Kaneko had spoken of "skyscrapers," but it wasn't until now that Eva understood the significance of that unusual word. She pointed out the uppermost tops of many buildings to Dagny.

"See how they appear to scrape the sky with their great height?" she said, but Dagny was looking in a different direction and crouched behind Eva. Looming high above the harbor was the unmistakable Statue of Liberty, her colossal size and presence even more imposing than Mr. Kaneko had described. He had told her that France had given Miss Liberty to America as a gift. At the time Eva was unable to envision a statue of such great size. She had seen larger-than-life-sized statues in towns and cities in the old country, but her most vivid imagination had not prepared her for the enormity and grandeur of this hundred-and-fifty-foot-tall woman who held a book in one hand and tall torch in the other. Liberty, as Mr. Kaneko called the statue, was a tower of strength and empowerment; the image of woman's superiority and motherly love; a welcoming goddess to strangers arriving in a foreign land.

"Mr Kaneko told me that the Statue of Liberty was brought across this very same ocean on a ship in three-hundred and fifty separate pieces," Eva said.

"I don't believe it," said Mats. "Such a feat would be impossible…you know how Mr. Kaneko likes to stretch the truth a little now and then." It was a mystery to Eva how such a puzzle of gigantic pieces could have been assembled right here in the middle of New York Harbor, but she still believed what Mr. Kaneko had told her. In America anything was possible.

Eva and Dagny stumbled down the wooden ramp as if they were

drunken sailors. Upon reaching the wooden deck they felt themselves swaying as if still aboard ship, and held tightly to each other to keep from falling down.

"Just a case of sea legs," said Mats, who looked a bit unsteady himself, planting his feet wider on the wooden pier. "It takes a while to get used to having the good solid earth beneath your feet again."

They found an empty spot on the pier and waited for Mr. Kaneko. Mostly happy faces passed by, but there were a few sad ones, too, especially the old carpenter with his homemade hammer and knife attached to his belt, carrying a weathered case in each hand. He nodded to Eva as his quiet wife looked up nervously from under a white kerchief and managed a faint smile. Eva had gained her trust one day when the woman sadly confessed that her husband's days on earth were numbered; they were going to Virginia to live out their lives with their only son and his family.

There was the stout, middle-aged lawyer carrying a black case, puffing to keep up with his spritely, thin wife, who appeared to be wearing every piece of jewelry she owned. Her neck, arms and fingers glittered from so much gold, silver and brilliant gems. Behind them the boisterous farmer from Skane rolled his millstone down the ramp followed by his heavy-set wife. She was bent over with heavy cloth bags slung over each shoulder, cautioning him to be watchful the stone didn't get away from him and fall into the sea. Two rosy-cheeked sisters stopped to say goodbye to Eva. They were strong, large-boned, fair-haired girls in their middle twenties who still had a long journey ahead of them, two thousand more miles to the west to Minnesota, where they expected to meet men needing wives who weren't afraid of hard work. Underneath their rugged exteriors, they were two of the jolliest girls on the ship. Eva wished them both good luck. She noticed, too, the many young girls who smiled at Mats as they walked by and how he politely tipped his hat and smiled to each one of them.

Looking up, Eva waved vigorously to Mr. Kaneko and Sayuri as they made their way down the ramp, oblivious to a row of men in uniform hanging over the railing. Perhaps the crewmen thought she was waving to them because all of a sudden they waved back in her direction. Their shrill whistling and shouting embarrassed her. When she turned to look away, Mats' gaze met hers, his mouth spreading into a wide grin at her reddening cheeks.

"I didn't know you made so many friends on board, Eva," he teased. Apparently she hadn't spent as much time alone on the ship as he'd supposed. She tried to explain.

"The crew was always friendly and polite. I didn't want to ignore them and appear snobbish," she said in her defense. Mats nodded slowly several times as if in agreement, but his smirk revealed that he was making fun of her. She ignored him and walked toward Mr. Kaneko and his fine camera.

He explained to Eva how the camera worked and told her to stand next to a weather-beaten post with the ocean stretched out behind her. He took several shots of her smiling face with the excuse that the light wasn't quite right. Then he took two of Eva and Mats together. Dagny, skeptical of the big black box, had been hiding behind Mats, and now Eva insisted that Mr. Kaneko take a picture of them together, too.

"May I take your picture?" Eva asked.

Mr. Kaneko showed her which button to press and looked around for Sayuri, who sat on her large trunk, looking agitated and anxious to be away from the whole scene. When he beckoned for her to join them, Sayuri ignored him and walked back toward the ship to talk with someone else. Eva couldn't help but wonder if Sayuri had noticed that Mats' things were missing from her trunk. This fleeting thought was quickly forgotten as Eva became more interested in Mr. Kaneko's camera. She looked through the lens to see what happened when she pressed the button. One fast click and it was done. She wondered if there had been time enough for the camera to see everything. Its workings befuddled her, but she knew that someday she would have a camera of her very own.

"Both of you...give me your addresses so that I may send copies of the photographs," said Mr. Kaneko. Eva was excited to have something to look forward to.

Mr. Kaneko took Eva's arm. "Remember now what I told you the other day about Boston and those yellow taxi cabs." She reassured him that she had only to give the taxi driver Ingrid's address and he would drive her directly to her sister's house.

The Train Ride

New York City was a fearsome, dirty place, full of poor, disheveled folks milling on street corners and in alleys eying the possessions of everyone who walked past. Eva was grateful for Mats' company, especially when it came to purchasing their train tickets, even though none of them could figure if the change he'd received back was correct. Mr. Kaneko had told him to pay with small bills instead of one large denomination because there was less danger of being cheated. He'd expected more money in return, but the few coins in his hand was enough to buy a cup of weak coffee and a stale doughnut for each of them.

The smell of burning coal filled the air and tiny cinders sprayed down on them as they hurried past the massive black locomotive that Mats called 'the iron horse.' Eva saw no equine resemblance in the big metal machine, with steam rushing out from its metal wheels and smoke gushing from the smokestack. She would much prefer to look at Mr. Kronberg's fine black horses or any of the magnificent work horses at the Lindholm estate.

Mats would be traveling later on a different train, so he had plenty of time to accompany the girls to their awaiting coach. They boarded the train and walked to where two empty seats faced each other. Still grateful for Dagny's help in getting his watch and money back, Mats gave her a quick, friendly embrace.

Then he took Eva's hands in his, looking solemnly into her eyes. His lips quivered, but he didn't speak. A sudden emptiness gripped his belly as he realized he might never see his sweet Eva again. A haunting sadness came over his face...like a little boy who'd lost a favorite pet and was trying to hold back the tears. He pulled her toward him and held her tightly in his arms for a long time.

"I'm going to miss you," he whispered, "more than you will ever know." His eyes were intense and penetrating as he took her face in his hands. She hoped he'd kiss her and he did, tender at first...and then so hard she thought her lips might bleed.

"Don't forget to write as soon as you get settled," he said in a voice almost too soft to hear.

"I will," she said, brushing a tear from her eye, as all too quickly he was gone.

Eva saw Mats walk past the window, his face hidden by a newly purchased fedora, a hat similar to the homburg that his father always wore to Stockholm. Dagny was better able to see Mats' face as he passed by.

"I think he is crying," she whispered. Tears welled up in Eva's eyes, too, as she strained for the last glimpse of him and then the awful sobbing began...tears that Eva thought would never end.

Dagny put her arms around Eva and felt her trembling. "I didn't think you liked him so," she said.

"I don't," said Eva through her sobs. "I mean...I do like him...but...I don't know why I can't stop crying." Others turned to look and they quickly found their seats. Dagny put her arms around Eva and gently rocked her until it was over.

"I don't understand it," Eva said finally. "Mats is the one leaving, but it was Karl I was thinking of."

"Perhaps you never rightfully grieved for Karl and it all came out now."

"You may be right," said Eva, squeezing her friend's hand. "I'm so glad you are here with me."

"Ya, I am too," said Dagny.

The train car was half empty, so that the girls each had their own seat with their belongings beside them. Eva rode backwards, facing Dagny, watching the many endless train tracks glinting in the afternoon sun. Slowly they narrowed, merging together into one, long thread. The tall buildings of New York City shrank until they faded into the sky and she struggled to keep her memories alive because they seemed to be fading, too.

Suddenly a black locomotive appeared, whizzing past in a great clatter and spitting thick smoke high into the blue sky. It was followed by several passenger cars, their windows full of silent, staring, faces flickering by like the click of a camera. Then it was quiet again until their train slowed down by a wooden platform. Slowly they approached the station where another train was stopped.

Passengers departed and others came on board. A young boy of about ten appeared in one of the windows of the other train. He reminded Eva of young Mats. When he made faces at her, she returned with a silly one of her own. Then a younger girl appeared in the same window holding a porcelain-faced doll in a satin gown.

"Look, Dagny, have you ever seen a more beautiful doll?"

Dagny glanced at the little girl and then turned back to look across the aisle. "I'd much rather have that floppy, red-haired doll in the seat across from us. She's much more cuddly."

Eva followed Dagny's eyes to a woman holding a large stuffed doll with red-yarn hair sticking out from a round, smiling face.

"So we have two red-heads on board today," said the woman. "But I must say, you are much prettier than my homemade rag doll." She smiled at Eva, who hadn't understood much of what the woman said and was hastily looking through her English-Swedish dictionary that Mr. Kaneko had so kindly given to her.

Finally she spoke...slowly, enunciating each simple word. "Pretty doll...you...make?"

"Oh, yes, this is the third one I've made, one for each of my granddaughters. Her name is Raggedy Ann...very popular in the United States now."

The woman talked very fast, each word running into the other and Eva closed the dictionary in frustration. A man in the seat behind Dagny spoke up. He was Danish, but knew enough Swedish to translate what the woman had said.

"Raggedy Ann..." repeated Dagny. "Raggedy Ann...I like the

sound of it, don't you Eva?"

Noticing that Dagny was watching her every move, the woman began unsnapping the doll's green checkered dress. "Every Raggedy Ann has a heart sewn on her chest with the words 'I love you.' Would you like to see it?"

The man intervened again with his Swedish translation, and Dagny was up in an instant, hovering over the woman, admiring the large, red heart shape with the words 'I love you' embroidered across the center of it.

Then the woman rummaged in her bag and pulled out a little book. "I have several of these. You may keep this one," she said, placing the book in Dagny's hand. "It tells the story of Raggedy Ann, and at the end of the book is a paper doll and clothes you can cut out to dress her in." Dagny opened the book and looked blankly at the first page.

"So many words," she said. "What do they mean?"

"Let me read it," said the man. "Then I can tell you the story." Dagny watched him turn the pages and after a while he closed the book.

"From what I understand," said the man in his best Swedish, "a famous cartoonist and writer had a daughter who found a handmade rag doll in her Grandmother's attic. Apparently the doll had no face, except one shoe-button eye, so the father took his cartoon pen and drew a nose and whimsical smile on the doll. Then the daughter went to her grandmother who sewed on a second button eye. She was named Raggedy Ann. From watching his daughter play with the doll and other toy friends, he began writing stories about Raggedy Ann."

Dagny listened eagerly to what the man said, then took the book, holding it close to her chest as if it might take flight and find another home. Eva saw the wonder of Christmas shining on Dagny's happy face and told her so.

"I don't remember many happy Christmases," replied Dagny, gazing abstractly through the smoky train window. "Last Christmas Mother gave me a small rag doll with no hair and faded clothes. In my eagerness to leave the strawberry farm, I forgot to bring her with me." This saddened Eva and she got up to sit beside Dagny.

"Shall we look through your book?" she asked, hoping to cheer her up. Dagny's fingers traced the likeness of Raggedy Ann on the cover. Finally she opened the book and the two of them took turns guessing what Raggedy Ann was doing and might be saying. At the end there were several pages of colorful dresses and white pinafores, both plain and fancy, with little tabs sticking out of each one. On the inside of the back cover was a full-length drawing of Raggedy Ann wearing her white bloomers and with the red heart on her chest.

The woman across the aisle had been keeping an eye on the two girls. Finally she leaned across the aisle with a sharp, pointed instrument in her hand. "Here are a pair of scissors if you'd like to cut out the doll and her clothes."

Dagny glared at the sharp, knife-like object, quickly closed the book and stared down at the floor. The man behind Eva came to their rescue again. "I have granddaughters who love to play with paper dolls." Then he explained about cutting out the doll and items of clothing, being careful not to damage the little tabs attached to Raggedy Ann's paper outfits because those were what held on her clothes.

Eva attempted to show Dagny how to cut out the cardboard picture of Raggedy Ann, but Dagny grabbed the little book, glaring at the scissors as if it was some deadly weapon. Eva understood how it was with her friend and let the matter rest, but she did say what fun it would be to play with the paper doll and dress her in the paper clothes.

"It would almost be like playing with a real doll," Eva said as a last resort. Dagny mulled this over in her mind for a while before reluctantly giving Eva the book.

"You do it," she said with great trepidation. Eva was happy to cut out the doll and all her clothes.

The picture of Dagny holding the paper doll and carefully arranging the clothes reminded Eva of the times she played with the little yarn doll her mother had made. Ingrid had received a similar doll, but she'd thrown her yarn doll in a corner saying it wasn't a real doll. Her mother's feelings had been hurt that day and she'd picked up Ingrid's doll and given it to Eva.

Playing with two dolls was twice the fun. Eva would speak for each of them. Sometimes they were two sisters who argued, but more often they were friends in a faraway land who lived in stone castles, wore fine clothes and had tea every afternoon.

Eva fell asleep on Dagny's shoulder. After a while she was aware of Dagny watching her.

"I think you were dreaming," said Dagny.

"How did you know?"

"My mother's face used to twitch when she dreamed," said Dagny, remembering back to those times at the potato farm when she and her mother had slept together in her room.

"Was my face twitching a lot?"

"Sort of a lot."

"Did I look happy?" asked Eva.

Dagny paused a moment. "Sometimes you scowled a little. Was it that same dream about Karl?"

Eva nodded as she looked briefly toward the window and leaned her head against the seat. In her dream she'd see Karl working on a hillside, across the lawn or in the dining room. Obstacles popped up every time...a row of trees, a barn, crowds of people. Only a few times could she almost touch him, but then Mrs. Lindholm was there, standing in the way and she'd awaken in lonely desperation.

"Today I dreamed Karl was on a passing train, his face appearing in each window as if he was trying to speak to me or ask a question. In the last window was Mrs. Lindholm looking at me with her cold blue eyes and smirking lips. My dreams always leave me with such a feeling of emptiness and longing."

All Eva had of Karl now was the ring. Looking at it usually brought her some comfort, followed by an overwhelming heartache. She turned her hand so the sun brought out its dazzling, translucent sea-green color and for a moment she felt him with her. She remembered her promise and silently said *I love you*, but the comforting mood was much too brief, interrupted by the noises around her and then Dagny's voice.

"I don't dream very much, but Dag used to dream all the time."

Eva turned quizzically toward her friend. "What do you mean?"

"Dag had bad dreams. Usually she was running very fast and would fall into a deep, dark place. She'd try to claw her way out, but more dirt and rocks would fall back in and she couldn't breathe. Gasping for breath, her heart beating loudly in her chest, she'd awaken to Mother asking what the screaming was all about." Dagny turned to the window with a bewildered, far-away look in her eyes. Eva immediately thought of Vidar in the potato shed that day, how suffocating his heavy body had been and what terrible things he might have done to Dagny...or to Dag, as she was called back then. Eva was confused by the two names, Dag and Dagny, but she didn't want to ask about that now and bring back bad memories. It seemed Dag was someone in the past who the new Dagny wished to forget.

"That was a frightening dream," said Eva, her own dreams not seeming that important now.

"I don't understand much about dreams," said Dagny. Then her face lit up. "But I do remember that Dag's bad dreams stopped when you came to the farm that day. That night I dreamed that an angel with long red hair came down and lifted me out of the black hole and carried me to a place of beautiful flowers." Then Eva understood.

"So Dag vanished with her dreams and you became Dagny again?"

"Something like that," said Dagny. "But you were that special angel that saved me."

"Believe me, I'm no angel," replied Eva.

"Well, I know it was you in that dream. You saved me in Gothenburg, too. From that day, I wanted to be just like you. I haven't had a drink or been with a man since then. I got me a respectable job and here I am!"

"I just happened to be in the right place at the right time," said Eva. "Sometimes we are put in places to inspire others, but you were the one who saved yourself and made all the right choices." Eva took Dagny's hand and gently squeezed it. "I'm so proud of you!" It was the first time Eva had ever seen Dagny blush.

Eventually the train moved into an area of intersecting roads and modest white houses with children playing in small, neatly fenced-in yards. People sat on porches watching the train and children stopped their play to run closer and wave. A bell clanged several times and then the train screeched slowly to a halt in front of a long, green building with white trim. The woman across the aisle waved out her window and began gathering up her things. She looked fondly at Dagny, who was busy playing with her paper doll.

"Thank you," said Eva in her best English. The woman responded with words that neither Dagny nor Eva understood. Dagny watched the woman walk away with Raggedy Ann peeking over her shoulder until the mop of red-yarn hair disappeared in the departing crowd. Dagny collected all the paper clothes and put them carefully in her book with the doll.

"I don't feel like playing anymore," she said sadly, looking toward the empty seat across the aisle.

The train moved forward again and Eva watched the landscape change to lovely pastoral scenes and gentle, rolling hills that were reminiscent of the farms in Sweden. Her eyes glanced to the sky where puffy clouds arranged themselves into various shapes, cottony figures that resembled flocks of sheep or rabbits sitting up in a field. Finally the clouds rose in a billowing mass and formed a huge white dragon. She pointed it out to Dagny. "All I see are clouds," she said, with heavy, blurry eyes. Then she leaned her head back on the seat, saying, "I don't much care for dragons."

Then on the lower hillsides Eva noticed real animals: herds

of black and white Holstein cows similar to ones that Karl had showed her while driving to Gothenburg. She pictured him in the barn that day with the cow. How gentle he'd been with the mother and calf...how gentle he always had been with her. She saw him in the milk room putting the puzzling new machine together, in the orchard cutting the shiny red apple into eight perfect pieces, and in the hay mow on Midsummer Eve while she looked up at him in the lingering rays of the golden sun. She remembered his funny stories that made her laugh out loud; how he'd gaze down at her in wonderment as if he'd just discovered something new and precious. She saw the love in his face and they would be drawn to each other with an embrace, a kiss or just walking hand in hand, enjoying the comfort of each other's silent presence, not needing to speak any words.

These thoughts filled Eva's eyes with tears. Lately she cried so easily. She thought it a weak and childish thing to do and promised herself not to ruminate on what might have been and to live in the present moment. They were wise words she remembered her mother saying years ago concerning the way wild animals survived in the forest. The moose and deer didn't worry about the past or future, savoring the present moment with awareness and fulfillment.

Dagny was sound asleep, so Eva brought out her knitting, a pleasant solitary activity that calmly occupied her mind. As the skies darkened and the sun dropped behind the hills, the yellow glow of lighted windows flickered in the distance like busy fireflies on a warm July evening. Each golden radiance reflected imaginary scenes to Eva...of families relaxing after a day's work, gathered together to eat a delicious meal, engaging in lively conversation or playing games and reading books. All this made her homesick and hungry, wishing she'd thought to purchase some bread and cheese for the long train ride. She closed her eyes and listened to the wheels of the train clicking against the metal tracks.

"I think the train is slowing down" said Dagny, her low voice awakening Eva from a sound sleep.

"Boston...South Station...Boston!" shouted the conductor as the train passed by a lighted platform where men waited with empty carts. A rush of passengers and their bags filled the aisles as they made their way to the front of the coach. Eva and Dagny collected their things and followed the crowd, gently nudged along by those behind them.

South Station was a smaller version of Grand Central Station in New York, but to Eva and Dagny the unsettling confusion was worse. They felt completely lost without Mats to guide them and blindly followed the meandering crowds through familiar odors of fresh bread and cooked meat.

Hunger drove them to an empty bench where Eva studied her Swedish-American dictionary under words for food and drink. She told Dagny to stay with their bags, then courageously walked toward lines of people waiting at a food stand. Behind the counter a man filled small bread rolls with sausage-like pieces of meat, passing them to outstretched hands while accepting their coins and bills. He worked brusquely, but efficiently, saying barely a word.

"Two hot dogs, please," said a young boy holding up a paper bill. After the boy departed with his food, Eva raised her hand and requested the same thing. The man's abrupt demeanor changed when he gave her the food. Her innocent beauty relaxed his stern face and he took time to show her the jars of mustard and relish.

"Your smiling face is enough payment," he said when she held out a dollar bill. When Eva insisted on paying, he waved her off with a smile and waited on his next customer. Embarrassed by the stares of other people standing in the line, she rushed back to join Dagny.

They learned later that this station was only for trains arriving from the south and departing again to southern destinations. If they wished to go north to Somerville, they must go to North Station, and were advised to wait until daylight to do so. Other passengers had taken up residence on several wooden benches and many were already asleep, so they did the same.

A Look at Somerville

Somerville was less than four miles outside of Boston. The first thing Eva did after stepping from the train was look for a yellow automobile with the word TAXI written in black letters. As if she'd turned a switch, a yellow streak whipped down the street screeching to a halt in front of them. The driver jumped out of the vehicle in a cloud of cigarette smoke, threw their bags in the trunk and opened the rear door. Eva immediately showed him Ingrid's address.

"You should have gotten off at the previous station," he said, taking a long puff on his cigarette and slowly exhaling. "Now I will have to drive you all the way back."

"Station…back," she said, pointing to the green building behind her and feeling rather proud that she recognized the words.

"Never mind…get in," he muttered, holding the flopping cigarette between his lips and motioning to the back seat. He'd met up with a lot of foreigners lately and didn't want to take time to try to explain everything.

The taxi jerked forward, stopped to let another car go by and took off, passing that car and a long truck. Then it took a sharp right turn and quickly turned right again. Horns honked and tires squealed as Eva and Dagny huddled close together watching stores, houses and tall buildings fly by the car windows. Finally the traffic thickened and the taxi slowed down. The driver seemed more relaxed now. His wavy black hair curled around the edges of a dingy yellow cap and she could see one of his dark brown eyes squinting in a little mirror on the windshield; she had the odd sensation he was looking back at her. Unnerved by this she slid closer to the door and stared out the window.

Gradually the attractive shops and neat houses changed to older structures in need of fresh paint and in various stages of decline. The taxi slowed to a crawl on a narrow road where grayish buildings stood three stories high and appeared to be attached to each other. Scrawny trees and bushes fought for space on tiny lawns where no flowers grew except for a few clumps of white daisies. The only other bright spots were occasional potted geraniums visible in some of the windows and three children riding bicycles at the end of the road. Eva could not imagine her sister living in such a place.

"Is this the right road?" she asked the man, showing him again the paper with Ingrid's address. He pointed to the number 31 on the paper and gestured to the building where the tarnished brass numbers 25-36 were nailed to the door. Then he opened the trunk and put their bags on the sidewalk. Holding the cigarette between his lips he muttered words that Eva didn't recognize, but his outstretched hand told her he was waiting for the fare. She fumbled in her purse and put a few coins in his hand. He looked at them and scowled.

"You owe me fifty cents more," he mumbled, holding up two fingers. "Two quarters." Again, his cigarette prevented her from understanding what he said. His wandering eyes made her uneasy and she gave him two nickels. He shook his head and with a smirk grabbed her wrist. Then he kissed the back of her hand with a too-long, wet kiss.

"Now we're even," he said with a grin that revealed uneven, brown-stained teeth. Stunned, she watched him hop into the taxi and speed down the road. Then she rubbed the back of her hand on her blue skirt.

"I think he likes you," snickered Dagny.

"He's worse than a rat," said Eva, picking up her bags, the redness of her cheeks caused more from anger than embarrassment. "No more taxis. From now on, Dagny, we will walk."

The front door opened into a small foyer showing two more doors with the numbers 25 and 26. Down a short hallway were two more doors with numbers 27 and 28. They followed an arrow pointing toward a long staircase and walked up to the second floor, dragging their bags behind them.

The door to apartment 31 was ajar. Eva walked into an empty room with faded pink wallpaper, but the windows and floor were sparkling clean, so she placed her bags in the middle of the room and told Dagny to do the same.

"Was that a child's voice?" asked Eva, peeking into a small kitchen.

"That scraping noise sounds more like a scurrying mouse to me," said Dagny.

"This kitchen is too clean to have mice. There isn't a crumb to be seen anywhere," whispered Eva. Then both girls heard the high-pitched laugh of a young child. Sitting in the middle of the adjoining room was an olive-skinned boy playing with a small, wooden toy horse. He was very much surprised and looked up at the women as if he'd been caught stealing cookies from the forbidden cookie jar.

"Gus, he...give to me," said the boy shyly, holding up the hand-carved horse. Eva took hold of Dagny's arm to get her bearings. "Gus is Ingrid's son," she told her. "I'll bet Olle carved that little wooden horse."

Dagny, the stronger one at this moment, took over with her limited knowledge of English.

"Where... Gus?" she asked. The boy shrugged his shoulders. Then his face beamed with pride, as he held up the little horse.

"Gus has real pony!" Eva thought to find her dictionary, but heavy footsteps sounded behind them.

"Michael, are you in here again?" said a woman's loud voice. The boy dropped the horse and ran to the woman. Her complexion was darker than the boy's, but Eva was certain they were mother and son from their round faces, dark eyes and hair. She collected her thoughts and slowly spoke in her best English.

"Ingrid Olson is my sister...do you...know her?"

"Ingrid...nice girl," said the mother in a heavy foreign accent, adding, "they move north." The word north was familiar to Eva.

"Where north?"

The woman shook her head and shrugged her shoulders. The boy tugged on her apron and mumbled. "Excuse...please...must go now," she said, taking her son's hand. Eva, noticing the horse had a broken leg and was probably left behind on purpose, picked it up and gave it to the boy. His smile said thank you as he cuddled the horse in his arms.

Eva looked in her dictionary for words beginning with the letter *p*. "Pony means small horse," she told Dagny. "I think Ingrid and Olle have moved to a farm north of here so that Gus can have a real live pony...that's why Ingrid never got my letter!"

The clouds had thinned by now, letting a few hazy rays of sun brighten up the surrounding grayness. Eva's mood was lighter, too, as they hurried back to the street corner, sitting on their bags while deciding which way to go.

"I'm so thirsty I could drink out of that puddle," said Dagny. Eva, feeling a bit light headed, suddenly realized that neither of them had eaten anything since the night before. To the left were more decrepit buildings, so they headed in the opposite direction toward some tall trees where two automobiles were parked on the roadside.

Behind the trees was a long rectangular building with *Diner* written above it. Through the small narrow windows were faces of happy people eating and talking.

"That building reminds me of a train car," said Dagny as Eva thumbed through her dictionary.

"Both *diner* and *dinner* have to do with eating," said Eva. "Let's go in."

The crowded room was noisy with lunchtime customers, men in working clothes and some in dress suits, but not many women.

"Seat yourself," shouted a girl walking by with a tray full of dishes. Eva spied an empty booth in the back corner and walked towards it. After they made themselves comfortable another waitress showed up.

"Something to drink?" she asked. The two girls looked up to her with questioning eyes. Their homemade clothes and stuffed bags sticking out from under the table told her these two were probably new immigrants, although the red-haired one seemed more clever than most.

"Coffee?" she asked, pointing to a filled pot on the counter.

"Two cups please...and two hot dogs," said Eva. She studied her dictionary until the waitress returned. "Where...is...hotel?" she asked.

A middle-aged man in a nice suit sat across the aisle. He heard Eva's question and turned to look at them.

"I take it you are new arrivals from the old country." The girls' faces brightened, thrilled to hear familiar Swedish words. He recommended a nice boarding house not too far away, but Dagny snapped her head around and spoke to him emphatically. "No boarding house...we are not that kind!" The man grinned and decided to take a different approach.

"I know a nice Swedish lady who rents rooms by the night or by the week, and she also serves meals. If you walk to the end of this street, you can get on a trolley. Just tell the conductor you want to get off near Mrs. Sandquist's house."

Mrs. Sandquist, a white-haired, grandmotherly woman with twinkling blue eyes, spoke fluent Swedish and took Eva and Dagny in as if they were her own daughters.

Their room was bright and clean. A breeze flowed through a window, billowing out the white lace curtains and bringing with it the scent of roses. The sun peeked through onto a sparkling wooden floor and flared across a quilted pink coverlet on the big double bed. Against the flowery wallpaper, a huge oak bureau waited to be filled, and a small, matching desk held writing paper and a pen. They were to share a large bathroom that smelled of lilac soap. Thick yellow towels and wash cloths hung next to an inviting, white-footed bathtub.

"Feel free to take a leisurely bath. The other guests are all away for the afternoon. Supper is served at six downstairs in the dining room." Then Mrs. Sandquist closed the door quietly on two extremely happy and excited girls who could barely wait for a long, hot bath. Their day had gone from hopeful to despairing and back to hopeful again in just a matter of hours.

The Trolley Ride

After supper five people, including Eva and Dagny, sat around an oblong table covered by a white lace tablecloth. Placed in the center was a vase of fresh daisies; two red candle holders on either side held glowing white candles. Everyone had eaten their fill of blueberry pie and was leisurely drinking coffee. The three other guests, speaking in their individual Swedish dialects, were greatly interested in these two new girls, asking them countless questions about their lives in Sweden and their voyage across the Atlantic. Eva also told them about going to her sister's vacant apartment, finding the little boy and the woman telling her that Ingrid had gone north.

"Where would north be from here?" she asked, looking at each guest for an answer.

"When I tell someone I'm going north, that means I'm taking the trolley to Arlington," said Mr. Johnson, a thin, elderly man with round, gold-framed glasses resting halfway down his rather long nose. Peering over them toward Eva, he told her that the town of Arlington bordered Somerville in a northerly direction.

The younger man sitting next to him chuckled. "To me, north is up in the mountains of New Hampshire where deer are plentiful and the bear hunting is good." His name was Ernest and Eva thought him to be in his forties, although he could have been younger. A beard always made a man look old, and his beard was quite full and rather bushy.

The third guest, a shy woman named Sigfrid, shuddered at the thought of New Hampshire. "Such a wild place it is...with deep, dark forests, raging rivers and wolves...and so cold and isolated."

Eva considered all three responses. She could not imagine Ingrid living in the same kind of isolation that she had run away from so many years before, so it seemed unlikely Ingrid would choose to live in New Hampshire. Dagny, on the other hand, was quietly enjoying her coffee thinking back to the Captain and his many adventures.

"To me, north means the North Pole," she blurted out so suddenly that she surprised even herself. Then all the guests sat back in gales of laughter, joking how it would be living with Santa Claus on the North Pole. Thinking they were laughing at her, Dagny grabbed a linen napkin and hid her face.

"Now you have embarrassed poor Dagny," said Mrs. Sandquist, who was refilling the coffee cups again. She put her hand gently on Dagny's shoulder. "I think your idea is best of all."

One by one, the humbled guests agreed with Mrs. Sandquist, who explained to Dagny that the Swedish Jultomten was called Santa Claus in America, and that he lived at the North Pole with Mrs. Claus, his eight reindeer and the many elves who helped make toys for Christmas.

"I'd like to go there, wouldn't you?" asked Dagny. The guests looked at each other and smiled.

"Well now, who wouldn't want to live near Santa Clause and all those wonderful toys!" Everyone nodded in agreement with Mrs. Sandquist, who now had earned a soft spot in the hearts of both Dagny and Eva.

That night Eva dreamed of Santa Claus, the cold North Pole and mountains with wolves howling in the deep forest. She woke up abruptly to see Dagny looking out the window, but the strange howling noise continued.

"A large red truck just went screaming down the road," exclaimed Dagny. Eva was too late to see the truck, but the sirens persisted for a long time.

The whole house was awakened and all the guests had gathered around the table by the time Eva and Dagny arrived for breakfast. This was unusual, they were told, because the three other guests normally trickled down to the table at different times in the morning.

"Well, how nice to have everyone together here for breakfast," commented Mrs. Sandquist. She noticed Sigfrid and Ernest were still a bit sleepy-eyed, but Mr. Johnson, always an early riser, was full of talk.

Sigfrid quietly sipped her coffee, Ernest ate his bacon and eggs more leisurely than usual and Mr. Johnson, who had not yet touched his oatmeal, was giving his opinion about where the fire engines had gone and telling of various house fires he'd seen in the past. Neither Dagny nor Eva had ever seen a building go up in flames and they quickly lost their appetites listening to Mr. Johnson's graphic descriptions of buildings burning, heroic firemen, people left with no place to live, injuries and casualties. Mrs. Sandquist scowled at Mr. Johnson, who finally got the hint and ate his oatmeal in silence. After that, the table was mostly quiet except for spoons clinking in bowls and various sipping sounds from the coffee drinkers. Mrs. Sandquist got the conversation going again.

"I looked up the names Oleson and Olson in the telephone directory, but there was no Ingrid or Olle in Somerville, nor in the surrounding towns."

Mr. Johnson saw the girls' disappointment and said he would inquire at the police station to see if they knew of any Olsons in the area.

"I ride the trolley every day just for fun. Why don't you girls join me today? It would be a fine way for you both to become acquainted with our great city."

Mrs. Sandquist was quick to explain that Mr. Johnson was a retired trolley conductor and very knowledgeable about the area. She suggested they all transfer to the bus at Arlington Heights and ride up to Lexington to see the famous statue of Captain Parker and the Common where the Revolutionary War began.

"I'll make a picnic lunch and you can all eat on Lexington Common," she added.

"A splendid idea!" said Mr. Johnson, who rose immediately from his chair and informed Eva and Dagny that he would meet them in the parlor in half an hour.

Mr. Johnson sat proudly in a green, overstuffed chair with his right hand resting on a carved wooden cane when the girls came downstairs. His suit, the best one he owned, was a bit threadbare at the elbows, but the smile he wore was fit for a king. Compared to his usual daily rides on the trolley, this one promised to be much more eventful. Today he had a mission, and he was excited about being accompanied by two lovely young ladies.

The trolley clattered along the narrow tracks, making frequent stops to let passengers on and off. Eva had forgotten her dictionary, but found that Mr. Johnson knew English quite well, though even he often had trouble keeping up with reading all the signs above the storefront windows.

At first, Eva took note of each structure as he described them: grocery stores and meat markets, pharmacies and stationary stores, places that sold clothes, shoes and household appliances, a bank, fire and police stations, a church, another bank, another church and various restaurants.

"I've never seen so many stores and buildings," exclaimed Eva.

"Well, there has to be for all the thousands of people living here."

"What is that large brick building with the white pillars?"

"That's the public library," he said. "Did you have one in your village?"

"Oh no, but our neighbor, Mr. Kronberg, had a library room in his house. And last year I worked for the Lindholm family and theirs was even larger.

"Well," he smiled, "you will be quite impressed with all the huge rooms filled with floor-to-ceiling racks full of books. I'd be happy to show you around sometime."

The stores soon gave way to private homes, although visible now and then were mills, factories and schools. Mr. Johnson suddenly became quiet, his head dropping into peaceful slumber. Eventually the trolley jerked to the left with a loud screech and he woke up as if he'd never been asleep. They had arrived at the transfer station at Arlington Heights, where they boarded a bus to Lexington.

The padded, plush bus seats were soft and cushiony compared to the hard wooden trolley seats, and the view through the windows soon grew greener and more residentially beautiful. Trees were more abundant and sprinkled between them were large, comfortable houses surrounded by well-manicured lawns and multitudes of colorful, blooming flowers and bushes. They passed by a long brick school and a massive stone church almost hidden by tall trees.

"This is the historic town of Lexington," said Mr. Johnson, pointing out the town hall and several other lovely brick buildings with white trim. The sidewalks were swept clean with only a few well-dressed men and women going about their business.

The bus stopped in the middle of Lexington Center to let off passengers and take on new ones. Mr. Johnson continued with his historical commentary. "This area was originally part of Cambridge and was called Cambridge Farms," he explained. "In 1713 it was incorporated as a separate town and called Lexington...perhaps named after an Englishman named Lord Lexington."

The bus continued by a movie theater, ice cream parlor, railroad station and gift shop.

"This is where we get off," said Mr. Johnson. All three had been sweating on the hot bus, but they had not been overly aware of the heat until now. The noonday sun beat down on them as they crossed the street toward a tall statue of a farmer holding a rifle.

"That's Captain John Parker. He commanded a militia of local farmers against the British soldiers in the famous Battle of Lexington." Mr. Johnson continued talking as they walked down a tree-lined footpath encompassing a large triangle of closely cropped green grass. The girls, not overly interested in hearing about battles and men fighting each other, listened half-heartedly to words they didn't understand, such as revolutionary, Minutemen, militia, British and Redcoats, and instead looked for a shady spot to have lunch. They sat under a large maple tree and ate the delicious ham sandwiches, pickles and peanut butter cookies that Mrs. Sandquist had prepared for them. Also enjoyable was the delightful coolness of a subtle breeze blowing across the great expanse of lush green grass.

"It's so peaceful and relaxing here on the Common," stated Eva, during a lull in Mr. Johnson's historical commentary.

"This place wasn't so peaceful back on April 19 in the year 1775, during the battle of Lexington."

"You mean soldiers might have died on this very spot?" asked Dagny, suddenly putting down her peanut butter cookie.

"That very well could be," he said. Then, to put the girls' minds at ease, he changed the subject. "What do you say we walk down town to Durands and get an ice cream cone?"

"Iced cream? What is that?" said Dagny.

"You will love it," said Eva. "I had some last summer at the Lindholms'. When the creamery wasn't able to take all the cream from the dairy, I helped Cook make ice cream. When we were done she let me eat the frozen cream from the beaters. It was the most heavenly food I've ever eaten...especially on a very hot day like this one."

The ice cream parlor presented another time of indecision for the girls. Three times Mr. Johnson had to read through the long list of flavors and finally he could stand it no longer and ordered his favorite, plain vanilla. Eva, fascinated with the more exotic flavors, finally decided on cherry almond. Dagny, remembering Bertil's farm, chose strawberry. Eating ice cream was like good medicine and banished all thoughts of war and men fighting each other. So far, ice cream was Dagny's favorite thing about America.

On the way home Eva noticed an adorable little house. A large white sign with black letters hung in the window. "The sign says FOR RENT," said Mr. Johnson, thereafter explaining the difference between renting and buying.

"Would someone like me be able to rent that house?" she asked.

Mr. Johnson snickered. "If you had money enough to pay the

rent each month." He didn't know how much that would be, but probably more than she could afford. Of course, he wasn't aware of the little bundle of bills she carried with her all the time beneath her shift; something she wasn't about to reveal to him now.

As they rode back through Arlington, Eva kept seeing the little house in her mind; the rows of neat shops on either side, how it set back from the sidewalk, and what might be a nice lawn if the tall, dead grass was cut. She envisioned the dark, grayish house painted white, the scraggly bushes neatly trimmed, and flowers blooming on either side of the front porch. On the grassy front lawn would be a wooden sign painted yellow with blue letters that read YARN SHOP.

"What are you smiling about?" asked Mr. Johnson.

"I was just thinking about that little house."

"It doesn't cost anything to dream, Eva," he replied dubiously, leaning his head back against the seat.

"I'm not just dreaming," she stated. "I'm thinking seriously about renting it." She was so emphatic that he sat up straight in his seat. His jaw dropped and she could see the whites of his eyes. "Well!" was all he could say. Then, he repeated to himself. "Well, well..."

No more words came from Mr. Johnson's mouth, but his mind was spinning. How could a girl fresh from the old country be able to pay that kind of money each month to rent a house? The whole idea was preposterous.

"Perhaps you should think about getting a job before you spend money that you probably don't have," he told her. "That house has been for sale for over a year. I hear it will need a lot of repairs."

Dagny took note of Eva's dampened spirit and spoke up.

"I can get a job, too...we can fix it up together!"

"That's kind of you, Dagny, but Mr. Johnson is probably right. It is just a silly notion." Eva turned to look out the window, but saw nothing but the little house in her mind. Mr. Johnson saw her disappointment and tried to make amends.

"It was not my intention to discourage you, Eva. I just wanted to prepare you for any unseen difficulties that might arise."

"There is much I don't understand and I'm grateful for your concern, Mr. Johnson, but I am not discouraged."

Mr. Johnson could not bear to see Eva's unhappy face and tried to cheer her up.

"Anything is possible these days," he replied. "If there is anything I can do, let me know."

Eva's sudden sadness was not only about the house. It was also about the baby. Lately, she had been prone to moments of foreboding...times when an all-consuming fear of bringing up a child alone overwhelmed her usual calm demeanor. How she missed Karl's comforting embrace and quiet strength. In her daydreams she often spoke to him and heard his familiar reassurance that all things usually had a way of working out for the good of all.

Sometimes these conversations were not silent and Dagny would look at her and smile. "You're talking to yourself again," she would say. Eva had been embarrassed at first, but after a few times she'd been able to confide some of her thoughts to Dagny, who understood completely. "I used to talk to Blix all the time back at the potato farm," Dagny explained. "I'd climb into his crib and he'd lay his head on my chest and fall asleep, but I just kept talking and felt better because of it." When Dagny said no more Eva didn't invade her friend's privacy. There were some things that couldn't be put into words. She supposed there were many people who carried little secrets hidden in their hearts for as long as they lived.

Eva's concern was how to earn money and at the same time care for this child that was growing in her belly. Ideally, she would see her dream materialize; a building large enough for a yarn shop and also ample living space to accommodate all her personal needs. One look at this house had convinced her that this was the ideal place to live and have a business.

The Little House

Eva spent a sleepless night making plans for the little house and wondering what it looked like inside. That's all she could talk about at breakfast the next morning. Mr. Johnson listened thoughtfully, finishing his oatmeal in silence. Then, having made the decision to do everything possible to make Eva's dream come true, he hastily excused himself from the table. He remembered seeing a telephone number in the corner of the FOR RENT sign.

By lunchtime he had called the owner and made an appointment for Eva and Dagny to see the house at three that afternoon.

"If you wish, I could go along as interpreter," he suggested to Eva. "Some sales people can't be trusted, especially around women, and having a man present might encourage honesty." That was true, of course, but his own curiosity about the house was foremost in his mind.

They arrived early and Eva could not wait to investigate the back yard. The house was larger than she had first thought. She envisioned room enough for the yarn shop downstairs and living quarters on the second floor, where two dormer windows looked out to the front and rear. A small shed was attached to the house and two crooked apple trees set on each corner of a fenced-in back yard. Dagny pulled out a clump of dead grass and scooped up some soil.

"A garden might even grow here," she said as the dark loam sifted through her hands.

When the owner arrived and unlocked the front door, Eva saw at once that Mr. Johnson had been correct when he said the house would need a lot of work. She was grateful he had remained silent and did not say, "I told you so."

The walls and ceiling needed new plaster and the floors were uneven and dirty. Huge gray cobwebs clung to the corners of the room, draping the hazy windows like dirty lace curtains. Nonetheless, Eva saw a perfect place for her little shop filled with shelves of brightly colored yarns. A trail of dusty footprints followed them into the back room where piles of old furniture, lumber and cardboard boxes littered the floor.

"You can have all this junk," said the owner with a sweep of his long arm, "as well as that old ice box and stove by the door."

There were two soapstone sinks on one wall and a small bathroom in the corner, but the wash basin and toilet were dirty and stained.

"A little bleach and elbow grease will fix that up in no time," he said apologetically. Then, feeling ashamed of the filthy conditions, he added, "in fact, if you want to clean the house yourself, I'll give you the first month's rent free." Mr. Johnson nodded his approval to Eva and she agreed.

They took a stairway to the second floor and Eva's imagination went wild again. At once she envisioned a kitchen on the sunny side of the large front room, the remainder being used for dining and possibly a small sitting area. There were three back rooms; a good-sized bathroom, complete with a heavily stained, footed bathtub, and two smaller rooms with mismatched single beds and sun-faded bureaus. Two soiled mattresses drooped against one wall with little gnawed holes that mice or rats had probably made to raise their families. When the owner asked if Eva wanted the old beds and bureaus, Mr. Johnson answered for her.

"Of course they do, but those mattresses aren't good for anything." The owner promised to take them to the dump.

On the way home Mr. Johnson explained about lawyers and contracts. He knew of a lawyer who spoke Swedish and said he would make an appointment.

The next day the three of them walked to Mr. Yman's office in Davis Square. He reminded Eva so much of Mr. Kronberg that she had no fear and trusted his every word. Once introductions had been made, Mr. Johnson excused himself and sat out in the waiting room. For this, Eva was grateful because she was able to confide to Mr. Yman about the money she'd brought with her from Sweden. He advised her to purchase the house outright, which would be much cheaper in the long run than paying rent each month.

"If you do buy the house," he added, "you will be required to pay yearly property taxes...in addition to the usual monthly expenses, such as electricity, fuel for heating, insurance and any necessary repairs." Eva knew about burning wood in the stove and making candles, but had not considered taxes and insurance. Still, she listened carefully, feeling confident that everything would work out all right. It was as if a higher power was in control, helping her ask the proper questions and make the right decisions...something short of a miracle.

"When can I buy it?" she asked, surprising both Dagny and Mr. Yman.

"As soon as I write up a contract, transfer the deed and have your payment, we will get together with the seller and do the necessary signings," he told her. "I'd say probably within a week or two."

"Oh, that long?" she asked. "I was hoping to get started on the cleaning right away."

Mr. Yman liked her enthusiasm and said he would speak to the owner.

Eva and Dagny cleaned the upstairs first, beginning with the bedrooms. So anxious were the girls to stay overnight in their new house, they decided to sleep on the floor, wrapped up in clean quilts that Mrs. Sandquist had said were too worn for her guests to use. She had also thrown in two soft pillows and some old towels.

"That was a lot of money you gave to the lawyer," said Dagny later in the evening as they lay awake on the soft quilts.

"Mr. Yman said buying the house is a good investment, but I do worry about all the other expenses."

"Mother gave me money when we left the potato farm. I still have most of it," said Dagny.

"You keep your money for now," said Eva. "We'll just take

one day at a time and see how things work out."

"Well, I promised to stay with you until after the baby is born and I intend to pay my way in the meantime."

"Helping clean the house is payment enough for now. Just you being here is a great comfort to me,"said Eva, rubbing her belly and thinking about the baby.

They were awake for a while, absorbed in their own thoughts. The moon had risen; it shone through the side window, gently spreading a wide ray of light across the room.

"I'm sweltering," said Dagny, getting up to open the window. Eva saw her gazing up to the moon and thought she was praying.

"What do you say to the moon when you pray?" she asked, but Dagny was caught unawares and didn't answer right away.

"I don't really talk to the moon," she said after a while. "When I see his face I know he is looking down on me and will take care of me in the night."

"He? So the moon is a man?" asked Eva.

"The moon has wisdom like a man, but the moon isn't a person."

"And the sun?"

"Mother used to say that Sunna, the sun goddess, rides through the sky in her chariot pulled by two horses, Arvak and Alsvid, so I think of the sun as a woman full of light and goodness. My prayers are simple," said Dagny. "But your book has many words. Does your prayer take a long time?"

Eva smiled in the semi-darkness. "Well, sometimes it takes a while to be inspired, but other times God's love is instantaneous."

Dagny was thinking where Eva's God was when the mean Augusta caused her so much trouble. But not wanting to make her friend sad by bringing up the past, she didn't say anything. At the same time, Eva was thinking of Dagny's difficult childhood. Were the sun and moon hiding behind clouds then? Dagny somewhat answered Eva's question without being asked.

"My prayers haven't always come true when I wanted them to. Have yours?" asked Dagny after a while.

"Not always," said Eva. It may be that we are not ready for

what we ask for...sometimes we must learn patience and work harder to be a better person before our prayers are answered."

Dagny came back to lay on her quilt, but she had one more question. "I can see the moon and sun, but you cannot see your God, so how do you know he is there?"

"I know God is with me always because I can feel his goodness, his power and his love," said Eva. "To me, God is an unseen presence and power, providing, guarding and guiding me to do what is right and good."

"It is the same with me. The sun and moon have been in the sky since the beginning of time. Even on a cloudy day when they are hidden from view, I know they are still there."

"So we are not that different, are we?" said Eva, yawning. "It's just that we see God in our own personal way."

"No, we are not that different," sighed Dagny, exhaling loudly with a big yawn of her own.

Under the pillow Dagny's hand felt the soft brush and a shower of guilt fell over her. If she didn't confess right now there would be little sleep tonight.

"I stole something from you," she blurted out into the quiet night.

"What do you mean?" asked Eva, rolling over on one elbow and looking straight at her friend.

"It's a long story, do you want to hear it all?"

"I love long stories," said Eva. "Not only that, but now you have aroused my curiosity and I want to hear everything."

Not sure where to begin, Dagny sat up on her quilt and scratched her head.

"Well...um...I'm not very good at telling stories."

"That's alright. Just take your time and pretend I'm not here," said Eva, lying back on her pillow with her hands folded across her chest. Dagny took a big breath, cleared her throat and began.

"Well, it was after mother and I left the potato farm that day. We got lost and ended up at your house. It was pouring rain and we went to the barn to sleep. The next morning I found a pail of milk in the springhouse. Mother and I were very hungry and hadn't had fresh milk and cream for a long time, so we ate all the cream with our bread and then drank all the milk." Dagny stopped talking and glanced over at Eva. "We shouldn't have eaten what didn't belong to us," she said with a sniffle.

Eva sat up and took hold of Dagny's hand. "Don't you worry one bit about the milk. I had already gone by that time and the milk would surely have spoiled if you hadn't used it up."

Dagny took another deep breath and continued.

"We had eaten too much and afterwards I ran behind the barn to throw up, but mother laid on the hay groaning with a bellyache. After a while she asked me to go to the house to find some mustard or salt to help relieve her belly. After I found the salt I should have left, but I didn't...I got nosy and went into your room. That's when I took your brush."

Dagny stroked the brush lovingly in her hand. "I just wanted something to remind me of you," and then she broke down and cried.

"It's all right, Dagny. I'm sure you were just curious. I would probably have done the same thing." She embraced Dagny and consoled her.

"I was going to put the brush back, but mother knew how much having it meant to me. She told me to keep it...that someday we might see you again and I could give it back to you." Then Dagny stretched out her arm to give Eva the brush.

"If I had wanted the brush, I would have taken it with me. I have another one, so I want you to keep it." She hugged Dagny again and all misgivings were forgiven and forgotten.

They both woke up to a piercing squeal, followed by loud banging and clanking coming from outside. Dagny jumped up first to look out the open window and saw a boy about her age carrying a large metal container on his back. She watched him walk to the curb and dump the contents into the back of a large truck.

"There's a truck out front with big red letters written on it."

Eva grabbed her dictionary, but the smell told her more than words. "I think he is taking garbage from the building next door," said Eva, but Dagny wasn't paying attention. She was focused on the boy, who had come back and was placing the empty container into a hole in the ground. Suddenly he turned around to look up at her.

"Hello, miss. Will you be having any garbage to pick up next week?" His face was pleasing to her, but not knowing a word he said, she backed up too quickly and hit her head on the window. By the time she looked again, he had walked half way down the driveway. She liked the way he walked and how his breeches were a little too tight. She craned her neck to watch him jump easily onto the rear of the truck.

"So, what did he say to you?" asked Eva with a smirk.

"I have no idea, but he has a nice smile and..." Dagny giggled and hid her face in her hands.

"Probably he told you what beautiful black hair you have."

"Oh, Eva. I got out of bed so quickly I never combed my hair!"

"To tell the truth, you look very attractive with your hair all messed up," confessed Eva.

Dagny looked into the cracked mirror and didn't recognize herself. She rather liked the way she looked, too. After that, she braided her hair a little looser, fluffing up the sides and top, before pinning it up softly around her head.

In less than two weeks' time the bushes were trimmed, grass mowed and the interior of the house was spotless. Mr. Johnson and Ernest plastered the walls and ceilings one weekend. They wanted no pay for their work, but Eva made certain there was plenty of coffee and treats, plus a big noontime dinner each day.

Adventuring Out

Eva had begun the ritual every morning of picking out a common English phrase from the back of her dictionary. She would read it to Dagny and tell her to speak those words to herself during that particular day. However, Dagny's mind was filled with images of the garbage boy and left little room for learning English.

It wasn't until the next Friday that all this changed. Mr. Johnson stopped in early that morning to tell Dagny he'd just seen a help-wanted sign in the butcher shop window. She had expected him to accompany her, but he thought it would be best if she went to the shop by herself to inquire about the job. Now she was ready to study some English phrases.

"I yam...loook for erk," Dagny said for the tenth time.

"Look at my lips," said Eva patiently as she repeated very slowly, "I... am... looking... for... work." It was difficult for Dagny to get her tongue around the letters and they never did come out exactly right. Mr. Johnson sat listening to her futile attempts and after drinking two cups of coffee decided he'd better accompany her to the market.

In less than half an hour Dagny came bursting through the front door shouting, "I got yob...I got yob!" She always had trouble pronouncing the letter 'J'.

"Not yob, Dagny," reprimanded Eva. "Say it correctly...job."

"It doesn't matter, I'm too excited now to speak English," she said in Swedish. "I begin work on Monday morning at six o'clock."

By mid-afternoon the August heat was suffocating. Eva opened every window in the house, hoping a cross breeze might blow through, but the outside, humid air was oppressive, bringing with it an army of hungry mosquitoes and flies. After closing all the windows, Eva and Dagny sat on the porch and ate cheese and jelly sandwiches, discussing whether to spend money on new screens for the windows or mattresses for their beds. They decided to buy one screen at a time, beginning with the small window on the east side of their bedroom.

"Now that we have a proper address I'm going to write a letter to Mats," said Eva. "I'm anxious to see the pictures that Mr. Kaneko took of us."

She intended to write only a few lines, but kept thinking of more to say. Dagny practiced writing her name, struggling to form each letter. She looked over to Eva, whose pen flowed swiftly and neatly across the page.

"Your writing is beautiful," said Dagny. "What does your letter say?"

"I told Mats how we tried to find Ingrid, about staying with Mrs. Sandquist and the day Mr. Johnson took us on the trolley ride and saw this house for the first time."

"I should probably write to Mother and Bertil," sighed Dagny.

Eva put aside her letter. "Of course...let's get at it right now."

"No, you finish writing. It takes me so long to print one letter that I forget what's in my head and get all mixed up. Anyway, I'm too tired to write anymore tonight."

Eva's letter to Mats was over four pages long. When she read it aloud in the morning, she thought it sounded silly, but Dagny listened eagerly to every word and said it was a lovely story. Eva slid a fresh piece of paper over to Dagny. "Are you ready to begin?" she asked.

"No!" said Dagny, "I think you should write it!"

"I will help you, but you are writing this letter," stated Eva firmly.

Almost two hours later, after many mistakes and scribbled pieces of paper, Dagny's letter was finished. Only three short sentences long, the large printed words took up the whole page.

"We did it!" said Dagny proudly as she held the masterpiece in her hands.

Eva put her hand on Dagny's arm and looked her in the eye. "No, Dagny, you did it...you printed these words all by yourself. I'm so proud of you."

"Mother and Bertil will be proud of me, too," said Dagny, wondering out loud how such a tiny envelope might find its way back to Sweden.

"Of course they'll get your letter," said Eva, "but it might take a month before you get an answer."

"We can take our letters down to the post office this afternoon," Eva continued. "They will make sure everything goes to the right place."

"Aren't you going to write to Karl?" asked Dagny, still thinking how far away Sweden was.

"You read my mind, Dagny, but I just don't know what to say or how to say it. And what's the use anyway. I told you how Mrs. Lindholm inspects all the incoming mail. She would never let Karl see a letter from me."

"Well, I think you should give it a try. You never know, perhaps his mother will be sick that day and someone else will sort out the mail."

"That would be too much to hope for," replied Eva as she sliced bread for sandwiches. "Let's have lunch and then I'll decide."

Eva took one small bite of her sandwich and chewed it for a long time. She could think of nothing now but Karl. Her stomach tightened into a hard knot and she put the sandwich on her plate. "I can't think of the right words to say," she told Dagny. "I do want Karl to know that I still love him...and that it wasn't my choice to leave, but..."

"No buts...just write that down on paper and be done with it," ordered Dagny. "You'll feel so much better by letting him know the truth." Eva began to write, but the words didn't sound right and the writing was uneven. "I'll finish this tomorrow," she said, folding it up and putting the paper in her pocket.

All afternoon she thought about Karl, but it wasn't until she was in bed and Dagny was snoring that the right words came to her. She quietly went into the kitchen and wrote the letter, returning to bed satisfied and falling immediately to sleep.

Mr. Johnson often found excuses to stop in and visit the girls. In his hand was usually a gift...some little thing for the house or a special baked treat from Mrs. Sandquist. Saturday was one of those days. His gift was an invitation from Mrs. Sandquist asking them to join the boarders for a roast chicken dinner the next day.

Being Sunday, Mrs. Sandquist wanted them to come early to attend the Swedish Church and meet the parishioners.

Dagny would have wished to sit in the very last row, but Mrs. Sandquist proudly led the girls to a pew near the front. All eyes were on the newcomers. Dagny looked neither to the left nor right, her eyes fixated on Eva's blue dress sashaying back and forth in front of her down the very long aisle. If she were to look up, she'd have seen that most eyes were also on the striking redhead in the blue dress.

It wasn't until they were seated that Dagny looked around at the beautiful colored windows lining the walls. Eva had seen the window pictures immediately upon entering the church and recognized each one of them.

"Aren't the window pictures beautiful?" whispered Eva. Dagny nodded approvingly, but the pictures meant nothing to her.

"That one is of shepherds on a hill overlooking the holy family, the next is Daniel in the lion's den and the third is Jesus preaching in a synagogue." Eva gestured to the other side. "That one is Moses holding tablets of the Ten Commandments, then Jesus with the loaves and fishes and finally the crucifixion." Dagny didn't understand any of it and looked away without commenting.

"They are stories from the bible," whispered Eva. "I'll explain more about them to you later."

Mrs. Sandquist gave Eva a hymnal and suddenly everyone rose and began singing. Eva had often heard her mother humming in the kitchen, and the first melody was one she remembered. Since the hymnal was in Swedish, she quickly found her place and fell into the rhythm of the song. By the second verse her voice was loud and clear, causing Dagny to gaze at her in amazement. Admiring Eva wasn't unusual for Dagny; almost every day she saw some unexpected surprise regarding her friend.

After the service, as everyone gathered downstairs for refreshments, a rather large and boisterous woman barged through the crowd and took Eva's hand.

"I'm Mrs. Bergstrom." Then she pointed to a distinguished looking man at the buffet table. "That tall man in the brown suit is my husband, Dr. Bernard Bergstrom...the best dentist in Somerville." It was apparent she was very proud of her husband as she continued rambling on, not giving anyone else an opportunity to respond.

"You must be those two lovely girls that Mr. Johnson told me about...the ones who are fixing up the old Clark place...and doing a fine job of it, too."

Finally Mrs. Sandquist was able to intervene. "Yes, Mrs. Bergstrom. May I present Eva Gunderson and her friend Dagny..." She couldn't remember Dagny's last name, but it didn't matter because it was Eva who had Mrs. Bergstrom's full attention.

"Mr. Johnson told me you are looking for work. Is that true, Miss Gunderson?"

Eva had only a chance to nod in agreement before two young girls came running toward them, the youngest pulling on Mrs. Bergstrom's lavender skirt asking if she might have a cookie.

"Oh, let me introduce my daughters. Emily is ten and Emma is seven...girls, this is Eva Gunderson."

Both girls looked at Eva in awe, but it was the youngest who asked about her hair. "Are you wearing a wig?"

"Emma! That isn't a very polite thing to say," said her mother. "You may have a cookie after you eat a sandwich." Then she dismissed both girls with a wave of her hand. "Now...where were we? Oh, yes...I'm looking for someone to help me with housework and to stay with the children after school. Would you be interested in doing that, Eva?"

Working Girls

Monday dawned sunny, and cool as a crisp autumn day. After seeing Dagny off to the meat market, Eva took the trolley to

Somerville. She was familiar with the area where the Bergstrom's lived and was looking for something specific that Mrs. Bergstrom had told her.

"It's a big white house with my husband's dentist office added on to the first floor. You can't miss it. There's a big tooth hanging in the front window."

Eva expected to see a picture of a tooth, but what she saw was a huge paper form that filled the window space complete with eyes, nose and smiling lips. This told her something about the proper Dr. Bergstrom: he had a sense of humor. Mrs. Bergstrom had also told Eva that there wouldn't be much to do today but look through the house, become familiar with their family routine and most importantly to get personally acquainted with Emily and Emma.

Mrs. Bergstrom led the way upstairs to an immaculate guest room...a bedroom furnished with well-preserved antique furniture and a beautiful heirloom quilt with little figures wearing sunbonnets appliqued on different colored squares of cotton cloth. She was quite out of breath and gestured toward an inviting blue-velvet chair.

"This is a Queen Anne chair that belonged to my husband's mother," she said proudly. "Please sit down and feel how comfortable it is." Then Mrs. Bergstrom sat on a straight-back oak chair beside a table whose top was inlaid with alternating light and dark squares of wood.

"This table is always ready for a game of checkers," she said with a hearty laugh that made Eva smile, even though she had no idea what checkers were. She looked around the room as Mrs. Bergstrom described the four-poster bed, elaborate carved mirror over a matching bureau and several old portraits of Dr. Bergstrom's parents and grandparents. As she delved into the history of each portrait, Eva decided her employer was very content to do nothing but sit and talk, wasting much valuable time discussing her knowledge of old cameras, photographs and something called daguerreotypes. Eva cared little about the many faded brown and tan photographs that seemed little more than pale sketches, feeling as though she wasn't earning her pay by relaxing in Queen Anne's velvety chair and twiddling her thumbs.

It wasn't until Mrs. Bergstrom ran out of things to say that she moved on to the next room, stopping briefly in the doorway of an untidy master bedroom with a quick apology for clothes strewn over chairs and the bed still unmade. Then on to the girls' room with toys and more clothes scattered about, and lastly a large messy bathroom with wet towels on the floor and a spotted mirror on the wall. All at once Eva's hands were itching to scrub and straighten up these three rooms, but Mrs. Bergstrom was already on her way down the hall spouting out more apologies and excuses.

"I haven't had any help for over a month," she complained, "and I've been so busy with my women's projects, social work and making sure the girls get to their dance class and piano lessons."

"It will take me no time at all to put the rooms in order," said Eva, standing expectantly at the top of the stairs.

"It's time for coffee, dear," she hollered back. "You can do that later."

Did Mrs. Bergstrom always put off working in favor of resting or visiting? Eva pondered this as she made her way to the kitchen.

It was no surprise to Eva that Mrs. Bergstrom ignored the unwashed breakfast dishes as she turned on the burner under the coffee pot and set four cinnamon buns on a plate, all the while telling Eva where the silver and dishes were stored, opening drawers to show the linens and towels and revealing pots, pans and cleaning aids in the base cabinets.

"Let's sit down while the coffee perks," she said. Although not a good housekeeper herself, Mrs. Bergstrom was quite explicit about what she expected Eva to do each day.

"First, make up the beds and tidy up the bedrooms, clean the bathroom and vacuum the hall and stairway. Then concentrate on the downstairs, washing the breakfast dishes, counters and floor, dusting and vacuuming the dining room, parlor, and front hall when needed."

"The girls come home from school a little before noon and there will be instructions for lunch if I'm away. The doctor will also be here for lunch and relaxation between twelve and one o'clock, and if you have time, there is always a pile of ironing waiting to be done until the girls arrive home from school around three fifteen."

She explained that being a doctor's wife was a busy one; besides her book club, and bridge club, she was also required to attend many other social events, church meetings and various luncheons in the area. At holiday times, she was busier and might need Eva's help on Saturdays. From the kitchen came the sound of gurgling coffee and she asked Eva to bring in the mid-morning snack.

The coffee was good, but the bun was too sweet for Eva's morning taste, although she managed to finish it by the time Mrs. Bergstrom had eaten the other three. It was no surprise that her employer's dress was stretched too tightly across her back and the little buttons in front were hard-pressed to stay in the buttonholes.

"I was thin and trim like you once," she said. "But that was before the children came along."

Eva's eyes immediately darted from the too-small dress to a stack of magazines on the floor.

"Do you read all those magazines?" she asked.

"I don't know why I subscribe to every new periodical that comes along," Mrs. Bergstrom said. "I supposed it is better than going out and buying a new dress every month like some women do."

Eva nodded in agreement, although she was shocked at the idea that some women might buy a new dress every month. They sat quietly for a while and then Eva heard Mrs. Bergstrom snoring. Quietly Eva brought the dirty dishes into the kitchen and went upstairs to the bedrooms.

Within a half hour she was back in the kitchen tackling the stack of dirty dishes leftover from breakfast.

A door closed and soon Dr. Bergstrom appeared in the

kitchen.

"Hello, Miss Gunderson. And how are you today?" he said, hanging his white jacket over a chair. It was lunchtime and Eva had no idea what to serve him. She said hello, dried her hands and was relieved to see his wife entering from the parlor. Dr. Bergstrom went directly to the refrigerator, took out some ham and cheese, grabbed a loaf of bread and started making himself a sandwich. Mrs. Bergstrom heated up the coffee and sat down with her husband. Apparently the doctor was quite capable of making his own lunch, which was a great surprise to Eva. In Sweden she had never seen a man lift a hand in the kitchen. She went into the parlor to dust and immediately noticed an opened magazine on Mrs. Bergstrom's chair. On the table next to it was a half-eaten box of chocolates.

Emily and Emma arrived home from school a little after three o'clock, changed into their play clothes and sat at the kitchen table watching Eva's every step as she prepared a snack of milk and cookies. Their mother sat with them drinking another cup of coffee.

"Sit down and join us, Eva," said Mrs. Bergstrom. "It will give you and the girls a chance to get acquainted." The girls spoke very good English and also understood many common Swedish words and phrases.

"Their father doesn't want the old language to be forgotten," said Mrs. Bergstrom. She was about to say more, but was interrupted by Emma.

"On every Wednesday we have Swedish night," she said, proudly, spouting out several Swedish words that didn't fit together. "And sometimes we wear our Swedish costumes."

Emily, apparently not as enthused as her sister, rolled her eyes as if all this Swedish stuff was something that had to be endured. Mrs. Bergstrom ignored her elder daughter and explained that on certain Swedish holidays they all wore their Swedish clothes and ate the customary foods for that particular occasion.

"It's a good way to make Swedish history come alive, don't you think, Eva?"

"I think it is a splendid idea," but before she could say more, Emma interrupted again.

"Mama...can Miss Gunderson come over on Wednesday night?"

"We'll see, dear. I'll have to speak with your father."

That put an end to that conversation and when they finished eating Eva went up to the girls' room so they could show her all their toys and games. Of course, Eva had already seen most of them, especially the ones she'd picked up and put away in the toy chest.

Eva got off the trolley near the grocery, bought some fresh green beans and a bag of potatoes, then walked the quarter mile home. She had eaten so often during the day that she wasn't at all hungry, but she knew Dagny would be starved.

Dagny came home tired and dirty, but the brownish-green bedraggled plants she held in her hand looked worse. She showed Eva the tiny new green shoots growing underneath the dead tops.

"The girl at the flower shop saw me looking at them and put the whole box in my hand. I shook my head because I wasn't going to pay one little penny for anything looking that bad. Then the girl put her hands up saying 'free...free' and pushed me out the door before I could set them down."

"If you pinch off the old leaves, they will look better," said Eva, hoping that the seedlings might have a better chance of surviving.

When Eva awakened on Tuesday morning, Dagny wasn't lying on her quilt and her clothes weren't on the chair. Either it was later than she thought or Dagny went to work earlier than usual. She put on water to heat for coffee, splashed cold water on her face and was getting dressed when she heard the squeaky brakes of the garbage truck. When she glanced out between the buildings, she saw Dagny planting flowers near the garbage can cover.

"That little imp!" thought Eva. "Those plants were just an

excuse to be out there when the garbage truck came." Today, though it was an older man with a beard walking up the drive and not the cute young man Dagny was expecting. She stomped up the stairs and was in a sour mood.

"Someone else picked up the garbage today," Dagny said dejectedly. Eva felt her disappointment.

"Maybe he's sick. He'll probably be back next week. Come have some breakfast and you'll feel better."

"I'm not hungry. I have to go to work," said Dagny, as she treaded heavily down the stairs.

Four days later Dagny came home, tired and dirty as usual, but this time her face was beaming with delight.

"You'll never guess what happened today!"

"Let me try," said Eva, rolling her eyes and pretending to think of something extraordinary that might possibly happen in a meat store. But Dagny was too excited to wait for Eva's response.

"Arne came into the store to buy meat today."

"Arne? Do I know him?" asked Eva, knowing full well who he was but not letting on to Dagny.

"He's that cute garbage boy. I actually spoke to him in Swedish."

While Eva was thinking about what to say next, Dagny was halfway to the bathroom and hollered back.

"He'll be here at seven."

Filled with nervous anticipation, Dagny picked at her food.

"Does my hair look all right?" she asked. Eva went over and tucked in a few loose ends of her braid and fluffed out the sides.

"Are you going somewhere special?" she asked Dagny.

"Just for a walk and maybe to ride the bus for ice cream."

Arne arrived promptly at seven wearing a clean shirt and trousers, his face scrubbed to a shine. When Dagny introduced him to Eva, he smiled bashfully, bowing politely in the old Swedish way. Honored by his respect, Eva was feeling more like Dagny's mother than her friend.

"Glad to me...meet you," he said with a slight stutter.

"I'm happy to meet you also," said Eva.

After a lengthy, uncomfortable silence, she added, "now you two have a nice evening."

"We'll be ba...back before da...dark," he stammered.

Eva stood by the window watching them walk side-by-side down the sidewalk towards the bus station. They were both looking straight ahead and she wondered if these two shy young people had much to say to each other.

After washing the supper dishes, she sat down at the kitchen table to knit. Good ideas often came to her while knitting and tonight she remembered a conversation with Mrs. Bergstrom about selling both Swedish and American yarns.

"You'd be kept in good business by just the ladies of the Swedish church," Mrs. Bergstrom had said with her boisterous laugh. "They'd probably be willing to pay any amount you ask to have yarn from the old country." She later found the address of a yarn supplier in Stockholm and gave it to Eva.

Eva wrote down the amounts and varieties of yarn that she thought might sell here in America. The list was long and very expensive with the freight added on...money that she didn't have right now. It would take weeks to hear back from the company and fears crept in about doing business overseas. What if she sent her money and never received the shipment? What if the yarn arrived damp and moldy? There were too many 'what ifs' and she put down her pencil in despair. Doing business overseas was too risky. What she needed to do was find a farmer who had sheep and make her own yarn.

Shadows were lengthening across the street and many buses had passed by the house, but there was no sign of Dagny and Arne. All traces of color vanished from Eva's view as the distant buildings merged with the darkening sky. One by one, the friendly glow of golden lights appeared in neighboring windows and the streetlights cast white circles on the sidewalk. It was way past time for the last bus to be arriving at the station. Eva turned on the porch light and went upstairs to get undressed. She waited by the window until a bus finally stopped. When two figures ran across the street toward the shop, she laid down on her quilt.

The front door opened and closed and then Eva heard footsteps on the stairs. Dagny tip-toed into the bedroom and sat by the window. After a while Eva's voice broke the quietness of the room.

"Did you have a nice time?"

"Ya," was all Dagny said.

Eva's head filled with precarious notions, but she said nothing and waited, listening while Dagny got undressed. Finally she laid down on her quilt.

"Arne wanted to talk with you tonight, but we thought you were asleep. He's very upset."

"About what?"

"That he didn't get me home before dark as he said he would."

Eva was greatly relieved and said, "I was a little worried that the last bus was late."

"Well...we went to Lexington Center to get an ice cream...and the bus broke down. We had to wait for another one. Arne wants to see me again next week but he's afraid you won't let him in the house again."

"I'm not angry with Arne. It wasn't any fault of his that the bus broke down. I like Arne. He seems like a very proper boy."

"Yes, he is," said Dagny with great relief and joy in her voice. "I'm going to marry him!"

"What? How can you say that? You barely know him."

"I know all I need to know," she said emphatically.

Eva was wide awake now and sat up straight on her quilt. "Is he the first boy you have ever liked?"

Dagny thought about the many sailors she'd met at the boardinghouse, the student and others. "I have liked a few boys, but Arne is different from all the rest."

"In what way?" asked Eva.

"It is hard to explain, but I'll try," said Dagny, rising on one elbow and taking her time. "First of all...I feel at ease with him. We can be quiet together and sometimes we speak at the same time. He makes me laugh and I like the way his eyes twinkle when he smiles at me...and he's kind and respectful to me and everyone we meet."

Eva wondered how much one can learn about a person in only a few hours.

"Well, those things are very important, but marriage is a big step from just going out for an ice cream."

"I know," said Dagny. "Most boys talk all the time and are too forward, but when I speak Arne listens, as if what I have to say is important. And he treats me as if I were...um...too good to touch." Then she added, "I had to hold my hands together tightly on the bus because I wanted to hold his hand so much."

"Does he care for you as much as you care for him?"

"I think so...the very last thing he did was kiss the back of my hand." Then Dagny lay back down on her quilt and there was no sound in the room...until Eva started giggling.

"What's so funny?" asked Dagny.

"It's a good thing today is Saturday."

"Why?"

"Because the market is closed tomorrow. You won't have to wash your hand until Monday."

Dagny chuckled. "I'm glad you thought of that." Then she sighed, slowly raising the kissed hand and gently pressing the back of it against her lips.

Arne

When Dagny came home from work the next Friday night, she had a look similar to when she had brought home the dying flowers; that same smirk spreading across her face like she had some big secret.

"Guess what I have?"

"Oh, Dagny, I'm not so good at guessing games. Let's see...is it more flowers?"

"Nope."

"Hmmm, is it something to eat?"

"Yes...and it was free!"

"Surely no one is giving away good food. It isn't spoiled, is it?"

"I'm sure it's fresh because I cut it myself," said Dagny, giving Eva a large package wrapped in white paper.

"Stew meat...how wonderful. There must be two pounds here!"

"Three, more likely," replied Dagny, explaining to Eva that because of the very hot weather no one had purchased much stew meat and the butcher said she could have it.

"I don't care if the weather is hot or cold. I always love a good stew," said Eva gratefully.

Arne knocked on the door early the next morning and peeked in. He stood on the threshold with an armload of fresh vegetables, but would not come in. First he apologized to Eva for keeping Dagny out after dark.

"I understand about unforeseen circumstances," she told him. "The bus breaking down was something you had no control over and I certainly do not hold you responsible for coming home late. Now, please come inside."

Only then did he enter the room, persuaded also, perhaps, by the delicious aroma of simmering meat wafting downstairs from the kitchen. Dagny had been standing behind Eva and now came forward to take the potatoes, carrots and onions.

"Arne grew all these on his own land," she said proudly.

"So you have a farm?" asked Eva.

"A small fa...farm," he said, "but I have pla...plans to have a mu...much larger one someday."

Eva noticed a tender look between Arne and Dagny. "Well, thank you very much. Now you two sit down and visit while I prepare these vegetables for the stew." When Dagny offered to help with dinner, Eva insisted that she stay downstairs and visit with Arne. "You can tell him all about the proposed yarn shop."

Dinner was a quiet affair. The room amplified the sound of

everyone eating and Eva knew from their second helpings that her stew and biscuits were a big success, as was the blueberry pie dessert. Arne put down his fork and smiled at Eva. He thanked her for the meal and then, as if he'd been thinking and planning what to say the whole time, started talking.

"Those bro...broken spokes in the ba...back room? I can ma...make new. Can make new ped...pedestal for ta...table top, too." Dagny bubbled with pride.

"Arne made furniture in Sweden and has his own woodworking shop."

"My, you are one busy young man," said Eva.

"Ya, I try to ke...keep busy." He stood up and bowed to both Eva and Dagny.

"I get tools." Then he spun around and disappeared down the stairs.

Arne returned on his bicycle, towing a cleverly made chest on wheels. When he and Dagny were rummaging through the junk pile for some pieces of wood, they found a broken seat.

"This goes with the spin...spinning wheel," he told the girls. Then he quickly put the broken pieces together to show them how it went together. "I can fix," he said, picking up his hammer.

Dagny hovered over Arne fetching whatever tools and materials he needed while Eva looked idly on. She definitely wasn't needed here.

"I feel like baking," she stated. "Do you like apple turnovers, Arne?" He looked up from his work.

"Ya, I like any...anything apple."

Later Eva brought down the coffee tray with a large plate of warm, crispy apple turnovers sprinkled with sugar and a small plate of cheese.

"Good," said Arne. "Bet...better than pie."

"I love the crust best," said Dagny. Eva passed the cheese and poured more coffee.

As usual Arne concentrated on eating and put away four

turnovers. Nothing compared to a guest who came back for seconds or thirds. So, for Eva, eating four turnovers was the sublime compliment.

"Very good," said Arne, pushing back his chair and rubbing his belly. "Now I have sur...surprise." He was looking at Eva, but Dagny was giggling and Eva wasn't certain who the surprise was for. Then Arne got up and went into the back room, returning with the complete and beautiful spinning wheel, with the seat attached.

Eva was speechless as she sat behind the wheel, blinking to hold back the tears, and felt the smooth, fine wood beneath her fingers. "You do fine work, Arne. Thank you so much."

"A little var...varnish will make it lo...look like new," he said.

Another Surprise

On Sunday Dagny was dragging her feet about going to church. It was as if she could not keep from staring out of the window.

"You seem uneasy today," remarked Eva. "Are you sick?"

Dagny turned suddenly and looked down at the floor.

"Arne invited me over for dinner today," she said. "I'm going to help prepare his special meal."

"And what might that be?" asked Eva.

"I don't know exactly," said Dagny. "Something he makes every Sunday and eats all week long."

Eva sat with Mrs. Sandquist at church and went to the rooming house for dinner before taking the trolley back to Arlington. When she arrived home she was surprised that Dagny and Arne were not there. She was happy to have some alone time and sat down to knit and make plans for her yarn shop. When two hours passed with still no sign of either of them, Eva considered taking a walk and casually stopping in at Arne's farm, then decided against doing that. Poking her nose where it didn't belong didn't set well with her, so she busied herself with making a fresh apple pie.

It was almost five o'clock when she spotted them from the upstairs window. Arne was on his bicycle pulling a small cart containing a very large bundle wrapped in dark cloth. Dagny walked briskly behind the cart trying to steady the bundle.

Eva ran to open the door as they carried the covered object up the porch steps and placed it in the middle of the floor, beads of sweat on their foreheads, their faces bursting with eager anticipation.

"It's for you, Eva. Open it!" exclaimed Dagny. "It was Arne's idea," she added, proudly looking at him with her hands on her hips.

Eva carefully unwrapped the bundle and couldn't believe her eyes. "Oh, Arne…a pedestal for my table top. How fine it is!" She knelt on the floor to inspect the beautifully grained oak wood, running her hands down the graceful curves that turned out slightly at the bottom into three rounded feet like lion paws

"Your craftsmanship amazes me, Arne," exclaimed Eva, brushing away her tears. "I'm overcome with gratitude. Thank you so much." Arne's pride soon melted into confusion when he saw Eva's tears.

"She always cries like this when she's happily surprised," explained Dagny.

He stood bashfully looking at the floor with his hands in his pockets, shyly accepting Eva's embrace and swift kiss on the cheek.

"So you had all this planned yesterday, didn't you?" said Eva.

Dagny and Arne smiled at each other, nodding in simultaneous agreement. Then Arne went over to inspect the table top.

"I can st…stain this to match ped…pedestal." Then he carried it into the back room. Already Eva was picturing the finished table sitting in the front window of her shop with a couple of ladies sipping coffee while deciding what color yarn they might buy. The yarn shop was beginning to take shape.

That night as they lay on their quilts, Eva thought about her eventful day and remembered she had not asked Dagny about her Sunday dinner with Arne.

"Is Arne a good cook?"

"Oh, yes," she replied. "He had a big chunk of corned beef simmering on the stove when I got there. He said he was making a boiled dinner." Then she explained that a boiled dinner was something like a stew except that neither the beef nor the vegetables had to be cut up in small pieces.

"While he worked on the pedestal, I washed the beets and threw them into the pot, scraped the carrots, peeled the turnips, onions and potatoes and dropped them all into the pot with the simmering meat."

"My goodness!" sighed Eva. "That's a lot of vegetables to eat in one meal."

"Arne does it that way so he has lots of 'leftovers.' Each day he warms up enough for dinner and on the last day he grinds up what's left and makes 'red flannel hash,' which he fries in a skillet. That's the part he likes best."

"Flannel? That's a new word to me," said Eva, turning to her dictionary. The definition varied from flattery and nonsense to a soft wooly fabric used in men's shirts and ladies' nightgowns. "Are you sure the word is 'flannel?'"

"That's what Arne said," replied Dagny. "It's the beets that make the hash red. Arne said he'd bring some over so we can have a taste."

From Fleece to Yarn

Dagny found an old cardboard box while rummaging through the trash pile. "Is this stuff any good," she asked, holding up some funny looking pieces of wood.

"Oh yes," replied Eva. "Those are spindles and bobbins used for winding yarn." Eva looked into the box and saw carders, combs, a packet of indigo dye and a box of potash alum used for setting dye colors. This was all new to Dagny, who didn't share Eva's little moment of excitement until Eva said, "all we need to do now is find some sheep."

"Are we going to raise sheep, too?" Dagny asked hopefully.

"No, we can't have sheep here, but there must be a farm nearby where I can buy fleece."

Eva got along very well with Dr. Bergstrom, who seemed to have no prejudices about women nor strict ideas about status or class. He seemed genuinely interested in all people and could speak intelligently on just about any topic. Eva supposed that was because he was a dentist and spoke to a variety of patients each day.

If his wife had a luncheon engagement, he and Eva usually ate their noontime meal together in the kitchen. She was surprised that first week of this familiarity, but soon looked upon him as a Mr. Kronberg replacement.

As the days went by she became less and less self-conscious about asking him questions.

"I'm looking for my sister, Ingrid Olson, and wondered if she or her husband, Olle, were ever patients of yours."

"Olson?" He thought for a moment. "I've seen a few Olsons in my practice, but no Ingrid or Olle Olson." Seeing her disappointment, he said he'd be happy to make inquiries about them with his other professional friends.

"They used to live on the outskirts of Boston," she said. "But I have reason to believe they moved further north."

"Well, that makes things a bit difficult. They might even be living in New Hampshire or Maine."

"That is quite possible," she said.

"I'll ask around and see what I can find," he told her.

Another day they talked about Sweden and how different her upbringing had been from his. He was raised in Stockholm and had the advantage of going to college. They also compared notes on their voyage to America and she confided to him her dream of having a yarn shop.

"Do you know any sheep farmers that might have fleece to

sell?"

"Fleece?" he asked. "So are you planning to spin your own yarn?"

"Yes. Doing everything myself will be a lot cheaper than buying yarn from a factory or warehouse. I actually enjoy the process of dying the wool and I love to spin."

"You surely are an enterprising young lady," he said, considering what she had told him about her life in Sweden and the fact that she already had purchased a house and wanted to start her own business. "I do know some dairy farmers. They might have some sheep or may know someone who does."

A few days later Dr. Bergstrom came to the kitchen for lunch with a long face. "Well, Eva, I spoke with a farmer yesterday. Apparently sheep are sheared in the spring, so it will be at least April before he has any fleece to sell."

Before Eva could express her dismay, the doctor's face lit up with a smile. "However, the farmer then told me about a man by the name of Dave Beckworth who lives in Bedford. His father used to raise sheep. They were sold two years ago, but the old fleece is still stored in a shed. It seems the fleece is taking up space that Mr. Beckworth needs for storing machinery and he would gladly give it away...and even deliver it free of charge."

Eva could not believe her good fortune and through Dr. Bergstrom, she agreed to have the fleece delivered on Saturday.

Dave was probably in his thirties, friendly and neatly dressed, but he did not understand Swedish. Through hand signals and the use of 'yes' and 'no,' he backed the truck up next to the shed and removed the cloth covering.

Eva was expecting to see white fleece, but this dirty gray mass was full of black specks, dead flies, dried manure and straw. Aware of her disappointment, he started to cover up the fleece, but she put her hand on his arm and said in English, "I take it." She would have to make do. Dirty or not, she needed fleece now and waiting until spring for new fleece wasn't an option.

Dagny scowled at the filthy mound in the truck. The hot

noon-time sun beat down on the fleece, which emitted a foul, rancid odor.

"No one will buy yarn made out of that," said Dagny disgustedly. "I'm going to visit Arne." Eva smiled to herself. She wasn't seeing the dirty fleece. In her mind were skeins of beautiful colored yarn that hadn't cost her a penny. However, over the next few days, Dagny's sour mood put a damper on Eva's plans, although nothing was mentioned about the fleece. They were both working during the day and tired when they got home, especially with the August heat and humidity. After a full day's work, heating up buckets of water and hauling them downstairs to fill tubs to clean the fleece was the last thing they wanted to do in the sweltering weather.

By Friday a cold front prompted severe thundershowers, replacing the stifling summer heat with the crispy coolness of autumn. Revitalized by the change in weather, Eva began the relentless task of unrolling the bundles of fleece and picking out the straw, seeds, dried bugs and specks of dried manure.

Not much care had been used when rolling the fleece. Stained belly wool and other contaminated parts had been rolled up with the larger, cleaner pieces, so that much sorting out had to be done, and the most soiled wool had to be discarded.

After a day or two Dagny felt obligated to help. They filled the tubs and let the fleece soak in cold water overnight in preparation for the hot water wash planned for the next day. All this was new to Dagny, but Eva was glad she had paid good attention to how her mother had prepared the fleece years ago.

Arne arrived on Saturday morning to find both girls hauling buckets of hot water from the kitchen stove to the large tubs in the back room. Eva added soap and gently poked the fleece with a long-handled wooden paddle until it was fully immersed in the soapy bath and then went back to the kitchen to heat more water. A second hot wash would be necessary, and possibly a third.

To sell high-quality yarn she needed fluffy white fleece without a trace of grease before the dying process could begin.

She inspected the fleece after the third rinse and still wasn't satisfied, but neither was she looking forward to boiling more water and carrying buckets down the stairs again. Already her back was aching and she sat down for a minute to rest.

It was then she noticed a bucket of steaming water dangling outside the window. She peeked out the door as Dagny untied the full bucket and replaced it with an empty one. Watching the empty bucket jerk upwards, she saw Arne looking down from the second-floor window with a satisfied grin on his round face.

"Isn't he wonderful?" exclaimed Dagny. "Now we don't have to carry hot water down the stairs and there won't be puddles on the floor anymore."

"You two surely are full of wonderful surprises," said Eva, as another steaming bucket was lowered on the rope. After the final rinse, they carried the dripping fleece outside to dry on lengths of chicken wire that Arne had stretched between the shed and back fence.

The next step was to dye the fleece. Eva's mother used boiled birch leaves for yellow, carrot tops to make a light green and spinach for darker green. For beige, she used yellow onion skins or boiled bark, red onion skins for light violet blue, beet water for red to deep pink, and strong black coffee for a rich brown color.

Elderberries grew along the back fence and made delicious jelly. Eva had picked enough clusters of these dark purple berries to know how their juice stained her hands. First she would get a deep purple color, then a pretty maroon by adding more water and finally various shades of pink.

On Sunday Eva sat in the last pew at church. She heard little of the sermon; her eyes were on the stained glass windows. She envisioned white fleece turning into all those brilliant colors and could barely wait to catch the trolley home to begin the dying process.

She was glad Dagny had gone again to Arne's for dinner. Quickly she changed into old clothes, poured herself a glass of milk and made a cheese and jelly sandwich.

Carefully she mixed alum with water in an old enamel pot, added juice from the strained berries and gently stirred in the fleece. After turning a deep purple, the fleece was rinsed in several waters and spread thinly on chicken wire to dry. "So far so good," she said to herself as she poured more water into the dye bath. As she expected, the next batch was not as dark as the first and she was satisfied with the lighter shade of cranberry. Then came a deep pink, a dusty pink and a very pale pink. She fluffed up each color and spread the fleece carefully on the chicken wire to dry, then went into the house to clean up.

When the first batch was dry she scooped up an armful and rushed into the front room to begin the third step of yarn making...carding the fleece.

Carefully, placing a small amount wool on one paddle, she gently combed the fibers onto the second paddle, back and forth, keeping the fibers neat and straight, until finally she was able to roll a length of continuous wool into a long, neat rolag. Over and over this procedure was repeated as her basket filled with fluffy, soft rolags ready for spinning. She would have continued without eating supper if Dagny hadn't come home with a pot of flannel hash. Dagny was intrigued by the basketful of colorful rolags.

"How soft they are...and such a beautiful color!" she exclaimed. "May I try?"

Eva showed her how to comb the fleece and then gave her the paddles. Poor Dagny's patience soon gave out. The soft fibers tangled, clinging together in a tight ball that couldn't be pulled apart. Frustrated, she threw the two paddles on the floor. "I'm worse at this than I am at knitting," she grumbled. "I'm going upstairs to heat up the hash."

"I'll be up soon," said Eva. Like her father, she believed nothing should go to waste, so she picked up the hard ball of fleece, loosened several fibers and finally was able to dislodge the rest. She carded them into a nice rolag and added it to the others. Tomorrow she would start spinning.

The front room looked more inviting now. Near the large window overlooking the street stood the round oak table and newly varnished chairs. Along the opposite wall was a long counter Arne built from old pine boards he'd found in the shed. In the middle of the room, under a single light bulb, stood the spinning wheel.

The wheel had beckoned to Eva ever since that very first day she found it in pieces under the pile of rubble. Sometimes, as she walked across the room, her hand spontaneously reached out to the graceful old 'machine.' Often her touch set the wheel turning. Was it trying to tell her something? Then she'd find herself speaking to the wheel, confiding her thoughts and secret dreams as if it was a cherished friend.

Eva would rather have stayed home on Monday to begin spinning than spend the day at the Bergstroms, but her loyalty and reliability won over such a frivolous idea. Alas, all was not lost when after school Emily and Emma attended a birthday party and Eva's desire came true. Sitting in the parlor listening to Mrs. Bergstrom for another couple hours was not what she wanted to do. Such idleness was a waste of good time and Eva could think of nothing else but going home to begin her spinning.

"If you have nothing more for me to do, I might as well go home and get some of my own work done."

"Oh," said Mrs. Bergstrom, turning up her nose. "Are you still cleaning that old fleece?"

"The fleece is all clean and dyed. I'm anxious to get started on my spinning."

"Well…you are really serious about this yarn shop thing, aren't you?"

"Have you forgotten that I'm planning to be open for business by the first of December?"

Mrs. Bergstrom was quite taken back. "I hope you will be able to help me for a couple days each week after that, especially on the days just before Christmas."

Eva thought about the baby and how tired she was at the end of each day. How long could she keep her rounding belly a secret? She was still embarrassed about her pregnancy; afraid of what people thought of an unmarried girl having a baby. She had heard the church ladies talk unkindly of such a predicament. Eva set aside all this and put on a brave face. "I'm sure we can work something out for the benefit of both of us."

That wasn't quite what Mrs. Bergstrom expected for an answer. "Good. We'll be expecting you and Dagny to join us for Thanksgiving dinner."

When Eva opened the front door, her heart beat a little faster. She sat down and put her hand on the wheel. "The time has finally come," she said aloud, as if telling her thoughts to the wheel. "We must work together now and spin this fleece into beautiful strands of yarn." The words were more like a prayer as her foot gently pumped the wooden treadle. The big wheel responded, turning slowly and steadily as her hands gently twisted the pink fleece into the desired thickness.

Eva found herself humming the old Swedish melodies like her mother had done so many years before. When the bobbin was full, she wound the soft pink yarn into a loose skein. She held the soft bundle in her arms as one might hold a newborn babe. Her vision had finally given birth. She had only to nurture her dream and watch the yarn shop grow into a reality.

It was almost time for Dagny to be home from the butcher shop, but Eva could not stop. She picked out more pink fleece and began spinning on an empty bobbin. Another hour went by. Suddenly Dagny burst through the front door, followed closely by Arne, who was grinning from ear to ear and holding a wooden box sanded smooth and varnished to a satin finish.

"Arne has something to show you!" Dagny's enthusiasm bubbled over like a boiling pot that couldn't be stirred down. "Remember that rickety box in the shed that was filled with old magazines and newspapers?" Eva nodded, but Dagny didn't give her a chance to respond. "We thought it would make a lovely container to hold your skeins of yarn." She watched admiringly as Arne placed the box on the counter, then spoke again to Eva. "There's more boxes in the loft. Wouldn't they look nice lined up in a row on the counter showing off all your skeins of yarn?"

"I think that is a wonderful idea," exclaimed Eva, eager to reveal a surprise of her own. She reached down into her yarn bag, picked up the precious skein of yarn and placed it gently in the beautiful box.

"How long will it take you to fill the box?" asked Dagny.

That wasn't the reaction Eva had expected, but she answered the question with optimism. "I might have it almost full in a week or so."

"That long?" said Dagny, with obvious disappointment. She had no idea of the time and patience it took to dye, card and spin the fine fibers of fleece into perfect strands of yarn. Even if Eva worked diligently every evening the box might not be filled in two weeks.

The Grand Opening

Each week Arne refinished three or four yarn boxes. He was meticulous about sanding, staining and varnishing them so they all looked identical. One by one the row of boxes on the counter grew. When there was no more space, he set another row of boxes on top of the first row and soon there were twelve empty boxes waiting to be filled. Eva spent every extra moment at the spinning wheel, sometimes staying up long after Dagny had gone to bed.

Spinning was akin to knitting when it came to opening up Eva's mind to creativity, but her mind wandered to other things, too. Karl drifted into her thoughts every day, sometimes briefly sweet and other times as a lingering heartache. There had never been a response from the letter she'd sent him, nor had she received a letter from Mr. Kronberg. She had expected to hear from Mats though; he'd promised to mail Mr. Kaneko's photographs. Dagny still held out hope that she would receive some word from her mother or Bertil, but she too was becoming discouraged. Eva knew that looking back did no good. She must focus on the future and for the sake of her baby put all her effort into the yarn shop.

November brought shorter days and cooler weather with gray skies threatening rain, perhaps even snow. Arne had told Eva of an October day the year before when six inches of snow fell on his late garden crops, the pumpkins sitting in the field with their jaunty white caps and the drooping carrot tops struggling under their heavy coats of snow. By afternoon the snow had all melted and the vegetables looked as healthy as before.

The picture he described of the drooping carrot tops reminded Eva of the great pines and spruce of Norrland after an all-night blizzard; how tired and sad the trees looked in the faint light of morning, their boughs hanging low and motionless under a heavy blanket of snow. There was no heat to the languid sun, though, until winter melted into spring. Then icicles clung to the branch tips, sparkling like lighted candles on a Christmas tree until the sun rose higher in the sky and the forest again came to life.

Looking out the shop window now, she saw no evergreens. All the trees had been stripped naked of autumn colors, their leafy garments now a dying blanket beneath their skeletons. Eva turned her back on the dismal outside scene and smiled to herself, revitalized by the vibrant atmosphere of the room, her very own yarn shop, complete now with Arne's boxes filled with yarn. Many skeins were made from her own homespun yarn: dark colors from elderberries, beets, blueberries, turmeric powder and indigo dye, and lighter dyes made in water boiled from cooking local vegetables, nuts, bark and grasses. Other boxes held yarn purchased from Sweden: multi-colored skeins of alternating colors, some heavy, tweedy mixtures of white, tan and brown, and many extra-fine balls of baby yarn in soft pastel colors. Also on the counter were numerous pattern books and a large assortment of knitting needles and crochet hooks.

Decorating the walls were scarves, hats and mittens she had knitted in spare moments to sell as gifts. In the corner of the window was a large square of cardboard she'd painted white. After the paint dried, she dipped a brush into indigo dye and carefully printed YARN SHOP. Below, in smaller letters, were the words

Grand Opening, December 1.

Dagny preferred to spend Thanksgiving with Arne, so Eva planned to go to the Bergstrom's alone. She helped Mrs. Bergstrom the day before, peeling vegetables and fruits, making pies, and staying with the children while their mother went to the hairdresser.

"Mama's getting her braid cut off today. She's having a 'perment,'" said Emma.

"Not a perment," said Emily. "Mama's getting a permanent wave." Not wishing to show her ignorance of this new word, Eva just smiled and said, "oh, that's nice."

Their father came into the room and the girls hushed up. "It's a surprise for Papa," whispered Emma into Eva's ear.

"Telling secrets again, Emma?" he asked.

"Yes Papa."

Because of the upcoming holiday, he had few patients today, so he told Eva she could go home.

Eva arrived early on Thanksgiving morning to help with dinner. She was met at the door by the wonderful aroma of roasting turkey and Mrs. Bergstrom's curly hairdo. She was all titters and giggles. "Do you like it?" she asked, fluffing out her hair and pirouetting around the foyer like a young schoolgirl. Emma stood in the doorway admiring her mother. "Doesn't she look just like a movie star?"

Eva, thinking that ***movie star*** must be something wonderful, replied, "you look beautiful and so much younger."

"That's what my husband told me," giggled Mrs. Bergstrom. With a little pink in her cheeks she added, "well, this isn't getting dinner ready, is it?"

Dr. Bergstrom gave a lengthy prayer before dinner, and Eva was reminded of Ingrid's letter describing her first Thanksgiving in America. She felt the same gratitude and added a little prayer for herself, that she and Ingrid would soon be reunited. There was barely room enough on the large table to hold the platter of turkey and stuffing along with the bowls of mashed potatoes, rich brown gravy, squash, corn, peas and creamed onions, plus a large basket of cinnamon rolls frosted with white icing. On a side table were apple, pumpkin and mince pies for dessert.

Dr. Bergstrom towered above everyone else, giving the impression of a quiet and powerful force. His hands, though, were different from those of other men Eva had known, very clean, almost feminine, with long tapered fingers and carefully clipped nails. He was a dentist, she thought to herself, and had his fingers in people's mouths every day. When he first looked at a person, did he see only their teeth...if they were crooked, missing or discolored? She swept her tongue quickly across her teeth and wondered if they looked dirty or had food lodged between them.

Mrs. Bergstrom went into a lengthy procedure of what was involved in having a permanent, the cutting, rolling and saturating of the hair with a very smelly substance. Eva understood little of it. The whole process sounded complicated and was probably expensive.

"Seeing all that hair falling on the floor was like getting rid of a heavy burden," said Mrs. Bergstrom, running her fingers through the tight curls. "Short hair makes me feel so...so free!"

Dr. Bergstrom glanced at his wife and shook his head. Eva noticed his eyes were smiling and that his wife was blushing again.

"I don't know why they call it a permanent," said Mrs. Bergstrom. "The curl doesn't last indefinitely. In six weeks I'll have to have a trim and four months later it will be time to get my hair curled again."

Emma sat next to Eva and stared at the small red ringlets framing her face and curly wisps of hair escaping from her thick braid.

"Do you have to get a permanent every four months, too?"

"No, I was born with curly hair," replied Eva. "I wish sometimes I could straighten it out somehow."

A touch of envy came briefly over Mrs. Bergstrom's face.

"Oh, you are so lucky to have natural curls, Eva...but poor

Dagny...she really should do something with that thin black hair of hers." This took Eva by surprise. She couldn't visualize Dagny with short, curly hair, but she said nothing.

Mrs. Bergstrom rambled on about how much easier it was having short hair. "Long hair is a lot of work...all that brushing...and such a chore to wash and dry. And it feels so good not to have to carry around a heavy braid on my head and have a headache at the end of every day."

Eva had to agree about that. "Oh yes," she said. "It is such a relief to take down my hair and give my head a rest in the evening."

Emma turned again to look at Eva, appraising the curly mass of red with one thick braid wrapped around her head several times. "Your hair must be very long," she said.

"Long enough to sit on and to keep me warm at night," she whispered for Emma's ears only.

"I want to see you sit on your hair and show us how it keeps you warm at night," said Emma in her shrill young voice that made everyone stare at Eva.

"Tomorrow might be a better time," Eva whispered to Emma. "Let's finish dinner so we can have some dessert."

Mrs. Bergstrom insisted that Eva come over on Friday morning. She was still in her nightdress, sitting in the pink-flowered chair with her feet on a matching footstool when Eva walked in.

"Are you not feeling well today?"

"I'm just recuperating from yesterday," said Mrs. Bergstrom, dipping her fingers into a new box of chocolates. "Preparing holiday meals is so mentally and physically exhausting. It takes a day or two for me to get back to normal." Eva immediately went into the kitchen to clean up from breakfast, but the room was as clean as she had left it the night before. Had no one eaten yet today?

"Would you like me to brew some coffee, Mrs. Bergstrom?"

"That would be fine, dear. Then come sit and chat until the girls come down."

As far as Eva was concerned, there wasn't much to talk about. Everything had been discussed in great detail yesterday and didn't need to be rehashed again today. In fact, there was no reason for her being here today, except to keep Mrs. Bergstrom company. This wasn't unusual. There had been many days like this. Eva was paid an hourly rate whether she worked or not, but time passed slowly sitting idly in the parlor. Mrs. Bergstrom needed a hobby to fill her idle moments. Although she'd seen no evidence of yarn or knitting needles about the house, Eva asked if she liked to knit.

"I tried it as a girl and failed, just as I did with sewing and needlepoint, much to my mother's dismay," said Mrs. Bergstrom, her hand hovering over the box of chocolates. She took one and offered the box to Eva, who kindly refused.

"Perhaps you were too young, or just not interested in knitting at the time," said Eva. She took a scarf she'd been making from the knitting bag she always carried with her on the trolley. She slipped the scarf onto a holder and showed Mrs. Bergstrom how to cast new stitches on the needle and how to knit the simple garter stitch.

"This is much easier than I remember," said Mrs. Bergstrom, excited to see the piece growing inch by inch. Since she was doing so well, Eva showed her another stitch.

"If you knit the stitches toward the front, the pattern will be flatter on the back; then knit the next row as you did before, alternating these two rows. This is called the stockinette stitch. Most basic sweaters are made in this manner."

Soon giggles and footsteps were heard from the hall.

"We want to see you sitting on your hair," said Emily and Emma in unison. Eva looked to their mother for approval.

"Calm down girls. The coffee's ready. Let's go to the kitchen for some of those yummy cinnamon rolls and then you can see Eva's hair." After the girls devoured their milk and rolls, they sat anxiously waiting for their mother and Eva to finish their coffee.

Then Emily and Emma took out the many hair pins securing

the long braid. Eva shook her head and ran her fingers through the tight waves to loosen them and sat on her hair.

"Wow!" exclaimed Emma. "Your hair is long...and very red!"

"So soft and curly, too," said Emily. "May I brush it?"

Eva luxuriated in drinking her second cup of coffee while the girls took turns brushing her hair.

"That's what I like about going to the beauty shop," said Mrs. Bergstrom. "It feels so good to have someone else wash and fuss with my hair."

"Ever since yesterday I've been turning it over in my mind whether or not to have mine cut," admitted Eva. "I get those headaches, too."

Mrs. Bergstrom was so excited, she didn't know whether to finish her coffee or immediately call her hairdresser.

"I'll see if I can get an appointment for tomorrow," she said, jumping up from the table. "And I'll make one for Dagny, too."

"Not tomorrow, Mrs. Bergstrom. I need more time to think about it...and also to talk it over with Dagny."

"Well, I'm going to call and see if they have an opening. You know what they say about striking while the iron's hot."

"Iron?" Ironing wrinkles from clothes was one thing. Eva definitely didn't want her hair ironed, but Mrs. Bergstrom was already dialing the number and Eva was left thinking this wasn't such a very good idea after all.

Mrs. Bergstrom had everything planned out in a matter of minutes. She would go as interpreter and meet them at the beauty shop at three o'clock tomorrow afternoon. Eva was in a state of flux, concerned that Dagny wouldn't want to go.

"Of course she will," said Mrs. Bergstrom. "There's not a woman alive who doesn't love making herself more beautiful."

Dagny's reaction was very favorable. She wanted to see Mrs. Bergstrom's new hairdo and was curious to see what a beauty shop looked like.

Unfortunately, her interest was short-lived. There was

nothing beautiful about the pungent smell greeting them at the door, nor did any of the women sitting in the row of chairs look very attractive with their hair slicked down after washing or rolled up with curlers all over their heads. The room was noisy with chatter and laughing.

After introductions, Mrs. Bergstrom and Dagny took seats along the back wall and Eva was taken to a black revolving chair in front of a long mirror. Dagny could see Eva's nervous reflection as the hairdresser unpinned her hair, but it was Dagny who winced when the long scissor blades touched Eva's braid. After covering her face, Dagny peeked through her fingers to see the hairdresser admiring the fat red braid that hung like a limp snake from her hand. After that she watched reddish ringlets floating to the floor as the hairdresser snipped, combed and snipped some more.

Eva's hair bounced gently on her shoulders when she rose from the chair, red curls framing her smiling face like a beautiful painting. Eva's transformation gave Dagny courage to take her turn in the revolving chair.

"No scissors!" she told the hairdresser, who immediately picked up a sharp razor and cut the thin braid before Dagny knew what was happening.

"Bangs would look good on you," said the hairdresser. "Then I can taper the sides and back to give your hair a little fullness."

Mrs. Bergstrom tried to explain all this to Dagny but much got lost in the translation.

"Here, let me show you," said the hairdresser, thumbing through a book of photographs.

Dagny saw a pretty model and pointed to her picture. "I want to look like her."

The result wasn't exactly what Dagny expected, but the haircut was flattering and she received raving compliments from Mrs. Bergstrom and Eva.

At first, whenever Dagny walked by the little mirror in the kitchen, she'd stop short to look back at the strange girl on the wall. Finally she grew accustomed to herself. Eva understood completely; she was guilty of doing the same thing.

The grand opening was a huge success. The morning dawned sunny and warmer than usual, bringing people out of their homes. Mrs. Bergstrom brought Emily and Emma. Members of her bridge club, church and other women of society trickled in throughout the day. But it was mostly common, everyday housewives who purchased the larger quantities of yarn.

Because Eva's blue dress didn't fit now, she wore a dark brown skirt with a loose-fitting green cardigan sweater unbuttoned over a white blouse, an easy disguise for her rounding belly. It was questionable how long she might keep her pregnancy a secret from the outside world. Anxiety over what people might think of an unmarried woman having a baby had compelled her to hide her indiscretion from others for as long as possible. In the very back of her mind was the novel Mrs. Lindholm had given her in the library; the sad tale of a pregnant girl who delivered her baby alone in an abandoned barn and later was forced to survive by stealing vegetables from farmers' gardens and foraging in the forest for berries and edible plants so she and her baby would not starve. Sometimes the image of this poor girl haunted Eva to the point where she would wake out of a sound sleep, her heart pounding in her chest, from thinking she was that very same girl, alone in the forest scavenging for food. In Eva's dream she was always looking back to see if Mrs. Lindholm was following her. Dagny's innocent excitement about having a baby in the house was comforting and little by little Eva's nightmares had lessened as she put forth all her mental and physical efforts into making the yarn shop a reality.

Eva stood by the door greeting her guests, the delicious aroma of fresh coffee leading them to the counter where Dagny stood nervously behind steaming cups and rounded plates of cookies, cupcakes and sliced almond cake. Since the stove was upstairs, it was up to her to brew the coffee and keep plates filled with baked goods. Slipping on the steps was her greatest concern and she wished Arne was here to lower the big coffee pot down on a rope as they had done with the pails of hot water.

Glowing compliments put Eva in high spirits. She lost all self-consciousness while helping customers choose patterns, yarn colors and correctly sized needles. As the day progressed everything became easier and she was able to relax and enjoy every moment, but at the end of the day when the last visitor was gone both she and Dagny were ready to go upstairs, put up their feet and relax in their little parlor next to the kitchen.

"I think the day went very well, don't you?" asked Eva as she counted all the bills and change.

"Ya...I've never seen so many people...much more than come into the butcher's every day."

"We took in a lot of money, too," said Eva. "Enough to buy two mattresses, order a new shipment of yarn and still have some left over."

A week later, the mattresses arrived. Arne had refinish the two old bureaus and beds that were in the upstairs back rooms and now the girls made them up with second-hand sheets and blankets that Mrs. Sandquist had so generously given them. Having separate bedrooms was a big change from sleeping on the hard wooden floor. At first they missed the camaraderie of lying side by side, where words flowed effortlessly as though one were talking to oneself. Now there wasn't time for conversation. Lying on a soft mattress was like floating on a cloud and they were usually asleep soon after their heads hit the pillow.

Christmas

The day before Christmas was one of Eva's busiest days in the yarn shop and she had to lengthen her morning hours over the noon hour in order to accommodate all her customers. She drank a glass of milk and made a peanut butter and jelly sandwich thinking she had been foolish to tell Mrs. Bergstrom she would come to help her this afternoon. She arrived only half an hour late, her tardiness unnoticed by the Bergstroms, who were busy decorating the Christmas tree.

By the time Mrs. Bergstrom came to the kitchen, Eva had two pies in the oven and was showing the girls how to make cookies. Emily and Emma were having fun rolling dough into little balls, and they had flour and bits of dough on their faces.

"Oh, girls you're getting flour and sticky stuff all over the floor!" shouted their mother disapprovingly.

"But Mama, we're helping Miss Gunderson," said Emma, as more dough slipped off the table.

"Don't worry about the mess, Mrs. Bergstrom. It won't take me a minute to clean up and the girls are having such a good time."

Emily stated matter-of-factly that they were making peanut butter cookies.

"I never heard of putting peanut butter in cookies?" said her mother, turning up her nose at the idea.

"One of my customers gave me the recipe," said Eva. "Since the girls love peanut butter, I...well, we thought to surprise you."

"Well, I surely am surprised," said Mrs. Bergstrom, looking at the bare kitchen counters. "It's getting late and the doctor will be surprised, too, not to have an apple pie for Christmas."

Eva felt reprimanded and didn't know what to say, but Emily was quick to set her mother straight.

"Miss Gunderson already made an apple pie, Mama. It's baking in the oven with the pumpkin pie."

"Oh...," said her mother, rendered speechless for a moment. "Well...that's nice. Now why don't you girls finish making those cookies while I wrap a few more presents to put under the tree." Emily and Emma giggled as their mother rushed out of the room. Eva repressed a smile and picked up a fork to show the girls how to make a crisscross design on the cookies to flatten them on the baking pan.

Dagny was already upstairs when Eva got home. "You don't mind if I eat at Arne's tonight, do you?"

"Of course, not," said Eva, although she was a little disappointed.

"I'm going to help him finish up...um...some Christmas things."

"Have fun," said Eva. "And merry Christmas to both of you."

Eva was on her second cup of coffee gazing out the upstairs window at the lights twinkling through the outside darkness. A half-filled trolley stopped to let passengers off. Under the streetlight she saw many laughing faces, their arms loaded with bundles. Tonight was Christmas Eve; it was also her birthday.

She hadn't mentioned this to Dagny. They had talked once about birthdays, but Dagny wasn't certain of the exact day of her own birth.

"Mother said I came to her in summertime when the sun was high and there was no night," Dagny had told her one time. Eva had seen a wistful look in her eye that day and had never mentioned birthdays again, but she'd made a mental note to celebrate Dagny's birthday on the next Midsummer Day, the longest day of the year.

Everyone's birthday had been a cause for celebrating in the Gunderson home. Eva's mother had made certain of that, treating each girl like a princess all day and making whatever she fancied for dinner. There was always a special gift and her favorite chocolate-frosted cake to share with the family.

She thought back to the happy Christmases in Norrland, which were more than just one day of celebrating. Cookie baking began on Saint Lucia's day and her mother made sure the festive spirit continued through the twelve days of Christmas. Perhaps this was because of her father's winter sadness that the season was begun so early and extended into January. This year Eva had been too busy and tired to make even one batch of cookies...until today. Emma and Emily had brought the Christmas spirit to her and she suddenly had felt the urge to bake cookies. Emma had dipped her finger into the peanut butter jar and turned around to see Eva watching her. That's when Eva told the girls about the peanut butter cookies and they'd immediately clambered around her asking if they could make some.

Reflecting on all this reminded her of the little bundle of cookies that Mrs. Bergstrom had given her before she had left that afternoon. She took them out of her knitting bag and ate one. There was something very compatible about sipping coffee between bites of the delicious peanut butter cookie. Her hand went back for another...and then another..."Happy Birthday to me," she said to herself and laughed, feeling not a smidgen of guilt about eating five cookies.

She left the rest of the cookies on a plate for Dagny and then she undressed for bed. Before turning off the light she opened up her leather Bible, the last present she'd received from her father, and read from the second chapter of Luke about the birth of Jesus.

Dagny was in the bathroom when Eva stretched her legs and stuck one foot outside the covers, pulling it in quickly to the warmth of her cozy nest. There was no need to get up early this morning, so she rolled over and dropped off to sleep. She awoke to Dagny scuffing by her door to the bathroom again.

"Are you feeling all right, Dagny?" The loud slam of a door was her answer, plus the awful sounds of groaning and retching. Eva rushed into the bathroom to see Dagny leaning over the toilet, pale and unsteady on her feet.

"I think I'm better now," she said, "but I'm a little dizzy."

Eva helped her back to bed, washed her face with a wet cloth and covered her with a blanket. Dagny slept until almost ten o'clock, drank some black coffee and was feeling much better when Arne arrived.

"I won't be going to the Bergstroms' today," she told Eva. "Arne said he'd stay with me so I wouldn't be alone."

Emily and Emma greeted Eva at the door and led her into the parlor, where Dr. and Mrs. Bergstrom were adding more gifts to the multitude of brightly colored packages already piled under the tree. Feeling guilty about her homemade gifts, Eva stuffed her puny donations under her coat.

"Aren't you going to put your presents under the tree?" asked the sharp-eyed Emma.

"Perhaps you can do that for me," said Eva, awkwardly retrieving the hidden gifts.

"Every year I say we aren't going to buy so much," said Mrs. Bergstrom apologetically. "The stores are full of such wonderful things, and I just can't say no to myself. But Christmas is for spoiling children, don't you think?"

"Of course," agreed Eva, who wasn't about to disagree with her hostess and friend.

Dr. Bergstrom knelt down in front of the tree and read the name tag on each gift before giving one to Emily and another to Emma to give to the appropriate person. Then, in a frenzy of commotion, the girls began opening their mountains of gifts, barely looking at one before tearing the ribbons and paper off the next. Eva was astounded at their haste and lack of appreciation.

In Sweden opening each homemade gift had been a special occasion where much time was spent carefully taking off the ribbon and paper to save and use again for next Christmas. Eva, the youngest child was given her gift first, while the oldest family member waited until last. Eva remembered her father shaking his gift now and then and guessing some outlandish thing that might be inside, and everyone laughing to think how a fishing rod or cow might fit in the small package. He would usually insist his wife open hers before he did, but she always preferred to be last. "You always forget, Gustav, that I am the oldest," she would whisper to him. For her, waiting in anticipation was as much fun as opening her gift. When Eva was a child, she never understood what her mother meant by "anticipating," but now, patiently waiting with only one gift in her lap, and secretly shaking it when no one was looking, she realized what her mother meant.

When it was her turn, she carefully untied the gold ribbon, smoothing and folding the shiny red paper before opening the little white box. Between two layers of cotton was a beautiful silver bracelet with an American flag charm.

"Charm bracelets are the fashion now," said Mrs. Bergstrom, holding out her left arm and shaking her wrist so the charms of her two bracelets clinked together in a melodious chorus.

"When something important happens, my husband always buys me a charm to remind me of that special event," she said, describing each one. "This wedding bell is when we were married and the little house is when we purchased our first home. Here's a little shoe for Emily and one for Emma with their dates of birth inscribed on each sole." By the number of charms on each bracelet, Eva surmised that Mrs. Bergstrom had already had more than thirty special occasions in her nine years of married life.

So many gifts, thought Eva...how many dolls can a little girl play with? There were also fine dresses, games, jewelry, ice skates and sleds... and then there were the homemade beet-dyed hats and mittens that Eva had knitted, now lost in the mound of wrappings and empty boxes.

For Eva, the highlight of the gift opening happened when Emily opened up one of her last gifts. She excitedly ripped the paper off, but her disappointment was evident when she saw the simply dressed rag doll.

"That's not a real dolly. She's too plain and her head's too big!" she exclaimed, throwing it across the room. Disturbed to see Raggedy Ann lying upside down on the floor, Eva immediately retrieved the doll.

Mrs. Bergstrom saw how gently Eva smoothed out the doll's dress and yarn hair, holding her tenderly as she might a fragile child. Emily noticed, too.

"Do you still play with dolls, Miss Gunderson?"

"Well, this doll is special," replied Eva.

All eyes were on Eva now. She flushed with embarrassment at what they must be thinking...almost a grown woman making a fuss about a silly rag doll.

Eva told them about the woman on the train, when she had left with Raggedy Ann and the forlorn look on Dagny's face.

Dr. Bergstrom was touched by the story and Mrs. Bergstrom

brushed a tear from her eye as Emily stared wide-eyed in amazement.

"I want Miss Dagny to have her."

"Thank you, Emily," said Eva. "I know Raggedy Ann will make Dagny feel much better."

After dinner, Dr. Bergstrom asked Emily and Emma to clear the table and help their mother in the kitchen. Immediately Eva rose from her chair.

"Please sit down, Eva. You are our guest today." She did as she was told, but would rather have busied herself in the kitchen than sat and be waited on.

"Now don't forget to come in to the office soon. It's important to have your teeth checked, especially when...ah...in your present situation."

Eva was speechless, but her startled expression confirmed his suspicions. He smiled and continued. "I don't know how to say this, but...my wife is very straight-laced about girls becoming pregnant out of wedlock."

Eva looked down, the familiar heat of embarrassment rising from her chest, the blush glowing in her neck and face. She brushed some imaginary lint from her sleeve and in a soft low voice said, "I didn't know it was so...so obvious."

"I'm sorry, Eva. Now I've embarrassed you." He cleared his throat and continued. "As far as I know, my wife hasn't noticed, but I thought I should let you know about her feelings on this matter."

The time had come when Eva could no longer hide the fact that she was pregnant. A sudden gush of strength surged through her body, removing all embarrassment and shame. Then she sat up straight in her chair and looked the doctor in the eye. "Thank you, Dr. Bergstrom, for telling me of your wife's feelings. Tomorrow I will inform her that I will be working full time in the yarn shop."

"I didn't mean that you would have to stop working here," he said with some regret.

"Well, I've been thinking about doing that for several weeks now, but I'll continue helping Mrs. Bergstrom until she finds someone to replace me."

Dr. Bergstrom reached into his jacket pocket and gave her a piece of paper. "Here's the name and address of a fine doctor who I know will take good care of you. The office is less than a quarter mile from your house."

Eva thanked him and put the paper in her purse. She decided to go home immediately after dessert.

Dusk had turned to darkness as Eva stepped off the trolley. Twinkling, bright-colored lights decorated many shops and houses on either side of the road. Through her own shop window she was pleased to see two figures sitting at the round oak table, their heads looking down as if playing a game or putting a puzzle together. She hid Raggedy Ann beneath her coat and went inside.

"Hello, it's just me," she announced, dashing across the room. Dagny looked up from their checker game. "Did you have a good time?" By now Eva was halfway up the stairs and hollered back. "Oh yes, very nice."

Eva barely had time to put Raggedy Ann on Dagny's bed and hang up her coat before the two of them came running up the stairs. Dagny went to the stove where a pot was simmering. "We made some stew from the beef I brought home yesterday. Would you like some?"

Although Eva had eaten a big dinner, being home encouraged her appetite. She ate a few spoonful's and commented how delicious the stew was.

"Ya," said Dagny, grinning at Arne, "We're good at making one-pot meals, aren't we?" He smiled at her and nodded bashfully.

After Arne had finished two bowlfuls he pushed away from the table, causing Dagny to immediately jump from her chair to stand behind him. She put her hands on his shoulders.

"We have a surprise downstairs for you," she announced excitedly. "Do you want to see it now?"

"The dishes can wait," said Eva. "You know how I love

surprises!"

Eva stood in the middle of the shop with her eyes closed. She heard footsteps walking away, then a commotion in the back room before heavy footsteps returned.

"You can look now!" said Dagny.

On the floor before Eva was a beautiful wooden cradle. At one end was a wooden hood with heart-shaped cutouts on each side. Arne's face was beaming as he briefly touched the reddish-brown finish, causing the cradle to rock back and forth. "Hard maple wood," he said, looking at her with pride. "Should never w...wear out."

"You are a fine craftsman," said Eva, "And I love the little hearts. Thank you so very much."

He blushed as Eva hugged him, his hands remaining at his sides, undecided about what to do next. "I should go now," he muttered, not knowing what else to say.

"It's early yet," said Eva. "Mrs. Bergstrom gave me half a pumpkin pie. I'll go upstairs and put the coffee on." When she returned with the pie and coffee tray, Dagny and Arne had just finished another checker game.

"He beats me every time," complained Dagny. Arne sat smugly watching her pick up the pieces and put them in the box. Eva noticed she was grinning and wondered if she'd lost on purpose.

The room was quiet but full of good feelings as they all enjoyed the delicious pie and coffee, although Dagny kept eying two little boxes to the right of Eva. One was wrapped in red paper and the other in plain brown. After they finished the pie, Eva poured another round of coffee. Then she gave Dagny the little red box.

"Mrs. Bergstrom was sorry you couldn't be there for Christmas dinner and wanted me to bring this home to you."

Dagny ripped off the paper, opened the box and held up a small silver chain. "What is it for?"

Eva fastened the chain around Dagny's wrists and held up her own arm.

"See, we have matching bracelets. Mrs. Bergstrom said charm bracelets are all the rage now. She thought it appropriate that our first charm be the American flag."

"It's beautiful," said Dagny. "I love how the silver sparkles in the light." After that, Eva gave Arne his gift. He fumbled with the paper and felt the soft wool of a scarf and matching hat. His artistic eye inspected the unusual pattern.

"I used a strand of tan and one of brown, then knitted them together to make that heavy, tweedy look," explained Eva. He thanked her and immediately put the scarf around his neck and the cap on his head.

"Nice and warm," he said. "Now I go home be...before snow falls."

Eva heard them whispering as they dawdled by the front door, so she said goodnight and went upstairs. Then she washed and dried the dishes, brushed her teeth and got undressed. Dagny still hadn't come upstairs, so she got into bed thinking to wait for her.

She was aroused from sleep hearing Dagny's squeals of delight upon finding Raggedy Ann sitting on her bed that Christmas night. Raggedy Ann was the best present Dagny had ever received. They slept together every night and she carried the rag doll wherever she went, except to the butcher shop where it might get soiled.

January

Despite the large number of sales on opening day, Eva had an extremely successful Christmas season, but two weeks into January she was lucky to have five customers on any given day. She was almost sorry now that she had given notice to Mrs. Bergstrom, who had found someone to replace her the very next week after Christmas. Already Eva missed Emma and Emily, but she kept herself busy dying and spinning the remainder of last year's fleece. Spinning was an opportunity to sit and relax without feeling guilty, a way of totally enjoying herself while accomplishing a necessary task.

Eva had sent out Christmas cards to Karl, Mats, the Kronbergs and her Aunt Anna and Uncle Lars. She had hoped the one to Karl might have accidentally slipped through to him, especially with the abundance of holiday mail arriving at the Lindholms. Now she was left wondering.

Every day she looked forward to seeing an envelope from Mats with the pictures Mr. Kaneko took the day they all landed in New York. She was also concerned that she hadn't heard from the Kronbergs. Mr. Kronberg was her only link to the Lindholms and she'd written a brief note about her hasty departure in hopes that he might somehow inform Karl. Mr. Kronberg, who was aware of Mrs. Lindholm's displeasure, would surely tell Karl the truth and hopefully give him her address.

One beautiful Christmas card still decorated her bureau. It was from her aunt and uncle in Minnesota. Under the printed message were a few lines written in Anna's flowery handwriting.

Dear Eva
We were so thrilled to find you are living in America and already have your very own yarn shop. What a very talented and industrious girl you are! We miss Jonas. He is attending music school in New York, but he does return to Minnesota for the summer and he took the train out for Christmas. We are very happy living by the lake. Lots of Swedes here, too. Lars is always busy with his boats and wood carvings and also does a little fishing. I have my garden in summer and do a lot of knitting and sewing during the long winter months. Here is a lot like Sweden and we feel very much at home. We hope you feel the same way living in Massachusetts.
Merry Christmas.
Anna and Lars.

On weekends and some evenings Arne came to build shelves and cabinets for the little room adjacent to the shop. He'd found a small stove in a second-hand store that Eva thought would be perfect for making coffee downstairs. In order to bring more customers into the shop, she advertised in the window that she was selling hot coffee, cocoa and various kinds of muffins. As time went on she added doughnuts, frosted yeast rolls, and cinnamon coffee cake.

Officer O'Leary, a robust, red-faced Irishman who had occasionally stopped in to check on Eva in the past was now a daily paying customer. His visits were welcome, even though the two had trouble understanding each other. It was a comfort to know he was out on the street, his presence preventing a lot of ne'er-do-wells from frequenting her shop, especially on very cold days when transients with no money needed a place to get warm. She had made the mistake of admitting a few of these poor souls and giving them something to eat, but to her dismay they had become regular visitors. Officer O'Leary had no trouble sending them away.

Many women stopped in, cold and tired from shopping, resting at the oak table with a warm drink. Gazing about the room at the knitted scarves, hats, mittens and afghans, they would be reminded of a gift owed to someone. Some bought already knitted items, but most were knitters themselves and were tempted by the boxes of beautifully colored skeins of yarn. Before leaving, it wasn't unusual for a woman to buy a half-dozen cinnamon rolls or muffins and sometimes a whole almond cake along with their skeins of yarn. There were winter days when more money came in from selling food and drink than from knitting materials.

No establishments were open in town on Sunday and it was good to lock the door and not think of entertaining customers for a day. Usually Eva would take a leisurely, hot bath in the morning, put a roast in the oven and enjoy the long trolley ride to church. She had been able to cover herself with a roomy, long coat and feel confident her little secret was still safe from Mrs. Bergstrom and her church-lady friends, but now her belly was much too large and she had dispensed with attending church.

Being pregnant had given Eva little inconvenience, but lately she welcomed the opportunity to get off her feet on Sunday afternoons and do nothing but knit, spin or study her Swedish-English dictionary. Dagny had begun to take more interest in cooking now, so Eva didn't need to be running up and down stairs tending the stove as much as before. Arne usually came over on Sundays to do carpenter work, and he kept them supplied with potatoes and other root vegetables.

Each day Eva had put off making the dreaded appointment at the doctor's office. Visions of that time on the ship plagued her, making her cringe at the thought of being undressed in front of a strange man. Her mother had never been to a doctor, although a woman from the village had come to help with Ingrid's difficult birth. Ingrid was born in summer when the roads were dry and passable, but such was not the case five years later on Christmas Eve when snow filled the path to the gravel road.

Eva had arrived earlier than expected, slipping out so quickly and effortlessly that her mother was sitting up in bed with Eva in her arms when Gustav came in from barn chores. He knew about the birthing of calves and wasn't afraid of doing what was necessary for his wife and child.

But Lexington was not like rural Sweden. Here there were stricter rules about pregnancy and childbirth, so Eva felt pressured to make the necessary preparations for the safety of herself and the baby. During a midwinter thaw, when the sidewalks were mostly bare of snow and ice, she walked the quarter mile to the doctor's office. A girl at the reception desk told her the doctor was busy and made an appointment for the next day. Now she had twenty-four more hours to worry about seeing the doctor, or rather, about the doctor seeing her.

But the next day she learned that all her anxiety had been for nothing. As she lay on the examining table, it wasn't a man looking down at her. Instead she saw the face of a kindly woman, old enough to be her very own mother.

"I'm Dr. White. How are you feeling today, Miss Gunderson?"

"Very well," said Eva with a sigh of relief. The doctor smiled, asked a few questions and gently felt her abdomen. Afterwards Eva remembered only that her baby should be arriving about the third week in March and to return in two weeks for another examination. She was given a booklet of questions and answers, but there were many words she didn't understand, so she put the book aside and forgot about it.

On Valentine's Day, Arne gave Dagny a small diamond engagement ring. Dagny loved sparkly things and was fascinated by the brilliant gem, often sitting by a sunny window admiring how the diamond made tiny rainbows dance on the walls and ceiling. For a few weekends she was inclined to daydreaming, sitting with Raggedy Ann in her lap and gazing at the walls absent-mindedly, often neglecting her work about the house. Eva understood how it was to be in love and let Dagny enjoy her newfound happiness.

Soon Dagny was back to normal and talking a blue streak. It was as if she had bottled up all her feelings and now the stopper had popped and all her words came tumbling out at once.

"I told Arne about that part of Maine where everyone lives in the old ways and speaks Swedish. He already knew about the place."

Eva looked up from her spinning. "Would he move away from his own little farm here?"

"Oh yes," said Dagny. "He said there are many larger farms for sale in New Sweden now. Can you believe we were thinking and planning the same thing without the other knowing?"

"An amazing coincidence that tells me you were made for each other," said Eva.

Dagny nodded in agreement. "Arne knows about history, too. He told me that in the year 1870 the state of Maine sent a man to Sweden to find farmers willing to settle in Northern Maine. I think the man's name was Thom. No, his last name was Thomas and he brought around fifty people to this place they called New Sweden. Each family received a cabin and one hundred acres of land. Two years later there were over six hundred Swedes living in the town of New Sweden."

Eva stopped spinning. "My goodness...you surely have learned a lot about New Sweden! How did you remember all that?"

"I listened hard because I want to go there so much. Living there has been my dream...just like your dream of owning a yarn shop."

"New Sweden sounds like a wonderful place. I wouldn't mind going there myself."

"Would you, Eva? Would you go with us?"

"You aren't thinking of moving soon are you?"

"Oh, no, said Dagny. "I promised to stay until the baby is born and how ever long you need me afterwards, but maybe after three or four months we could all go together."

But Eva put such thoughts to rest. "The yarn shop is pretty well established now...and there is Ingrid...I will not rest until I find her." Eva thought about Karl, too. No, she couldn't go that far away. There was that preposterous notion in the back of her head that he might eventually come looking for her, but Eva didn't confide this silly, wishful thought to Dagny.

"I understand," said Dagny, sliding back comfortably in her seat. "Arne says there are hundreds of miles of flat land in Aroostook County suitable for growing potatoes. I'll tell you one thing, I never thought I'd ever plant another potato!"

Like dark clouds predicting rain, silence passed over them...a moment when both girls were back in Sweden, with brief thoughts of the potato shed and Vidar reminding Dagny how grateful she was for being freed from all that...thankful to Eva for intervening that awful day.

"You will always have a home with Arne and me if you ever need one."

Eva blinked away the tears. "That is kind of you to say. Your thoughtfulness means so much to me," she said, rising from her seat to embrace her dearest friend.

During the last week in February Eva slipped on the stairs and turned her ankle. Dagny insisted on quitting her job and helping Eva full time in the yarn shop. Eva hadn't been to church for many weeks when Mrs. Bergstrom glided through the door with two other church ladies.

"We've missed seeing you at meeting and thought you might be sick," she said with outstretched arms.

Eva had been spinning and rose to greet her friend. Mrs. Bergstrom's eyes instantly fastened on Eva's protruding belly with a combination of shock and disgust. Eva remembered what Dr. Bergstrom had told her and walked behind the counter, but the damage had already been done. Mrs. Bergstrom hastily turned around and informed her friends that she had forgotten about an appointment. She was in such a tizzy to get out of the shop that she bumped into the door and her hat went flying off her head. She never looked back and rushed out the door without it.

The church ladies stood awkwardly in the middle of the room as if not knowing what to do next. Eva put on her bulky sweater, set the coffee tray on the table and asked them to sit down. Glad to get off their feet and relax, they accepted her offer. Eva showed them some new pattern books and they each bought enough yarn for a small afghan.

Dagny broke out in uncontrollable laughter as soon as the door closed behind them. "I'll never forget that surprised look on Mrs. Bergstrom's face the minute you stood up!"

"She will tell everyone and I'll never be able to set foot in that church again," said Eva with regret.

"Soon this will all be forgotten and they will have someone else to talk about," said Dagny. Eva sat down heavily at the oak table and sighed. Dagny picked up the flowery hat and set it lopsidedly on her head, then walked over to Eva with two pieces of almond cake. In her most sophisticated Mrs. Bergstrom voice she said,

"My dear, don't you think it's time for a bit of coffee and cake?" Seeing Dagny in that ridiculous hat broke Eva's gloomy mood.

"Oh, Dagny...you sure do know how to cheer someone up!"

Karla

1935 – 1953

The Bus Ride

Karla took two days to come into this world. She was born on the sixth of March and weighed eight pounds. Like Ingrid, she cried from her very first breath. Eva's milk was slow coming down and Karla fussed constantly. However, in three days she had enough milk for two babies and as Karla nursed one breast, milk poured from the other.

So why was Karla crying all the time? The doctor said it was merely colic and told Eva to walk her around the room until she stopped crying. Eva held her constantly and walked around the house jiggling her up and down. At night they slept together in Eva's bed so she could just reach over and put her hand on Karla to soothe her. Often Dagny did the same in order that Eva might get some rest.

Eva was blessed to have Dagny at home with her every day to help prepare meals, wash dishes and make the beds. When someone came to the shop, Dagny was the one who ran downstairs to wait on customers. If Eva needed a nap, Dagny took Karla out to the porch or in the back yard. Soon Eva was downstairs again and from then on, both girls shared the responsibilities of home, shop and caring for Karla.

The first time Dagny removed Karla's diaper she saw a big, red blotch on Karla's thigh. She was trying hard to rub it off when Eva walked in.

"It won't come off, Dagny. It's a birthmark."

Dagny stared at the irregular, spidery looking mark that covered nearly a quarter of Karla's upper thigh and thought it a bad omen.

"Is she marked because of you and Karl...that you and he....well, that you weren't married and..."

Eva interrupted and explained that the doctor had told her not to worry. It wasn't her fault or the result of anything she had done and that birthmarks happened more often than most people realized. A lot of birthmarks were hidden by clothing and many faded over the years or just went away, he had said.

"I'm grateful it isn't on her face or some other exposed place," said Eva as she pinned on the clean diaper and wrapped Karla in a blanket. Dagny was still troubled and several days went by before she went near Karla again. One afternoon when Eva was napping, she picked up the screaming Karla, who stopped crying instantly and looked up to Dagny with a big toothless grin.

"Who are you talking to?" asked Eva, sleepily rising from her bed.

"Karla just smiled at me! I was telling her how beautiful she is."

"She smiled at me this morning, too," said Eva. "I was thinking how powerful a smile is, how such a joyful connection can bond two people together in an instant."

Karla's smile had momentarily made Dagny forget about the birthmark and over time she wasn't bothered by the sight of it.

A long spell of rainy weather finally subsided and the first of May dawned sunny and warm. Karla was sleeping longer during the night, so that Eva was able to get three hours continuous sleep before needing to get up to feed and change her. However, the baby still cried a lot during the day. Eva had been housebound for too long and suggested to Dagny that they all go for a ride to Lexington Center.

At the bus stop Karla began to squirm, her face puckered up and big tears fell down her cheeks. Eva was about to return home when the bus driver opened the door and smiled down at them.

"A bus ride is all she needs," said the driver convincingly. "I'll bet she'll be asleep in less than five minutes."

Eva had her doubts about that, but as soon as they sat down and the bus started up a miracle happened; Karla stopped crying, looked around, grinned at her mother and fell into a deep sleep.

She was still sleeping when they reached Lexington Center, so Eva and Dagny decided to ride all the way to Bedford, the end of the line. The landscape changed quickly from blocks of stores, to moderate-sized homes and then to large farms with open fields and cows grazing in green pastures. Eva immediately thought of Ingrid and searched the countryside for signs of a pony, but to no avail. All too soon they were back among tidy small homes and rows of stores until the bus stopped in the town of Bedford. The driver said he would be in the station for about ten minutes and they could get out and walk around until he came back. Karla wrinkled up her face and started moving her arms, so Eva thought some fresh air and new scenery might calm her down.

"Let's walk for five minutes, then turn around," said Eva. On the way back Dagny carried Karla. When they approached the hardware store a man came out with a bag. He looked at Eva, tipped his cap and said, "Hi beautiful." Eva ignored him and walked faster. A minute later he passed them in a gray car, smiling and waving out the window.

"He's a fair looking boy," teased Dagny. "Might even be Swedish."

"What do you mean by that?" questioned Eva.

"Well, you were blushing a little, so I thought you might have liked him."

"I have no time for a man, especially for one so forward as that," stated Eva emphatically.

Dagny held the sleeping Karla on the ride back. Eva's eyes grew heavy and she slept all the way home. From then on, whenever Karla was extra fussy, they rode the bus to Lexington Center, bought an ice cream cone and walked to the common until the bus returned from Bedford.

Trip to Boston

It was surprising to both Eva and Dagny how Karla responded so naturally to Arne, and how the feeling was mutual. On Sundays Arne would come to the upstairs parlor and amuse Karla while the girls prepared dinner. She'd lie in his arms grinning up at him as he spoke to her. Often when she got fussy he'd bring her downstairs, bouncing her up and down with every step. Today was sunny and warm. Eva looked down from the upstairs window as Arne took long strides up and down the sidewalk, the top of Karla's head peeking contentedly over his shoulder.

"Have you noticed how Arne doesn't stutter when he talks to Karla?" said Eva while they were preparing dinner. Dagny continued peeling onions and didn't answer. She had been quiet all morning. There was something unusual in the air, but Eva couldn't put her finger on the cause.

"Your face is a bit flushed. Do you have a stomach ache or fever?"

"Neither," said Dagny, a tear escaping from her eye.

"Then why are you crying?"

"I'm not crying," said Dagny. "Onions make my eyes run."

"Do onions cause silence, too?" asked Eva.

"I've been thinking all morning how to tell you, but I can't find the words."

Eva put her hands on Dagny's shoulders. "You know you can tell me anything. Now sit down and get whatever it is off your mind."

They sat beside each other for a brief, quiet moment with Dagny looking down at her lap. When Eva reached over to touch her hand, Dagny's tongue let loose.

"Arne wanted me to tell you...he sold his property and farm equipment. A lawyer is making final arrangements for purchasing a farm in New Sweden."

"That's very good news," exclaimed Eva. "When will you be leaving?"

"Soon...if it's all right with you."

"I'm back to feeling like my old self now," said Eva. "You may leave whenever you wish."

Dagny fidgeted in her seat and twiddled her thumbs. "He wants to be in Maine in time to put in a garden and plant some fields of potatoes."

Eva grinned. "Sounds like all you have to do now is to get married!"

Dagny covered her face with her hands and then confessed that they had gotten married yesterday.

"So that's why you were so late coming home last night. And you didn't tell me until now...you little imp!"

"Now I've spilled the beans," said Dagny regretfully. "We weren't going to tell you until after dinner."

"That's all right," said Eva as she embraced her friend. "I'm so happy for you. When you and Arne tell me this afternoon I'll be twice as happy for you both."

After dinner Arne brought a rocking chair upstairs on his back, the only piece of furniture he hadn't sold. It was one of the first things he'd made when he came to America and now he wanted Eva to have it. It was the most comfortable chair she'd ever sat in.

Importing yarn from Sweden was too expensive. Mrs. Sandquist had told Eva of a place in Boston that sold yarn in large amounts at wholesale prices.

"I'd get lost in Boston," said Eva. "All those narrow winding streets and scary underground trains."

"I went to school there and worked in many of the stores, so I know my way around the city," said Mrs. Sandquist. "I'd be glad to go with you. Why don't you bring Dagny, too?"

When Eva told this to Dagny, she declined. "I'd like to go, but wouldn't it be easier for you if I stayed home and took care of Karla?"

"No, I want you to come. You and Arne are leaving for Maine in three days and this will be our last chance to have fun together."

After deliberating, Dagny came up with an idea.

"Perhaps Arne could look after Karla. He's planning to come over anyway to work in the back room."

Eva was filled with indecision about leaving Karla. How would Arne know what to do if an emergency arose? "I don't think I should go to Boston at all," sighed Eva. "It would mean leaving Karla for most of a day."

"With Arne here, I'll bet Karla won't miss you one little bit," said Dagny.

"Well, she is taking two good naps every day now," said Eva. "I'll think on it."

The next day Eva gave Karla a good feeding and placed her in the cradle, then instructed Arne about giving her some cow's milk if she got fussy later. She also gave him a little cloth with sugar tied in it.

"Don't forget to get all her burps up, and if she's still fussy you can give her the little sugar tit to suck on. It should pacify her until we get back."

Eva put a *closed* sign in the window so Arne wouldn't be bothered by customers and told him to lock the door.

Everything went smoothly until Arne stopped working to eat his lunch by the shop window. As he finished drinking his coffee, a sailor looked in and tapped on the window. Arne hoped the man would go away, but then the door knob jiggled, followed by a loud knocking. Karla began whimpering.

Since the sailor had already seen him, Arne couldn't very well pretend he wasn't there, so he picked up Karla and opened the door.

"I'm Mats Kronberg," said the sailor, offering to shake Arne's hand, who dared not put out his hand for fear of dropping Karla.

"Is Eva home?" he asked, poking his head in to look around the shop. "She and I were old friends back in Norrland. Did she ever speak of me?" He spoke in Swedish, so Arne immediately felt more comfortable and backed up so Mats could enter.

"No, I ne...never heard her sp...speak of you. Sh...she's gone to Boston."

"Gone to Boston?" exclaimed Mats. "I just came from there." He thought it ironic that he had been traveling from Boston at the very same time Eva was going there. What were the chances of that happening...one in a million? Already the stakes were against him today.

Arne was more concerned now with Karla. She began wiggling her arms and legs wildly like she always did when she wanted him to lift her high in the air above his head. He took the hint and she giggled from excitement as he lifted her up and down in his large hands.

"That's my good girl," he said, smiling at her. She squealed with joy as he lifted her high above his head again and again. Then she nestled in his arms.

Mats studied the baby. She was definitely the image of Eva with her reddish-blonde, curly hair and rosebud mouth. He counted the months since he'd last seen Eva and his calculations didn't come out right. But babies sometimes come a month or two early, he surmised, and thought no more about it.

"I can see she looks just like her mother," said Mats, hoping to get more information from this rather short and muscular man whom he thought must be Eva's husband.

"Ya, she da...does for sure," said Arne, lifting Karla up one more time until she giggled. Then he placed her in the cradle and began rocking it slowly back and forth with his foot.

"That's some fine piece of work you've got there," said Mats, feeling the smooth finish and inspecting the dovetailing, scalloped edges and cut-out heart designs of the cradle. "I've done a bit of woodworking myself, but nothing as nice as this."

"Ya, I ma...made it for Karla," he said proudly.

As Mats bent over, an envelope fell from his pocket onto the floor. "Oh, I almost forgot...intended to mail these pictures to Eva but never got around to it." He gave the envelope to Arne. "You can look at them if you want."

Arne went over by the window and sat down at the old oak table, where he studied each photograph. He put them all back in the envelope except for the one of Eva and Dagny, both with wide smiles, waving in front of a big ship. Dagny wore her white kerchief and Eva had on the straw hat Karl had given her. Mats stood behind Arne looking down at the photograph admiring the stunning likeness of Eva.

"Your wife is a beautiful woman, isn't she?" said Mats. He

was referring to Eva, of course, but Arne couldn't take his eyes off Dagny.

"Ya, she sur...surely is," replied Arne, holding the picture a little closer to his face.

Mats glanced at the clock on the wall. He had thought to take Eva out to dinner, but that wasn't going to happen today. He was hungry and had to be back to the ship before six. "Well, tell Eva I'm sorry I missed her. I'll come around again sometime."

Arne looked up, raised his hand in farewell and went back to admiring the photograph of his sweet Dagny.

It was almost suppertime when the girls burst into the shop full of laughter and giddiness, each carrying two large bags of brightly colored yarn. Dagny ran out back to tell Arne about their wonderful trip to Boston and Eva sat down to nurse Karla, who had suddenly awakened and was screaming at all the commotion.

Karla nursed aggressively and Eva's painful breasts exploded with a rush of milk that soaked her shift. She grabbed a clean diaper to protect her bodice and laid her head against the back of the rocking chair. It had been an exciting and busy day and she was exhausted. As it turned out, Boston wasn't the dirty, crowded city that she remembered. Mrs. Sandquist had pointed out historical landmarks, museums and restaurants with foods of many different countries. Today she had seen the hustle and bustle of happy throngs of people and interesting store windows that made the girls stop in wonder at the lovely, colorful displays.

After a while Dagny and Arne came in from the back room and sat at the oak table. Arne gave Eva the envelope. He told her a man in uniform had brought them, a sailor from Boston.

"His na...name was M...Mats." Arne couldn't remember his last name, only that he was an old friend from Norrland.

Eva's mouth dropped. "Mats came here today?"

The envelope slipped from her hand and fell onto the floor. She was devastated thinking she'd missed seeing Mats. Why was he in the Navy? What happened to his plans for college? Did he marry Jenny? There was so much she wanted to know. Arne picked up the envelope and took out a photograph.

"Look here. This g...girl looks j...just like you," he said to Dagny.

"It is me!" she said. Then she explained about the other pictures and the many people she had met on the voyage to America. Dagny's joyful voice sounded far away to Eva, its resonance fading into the remoteness of another time. Eva was drowning in her own sad thoughts. Her wonderful day had paled now. She wished she'd never gone to Boston today.

Karla had fallen asleep in her mother's arms. Dagny and Arne's soft voices flowed in from the back room and Eva wondered, too, if she had also drifted off to sleep. She put Karla in the cradle and buttoned up her dress. Only then did she sit at the table to look at the photographs. It was a very long time before she was able to put down the picture of her and Mats standing on the pier. How happy they both looked, full of hopefulness and big dreams for the future.

Eva's first visit to the dentist had been during the last week in November, just before the grand opening. Now it was the last week of May; time for her six-month checkup. She had been dreading it for weeks. Not so much fearing she might have another cavity, but worrying about the possibility of running into Mrs. Bergstrom and what the outcome of that might be. They hadn't seen each other since that embarrassing day Mrs. Bergstrom had come with the church ladies. Her flowered hat still decorated the shop wall. If Mrs. Bergstrom wanted her hat, she could come and get it herself.

Emma was playing on the rug in the waiting room and ran excitedly toward Eva when she came through the door. "Oh, Miss Gunderson, I've missed you so much." Emma was fascinated with Karla and the feeling was mutual.

"Are you babysitting again?" she asked. Eva told her that in a way she was babysitting and quickly changed the subject.

"How come you aren't in school today?"

"I had the chicken pox," she said as proudly as if she'd won a special prize. "I'm over it now, but I have to stay out of school for the rest of the week."

The kind receptionist offered to hold Karla during Eva's examination. Dr. Bergstrom was delighted to see them both, complimenting Eva on her beautiful, healthy baby. He asked about the yarn shop and Eva wondered if his wife had told him about that troubling day. As she was rinsing her mouth from the cleaning, she heard Mrs. Bergstrom talking in the waiting room. She had been shopping and was here to pick up Emma.

"What an adorable baby!" came Mrs. Bergstrom's loud voice from the receptionist's desk. Eva could hear her cooing and talking baby talk, but when Eva came in to pay her bill, Mrs. Bergstrom knew in an instant who this beautiful child with the reddish-golden hair belonged to.

"Well, Eva! What a surprise!"

"Hello, Mrs. Bergstrom," said Eva, wondering what to say next. She was saved from uncertainty by Emma.

"Can Miss Gunderson have lunch with us, Mama? Please?" pleaded Emma.

"Maybe some other time, dear. I'm really in a hurry today."

"You promised we'd eat at the dairy bar and I'm not leaving without Miss Gunderson."

Dr. Bergstrom soothed the situation over by insisting they all go out to lunch together. His wife dutifully complied. He was quite the diplomat and the meal was not nearly as awkward as Eva had feared. In fact, she was invited over for dinner the next Sunday, after a little prodding from Emma. Eva politely refused because she was going to Mrs. Sandquist's. Mrs. Bergstrom seemed not at all disappointed.

July Surprise

Midsummer was like any ordinary day in America, although a few of Eva's Scandinavian customers mentioned how they still celebrated the festive holiday by preparing special foods remembered from the old country and dressing in their native costumes. Eva was tempted to make a braided yeast bread with cherries, raisins, nuts and white frosting, bake a ham and some scalloped potatoes and even put on her mother's dress, but Karla was too young to appreciate any of that. Eva, feeling little Swedish spirit this year, ate leftovers for dinner.

Eva felt a great loss after Dagny and Arne moved to Maine. They were like family, filling her house with joy and laughter. Now it was mostly an empty shell of silence where she welcomed each little whimper or loud cry from the cradle; anything that revealed life still existed. She had immersed herself in the yarn shop and in caring for Karla, who had changed from a helpless baby into a real little person with funny expressions and adorable ways of her own.

There were times when she sorely missed Dagny. After becoming engaged, Dagny had been eager to learn more about cooking and baking. Eva had taught her much about mixing up bread dough, making corn bread, cutting out biscuits, and putting special meals together that weren't cooked in one big pot. Boiled dinners and stews were fine for busy days, but there was more to eating than beef and root vegetables. Eva took time to show Dagny how to fry fish, roast a chicken, a loin of pork and a leg of lamb, and told her what her mother had said about variety spicing up one's life when it came to pleasing a man and his stomach.

Desserts were a problem for Dagny, especially Arne's favorite, apple pie, which needed a flaky crust and a filling of apples baked just right...not too hard and not soft like applesauce. Dagny did become proficient in making peanut butter cookies, as long as she remembered to take them out of the oven before they were burned to a crisp.

Almost two months had passed and still no word from New Sweden. Eva understood the work involved in setting up a new home, planting a garden and readying fields for potatoes. Knowing Dagny's lack of skill in writing, Eva hadn't expected to receive a long letter, but hoped to hear a few words about their journey through Maine, what their farm looked like, and to learn their street address. She pictured Dagny out in the fields working beside Arne and wondered if they'd bought an ox or horse to help them plow and cultivate the land. At the end of the day she could see them in the kitchen preparing dinner together just as they had done at Arne's house so many times before.

After putting down Karla for the night, Eva remembered how she'd wanted to celebrate Dagny's birthday on Midsummer. She wrote a letter reminding Dagny of this, and wished her a happy birthday. She told her about the neighbor who had given her an old carriage and how once a week she pushed Karla down to Arne's old place to buy vegetables. The old couple who lived there were friendly and hardworking. They also had hens and a cow, so she was able to buy fresh eggs and milk there as well.

When it came time to address the envelope Eva realized she didn't know Arne's last name. Perhaps it wouldn't be necessary. How many married couples in New Sweden would be named Arne and Dagny? They weren't the commonest of names. When she asked the postman, he thought the letter would probably reach its designated destination, regardless of no last name or street address. He knew of such cases, and since New Sweden was a very small town, he told her not to worry.

In the storeroom Eva found a pair of matching, framed pictures that were faded and water stained. She cleaned the glass and polished up the frames, replacing one of the old pictures with the photograph of her and Mats, and the other with her with Dagny. They hung in the kitchen above the table where she and Karla ate their meals. To look at them brought her happiness, unless she dwelled too much on what lay behind one of those carefree smiles, her own. Eva's outward smile showed promise and optimism, masking a fear of the future and remembrances of a lost love. Eva had no pictures of Karl, except for the album saved in her head of all their special times together. However, little by little many of these images were diminishing in clarity as newer ones fought to replace them.

The ring gave her great comfort and when she gazed into the

vibrant colors she saw Karl as he was that day he slipped it onto her finger. That last moment in the breakfast room was still vivid in her heart and mind, Karl's handsome, fair face looking down at her own with loving eyes and bright hopes for the future.

"It would please me to know you are wearing my ring. It is said the stone inspires love," he had told her. Then, after a brief, tender kiss, he'd said, "I love you," and she'd told him she loved him, too.

"I won't take this ring off until I see you again," she had said. Then Karl had taken her face in his hands, saying, "promise?" And then she'd given him that promise. Eva often thought about that day, remembering her promise, trying to convince herself that someday they would meet again. Until then, the ring would never leave her finger.

The day came when Eva finished spinning the last batch of carded fleece. She felt much optimism looking around the shop at the full boxes of colored skeins on the counter, and knowing that the base cabinets were full of surplus yarn. Summer hours at the shop were ten to four, which gave her more time in the morning to care for Karla and to work in the garden in the late afternoon. If a customer showed up before or after shop hours, they were not turned away.

Arne had dug up part of the back yard where the sun shone most of the day, and planted many of the root vegetables he'd grown on his own little farm. Eva later added above-ground vegetables such as green beans, cucumbers, squash and a patch of corn near the back fence. The garden provided a change of pace for Eva and fresh outside views for Karla, who at first sat in the shade of an old apple tree mesmerized by a pair of robins flying in and out as they cared for a nestful of hungry babies.

As Eva cultivated the rows and pulled out weeds, she sometimes thought of her mother's words...weeds in a garden were like problems in one's life.

"Life is like a garden," her mother had said one day. "Troubles are like weeds. Though small at first, they can eventually shade and overpower the delicate flowers. It is best to work a little every day cultivating harmony, weeding out obstacles when they are small enough to be eliminated quickly and easily."

Eva remembered how her parents had been so sad and full of guilt after Ingrid had fled to America without saying goodbye. On the other hand, Eva had been happy for her sister, who had run away to that exciting place called America. She remembered only the guilt of not feeling sad. With Ingrid gone, Eva didn't have to live in the shadow of her sister's demeaning influence, who had been like an obnoxious weed overpowering the flowering Eva. She had thought of Ingrid's departure like pulling out a troublesome weed. It was then that Eva had wanted to be the most beautiful flower in her mother's garden, hoping to spread joy throughout the saddened house. However, trying to be that cheerful, inspiring flower hadn't been an easy job. Time had changed everything and everyone. She was a different person now and missed Ingrid very much.

While hilling up the potatoes, her mind always went to Arne and Dagny, who probably had many acres of potatoes to care for. At most other times Eva remembered Dagny as she looked that last day, holding Raggedy Ann carefully under one arm and a stuffed pillowcase over her other shoulder. Dagny had insisted on carrying Raggedy Ann. "How can she breathe closed up in a stuffy old bag?" she had said quite seriously to Eva. Walking down the sidewalk that morning beside Arne, Dagny looked more like a daughter than a wife, but Eva knew they were both deliriously happy and that was all that mattered.

In July Dave Beckworth stopped in to see if Eva needed more fleece. A farmer in Bedford had bought a flock of sheep and had recently had them shorn. Remembering all the work involved in washing fleece, Eva was tempted to say no, but the old days of Norrland came to mind, those frugal times when food and money were scarce, and her sensible, thrifty nature caused her to reexamine the shop's inventory, the cost of purchasing additional yarn from Sweden, and the expense of making another trip to

Boston. There was no question that buying more fleece was the only way she could make a substantial profit.

Eva's situation had also changed. She was alone now, with the full responsibility of caring for Karla. No longer did she have financial help from Dagny, nor were there any more end-of-the-week donations of leftover meat from the butcher and Arne's generous gifts of vegetables. He had been so much help, too, remodeling the downstairs and making any necessary house repairs, just for the price of a good home-cooked meal. All maintenance was up to her now, and hiring someone to fix a leaky roof or faucet would be costly. This house was her home and the yarn shop her only means of support. There was no decision to consider; she definitely needed more fleece. Plans were made for the fleece to be delivered the next Saturday.

Eva was picking peonies from a bush near the driveway when the truck pulled in. An old man was driving and Dave waved from the passenger seat. A young boy around two years old sat between them trying to keep ahead of a dripping ice cream cone. Dave helped the boy down from the truck and approached Eva. "This is my son, David."

She knelt down to say hello to the boy and he answered by holding up his cone as if intending to share it with her. "Ice ceeem?" he said proudly. They all laughed because there was barely any ice cream left, except for all the dribbles on the cone.

While the men unloaded the fleece, Eva took David into the back room to wash his sticky hands and face before introducing him to Karla. Eva grabbed one of the little balls she'd made out of yarn scraps and told David to sit on the floor. She sat behind Karla to support her and rolled the ball to David, motioning for him to roll it back. Karla laughed as the ball touched her leg and David was amused by that. Eva took Karla's hands in hers, pushing the ball to David, and he rolled it back to Karla, whose giggles made David laugh uncontrollably. Time passed quickly and when the truck motor started, Eva invited the men in for refreshments. They wanted only a cold drink of water, so they all relaxed on the back steps.

"Nice looking garden," said Dave, admiring the tiny cucumbers growing on the vigorous green plants.

"I planted too many seeds," replied Eva.

"Well, you could always sell some. Mine got that black rot, so I know my wife will be buying cucumbers for making pickles."

Eva's constant study of the English language was paying off. She understood most of the conversation and was able to respond intelligently except about the black rot. The old farmer was agreeing with Dave and began talking about the hot weather and its effect on sheep. Eva was reminded of the hat she'd made for Dave and ran back into the house to get it.

Little David was immediately curious about what was in the paper bag, so she told him to give it to his father. But something got lost in the translation and little David put on the hat and began running up and down the rows of vegetable plants. Eva explained to Dave that the hat was made from the fleece he brought last year and she'd made it for him.

He thanked her and called his son in from the garden. The hat was much too big for little David and kept slipping over his eyes. Everyone laughed, including David, who just pushed the hat back so he could see and insisted on wearing it, even though the temperature was close to ninety degrees.

Meanwhile, the old farmer had been observing Eva. "You remind me of one of my neighbors," he said. "She doesn't have red hair, nor does she look like you, but there's a resemblance I can't explain… something similar about the eyes, the turn of your mouth and the way you react to things." Eva understood bits and pieces of what he said.

"She's older than you, a bit plump with very yellow hair, but your accent is similar."

Eva listened politely until he said, "her name is Ingrid."

Eva was on the edge of the step now, dumbfounded, her face pale and eyes wide open, causing Dave to ask if she was feeling all right. Tears rolled down her cheeks.

"I have sister, name Ingrid. Where is?"

"Bedford...about two miles north of the village," said the old farmer. "Her husband is Olle Olson and they have two children."

"And a pony?" she asked, almost in a state of shock.

"Yup. The young boy does have a pony."

A quietness fell over the porch, as if the slight breeze had blown away any words. Eva stood, teetering on the step. Dave took her arm.

"Well, I'd say this deserves some sort of celebration!" he said. "Why don't we get in the truck and visit the Olson place!"

"We go see Ingrid?" said Eva softly, walking as if in a trance.

"Karla come, too?" said young David as he tried to lift her off the ground.

Dave helped Eva and Karla into the truck and jumped in the back with his son. The old farmer started the engine, talking a blue streak, but Eva could think of nothing but finally seeing her sister. When the man's voice grew louder, she would look at him and nod, her beautiful smile keeping him in a good mood. Her heart beat faster as they passed through Lexington Center and started on the familiar road to Bedford.

They turned into a long gravel driveway where a white house hid behind three large maple trees. Under the middle tree a young girl sat on a swing watching the approaching truck. A man pushed a lawn mower between the house and a large field. Then Eva saw the pony, brown and white, cantering across the pasture with a child on its back.

Eva opened the door before the truck came to a halt as the little girl came running toward them.

"You must be Nina," said Eva, noticing her reddish hair. The little girl nodded her head yes.

"I'm your Auntie Eva. Is your mama home?"

"Mama's over there," said Nina, pointing between the house and garage, "in the garden."

Ingrid was weeding carrots and wasn't too happy about it either. She was swearing in Swedish as Eva made her way down the rows of vegetables. When Karla began to fuss, Ingrid turned around, shielding her eyes from the sun, stunned to see the tall red-headed girl coming toward her. She dropped her trowel and ran toward her sister.

"Eva! I can't believe what my eyes are seeing!" They hugged tightly, neither wanting to let go, each jabbering in their native tongue, while poor Karla, squeezed between them, protested with loud screams and a very red face.

"Now who is this little cutie?" asked Ingrid. "I can tell she's a Gunderson!"

"This is my daughter, Karla."

"Come, let's sit on the bench," said Ingrid. "I'm a bit weak in the knees."

Just then young David came running around the house hollering, "Karla cry? Karla all right?"

"Yes, David, Karla is fine," said Eva, putting her arm around him as his father walked toward them.

"Dave, this is my sister, Ingrid. Ingrid, this is David Beckworth, little David's father."

"Is he your husband?" whispered Ingrid, as Gus and Nina, accompanied by Olle and the old farmer, joined them.

"Oh no. Just a friend," confided Eva. "I'll explain later."

Ingrid took over with the introductions and invited everyone to the porch for refreshments. Olle lagged behind, saying he had to finish mowing the lawn. Ingrid scowled at her husband. For some unknown reason, he looked embarrassed, but Ingrid ignored him. Eva saw their exchanged looks, feeling all was not well between them. Olle looked vaguely familiar. It didn't take her long to realize that he was the same man who had spoken to her at the hardware store and waved to her and Dagny from his automobile. He had apparently remembered her, too.

"You two have a lot of reminiscing to do," said Dave, picking up his son, who squirmed and cried to get out of his father's arms. "Not only that, it's past David's nap time."

"I can come back later to bring you home," the old farmer told Eva. She thanked him and said she would be happy to ride the bus home. Gus told his mother he was going to ride his pony and he followed the men back toward the truck.

Nina played with Karla on the parlor floor while the two sisters sat together on the sofa getting caught up on their separate pasts. After Nina and Karla fell asleep on the rug, the nonstop talking continued until both Olle and Gus came in starving for something to eat. Ingrid looked at the clock on the wall, astonished to see that it was after five o'clock.

"I'll get supper cooking right away," she said to Olle, who followed her into the kitchen demanding a cup of coffee. Nina had awakened and Karla looked around at the unfamiliar surroundings and began to scream. Eva felt her breasts swelling. It was past feeding time. She could see Olle sitting at the kitchen table drinking coffee and smoking a cigarette, so she found a comfortable chair in the corner to let Karla nurse. It felt good to lean her head against the back of the plush chair and unwind.

Eva was surprised by how quickly her sister prepared the fine meal of fried chicken, mashed potatoes and fresh green beans from the garden, all the while keeping up a line of chatter and not letting Eva lift a hand to help. Supper was an interesting mixture of family interaction, Gus and Nina picking at their food and squabbling between themselves, Olle telling them to be quiet and ordering them to eat everything on their plate, while Ingrid cautiously tried to smooth everything over while maintaining pleasant conversation with her sister. Olle's combative demeanor had much improved after his belly was full and he took kindly to Ingrid's suggestion that he drive Eva to the bus station.

He had been taken aback upon seeing her today and wondered if she remembered his face from before. Her expressive features told him she did. Had she said anything to Ingrid? He knew how women gossiped. But there was nothing he could do about all that now. The physical exertion of mowing the lawn, with the help of a couple of beers, had eased his mind somewhat through supper and now he sat in the car watching the two sisters walking hand-in-hand toward him. Karla bounced on Eva's outside hip and Olle could not help but notice Eva's full skirt dancing around her two shapely legs. He looked away, inhaling deeply on his cigarette and exhaling slowly, hoping to divert his erotic thoughts.

Eva recognized the gray car, but she had no choice about accepting the ride; she was emotionally tired and two miles was too far to walk while carrying Karla and her heavy bag. As they backed down the driveway, she rolled down the window to wave to Ingrid and the children, leaving it open for the cloud of smoke to escape. Two miles seemed a long time in the strained silence of the car. Eva mentioned how nice their house was and she said a few other things that he agreed with or just nodded his head to, but when he said no more she babbled to Karla about mundane things to fill the void until finally the station came into view.

"I certainly do appreciate you giving me a ride, Olle."

"Don't mention it," he said, savoring her sweet smile.

"Don't mention what?" she asked, wondering what she wasn't to comment on.

"Nothing. That's just an American saying that usually follows a thank you."

"Oh," she said opening the door. "Well, goodbye until Sunday. Ingrid said you'd be here at noontime to pick me up."

"I'll be here Sunday at noon then," he said most agreeably, his over-engaging grin causing her to hurry into the station.

Sleep evaded Eva that night as she lay in the soft darkness recounting Ingrid's every word, Gus and Nina's happy faces and the uncertain behavior of Olle. He wasn't her idea of a typical married man, but perhaps marriage was different in America. Putting his actions aside, this had been one of the happiest days she could remember.

Olle

Eva and Karla rode the bus to Bedford every Sunday. On the fourth trip there was no sign of Olle's car, so Eva started walking, cradling Karla in her right arm while carrying a satchel with her knitting and a change of clothes and diapers for Karla in her other hand. At first the tree-lined sidewalk offered much shade from the August heat, but after they turned left at the fork in the road, only large fields spread out everywhere around them. The unrelenting sun made Eva wither like the shriveled weeds and drooping daisies struggling to stay alive by the side of the road. What's more, she'd forgotten to bring Karla's bonnet; the baby's face turned red and sweaty as she squirmed in Eva's arms.

A yellowish-brown dog trotted out of a field and stopped ahead of her, its profile more fox-like than dog, although larger than any fox she'd ever seen in Norrland. It ran across the road and sat watching her rather intently as she stood very still and debated whether or not to continue or go back to town. Then the dog's eyes shifted to a place beyond her and she turned to see a gray car approaching. Soon she was looking at Olle's smirking face through the open window.

"Hop in." he said. "Sorry I'm late."

By the time she settled herself and Karla in the seat, the dog had run into the field, but she could see its pointed ears and rounded head above the tall grass. She carefully picked her English words because Olle rarely spoke Swedish now that he was an American.

"See the dog?" She said pointing into the field.

"That's no dog," he said. "It's a coyote. If I had my gun I'd shoot it."

"Are they dangerous?"

"Oh, ya…you were lucky to get out of there alive. Good thing I came along when I did."

"I don't understand. Could tell me in Swedish?" she asked. Olle took a long puff from his cigarette and slowly repeated the words in Swedish.

"I was just making a joke," he told her. "Coyotes have been known to steal family pets like cats and small dogs. Usually they are harmless, but if they are rabid they become aggressive and their bite can be deadly, so it's best to keep a safe distance away."

Eva was more comfortable now, not having to think a long time before saying proper words in English. He told her that he and Ingrid had learned English from a school teacher who lived next door. They thought that was the proper thing to do because the children would be speaking English in school.

"Well, you both speak English very well, Olle, but I'm glad you haven't forgotten the old language."

"We try to use English around the children, but when we have Swedish guests, we revert to Swedish and mix things up a little, especially if there is something that the children shouldn't hear." Olle chuckled. He was in a good mood today and the ride was short and pleasant.

It appeared he was a good provider. They had a fairly new automobile, Gus had his pony and Nina her dolls. The lawn was always mowed and neatly trimmed around the trees and house, which was newly painted and well furnished inside. Ingrid was a fine cook, preparing every Sunday meal with expensive cuts of meat, plenty of freshly cooked vegetables, tasty fruit sauces and delicious desserts.

As they turned into the driveway Eva propped Karla in front of the window so she could see Gus and Nina running across the lawn toward them. She immediately giggled, wiggling her arms and legs, squirming to get out of the car. Ingrid stood waving in the doorway and Eva hurried up the stone path.

When Olle walked into the kitchen he seemed different. He had left his pleasant demeanor parked in the garage with the car. As soon as he faced Ingrid he was in a grumpy mood, short-tempered and critical that dinner wasn't ready. Turning on his heels, he stomped out to the porch.

Ingrid sighed, rolled her eyes and mashed the potatoes with gusto. Eva could see Olle through the kitchen window brooding. He lit up another cigarette, leaned his head against the wooden rocker and closed his eyes. Something was in the air and Eva surmised it wasn't just because dinner was late.

As Ingrid carried bowls and platters of food to the table she asked Eva to inform Olle it was time to carve the roast. Eva did as she was told and was surprised when Olle grinned up to her from the chair...that same knowing smile that seemed just for her. She preferred to think it was because he was happy that dinner was ready.

It was apparent Ingrid wanted to please her husband by satisfying his stomach, but he usually ate without saying much. Perhaps he was raised that way, but Eva thought his moody silences were more than that. Unless he had a complaint, he rarely spoke directly to Ingrid. When Olle wasn't in the room, Eva often noticed that Gus ran to his mother with a message from his father, and vice versa. It seemed odd that she'd never heard a loving word between them, nor had she seen them being affectionate in any way.

At the table, as well as other times, Ingrid monopolized the conversation, speaking when necessary to the children in English, but mostly chatting with Eva in Swedish. If Olle spoke, it was to criticize the children for their manners or for playing with their food. An unsettling cloud of silence usually followed his faultfinding until eventually giggles erupted between the children. Ingrid couldn't help but smile and soon she and Eva were chatting again.

Eva was uncomfortably embarrassed for Ingrid, who tried to make light of her husband's attitude and tried to soothe the troubled atmosphere with cheery little comments. Eva, too, tried her best to fill in the dead spots with talk of Karla, the yarn shop and some of her more interesting customers. Even Olle laughed about the day Mrs. Bergstrom came in and saw the pregnant Eva. In fact, Olle took notice of Eva every time she spoke and often she caught him looking at her for no apparent reason. He came into the parlor once when she was nursing Karla, standing for a long time in front of the bookcase before choosing a book and sitting down across from her. He pretended to be reading, but she knew he wasn't most of the time. After that she made it a point to avoid being alone with him. However, that was impossible when it came time for her to go home.

In late September when the days were shorter, it was almost

dark one Sunday when Olle backed the car out of the garage. He popped the cap on another bottle of beer and watched the two sisters talking by the front door. Eva was slim and taller than Ingrid, whom he thought looked rather dumpy in comparison. Eva was a knockout all right in that blue dress...and smart, too: only in America for a year and already the owner of her own business. And that red hair...he'd heard the men talk about a redhead's temper and how aggressive they were in bed. He looked the other way and sipped his beer.

When Eva opened the car door, Ingrid was talking.

"I can't wait to see the yarn shop. Perhaps we can come down next Saturday. Would that be all right Olle?...Olle?"

"Sure. Saturday will be fine," he said, not wanting to refuse his wife in front of Eva.

Nina had ridden down to the bus stop every time Eva came to dinner. She liked to sit between her father and Auntie so she could hold Karla, but tonight her father insisted she stay home. He told her he had to visit a friend in Arlington and it would be past her bedtime when he got back. This was news to Ingrid, but he sometimes drove out after supper to see about a woodworking job somewhere. She put her arms around Nina, consoling her with the promise of a story before bed. Eva held Karla up to the open window, making her arm wave.

"See you next week, Auntie," hollered Nina, waving back.

"You don't look like any of my aunties back in Sweden," said Olle, turning to grin at Eva. She chose not to respond to his implication and talked matter-of-factly about her own aunt, her father's only sister.

"I have one aunt. Her name is Anna, but I've never seen her. She married a boat maker and they live in Minnesota now."

"Minnesota is okay, but California is where I'd like to live...if I wasn't married, that is."

Eva didn't want to pursue that line of conversation either, and ignored it. As they approached the bus station, she put her pocketbook and diaper bag over her arm and lifted Karla to her shoulder, but Olle continued driving past the station.

"Go back. That's my bus!" she shouted.

"No sense paying for a bus ride when I'm going right by your house anyway."

That seemed like the sensible thing to do, but now Karla was whimpering. Eva had planned to nurse her on the bus and now she hoped the motion of the car would put her to sleep. But Karla clearly wasn't happy and bawled louder than before. Even though darkness had settled in, nursing Karla in the car with Olle sitting beside her wasn't something she wanted to do. He seemed annoyed with Karla's crying and Eva wished she'd insisted on taking the bus.

Finally she placed a clean diaper over her bodice, unfastened several buttons and held Karla to her breast. The baby was hungry and nursed vigorously, embarrassing Eva, who searched her mind for something to talk about to mask Karla's little sucking noises.

"Bedford is a lovely town. Reminds me a little of Sweden, don't you think?"

"Ya, maybe," he said...and then the dreaded silence lingered on as Karla continued to nurse.

Olle had always taken pleasure in watching Ingrid breast-feed Gus and Nina, and the sensual sounds of the baby nursing at her breast always aroused him. Envisioning Eva in this way had the same effect. He finished his beer and threw the empty bottle behind the seat.

Finally Karla fell asleep and Eva buttoned up her bodice. She could see Olle's serious face as the lights of Lexington Center flickered into the front seat, as if being turned on and off by some magical switch. Then they were in the dark again. Finally she saw the white pillars of the Sacred Heart Catholic Church.

"Just a mile on the right," she said.

"I know where you live. I've driven by your house before."

Olle pulled up in front of the shop door, turned off the engine and lit another cigarette.

"So you like living in Lexington?" he asked, leaning against the door to observe her better.

"This location is good for business," she replied, "but I miss the lakes and mountains of Sweden."

"You'd like New Hampshire then...how would you like to take a ride up to Lake Winnipesaukee next weekend?" Again he took her by surprise.

Then he hastily added, "Ingrid could make a picnic lunch. It will be a little cool for swimming, but the kids will have fun playing in the sand and it would be a nice change for you and Karla."

"Winnipesaukee? That's an odd sounding name."

"Just an old Indian name that has two meanings. One is 'beautiful water in a high place' and the other is 'smile of the great spirit,'" he told her. "It's the largest lake in New Hampshire...has over two hundred islands."

"Do Indians live there now?" she asked, remembering the story of how friendly natives ate with the Pilgrims on the first Thanksgiving.

"I doubt it. Rich folks have summer homes there, spending their time lying out in the sun and riding around the lake in speed boats. Most of my friends go up for the fishing."

Eva could see Olle's silhouette from a streetlight behind him. The same light shined in on her arm and reflected on Karla, so she supposed her own face was not in total darkness. She felt him watching her, but she saw only the red glow at the end of his cigarette when he inhaled. A sudden impulse caused her to reach for the door handle.

"So, would this Sunday be good for you?" he asked, crushing out his cigarette in the ashtray.

"Going to the lake sounds lovely, but..." Before she could open the door, he reached over and put his arm around her. "How about a goodnight kiss for your brother-in-law?" he whispered softly in her ear.

His left hand touched her hair, caressed her neck and attempted to pull her toward him. His breath smelled of beer and she attributed his behavior to drinking too much. When he bent forward for the intended kiss, she placed Karla between them, who immediately awakened and fussed enough to put an end to

Olle's impassioned plan.

Eva thanked him for the ride and quickly got out of the car.

"See you next weekend," he said.

"You'll be bringing Ingrid down on Saturday?" she asked.

"Right," he said. "Then we can make plans for Sunday."

"Perhaps," she replied, slamming the door a little too loudly.

Olle's car was still parked outside when Eva closed the shop door. In the darkened room she sat at the oak table to nurse Karla back to sleep. The headlights came on and suddenly the car made a sharp turnaround and headed back to Lexington. Arlington was in the opposite direction, so she doubted he had any intention of visiting his friend tonight.

Olle's behavior was repulsive to her; she was his wife's sister, for goodness sake. She had felt like telling him off, but decided against it. Eva knew that too many beers had that effect on men. While serving at the Lindholm's many weekend parties, she had observed how liquor made Gunnar and other male guests more daring and careless with their words and hands. She would have to be careful from now on to not be alone with Olle, especially after he'd been drinking. And in the future, she would insist on taking the bus home.

Ingrid Visits the Yarn Shop

When Ingrid arrived at the shop on Saturday she announced that Olle would be back later. He and his boss were meeting at the lumber yard. Then, so the children wouldn't hear, Ingrid whispered in Eva's ear, "I'm just as glad. I'll enjoy myself more without him." Eva made a mental note to have a serious talk with Ingrid, but for now she showed them around the shop.

"Remember, Eva, how everything I ever started to knit ended up in a tangled mess?" Ingrid said. Eva gave her that knowing look as Ingrid continued. "How stupid I was back then. All I wanted was to get away from the cottage and live in the village.

What I wouldn't give now for some of that peace and quiet."

"I'm sure you have more patience now," said Eva. "I could get you started on a scarf or simple afghan if you wish."

"I did finish a couple of sweaters for the kids a year or two ago. They didn't notice my dropped stitches or when I knitted two stitches together or the sleeves didn't fit right."

Eva picked out a skein of dusty pink. "Would you believe this color came from water that beets were boiled in?"

"You are so creative, Eva...so soft it is...and such a beautiful shade of pink."

Eva went on about the common vegetables, leaves, bark and other dyes she used. She told Ingrid about the first load of fleece, how dirty it was and the hard time she and Dagny had picking it over and washing it many times before being ready to dye, card and spin.

"Who is Dagny?"

"Oh," said Eva. "I never mentioned her in my letters?"

"Not that I remember."

"Well, Dagny used to live in Norrland...on that potato farm north of our cottage where Papa always brought the cow to be bred," said Eva.

"You mean where the 'strange one' lived...that boy who dressed up in girls clothes?"

Gus and Nina's ears perked up when they heard mention of 'the strange one.' They came closer to hear about the country where their mother had come from. It was then Eva decided to tell Dagny's story as if it were an old folk tale.

"Let's all sit down at this round table," she said to them, "and I'll tell you a story."

"Once upon a time, there was an ugly giant who live on a potato farm deep in the forest of Norrland. His name was Vidar, but everyone called him Potatohead because his face was brown and speckled like many potatoes are."

"One day a woman named Suvi and her daughter Dagny met Vidar on an old forest road. They had come down from the north and were tired and hungry. He was stingy and not one to give food away, but on this day he offered the woman and child a drink of cold milk and some fresh bread."

"It wasn't their well being he had on his mind. Vidar's eye was on the beautiful horse that carried these two travelers. When he offered a fair price, the woman said she wouldn't sell her horse for any amount of money. But Vidar wasn't one to be refused. He needed a strong steed for hauling trees from the forest, plowing fields and harvesting his potatoes. He also wanted to show off this magnificent horse to all the local farmers; men who had refused to sell him either ox or horse because they'd seen Vidar kick the village dog many years before."

"He didn't get the horse, did he?" said Gus, who was thinking of his own pony and the poor village dog.

"Well," said Eva, "he did and then again, he didn't."

"Vidar decided to offer the mother and child a place to live. This way he would have use of the horse and also have a woman to cook his meals and work in the potato fields. He told the woman about his farm and all the vegetables and fresh moose meat he had and the fine wooden house with a warm stove. A cool breeze reminded Suvi that winter would soon be here and they could no longer sleep under the trees or in a farmer's drafty barn. Where would they find food when the snow lay two or three feet in the forest and fields?"

"So Suvi agreed to live in his house and immediately Vidar took the reins and led the horse up the path that led to the potato farm. But Suvi didn't trust Vidar. He had a mean and lustful look in his eye, so she told Dagny that from now on she would be called Dag and that she would wear only boy's clothes."

"What is lustful?" asked Gus. Eva blushed and looked at Ingrid.

"Naughty," said Ingrid quite matter-of-factly.

"But I thought only children were naughty," Gus replied. Both Eva and Ingrid were relieved when Nina interrupted and said she wanted to hear more about the ugly giant. But Eva didn't know where to go next with the story. She couldn't tell all the horrible things that Vidar had done to Dag and Suvi and how they had tried to run away and he'd chained them like dogs inside the barn. Nor could she speak of the day she went to the farm to buy potatoes and Vidar had grabbed her arm and dragged her behind the potato bins...and...

"Are you all right, Eva?" asked Ingrid.

"I'm fine. Let's see now, where was I?"

"Vidar was being naughty," piped up Nina.

"Oh, yes. Well, one day Suvi and Dag had enough of Vidar's mean ways. They took the horse and rode through the forest until they came to the village church, where they were given clean clothes. Dag was happy to wear skirts, blouses and pretty dresses again and to be called by her given name of Dagny. They worked on a strawberry farm for a while and then Dagny got a job in the city of Gothenburg. The strangest part of the story is that both she and I were on the same ship going to America. We became very good friends and she stayed here in this very house to help me until after Karla was born."

"Well, that was a fine story, Auntie Eva," said Ingrid, smiling at her two children.

"I'm glad mean Vidar didn't get to keep the horse," said Gus.

"Me, too," said Nina, "but Vidar was very scary."

"Yes," said Ingrid, "but like all good stories, this one had a happy ending."

Then Nina and Gus ran over to inspect the yarn boxes.

Ingrid took this opportunity to whisper in Eva's ear, "so what about 'the strange one' and the pink dress?"

Eva whispered back. "It was the villagers who made up the story of 'the strange one.' They didn't know the whole truth about Dagny and why she wore boy's clothes. She was so desperate to wear dresses that she'd go to the lake, wash herself in the cool water and put on her mother's pink dress. Sometimes she liked to dance around on the beach and other times she would just run freely through the forest."

"Now I feel so sorry for Dagny," said Ingrid. "She must have had a hard life."

"Yes, she did. Norrland is a hard and rugged place," sighed

Eva, thinking about her last winter at the cottage. Then both sisters sat in solemn remembrance of the old days. Eva took Ingrid's hand and spoke softly. "We had some wonderful times, too. Let's try to remember them."

"I want this one," shouted Nina suddenly, holding up a mixed skein of lavender and purple.

"Maybe when you are older," said Ingrid. Nina pouted and scowled at her mother.

"Auntie said she'd show me how to make a dolly."

"Remember the yarn dolls Mama made out of scrap yarn, Ingrid? How she wound tan-colored yarn around a book, tying one end for a head and the other into legs?"

Ingrid sighed again. "I remember hiding them under the bed because they didn't look like the dolls in the village store...all the work that Mama did and I never appreciated it." She turned toward the window, dabbing the corner of her eye.

"Well, you wouldn't mind then if I gave Nina that skein of yarn, would you?"

Ingrid shook her head. "No, I wouldn't mind at all."

"Whoever wants cookies and milk, come with me!" shouted Eva as she climbed the stairs to the kitchen.

After Gus and Nina finished eating, they played on the parlor floor with Karla, while Eva and Ingrid talked over a second cup of coffee. It was then Eva was able to fit together a few key pieces to the puzzle about Olle and her sister.

Ingrid told her that after Nina was born she had a stillborn baby. It was a devastating experience and after that she didn't want to become pregnant again. As a result she'd brushed off Olle's romantic advances.

"At first he understood how I felt. He thought I'd get over it, but I just couldn't. Then he got moody and distant...went for long rides in the car alone so he wouldn't have to talk to me. You probably can tell things aren't right between us." Eva nodded sympathetically and Ingrid continued. "Later I tripped on the cellar stairs, hit my head and injured my arm. I couldn't write or remember anything for a long time and Olle thought I was faking it all…because I still wouldn't let him touch me."

Eva was heartbroken for her sister, but at least now she understood the tension between the two of them and the frustration that led Olle to drink and seek affection elsewhere. Eva told her about a magazine one of her customers had left on the counter.

"There was an article about birth control that caught my attention. I couldn't understand all the words, but maybe you'd like to read it sometime. I remember it mentioned how to avoid getting pregnant…something to do with counting thirteen days from the next bleeding to find out the day that pregnancy will occur. Apparently the system works if you bleed out regularly each month, which I don't. I'm usually a week later than the month before."

"My period comes every month like clockwork…every twenty-eight days," said Ingrid.

"Perfect!" exclaimed Eva. "This method should work quite well for you, but speak to your doctor before trying it."

"I couldn't do that!" exclaimed Ingrid. "I'd be too embarrassed."

"You must find a way to bring love back into your hearts, Ingrid. For the sake of your marriage, please promise me you'll talk to your doctor."

"Well, I don't go to doctors much…just at birthing time…and then I usually just talk to the nurses."

"So, you would be more comfortable talking this over with a woman?"

"Most definitely," said Ingrid.

"Well, my doctor is a woman…very grandmotherly. Her name is Dr. White and she has an office just down the street from here." Ingrid sipped her coffee and didn't say anything.

"We could go right now and make an appointment," said Eva, eager to get this whole thing settled.

"Well…I need more time to think on it."

"Promise me you'll try to see Dr. White next week."

Ingrid fidgeted in her chair and couldn't make any promises.

"You'll be much happier if you do...and so will Olle." Eva chuckled. "Once Olle knows why you are going to the doctor, I'll bet he'll take the day off from work to celebrate."

"Oh, Eva! How you talk!" Ingrid didn't blush very often, but she did then.

Eva got up from the table and went into her bedroom to get the magazine.

"Take this home and read the article. Then we can work something out."

"Daddy's car is parked out front," said Gus excitedly about an hour later. "I can hear him honking."

"Tell him we'll be right there," said his mother.

"I want to stay and play with Karla," said Nina, pouting and not moving an inch.

"I think Karla has other plans," said her mother. "Looks like she's fallen asleep."

Eva reminded Nina that she and Karla would be visiting them in another week and gave her a bag of cookies.

"What do you say, Nina?" prompted her mother.

"Thank you, Auntie. Are they all for me?"

Eva laughed. "I think there are enough for you to share."

"Okay," replied Nina.

Ingrid said nothing about driving to the lake on Sunday and neither did Eva.

Thanksgiving

Ingrid struggled part way through the birth control article and gave up. She didn't think such a theory could be trusted. She believed things took their course and the only way to fool nature was not to give in. No promises were made to Eva the next Sunday, nor the next about going to see the doctor. Eva had done everything she could think of, short of taking Ingrid's hand and dragging her down the sidewalk to the doctor's office.

October brought cooler weather and business at the yarn shop picked up considerably. Children were in school now, leaving mothers with more time to knit, especially for Christmas, which was little more than two months away. This all worked together to make Eva's October profits double those of any month so far.

The yarn boxes that Arne had refinished were less than half full by November and the base cabinets were empty. Since all of the vegetables from the garden were either canned or put in the cold room, Eva now had more time to work on the new fleece, even though Karla was beginning to crawl and getting into all kinds of mischief.

She was surprised on Saturday afternoon to see Mrs. Bergstrom and Emily.

"We just left Emma crying at a neighbor's house," said Mrs. Bergstrom. "Can you imagine she would rather have come to see you than go to her friend's birthday party?"

Eva was flattered to know this about Emma, wondering at the same time if Mrs. Bergstrom might rather have been somewhere else than here.

"Well, I'm so happy to see both of you," said Eva, smiling especially at Emily. Mrs. Bergstrom looked around the shop as if searching for words and picked up a skein of green yarn.

"I was thinking of knitting a sweater for the doctor," she said.

"Cardigan or slipover?" asked Eva.

"Slipover. I don't want to bother making buttonholes. They never come out straight and neat anyway."

"How many skeins will you need?" asked Eva.

"That's what I was wondering. Usually I run out of yarn and have to buy more. By then the dye lot is different and the new skeins are a little lighter or darker in color."

"Well, I suggest you buy a few extra skeins and if you have any left over, you may return them and get your money back." Eva looked over to Emily, who was seriously pondering some multi-colored skeins of yarn at the end of the counter. "Do you know how to knit?" Eva asked, but Mrs. Bergstrom was quick to answer for her.

"She tried it years ago, but never got the hang of it."

"But Mama, you always got upset with me when I slipped a stitch or knit two stitches together."

"Well, you didn't seem all that interested anyway...and I was...well, you know how busy I am.

"That reminds me, Eva. The doctor wanted me to...rather, we would like to invite you and Karla to come for Thanksgiving dinner."

The invitation surprised Eva, but she kindly accepted. She wouldn't be going to Ingrid's because they spent Thanksgiving with Olle's boss, something they did every year.

"Dagny can come, too," said Mrs. Bergstrom looking around. "By the way, where is she?"

"Dagny was married last spring and lives in Maine now."

"Married? Such a plain girl...I hope she got a nice husband."

"Arne is very kind and hardworking," said Eva. "Almost every piece of furniture I have was refinished or completely made by him."

Mrs. Bergstrom glanced around the room. "Really now...even that table with the intricate pedestal feet?"

"I found the table top in the storeroom. Arne made the pedestal and refinished the table top to match."

"Hmm...well, looks like Dagny did all right for herself." Then Mrs. Bergstrom looked at Eva as if she was about to say more, but bit her lip and remained silent. The thought crossed Eva's mind that Mrs. Bergstrom might be curious about who Karla's father was and if Eva was to be married soon, too, but she decided not to say anything about it. Eva then showed Emily a pattern book for beginners, pointing out a few items she could make using the simple garter stitch.

As Mrs. Bergstrom paid for her yarn Emily put three multi-colored skeins of pink, beige and light green on the counter. "What are you going to do with that?" said her mother disapprovingly. Emily was undaunted by her mother's negative attitude.

"Miss Gunderson told me this yarn came from Sweden, so I'm going to make a...something special."

"Well, if you want any help from me, you'll have to wait until after the holidays," retorted her mother.

"But that will be too late; it's going to be a Christmas present."

Eva put her arm around Emily's shoulder. "Perhaps I can show you how to knit on Thanksgiving. I'm sure you can have it finished before Christmas."

"Oh, all right," said her mother impatiently as she rummaged through her purse for more money.

Eva brought an apple pie and an almond cake for Thanksgiving dessert. It seemed good to rekindle her friendship with the family and she felt quite at home. Emma took over with entertaining Karla while Eva helped Emily cast stitches of yarn onto her needle and then instructed her how to knit the simple garter stitch. Emily had some trouble at first. Some stitches were too loose, while others too tight, but Eva told her to relax and she soon got the hang of it.

"You're doing great," said Eva. "No more practicing. Let's get going on the real thing."

"It's a present for Mama," whispered Emily. "Let's go up to my room."

With just the two of them alone in her bedroom, Emily did much better and before long had knit three inches of her scarf.

"You are a born knitter," said Eva, giving Emily a hug. "I'm going downstairs to help your mother and I'll be back in a while to see how you're progressing."

Karla was asleep on the parlor rug, so Eva covered her with a small blanket. Dr. Bergstrom was carving the turkey and Emma stood by him nibbling on little pieces of meat. Mrs. Bergstrom had just opened the oven door and put in two pies to be baked. Steam rose from two large pots on the stove and Eva lifted one of the covers. "These potatoes are done, would you like me to mash them?"

"We usually have riced potatoes on holidays," said Mrs. Bergstrom. "If I can find that darned ricer." Eva finally found it in a base cabinet.

"Can I help squeeze the potatoes?" asked Emma, as she watched Eva deftly manipulate the cumbersome metal utensil. The ricer was too big for Emma's small hands, but Eva let her have a try. Ricing wasn't as easy as it looked and when Emma tried to squeeze the handles together, the ricer, full of potatoes, slipped from her hand and fell to the floor.

"Now look what you've done, Emma!" exclaimed her mother. "Get out of the kitchen and go play."

"I'm sorry, Mrs. Bergstrom. It was my fault." said Eva. She smiled down at Emma. "I should have known she was too young to handle the ricer. I'll clean up the mess."

After Eva riced all the potatoes, she drained the squash and began mashing it with butter and brown sugar. Dr. Bergstrom was still carving the turkey when Emma returned to the kitchen.

"Can I have the drummer, Daddy?" Before he could answer, her mother corrected her.

"How many times do I have to tell you, Emma, it isn't a drummer. The turkey leg is called a drumstick."

Her father winked and said he had saved one just for her.

"Where's Emily?" she asked as Eva returned carrying Karla in her arms.

"She's upstairs. I told her I'd be back to check on her knitting. Let's you and I go up together and see how she's doing."

Emily had another three inches added to the scarf, with just one little slipped stitch that Eva was able to quickly fix. "Knitting is fun," said Emily. "I could knit all day long."

"I know just how you feel," said Eva. "I remember winter days when I've done just that."

"I could never sit for that long," said Emma, already waiting in the doorway to go back downstairs.

After dinner when the dishes were washed and dried, they all moved into the parlor. Emily and Emma were playing with Karla on the floor when Mrs. Bergstrom jumped out of her chair.

"I almost forgot!" she exclaimed as she gave Eva a small box wrapped in colorful paper with a large pink bow. Emma was all giggles as Eva unwrapped the little bundle, opened the box and looked between two layers of cotton.

"It's for your charm bracelet!" announced Emma as soon as Eva picked up the little silver charm. "See, it has Karla's birthday written on the bottom of the shoe." Eva, not a big jewelry person, was relieved that she'd remembered to wear the charm bracelet today and Dr. Bergstrom was able to quickly attach the little silver shoe.

"Thank you so much," Eva said, moving her arm so her two little charms clinked together.

Eva was surprised to see Emily the next Saturday afternoon.

"I was pestering Mama about coming to see you, but she was too busy. Guess I got on her nerves cuz she said I was almost eleven now and was old enough to take the trolley by myself if I wanted to...so here I am."

"I'm delighted to see you. Did you bring your knitting?"

Emily reached into her bag and shyly showed Eva the nearly completed scarf. Eva could find no dropped stitch or added stitches. Every stitch was the same size and the edges of the scarf were straight and even. She held it out to its fullest length. "I can't believe you've done all this since Thanksgiving and with not one mistake!"

Then Emily confessed she'd taken out two rows because a stitch had slipped off and made a little hole in the scarf.

"You fixed it all by yourself?" asked Eva.

"Sure. I knew how to do it from watching you," said Emily proudly.

"You are some smart girl!" All of a sudden Emily seemed all grown up. The knitting experience had given her a new confidence.

"I think the colors are beautiful together," she said shyly, admiring the scarf. "Do you think Mama will like it?"

"Of course. She'll be so proud of you!"

"Is it long enough now?" asked Emily, hoping that it was. Eva put it around her neck and looked in the mirror.

"I think this will be just fine, especially after we put fringe on it."

"Fringe? What is that?"

Eva showed her an afghan hanging on the wall with long strands of yarn looped together to make a finished border.

"It is quite simple to do, and it will make your scarf look very fancy."

"Mama loves fancy stuff," remarked Emily. Then she confided to Eva that her mother was not doing as well with her father's present. So far she had knit only twelve rows of ribbing and at that rate the sweater wouldn't be done until her father's birthday next summer.

"When your mother bought the yarn I had a feeling she might be too busy to finish it before Christmas. A man's sweater takes a long time to knit." Eva cut a short length of yarn and gave Emily the scissors. "You may cut about forty more of these eight-inch-long pieces and then I'll show you how to fasten them to the scarf." The bell tinkled as a customer came through the door and at the same time little cries came from the cradle.

"I'll go play with Karla," said Emily.

By mid afternoon the scarf was finished, complete with fancy fringe. This had been an interesting day. Having Emily for company had been a bright spot in Eva's dreary November afternoon, a fresh face, curious, helpful and eager to learn. In the absence of Emma, Emily was more outgoing and took the initiative of looking after Karla when Eva was busy. The next Saturday when Emily returned for another visit, she stayed with Karla while Eva went downtown to do an errand.

"I like being here with you," confided Emily. Eva was flattered, but also wondered if some of Emily's enjoyment came from the money she received from babysitting Karla. It didn't matter. Leaving Karla with Emily gave Eva an hour or two of freedom on Saturday afternoons. Shopping was much more enjoyable without having to worry about a baby carriage, clean diapers and a fussy baby, especially in rainy or very cold weather.

Christmas Surprise

Eva and Ingrid had made plans for Christmas back in October, the same day they'd first talked about the birth control matter, but neither had seen the other since then. It had been arranged that Eva and Karla would go to Bedford on Christmas Eve day and stay overnight, in order to be there early on Christmas morning when the children opened their stockings. During the first week in December Eva received a Christmas card from Ingrid with a short note reminding her of this.

Dear Eva,

We are all looking forward to having you and Karla here on Christmas Eve and hope that you will stay overnight as we planned. Because you will be bringing extra clothes and such, Olle will drive down to pick you up around three on Christmas Eve day. If that time isn't convenient, let me know. Gus and Nina are excited that you will be here on Christmas morning when they open their stockings. I have a little stocking for Karla to hang up, too.

I must tell you that things are much better between Olle and me. He drove me to Dr. White's office and sat in the car with the children during my appointment. (And, yes, we did celebrate that night!) Thank you for showing the article to me and pressuring me to see Dr. White. She explained everything to me and was so sympathetic and understanding. Our home is certainly much happier now.

I started making Christmas cookies during the first week in December…those delicious ginger cookies that make the whole house smell so good. I like to make many different kinds of holiday cookies so I can bring them to friends and still have plenty for guests and my hungry family.

Looking forward so much to your visit.

Love,

Ingrid

Eva was relieved to hear that things were better between Ingrid and Olle, so with no hesitation she wrote back saying she would be ready at three o'clock and would be bringing some special lemon tart cookies and almond cake.

She had a short Christmas card list: Anna and Lars, Dagny and Arne, Ingrid and Olle, the Kronbergs, Mats, the Bergstroms and one to Mrs. Sandquist and her boarders. There hadn't been a word from Mr. Kronberg, which was troubling because she had written three letters and none had been returned. She had hoped that by now he would have visited the Lindholms and been able to explain to Karl why she had left so suddenly for America.

Emily came on three successive Saturday afternoons to sit with Karla, allowing Eva to be free to spend more time with her customers and also to go Christmas shopping. Emily was interested in the yarn shop and had been very observant when customers came in, so she was quite capable of helping them if Eva was not there.

Olle arrived promptly at three on the day before Christmas. Eva had been ready for over an hour, feeling uneasy about seeing him again and wondering what to say, but he was more nervous than she as he politely carried her bags of clothes, gifts and food to the car. He held the door for her and Karla to get in and his genuine smile put her at ease. After he got behind the wheel, he turned a serious face to her.

"First I must apologize for...um...things I said to you and the way I acted after I drove you home that time. It wasn't like me... and I'm very sorry." The deep regret showing in his face made Eva want to hug him, but she chose not to do that.

"Knowing you'd been drinking, I didn't take your actions seriously," she said, changing the subject to Christmas, then the yarn shop and Karla, who was fascinated by the steering wheel and kept wanting to sit in Olle's lap. Finally Karla gave up and fell asleep.

Eva walked through the front door into the delicious aroma of roasting pork and the excited greetings of Gus and Nina.

"Come see the cookies we made!" shouted Nina, taking Eva's hand and pulling her toward the kitchen. "We didn't really make them," she confessed. "Mama cut out shapes of Santa and reindeer and stars and then we sprinkled them with colored sugar!"

Eva remarked how beautiful they looked and said she couldn't wait to eat one, but Nina scowled and spoke very seriously. "I think we will just look at them."

"I'm gonna eat the ones I decorated and you can have all of mine you want!" said Gus emphatically to Eva.

"Merry Christmas!" said Ingrid, with a warm hug that included Karla. "Look at you, Karla, in your beautiful red dress!"

"It's just a simple knitted outfit I fashioned out of some leftover red yarn…cheaper than buying something at the store." Eva said apologetically.

"You are so clever, Eva. Remind me to give you that box of Nina's outgrown clothes I told you about the last time you were here." Karla jabbered and wriggled in Eva's arms and everyone went into the parlor.

A warm fire crackled in the fireplace and sprigs of evergreen lay on the mantle with two large white candles burning brightly at either end. A large spruce tree stood in the middle of the room decorated with shiny, colored ornaments and strings of blue and yellow Swedish flags. At the very top a smiling white angel looked down as Olle lit the many white candles attached to the branches and everyone looked in glorious wonder at the enchantingly beautiful tree aglow with a fairyland of twinkling lights.

Then they all held hands and sang the old familiar Christmas songs, circling around the tree in the traditional Swedish fashion. Karla giggled with joy between Ingrid and Eva as they gently lifted her up and down as if she was dancing, too. Even Olle was singing, smiling tenderly at his wife. Yes, everything was back to blissful normalcy in the Olson home.

The New Year brought extreme cold and much snow to eastern Massachusetts, preventing many customers from coming into the shop. There were those habitual knitters, of course, who could never bear to run out of yarn. Like the reliable postman, who delivered the mail every day no matter how bad the weather, these fervent knitters trudged through snow, slush and frigid temperatures to replenish their diminishing stockpiles of yarn.

With more time to spend on Karla and spinning, she also found moments to think about Dagny and Arne and dwell more on the past. She hadn't heard a word from Dagny. Even though she knew Dagny had never had much interest in learning to read and write in Swedish or English, Eva had hoped to receive a Christmas card.

She was very disappointed when the card she had sent to the Kronbergs was returned with 'not at this address' written on the envelope. This was odd because she thought everyone in Norrland knew who Mr. Kronberg was. She considered writing to Mats inquiring about his father, but decided to wait in hopes that a card from him might still arrive.

She received cards from Ingrid, Mrs. Sandquist, The Bergstroms and Anna, whose beautiful card pictured glittering silver snow falling on a forest cottage. Snow-covered mountains rose in the distance and in the foreground were a mother moose and her yearling looking toward the little house. The card glorified the top of her desk and memories of Norrland swept over her at every glance. Alongside the card was a most treasured gift, a colored photograph of Anna, Lars and Jonas. It was almost a portrait, showing only the upper portion of their bodies with very clear, smiling faces. Anna was round faced with twinkling eyes that reminded Eva of her father. Anna's notes were always informative and beautifully written with a flourishing hand.

Dear Eva,

How sad it was to hear of my dear brother's passing. The last time we saw each other was just before Lars and I left for America. We traveled back to that familiar cottage and saw how attractively your mother had decorated the walls with paintings and other womanly objects that make a house a home. Ingrid was about five and you were just a small bump on your mother's stomach. And now you are a mother with a baby of your own! How quickly time passes.

Jonas was almost seven at that time. Now he is all grown up, finished college and is playing violin with the symphony orchestra in Minneapolis. We are so proud of him.

We are so proud of you, too! Raising a baby alone and also the owner of a yarn shop! You are an amazing young woman. I enclose a photograph of Jonas, Lars and me taken last summer by a friend who is a professional photographer. We are all sitting in one of Lars's latest canoes. You can see a corner of our house with the lake and mountains in the distance. Looks a bit like Sweden, don't you think? We love it here. There are many other Swedes in the area, as well as Germans and French from nearby Canada.

I was delighted that you finally found Ingrid and that she lives only a few miles away from you. Give her our love.

We wish you, Karla, Ingrid and family a Merry Christmas and Happy New Year. Please write soon.

Love,

Anna

Through study and conversation with her customers, Eva picked up a lot of English words and phrases. She had improved her writing considerably by carefully practicing many of the techniques she found in the book that Dr. Bergstrom had loaned her on proper English writing. She practiced writing every day and still kept the habit each morning of learning a new word or phrase from the old Swedish/English dictionary that Mr. Kaneko had given her.

1936

In February Dave Beckworth stopped by with his wife, Rebecca, and little David. After the Beckworths admired the beautiful skeins of yarn, they all sat down for refreshments. Eva took a liking to Rebecca right away.

"I tried knitting as a child, but failed terribly," Rebecca said, glancing around at the many knitted items hanging on the walls. "Do you by any chance offer knitting classes? A neighbor of mine would like to learn how to knit and I'd like to try my hand at it again, now that I'm older and have more patience."

"I'd be delighted to teach you both," said Eva. "Tuesdays are usually slow, especially in the morning. How about ten o'clock next Tuesday?"

This was exactly what Eva needed to bring more interest into the shop. Word spread quickly and by the first of March there were six young women sitting around the large, round table in various stages of learning how to knit. They brought their young children, who all played together with Karla in the corner of the shop.

On March sixth Eva invited Ingrid, Gus and Nina for Karla's first birthday. Also in attendance were five of the knitting club members and their children. Twelve rambunctious children sat around two tables pushed together for the occasion. Eva had gone all out with special napkins, little party hats and individual bags of candy, as well as ice cream and a large birthday cake she had made and decorated with white frosting and twelve pink roses, one for each child. Of course. Rebecca was there with David, now a big boy of three years old. He was mature for his age, a little man already, polite and serious, always going out of his way to please Karla and looking out for her safety. He saved his pink rose and gave it to her. His reward was to see her smile, which she did before popping the whole rose in her mouth.

Two days later the mailman brought a special letter addressed to

Eva and Karla...no last name, but the address was clearly written on the envelope in large, mismatched letters. Eva ran immediately to the window and opened it.

Deer Eva
My frend help me to write letter. Sorry took so long. Been busy. Here is more like Sweden. Small house of 4 rooms. Arne work with lumber mil. Very good husband. He is more than I xpect. We have baby girl named Annika in Febuary. Over 9 pounds and cry like Karla. I had no milk for Annika so Arne bought us a cow. She is gentl and frendly. Lots of snow in felds, but warmer today.
Dagny

The letter was in Swedish, printed in deliberate lettering, and much too short. There was so much more Eva wanted to know, but she was thrilled just the same and read it over and over. So Arne is a good husband and he is more than she expected. Reading this made Eva smile. She thought they would be compatible and it was nice to hear that their marital life was satisfying, too. She sat down immediately to answer Dagny's letter.

March 8, 1936

Dear Dagny, Arne and Annika,
I've been a little worried about you so was so pleased to receive your letter and know that all is well.

Congratulations to you and Arne on the birth of Annika. Such a pretty name. A gift will be in the mail soon. I was sorry to hear that you had no milk for little Annika, but boiled whole cow's milk should be fine. Soon you will be able to add some cream of wheat with a bit of finely mashed applesauce for her supper and she should sleep longer. Remember how that worked for Karla and I was finally able to get four hours of uninterrupted sleep?

I have great news. I found Ingrid. She lives just a few miles from the bus terminal in Bedford, so we see each other often. Karla and I spent Christmas Eve and Christmas Day with Ingrid, Olle, Gus and Nina. It was the best Christmas ever.

I must also tell you that I am friendly again with Mrs. Bergstrom and we spent Thanksgiving at their house. Her daughter Emily comes often and babysits so I can spend more time with customers and also do errands. She is very helpful and dependable.

Remember Dave Beckworth, the man who brought that first batch of dirty fleece? His wife, Rebecca, wanted to learn how to knit, so that has started me on a new venture, knitting classes.

Remember those girls who hung around in front of the drug store last year? They still congregate there waiting for their boyfriends to walk by. I thought they might be better off sitting in my shop learning how to knit as well. Emily doesn't know them, but she did offer to go over and give them each an invitation for one free knitting lesson. Three of the girls shook their heads and crumpled up the invitation, but a fourth girl folded up the paper and said she'd ask her mother.

I still miss you both and every time I sit in my rocking chair, look at the boxes full of yarn or put Karla to bed in the beautiful cradle I think of you both.

Members of Rebecca's knitting club brought their children to celebrate Karla's first birthday. One of the women brought her camera, so I'm hoping to have a good picture to send to you next time. Ingrid, Gus and Nina were there, too, so hopefully there will be a good photograph of them also.

I enclose a picture of Karla and me that Dr. Bergstrom took on Thanksgiving. I would so love to have a photograph of the three of you. Surely there must be someone in New Sweden who owns a camera.

Love to you all,
Eva

The knitting groups were the perfect social event for both Eva and Karla and the days passed quickly into June.

The warm days of summer brought another dry spell in yarn sales, but Eva expected this and relished the free time to spend planting and caring for her garden. The mothers' knitting class dwindled down to almost nothing during the hot weather, too, although Rebecca stopped in often to visit, helping Eva with her

English while David and Karla played on the floor nearby.

Soon it was September. The cooler weather was always a good incentive for women to think about knitting again, and this year she had a wonderful group of four, older, grandmotherly women who came to knit together. They all were accomplished knitters merely wanting a good excuse to get out of their homes and enjoy the company of other women their age. Eva provided the coffee and they took turns bringing refreshments. All this proved profitable for Eva, too, since they all contributed money for her services and most of them were knitting large afghans that required dozens of skeins of yarn.

One Saturday afternoon two of the girls on the street corner came in for a free lesson. Emily was there that day with a friend of hers, too, so that was the beginning of Eva's younger class, which over the weeks grew to seven lively, talkative girls of eleven and twelve years of age.

Four days after Christmas a card arrived from Dagny.

Dear Eva

Thanks for prity blanket for Annika. In November came a boy named Albin. Weighed over ten pounds and I had milk for two babies. Annika want to nurse every time Alvin does but she like cow milk better. She just want to cuddle. The old folks here speak and write Swedish, but school children know both English and Swedish. My friends daughter teach me English, but was too hard for me. She help me write too. So glad you find Ingrid. Thanks for picture. Karla so big and pretty. We had big midsummer celebration last June with song and dance and most everyone bring potato salads to eat. I remembered how you make potato salad and brought that. No one else had crispy bacon in their salad, so mine was big hit. That pleased Arne. I send picture someone took of us. You can see that Arne's buttons are bursting with pride. That's what he said…but I think it is my cooking. I'm a little skinny. Our potato crop did very well this year and Arne cut trees to make field for next year. Was12 below zero yesterday. I stay inside all day with children. Only 9 below today and not so windy.

Merry Christmas to you and Karla.

Love

Dagny

January 3, 1937

Dear Dagny,

Two babies in one year! How very busy you must be with two more little mouths to feed and all those diapers to wash. Thanks for sending the nice photograph. You all look so happy. Annika's hair looks light-colored like Arne and Alvin's dark like yours.

I'm glad your potato salad came out so well. Nothing like a hungry husband to make his wife a good cook! Delighted to hear your potatoes did well. I planted a garden last summer, too. Karla found something else growing in the squashes, a tiny kitten. I gave him a little milk one day…and the next…and soon he was a permanent resident. He is mostly gray and white with one completely white front leg that looks like he stepped into a can of white paint. Karla says he wears a stocking, so he has the Swedish name for stocking, Strumpa, which suits him just fine.

My goodness, it does get cold up there in northern Maine. We had snow two days before Christmas, the first snow Karla had ever seen and we went out early in the morning to make a snowman. Well, I did most of the making while Karla watched and ate snow! I put an old green knitted hat on his head and a bright red scarf around his neck, so he is looking very festive.

I made a boiled dinner last week and thought of you both every night we had a meal of it. Karla loves the red flannel hash.

I keep busy following Karla around. She speaks very well if she takes the time to slow down, but mostly says 'Mama,' 'I want,' 'me hungry' and 'no' which she hears me say to her so often!

Mrs. Bergstrom and Emily have come to visit several times. Mrs. Bergstrom needed help with a sweater she was knitting for her husband. I don't know if he received it this Christmas or not. When Emily saw me crocheting an afghan, she wanted to make a similar one for her parents' parlor to match their new maroon and gray sofa. She crocheted individual squares at home and then sewed them into long strips when she came to class each week. She is persistent and meticulous, surprising even me when she had the afghan finished in time to give it to her parents for Christmas.

I will be sending you a package in honor of your two babies. Hope you had a merry Christmas. Happy New Year to you, Arne, Annika and Albin.

Love,

Eva

True to her word, Eva sent Dagny two little charms for her bracelet: two silver shoes, one with Annika's and the other with Albin's birthdate. In February she received a short thank you note saying the charms had arrived and that everyone was in good health.

During the last week in May Eva planted a large garden that kept her busy all summer weeding, picking and preparing the vegetables for canning and cold storage. "Where did the time go?" she thought, admiring the shelves in the back room. This year there were double the amount of canned goods preserved than last year. Jars of green beans, peas, tomatoes and corn, plus many varieties of fruits and pickles decorated the storeroom wall with a rainbow of colors, including luscious shades of green, red, yellow and dark blue. The storage bins in the cold room overflowed with potatoes, carrots, cabbages, squashes and beets. Gardening was a lot of work, but the satisfaction of gazing at all that wonderful food ready for winter eating was more than worth it all. Autumn turned into winter, but Christmas brought no word from either Dagny or Mats. Karla turned two in March and soon it was time to plant another garden.

The Great 1938 Hurricane

The weather forecast on the morning of September 21 was for gale winds along the Atlantic Coast near New Jersey and by four o'clock in the afternoon the eye of a hurricane had made landfall near New Haven, Connecticut. Within an hour Eva noticed the sky had darkened, sprinkles of rain spattered the windows and the maple trees across the street swayed back and forth in the gusty wind.

One after another, women came in buying large quantities of yarn, such as when people flock to the grocery store to stock up on food just before a big snowfall. Perhaps this little gale was more than Eva anticipated. Each woman had a different version of the expected weather.

"Just a little wind and rain," said one.

"I heard a hurricane is heading for western Massachusetts," said another.

"It's following the Connecticut River into Vermont," said a third woman. "Already done a lot of damage in Rhode Island and Connecticut."

The first woman stayed for a long time deciding what colors she wanted, as did the second, but the last one bought an armful of blue skeins and was the first to leave. "Better hurry up. I think its gonna be a bad one here, too," she said before slamming the door behind her.

When the shop was quiet again, Eva stood before the window holding Karla in her arms. The weather had grown worse and lightning streaked across the southwestern sky. A bus, with headlights dimmed by the pelting rain, inched its way up the street and passed the shop without letting anyone on or off. The sidewalks were bare except for a man holding on to his umbrella that had turned inside out, the wind almost knocking him off his feet. Finally he disappeared into a nearby store.

She had just finished reading Karla a story when the lights went out. Eva lit a candle and they had a cold supper, but the lightning strikes were brighter and the loud thunder scared Karla. "Why don't we sleep together tonight," said Eva, placing her daughter in the big bed. Karla forgot about the loud noises and shrieked with joy. When they lay under the covers Eva said their little nightly prayer.

"I know that God is where I am
Beneath, around, above
Providing, guarding, guiding
Encircling us in love."

Karla fell almost immediately to sleep in her mother's embrace, but Eva lay for a long while listening to the rain pelting against the window panes. The wind roared outside, threatening to lift the roof off the house. But as her prayers strengthened, the storm subsided. Everything stayed intact and in the morning Eva awakened to a great silence. The view from the upstairs window showed no activity on the street, except for two men evaluating the plight of a big maple across the street that had blown over and leaned precariously against an electric pole. The wires dipped low from the weight of another tree and the men shook their heads before walking away through the broken branches and wet leaves strewn over the road. There were no buses and no electricity; breakfast was cold cereal, milk and a shared apple. Eva missed her morning cup of hot coffee.

She was actually looking forward to Officer O'Leary's visit today, which didn't happen until after she'd put Karla down for an afternoon nap.

"Everything okay here?" he asked, poking his head through the door.

"I'm so glad to see you, Officer O'Leary, come in and sit down." Red-faced and out of breath, he removed his cap and sat down by the window appraising the dismal outside scene.

"Probably won't have any power today or bus service either. Too many wires and trees down everywhere."

"That won't bother me," said Eva. "I've gotten along with candles before, but we always had a wood stove to cook on…and to make coffee."

"That's what's missing," he said with a grin, "that wonderful smell of coffee brewing."

"I'd be happy to get you a glass of milk and one of yesterday's muffins."

"Thanks anyway. I'm all set...just had a sandwich at the station." Then his face grew serious. "They're saying this is one of the worst hurricanes in New England history. Not so much here, but in western Massachusetts, around Springfield, the damage is pretty bad. South of here in New Jersey and Rhode Island it's worse than anywhere else...hundreds of casualties and injuries."

"Did you say hundreds?" asked Eva.

He nodded. "The final count could be three or four hundred."

Eva was awestruck. She had never heard of anything like that ever happening in Sweden and could not comprehend how so many people could be affected by the wind and rain.

"I hear the shoreline is eroded and many houses collapsed into the ocean. Rivers running through cities and towns overflowed their banks, flooding streets, stores and homes, and the wind knocked trees down on everything in its path." He glanced out the window again at the fallen trees. Five burly men with axes and a long two-man saw were lopping off branches and sawing up large limbs and tree trunks into small chunks.

"I always feel sad when a tree dies or is cut down," said Eva.

"It's a sad day for a lot of people today...very sad..." he said. Then he pushed back his chair. "Well, now that I know you and Karla are all right, I should go and keep checking on everyone else on my route." Eva thanked him for stopping in and hoped he would return tomorrow.

She couldn't remember a time when she had absolutely nothing to do as she did that afternoon. Everything these days depended on electricity...everything but her spinning wheel.

By the time Karla came scuffing down the stairs, Eva had finished spinning a skein of light green yarn.

When the electricity was finally restored, Officer O'Leary resumed his regular rounds and stopped into the shop every morning.

"Lexington fared pretty well during The Great New England Hurricane," he said. "That's what they call the storm around here, but some call it The Yankee Clipper and those south of here say it was The Long Island Express." Eva understood about New England and hurricanes, but the second two names meant nothing to her and she just nodded in agreement.

He took a few sips of coffee and continued. "Regardless what it is called, this was one of the worst storms ever to hit New England. Over one thousand miles of eastern shoreline was affected. Over nine thousand homes and buildings were destroyed and twice as many damaged. Around six hundred people perished in the storm and more than that were injured."

"I had no idea it was that bad," she replied sadly.

"There was one funny story in the paper about Katharine Hepburn."

"Who is she?" asked Eva.

"Miss Hepburn is a very famous actress in the movies and on stage. She got an Academy Award for best actress in Morning Glory, but I think her best movie so far is Little Women. I think you would like that one." Eva, who had never been to the theater or to a movie, just smiled, reminding Mr. O'Leary about the funny story in the newspaper.

"Oh yes..." he continued. "Well Katharine Hepburn has...rather she did have before the storm, a large family home on Long Island Sound. It was completely destroyed and washed away into the ocean. Her mother and servants were there at the time, but were able to get away and no one was hurt. While inspecting the rubble where the house once stood, Miss Hepburn saw her bathtub setting on the beach. In a playful state of mind, she hopped in the tub and posed for the camera." He laughed so hard that Eva saw a most indecent image in her mind, but when Officer O'Leary came in the next day and showed her a newspaper with the photograph in it, she was relieved to see Miss Hepburn fully clothed and smiling happily in her tub.

Eva was deep into the Christmas spirit this year. To make the shop more festive she bought a large spruce tree early in December and splurged on a box of colored lights and tinsel. In her hasty departure from the Lindholms, many cherished items had been left behind in the wooden chest, including the old ornaments she remembered as a child: little porcelain figures of forest animals, tomtes, angels, strings of tiny Swedish flags and the metal candle holders that clipped to the tree branches. To save on expenses, she baked dozens of cookies that were cut into gingerbread men, Santas and stars, decorating them with white frosting and colored sugars to hang on the tree. When a child came into the shop, they were allowed to pick their favorite cookie to eat or take home.

Karla was almost four years old. In some ways she acted twice her age, especially with speaking and behavior. She didn't miss a trick and wasn't one to take a back seat to anyone.

"I want a cookie on the tree," she said after several children had picked their favorite ones.

"Those are for our guests, Karla. You can have any cookie you want from the plate on the table."

"But I want that one," she insisted, pointing to one halfway up the tree. Eva was equally determined and took an identical cookie from the table.

"Here, this gingerbread man is just like the one on the tree," she told her daughter, who took the cookie and inspected it.

"The one on the tree is bigger and more pretty," she said, holding out the cookie in her hand. Eva was beginning to lose her patience and wasn't about to give in.

"You eat the one I gave you or you will have none at all!" Karla pouted and sat down on the floor scowling at the unwanted cookie she still held. Eva thought that was the end of it and waited on a woman who had just come into the shop. Karla continued to sit on the floor gazing up at the coveted gingerbread man hanging so deliciously on the tree.

Suddenly Eva heard a big clinking thud and turned around to see her beautiful Christmas tree lying limply on the floor while a very surprised Karla stood looking at the broken half of the large gingerbread cookie in her hand, the top half still dangling from the tree.

"I don't want that one after all," said Karla holding up the bottom half of the cookie for her mother. Eva took it and Karla ran upstairs crying.

"Oh dear, now the child is all upset," said the woman sympathetically.

"My daughter will be just fine," replied Eva as she picked up the tree and righted it in its stand. "No harm done to child or tree. And Karla learned a good lesson."

Now that the little episode was over, Eva showed her customer another skein of yarn. "I think this color will go perfectly with the one you picked out. What do you think?"

"They complement each other beautifully," said the woman. "I'll take ten skeins of each color."

When Eva went back upstairs, Karla was sitting on her bed, red-eyed and sniffling.

"I sorry," said Karla, as Eva wiped her daughter's face with a soft cloth.

"Shall we have some milk with our cookies?" asked her mother. Eva had removed the upper half of the cookie from the tree and placed it on the table with the bottom half. Karla's original cookie, which now appeared larger and had more sprinkles, lay beside the broken one.

"You can pick which cookie you want to eat," said her mother. Karla looked longingly at the larger, prettier cookie, but took the broken one instead. Taking everything into consideration, Eva thought this had been a very good day.

Eva's Christmas card list had more than tripled with the addition of each knitting class member, so her walls were decorated with all the lovely cards she received that year. There was one card that wasn't very festive, a drawing of a ship in black and white, but she put it on the wall with the others because it was from Mats. He wrote only a few lines; wishing her a Merry Christmas, saying he was in the Navy and stationed in California. His address was different from the one she had been using, so she sent him another card telling him she hadn't heard from his father and asking if his parents had moved from the farm.

1939

Dagny's card didn't arrive until well into January.

Dear Eva
Hope you had nice Christmas. Thank you for pretty card with jolly Santa. Annika carry it round the house all day saying Santa coming…Santa coming. We have Christmas tree with presents Arne made for Annika and Albin…little carved horses for them to play with. Axel too small for presents. He was born in October. I was sick with Axel and think he come too early. He was puny baby of only 6 pounds and my milk didn't come down. When it did, my breasts were sore and Axel was fussy nurser. Now we are doing fine, but he cries a lot. Thank you for the knit hats and sweaters for Annika and Alvin. They are beautiful and Annika loves the kitty on hers. It was warm enough not to wear jackets to church last Sunday, so everyone say how cute they look in their new sweaters. I wore my bracelet and the children love to hear the charms clink together. So do I. Had over three feet of snow before Christmas, but that is good. Folks need snow to ski and drive sleighs. Arne bought horse to help in woods and fields. He found old sleigh in barn, fixed the runners and painted it red. So we go to town in style. Last autumn he build 2 more rooms in back of house. Sorry letter is late, but had to wait until Stina come to help.
Happy New Year.
Love,
Dagny

It was quite a surprise to hear of Axel's birth. Eva felt sorry for poor Dagny with three very young children to care for now, although Dagny hadn't sounded discouraged. She had always taken everything in stride in the past and probably would continue to do so.

Eva looked around the room at the many items displayed for sale and picked out a blue blanket for Axel. She wondered if Arne had a hand in naming the children…all with names beginning with the letter 'A'. It wasn't unusual to do that. Besides Emily and Emma, there were several families in town whose children's names began with the same letter. Others had names that began with the same sound like Laura, who named her children George, Joseph and Julia.

Eva thought for a while about a boy's name that began with 'K', but she couldn't get beyond the name of Karl. He came vividly to her mind and she felt that empty hole in her stomach again. It was foolish for her to feel that way after almost four years. He was probably married to someone else by now. She took a deep breath and went to her desk to write to Dagny.

January 11, 1939

Dear Dagny,

I was so very happy to hear from you today and had to sit right down and answer your letter. I love the Christmas card you sent with the glowing fireplace and the tree decorated with candles and glistening red and gold balls. It is hard to imagine you with three babies already. So happy to hear you have a horse. You always did love horses. I'm sure the children will enjoy riding on his back next summer. Has it really been two years since we last wrote to each other? Time surely flies by when one is busy. I'm trying to think back about what has happened since then.

I'll start with the yarn shop, which is doing even better than last year. I am selling twice the amount of yarn as last year and two more knitting classes have been added to my already busy week.

I was thinking about New Sweden and all the potato salads you wrote about at the Midsummer holiday two years ago. I had this funny picture of about two dozen platters of salad all looking exactly the same lined up in a row on a very long table. I laughed until tears rolled down my eyes just thinking about it, but I suppose each woman has her own special way of preparing her family's favorite salad, so hopefully there was a good variety of dishes.

I must tell you about the big time Ingrid had last Midsummer's Day. She keeps all the old Swedish traditional holidays and on the weekend closest to the summer solstice invites all their friends and neighbors to come for a great feast with singing and dancing around the maypole. There were several couples of Swedish descent and one that was married to a Norwegian. Of course, he was the brunt of many Swedish/Norwegian jokes, but he was a very good sport about all the jesting.

Rebecca and Dave Beckworth were invited, too. If it wasn't for Dave, I might have never found Ingrid. Karla was happy that little David was there to play with. Rebecca's cousin, Samuel, was visiting them from New York, so he came, too. We are about the same age, so I was happy to instruct him in the traditional ring dancing around the maypole. He was very nice and polite.

Ingrid may not be a good knitter, but she is a clever seamstress and had made authentic Swedish folk costumes for herself and Olle and the children, including one for Karla. I wore the same one as I had at the masquerade party aboard the ship.

The next Sunday Rebecca, Dave, David and Samuel dropped into the yarn shop and we all drove to the Boston waterfront to eat at the famous Durgin Park Restaurant. It was crowded but the food was delicious and plentiful and the atmosphere relaxed and cozy. The restaurant has been in business since 1827and the Yankee food menu is almost the same as back then. One of their most popular meals is corned beef and cabbage, very similar to Arne's New England Boiled Dinner. Their fresh strawberry shortcake was heavenly!

Samuel is very nice and Karla loves him. I'll tell you more later. Karla is crying upstairs and I must tend to her.

Love,

Eva

Eva was greatly surprised to receive a letter from Dagny in February. Thinking something dreadful must have happened, she tore open the envelope and scanned quickly down through the short paragraph. She saw at once that everything was fine. She realized that this prompt reply was due to Dagny and Stina's curiosity about Samuel. They wanted to hear more about him.

Dear Eva

Stina come to visit same day as your letter, so she read it to me right away. We laughed at what you wrote about the potato salads. I tried a few of them and they all tasted the same. Men do not care. They eat anything set in front of them. Some meatballs would have tasted good. I might make some next year after we butcher the steer. We are all well. Very cold the first week in January and then warmed up to snow three feet and then another foot after that. Arne shoveled a path to the barn and the high banks of snow are like mountains that we can't see over. Stina and I want to know what else you meant to say when you wrote…Samuel is very nice…I'll tell you more later. Is there more to tell about Samuel? Write back soon.

Love,

Dagny

February 24, 1939

Dear Dagny

So you are curious about Samuel? Sorry to say I have nothing very exciting to tell you, but I'll continue with my story. As I wrote before, Samuel's family lives in New York City, but not in that crowded and dirty section of New York that we saw. Remember those tall buildings in the distance that seemed to touch the sky? They are indeed called 'skyscrapers' and he and his family actually live on the top floor of one of those buildings that overlook a large patch of green called Central Park. I'm certain I wouldn't want to look down from their windows. I always got dizzy in the haymow of our little barn in Norrland!

Well, back to Samuel. In September he returned to Cambridge. He attends Harvard College. He said he often takes the trolley from there to Arlington. It is relaxing and he can think better, do a bit of studying and get away from the hustle and bustle of college life. When he found out I live close to the turnaround, he walked over to say hello. Now he has a realistic destination and often stops in on Sunday afternoons.

The first time he came we ate at that little diner near the meat market and then walked around the square. To return the favor I invited him for dinner the next Sunday and he stayed until it was time to take the last trolley back to Cambridge. He was very interested in hearing about my life back in Sweden and how I happened to open a yarn shop. He's smart, funny and very patient in helping me with my English.

It was around the middle of December when I accompanied the Beckworths to Cambridge. We met Samuel there and took a tour of Harvard University. There is a statue of John Harvard, a minister for whom the university is named, and if one wishes to rub the statue's foot, it will bring good luck. I felt a bit foolish doing that, but I can always use a bit of good luck!

We went to a luxurious restaurant and had two kinds of wine, a cup of onion soup, a lovely salad and delicious tender little beef steaks wrapped in bacon with rice and broccoli. Samuel insisted on paying for everyone's dinner as a special holiday gift since he would soon be returning again to New York.

Rebecca told me later that Samuel's family is very wealthy. His father is a successful lawyer and his mother inherited a great amount of money. I haven't seen him since he went home for the holidays.

Hope you are having a good winter.

Love,
Eva

Within a few days a letter arrived from Mats.

Dear Eva

Sorry I haven't written sooner. My life has been in turmoil lately and things are just beginning to return to normal, as if life in the Navy is anything near normal. Yes, my parents did sell the farm, then Father died and Mother moved in with Johan and his wife. They have a house, small barn and several acres outside of Stockholm, enough so Mother can have her three most favorite goats. They help get her mind off other things and she seems to be coping quite well.

I was fortunate enough to get a furlough long enough to make the trip to Sweden and back, but I couldn't spend much time there after the funeral. The Lindholms were in attendance and Mr. and Mrs. asked about you, but Augusta immediately departed with one of her elite Stockholm friends and I never saw her again. Anders was telling me about the new cheese plant he and Karl set up after their trip across Europe several years ago. Karl practically lives at the cheese plant, even though he got married last summer. I can't imagine shy, studious Karl, ever getting married, can you?

Eva's body went limp upon learning of Karl's marriage, but she continued reading.

Karl and his wife were there. Anders introduced me to his wife, who's named Marta, but Karl wouldn't talk to me and walked away. 'Don't mind Karl, he's just in one of his moods again' said Marta, who was eying some guy to her left at the same time. Anders just shook his head and tried to keep the conversation going. You wouldn't like Marta. She's just like Jenny, arrogant, selfish and domineering. Hopefully she won't be cheating on the outside like Jenny did with me. At least Jenny and I never got married and I was able to join the Navy and forget about her.

Karl did pull me over later, practically dragging me to an empty table under one of the big pines in the back yard. He had half a glass of vodka in his hand and took a big swallow. Then he said something I'll never forget. 'You Bastard, Mats, why did you take Eva off to America?' I told him I had nothing to do with you leaving, that I'd stopped in to say goodbye to his mother and the next thing I knew the three of us were sitting at the breakfast table together and some incompetent maid was serving us dinner. I told him how dumbfounded I was to hear you would be accompanying me to America and that it seemed a big surprise to you, too. I also said how sad you seemed to be leaving Sweden and how I got the impression something bad had happened between you and his mother, but you'd never offered any explanation and I never asked.

You should have seen his face go pale. He sat down and put his head in his hands. Heck, for a minute I thought he was going to cry. 'You didn't marry Eva?' he asked after a while. I told him it wasn't my intent to marry you, that I had gone to America to marry Jenny Almgren and attend architectural school, but none of that panned out. He took another sip and asked if I'd seen you lately. I told him I went to see you once and was surprised that you were married and had a baby so soon after arriving in America. He looked at me like he'd seen a ghost, finished that glass of vodka and went stumbling back to the house. I didn't see him again.

Well, I guess this brings you up to date on what I know.

As ever,

Mats

Eva read the last three paragraphs over many times before she got it right. Even then, the sad news of Karl was difficult to accept. This was not the old Karl she remembered with such fondness. There was one other question she had. Where did Mats get the impression that she was married?

The room had darkened somewhat, although the sky was a deep blue and the setting sun marked the tops of the maples across the street with a golden line as if painted with an artist's brush. Eva did not know how long she had been sitting in front of the window, but she could feel where the tears had dried on her cheeks. Strumpa was asleep in her arms and she heard Karla's voice.

"What's the matter, Mama? Is Strumpa sick?" Eva managed a brief smile.

"Strumpa is fine. Why don't you give him his supper while I go to the storeroom for vegetables."

Eva shut the door and sobbed until there were no more tears, reproaching herself for never having told Mats the truth about her and Karl. She had tried to be strong, always hiding her true feelings, and had been too ashamed of her pregnancy to share that burden with Mats. Now it was too late. Karl would never know the real story behind her hasty departure, that it had all been his mother's idea to keep them apart. If she had told Mats, he would have been able to tell Karl the truth and things might be different now. At least he would know he had a daughter.

Eva barely ate half of her supper. After reading a story to Karla and tucking her in, she went downstairs. Writing to Mats was the only way she could stop her thoughts from assaulting her brain. Already her head was aching and she had no idea where to begin. She started a letter five times before filling one page. Finally she rose from her desk and went upstairs to bed, but the writing continued in her head for hours before she finally drifted off into a restless sleep.

She felt better in the morning but was still undecided about what to say to Mats...or what not to say. What could be gained by rehashing the past? Karl was married now. She needed to forget him. Instead, she wrote Mats a short note of condolence regarding his father's death, recalling some of the more memorable times she had spent with the wonderful Otto Kronberg.

The Visitor

It was a blustery March afternoon and the thermometer read thirty-five degrees. Eva stood by the shop window watching the gray clouds gathering in the west, remembering what Officer O'Leary had said yesterday about how it wasn't uncommon to have a blizzard in March. He also said it often snowed in April and a few flakes had been seen even in May. She'd had enough of winter and hoped his prediction wouldn't come true.

The sun came from behind the clouds just as a white delivery truck caught her eye. It slowed down and finally came to a stop in front of the shop. Hopefully it contained the delayed shipment of yarn she'd ordered from Boston. At the same time she noticed a woman crossing the street, her head bowed against the wind, carrying two heavy cloth bags woven in a familiar Swedish pattern. Being so close to Boston it wasn't uncommon for misplaced immigrants to be wandering the streets of Somerville and sometimes in Arlington, but rarely were they seen in Lexington. When the woman hesitated outside the shop window Eva noticed something familiar about the tired eyes and weathered face looking back at her, but couldn't remember where she'd seen her before. As the deliveryman approached with two large boxes, the woman went around him and continued walking down the sidewalk, gently pushed along by a slight breeze.

Had there been no one else in front of the yarn shop the woman might have gone in, for the number on the door was the same as the one printed on the envelope she carried in her pocket. Instead she stepped into a nearby alley and stood near a brick wall where a large patch of sunlight warmed her tired bones. The breeze followed her into the alley, whipping up whirlwinds of paper and dirt around a trash barrel as she pulled the too-tight jacket across her chest.

She fished in her pocket for a cigarette, but the wind extinguished the match. It took three tries to light it. Inhaling deeply, she leaned her head against the still-warm bricks, closed her eyes and exhaled slowly. She hadn't always smoked. Once in a while her lover had smoked a cigarette. He had said it calmed his nerves. She was heartbroken when he died. Overwhelmed with grief, she had turned to his box of cigarettes to sooth herself. Smoking one cigarette had provided some relief, but that had soon worn off and she'd needed another one...and another. Before long she was smoking twelve cigarettes every day to free herself of sadness and uncertainty of the future.

It had been a long trip from New York to Boston. She knew few English words. Because she had no money for train fare, she was forced to walk and hitch rides from city to city and town to town until finally arriving in Lexington. Just as she crossed the street the sun came to her aid, peeking through a hole in the cloudy sky. It had shined brightly for a moment to reveal a red-haired girl in the window and the woman had known at once she had found the place she'd been looking for. She inhaled deeply again and the corners of her mouth softened. She could wait another few moments until the delivery boy was gone. Then she would walk through that same door and hopefully find peace again.

These quiet moments were interrupted by a gray and white

cat scampering toward the sidewalk, its right leg almost completely white as if it wore a stocking. The cat sat down in a patch of sunlight and commenced to meticulously clean his fur with long, thoughtful licks, his eyes blissfully shut in the complete enjoyment only known to cats. Suddenly he jumped to his feet and dashed back down the alley, followed by a very young girl intent on capturing the startled animal. Then the girl tripped and fell, looked at her hand and began to scream. The woman dropped her cigarette, stomping it out with her foot, and knelt down to comfort the child. She brushed the fine gravel from the little hand, kissed the soft palm and thought of her own child as she held the whimpering little girl in her arms.

It was then Officer O'Leary saw them and rushed down the alley. Roughly grabbing the woman's arm, he picked up the child and marched them both toward the sidewalk. The woman tried to get away, but he held her more firmly, ignoring her foreign protests. She fought and kicked, making him more determined to bring her to justice.

He'd observed the vagrant woman roaming about the street earlier and thought she was up to no good. Just before Karla went missing from the yarn shop, he'd seen the woman sneak into the alley and that was the first place he looked. Seeing her with the child was enough to officially accuse her of kidnapping.

By now Karla was screaming again and Eva came running toward them from the porch. She took her daughter from Officer O'Leary, who was red in the face and quite out of breath. He still had a tight hold on the woman's arm and told Eva he'd caught her in the act of abducting Karla.

Eva didn't comprehend all of what Officer O'Leary said, but the woman babbled in a familiar Swedish dialect and finally Eva understood enough to believe the poor woman was innocent.

"We can discuss this better inside," said Eva, gesturing for them to follow her. Then she tried to explain to Officer O'Leary that Karla had probably followed Strumpa into the alley and that the woman just happened to be there and was merely comforting her daughter.

"Well it didn't look that way to me and I never saw any cat," said Officer O'Leary in his defense. Eva turned to quiet her daughter.

"Where is Strumpa?" she asked, brushing away tears and smoothing Karla's hair.

"Strumpa out," said Karla, pointing to the shop door.

"I'll bet Strumpa ran out through the door when the delivery man came in with my yarn boxes and then Karla ran out after Strumpa," said Eva.

"And then this woman grabbed her," said Officer O'Leary, who still kept a firm grip on the old woman's arm. Being inside with Eva, the woman had calmed down, her hopeful eyes searching the room.

"I want to see my Dagny," she cried. Then everything became perfectly clear to Eva.

"You are Suvi, Dagny's mother," she exclaimed, very much surprising Officer O'Leary, who slowly released his prisoner.

"You know this woman?" he said deflatedly, realizing his insignificant status in this matter. Eva tried to smooth things over.

"Please sit down, both of you, and I'll get us all a cup of coffee." Officer O'Leary didn't have to be asked twice about having coffee.

The famished woman drank the first cup down all at once and Eva promptly refilled it and brought in some frosted buns. The woman looked at the plate as if she'd found a pot of gold, and when Officer O'Leary helped himself to one and then another, the woman gingerly picked one up and nibbled at it. Eva smiled at her.

"You may have all you want. There's plenty more in the other room," she said reassuringly in Swedish. Suvi nodded and whispered to Eva, "is Dagny here?"

Eva briefly told her about Arne and how they had married and moved to Maine. Officer O'Leary looked around, not knowing what was being said. The women were smiling. Were they talking about him? He was embarrassed that he had made something out of nothing. It was time to go, he thought, and pushed himself away from the table.

"Have a good afternoon ladies," he said, tipping his cap and walking across the room.

"Thank you for bringing Karla back," shouted Eva, but he kept walking, raised his left hand in acknowledgment and shut the door behind him.

"Is Maine far from here?" asked Suvi.

"I can show you exactly where she lives," said Eva spreading a small map of New England on the table. She put her finger on Lexington and then slid it way up to New Sweden in northern Maine.

"You may have this map," she told Suvi and then she wrote Dagny's address on the top right hand corner.

"I saw a big map once of Sweden," said Suvi. "This map smaller...not so far."

Eva knew maps came in different sizes and that distances appeared shorter on some and longer on others. New Sweden was very far away, but she didn't want to discourage the woman. "Promise me you won't tell Dagny that I'm coming," said Suvi. "I want to surprise her."

"I promise," said Eva, "but have Dagny write to me so I know you arrived safely."

Suvi glanced out the window. "There is still light. I should leave now...get a few miles under my feet before dark."

"It's much too late to be starting out now," said Eva. "I suggest you have supper with us and get a good night's sleep. In the morning we can find out where you can get a bus to Maine."

The mention of supper got Karla's attention. "Can we have pisketti for supper?" she asked.

"Not pisketti, Karla. Say the word correctly; it is pronounced spaghetti."

But *spaghetti* was too much for Karla to get her tongue around, so she asked, "can we have some?"

Suvi fidgeted in her seat, picking at her fingers as if anxious to leave immediately, so Eva did not press Karla any further.

Seeing Suvi's dirty hands, and matted hair that probably hadn't been washed for weeks, Eva had an idea that might keep Suvi here until morning.

"I have a lovely tub upstairs," said Eva invitingly. "Wouldn't you like to soak in a nice hot bath before supper?"

Suvi turned around slowly as if considering the idea, so Eva continued. "Then you can spend a restful night sleeping in Dagny's old bed."

Suvi smiled and the fidgeting stopped. "I'd like that," she said.

Eva awakened earlier than usual the next morning, but not early enough. When she went to Dagny's old room, the bed was neatly made and Suvi was not there. She ran downstairs calling Suvi's name, but there was no sign of her there either. Standing outside on the sidewalk she looked up and down the wide road, seeing no one but a young boy on his paper route riding his bicycle in the opposite direction.

Eva walked despondently into the house. She had planned to have a hearty breakfast for the three of them and to give Suvi money for her bus ticket to Maine.

Now she would have to wait until a letter came from New Sweden to know if Dagny's mother arrived safely. She said a prayer for Suvi every night until the middle of April.

Dear Eva

My mother say you were so kind to her and she tell me to write that she is here. That was two weeks ago when we all had fevers or bad coughs. Mother took care of us and I am feeling good now. She told me that Bertil fell sick and died before he could answer my letter. His wife took over farm and mother had to leave. Bertil gave her money before he died and say for her to buy ticket to America and find me. She loves babies and is big help to me, but say Arne and me sleep apart so we don't have more. Maybe for a few days, but we like to play under the covers. Still have snow in woods and some along stonewalls. Roads are muddy and hard to get to village, but have plenty food in cold cellar and fresh eggs from hens. Cow had nice heifer calf last week. How is Samuel?

Love,

Dagny

April 23, 1939

Dear Dagny ,

I was so happy to hear from you that your mother arrived safely. She must have been so surprised to see her three new grandchildren!

Ingrid had us up to her house to celebrate Karla's fourth birthday. She can run faster than me and thinks it is fun to grab something and have me chase her around the shop, but she is usually very good. When customers come in 'my official greeter' is always first to show them her favorite colors of yarn, which change from time to time, but are now various shades of purple.

The snow here is all gone now except for a little under the trees on the shady side of the shed. In the front yard, my crocus and daffodils are peeking through the ground and it won't be long before the peony shoots will be doing the same. I hope you have some flowers up there, too.

My garden did very well last year, but now all my vegetables are used up except for a misplaced bag of potatoes I found last week with long sprouts growing out of them. They are a little soft, but still nice and white inside. I hadn't thought of it before, but do you have a big problem with all your potatoes sprouting?

I haven't seen Samuel since we went out to dinner last December. He never did return to Harvard after Christmas. Rebecca said he is helping his father with some work involving the Jews in Poland and Germany. He hasn't written to me, but Rebecca received a letter in February where he asked her to say hello to me. I really did enjoy his company and I thought the feeling was mutual, but you never know about men sometimes. A few men wander into the shop now and then, but when they see Karla they don't stay long. That shopkeeper at the gift shop still stops in every month or two to buy mittens and hats and always sits down for coffee and something to eat. I think he is married, so I am courteous, but not too friendly. He loves to talk, especially about the new movies at the theater. Someday I would like to go see a movie. Do you have a movie theater up there?

Say hello to your mother and Arne and hugs for the children.

Love,

Eva

In June Eva sent Dagny a birthday card. She enclosed a silver shoe charm with Axel's date of birth to add to her bracelet. Eva's bracelet now had four silver charms, given to her as Christmas gifts from the Bergstroms. In addition to the American Flag and the shoe with Karla's date of birth, there was one of a little house and another with crossed knitting needles in a ball of yarn.

Samuel

Another summer, another vegetable garden. The month of June had just the right amount of sun and rain to warm the ground and nourish it. The plants thrived and Eva found herself involved in canning and preserving all kinds of vegetables and fruits. As usual, the knitting clubs wound down for the summer, except for the older women's group, which continued to meet every Wednesday afternoon. These women were a wise, happy bunch and she enjoyed listening to their banter, especially reminiscing about the old days when they were newly married and raising their own children. Although the mother's group would not return until September, Rebecca usually stopped in on Monday mornings to visit, sometimes knitting and other times helping Eva with her English while David and Karla played.

Today they sat over coffee and almond cake, while Rebecca read over a letter Eva had written.

"You are writing so beautifully now, and only two little mistakes. Sometimes you get 'would' and 'wood' mixed up, but other than that everything looks fine." Rebecca was curious about the real reason why Eva had left Sweden and came to America. She had commented once about Eva's beautiful ring and seen the wistful look in her eye when she'd said it was a gift, but Eva had immediately started talking about something entirely different and Rebecca never asked about it again. They had become closer of late and Rebecca hoped Eva would let her defenses down and reveal more of her past.

"There's something so comforting about a hot cup of coffee, don't you think?" asked Eva.

"Oh yes, especially with this delicious cake of yours! Is it an old recipe from Sweden?"

"My mother showed me how to make it one Christmas when she received a packet of almonds, but it is even better to add some almond extract along with the nuts." Eva had a far-away look in her eyes and continued. "When I worked in the Lindholm kitchen, there was a cabinet full of all kinds of fragrant oils and spices. Almond extract was perfume to me and sometimes I'd put a drop on the inside of my wrist so I could smell the wonderful fragrance when I got back to my room."

"Cook asked me to make something for dessert one day, so I went a little heavy on the almonds and extract. After dinner Karl came into the kitchen for another piece of cake and Cook told him he'd have to ask me. When I gave him the plate with the slice of cake on it, he sat down and asked me to share it with him."

"Who is Karl?" asked Rebecca curiously. Eva sat up straight in her chair as if roused from a dream.

"Oh, did I say Karl?" Now Eva felt obligated to explain more to Rebecca about the Lindholm family. She started with how kind and understanding Mr. Lindholm was and then went into great length about Mrs. Lindholm's deceitful scheme for Eva's sudden departure. "They have two sons...Gunnar, who I'd rather forget, and Karl...who I will never forget. Karl is...he's Karla's father," said Eva, ending with a solemn whisper, "but I'm just married to a sweet memory."

"Mrs. Lindholm was a little wicked, wasn't she?" remarked Rebecca. "Dave's mother didn't like me either at first. She wasn't too happy about Dave marrying a Jewish girl, but I finally won her over and now we are very good friends."

Eva had been brought up in the Lutheran faith. She knew that Jesus was a Jew, but she had thought little about the differences between Jews and Gentiles. With so many religions in the world she thought everyone had a right to practice the faith in which they were raised.

"I'm Lutheran and you are Jewish," said Eva. "We get along very well. I don't understand why one's religious beliefs make any difference."

"I certainly agree with you, Eva. Sometimes I don't understand it either." Rebecca thought a moment. "There are a lot of similarities between Jews and Christians, but there are many differences, too. Those dissimilarities are the reason Samuel has been so busy lately." Rebecca hesitated, not wishing to say why Hitler called the Jews an inferior race. "Samuel has been flying back and forth to Europe. Seems like there are grave racial troubles in Poland and Germany." Rebecca brushed a tear away. This news surprised Eva. She wanted to know more about Samuel and why her friend was sad, but Rebecca suddenly called out to her son.

"Help Karla pick up her toys, David, we have to go now." Then she turned to Eva. "I have some shopping to do. Dave is on vacation this week and he thinks a trip to the mountains would be good for both of us. He wants to go camping in New Hampshire. There's a place near Lincoln that raises sled dogs and they have live bears there, too. Frankly I'm not too excited about sleeping overnight in the forest, but Dave thinks it would be good for David."

"Have fun," said Eva, "but be careful around those bears."

They hugged a little tighter than usual, but Eva didn't know if it was due to the troubles in Europe or camping in the woods.

In August a man in a dark suit and black felt fedora came into the shop. Eva's first reaction was one of fear, but when he took off his hat and spoke she was relieved to see her dear Samuel. He'd lost weight and grown a mustache, but it was more than that; his laughing eyes were sad and his whole demeanor much too serious. How could a boy become a man so quickly, she thought to herself. He'd changed from a carefree college student into a man with a solemn purpose.

Then he embraced her gently and whispered in her ear, "you don't know how I've missed your beautiful face and cheerful ways." This was so unlike the old Samuel. She was almost anticipating a kiss when Karla came running out from the back room, leaving what might have happened between them that moment a great mystery.

Karla was an outgoing and lively four year old, but upon seeing the serious stranger she stopped in her tracks and hid behind her mother's skirt.

"Don't you remember Samuel?" asked Eva. He removed his jacket and lowered himself to Karla's height, but it wasn't until she heard his voice and saw the old familiar smile that she dared venture forth to accept him.

"It's probably too cold for ice cream today," he said matter-of-factly.

"Oh no," replied Karla very seriously, "not too cold for ice ceem."

"What do you say we go for a ride in that shiny black car out front, drive to a nice restaurant and then buy an ice cream cone?"

Karla ran to the window. "Mama, Mama, look at that big car!"

"What a beautiful automobile. Is it yours?" asked Eva.

"It's my father's," he admitted. "We had to come to Boston on business and he is visiting relatives today, so I borrowed the car for the afternoon."

Eva was glad to see a bit of the old Samuel return as they drove back through Arlington.

"I thought we'd go to that little place in Cambridge again," he told her.

They were both in the mood for beef, so Samuel ordered them each a tenderloin steak wrapped in bacon with mushrooms and onions, but first they had a bottle of wine and a nice salad.

"This is the first good meal I've enjoyed in a long time and I owe it to this fine company," said Samuel, raising his wine glass in acknowledgment."

"You do look a bit thinner than last time I saw you," said Eva. "I think you've been working too hard and not getting enough sleep." She sounded like his mother and he told her so in a kindly manner, but he added that he and his father had been very involved with concerns overseas.

"I'll tell you more later," he said, and like Rebecca, he looked away briefly and talked about more pleasant things. Eva brought him up to date on the yarn shop, knitting clubs and her garden, but the conversation became strained as they each tried to avoid Samuel's secret work in Europe. Karla dawdled with her ground beef, trying to hide the peas under her mashed potato, but her mother's glaring eye warned her there would be no ice cream if she didn't finish her meal. Finally the dirty dishes were cleared and they all had ice cream cones dipped in tiny chocolate pieces.

On the way home Karla fell asleep in her mother's arms and Samuel stopped the car under a huge weeping willow tree overlooking a small city park. When he turned off the ignition, an overwhelming silence filled the car and he rolled down his window. A comforting breeze brought in the sound of chirping birds and laughing children playing in the park. Samuel rested his head on the back of the seat and they watched families strolling along the dirt paths while boys and girls played ball and hide and seek. Finally he turned to Eva.

"I almost didn't come to Lexington today." He hesitated, almost reluctant to continue. "I wanted to see you and tell you something, but I was afraid that..." Eva saw him look down at the steering wheel, rubbing the shiny surface as if this might help him find the words that had escaped him. She bent forward in her seat to catch his eye.

"You can tell me anything, Samuel. You must know that by now," she said convincingly. Then he turned sideways in his seat to face her, speaking almost in a whisper, as if someone close by might overhear.

"In Europe there is great unrest, especially in Germany and Poland and also in France and Italy. There is even talk about war...a war that might be of world-wide proportions."

"War?" exclaimed Eva. "Everything is so peaceful here, surely it won't come to America."

"Now I've worried you. I was afraid of that. I don't mean here in America...at least not right now, but it is an entirely different story in Europe, a tragic story that will end many lives."

"In Sweden, too?"

"No, not so much in Sweden. They are one of the few neutral countries that try to get along with both sides in a war. There is a radical group in Germany called Nazis who think they are superior to everyone else. An evil man named Hitler is their leader and he has built up a regime to acquire more land, and to form, what he calls, the perfect race."

"Rebecca did mention something about racial problems to me recently," said Eva, "but I didn't understand exactly what racial meant, and then she began talking about something else."

"Well, in Hitler's prejudiced mind, the Jews are inferior to the white race and he doesn't want any Jews in his country or anywhere else for that matter. Already he is preventing them from having driving licenses, or attending concerts and theaters, and many have been required to hand over all their gold and silver to the Nazi government. There's even some talk that those Jews who do not flee the country may soon be...um... eliminated."

"Eliminated?" Eva was trying to think of what that word meant and Samuel tried to explain without being too explicit, but there was no other way to say what he saw coming.

"Jews will be removed, banished from their homes and country, or worse than that...put to death." Eva's eyes widened and her mouth dropped open.

"How can Hitler eliminate a whole race of people? That's

impossible for one man to do!"

"He has armies of men under his command who are carrying out his evil plan in many different countries. I have been there and seen it with my own eyes. I'm working behind the scenes for an organization that tries to rescue Jews and get them to a safe place."

"What you are doing sounds very dangerous. Not only am I concerned about the war, but now I'm going to worry about you."

"My intention isn't to worry you," he said, taking her hand in his. "There is nothing you can do about the war… and worrying is a waste of time."

"I don't know why people just can't get along with one another and let each think or believe what they may. All it takes is a little patience and understanding," said Eva. "Inside we are all quite alike, don't you think?"

"Yes, I agree with you, but unfortunately Hitler does not." Then he went on. "I'm telling you all this so that you can prepare yourself and take certain precautions with your business. In wartime there are shortages of food and other necessities because of the great demands of the military. You should stock up on canned goods and items like sugar, flour and coffee…plant a large garden and preserve your own food."

"I've already canned a lot of vegetables this year," she said. "Perhaps I should sell the yarn shop and get out while I can. But I really don't want to do that."

"Actually you are in a very good business," he said with a hint of a smile that relaxed her somewhat. "If there is a shortage of clothing, women will be more apt to buy yarn to knit warm clothes for their family and if there is a fuel shortage they will be making more sweaters and those knitted blankets…what are they called?"

"Afghans. Yes, it takes a lot of yarn to make an afghan," she added.

"I would suggest you order extra supplies of yarn and products associated with knitting. Yarn should keep very well for years if stored in a clean, dry place, especially if you add a few mothballs to keep the pests out. You might want to buy extra fleece next year, too, and dye it in an olive-green color suitable for the army. Mothers and wives will probably want to knit warm scarves and hats to send to their sons and husbands in the military."

"Well," she sighed, "I guess I won't be sitting around wondering what to do with my time, will I?"

"No, but I can't see you doing that anyway. Better to be prepared, just in case." Samuel's sad eyes gazed into hers and she felt his hand on her cheek.

"I know it wasn't easy for you to tell me all this, but I'm glad you did," she said with her disarming smile.

"I think I'm falling in love with you," he said so tenderly she almost cried. She was mesmerized by his brown eyes. They had a sparkle to them like a sprinkling of fine gold dust. Then suddenly he kissed her, soft and wet, then more forcefully so that Karla wriggled in her mother's arms. Eva was almost glad for the intrusion and pulled away as Karla sat up and rubbed her eyes. "Can we play on the swings?" she asked.

"I'll race you to that fountain," said Samuel, opening the car door. Eva laughed as he lifted his legs high in the air, taking little baby steps so that Karla might beat him across the lawn. Samuel was that young boy again, the one Eva remembered from before.

There was no more talk of war that day, nor was there another kiss. Eva had a soft spot in her heart for Samuel, but his kiss had not moved her to passion like Karl's had.

Talk of War

In the weeks that followed Eva thought a lot about war and the future, of Sweden and Karl. What about Mats? She had received a Christmas card from him last year with a brief note that he was in California. She thought of Mr. Kaneko's two rivers, how Mats' river ended abruptly…and now he was on a Navy ship somewhere in the Pacific Ocean.

Practicality set in. She immediately ordered a large shipment of yarn with the company from Sweden, ordered extra yarn from the wholesale place in Boston and spent more money at the grocery store stocking up on canned meats, coffee and items needed for baking breadstuffs.

She bought a dozen packets of olive-colored dye and ordered more fleece.

Emily began stopping in more regularly; not to knit or babysit, but to talk. Little by little she confided little personal bits of information to Eva, things that should have been discussed with her mother. Emily was fifteen now and she had a boyfriend that she liked very much, but he was Catholic and her mother would not allow her go out on a date with him.

"Mama told me to find a nice Protestant boy and even suggested a few that went to our church," said Emily. "I've known those boys all my life and feel more like their sister than a girl friend."

"I don't know much about other religions, but I'm sure your mother must have her reasons," replied Eva.

"Mother has reasons about everything!" pouted Emily.

"Well, mothers usually know what's best for their children...at least they think they do, so for now I'd try to abide by what she says."

"But you don't know how it is to really like someone that you can't have for a friend," said Emily, scowling and almost angry that Eva was siding with her mother. Emily's face softened and she looked up to Eva, tears running down her cheeks. "We really love each other."

Eva understood completely and took Emily in her arms.

"Oh Emily, I do know how it feels not to be able to be with the one you love."

"You do?" said Emily, pulling away to look at Eva's troubled face.

"I was fifteen and in love once, too."

"Really?" Now Emily wasn't so caught up in her own problem and was willing to listen. Eva told her only what she thought Emily should know about her, Karl and Mrs. Lindholm. "So

Karla's father is still in Sweden?"

"As far as I know he is," said Eva. "I've never seen nor heard from him since I came to America."

"Oh, that's awful," said Emily. "At least my boyfriend and I can see each other at school and talk sometimes. I guess I should be grateful for that."

"You have a very mature attitude, Emily. Being grateful can often be a stepping stone for something better. We don't always know what is best for us."

On September 1 Officer O'Leary came rushing through the shop door showing her the newspaper headline that read NAZIS DROP BOMBS ON WARSAW.

"What is Warsaw?" she asked.

"The capitol of Poland," he said. "Hitler has invaded Poland."

"I'd heard there was trouble between Germany and Poland," she replied, "but I was hoping they'd straighten out their differences."

"There's more than two countries involved! I hear Britain and France are getting in on it, too." His plump cheeks were as crimson as two ripe apples. "Hitler and his Nazis want to take over all of Europe."

"Why don't you sit and calm down. I'll get you some coffee."

"Can't stop today, Eva...Gotta go spread the bad news. "Thanks anyway," he said, slamming the door shut.

In December Eva received a Christmas card from Dagny, whose printing was much improved.

December 1939

Dear Eva,

We have 2 cows now and one heifer born last June. She is only baby born here this year and I am glad of that. I have my strength back and feel good as new. Axel is growing big on my milk and still nurses like a hungry calf. Annika is almost four now and likes to play with dough when I make bread. I must mix up extra because she love to eat uncooked dough. She get flour in hair and dress but all washes out so I not care. It same when she makes mud cakes outside in summer, but I spank when she eats them. Who knows what is in that wet dirt. Albin is three now. He never did crawl. One day he just get up and walk and follow Arne wherever he go. Nice to see Arne plowing with Albin sitting proudly on back of horse. Arne says Albin be some farmer when he grow up and I think so to. Arne found shelves of old preserves in cellar of barn. He dump out spoiled food and save jars, so Mother have job washing them all. She is good. She help in garden and with jarring up food for winter. Together we put up over four hundred quarts vegetables and pickles and four dozen jars of blueberry jam. Lots of blueberries grow in Maine. How are you and Karla, the Bergstroms and Samuel? Do you ever hear from Mats? Merry Christmas.

Love,

Dagny

December 30, 1939

Dear Dagny ,

Happy New Year! Karla and I are fine and I'm so glad to hear that all is well with you and your family. How I would love to see you all!

I haven't seen Mrs. Bergstrom lately, but Emily comes to visit often. Emily is fifteen and she and her mother aren't getting along very well because Emily wants to go out with a Catholic boy. There are probably not many Catholics in New Sweden, but in Massachusetts there are a lot of Irish, especially in Boston and surrounding areas, and most Irish are Catholic. I don't understand the difference between Protestants and Catholics, but we worship the same God, so what is there to be upset about? Officer O'Leary is Irish. I questioned him, but we don't understand each other very well. When he said Catholic was the only religion, I didn't argue. I suppose everyone thinks their own religion is best.

I did some canning, too, but not as much as you. Of course there is only Karla and I here to feed. I have almost two hundred jars of vegetables, mostly green beans, peas and corn, plus a dozen pints of cucumber pickle and over a dozen jars of elderberry jelly.

I've been busy with a new load of fleece. It was fairly clean, so the washing wasn't a big problem, but the whole process is time-consuming. I have it all dyed and carded, with more than half yet to spin.

We had another lovely Christmas at Ingrid's. She goes all out with food and gifts, but not such lavish gifts to the children as the Bergstroms. I was able to buy store gifts for Gus and Nina, instead of the customary knitted hats, mittens and sweaters I've given in past years.

Mats never did marry Jenny. I don't know what happened, but he is in the Navy now. Oh yes, Mr. Kronberg died. When Mats went back for the funeral, he saw Karl. How stupid of me to never tell Mats the whole truth about why I left Sweden. If I had, Karl would know it wasn't my idea to come to America and perhaps things would be different. It makes me sad to dwell on 'if only I had done this or that,' so I try to live only in the present, something my mother told me to do years ago.

Samuel came to visit in August. He is busy in New York and Europe working for his father.

Love,

Eva

Since everything was going so well with Dagny, Eva decided not to say anything about the troubles in Europe or about a war that might never come to America.

1940-1941

On April 9, 1940, Officer O'Leary rushed into the shop telling Eva that Germany invaded Norway and Denmark.

"Why does Hitler bother with Norway?" she asked. "There's not much more than mountains and lakes there."

"Perhaps because Norway has so much coast line on the

Atlantic," he said, "but I suspect he needs Norway's vast iron ore mines to make tanks and arms for the military."

"What about Sweden?" she asked. "Will they invade there, too?"

"Haven't heard anything about Sweden, except they are staying out of the war...something about them being neutral."

After he was gone, Eva looked up the word 'neutral' and felt better about Sweden not taking sides in the war. With everything else on her mind, she didn't want to think of Karl having to fight against that awful Hitler.

In May Germany invaded Holland, Belgium and France. Officer O'Leary talked of men named Churchill and de Gaulle and others whose names meant nothing to Eva. She had never heard of Belgium before, so she bought a round globe on a wooden stand that showed every country in the world in beautiful color. She continued to stock up on flour, sugar, coffee and canned milk, bought herself and Karla new shoes and boots and ordered another shipment of yarn from Boston. On August 23, Germany bombed London. Two days later Britain bombed Berlin.

The next day Eva received a smaller 'bombshell' from Dagny, but this was an event of much happiness.

August 1940

Dear Eva

We have 2 more babies in July named Arvid and Astrid. Only 6 pounds so they come fast. Arne so proud. I feel good, but spend much time nursing. Arne make sling to hold baby, so I can walk around and do work. You not need to send sweaters for Arvid and Astrid. Have ones you gave to other babies. Mother is fine and sews quilts, so we have plenty to keep warm.

We have very big garden and more fields planted to potatoes. Got another heifer calf from cow, so have 4 cattle and 2 work horses and Arne buy bred sow and she have 12 fat piglets. Arne wants to roast one soon, but I think little ones too sweet to kill and eat, but he say meat is sweeter, too. We do like pig meat. Arne plan to add another room out back of house.

Arne is very Lutheran and so am I now. Are we at war with the Catholics?

Love,

Dagny

August 25, 1940

Dear Dagny

What a surprise to hear that you had twins! How I wish I could see them. Don't forget to send me a picture of your growing family.

Oh, no, we are not at war with the Catholics. The war is between several countries over in Europe, but as far as I know Sweden isn't involved in it.

When I last saw Samuel he told me his work had something to do with the war and he suggested I stock up on yarn for the shop as well as special foods such as flour, sugar, coffee and other necessary items needed to make breadstuffs, as well as making sure I have a good sized vegetable garden each year. I wonder if I should keep a few chickens out back, too! I'd love to have a cow for milk but there is no room for pasture and feeding her would be expensive. It seems to me that you and Arne are very self-sufficient and can do quite well without depending on stores for survival in case of war. I don't intend to alarm you, but it doesn't hurt to be prepared for an emergency.

I went to the jewelry store and they didn't have any shoe charms, but I saw a silver toy bear charm and a rattle that actually makes a sound. Maybe they will have more shoe charms later, but let me know which you would like so I can send them to you for next Christmas. Samuel gave me a charm for my bracelet, the outline of Sweden in blue and yellow.

I have expanded the little garden plot so that most of the back yard is planted with potatoes, carrots, beets, corn, tomatoes, cucumbers, peppers and onions, so I keep busy.

Love,

Eva

The last day of August a package was delivered from New York.

Inside was a radio with a letter from Samuel explaining the various knobs for adjusting volume and searching for different stations. He said that listening to music gave him much pleasure and took his mind off of the war.

Eva plugged in the radio and turned it on. The sound of music floated through the room and she learned later the song was called *In the Mood* by Glenn Miller. It had definitely put her in a better mood, but she was mystified how voices and sounds changed by merely turning a knob. This reminded her of the magical time in Mr. Kronberg's library when she opened the music box and wondered where the orchestra was.

News about women's issues interested Eva, although she was shocked to learn that twenty-four thousand women from age eighteen to thirty-five were serving in the British Army. Many women were disappointed to find themselves doing just what they had done at home, cooking, cleaning and clerical jobs, although there were some closer to the front lines working as nurses, journalists and news reporters. The radio continued to talk about rationing. For almost a year now England had rationed butter, sugar, bacon, meats, cheese, preserves and tea, and each person was limited to one pair of shoes each year.

Alone with a young child she would have to do what she could on the home front, but she knew not what that might be. In the meantime she would prepare fleece and dye it the appropriate color for her customers to kit warm clothing for the soldiers.

On September 7, the Germans bombed London and surrounding English cities. Every day Eva heard of new countries involved in the war; names like Libya, Greece and Iraq, and others with odd sounding names like Yugoslavia, Ethiopia, Somalia and Bulgaria. It was difficult to keep track of who was battling whom, yet every country appeared so small and peaceful on her little round globe. The relaxing music on the radio was her only means of escape from the daily deluge of sad events described in the local paper, by Officer O'Leary and her customers. The green leaves turned yellow, red and orange. Then they fell to the cold ground, becoming a dull brown carpet that was soon covered by an early winter snow. Christmas came and went and the New Year arrived quietly. Nineteen hundred and forty-one was a repetition of the previous year...until December.

The War Accelerates

On December 7, 1941, there was no music. Every radio station shouted out the news that the Japanese had launched over one hundred planes and attacked Pearl Harbor. Over a thousand American sailors were lost on the battleship U.S.S. Arizona, and eight other battleships were sunk or disabled with over two thousand casualties. It was disturbing news and even more so after Eva located Pearl Harbor on the globe and saw how close it was to California.

The next day President Roosevelt declared war on Japan. That night Eva woke up in a sweat. She'd been dreaming that she was rowing frantically through a thunderstorm in the ocean toward a small boat that kept dipping in and out of sight in the high waves. Every once in a while she saw Mats' face, but his boat drifted further and further away. She rowed faster. Then a bolt of lightening struck the place where Mats had been. A glimmering light rested on the horizon as pieces of splintered wood floated past her. Then the light blinked out and she was alone in the darkness. She awakened with insurmountable dread that she would never see Mats again. Before her morning coffee she wrote a note on Mats' Christmas card, addressed it and put it out for the mailman to take that day.

On December 11, America declared war on Germany and Italy. Rebecca received a letter from Samuel telling her about Hitler ordering all Jews to wear a visible, yellow Star of David on their clothes so they'd be immediately recognized as Jews by the Nazi soldiers patrolling the streets. She said most Jews had lost their government jobs and many had been driven from their homes and placed in special Jewish settlements. Samuel was in an undisclosed place in Europe helping Jews who had fled their homelands. He said rationing was getting worse in England, reminding her to keep stocking up on food and other essentials and for Eva to do the same.

Eva received Christmas cards from Mrs. Sandquist, the Bergstroms and members of the older women's knitting group, who all looked upon Eva as their own daughter and Karla as a granddaughter. Rebecca and Dave sent a religious card of the three wise men looking up to a large glittering star. A card from Anna had a short note saying there was not much call for Lars' boats and carvings, but they had enough savings to keep them going and Jonas was still playing in the symphony orchestra. His music soothed the hard times, just as the radio songs did for Eva.

Just before Christmas a letter came from New Sweden.

December 1941

Dear Eva

I like the little shoe charms with the dates on them. That way I can keep track of all the children's birthdays. Don't know what I would do if Mother was not here to help me. Five children is a lot of work, especially with the twins and the older boys running around and getting into mischief. Annika is almost six and loves to help, but sometimes her help is more bother. Her heart is in the right place though, so I try to be patient. We didn't put up so many jars of vegetables last summer. The days weren't long enough with everything else that needed to be done. Arne is working in the woods with horses this winter, clearing more land. Mother and I will again take turns watching the children and harvesting more potatoes next year. We all have had a healthy year up until the first week in December when one by one we all came down with colds. I felt good enough to put up the Christmas tree and decorate it, but didn't do much extra baking. No one felt like eating much anyway, except for Arne who has a big appetite even when sick. He loves a big bowl of soup or stew, so easy to make up a big pot and everyone can eat how much they want. Arne sometimes discusses politics and war with the men in the village, but it goes way over my head. I have enough to do to keep peace between my fighting boys. Thanks for the pretty card. I didn't send out Christmas cards this year. How is Samuel? And Mats? I have the picture of you and me in a frame on the wall in the parlor. I am getting better at writing thanks to Stina.

Love,

Dagny

Dagny seemed unconcerned about the war. It was as if her little town in the northernmost part of Maine was isolated from the bad news. Farmers were more self-sufficient than city dwellers and probably weren't affected so much by food shortages.

1942

January 5, 1942

Dear Dagny

I was sorry to hear you were all sick with colds and hope that everyone is now back to feeling healthy again. You are the one who has to take care of everyone else, so you must be extra good to yourself and not do so much. I don't believe in being a slave to my house like some of my customers who must dust every day, wash windows once a week and run around with an old toothbrush trying to clean every tiny nook and cranny. I know Arne is good to you, but YOU must take time once in a while to do something special for yourself, even if it is an extra-long relaxing bath. Think of it as a mini vacation.

Karla had two bad colds last year and I had the sniffles a few times. She recently had the chicken pox. She started school in September and who knows what other germs might be hopping from desk to desk with thirty children closed into one room for all day. Karla loves school, especially reading. Of course I've been reading to her every night since she was about two years old. Now she goes to sleep hugging her favorite book under one arm and the fuzzy bear that Ingrid gave her under the other. By the way, I found Karla chewing on something one day. It was one of the bear's eyes! I quickly took it out of her mouth, removed the other eye from the bear and threw them out. She could have swallowed or choked on them. She still loves the bear and doesn't seem to mind that it has no eyes. You might want to check any stuffed animals around your house to be sure they are safe for your little ones.

The yarn shop has done well this year, probably because I didn't go to the expense of buying a lot of yarn and bought fleece instead. I was wishing you and Arne were here to help me with the buckets of hot water! Thankfully the fleece wasn't very dirty.

We went to Ingrid and Olle's again for Christmas Eve and Christmas Day. The house looked beautiful and the meals were delicious. Olle bought some piglets last spring and had one butchered and cured in time for the holidays, so there was plenty of roast pork and ham for lunches and dinners, as well as bacon for breakfast. You know how I love bacon!

Samuel is in Europe on business. He told Rebecca that we should stock up on food and other essential store items, so you might want to do the same in case there is a shortage because of the war. I haven't heard from Mats lately. Last I knew he was in the Navy and still stationed in California. We are in good health and trying to live life as normal as possible. Hugs to all of you.

Love,

Eva

As the year wore on, Officer O'Leary came into the yarn shop so often that whenever Eva saw him pass the window, she began to feel like locking the door to keep from hearing more bad news. She did this one day in May and felt guilty, wondering all afternoon if he might have had something good to say. She decided it was to her advantage to keep abreast of all news, good or bad, to better plan for herself, Karla and her customers. The next day she invited him in for coffee.

"Well, rationing has begun," he said, opening up a small booklet. It was a ***sugar book*** stating that from now on everyone would be limited to one-half pound of sugar per week. "And that's not all. There's talk of everything being rationed before the end of the year."

Eva had stockpiled over a dozen five-pound packages of sugar, but she didn't tell this to Officer O'Leary. She noticed he used only one teaspoon of sugar instead of two in his coffee, but he took a bite of cookie with each sip.

"There's talk of rationing shoes...each adult and child will be allowed only three pairs of new shoes each year, but the stores are already running low on regular sizes, so you'd better get to the store real soon."

"Who needs three pairs of shoes?" asked Eva. "One pair usually lasts me much longer than a year," she said.

"Well, my wife must have shoes to match all her pocketbooks, which seem to be a different color for every day of the week."

Eva laughed. "I've seen shoes walk through the shop door in every color of the rainbow, but I only buy black ones. They go with everything."

"I usually have my shoes resoled so they last another year or two," he said, "But my wife must buy new ones to keep up with the latest styles."

"I bring mine to the cobbler, too. My father always brought our shoes to the village each year to be repaired. Then he bought rubber patches to put on the tears and holes in our boots."

"I can see you are a very practical young lady," he said. "Maybe the war will make my wife think twice next time she goes shopping, but I doubt it." His mouth stretched to a grin. Officer O'Leary was proud of his stylish wife. He took a last sip of coffee and pushed back his chair. "Better stock up on coffee," he said. "By the way, the war effort needs more metal. They want everyone to save their used tin cans, but remember to rinse them out good."

"Is someone going to collect them?" she asked, but he had already closed the door.

Eva kept busy dying fleece for olive-colored yarn. Spinning this drab color was monotonous, but it was all put to good use as mothers and wives began knitting vests for the soldiers. These very warm, heavy vests involved knitting two strands of yarn together to keep out the cold. Knitting for the soldiers made the women feel good. It was their way of contributing to the war effort.

Emily rode up on the trolley one Saturday with her girlfriend. They wanted to knit scarves for the soldiers. Again Eva was aware of girls on the street with nothing better to do than gather in little groups and wander about the neighborhood during the summer vacation. She put a sign in the window, ***Knitting keeps idle hands busy***, and underneath in small letters, ***knit a scarf and keep a soldier warm***. Within two weeks there were nine girls knitting scarves.

Eva had been curious about Emily and her boyfriend, but hadn't had a chance to talk with her alone. However, she didn't have to wait long. Young girls love to chatter, and from the knitting group Eva soon overheard the news that Emily had broken up with the boy she had been "in love with" and since then had dated many others. They were a boy-crazy bunch, dating seriously for a couple weeks, breaking up and moving on to new boyfriends.

In August Eva received a letter from New Sweden.

August 1942

Dear Eva

I thought of what you said about being good to myself. I must say that not being pregnant was a fine vacation and I did enjoy a few long soaking baths. In June we welcomed a little girl named Anna. She is the perfect baby. I feed her, she sleeps, feed her again and she sleeps until the next feeding. And she sleeps through the night. Arne is so good to me. We got a good price on our potatoes last year, so Arne bought another horse and hired a man to help work in the woods and also in the potato fields so I don't have to be outside so much. The men are not above picking peas and beans either which is a big help to Mother and me. I think of you often, too, but I don't miss cleaning the fleece…although I've done dirtier work here at times. We have had such good luck and I wouldn't trade my life here for anything, but it would be nice to see you and Karla again. With Samuel in Europe and Mats in California, you will never get married. Stina says both places are far away from here, and far away from you, too. If there isn't anyone you like in Lexington, we could introduce you to a nice widower who lives down the road from here. He owns the hardware store in the village and has red hair, too.

Love,

Dagny

Reading about Dagny's thoughts on men made Eva laugh so hard she cried. Eva thought, ***she is so happy with her sweet Arne that she wants everyone to be married and have the same happiness.***

Eva didn't need to be married to be happy, although when she thought of Karl, happiness took on a new dimension. She guessed there were many levels of happiness in one's life. She had accepted her present situation and tried to make the most of it.

Rubber overshoes were rationed in October of 1942 and on November 29 coffee was rationed to one pound per person every five weeks. Eva had already dispensed with the sugar bowls and cream pitchers, preparing an individual's coffee the way she knew they liked it…although she did notice on occasion that a customer often reached into their own pocket for extra sugar they had brought from home. Many had given up sugar and cream altogether. Eva, who had always enjoyed her coffee with a lot of cream and a little sugar, now drank her coffee black.

She had a fair stockpile of coffee in the back room, but coffee lost its freshness after a while and there wasn't enough to get through the winter. Now she would have to figure out some way to make it last longer. She started by putting one less spoonful in the pot. A month later she skimped a little more. Sometimes a customer gave her leftover coffee when they received their new supply. Others, who didn't drink coffee, left ration coupons under their plates for her to use. Rationing affected people in different ways. Some became more possessive and stingy, while others shared and looked out for their neighbors and friends. Flour and fish were now rationed, as well as all canned goods. Kitchen fats could be turned in for extra rations of beef at the butchers.

One snowy day an elderly man stuck his head in the door and looked around. Eva thought he might be the husband of a woman picking out yarn and asked if he wanted a cup coffee. He readily accepted her offer and sat at a table by the window. When the woman left, he went over to Eva as if he had some big secret to reveal.

"I want to learn how to knit," he whispered, looking cautiously over his shoulder.

Eva was relieved and a bit amused, but quickly grabbed some needles and yarn, sat the man in a corner and cast on a short row of stitches on the needle.

"My name is Edgar Josephson. My wife passed away last year. I just don't know what to do with myself." Eva listened sympathetically as he rambled on. "I usually walk around town after breakfast visiting my friends. One day I saw your sign in the window about knitting for the soldiers, but I was too embarrassed to come into a woman's shop. I wanted to do something for the war and knitting for the soldiers seemed like a good idea for an old fogy like me. Today something made me come in." He smiled at her. "I think it was the smell of this wonderful coffee I'm drinking."

"I'm delighted that you came in. We'll begin with the simple garter stitch," she said, knitting the first row of stitches while explaining about the needles and yarn. Then he took over, rather clumsily, but did fairly well until two women entered the shop and several stitches slipped off the needle when he tried to hide his work under the table.

"Finish your coffee and I'll put the stitches back on after the women leave," she whispered in his ear.

In the meantime, Karla came home from school, saw that her mother was busy and ran upstairs. It wasn't long before she was sitting on the bottom step studying the strange man sitting in the corner. Edgar caught her eye and winked, but Karla looked away. Then she slowly peeked back again.

"Are you the little princess who lives upstairs?" he asked, a big grin spreading across his face. Karla's eyes looked big with wonder. Then she nodded and smiled.

"A little princess used to live at my house," he said. "She grew up and became a queen."

"Does she live in a castle?"

"Well, she calls it her castle. Actually she lives on a ranch in Texas."

"A ranch?" asked Karla. "Does she have lots of horses?"

"Yup...lots of horses and cattle."

"I have a horse!" said Karla. Then she ran back upstairs.

When Karla came back the two women customers were gone and Eva was putting a glass of milk and a plate of cookies on the table. "Karla, this is Mr. Josephson."

"Santa gave me this horse," said Karla proudly, showing off the small wooden carving that Olle had made for her one Christmas. It was a simple outline of a horse with thick legs and no tail, but it was one of Karla's favorite toys.

"What a fine, sturdy little horse," said Edgar. "I'll bet he can do a full day's work."

"He doesn't work," stated Karla, emphatically. "He's a orminent."

"Or-na-ment," said her mother, emphasizing each syllable. Karla frowned and thought a few seconds.

"He makes me happy just to look at," she said, holding the little horse in one hand and picking up a cookie with the other. Edgar could barely take his eyes off the cookie plate.

"Peanut butter cookies are my favorite," he said wistfully. "My wife made a batch every week."

After a lengthy silence, Eva asked him if any of his friends were interested in knitting.

"Well, there's an old guy who just moved in next door. I hear he does cross-stitch pictures...pretty good ones, too."

When Eva finished putting the dropped stitches back on the

needles she gave them back to Edgar.

Karla put half her cookie on the table and stared at Edgar. "I didn't know men did knitting," she said.

"Anyone with two hands can knit," said her mother sternly. "Now why don't you go upstairs and play while Mr. Josephson and I finish talking."

"Okay," said Karla, finishing her cookie and grabbing another.

"If your new neighbor enjoys cross-stitching, I'd say he'd be a very good candidate for knitting," said Eva after Karla had gone upstairs.

"Ya...he's kind of fussy about things. Always takes his shoes off before coming into his house...and everyone else's house, too."

"That's very considerate of him," said Eva.

"Probably his wife's idea. She's more particular than he is."

Eva smiled. "Anything to keep peace in the family, I suppose."

"You got that right." Then he became misty-eyed. "My wife used to annoy me with all her...um...idiosyncrasies." Eva had no idea what that long word meant, but nodded her head as if she understood. He began to knit again, continuing to look down as he spoke.

"I should have been more caring to her ways...more understanding about her needs, but I was too selfish...only thinking about myself. Now all I feel is guilt." Eva did understand what he was saying now. She had felt the same way when she was taking care of her father.

"I'm sure you did the best that you could at the time. Sometimes it is only later, when we are away from a situation, that we can see how we could have done things better."

"Ya...that's just how it is," he said, looking up at her.

"Now I've dropped more stitches," he said in frustration. Eva picked up the dropped stitches and carefully put them back on the needle.

"If only all our mistakes could be fixed so easily," he said.

She put her hand on his arm. "I think the best we can do is to learn from our mistakes and try to not repeat them. If we dwell on past mistakes, we won't move forward."

"You are a wise young woman," he said. "Thank you for making me feel better."

About two weeks later Edgar came back with another elderly gentleman.

"This is my new neighbor, Fred. He wants to knit, too. But is there a time when the shop isn't busy?" asked Edgar.

"He means when women wouldn't be around to see us knitting," added Fred. "We have a couple guys that want to come, but they don't want any women around making fun of them...if you get what I mean."

"I understand," said Eva. "I do have a woman's group that comes on Monday morning and some teenage girls who come on Saturdays, but women are apt to stop in anytime."

The two men looked at each other, scratching their heads, and thinking this wasn't a very good idea after all. Eva finally had a suggestion.

"During the winter I close early. You could come any day after four o'clock."

Edgar glanced at the window. "It gets dark outside around that time...anyone walking by could see us real good in here with the lights on."

But Fred had a comeback. "That's why some windows have heavy curtains, Eddie."

Eva nodded in agreement. Her light, see-through nylon curtains helped diffuse the sun in the daytime, but she knew if anyone stood close enough to the window at night they would be able to see figures moving about in the shop.

"You won't believe this," said Eva. "I bought a pair of drapes last fall, but haven't taken the time to buy a rod to put them on."

Fred got up from his chair to examine the window.

"Well, then, it's settled. Since you're kind enough to have us old geezers meet here every week, the least we can do is put up a pair of drapes. Got a yardstick?" he asked.

"No," said Eva, "but I do have a ruler."

Fred measured the window, allowing for several inches on

each side.

"I'll pick up a track and some cord tomorrow and we'll get those curtains up for you."

Later in the week they returned with two friends. Between the four of them, they had the track and curtains up in fifteen minutes and the rose flowered drapes slid smoothly across the window, separating all those inside from any curious eyes on the sidewalk. Now the men were satisfied no prying women's eyes would see them knitting and Eva was delighted to have privacy in the shop, especially with Karla at an age where she might be running around with nothing or next to nothing covering her in the early mornings or at bedtime.

Within a month there were six elderly men sitting around the table knitting: Edgar, Fred, Harold, Emil, George and Harbo. The round table was a bit crowded, especially at coffee time, so the next week Harold, Fred and George brought in a table and two chairs from a second-hand store. They had sanded and varnished the three pieces to make a matched set.

Then Edgar went back to the porch and rolled in a child's bicycle he had purchased at the same store. He picked up the excited Karla, set her on the seat and pushed her around the shop.

"Go faster," she hollered, so he steered the bike into the storeroom. He took off at a fast run to the cheers of his five buddies. After much huffing and puffing, Edgar gave the bike to Harold, who almost immediately had a very red face. Each man had his turn until Eva finally intervened and made Karla work the pedals herself, which wasn't as much fun.

"We will practice tomorrow and improve your balancing skills, but now the men must tend to their knitting." Karla pouted and stayed in the storeroom while everyone else returned to the shop.

Harbo didn't drink coffee, so every five weeks when he bought his rationed pound of coffee, he donated it to Eva. Emil and his wife, Olga, were both on diets and were cutting down on sweet desserts, so Eva was the recipient of their extra bags of sugar. George, who lived on the old family homestead with his wife,

Ann, had been a dairy farmer all his life and still had three cows left from the old herd. During the past summer two cows had calved, leaving him with an abundance of fresh milk. He sold some milk at the farm, but every week when he came to the shop to knit, he gave Eva a quart of fresh milk, some nice rich cream or a pound of butter.

Eva loved each one of the men, accepted their individual eccentricities and rarely asked personal questions. She had been curious about Fred, though, who was the only one who took off his shoes before entering the shop. Harbo, who was a bit of jokester, often made references to Newfoundland, where Fred had been born and raised.

"By the way, Fred, did you ever tell Eva about your father's boots."

All the men stopped knitting and began to chuckle.

"Okay, what's so funny?" asked Eva.

"It's a long story," remarked Fred. Karla overheard the conversation and when she heard the word *story* she came back to the shop and sidled up to Fred.

"I like long stories," she told him. He picked her up and put her on his knee. Eva could see he was in one of his story-telling moods, so she set some almond cake on the table and poured another round of coffee for the men and milk for Karla and Harbo. Fred cleared his throat and began.

"Once upon a time, when I was a little boy, I lived on a farm in a bleak and rugged place off the coast of Canada called Newfoundland. My father was as stern and unyielding as the rocky coastline of that remote, wild island and ruled the barn and house. No one could tell him what to do or how to do it. Mother was from a nearby village. She tried to keep the cottage neat and clean, but she knew from the first day she came here that she was up for a challenge."

"'Leave those filthy boots outside,' she'd say. But Father would clomp across the floor paying no attention to her and sit down in his chair demanding something to eat. When he was finished and went back outside, she'd sweep and scrub the floor, which would be spotless until he returned. Between breakfast, morning tea, dinner, afternoon tea and supper, Mother did a lot of cleaning and complaining, but neither did much good."

"Conditions were worse in winter. Ice froze everywhere, especially on my father's boots. But it wasn't just frozen water on his boots. It was...," Fred glanced at Karla, "all that smelly soft stuff in the barn that farmers are always stepping in. Mixed with layers of straw this soft stuff froze on his boots." Everyone laughed, including Eva, who knew what he was referring to. Karla didn't understand, but she giggled, too.

"It was the coldest day of the year and my father had to come into the house almost every hour to thaw out in front of the fire, but the muck and straw on his boots didn't melt; it just kept building up and his boots grew heavier. He could barely lift his feet when he came in at three o'clock. He was tired and cold and pulled his chair so close to the fire that his boots were resting on the grate. By now my mother had ceased to tell him to take off the filthy boots. She gave him some tea and went back to the kitchen to prepare supper."

"Father usually drank his tea and then went back outside, but this day he laid back and fell asleep, not waking up until he smelled burnt leather and felt a hot, burning sensation on his feet. The hot fire had dried out the muck and the straw and somehow his boots had caught on fire. His loud hollering made mother and me rush into the sitting room and my father was hopping around trying to put out the fire. 'Get outside in the snow, you fool,' my mother shouted. He stood in the middle of the room, the flames licking the length of his boots, looked at us and dashed outside."

"Afterwards he walked gingerly into the house. His burnt socks were black and steaming and he threw them and what was left of his boots into the fire. My mother looked at him crossly. 'You could have burned the house down.' My father looked like a whipped dog. When mother turned to go back to the kitchen I saw a wide smile of satisfaction on her face."

"He never wore his boots in the house again, always leaving

them in a cubicle by the door. I did the same and have never worn my shoes in the house since that day."

Karla turned a serious face toward Fred.

"Did your father's toes get burned?"

"I remember they were pretty red and sore. Mother slathered lard all over them for several days, but he never complained...he didn't dare to say a word."

Everyone laughed when Karla unbuckled her shoes and placed them by the door beside Fred's.

It wasn't long before the men finished their olive-colored scarves and were ready to tackle knitting hats, and later vests.

Karla mastered the art of riding a bike very quickly and graduated to the great outdoors. Eva tired quickly running beside her on the sidewalk and lesser traveled roads, so it wasn't long before she found a cheap woman's bicycle at the second-hand store. They liked to ride down the dirt road to Arne's old farm where they carried vegetables and eggs and sometimes a plucked chicken home in the wire baskets of their bikes. Sometimes as a special treat they rode to another farm that sold ice cream in sugar cones. These were happy times that Eva would later look back on with great fondness.

Two Years Later

By the year 1944, Doris Day was singing *Sentimental Journey* on the radio. This song was Eva's favorite. She would find herself humming it all night long. Another favorite was Frank Sinatra's *Put Your Dreams Away for Another Day.* She was used to putting away her dreams, but sometimes, especially when spinning or knitting, she pulled them out to relive again.

Rebecca stopped in one morning saying she had heard from Samuel. He hoped Eva was well and wanted her to know about a Swedish diplomat named Raoul Wallenberg who was saving Jews in Hungary. Because of Sweden's neutrality, he was able to give the Hungarian Jews official protection papers and hide them in Budapest houses that flew the Swedish flag. There they were safe from the Nazis. Eva was very proud of this brave man and her former homeland of Sweden.

On November 7, 1944, President Roosevelt was elected for his fourth term and the war continued into the winter.

Eva was grateful for her men's and women's knitting groups, both for the diversion of their wonderful presence and company, and for the many food gifts they continued to bring to the shop. They were glad for a place to meet with their friends and enjoy the cheery atmosphere of the shop, giving everyone a chance to forget about the war for a couple hours or so.

President Roosevelt died on April 12, 1945, and Vice President Harry Truman became president. Surprisingly, on April 30, Adolph Hitler committed suicide, and Germany surrendered on May 7. The war ended in Europe, but now the radio concentrated on the Japanese.

On August 6, the United States dropped an atomic bomb on Hiroshima, practically wiping that Japanese city off the map. Seventy-five thousand people were killed. Eva could not fathom a bomb of such magnitude that would demolish a city much larger than Somerville. Two days later another bomb was dropped on Nagasaki, killing just as many Japanese. She thought about Sayuri and Mr. Kaneko. The Japanese surrendered. Fifty-seven nations had been involved in this six-year-long war. The war was over and the people of America celebrated.

When Eva suggested having a party at the yarn shop, every man and woman from the knitting clubs came with their wives and husbands. Emma and the young girls brought their boyfriends, neighbors dropped in, as did the Bergstroms, Ingrid, Olle and the children. Everyone brought something...sandwiches and casseroles, breads and cheese and all kinds of desserts. The Andrews Sisters were singing ***Boogie Woogie Bugle Boy*** on the radio. It was Karla's favorite song. She took Eva's hand and began dancing, and soon the tables were pushed back and everyone was doing their version of the boogie woogie. Even old Edgar was dancing with the widow Johnson.

The Beckworths didn't come. When Rebecca didn't show up for Monday knitting club, Eva took the bus to Bedford. No one answered her knock on the door. Walking around the house, she saw Rebecca in the backyard lying in a hammock.

"Oh, Eva. I didn't know you were here...and to think you caught me napping! Come into the kitchen and have a bite to eat." Rebecca seemed disoriented, but managed to pour two glasses of lemonade and arrange crackers and cheese on a plate.

"I haven't been sleeping well," she admitted after a long silence. "All this talk about hundreds of thousands of war casualties and the many wounded who are coming home. You've probably heard about the atrocities to the Jews. The death marches, the concentration camps and the gassing of..." Rebecca's hands flew to her face and she began sobbing.

Eva put her arm around her friend to comfort her. "I know," whispered Eva. They held each other for a long time.

"No one has heard from Samuel in almost a year. Other helpers have had miserable ends," Rebecca said. "There's talk he might be... dead."

Eva was stunned at the news. Rebecca went over to the sink, splashed her face with cold water and turned around, forcing a smile.

"Enough of that. Lets go for a walk and get some fresh air."

They walked through the garden and past the little barn. Seeing two heifers and a calf in the pasture brought back fond memories to Eva and she talked a little about her days at the Lindholm estate, but only the happy times. Hearing this was good medicine for Rebecca.

"David is in 4-H now. He won that darker Jersey as a calf three years ago and buys hay, grain and sawdust from money he earns on his paper route. He loves to fuss with the cattle, showing them in the fair and winning blue ribbons every year." Eva was impressed. She hadn't seen David much since he began elementary school in Bedford. Now he and Karla each had a new circle of friends. However, Bedford was a very small town and had no high school. Students going into seventh grade were bussed to Lexington from seventh to twelfth grades. Now that David was twelve and Karla ten, Eva supposed he would be going to Lexington Junior High next year.

"I remember how David used to dote on Karla, sharing toys and picking her up when she fell down." Rebecca laughed. "He's still a very caring boy and very responsible with his cows."

"Karla loves animals, especially horses," Eva said. "We don't have room for a horse, so I take her over to Watson's Stables every Saturday to ride, even though it costs $2 an hour."

"I used to ride horses, too, a long time ago," said Rebecca, chuckling to herself. "Farm horses that my grandfather used for plowing and cultivating his vegetable fields. Not the usual riding horse type. They were Belgians with large gentle heads and broad backs that were difficult for my short legs to grip around and I'd have to hold onto their long manes to keep from sliding off."

Eva smiled at the humorous picture Rebecca painted and remembered Karl with his beautiful work horses. "I'd have to say cows are my favorite animal, but I used to love seeing the big horses at the Lindholm estate pulling large loads of hay across the field to the barn." Eva grew thoughtful then, and Rebecca continued.

"David wants to be a veterinarian. Several years ago he read an article in some kid's magazine about a doctor who traveled from farm to farm treating the farmers' sick animals. Ever since then that's all he can talk about."

"That's an interesting coincidence," replied Eva. "For the past few years I've subscribed to the Jack and Jill magazine for Karla to read. She loves getting something in the mail. Karla usually thumbs through the pages and then leaves it on the table...unless she comes across a picture of a horse or story about horses. Then she takes the magazine to her room and I never see it again. She was very impressed by an article about The Frontier

Nursing Service. Have you ever heard of it?"

"No I haven't, but nursing is a very good career for a young girl, don't you think?" Eva thought back to when she had cared for her father...all the heavy responsibility she'd felt, the frustrations, and the feelings of guilt she'd had afterwards.

"I wouldn't make a very good nurse," she sighed. "But nursing isn't what interests Karla. The service has couriers, young girls on horseback, who ride through the hills of a place called Kentucky delivering supplies to remote clinics. They also groom and care for the horses. Karla can't wait until she is sixteen so she can apply to work there."

"It sounds exciting to me," said Rebecca.

"Do you know anything about Kentucky?" asked Eva.

"Ah...the land of hillbillies and moonshine!" Rebecca laughed, then saw the serious look on Eva's face. "Oh that's just a joke. Actually Kentucky is a beautiful place of luxurious mansions and sprawling horse farms with white fences that go on for miles and miles."

"Sounds lovely. Is it very far away?"

Rebecca thought for a moment. "Hmm...probably a good two-day trip on an overnight train."

"Oh my...that's a long way," remarked Eva.

"Well, you don't have to worry about that now. In five years Karla will probably change her mind a hundred times or more. That's what I did...everything from wanting to be a movie star to teaching school. There are so many options for women these days. She might even want to take over the yarn shop."

"That would be nice, but I don't think she'd consider that."

"Life is uncertain," replied Rebecca. "You never know what tomorrow will bring."

Eva came home with a fresh bottle of milk and a pound of butter that Rebecca had made from extra cream. She wouldn't take any money for it, so Eva asked her to stop in at the yarn shop sometime and pick out some skeins of yarn.

At breakfast the next morning, Karla remarked how delicious

the toast was. "This is great tasting butter."

"Rebecca gave it to me yesterday. David has cows and they sell milk and butter."

"David makes butter?" replied Karla with her silly high-pitched laugh as if butter making was only woman's work.

Eva finished pouring two glasses of milk and then replied, "No, Rebecca is the one who makes the butter."

Karla turned her nose up after the first sip of milk. "This milk tastes odd, sort of like the smell of a cow." Eva hadn't noticed; to her it was cold, fresh and delicious. Karla's glass remained nearly full on the table. "For goodness sakes, Karla, just finish your milk. It's better for you than the pasteurized kind."

"You finish it then. I'm gonna be late for school." Karla then picked up her books and stomped out the door. This was the first time Karla had spoken this way to Eva, who thought at the time that her daughter was acting much like Ingrid had in the old days. Eva never had talked back to her mother in this way. She hoped it was just a one-time thing and not some 'Ingrid streak' developing in her daughter.

That afternoon the mailman brought a letter from New Sweden.

August 1944

Dear Eva

On the first of August we have another big boy of eleven pounds. We name him August. My belly was so huge we thought he would come a month earlier. Midsummer was a beautiful day with nice cool breeze, so I enjoyed the slow dancing and good food and getting together with town folk. Arne had a proud smile when the men joked about what a good breeder I was, but I was feeling more like a big cow and couldn't face them. August cried being birthed and is still crying unless I carry him around all day in the new sling that Arne made for me. Mother say he is quiet when he can hear my heart beating and I think she is right about that. She laugh at the thought of me still carrying him around when he is 6 years old and I have to laugh, too. Everyone else is healthy and busy in the potato fields picking potato bugs off the plants. Annika is 8 and big help setting the table, clearing the dirty dishes and loves to play with soapsuds in the dishpan, but not so good at scrubbing dirty pans. She smart like Arne and loves school. Teacher say for her to skip third grade and go to fourth grade in September. Stina likes reading. She has no children and has always favored Annika, teaching her early to write English words and bring little books for her to read. Arne just come in from fields for snack. He say hello. I go now.

Love,

Dagny

Karla 1949

Karla and her fourteen-year-old friends sat around the large oak table supposedly doing their homework when Rebecca and David dropped in unexpectedly. Eva was aware of girlish giggles and hushed tones of conversation in the background as she put a pound of butter in the small refrigerator she kept downstairs. David stood awkwardly behind his mother. He was a head taller than Rebecca and he'd developed a muscular frame. Eva could see one strong forearm and the car keys he held firmly in his hand. "When you came in, I wondered who that handsome young man was behind you," she said, smiling at David.

Rebecca glanced back proudly at her son. "David is learning to drive, so he brought me over today."

"Oh, my, almost sixteen already?" said Eva. "I can remember when you were only four." David smiled, his eyes shifting briefly toward Karla and then back across the room.

As far as Eva could tell, Karla hadn't acknowledged her guests, but she didn't say anything, thinking it better not to make an issue of her daughter's rudeness. The girls looked busy with their homework, talking amongst themselves in low tones.

Eva motioned toward one of the other tables. “Please have a seat. I’ll get the coffee tray. Would you like milk and cookies, David?”

“I’d rather have coffee,” he replied. “If you have enough.”

“So you’ve outgrown milk now?” said Eva playfully.

He grinned shyly. “No, Mom still makes me drink a glass with every meal at home.”

Eva heard the girls tittering in the background and hoped they weren’t making fun of David. Karla’s quick glance was met with Eva’s slight scowl and she knew her mother was upset... probably because she didn’t go ‘gaga’ over David, who she noticed was helping himself to the chocolate chip cookies. Eva got her daughter’s attention again. “There’s more cookies on the counter if you and your friends want some.” When Eva sat down to chat with Rebecca, David was engrossed in his Driver’s Manual, although he did look up when Karla got up to get a plateful of cookies.

Karla never mentioned David’s name, so at suppertime Eva did.

“I can’t believe how tall David is, and already driving a car. Rebecca told me that he belongs to 4-H and has shown his cows and calves at various fairs and won a lot of blue ribbons.” The curtain of silence that followed seemed to end the conversation. It felt as if Eva was talking to herself, but she continued.

“David is an A student and wants to be a veterinarian.”

Finally her daughter responded. “That's why he always has his nose stuck in a book at school. I don’t think he goes out for any sports, does he?”

“I have no idea. I doubt he has time for such frivolous activities”

Karla rolled her eyes. "Playing sports isn't frivolous. It builds character."

“Perhaps so,” said Eva, “but you could have had more character and respect by being a little more sociable this afternoon.”

Karla sighed. "I had to pay attention to my own friends."

"It would have been polite if you'd at least said hello to him."

"David and I might have been friends when we were little, Mama, but we have nothing in common now."

Eva had said what was on her mind. She didn't want an argument and decided to let the subject drop.

It was two years later before David's name was mentioned again. Karla was fifteen. Entering high school was the steppingstone from Karla's childhood. Gone were the horse collection, the cowboy boots, the weekly horseback riding and the Roy Rogers movies. Until recently Eva had been her daughter's best friend, but now Karla had transformed into a giggly, boy-crazy adolescent whose clothes, hair style, bright red lipstick and nail polish were identical to those of her three friends who all lived for Friday night at the roller skating rink and went to every romantic movie on Saturdays. Karla rarely confided in her mother anymore.

Walking down the sidewalk, the four girls looked alike. It was only when the sun caught Karla's very blonde head that Eva knew which one was her daughter. She was pleased that Karla still brought her friends to the shop after school and she made sure there was plenty of milk and cookies, brownies or cake on hand for an afternoon snack. Marilyn, Joanne and Judy seemed like nice girls, always politely saying hello before dropping their books on the old round table by the window and becoming absorbed in their own little world of laughter, gossip and whispers about more intimate subjects. Eva enjoyed their frivolous comments, references to teachers, boyfriends, their parents and all the foolish things that modern teenagers talked about these days, something she had never experienced during her own secluded youth in the forests of Norrland.

Karla was always willing to wait on customers, and sometimes Eva took advantage of the girls being there to leave the shop and do errands. One day she was gone longer than expected. Four wonderingly expectant faces turned to look in Eva's direction as soon as she walked through the door. After exploding into a round of giggling, Karla stopped long enough say that some guy had come in looking for her.

"He's really nice looking, for an older guy," said Joanne.

Eva was hoping it might have been Samuel. "Did he have dark curly hair and long black eyelashes?"

Judy piped up and said he was blond and blue-eyed.

"And he had big muscles that bulged out when he crossed his arms over his chest," added Karla. Eva grew weak and sat down dejectedly; she had missed seeing Mats for the second time.

After a round of giggles, Marilyn said, "he leaned against the wall grinning at us all and asked which one of us was the shop keeper's daughter, but we all shrugged our shoulders to keep him guessing."

Karla spoke next. "Then he walked slowly around the table looking us over one by one and said, 'I wonder who it might be'...until I started blushing like crazy."

"He told us that we were all very pretty," continued Karla, "and then he pointed to me."

"'Yes, you are definitely the one,' he said. "I could feel myself getting redder and redder because he was looking right at me with a silly lopsided grin. Then he told us he'd be back later, but I forgot to ask his name."

All eyes were fastened on Eva in the all-too-quiet room as the girls waited for her to reveal who the mysterious stranger was. Lost in thought, she mumbled softly, "his name is Mats Kronberg...an old friend of mine from Sweden."

After Karla's friends left, she was visibly concerned and spoke to her mother. "Is he my...my father?"

"Heavens no!" exclaimed Eva. "We were neighbors. Our fathers were very good friends."

Karla seemed neither relieved nor saddened by the revelation and resumed her studying.

"Did Mats say what time he'd be back?"

"No," said Karla. "I think he said something about going to dinner, but I don't know if he meant with us or not." Eva was excited thinking she would finally see Mats again and went upstairs to put away the groceries. This gave her a chance to be alone with her thoughts. She and Mats had lost touch with each other over the war years. He had made such big plans for himself...getting married and being an architect. And then everything had changed for him. She felt a rush of heat envisioning Mats in his uniform and thoughts of long-ago brought the familiar fluttering in her stomach. For a while she was that young girl back in Sweden.

Her overwhelming sense of anticipation simmered down somewhat when she heard Karla's footsteps on the wooden stairway. Eva went into the bathroom, splashed cold water on her face and looked in the mirror. Her face and neck were flushed and she tried brushing off this foolishness by talking out loud. "I'm an adult now. I'm Karla's mother and I'm too old for this blushing nonsense."

"Are you talking to yourself again?" she heard Karla say.

"I was trying to decide whether to start supper cooking or wait and see if Mats comes back. It's awfully hot up here in the kitchen tonight."

"Why don't we go down to the porch and wait," said Karla. "It will be cooler there."

As the minutes ticked by on the porch, Eva became uneasy. "Well, I might as well be spinning as to be sitting out here twiddling my thumbs and accomplishing nothing."

They both went back inside and Karla picked up her algebra book to work on problems she knew were wrong. Finally she put the paper away and called it good enough. She couldn't concentrate anyway. Her mind was on Mats, too. She thought her mother liked him, but it would suit her if he didn't show up tonight.

"At first I was sort of hoping Mats was my father, but I'm glad he isn't," said Karla. Her comment surprised Eva, whose fingers pulled away from the yarn and fell to her lap.

"You don't like Mats?"

"Oh, he's nice enough and very good looking, but he has those roaming eyes. Anyway, you know about sailors...they have a girl in every port, and I'm sure he does!"

Eva nodded in agreement, remembering Sayuri and how Mats liked watching the girls on the ship. She resumed her spinning while Karla sat by the window looking out.

"Mats was carefree and fun loving, always trying to make me laugh or blush," recalled Eva. "But I never fully trusted him as far as other girls were concerned. I've met a lot of American men and they are the same, but your father was different. He was gentle, yet strong, usually serious, but he often made me laugh out loud with his stories of animals...and he had a caring heart. From the beginning I knew I could always trust what he said or did."

"I wish you had a photograph of my father. Do I look like him at all?" asked Karla.

Eva sat back to remember Karl's handsome face. "You have his blond hair and thoughtful, caring eyes...that blue-green color of the rising waves just before they tumble back into the sea. And you have his warm smile. He is the most genuine man I ever met...besides your grandfather and Mr. Kronberg, of course."

Eva had told Karla little things about her father through the years, but tonight Karla listened in earnest. Eva thought back to just a few hours ago when she was upstairs with her mind full of Mats and her great desire to see him. Now, remembering Karl so fondly, she was embarrassed for thinking those thoughts.

"I'm rather glad Mats didn't come back tonight, too," she said emphatically, not disclosing what she had feared might have happened if he had. Would she have been so thrilled to see him that she might have engaged in something foolish? The thought almost terrified her now.

"Mom? Did you hear what I said?"

"Sorry, honey, I didn't hear anything but my own thoughts."

"Can we go to Sweden some day? I'd like to meet my father."

"I wish he could meet you, too," said Eva. She didn't want to discourage her daughter, nor did she wish to encourage a trip that might not turn out the way they expected. How would such a meeting take place? Karl was married now and she didn't know where he lived. She supposed there might be a way of finding out, but what if he still lived on the family estate? Surely his mother would not allow her in the house. Such a meeting would bring up more ugly stories to tell Karla about her year working at the Lindholm Estate. It was possible that even Karl would not want to see either of them and that would be even harder to accept. The whole idea needed a lot of thinking and it was already giving her a headache.

"Maybe next summer?" asked Karla.

"I don't know," said Eva. "A trip like that would need a lot of preparation. Either I'd have to close the shop or find someone responsible enough to tend the business while we're gone."

"Closing the shop would be a good idea," said Karla. "I think a vacation would do you good."

"We'll see," said her mother, but the whole idea of going back to Sweden made Eva nervous.

About a month later a letter came from Mats.

Dear Eva,

I'm on midnight watch. Real slow out there on the Pacific tonight…nothing like it was during the war, so I have some spare time to write.

Sorry I missed seeing you last month. It was fun talking with Karla and her friends. She's a knockout, just like her mother! I intended to come back later, but the guys had other plans and we had to be back in Boston before midnight or we'd be AWOL and I can't be accused of doing that again!

We shipped out to California the next day and spent a few days lying out on the beach before beginning maneuvers in the Pacific again. I'm telling you, this is the life. I'm glad now things worked out the way they did with Jenny and architectural school. I'm not made for inside work and my English was never very good, although I've learned a lot in the Navy…including some not so good English, too! Joining the Navy was the best thing I ever did. I don't think I'm made for marriage, either.

I think of you now and then, as a child in your cottage back in Sweden with your red hair going all which-a-way, as a lovely young girl kneading bread in the kitchen, milking your cow in the barn and the good times we had on the ship. You must be more beautiful than ever now. Gee, I'm getting a rise just thinking about you.

Hey, don't let your husband read this. I remember him at the shop that day you went to Boston. He surely doted on Karla and did a fine job making her cradle, but somehow he just didn't seem your type. But what do I know? There's someone for everyone, right?

One more thing. Johan writes once in a while to keep me posted on Mother and my other brothers, who are all fine, by the way. Well, in his last letter he mentioned Karl. Word has it that Karl got divorced from his wife and went to Stockholm to attend a big university there for four years. His brother, Gunnar, finally got married and took over the home place. And you won't believe this… Karl sold his share of the farm and went to America to get a doctorate or something like that. Always sort of pictured Karl as a doctor, didn't you? Thought you might like to know.

Write back soon.

As Ever,

Mats

Eva was ecstatic about the news of Karl. She had been worried about his drinking and the unhappiness that might have caused it. In that respect she had included him in her prayers every night. Now, sitting at her desk, endless tears of joy tumbled down her cheeks, causing numerous inky splats on Mats' letter. It didn't matter; she had read his letter so many times that she knew the last paragraph by heart.

The letter sounded so much like Mats that it made her laugh, especially because he had assumed she was married to Arne. Mats was always jumping to conclusions. She must write to Mats, admitting her former relationship with Karl and that Karla was a result of that liaison.

But for now, Eva could not get over the fact that Karl was a doctor. She remembered how tender and caring he had been when he took the glass sliver out of her hand, how patient he had been with the cows and knowledgeable about treating their diseases and injuries, how precisely he had cut the big red apple into eight perfect slices that late summer day in the orchard.

She was comforted by these happy memories and gladdened by the thought that maybe Karl might still be somewhere in America. She spun her globe around to the great United States. Karl could be anywhere from New York to California, from Wisconsin to Texas. America was such a huge place. Sweden had seemed large when she lived there, but on the map it was very small in comparison to America. A disheartening thought occurred to her. If Karl was still in America, she might never find him. There would have been a much better chance of finding him in Sweden.

Sophomore Revelations

High School presented new problems and situations that affected both Eva and Karla. Eva missed the lively conversation and silly antics of her daughter's friends who, because of numerous after-school activities, now seldom frequented the round table by the window. Karla also stayed after school for French Club, Drama Club, Chorus and a feeble attempt at field hockey practice. Although she still enjoyed riding a horse once in a while, Karla had to finally admit she wasn't cut out for competitive sports and she soon gave up on field hockey. Spectator sports was another thing entirely; not a week went by that she and her friends were not cheering for their high school football team…or so Eva thought.

"So, tell me about football," Eva asked after the first game.

"I had a great time," said Karla. "Michael said 'hi' to me."

"Who is Michael?"

"He's Captain of the football team," replied Karla. "And the cutest guy in school."

"Wasn't he playing in the game?"

"Sometimes he was, and sometimes he was on the sidelines."

"So, what is the point of football?"

"Well, the guys run back and forth throwing or kicking a ball across the field trying to make goals, I guess. I don't watch the game so much. I go to be with my friends and walk around hoping to see the guys on the team."

"Let me get this straight," said her mother. "While the game is going on, you walk around with your friends hoping to see the players, but you don't watch them play football?"

"Sometimes we watch, but you can't see their faces when they're wearing helmets."

"Oh, I see," said Eva finally, even though she didn't understand at all.

Lately Eva found herself wasting much time looking out the window, hoping someone would come in to buy yarn. Tending shop was like missing a bus and the ensuing frustration of waiting for the next one to arrive. She had to admit she was bored. Karla was in school, the various knitting groups had dissolved and all of a sudden her days were empty and far too quiet, unusual for someone who usually loved quiet.

Sad as it was, wartime had held an exhilaration and anticipation that was difficult to describe. The unknown element that war created tended to bring people closer together, promoting more amicability, patience and understanding between even the most difficult and demanding personalities. Somehow everyone had been set on more common ground and their dissimilarities had not seemed so important.

Fortunately, almost all of the drab, olive-colored yarn had been used up and sales of brightly colored yarns were increasing. However, many customers didn't have time for coffee and gossip as they had before, and Eva knew the reason why. Television had entered the parlors and living rooms of many people, making it unnecessary for them to go out to their friends and family for entertainment. Women found it easier to sit at home and amuse themselves by watching talking images on a screen. Where did these images come from? These large picture boxes with radio-like voices were a puzzle to Eva. She still hadn't figured out how music came over her radio.

Every day she heard glowing accounts of the advantages of having a television in the home, especially the seven words: "Now we know where our children are."

She had stupidly asked a customer where the children were now and the customer had said, "home watching television, of course."

Eva was quick to speak her mind against children sitting in one spot for hours with their eyes fastened to moving images on a screen when they should be outside playing and getting exercise or helping about the house. Watching television stole precious hours from women as well...especially mothers who should be teaching their children how to read and write or showing them the correct way to perform household chores. How many women put aside their daily household routines to sit idly in front of an amusement box? Some even said they watched programs as a family while eating supper. Eva was not about to buy anything that replaced good conversation and the enjoyment of a fine meal. It was enough to put up with the radio blaring out the latest songs in Karla's bedroom at night.

Eva had first seen a television set at the Bergstrom's. She had sat silently for a short time and then made an excuse to leave. Mrs. Bergstrom had looked up and waved goodbye, making no attempt to see Eva to the door.

Emily hadn't been to the yarn shop for a long time. Eva had refrained from asking about Emily since the time Mrs. Bergstrom sadly revealed they weren't speaking to each other. That was about a year ago when Mrs. Bergstrom had dropped into the yarn shop.

She had come in alone, and not in the best of humor. As she had walked from bin to bin picking out skeins of yarn, it was evident that her dress fit too snug around her widening waist and

Eva had hoped the small buttons on her tight bodice wouldn't give way under the strain of her abundant breasts.

Placing an armful of yarn on the table, Mrs. Bergstrom had made herself at home in Eva's large wooden rocking chair. "It feels good to sit down," she had said, sighing heavily. "So, how is Karla these days? I don't suppose she's old enough to be interested in boys yet." As usual, Mrs. Bergstrom hadn't waited for Eva's response. "Why is it that Protestant girls are so taken in by Catholic boys? First it was Emily, and now Emma is going through the same phase. I hope you don't have this problem with Karla."

Busy preparing the lunch tray, Eva hadn't answered soon enough for her visitor.

"You do understand the dangers of girls dating Catholic boys, don't you, dear?"

One had to be careful not to offend Mrs. Bergstrom by disagreeing with her, so Eva had poured the coffee while thoughtfully choosing her response. "I think marriage should be between people of the same faith, but I have friends of many different religious beliefs. Is dating a Catholic so serious?"

"Well, of course it is!" Mrs. Bergstrom had snapped, her eyes wide and glaring. "Dating leads to all sorts of predicaments. You know how teenage boys are these days. What if the girl becomes pregnant?" Then she had blinked and looked around the room. Of course this was something Eva did know about. Had Mrs. Bergstrom suddenly remembered?

"Well, I've always forbidden my girls to go out with Catholic boys, and I'll tell you why." Mrs. Bergstrom had cleared her throat and continued. "The Catholic religion is very strict about their members marrying outside their faith. If you or I, heaven forbid, wanted to marry a Catholic, we would have to take instruction in Catholicism and promise to baptize and raise our children in the Catholic religion."

As Mrs. Bergstrom had continued her one-sided conversation against Catholics, her comments had triggered the memory of a similar discussion that Eva had heard between Mr. Kronberg and her father. They had been adamantly discussing the dangers of Lutherans associating with Catholics, especially between men and women contemplating marriage. They had both agreed that none of their children would ever marry a Catholic, and she remembered how they had laughed afterwards when Mr. Kronberg said, “well, Gus, we don’t have to worry much about that, do we? They wouldn’t be able to find one around here anyway.”

Eva hadn’t understood any of this until now. Surely she wouldn’t consider going against her father’s wishes and she had found herself heartily agreeing with Mrs. Bergstrom.

“Well, good! I’m glad you have decided on the right course.”

But it had seemed perplexing to Eva how she might tell the difference between a Catholic and a Protestant.

“Mrs. Bergstrom, do Catholic boys look different from other boys?”

“No…they look just like us, especially the fair Irish, but you can tell once you know their last name. Irish names usually begin with ‘Mc’ or ‘O’, as in O'Donnell or O’Connor. Italian names might begin with ‘De’ and end with ‘i’ or ‘o’. French names are harder to figure out…they just sound very ‘French’. Many French names end in ‘ette’ or ‘eau’. Of course there are exceptions to every rule. There are other Irish names like Kelly and Riley and I’m sure it is the same with the French and Italians.”

“I’m so confused,” said Eva despairingly. “I’ll never be able to figure all that out.”

“Don’t you worry now. Just call me on the telephone. I know a Catholic name when I hear it.”

“But I don’t have telephone.”

“Well, I’d say it’s high time you got one. How can you run a business without a telephone?” Eva hadn’t had an answer for that.

The subject of religion came up occasionally in the shop. Eva learned that most of her Protestant customers would not allow their teenagers to date Catholics either. Ingrid thought the idea silly, but then she and Olle didn’t seem very religious and only went to church on Easter Sunday. Rebecca had experienced a somewhat similar problem when she was growing up in New York. Her parents had expected her to marry a nice Jewish boy, but she had fallen in love with Dave. After graduating from college, they had eloped.

Eva handled each day as it came and didn't worry too much about her daughter. Karla was pretty level-headed and easy to get along with. They'd never had any serious disagreements, that is until after Ingrid talked Eva into buying a telephone.

"Then we can talk every day. Won't that be fun?" she remembered her sister saying. Eva thought it an extravagant expense until Ingrid said how much easier and quicker it would be to order all her yarn and business supplies by telephone. Olle informed her she could also deduct these calls on her income tax as a business deduction.

For the first week conversing with Ingrid every morning was fun, but soon monotony set in and Eva grew tired of hearing every cute thing that Gus and Nina did, listening to Ingrid's plans for the day and the rehashing of every television program that she and Olle had watched the night before. Sometimes Eva didn't bother to answer the phone, but the constant ringing was annoying. Of course if a customer was there Eva would promptly excuse herself, allowing Ingrid to talk for a few minutes before telling her a customer was waiting. Ingrid didn't take kindly to these abrupt endings and over time she stopped calling every day.

It wasn't long before Karla took over the telephone after school, evenings and weekends, its jarring ring often startling Eva from her peaceful thoughts, a book she was reading or even from sleep. Strange voices invaded their home, mostly those of young boys with whom Eva was not familiar. Often Karla spoke in hushed tones with her back towards her mother and, after hanging up the phone, she'd go back to her homework without saying a word. Their chummy mother-daughter nighttime chats were a thing of the past, the friendly atmosphere evaporating into secretive silence.

One evening Karla appeared overly engrossed in homework.

Eva knew she wasn't studying; the pages of her book never turned. But Eva continued with her sewing until a muffled voice came from behind Karla's history book.

"Michael wants me to go to the movies Saturday night. Can I go?"

"Who is Michael? Does he have a last name?"

"O'Reilly."

'O'...an Irish Catholic for sure, thought Eva, visualizing Mrs. Bergstrom's adamant face as clearly as if she was sitting in this very room.

"You can't go to the movies with anyone named O'Reilly."

"You're joking, right?" said Karla.

"No. I'm quite serious."

"What's wrong with the name O'Reilly?"

"It's a Catholic name and I will not allow you to date any Catholic boys."

"Mama! That's outrageous! Johanne is Catholic and I go roller skating with her every week."

The time had come for that conversation Eva had been putting off about why Karla shouldn't date Catholic boys. Even though she had rehearsed her little speech many times, she still was not prepared to lecture her daughter on a subject she didn't fully understand herself.

Karla listened attentively at first and then sat in disbelief, her face flushed and defiant.

"I just want to go to the movies. I'm not going to marry him!"

"I'm sure there are lots of nice Protestant boys who'd love to take you to the movies if you'd give them a chance. David Beckworth for one. At least we know he's from a fine family."

"David? I don't want to be seen at the movies with him! I want to go with Michael. He's on the football team and one of the most popular guys at school."

"What's popular got to do with going to a movie?" asked her mother.

"You don't get it, Mama. It's all about being seen with the right boys. If you want to be popular you have to date popular boys. I can't be seen going out with a 'nobody'."

Eva didn't understand all this popularity talk and Karla's pleading got her nowhere.

"So, what am I supposed to do, ask each guy what religion he is before accepting a date?" said Karla sarcastically. "And what do I tell Michael, that my mother won't let me go out with you because you are Catholic? I'd be the laughing stock of the school."

"Tell him whatever you want, but I forbid you to go out with Michael and that's the end of it."

Karla slammed her history book on the table and stomped into her bedroom.

For several days Eva received the silent treatment. Karla's uncooperative attitude and moodiness continued, as well as occasional outbursts of temper. Eva held her ground against her daughter's defiant behavior, but as time went on she grew concerned with the widening gap of stubborn silence growing between them.

As an obedient, amenable child, Eva had always respected the authority of her parents, accepted their views, and abided by their rules...rules that were made for her safety and wellbeing. It had never occurred to her to argue against their beliefs and opinions. So why was Karla acting like this? A little voice in her head said, because she is just like Ingrid. Eva remembered how Ingrid had hurt their parents by running away. Thinking about this frightened her and she considered changing her mind, but Mrs. Bergstrom's words came sharply to mind and she stood her ground.

Karla continued to be the moody, stubborn stranger who responded in one-word sentences, a shrug of her shoulders or a rolling of her eyes. She tried to avoid her mother as much as possible by arriving home late from school, sleeping until noon on Saturdays and complaining of Sunday morning headaches to elude church.

"You're prejudiced, Mom, and that's a bad thing," Karla told her mother one day. Eva heard the word prejudiced, but it was the

Mom word that got her attention. All of a sudden, she wasn't Mama anymore...she was Mom!

Eva remembered hearing Rebecca and Samuel say the word prejudice, but to her that meant Hitler's dislike of the Jews and the fact that he thought they were an inferior race. She had no dislike for Catholics or Jewish people, nor did she think either was inferior to her or anyone else.

"I'm not prejudiced, Karla. I would just rather you dated Protestant boys."

Karla thought for a moment. In history she had been studying the problem of prejudice in regard to Negroes and Caucasians. "Okay, Mom, then you would have no objection to my dating a Negro boy... as long as he was Protestant. Right?"

Eva had seen Negroes in books and in New York City, but dating one was something she had never considered.

Karla had a smug look on her face that made Eva suspicious. Karla's question had caught her mother off guard and for a moment Eva was at a complete loss for words. Then the telephone rang and she hastened to answer it. For once Eva welcomed Michael O'Reilly's voice and held out the receiver for Karla. "It's for you."

Eva got ready for bed and read for a while, but she wasn't able to concentrate and turned off the light. Indecision was like a thief, robbing her of a good night's sleep. Alone in the overwhelming darkness, she battled with her thoughts. Was all this bickering worth the constant agitation and disruption of their daily routines? Are the differences in religion so important in life that they should split families apart? Was she doing the right thing by restricting her daughter? Karla had once called her pig-headed. This pig-headed image was not an attractive one. Eva finally put all her troubles in God's hands and fell asleep.

Eva awakened early and sat by the upstairs window overlooking Main Street. The misty grayness of early dawn slowly gave way to muted shades of blue and green. Then the sky, as if painted by the rays of the sun, became suddenly swathed in a brilliant blue. Slowly the sun brushed the tree tops and brightened the roof ridges. The shiny chrome top of an early bus sparkled in the sun as it stopped to drop off a couple of men in dirty work clothes, probably on their way home from the night shift. Three well-dressed businessmen with briefcases waited to board the bus. Although these men had different jobs and did not wear similar clothes, they were all hard-working men and deep inside they were in all probability pretty much alike. What difference did it make if they were Catholic or Protestant?

The dawn had brought a new discovery to Eva, but she was still reticent about altering her decision in regard to Karla dating Catholic boys. She didn't want to offend Mrs. Bergstrom, but neither did she want to push her daughter away and hamper their good relationship. Fortunately Karla was late getting up that morning and in her rush to get ready for school hadn't mentioned their discussion of the previous night. Indecision filled the idle moments between customers that morning, until Eva's answer walked into the shop disguised in the form of a little old lady from the Swedish church.

"How is Mrs. Bergstrom? I haven't seen her in quite a while," asked Eva, after they had dispensed with the usual formalities and comments about the weather.

"Not too good," said the woman. "Hasn't been to church since...since Emily eloped with that Joseph Kelly."

So, that's why Emily hadn't been to the shop lately. The woman said no more about the matter and became engrossed in choosing appropriate colors of yarn for an afghan she intended to knit.

So Mrs. Bergstrom's theory hadn't worked. Keeping Emily from seeing the one she loved had only increased her desire to be with him, and they had resorted to extreme measures. Everything became clear to Eva now. The burden of guilt immediately fell from her shoulders as she decided to release her tight rein on Karla.

Eva was at the spinning wheel when Karla came in from school.

She dropped her books on the table and rummaged through the refrigerator for a snack. She was annoyed that her mother was humming a happy folk tune and took it as an intentional insult.

"Does it make you happy to be so mean to me?"

The humming and spinning stopped immediately and Eva was on her feet. The good news she had prepared for her daughter had now exploded into fragments too small for her to remember and she went directly upstairs to put her thoughts together.

To set a pleasant atmosphere for the evening. Eva had planned to make Karla's favorite meal of American Chop Suey and then inform her of the good news, but Karla's mood was so sour and disrespectful that Eva made the ground beef into hamburgers instead.

When Eva stood at the top of the stairs announcing that supper was ready, there was no response. "Are you downstairs, Karla?"

"Of course I'm downstairs," shouted her daughter indignantly. "I'll be up in a minute."

Eva had finished eating her burger and was at the sink washing dishes when she heard Karla's footsteps on the stairs. Eva made no move to warm up the cold hamburg patty, and went to her bedroom to read. She heard the fry pan clink on the stove and the sizzle of the warming meat. It wasn't long before Eva smelled something burning. She resisted the impulse to prepare a new burger until Karla's screams rushed her back into the kitchen.

"Oh, Mom, it really hurts," said Karla through her tears. Eva ran cold water over the burn and bandaged Karla's hand. Then she turned the radio on to soft music and led Karla to the sofa. When she put her arm around her shoulders, Karla cuddled against her like a frightened child, and when the phone rang neither one rose to answer it.

"Maybe that was Michael," said Eva after a while.

"I don't want to talk to him tonight."

"I've been thinking about the past few weeks..." said Eva. Then Karla broke in.

"I've been thinking, too, about how childish and selfish I've been...I'm the one who has been pig-headed and stubborn and I'm sorry that I talked back to you."

"America is a wonderful country," said Eva. "It is filled with peoples of every religion, every color and culture. We all must get along, understand each other and respect each other's beliefs. So, what I'm trying to say is...what is most important is the goodness inside a person, not what church they go to." She kissed her daughter on the cheek. "You may go out with any boy you wish, regardless of their religious beliefs, as long as you respect him and he respects you."

Karla went to the movies with Michael on Saturday night, but he never called again. Eva wasn't disappointed and neither was Karla.

"Michael is such a jerk," Karla said emphatically one evening at suppertime.

"I'm guessing being a jerk is not very complimentary," said her mother.

"That's right. A jerk is a guy who goes out with a girl once and if she doesn't give him what he wants, he goes after another one."

"What did he want?" asked Eva, innocently.

"Um...do I really have to explain?" Karla's face was turning a little pink.

"Oh, now I understand...he wanted to kiss you, didn't he?" It was more of a statement, rather than a question, but Karla's cheeks reddened when she said he wanted more than a kiss.

"Anyway I like Billy DeAngelo now. He's on the football team, too."

Eva couldn't help but see in her mind the 'De' prefix of Billy's last name, remembering that Mrs. Bergstrom said it was an Italian name. But all that didn't matter now. Eva grinned. "So I'm guessing he's real popular."

"One of the most popular guys in the whole school," remarked Karla. "And he drives a convertible, too! He wants to go to the drive-in on Saturday."

"Is that the name of the movie theater?" asked Eva.

"Well sort of. It's called a drive-in because you can drive your car in front of the big screen and watch the movie in your car."

"Oh..." said her mother. All of a sudden, having her daughter alone in a car with a boy for an hour or more seemed a lot more serious than dating a Catholic. "I'm not sure about drive-in movies, but I trust your judgment... that you will act properly and do the right thing."

After that, Karla had her share of boyfriends, but nothing serious, although she still liked the popular Billy DeAngelo. On Friday nights she and her girlfriends still went bowling or to the roller skating rink. At first the boys would hang around the outside of the rink in small groups watching as the girls showed off their skating skills. Then one by one they'd skate out to the girl of their choice. Karla was a natural skater. Skating backwards gave her the opportunity to look the boys over and they'd wink or smile at the cute blonde with the smooth graceful turns. More often than not, there was usually some boy skating behind her pulling her long pony tail, wanting to take her hand around the rink. Karla's boyfriends usually made it through a week or two or even a month; change and variety tended to be the trend of most teenagers.

A couple of times Karla saw David at the rink, but he was with another girl she didn't know, probably someone from Bedford. David was a traffic monitor, so she saw him often at school. At times she offered him a little smile, but usually pretended to be occupied with something or someone else.

Rebecca had told Eva about David working last summer at a veterinary clinic in New Hampshire, and how he'd saved enough money to buy a good used pickup. Karla stayed after school one afternoon to work in the school library on an English report and had just missed the five o'clock bus. A drenching rain soaked through her thin sweater. When a red truck stopped, even though it was David, she welcomed a ride home. Eva was delighted to see his truck outside the shop, and even more pleased when it lingered for ten or fifteen minutes before Karla came running up the porch steps. Eva found it difficult to bite her tongue and not ask any questions about David as she hung up Karla's soaked clothes and wrapped her in a large, thick towel.

"I was working on my English project and didn't realize the time and that it was raining. David was kind enough to give me a ride home."

"How is David?" asked Eva, hoping to learn what they had talked about.

"He's okay. David is always okay. He never changes."

"How is your biography of Thomas Hardy coming along?"

"Good," said Karla. "Hardy wrote a lot of novels and poetry and it took me a while to decide on which two books to report on." She showed her mother the two she'd picked out.

Eva opened up *Far from the Madding Crowd* and looked briefly through the pages of fine print. "It would take me over a year to read just this one."

"No, it wouldn't, Mom. Once you got into it, you wouldn't be able to put it down."

"Well, I can't spin and read at the same time, so Mr. Hardy will have to wait. I barely have time to read my Bible." Karla picked up the second book, *A Pair of Blue Eyes.*

"I'm going to read this one first. The librarian told me the plot is based on Hardy's courtship of his wife. She said reading that one first would give me a better understanding of Hardy's character and personality, especially when it comes to comparing the two books for my report."

Karla was getting ready for bed when she happened to mention that David was taking her to the movies on Saturday night. "I've been wanting to see *She Wore a Yellow Ribbon* and he said he wanted to see it, too." Eva's delightful surprise was evident in her raised eyebrows and Karla was quick to remind her mother that it wasn't really a date. "I don't want you to get the impression that he's my new boyfriend or anything like that."

"I thought you didn't like cowboy movies anymore,"

commented Eva.

"Mom, this is a Western drama, not like those silly Roy Rogers movies with dopey singing and more or less the same stupid plots."

"I see," said her mother, trying to suppress the urge to smile.

The Day at Craine's Beach

One of the cute boys at the skating rink called to ask Karla to go out on Saturday, which caused a minor dilemma. Eva, overhearing Karla's responses, didn't approve of the way the conversation was turning.

"I could probably get out of it. He's just a friend," said Karla glancing at her mother who stood with hands on her hips glaring and shaking her head. Karla covered the receiver. "It's Danny and I'm going out with him on Saturday…David won't mind."

Eva, not the least bit happy, waggled her finger at Karla. "When you agree to go out with someone, you don't change your mind if something better comes along. That isn't the right thing to do. You can go out with Danny another time."

"But, Mom…"

"You tell him no…right now!" demanded her mother.

"Sorry, Danny, but I'm busy this Saturday. How about next week? …No, I can't get out of it. I've already promised someone else." Karla stood with the receiver dangling from her hand. "He hung up on me!"

"It's not your fault. That's his problem. You did the right thing," consoled her mother.

"Now he's mad at me and probably won't ever ask me out again!" mumbled Karla.

"Well then, he was very rude to hang up on you and you are better off without him. Karla walked into her bedroom and shut the door a little bit too loudly.

About an hour later Karla appeared in the kitchen.

"You were right, Mom. I should have told Danny 'no' right away, but he kept pressing me to get out of my date with David and I just got carried away with the idea. And then he had the nerve to say, 'Suit yourself then. You might not get another chance.'"

"He's an arrogant one, isn't he?" commented her mother.

Karla nodded. "As if I'd ever give HIM another chance!"

Eva stayed up to wait for Karla to come home on Saturday night, as she always did when her daughter was out on a date. She was spinning when she heard the truck pull up and finished the skein she was working on. After a half hour there was no sign of Karla, which Eva considered a good sign. She left the porch light on and went upstairs, slipped into her nightgown and brushed her hair. The moon was nearly full, illuminating the wide street below, which tonight appeared as a gentle river flowing beneath her. David's truck, the only vehicle in sight, could have been a small boat moored by the shore.

A door slammed and laughter drifted up from the sidewalk as two figures walked toward the house. Two hours had gone by since the truck had driven in. Eva smiled and went to her bedroom. Finally she heard Karla coming up the stairs. She was actually humming a happy tune as she walked past her mother's door.

"How was the movie?"

"The movie was great. I had a good time." Eva heard footsteps enter her room and saw Karla's silhouette in front of the moonlit window.

"It's a beautiful night out there...almost like summer," remarked Karla.

"That's just what I was thinking."

"We went to Howard Johnson's afterwards, and...you won't believe this...David likes to eat fried clams with ice cream just like I do!"

"Well, that surely is a strange coincidence."

"That's what I thought," said Karla, yawning. "Gosh it's late,

I've got to go to bed."

"I'm sleepy, too," said Eva. "Good night, honey, and sweet dreams."

"Thanks, Mom...sweet dreams to you, too." Eva had a good feeling about tonight. She was already having sweet dreams about her daughter and David Beckworth.

One warm, summery day in late April Billy DeAngelo's black convertible came to a screeching halt in front of the shop. At the time Karla was filling the yarn boxes, and hurried upstairs to check her hair and lipstick. The door opened, revealing the handsome Italian boy with dark curly hair, a flashing smile, and a confident stance, the picture of teenage popularity complete with the backdrop of automotive extravagance. Eva had caught glimpses of him before, speeding past the shop with other girls, their hair flowing in the wind, holding their coat collars high around their necks in the too-cool spring air. Now face to face, she saw the reason for her daughter's attraction, and her own suspicion that this boy was big trouble.

"Is Karla home?" he asked, swaggering around the shop and taking everything in.

"She's upstairs. I'll tell her you're here. Please have a seat," Eva said gesturing to the table by the window.

"I didn't know Karla had a sister," he remarked, giving Eva the once-over.

Eva, who was taken by surprise, stopped at the bottom step and turned around.

"Karla doesn't have a sister," she replied. Slightly embarrassed, and thinking she should have ignored his remark, she hastened up the stairs.

"Are you feeling okay, Mom. You look a little flushed."

"I'm fine. Just a bit winded from running up the stairs."

"What do you think of Billy?" whispered Karla.

"He seems nice, but I hope he's a good driver. You won't let him drive too fast, now, will you?"

"Oh, Mom...like I'm going to tell him how to drive. You don't tell a guy to slow down...not when it's about driving a car anyway..." What Karla inferred worried Eva as she sat by the window looking down at the bobbing blonde ponytail and curly black head in the front seat of the black convertible. The car slowly turned out into the traffic and drove off. Eva said a prayer for their safety and busied herself with knitting. She was still knitting when the front door slammed shut and she heard Karla's footsteps hurrying up the stairs.

"Now look who's red-faced!" said Eva.

"Oh, Mom, I must be dreaming. You'll never guess what just happened!" She was out of breath, her face still flushed and eyes sparkling with excitement; a spinning top that was wound too tight.

"Billy just asked me to go to the Senior Prom with him! Can you believe that?"

"When is the prom?"

"The first Saturday in June!" said Karla, striking a dramatic pose in front of the large, round mirror above the sofa. "What color gown should I get? Blue?"

They were a twosome now, going to the movies, or for an ice cream cone at Buttricks, or just sitting in the car in front of the shop for a couple hours talking. It was evident that Karla was infatuated with Billy and wanted to be with him all the time. Or was it Billy who wouldn't let Karla out of his sight? His controlling nature had spun a web around Karla, isolating her from her friends.

It had been more than a month now since Karla had gone anywhere with Joanne, Marilyn or Judy. They'd called many times but Eva feared that Karla wasn't returning their calls. She advised her daughter not to abandon her friends, but Karla's response was unsympathetic. "I see them all day long at school. It's about time they got boyfriends, too." Eva recognized Karla's defensive attitude; it was reminiscent of the "you can't date Catholics" era. Eva didn't want to go back there again and passed on further comment.

One afternoon after Billy's car sped away noisily from the shop, Karla told her mother about another annual event, Senior Day at Craine's Beach. "It's this Saturday, and all I have to bring is a picnic lunch and a bathing suit."

"Where is this Craine's Beach?" asked Eva.

"Near Ipswich...about twenty miles away," replied Karla.

Since David was also a senior this year, Eva called Rebecca to learn more about the place.

"We've gone there many times," Rebecca told her. "It's a nice, peaceful spot to sit and watch the waves come in off the Atlantic Ocean. Of course the water is freezing this time of year, but there's a lovely, sandy beach, about seven miles long, known for its beautiful sand dunes. Across from the beach is Plum Island, a wildlife reserve for migratory birds."

"Sounds like sort of a romantic place," commented Eva.

"It is, but there will be a lot of kids there, so I wouldn't worry. David says the guys are going to play beach volleyball, have a dip in the ocean and lay around on the beach soaking up some sun."

"Well, I feel better knowing that David will be there," said Eva.

Karla wanted a new bathing suit. Her old ones were too small and had consisted of a tank top and matching shorts that were long enough to cover her birthmark. She looked through all the one-piece stretchy suits and found one with a short skirt that came half way down her thigh. It just covered her birthmark.

Members of the senior class and their friends were scattered across the beach in groups of all sizes, each clique keeping much to itself. Some were sitting or lying on blankets sunning themselves, while others were playing games on the sand or frolicking in the ocean. Above all were the hot sun and squawking gulls.

Karla and Billy sat briefly looking out to the sea, but as more of his friends arrived, he ranged from blanket to blanket getting together enough guys to play a game of beach volleyball. Their girlfriends were mostly cheerleaders, who chatted and laughed amongst themselves. They all ignored Karla until a girl named Helen stopped to say hello before being dragged away by her boyfriend. Karla felt like an outsider in this elite group, who she thought tolerated her presence because she was with the quarterback of the football team.

She watched the boys run back to the parking lot and then return with cold beer and cigarettes. When Billy sat down on the blanket he offered her a beer. She took a little sip, but that was enough; she didn't like the taste of it and reached into her basket for a bottle of ginger ale. Two other couples joined them and others moved their blankets closer to get in on the fun. Billy seemed to attract people like an over-ripe banana attracts fruit flies.

Most had a beer in one hand and a cigarette in the other and the conversation soon turned to telling dirty jokes. Karla was definitely feeling out of her element and had nothing to contribute to the conversation. She wasn't hungry, but for the sake of something to do she reached into her basket and began eating an apple.

"Hey, you guys, let's go swimming," hollered Billy, grabbing Karla's hand. He pulled her up and nearly dragged her to the water's edge. Then he picked her up, ran into the water and dumped her into an incoming wave. She rose to the surface with water stinging her nostrils and throat, realizing for the first time how salty ocean water was.

"Can't you swim?" said Billy after she'd finished coughing.

"Not very well," she said, not wanting to admit that she could not swim at all. He dove into the water and rode a wave to the shore. Then everyone did the same. It looked like fun, and it was, until she got closer to the shore and her mouth filled with a mixture of salt water and sand. She spit out the grit and went back to rinse her mouth out with ginger ale, then stretched out on the blanket thinking she would have been happier if she'd stayed at home today.

Finally the kids returned to their blankets. Billy had forgotten to bring his lunch, so Karla shared the rest of hers and then he begged more from his friends. The girls sunbathed and the boys drank more beer. She heard them talking about school, what they'd be doing this summer and about what college might be like. Music from Billy's radio lulled her to sleep. Then she awakened with a jolt as Billy tickled her feet. Other boys were tickling their girlfriends and everyone was laughing and roughhousing until Billy noticed Karla's exposed thigh. This had been her worst fear, that he or one of his friends would see her birthmark.

"What in hell is that?" he shouted, staring at the purplish-red blotch. Karla heard a girl gasp and another say it looked like a red jellyfish. Karla wanted to run behind the dunes and escape the probing eyes and repulsive looks, but she couldn't move. She wanted to explain, but she had no voice; her throat had tightened up and tears welled up in her eyes.

Billy took several steps backwards, standing aghast with his friends who all viewed her as some kind of side-show freak. She saw disgust written all over Billy's face. Then Helen came forward.

"Quit gawking. Haven't you ever seen a birthmark before?" Then she knelt beside Karla, rearranged her skirt to cover the blemish and put her arm around her waist.

"Let's go for a walk," she told Karla. It was almost a command, and Karla obediently stood up and followed her down to the water's edge. For a while they walked side by side in a silence broken only by the small, rippling waves bubbling around their feet.

They came to an outcropping of rocks and climbed to the top to enjoy the cool, refreshing breeze blowing in across the water.

"By the time we get back they'll have forgotten all about it," said Helen sympathetically, but Karla felt as if her whole world had fallen apart.

"Not Billy," said Karla. "Did you see that awful look on his face? He won't ever want to be seen with me again."

"Well, good riddance. You're better off without him," said Helen with some authority.

"What do you mean?" asked Karla.

"I dated him for a while. He's just out for what he can get, and usually doesn't give up until he gets it, if you know what I mean. I wouldn't give in to him and he finally stopped calling." Then she told Karla how he got a girl pregnant last year, a girl from Waltham who had to leave school and put the baby up for adoption, and how Billy had denied any responsibility and went on his merry way. "I could never give a baby of mine away, could you?" asked Helen.

"Frankly, I agree with you that it's better to say no in the first place than to risk becoming pregnant and having to make such an important decision." Karla thought of her mother, how she must have felt when finding out she was pregnant, and how brave she was not to give her away. Some day she would ask her mother more about that.

They sat together on the edge of the rocks, their feet dangling over the side, watching the waves tumble toward them and listening to the gulls calling to each other. "This surely wasn't my lucky day," said Karla after a while.

"Well, the day isn't over yet. Most days are a mixture of good and bad, so there's no such thing as a totally unlucky day."

"So, I should be expecting a little bit of good luck?" Karla laughed. "I sure could use some right now."

"Actually I don't believe in luck," said Helen. "Luck is leaving your destiny to something else besides yourself. I like to feel I have power over what might or might not happen to me."

"You mean the power to make good things happen?" asked Karla.

"Something like that," said Helen. "Once in a while I do have a lousy day, but then my mother reminds me to be grateful for the good things around me, even if it is just a clean, soft bed to sleep in at night."

"I'm grateful to you for being here today," said Karla. "And for stepping up to help me when no one else cared a hoot."

"Well, they were all so rude. I couldn't just stand there and do nothing."

"I still think luck and chance have played a role in my life." said Karla. "See that guy way over there jogging next to the water? Now he could be good luck or he could be bad luck, but we don't know which just yet. It sort of depends on his intentions."

"Or our expectations," said Helen.

Karla laughed. "I just hope it isn't Billy DeAngelo."

"Well, I think hope does enter the equation," said Helen. "It's best to be optimistic. Perhaps he's Prince Charming coming to rescue you and whisk you away to his castle."

Karla nodded hopefully. "I could use a Prince Charming right now."

"Look, he's turning this way," said Helen. "Think positive."

"I'm trying," said Karla, shielding her eyes from the sun. "He looks much taller than Billy, who I suspect is probably into his second case of beer by now."

"You are right on both counts," replied Helen.

Karla set her face toward Plum Island and the circling seagulls and filled herself with good thoughts.

"I think it's David Beckworth. He rides the same bus as I do," said Helen. "He's looking pretty good in those bathing trunks, don't you think?"

Karla's head swiveled around to see David's long, muscular body inching closer to them. Finally he stopped in the shade of the protruding rocks and looked up to her. The sleeves of his white shirt were rolled up to his elbows and the unbuttoned front revealed a sprinkling of curly dark hair on his tanned chest. Her eyes slipped down briefly to his tight trunks, then back to his concerned face.

"Are you okay?" he asked.

Karla felt the cool breeze, yet all of a sudden she was very warm and sweating. "I'm feeling better, thanks," she said.

"You're blushing, Karla," whispered Helen, after watching their friendly exchange. Helen stood up and said to David, "Chances are she'll be fine now." Then she jumped off the rock and looked up to Karla. "I'm going to see how my *chances* are at getting a cold drink. If, by *chance*, you need a ride home, let me know."

"I will," said Karla. "Thanks for everything, Helen."

It didn't take long for David's long legs to scramble up the rocks. He sat down beside her and they watched Helen walk across the sand toward the minuscule spot where the seniors had staked out their private space. Helen's forceful use of the word 'chance' and 'chances' prompted David to ask what was up with all this chance stuff.

"Oh, nothing. We were just discussing the probabilities of luck and chance."

"So, how are my chances for spending an hour or two with you this afternoon," he asked, grinning down at her. She squinted up to look at him and smiled.

"I'd say your chances are very good." When her hand happened to brush against his arm, he slowly took it in his and gave it a gentle, comforting squeeze. Then she leaned her head against his shoulder and looked out toward Plum Island. She felt safe and strong, all thoughts of Billy and his rude friends melting away in the warmth of David's company. For a while neither knew what to say, but strangely they were both content with each other's silence.

"Actually, I don't believe in chance," he said finally. "I like to think that I'm in control of the events in my life."

"That's just about what Helen was telling me."

He laughed. "She's in my psychology class."

"Helen was the only girl who took pity on me today."

"Well, I'm sorry I wasn't there. I'd have knocked some sense into him."

"Really?" exclaimed Karla, looking straight into his caring brown eyes. "You would have smacked him?"

"You bet I would have. I almost did when I heard him ranting and raving about the...the incident."

"You mean he was telling everyone else about it?"

"You know Billy. He can't keep his mouth shut, or anything else, for that matter."

Karla blushed at David's reference and looked down to her

lap. Her birthmark was exposed and she hastened to cover it with her skirt.

"You don't have to worry about that with me," he said, gently laying his hand on her thigh.

This gesture touched her in several ways. First was the sensual thrill of it, but most important was the fact that he actually put his hand on her birthmark and it didn't repulse him. She saw David in a different light; she saw love in his face and she felt that love.

She watched him remove his shirt. "You'd better put this on. You're getting quite a sun burn." He put the shirt over her shoulders and his arm lingered on her back long enough so that she thought he might kiss her, but he leaned back on his elbows instead and looked out across the water. Her eyes glanced at the curly black hairs scattered across his tanned chest and how they disappeared beneath his trunks. His voice caused her to look back toward the sea.

"I've been to Plum Island," he said. "Some of the sand dunes are over fifty feet high and the strong undertow can sweep you out into the ocean if you aren't careful." He knew about the plum shrubs and the sanctuary with many varieties of migratory birds. He talked about plovers, egrets and herons, the Canadian geese and snow geese, the falcons, osprey, and mallard ducks. People also lived on the island, as well as red foxes and white-tailed deer. He pointed to another outcrop of rocks not too far away. "See those big birds over there with their wings outstretched? They're cormorants...ducks that have to dry their wings after diving for fish in the deep water."

Karla looked at him in amazement. "How do you know all this stuff?"

"I read a lot," he said. "Mostly about animal life and history."

"What kind of history?"

"All kinds. United States history, world history...anything that has to do with people and events of the past. You know how they say history repeats itself? Well, it's true. You can almost predict the future by reading about the past."

Karla was impressed with David's intelligence and solicitude. It amused her to compare his maturity to Billy's childish behavior.

He pointed toward the west, and her eyes followed the muscular line of his tanned arm to where his index finger touched the clouds. "See those thunderheads over there? I'll bet it will be raining in less than an hour. We should be heading back," he said to her.

He jumped down from the rock in one leap and held up his arms to help her down. At this point she was willing to follow him anywhere. She put her hands on his shoulders and he caught her around the waist and set her carefully on the sand. She had to be content with his smile, as he took her hand and led her to the water's edge. Tiny bubbles rushed in from the incoming tide, swirling around their feet as they walked slowly up the beach. She felt very connected to him and there was no need to talk. Every once in a while he'd gently squeeze her hand and look affectionately down at her, causing strange, but not unwelcome sensations in her belly. If he kissed her right now and wanted more, she might have given in to him. It wasn't like her to be thinking that way. Remembering what she and Helen had discussed, she brushed away these thoughts, but she kept asking herself if this is how it felt to be in love. Best to put her mind on something else.

Many of the senior class were still on the beach to their left and some were in the ocean playing water polo with a huge plastic ball.

"Did you leave anything on the beach?" he asked.

"Just my paper lunch bag and an empty ginger ale bottle. Billy can take care of that. He ate most of my lunch anyway."

"You're kidding me!" exclaimed David.

"No, I'm not kidding. He forgot to bring anything to eat."

"If you're ready to leave, I can drive you home."

"I'm ready!" she said without hesitation.

On the way home they stopped to get a cheeseburger, fries and a root beer, but David had not taken the road to Lexington. Instead he went north to Bedford. At first she thought they might be going to his house.

"I thought we'd go to Bedford Airport and watch the submarines," he said with a silly grin. Billy had driven her there once before in his convertible for the same reason. They had parked on a hill overlooking the airport, but she had seen no submarines. Billy had what the girls called "Russian hands and Roman fingers" and it didn't take Karla long to figure out that it's meaning was more like "rushing hands and roaming fingers." She had resisted and he'd gotten mad and driven her home.

She felt different with David, who already had his arm behind her head on the back of the seat. Every once in a while she felt his hand on her hair and it made her tingle inside.

Always the thoughtful one, he asked how her sunburn was.

"Oh, fine," she lied. He touched the side of her face.

"Your cheek is very warm and I can feel the heat on your back through my shirt," he said. Her back was very tender, but she wouldn't admit to it. Instead she came up with a witty reply.

"You just make me feel warm all over," which was partly the truth. His hand caressed her neck. His nearness made her yearn for more and she turned to look at him. The soft light of the moon highlighted her warm smile and he kissed her gently on the lips. She couldn't help but kiss him back. He leaned closer and kissed her with more passion, but then he suddenly pulled away, brushing away a lock of hair to look into her eyes.

"I've wanted to kiss you ever since that day I picked you up in the rain," he told her.

She had been kissed before, immature unemotional dry pecks or slobbery ones that made her want to wipe her face. Billy thought he was a good kisser, but she had never had the great desire to kiss him back as she did with David. She felt deliriously happy and was content in his gentle embrace. Then he looked down at his watch. "I still have barn chores to do tonight," he said, tenderly taking her face in his hands for one more sweet kiss. Then he started the truck, took her hand in his and drove back to Lexington.

Eva made Karla lie down and placed cool, wet cloths on her daughter's sunburned back. The bed sheets felt cool at first, but after a while they radiated heat from her body and the slightest movement was painful.

"So, did you have a good time at the beach?" asked her mother after the cold compresses had given her daughter some relief.

"Not in the morning so much... but as the day went on things got better and better."

Not wanting to pry about the morning, Eva asked if she wanted some beans and hot dogs.

"No thanks, David and I already ate, but I would like a glass of cold water."

"David brought you home?"

It was then Karla explained to her mother about her day at Craine's Beach.

Billy conveniently avoided Karla for the next few weeks. It was apparent he would not be taking her to his senior prom. David, who was also a senior, asked her to go with him. Afterwards they went their separate ways for the summer, he to the veterinary clinic in New Hampshire and she waitressing in a restaurant in Somerville. But every night Karla wrote him a letter and almost every day a letter came in the mail from David.

Within a matter of weeks Eva received a letter from Mats.

June 20, 1952

Dear Eva

Haven't heard from you since that VERY short note on your Christmas card. When was that, three or four years ago? Perhaps it is me that owes you a letter. So much has been going on here that I can't keep up with myself.

Hope you and your family are in good health. Imagine business is pretty good now that the war is over and people have money to spend. Love it here in sunny California. I hear they had a lot of snow in New England last winter. I'm glad I don't have to put up with all that cold weather.

You really should think about visiting California. You'd love it…summer all year long.

How old is Karla? She must be in high school by now. How the time flies.

I'm still waiting to hear why you left the old country in such a big hurry.

Oh, I met a gal last year. She's from the state of Vermont. Came to California to work for the summer and decided to stay. Haven't gone out with anyone else, so I guess you'd say we're a 'couple' now. I'll be retiring in a few years, so it's about time I got married and settled down, right?

The young guys call me The Old Viking. I guess I am getting older, but I don't feel any different. Life is good and I hope it is good for you, too.

As Ever,

Mats

Eva rummaged through her desk and found the letter that Mats had written after his visit to the shop three years before. It made her laugh all over again reading about him thinking Arne was her husband. It was time to set him straight on how things really were and the real reason why she had left Sweden.

June 30, 1952

Dear Mats

It pleases me to know you are content with your life in the Navy. Sounds like you've settled down a little and made 'that meandering river' run straight again.

Business has been very good since the war, although this month has been rather slow. June and July are always the worst months for sales. Who wants to knit in the heat of summer? Still have my garden to keep me busy.

Karla will graduate from high school next year and hopes to go to Plymouth Teachers' College in New Hampshire. She is a very good student and hopes to receive a generous scholarship, which should help out a lot.

I just read over the letter you sent three years ago. It's about time I set you right about a few things. First of all Arne is not my husband. He is married to Dagny and was babysitting with Karla that first day you came to the shop. Arne does fine woodworking and was a great help in getting my shop ready for customers.

He and Dagny live in Maine now. At last count I think they had seven children, but I might have missed one. Their children's names all begin with the letter 'A', so it's hard for me to keep them all clear in my mind. I kept quite busy with Karla and the shop and can't imagine seven children running around…and two of them twins!

I am not married, nor have I ever been. Remember that night on the ship when I told you I loved someone else? Well, that someone else was Karl Lindholm. Mrs. Lindholm knew something was going on between us because she caused trouble for me when Karl and his father went on vacation to southern Europe. The next thing I knew I was out the door and on my way to America with you.

If you haven't guessed it already, I will tell you now. Karl Lindholm is Karla's father. It wasn't Sweden I cried for on the ship; my tears were for Karl.

When I learned of my pregnancy I didn't know what to do. I wrote to him several times, but my letters were never answered. I didn't think he would see any of them anyway because Mrs. Lindholm always intercepted all mail coming into the house. I also wrote to Cook and your father. I thought if they knew the truth they would tell Karl and somehow things would work out. I never heard from Cook and your father's letters were returned to me unopened.

After all these years, Karl is still in my heart. I'm glad he has turned his life around. Do you know if he is still in America, or has he returned to Sweden?

It pleases me, too, that you have found happiness in California and that you have someone special in your life.

Love,

Eva

In November Eva heard from Mats again.

November 3, 1952

Dear Eva

It wasn't until late October that I received your letter of June 30. The envelope was pretty beat up when I finally got it. There must have been a mix up when I got shipped to Virginia Beach. As you can see, I have a different address now. When I found out I'd be having a desk job in Virginia, Mona and I decided to get married. Since I'm no longer aboard ship, we have rented a nice apartment on the fourth floor overlooking the Atlantic Ocean. I'll be retiring in a few years and then we might move up to Vermont to be nearer her father. He used to have a big farm, but has sold much land for house lots. Mona told him to save a spot on the knoll for us to build a house on, so that sounds like a good idea to me.

Strange how our life has been…me thinking you were married…then getting married myself…and now finding out that all the time you weren't married at all. Sometimes I think how things might have been, but apparently the big plan didn't include for us to ever be together. Don't get me wrong…I'm a happy man. I've had a heck of a good life and I'm lucky to have a woman who I love and who loves me. Maybe by Christmas I'll have a picture of the two of us to send to you.

Wow, what a shocker to hear about you and Karl! I would never in a million years have thought that you, the bashful young girl from Norrland, and Karl, so quiet and serious, would ever…well, you know what I mean. He was some lucky guy!

As Ever,

Mats

In December a Christmas card arrived from Anna with exciting news.

December 12, 1952

Dear Eva

As you know Jonas married his high school sweetheart, Carolyn, a year ago last November and they now live in Massachusetts where Jonas was offered a fine violin position with the Boston Symphony Orchestra. Well, I am pleased to tell you that Lars and I are now very proud grandparents of a sweet little girl. Her name is Annabelle, a combination of my name and Carolyn's mother, Bella. We miss them all dearly and are contemplating moving to a place called Cape Cod in Massachusetts. Jonas and Carolyn have a summer home there in the town of Barnstable where there is fishing, lobstering and clamming, and also a great demand for wooden maritime carvings.

We are sad to leave beautiful Minnesota, but excited to move on and be close to our son and family, and also to be nearer to you, Eva! First we must sell our house, which probably won't happen until next spring or summer. In the meantime, we have much to do with packing up all our belongings collected over the years. You might find Jonas knocking on your door sometime soon! How I would love to see that meeting! Merry Christmas and may the New Year bring us together.

Love,

Anna

Eva immediately got out her map of New England and spread it across the counter.

"I can't find any place in Massachusetts called Cape Cod, can you, Karla?"

"I think Cape Cod is a peninsula," said Karla. "See this long hook of land stretching out into the water?"

"Oh my, that looks a bit scary. Are you sure people live out there?"

"There are kids at school whose parents have summer homes on The Cape. I hear it is very beautiful." Karla ran her finger along the long narrow outcropping of land searching for a place called Barnstable. "Here it is," she said. "Barnstable isn't too far from the mainland of Massachusetts. I'd guess maybe a hundred miles, more or less, from here."

Annika

Eva and Karla spent Christmas Eve with Ingrid and Olle and went to Rebecca and Dave's house for Christmas Day dinner. It was the day before New Year's when Dagny's Christmas card arrived. When Karla came home from David's, Eva met her at the door with the exciting news.

"We finally heard from Dagny and guess what?"

"She didn't have triplets this time, did she?" joked Karla.

"No more babies, but here, let me read what she writes about Annika." Eva scanned the rather long letter until she came to Annika's name.

"Here is what Dagny says: 'Annika has been very big help to us all these years. As you know she skip a grade in early school and graduate from high school this year. She very shy and not keen to leave New Sweden to live in city, but Arne and me think change would be good for her. I remember how I look up to you and how you help me do better and we think you be good for our Annika. What I mean is could Annika come down next June or July to help in yarn shop? Then you have more time to spend spinning or doing what you please. If she like it and is good help, she can stay. If you don't need help, maybe you can get her work somewhere else? She good with cooking and cleaning and loves children.'"

"Wouldn't it be fun to have Annika visit us this summer?" exclaimed Eva. Karla was not so enthusiastic, but managed a casual "I guess so." Karla did not like surprises, especially when it might invade on her privacy, and she was usually good with excuses.

"I'll be waitressing again and won't be around to do stuff with her, and where would she sleep, with me in my bed?"

Her daughter's reaction wasn't what Eva hoped for. Karla, an only child, liked her space and wasn't always willing to share. Perhaps in time she would see the positive side.

"Well, I don't have to give Dagny an answer today," she said. "We can live with the idea for a while and see what develops."

Karla's face relaxed and she returned to her homework, but after several minutes she turned to her mother. "I didn't mean to put a damper on everything, Mom, but I'm really stressed out about my grades."

"I know you are, honey, and I understand completely. Things have a way of working out."

Eva didn't have to wait as long as she thought. In a letter, David told Karla about a resort near the veterinary clinic that was looking for waitresses for the next summer season. He'd seen the announcement on the college bulletin board and thought she might be interested. He also enclosed an application for employment which had a deadline of February first. Being within a few miles of David all summer was very appealing to Karla. This time the shoe was on the other foot and it was her mother who came up with excuses.

"If you're in New Hampshire until September, there won't be much time to shop and do what needs to be done before you leave for college."

"Well, I don't really have that much to do," said Karla. "I'm sure I'll have some time off at the resort to go shopping." Eva was hard pressed to think of more arguments, but she made a feeble attempt.

"You won't know anyone at the resort...and where would you live? I'd feel better if one of your friends worked there with you."

"Oh Mom, there are a lot unknowns at college, too, but you didn't seem worried about that before." Then Karla had an idea.

"If I'm away during the summer, Annika could have my room all to herself and if she turns out to be a help to you, maybe she would stay longer and be company while I'm away at college." Eva considered this, but didn't say one way or the other. Then Karla added, "then I wouldn't be worrying about you being all alone in the house at night."

"I don't mind being alone at night, but I do know I will miss you. I agree, though, that it would be nice to have someone to talk to and fuss over while you're away."

Eva wrote a short note to Dagny.

January 25, 1953

Dear Dagny

I would love to have Annika come here next summer. Karla may be working at a resort in New Hampshire, so Annika will have your old room all to herself. I won't need a lot of help, but maybe she can work here mornings and get another job for afternoons. I'm always seeing 'help wanted' signs in the store windows, so finding a part-time job shouldn't be a problem. Karla will be attending Plymouth Teacher's College in the fall, so her room will be available next year as well. I look forward to having Annika's company while she is gone.

Let me know when Annika will be arriving.

Love,

Eva

Dagny wrote back in May saying Annika would be graduating on June eleventh and that she would be coming to Lexington by bus the next week. Enclosed was a blurry photograph of Annika. Her eyes were squinting from a too-bright sun, her mouth pinched in a stubborn pout. Annika's expression told Eva that whoever was taking the picture had taken much too long and that Annika probably had more important things to do than stand idly in the hot sun. A kerchief covered her hair and she seemed very thin. The photograph, with a hazy field and a hint of pale trees in the background, had an old-fashioned quality reminiscent of photos of country girls she'd seen back in Sweden.

David came home from college in time to accompany Karla to her senior prom and see her graduate from high school. Annika still hadn't arrived by the time Karla left for her summer job in New Hampshire.

Each day Eva expected to see Annika. One day when she was alone in the shop the door opened and a young man walked in.

He had reddish-blond hair and a big grin that immediately spread across his handsome face.

"Eva!" he said excitedly. "I would have known you anywhere. You are the spittin' image of my own mother years ago."

"Jonas?" shouted Eva, running toward him with a fond hug. "But what is this spittin' image you speak of? I hope it is something good."

He laughed. "I said that without thinking. Tis only an expression that means exact likeness. You have the same curly red hair and beautiful skin of my mother. And you look very much as she did in her wedding picture over twenty years ago."

"No one ever told me that my father's sister had red hair," she said in amazement.

Eva's mind was suddenly relieved. All of Ingrid's teasing and suggestions about The Finn immediately dissolved into nothingness. "Where are my manners," she said. "Please sit down and have some coffee."

"Mother told me about the yarn shop," said Jonas, admiring the attractive wooden boxes filled with colorful yarn. "It is much larger and finer than I imagined."

His compliments filled Eva with pride as she poured the coffee and sat down comfortably beside him. Conversation flowed like sweet wine. It was as if they had known each other all their lives. Eva told him about her life in Sweden and he shared stories about his mother that were unknown to her. She had forgotten that Anna had been only ten years old when her father was born. Their mother had died soon after that and Anna had raised her brother as if he were her own son. Eva had a renewed respect for her only aunt and was anxious to meet her.

"My parents have sold their farm," he told her. "I've found them a small house near my summer place. It's in East Barnstable, a settlement of Finnish immigrants who came years ago to work in the cranberry bogs. The locals call it Finn City, but my Dad says he will surely fit in there, since his grandmother was Finnish."

Eva was excited. "Will they be moving there before winter?"

"I think they will. My father can hardly wait. The little house sets on the shore overlooking Barnstable Harbor. He's anxious to go fishing and lobstering."

"Lobstering? What is that?" she asked.

"Setting out traps for lobsters." When Eva still didn't understand, he continued. "Lobsters taste much like crayfish. You must have had crayfish in Sweden."

"Oh yes! I remember every August when Papa set out little traps in the lake and we'd get hundreds of crayfish. Mama boiled them in a big pot of hot water and we'd spend the afternoon stuffing ourselves with those little critters."

"Well, you will have to come down to Barnstable sometime and we'll have a lobster feast. If you like crayfish, you will love lobsters. They are much larger than crayfish and sweeter tasting."

"My mouth waters just thinking about it," she replied.

The late afternoon sun filled the room with a warm glow as they finished their third cup of coffee. Jonas told her about playing with the Boston Symphony and how on summer weekends he travels around New England playing the violin and accordion with a small group of Scandinavian musicians at fairs and for folk dancing.

"Thank you, Eva, for your kind hospitality. I must be on my way to Topsfield if I'm to get there in time for the festivities."

"I've enjoyed your company so much," she said. "I do hope you will stop in again so you can meet Karla." He left her with the wonderful thought that perhaps next time he would bring his parents for a visit.

Usually customers walked right into the shop, a tinkling bell sounding their arrival, but on this day there was only a feeble knock, one Eva might not have heard had she not been on the same side of the room. She opened the door to find an exact replica of the girl in the photograph that Dagny had sent.

Annika stood silent and solemn, almost sullen, appearing a bit bedraggled in her kerchief, dark skirt and stained blouse, looking as if she'd just stepped off the boat from Sweden. Her shoulders slumped from the two heavy bags she carried by her sides. But her feet, spread a good distance apart, were planted firmly on the porch mat. She reminded Eva of a wilting rose bud, unsure of unfolding its petals, afraid to reveal its inner beauty to the world, but Annika's solid stance told her this girl intended to make the best of her plight.

"Oh, Annika, I'm so glad to see you. Come right in," exclaimed Eva as she hugged the girl tightly. Annika stoically accepted Eva's embrace, but remained standing apprehensively just inside the open door with her arms hanging limply by her sides still gripping the two blue and white homespun bags. Her expression never changed as she gazed about the room. Eva guessed from hugging the girl that she was in dire need of a bath, but first they would have some light refreshment.

Eva sat across the table from Annika, who perched on the edge of her seat like a bird ready to take flight. Either Annika was extremely bashful or, as Dagny had suggested in her letter, Annika had not been overly willing to leave New Sweden.

"Would you like milk or coffee? Or perhaps some cold lemonade?" Annika's eyes dropped to her lap and she muttered the word 'coffee' without looking up. But she was not shy about adding two heaping spoonfuls of sugar and about half the pitcher of cream to her cup before drinking it down almost in one gulp. Eva poured another cup, refilled the cream pitcher and brought in a plate of almond cake. Annika snatched a slice, cramming it into her mouth, and finished her second cup of coffee. Eva wondered if she'd had anything to eat since leaving New Sweden and poured her another cup. Annika seemed more relaxed then, nibbling on another piece of cake as her eyes darted back and forth along the rows of colored yarn on the counter.

"Your mother and father found those old boxes under some rubble in the storeroom and refinished them to hold my skeins of yarn. Aren't they lovely?" said Eva.

Annika nodded her head and looked down. Her hands had fallen to her lap and Eva noticed her thumbs rubbing against each other. Had the mention of her parents agitated the girl in some way?

"I hear you are the knitter of the family. Did your grandmother teach you?"

Annika shook her head, mumbling something about Stina.

"Oh Stina. The neighbor who helped your mother write letters to me?"

Annika nodded again, but did not look up. Hoping for a more positive response, Eva suggested they do some knitting in the evening after Annika settled in. Eva saw the glimmer of a smile, but at the same time she noticed Annika's missing front tooth, something she hoped Dr. Bergstrom might be able to fix. Improving Annika's dour attitude might take longer, but with love, understanding and a lot of one-on-one time, Eva was ready to take up the challenge.

She showed Annika around the yarn shop and then they went upstairs to Karla's bedroom.

"Karla is away for the summer, so you will be sleeping in her room. You may put your things in the bureau while I draw water in the tub." Annika was smitten with the idea of having a bedroom all to herself. When Eva returned to the bedroom, Annika was still standing in the same spot absorbing the pretty, quilted pink bedspread, large bureau of drawers and especially the vanity where most of Karla's perfumes and cosmetics were lined up in a row across the glass top. Annika quickly put her bags on the bed and began pulling items out.

"You can put them away later," said Eva. "Your bath is ready."

Annika promptly turned around, looked Eva sternly in the eye and spoke with much authority. "I already took my bath on Saturday. Today is only Wednesday."

Eva understood. Back in Sweden her family had taken their weekly baths on Saturday nights, too, but she had washed up daily in a small enamel basin beside the pump in the kitchen. With so many children in her family, Eva wondered if Annika had ever enjoyed a long, relaxing private bath.

She took Annika's arm and gently walked her into the bathroom. "I've already drawn the water, so you might just as well take a nice, leisurely bath while I prepare supper."

The room smelled like a rose garden, but it was the long white tub full of sparkling bubbles that changed Annika's mind, as Eva knew it would.

Eva was frying meatballs when Annika walk into the kitchen completely dressed in the very clothes she'd arrived in. Somewhat shocked, Eva swallowed her words and put supper on the table. She would deal with the dirty clothes after Annika went to bed.

Annika dove into her plate of mashed potatoes and meatballs like an osprey after a big fish. Eva was glad she'd prepared enough for three people and took great delight in watching the famished girl consume the fine meal she'd prepared. Annika had removed her head scarf, revealing greasy, dull blond hair pulled back into a too tight braid...another problem to be dealt with.

"Let's wash your hair and then we can do some knitting," Eva suggested after the dishes were done. The promise of knitting caused Annika to reluctantly agree to the hair washing.

Eva dried Annika's hair with a towel and brushed it until mostly dry. Her hair, a little darker than her father's pale yellow, was a beautiful golden blonde...the color of yellow maples in late fall. Eva braided the thick strands loosely and tied them with a piece of thick blue yarn. The newly washed hair now had a slight wave that framed her face like a golden halo. She looked one hundred percent better already.

Eva didn't have to ask twice about going downstairs to pick out some yarn. Annika chose a multicolored blue skein and set to knitting right away, her needles clicking with speed and accuracy on an intricate, lacy pattern. Eva remembered Dagny's futile attempts at knitting and spinning, deciding Annika had gotten her creative talents from her father's side of the family.

The scarf was about ten inches long when Eva noticed Annika's hands slowing down considerably, her eyes heavy with sleep and head nodding. It was only seven o'clock when Eva helped her up the stairs. After cleaning up the bathroom, Eva looked in to see Annika already sound asleep. She picked up the dirty clothes, washed them and hung them up to dry.

Slowly Annika adapted to her new surroundings, though she still remained uncommunicative. The elegant, lacy piece she had started that first night wasn't a scarf at all. Quickly other strips were added and sewn together to form a beautiful afghan that reminded Eva of the various shades of blue and purple of the Swedish mountains and lake in Norrland.

Knitting brings out the spirit of a woman's creativity. There is no end to the ingenious way stitches may be combined to form new and interesting designs, and when two women knit with each other, there is the added benefit of camaraderie, somewhat like when mother and daughter or grandmother and granddaughter do a simple task together, such as washing and drying the dinner dishes. In such an instance a closer, more special bond often develops. Many a problem had been solved in that peaceful time as Eva and Karla had stood working by the kitchen sink together. Sooner or later conversation brought out thoughts deep inside one or both of them; words were spoken that might not ever be said otherwise, just because at that special moment, the door was open for talking and listening.

Eventually Eva made this same connection with Annika as they sat around the table knitting in the comfort of the kitchen or sitting room, each occupied with their individual thoughts, until one or the other spontaneously blurted out a question or comment that often evolved into a meaningful or enlightening discussion.

When a letter arrived one day from New Sweden addressed to Annika, Eva thought it strange that she never revealed any of its contents. Eva waited until that evening to inquire about the letter.

"So, how is your mother coping without your good help?"

"Fine, I guess. Mama always manages. She rarely complains," replied Annika with a note of finality that prevented Eva from probing further.

There were so many questions Eva wanted to ask pertaining to life in New Sweden and how it was growing up with so many brothers and sisters, whose care probably fell to Annika much of the time. However, Annika's guarded demeanor prevented Eva from probing into aspects of her life. Eva needed only to have patience, mixed with understanding and love, and hopefully this bashful country girl would open up to her. The clicking needles were often the only sound in the peaceful quiet room that seemed to wait breathlessly for words to be spoken.

"It wasn't my idea to come here," announced Annika out of the blue one evening. Eva put down her knitting, but Annika's hands seemed busier than ever. Thinking to break up the mysterious tension filling the room, Eva thought to make a pot of coffee, but decided against doing anything to hamper Annika's train of thought and began to kit again.

"Mama said it would be good for me to have a change."

"Yes, we all sometimes need to get away from the humdrum of daily life."

"Humdrum?" asked Annika.

"Just another word for monotony...or having to do the same boring routine day after day."

"There was a lot to do on the farm," replied Annika. "But there were other things I wanted to do, too."

"Like what?" said Eva, putting down her knitting again.

"Oh, just silly stuff," said Annika rolling her needles into the piece she was knitting. "I'm tired. I think I'll go to bed now."

A light was still on in Karla's bedroom when Eva came upstairs about an hour later. She peeked in to see Annika sitting up in bed with a pencil and paper.

"Are you writing to your mother?"

Annika didn't know what to say and covered the paper with her hands. She didn't want to lie but she didn't want to tell the truth either. "I'm just scribbling," she said crushing the piece of paper into a tight ball.

"Well, goodnight, Annika, I'm going to bed."

Annika turned out the bedside lamp,pulled up the covers and

said goodnight.

Eva found the scrunched up paper under the bedside table the next day. Carefully she smoothed out the wrinkles and began reading.

The Dandelion Chain

Children running through the field
Dancing in the sun
Laughing and tumbling
Having lots of fun

Dandelions everywhere
Let's make a golden chain
To decorate our hair
Before it starts to rain

Eva had noticed Annika walking around the garden yesterday morning picking dandelions. Then she had sat on the back porch steps and woven the blossoms and stems into a chain, only to leave them wilting in the sun. Annika had been pleasantly surprised to see the revived flower chain floating in a bowl of fresh water that Eva had arranged on the table.

"I used to pick daisies in the fields back home in Sweden," remarked Eva. Stella would follow me around and when I'd gathered enough we'd lay under the birches and I'd make a daisy chain. That is, unless Stella grabbed it before I was finished. Then I'd have to pick more daisies."

"Who was Stella?"

"Stella was a cow…my faithful, understanding friend I turned to when troubles arose."

After Eva finished telling stories about Stella, Annika looked up a bit puzzled. "Our cows weren't friendly like that. They always switched their nasty tails in my face every time I milked." Eva chuckled.

"I remember Stella doing that, too, especially when she'd just dipped her tail in some liquid manure." Then they both fell into laughter remembering other such mishaps in the barn.

Eva and Annika had found some common ground.

"Cows are okay, I guess," said Annika. "But I much prefer something I can cuddle up with in bed...like a cat."

The next day Eva saw another piece of paper lying upside down on Karla's bedside table.

My Kitty

I have a little kitty
All brown with spots of white
She follows me around all day
And sleeps with me at night

Her name is Fluffy Muffy
She has such nice soft fur
I tell her all my secrets
And they are safe with her

Sometimes we'll play a game
Where I will run and hide
Or I'll put her in a basket
And take her for a ride

She likes to get behind me
When I'm sitting in a chair
Playing with my yellow braids
And messing up my hair

When I rest or read a book
She'll jump into my lap
Then curl into a little ball
And take a nice long nap

Strumpa had died several years ago, but Eva remembered Rebecca saying recently that one of their barn cats had a litter of kittens in April. While Annika was in the bathroom, Eva went down to the shop to make a telephone call.

"Hello, Rebecca. Do you have any kittens left?" she whispered into the receiver.

"Sure do, how many do you want?" came Rebecca's loud voice.

"Just one," said Eva. "If you're going to be home for a while I could grab a bus and come over right now."

"Fine with me," said Rebecca. "I'll put the coffee pot on."

Rebecca had heard Eva speak fondly of Dagny and was delighted to meet Annika, who still wore her white kerchief, rather long, plain, blue cotton skirt, and a light-colored blouse. The three of them sat around the kitchen table drinking coffee and eating cinnamon doughnuts, but Annika had retreated back into her solitary shell and had not said anything but "how do you do." As yet, Eva had said nothing to Annika about the kittens.

"Well," said Rebecca. "Shall we go to the barn now?" She and Eva stood up, but Annika didn't move, except to take a bite of doughnut.

"Rebecca has a litter of new kittens in the barn, Annika. Would you like to see them?"

For a split second, Annika's face broke out into a most agreeable smile. Then she covered her mouth, stood up and nodded with great expectation. Rebecca, ignoring Annika's missing tooth, quickly led the way to the barn, telling her about each one of the kittens. Annika wasted no time selecting the one she wanted. Just like in her poem, she chose the brown one with two white spots and called her Fluffy Muffy.

From the first night, Fluffy Muffy slept curled up under Annika's arm, following her from room to room during the day and playing among the plants when Annika worked in the garden.

One evening after Annika went upstairs, Eva saw the kitten playing on the bed with a small ball made of odds and ends of yarn. Annika was leaning on her pillow with pencil and paper.

"Are you writing another poem?" Eva asked.

"Sort of," said Annika. "When I was weeding today I got to thinking of our garden back home. I thought I'd write down the words before I forgot."

"May I read it?" asked Eva. Annika reluctantly gave her the paper.

My Garden

My garden is a busy place.
So many plants, so little space

As I wander down the row
There's barely room to work my hoe

I see the footprints of a deer
And wonder who else has been here

Sunflowers growing everywhere
Bees collecting here and there

Every night and every morn
Pumpkins running through the corn

Goldfinch swiftly waving by
A coneflower lures a butterfly

Time to pick a row of beans
And fix myself a bowl of greens

Slice up some red tomatoes
And boil a pot of new potatoes

But first I'll have some cold iced tea
And cool off under the mulberry tree

"Your words and rhymes paint beautiful pictures, Annika."

"It's one I remembered from last year."

"I think you're a natural poet!"

"Mama thinks poetry is a lot of foolishness," was her reply.

"So, you've written other poems at home?"

"Oh yes, but I think Mama threw them all away."

Suddenly things came together in Eva's head. Dagny, so practical and work-oriented, probably thought such frivolous writing a waste of time, time that should be better spent helping with the children or farm chores. Eva made up her mind to give Annika ample opportunity for writing and furthering her talent.

"Maybe if you think real hard, they will come back to you."

"Maybe," was all she said.

Eva sat down on the bed and looked Annika in the eye. "I want you to keep every poem you write in this little drawer in the night table. Some day you might be able to get them published, perhaps as a children's book."

Annika's eyes sparkled with delight. "Do you really think so?" she asked.

"I do know one thing, Annika. If you want something bad enough...if you really have a passion for writing...nothing is impossible."

Annika was up with the sun every morning working in the garden before breakfast and then asking what her duties would be for the day. Eva was hard pressed to keep the girl busy. She had purchased fleece in the spring and began showing Annika how to prepare the fleece for washing... the hot and cold rinses, the dyeing and carding. She was much more efficient than Dagny, meticulous about cleaning the fleece and she enjoyed the dying process as much as Eva. Handling the carding boards came naturally to her, as did the final step of spinning. Both gardening and spinning gave Annika time to write poems in her head and she always had a pencil and paper in her apron pocket to write down her ideas without any feeling of guilt.

One day a boy from the Somerville church stopped in to

deliver some packages.

"Is that you, Tim?" asked Eva, recognizing the young man. He had grown nearly a foot taller than the last time she had seen him.

"Hello, Mrs. Gunderson. How are you today?" he said with a wide smile.

"I'm fine. Haven't seen you since...since you went away to school last September."

"One more year at Hesser and I'll have a real job," he said glancing around the room, his eyes stopping to look at the young girl behind the counter, who, at that very same moment, was staring directly back at him. Annika quickly looked down, pretending to read a brochure. Eva, not missing a thing, introduced them to each other. Annika looked up and said "hello," hiding the bottom half of her face behind the paper pamphlet. Tim smiled back, noticing her golden braids and smiling blue eyes.

Annika disliked going out in public, but after a few weeks she did consent to attend church. If Eva had asked her what the minister preached about that morning, Annika would have had no clue. She had been preoccupied after the second hymn by the young boy who sat two rows ahead of them at the very end of the pew. She never did see him full face, but the shape of his head, the brown hair with flecks of gold and the fleeting glimpse of his profile told her it was Tim. He didn't notice her and after the final hymn had slipped out of the church.

Mrs. Bergstrom seemed to have gotten over Emily's elopement and had resumed her old, busy-body ways again, although she never talked about her eldest daughter. After the service she cornered Eva in the reception room downstairs. "I suppose you've heard about the church social. We're having something new this year, a penny sale. All the businesses are donating gifts and I thought perhaps you might have a little knitted thing hanging on your wall you might donate."

"I have a small green afghan. Would that be suitable?"

"That would be lovely," said Mrs. Bergstrom. "And don't forget to bring a boxed lunch for the auction."

Annika had not paid much attention to their conversation; she was scanning the crowd hoping to see Tim. Mrs. Bergstrom then turned to Annika. "Who do we have here?" she asked, looking the plainly dressed girl up and down. "Another newcomer from the Old Country?"

Annika was still dressed in her best blue skirt and white blouse, but today her long golden braids had been arranged neatly around her head by Eva.

"Mrs. Bergstrom, I'd like you to meet Annika, Dagny's eldest daughter." Annika curtsied politely and said, "How do you do." Mrs. Bergstrom looked aghast at Annika's missing tooth for so long that Annika's hand went directly to her mouth and her cheeks turned apple red.

"Annika is helping me in the shop for the summer," said Eva, putting her arm around Annika's waist for a little moral support.

"Where is Karla?" asked Mrs. Bergstrom, as if Eva's daughter was a better choice than Annika for waiting on customers in the shop.

"She's working at a resort in New Hampshire and plans to attend Plymouth College in the fall."

"Well...how nice." For a moment Mrs. Bergstrom seemed lost in thought, but then Emma and Dr. Bergstrom came over to say hello. After introductions, Emma, now a grown woman of twenty-seven, engaged herself in conversation with Annika and brought her over to the food table.

"How sweet of Emma to take Annika under her wing like that," said Eva.

"Yes," said Mrs. Bergstrom. "You know my Emma...always looking out for lost souls, stray dogs and such."

Dr. Bergstrom noticed Eva's confusion about his wife's reasoning and suggested they all go get something to eat. Fortunately, Mrs. Bergstrom found someone else to talk with and Dr. Bergstrom was able to talk with Eva alone.

"Please excuse my wife. Sometimes she doesn't know what she's saying." Eva nodded as if she understood.

"So, Annika is Dagny's daughter?" he asked.

"Yes, Annika is the eldest of seven children."

"Well, she seems like a sweet young girl. I'd like you to bring her into the office sometime."

Eva shrugged her shoulders. "I asked her once about coming to see you, but she would not consider it. I think she is afraid of dentists."

"Well," he said. "If she doesn't come in soon to have some work done, she may find herself wearing dentures at an early age."

"Is there something you can do about her missing tooth?" asked Eva, expectantly.

"Of course. I can make her look as good as new."

Annika was busy the next week carding fleece and working in the garden, her mind busy writing poems in her head. At night she wrote down her thoughts on paper and showed them to Eva.

Be as the Wildflowers

When dark of night gives way to morning
And twinkling stars dull in the dawning
Far below, earth's life is yawning
Sheltered by a bright blue awning

Whose heads are those bent low with dew
Who fail to see a sky so blue?
Buttercup, daisy and dandelion, too
Wake up and greet this day anew

Life is good and we make it so
By seeking God if we're feeling low
We must walk where He does go
Nourished by His love we grow

Do not despair what this day may bring
Like vine and rock that steadfastly cling,
We must hold on, look up and sing
Of peace and joy our prayers bring

So like the flower and grass that grow
That seek the sun and winds that blow
Let love in your heart and you will know
That God is with you wherever you go

Annika was up early the next Saturday. She seemed restless and uneasy, looking up anxiously each time the shop door opened. Eva thought perhaps she was hoping Tim would drop in, but said nothing and continued with her work. Finally Emma came dashing through the door, all bright-eyed and excited to see Annika, who Eva noticed was now more relaxed and apparently very happy to see Emma.

"Are you ready for our big adventure?" asked Emma, rushing to take Annika's hand. Then, realizing Eva knew nothing of their plans, Emma explained.

"Perhaps I should have asked you first, Mrs. Gunderson. Last Sunday I invited Annika to spend the morning at our house. If it is okay with you, I'll have her back soon after lunch."

"I think that is a wonderful idea, Emma. Annika can stay as long as she wants to."

Emma had planned a fun morning. First they had coffee and muffins in the kitchen, then went upstairs to Emma's bedroom where lots of cotton dresses, blouses, and skirts lay neatly across the bed.

"These are all much too small for me. I want you to pick out whatever suits your fancy."

Annika didn't know what to say or where to begin, so Emma, always the impatient child of the family, picked up a dress to show her. "I always loved this one," she said. Annika's eyes grew wide looking at the bright blue dress as she shyly put out her hand to touch the matching bow and sash. When Emma suggested trying it on, Annika self-consciously backed away. Emma instinctively knew what the problem was and led Annika over to a full-length mirror.

"Let me hold the dresses around you so we can see which ones will fit and what colors you like best." Emma did this with each piece of clothing. Then Annika removed her heavy brown shoes and tried on several pairs of Emma's more modern styles.

Emma put a pair of black, low-heeled pumps and a pair of brown laced shoes in a bag and neatly placed a brown coat on top of them. Then she folded up the sweaters and dresses and put them in a second bag.

They met Mrs. Bergstrom in the hall. "Not in the office today, Emma?"

"I took the morning off, Mama, don't you remember?" One glance at Annika and Mrs. Bergstrom did recall something about the girl coming on Saturday. Emma rushed Annika down the hall before her mother spilled the beans about the real reason for Annika's visit today.

Emma was a dental hygienist and worked for her father. She had her own little office with a small window overlooking the back yard. Already knowing Annika's fear of dentists, Emma had tried to make her professional office more homey by covering the black and chrome dentist chair with a colorful quilt and placing a freshly picked bouquet of pink peonies to soften up the hardness of her metal desk.

Emma had thought of everything, even remembering to pull the shade in front of the big white tooth sign that hung so noticeably in the front window of the house and was highly visible when crossing the street from the trolley car.

Emma rushed Annika past the waiting room to another door which led to her private office; all the while engaging in a long line of chitchat, describing each painting hanging on the wall. Then she showed Annika a small book of poetry called *A Child's Garden of Verses.*

"I have two copies of this famous book," said Emma. "And

since you enjoy writing poetry, I'd like you to have this one." Annika opened up the little book, commented on the beautiful illustrations and thanked her. Then Emma got down to business, but first she took Annika's hand in hers.

"One of the things I do here is clean people's teeth." Then she smiled and gently squeezed Annika's hand in hers. "Would you let me clean yours?" Annika was dumbfounded, but she liked Emma and trusted her.

"Will it hurt much?" she asked.

"It won't hurt at all, and the tooth powder tastes like peppermints."

Annika sat on the pretty quilt and rested her head back against the chair. The cleaning was very enjoyable. After Annika rinsed her mouth, Dr. Bergstrom came in. So that he wouldn't look too professional, Emma had suggested he not wear his white jacket. Therefore he looked much as Annika had seen him at church, wearing a white shirt and striped tie. He began talking about the weather, asking Annika about school in New Sweden and how she liked living in Lexington.

"You don't mind if Papa looks at your teeth, do you?" asked Emma, taking hold of Annika's hand again.

"I guess not," mumbled Annika, looking up at the kind face of Dr. Bergstrom. She could hear Emma's reassuring voice as she felt Dr. Bergstrom's gentle hands in her mouth.

"I can make you a new tooth, would you like that?"

Annika nodded.

"I'm going to take an impression of the front of your mouth," he told her. "This is so I will know the right size to make your new tooth and be certain it will fit perfectly." Annika pushed herself back in the chair as something very soft and cool touched her gum. Dr. Bergstrom kept up a line of idle chatter, smiling and joking for a moment or two. "All done for today," he said at last. "See you next week."

Eva noticed a new confidence in Annika the very afternoon she came home with her new tooth. She was more outgoing and genuinely happy, greeting customers openly when they entered the shop and offering to help them.

A few evenings later, after Annika had sewn the last knitted strip onto her afghan and edged it with a finishing border, she folded it neatly and held it up to Eva.

"This is for you," she said with a hint of her old shyness. Eva's grateful admiration brought forth the sweetest smile from Annika and she couldn't resist hugging the girl. This time Annika returned the embrace and they held each other until she was aware of Annika's tears.

When Eva asked if anything was wrong, Annika was smiling. "I always cry when I'm happy."

"You know something, Annika? So do I." Another bridge had been crossed.

Sometimes Annika remembered poems she had written before. One that Eva especially loved reminded her of Norrland.

"I don't remember if I got all the words right," said Annika. "But this is one I wrote last winter."

October Snow

Icy winds blow back and forth
Clouds gathering from the north

A snowflake here, another there
Ballerinas in the air
Chickens darting everywhere
Dogs and horse don't seem to care

Snow falls on field and cow
Get out the shovel and the plow

Put on your boots and knitted hat
Make a snowman tall and fat
Eyes of coal and a carrot nose
Our hands and feet are nearly froze

A cozy fire of oak and pine
Makes us warm and feeling fine.

"You make everything sound so real. I can just picture the animals outside in winter, the snow falling and making a snowman," said Eva. "Are there more from last year?"

"There were many more, but I can't think of them until something happens to remind me."

Annika was excited about attending the church penny sale and lunch auction.

"Do you think Tim will be there?" asked Annika, shyly.

"I have a good feeling that he will be." They were decorating the outside of their boxes with ribbons and flowers from the garden. Inside the boxes were containers filled with potato salad, ham, cole slaw, cornbread and raspberry turnovers. Also included were silverware, two fancy plates, napkins and cups for lemonade.

"I remember Mama fixing a pretty boxed lunch. She hid it under an old tablecloth so Papa wouldn't see, but once at the church Mama's face always gave her away and he knew which box to bid on."

"Yes, I remember your mother wasn't good at hiding her feelings."

"And neither was I," said Annika. "At least not for the past couple years. I was always walking around with a pout on my face and Papa would try to do silly things to make me smile."

Eva thought probably Annika's unhappiness had been a mixture of several things: her broken tooth, too much farm work, caring for younger bothers and sisters, and not being able to fulfill her dream of writing poetry. In a very short time Annika's life had changed. Now she was an attractive young girl, more at ease socially, flourishing with her poetry and genuinely feeling good about herself.

Eva braided Annika's thick hair in two fat braids forming a golden crown around her head, fluffing up the top and sides for a softer look. She also searched through Karla's extensive array of bright red lipsticks, finally finding an unused tube of light pink to highlight Annika's rather thin lips. Because she smiled more often now, her blue eyes sparkled, giving her face a joyful radiance. Annika seemed very pleased with herself as she slowly descended the stairs in Emma's blue dress and shiny black shoes, although she stumbled on the next to last step and almost dropped her beautiful boxed lunch.

"I guess I need a bit more practice in these fancy shoes," she said with a slight blush.

"I know just how you feel, Annika. I'd worn nothing but flat tie shoes until after Karla was born. Finally the yarn shop showed a good profit and I desperately needed some new clothes and shoes. I was feeling a bit over-confident in my new high-heels and tripped in plain sight of everyone passing by on the sidewalk. I was so embarrassed when a gentleman came to help me up and commented on my skinned knee and big hole in my silk stockings."

The penny sale was first on the agenda. Everyone milled around the many tables putting tickets in front of items they wanted to win. Then they sat in folding chairs in the middle of the room as members of the church took turns calling out the winning numbers. Annika's number was called twice, earning her a flowered apron and a glittery necklace of tiny bright crystals that she had spent more than half her tickets on. Eva was lucky, too. She won a lovely pen and pencil set, a black leather handbag and a medium-sized, light-blue piece of luggage.

Then bidding began on the array of boxed lunches lined up on a long table along the front of the stage. Annika glanced around the room for Tim, but saw mostly bored middle-aged husbands with their wives, small clusters of schoolboys of all ages and a group of elderly men sitting together who were also looking around the room. Then she noticed Tim standing near a curtain at the rear of the stage.

Annika could not help but smile, sitting up a little straighter when her lunch basket was placed on the podium for bidding.

Tim noticed this and disappeared from the stage. But his absence made Annika anxious as one of the elderly men started bidding, then another voice raised the bid. Annika bit her lip as another bid was heard. The old man bid again and another voice raised it immediately.

"Going once...going twice!" said the auctioneer. "Young man, you have bought this fine looking basket." Annika closed her eyes and took a deep breath. She opened them when Eva nudged her arm.

"Isn't that Tim walking up to pay for your basket?" she asked. The auctioneer looked at the name tag and said, "Is there more than one Annika in the room today?" Annika wasted no time in standing up to claim the basket was hers. Tim ushered her outside to sit on a wooden bench under the large weeping willow tree.

When the bidding was over most of the couples sat together in the church to eat their lunches, including Eva and the old man who owned the flower shop. For a tall, thin man in his seventies, he surely had a ravenous appetite. Eva made the best of it by being friendly and gracious, eating very slowly to make certain he had enough to eat and that he had an enjoyable time. He must have been impressed because he sent a large bouquet of roses to her shop the next day.

Annika sat down that evening and wrote to her mother, telling about Tim and the church social and that she was very happy working in the yarn shop. After that Eva and Annika went to church every Sunday. Sometimes Tim came back for dinner and soon he and Annika ventured out on their own for long walks and bus rides to get ice cream.

Several days later Annika showed Eva a poem she had written.

A Smile

There's nothing like a broad sweet smile
From stranger, child or friend
It only takes a moment

To make your troubles end

A smile can mean so many things
I care, I understand
I love you, I respect you
I'd like to hold your hand

A welcome to a stranger
Appreciation of a friend
A silent hello, how are you
A quarrel on the mend.

Have you ever noticed
When you smile at someone new
You usually get a smile right back
And sometimes you get two

Remember now, you have a choice
To smile or look away
If I were you I'd choose a smile
To brighten up the day

"That's lovely. It is so good to see you smiling, too," said Eva.

Annika looked down and turned bright pink. "It's all because of you."

"No, Annika. These poems are expressions of you and how you have progressed by being here. By working in the shop, going to church and meeting Timmy, you have blossomed like a beautiful flower."

"But you have been such an encouragement to me."

"Living and growing is a result of your upbringing and all the people and circumstances you meet in life. I am just a small part of that. You have a great talent and I'm so proud of you."

Summer moved on through the month of July and into the middle of August, but the best thing was that Annika had been released from her cocoon of shyness and transformed into a beautiful social butterfly. Eva could take only part credit for this. She knew what Emma and Dr. Bergstrom had done, and that it was Tim who had set her free from the past.

"Tim is so different from the other boys I've known who always poked fun at my shyness and made me feel worse. Tim is patient with me, tells me funny jokes to make me laugh. When I'm very quiet, he just holds my hand and we enjoy a sweet silence. I never feel pressured to talk and we always feel comfortable with each other, and now my words and feelings just flow like sweet cider."

"Tim is a good boy. I'm delighted that you've found some happiness."

The telephone rang. It was Karla.

"David just called me. He's been accompanying one of the doctors on farm calls this week. I think his name is Dr. Anderson. He owns a bed and breakfast place called The Swedish Farm. The neat thing is that he also has a small herd of Swedish cattle. David thought you might like to go up and see the place."

"Well, I don't know, honey...Annika is still here and..."

"That's the whole point, Mom. We should go before Annika goes home, so she can watch the shop for you."

"I'm not sure Annika is going home. She's adjusted very well to working in the shop and she's met a nice young man and..."

"It doesn't sound like you really want to go."

"Well, you know me. I've got to have time to think things over before making a decision."

"Hmm...well, call me back tomorrow. We were thinking about going up during Labor Day weekend. I have to work on Saturday and Sunday morning, but David has that weekend off because his cousin's wedding is on Saturday. He said he could pick you up on Sunday, then come here to get me and we could all drive up in my car and see the place." There was no sound from the other end of the line. "Are you still there, Mom?"

"I'm still thinking," said Eva, "I'll have to talk it over with

Annika."

"Let me know tomorrow so I can make reservations for Sunday night."

"Okay. I'll call you back tomorrow."

Annika didn't balk at the idea of minding the shop by herself and encouraged Eva to go.

After thinking everything over, Eva was almost looking forward to seeing what this wild place called New Hampshire looked like.

Labor Day weekend started off rainy and cold, but by noontime on Saturday the sun poked through the clouds and the weather turned warmer. Annika was halfway down the stairs carrying Eva's suitcase when a man walked across the room toward her. "Is that you, Karla?" he said uncertainly to the very blonde girl.

"No," she said. "Karla isn't here. Would you like to talk with her mother?"

"Actually, it is her mother I came to see."

By now Eva was at the head of the stairs looking down on a man with light-colored hair and a goatee who looked very much like a young Otto Kronberg. However, large sunglasses covered his eyes and she thought him quite mysterious. Slowly descending the stairs, her hand gripped tightly on the handrail as the man took of his glasses. Then he looked up to her with that old familiar lop-sided grin and in a hushed voice said "Eva...Oh my sweet Eva".

He ran up the stairway two steps at a time and she stumbled into his arms for an embrace reminiscent of Mr. Kronberg's famous bear hugs. She felt immediately loved and safe and young again.

"Let's go downstairs before we fall," she said. Then he picked her up and carried her back down, while poor Annika stood transfixed at this blushing woman who was acting more like a teenager than her more serious employer.

Mats seemed taller than she remembered and more mature. There was a rugged handsomeness about him. His tanned face was creased with lines about his eyes and mouth, probably due to being out in the sun and wind too much, but his presence still took her breath away. Suddenly aware of Annika standing in the background, Eva straightened her skirt and smoothed her hair.

"Annika, this is my old friend from Norrland, Mats Kronberg. Mats this is Annika, Dagny's eldest daughter. She's helping me out for the summer." Annika smiled shyly as Mats took her hand.

"And how are your mother and father?" he asked Annika.

"Probably busy as ever," was her reply. Then Mats turned quickly to Eva again.

"You haven't changed, Eva...except that you are even more ravishing with short hair."

For a brief moment words escaped Eva. She felt the old heat rising from her chest and tried to curtail the inevitable blush that had plagued her as a girl.

"Well, sit down, Mats, while I make some coffee."

"Mona is in the car, Eva. I'd like you to meet her." Then he rushed out the door. It was as if Mats had suddenly remembered he had a wife and Eva smiled at the thought.

The three of them sat at the pine table in front of the shop window, as Annika brought in a tray of coffee and pastries.

"Please join us, Annika," said Eva. "We have lots of stories to tell you about your mother and our voyage together across the Atlantic."

It wasn't long before Annika was comfortable with this gregarious man and his new, young wife, whom Eva guessed might be ten years younger than Mats.

"If you had come tomorrow, Mats, you would have missed me again," said Eva. Then Mats had to tell Mona about the times he had come to the yarn shop and Eva had not been home.

"So, where are you off to this time?" he asked.

"Well, to make a long story short, Karla's boyfriend has been working with a veterinarian in New Hampshire. I think she said his name is Dr. Anderson. He has some Swedish cattle and we're going up to see them tomorrow."

"I know Dr. Anderson!" piped up Mona. "He used to test our cows for brucellosis and I thought he was the most handsome man on earth. That was probably seven or eight years ago. I was nineteen at the time and had a real bad crush on him." Mona took Mats' hand and smiled. "That was before I went to California and met Mats."

"What is this 'bad crush' you speak of?" asked Eva quite innocently. Mats answered in a playful manner, as if he was somehow getting back at Mona.

"Crush means a great desire to be with or want to kiss someone special," he said to Eva. "Sort of the way it was with me when I used to go to your house back in Sweden." Even though that was twenty years before, there was a brief look of longing in Mats' eyes that made Eva's face flush again. She turned and looked away.

Mona raised her eyebrows and regarded Mats, who grinned back and said, "but that was before I met you."

"Well, to get back to Dr. Anderson," said Mona. "Besides being very good looking, he was also very professional and caring. The last time I saw him was when my favorite cow, Ginger, calved and cast her withers. She was half Holstein and had been bred to a big Charolais bull who threw very large calves. Dr. Anderson knew I was upset. He told me not to worry, that he would take care of everything and that Ginger would be fine."

"Did everything turn out all right?" asked Eva.

"Oh yes. I can still see Dr. Anderson's kind blue eyes and charming smile when he told me to rub Ginger's head, but I couldn't help but watch how carefully he washed her uterus and covered it with sugar; I knew because he told me exactly what he was doing. After he put the uterus back inside of her, he said he was going to sew her up. I thought he was joking until afterwards when I looked and saw the neat row of stitches running up her bum."

"Doctors can do some marvelous things these days," said Mats thoughtfully. "I saw a lot of miracles during the war...and I saw a lot of other stuff, too." The room grew quiet, except for everyone sipping their coffee. Eva thought about Samuel and all the bad things she'd heard during the war. Then she rose from the table to get more coffee.

Annika was showing Mona some green yarn when Eva returned.

"Do you knit?" asked Eva.

"I'm not good working two needles, but I do enjoy crocheting." said Mona, "I was thinking I might make a baby blanket."

Eva brought Mona to another part of the store. "This yarn is very fine and soft, perfect for baby things." Eva glanced at Mats, who had a silly smirk on his face.

"I just skipped my period," whispered Mona, "so we're hoping to have a baby next spring." When she opened her purse to pay for the yarn, Eva would not take the money.

"Think of this yarn as my gift to you and Mats."

The Swedish Farm

Across the Massachusetts-New Hampshire border, the landscape became more rural and hilly. David and Eva met Karla at the resort where she worked and had lunch in the dining room overlooking a peaceful valley where small farms dotted the banks of a wide river. The noontime sun glinted brightly on the metal barn roofs, highlighting herds of black and white cows against the lush green pastures. Already Eva was liking New Hampshire.

They'd been traveling for a while through small towns and villages. Suddenly, rising above the trees was a mountain with a rocky nob on its summit.

"That's Mr. Chocorua," said David, as he turned left on a dirt road and stopped by a clump of white birches. A small bridge divided two small lakes where people were fishing and canoing.

"If you both stand on the bridge I'll take your picture," he said. "It's one of those things everyone does when they come here." Eva could see why. The lake was a brilliant blue and the breeze made little whitecaps ripple across the water. Birches, willows and maple trees dotted the shore, and behind all this rose Mt. Chocorua, painted a purple blue with its rocky peak jutting up against the puffy white clouds and pale blue sky.

"The scenery only gets better," said Karla as they returned to the truck.

They rode through more villages, the winding, narrow road crossing brooks and rivers and tunneling through thick groves of pine and spruce. The air smelled like Sweden and many times Eva thought she'd been here before. Around the next bend of the road was a gorgeous panorama of hills and valleys, and behind them were the mighty peaks of the White Mountains.

"That's the Presidential Range, named, of course, for many famous United States Presidents," said David as he turned into a rest area. He pointed to each peak, calling them by name. "Mount Jefferson, then Mount Adams and Mount Madison...all over five thousand feet above sea level. The tallest peak, over a mile high, is Mount Washington. It's the one with weather antennas on the summit."

"How in the world did they get those antennas way up there?" asked Eva. Karla laughed and told her there was a road that went up the mountain on one side and a train on the other.

"You are joking, aren't you?" said Eva, not believing a word her daughter said, and neither David nor Karla could convince her that either was true. "Why are mountains only named after men?" asked Eva.

"You know, I never thought about that," replied David. "For the moment I can't think of one single mountain named after a woman."

Karla slipped her arm through David's and smiled up at him. "That's because they're so big, handsome and rugged looking."

"Sounds like a good reason to me," said David with a wink as he started up the car again.

For a long time the road followed a meandering river, snaking through the tall trees on either side, once in a while revealing the lesser mountains and foothills of the great White Mountain Forest. Then more open spaces appeared and David pointed up to the right.

"See the cleared patch of land halfway up that mountain? That's where we're headed."

As they got closer Eva squinted at the rectangular green patch. The sun had peeked through the clouds to reveal a bright yellow building. "I thought a bed and breakfast house would be larger than that."

"Mountains have a way of making everything appear smaller," said Karla.

"Of course, that mountain isn't as high as those five-thousand footers," said David, "but it looks like a fairly good climb to me. Everyone around here calls it Anderson Mountain. I guess the doctor owns most of it." Eva was impressed...until she looked down at her high heels. "We don't have to hike up there, do we?"

David laughed. "There's a nice gravel driveway all the way to the farm, but if you want to go hiking, I hear there's a pretty good path to the summit."

Half an hour later they turned onto a dirt road leading to a narrow, gravel driveway that wound its way through the thick spruce and tall pines that arched tall on either side, sheltering the narrow road. Eva rolled her window down and the sweet, woodsy scent brought back pleasant memories of walking through the forest back in Norrland. The old Ford struggled around the sharp curves and she knew they were climbing up a pretty steep grade.

Beyond the forest Eva saw a splash of light, a field, and then the long yellow house on the hill, a wide porch running across the entire front with a row of blue rocking chairs partially filled with guests. A welcoming blue and yellow Swedish flag waved beneath a larger American flag in the center of a circular garden of marigolds and chrysanthemums. Her eyes followed the gentle slope of grass down to a small, yellow barn. Eva sat at the edge of her seat shielding her eyes against the bright sun, trying to get a better look at some cows standing under a spreading maple tree. One cow stepped out of the shadows and another followed, each grabbing mouthfuls of grass in the lush pasture. Karla heard her mother gasp.

"What is it, Mom?"

"Stella...my sweet Stella!"

Eva opened the car door, jumped out and ran down the hill, stopping part way to remove her high-heeled shoes.

Karla glanced at David curiously. "I think Mom is having another 'Swedish moment.'"

They followed Eva down the hill, watching her run toward the startled group of cows. A few of them lowered their heads and stepped back a few paces, but one of the larger cows ambled over to the wire fence. Eva put her hand out and the old cow reached her head forward so Eva could pat the side of her soft, red cheek. She had the same sweet disposition and exact markings of her beloved Stella. None of the cows were Stella, of course. She had known that was impossible from the beginning. It was just that she had suddenly been reminded of Norrland and for a moment had been briefly taken back there.

Finally, a bit embarrassed by how silly she must have appeared, Eva waited for Karla and David to catch up with her.

"At the rate you were running, Mom, I fully expected to see you jump the fence!"

"I really don't know what came over me," she replied, leaning against the fence post and struggling to put her shoes back on. The old cow nudged her hair and Eva reached back to scratch her ears. "She reminds me so much of my Stella."

Someone else noticed the young woman with the red hair. He nearly dropped the milk pail he was washing while looking out the milk house window and saw her running down the hill. He had looked away, then and rubbed his eyes. They were always playing tricks on him, these eyes that saw what his mind was thinking. Now a young couple were standing in the same spot. He was seeing things again. He sat down on an empty milk can with his head in his hands and remembered that dreadful day he came home and found his true love gone.

Upon hearing of his beloved's unexpected departure to America and probable marriage to a mutual friend, all of his hopeful dreams for their future were shattered. He had spent that night sleeping in her old bed. In the morning he had noticed a wooden chest and looked inside. It seemed curious that she would have left behind such a fine chest, one still filled with her personal things. Not understanding why, he had carried the chest up to his room. Just its presence made her seem closer to him and that was reason enough.

Afterwards he had put all his energy into the cheese plant, even sleeping there most nights, where he could avoid his mother's insistence that he meet and marry a woman of noble status, and also to avoid attending her lavish weekend parties. Even so, once in a while a father would bring a daughter down to see the plant, but the visits were only a guise. Most women did not enjoy the cool, sterile environment and the smell of sour milk. One had shown some interest in all the stainless steel equipment and had praised the taste of his cheese, convincing him to take a walk around the premises. He had not wanted to marry the woman, but her persistence, as well as the strong encouragement from his mother, had eventually worn him down. In the end it had been easier to give in to both women.

He learned later that his wife had been more enamored with the majestic house than with him, creating a loveless marriage that seemed a convenience for them both for a year or two. Then liquor took over his existence. Rather than eating in the main dining room, he would sometimes sneak into the kitchen to bring food back to the cheese house, taking with him a full bottle of vodka or other spirits. Sometimes he would find Cook still working by the stove or kneading dough for the morning bread. It was on one of those occasions that he had confessed his love for the kitchen maid. Cook admitted to knowing about their love affair, and told him she had even found excuses to bring them together. Then Cook had told him about his mother's accusations against the young maid and how Cook had thought the so-called stolen brooch had been planted in the girl's bureau. Cook also confided her suspicions that the girl had known nothing of his mother's devious plan for her sudden departure for America.

Sometime later he had attended a friend's funeral. The man's son had come home from America, the very one who had taken his beloved away. That day he had found out his love and this man had never married. But it was too late, he'd learned, because by then she was married to someone else and already had a child.

He had sat on the little bed in the cheese house that night contemplating the miserable circumstances of the past few years, drinking until he fell back on the mattress in a drunken stupor. He had repeated that routine for a week or so, until everything suddenly became clear as crystal and he knew he must turn his life around. He sobered up enough to go back to the house, take a hot bath, put on his best clothes, and carry the wooden bridal chest out to the car along with a favorite painting.

Then he had confronted his mother, who finally admitted to everything. By then the whole house was in turmoil, but he'd ignored the confusion and stuck with his plan. He told his wife he wanted a divorce and informed his father he was going to the Swedish University of Animal Sciences.

While in his fourth year at the university, he had corresponded with one of his father's friends in America, who suggested that he come to the United States to continue his education. In one letter this friend wrote: "Your grades are exceptional and my colleagues at Cornell University have suggested that you apply for a scholarship in veterinary science for next year."

When he had been divorced for two years and had recently sold his portion of the family estate to his brother, another letter had arrived from his father's friend with a most interesting invitation: "I am semi-retired from my veterinary practice and am now living in New Hampshire, a beautiful, rural, mountainous area where at every turn I am reminded of my old Sweden. I still have close ties with my old college comrades and nothing better to do than entertain you in my home and accompany you to Ithaca, New York, whenever you decide to come."

He had received the blessings of his father, but there was also the small herd of Swedish cattle that he still held close to his heart; heifers from the Old Swedish Breed cow that he'd bought from Otto Kronberg years before. Still having contacts with the old shipping company, his father had told him there would be no problem shipping the cattle to America when he was ready for them.

Karl had sailed to America, leaving the name ***Lindholm*** behind. As Swedish boys often did, he took his father's first name and added the word ***son***. He had become a new man and he had a new name. He then enrolled at Cornell University, College of Veterinary Medicine, in Ithaca, New York, as Karl Anderson.

From the milk room he had a clear view of the house and tonight the scene was especially beautiful. The late afternoon sun put a golden glow on the long yellow house, painting the pines behind it a rich green and the maples an orangish red. Behind it all was a blue sky with white puffy clouds. Karl finished his work in the milk room and went to the cheese house. He removed the curds from the cheese press, rubbed the outside with salt and wrapped it in a sterile cloth. For reasons he couldn't explain he was feeling unusually happy tonight.

He always walked along the stone wall on the beaten path that led to the far end of the house. From that distance he wouldn't be recognized by the guests and could easily slip into the private door of his room, remove his smelly farm clothes, shower and change into something more presentable for dinner.

David, Karla and Eva stood for a while watching the cows and admiring the mountains rising from the valley beyond the pasture. Then they walked back to the house to see about their room and freshen up before dinner.

An older woman greeted them at the door. Framing her cheerful round face was a very long braid of grayish-blond hair.

Adding to the quaint atmosphere was her folk costume, a long-sleeved white blouse, blue vest and skirt, with a red-and-blue striped apron tied around her rather thick waist – similar to the apron Eva's mother had worn.

"Come with me," she said with a slight Swedish accent, telling them how she filled the many jobs of housekeeper, cook, secretary and sometime hostess when Dr. Anderson was not at home or working outside. She stopped by an arched doorway that revealed a large, rustic room with pine paneling, numerous shelves laden with books, many small tables and comfortable-looking, overstuffed chairs. Most impressive was the magnificent stone fireplace that took up almost half the wall directly across the room.

"Perhaps you come back here in an hour or so for coffee, ya?" she said invitingly, before continuing on down the hall to show them to their rooms. "By the way, my name is Sonja and if you ever need anything, I'm never far away."

A table was set just inside the arched doorway with two red candelabras, each illuminated by half a dozen white candles. In the center of the table was a vase of late summer flowers with a large basket of shiny red apples on one side and a Swedish flag made out of cupcakes on the other side. Yellow-frosted cupcakes formed the cross and blue-frosted ones made up the background. There were several wooden boards with sliced cheeses and plates of assorted crackers and crisp breads. A large tray rested at each end of the table with a pewter coffee pot, creamer and sugar bowl. Around them were bone china cups and saucers and luncheon plates with colorful Swedish folk designs painted on them. Eva poured a cup of coffee for David and one for Karla before helping herself.

"I remember frosting cupcakes for a flag just like this," she told Karla. "It was Midsummer and Cook made enough cupcakes for two flags. I had to frost them all and arrange them perfectly on two large trays."

"It's a lovely decoration," said Karla, "too pretty to spoil by removing one of the cupcakes." Eva heartily agreed and helped herself to some cheese and crackers. Other guests were milling around talking, drinking coffee and filling their plates from the table. When a heavy-set man reached over and grabbed three cupcakes Eva decided they might as well each have one, too. David, who was always hungry, set two of them on top of his mound of cheese and crackers and they all went over to a small table by the fireplace to sit down and eat.

Eva took a long sip of coffee. "I haven't tasted coffee this good since...."

Karla put her hand on her mother's arm. "Let me guess...since you left Sweden."

Eva sat back and smiled at her daughter. "Okay, I get the message. I know I'm being foolishly nostalgic and I apologize, but there's something about this place that's so familiar. I feel as if I've come back to my roots. And this cheese is so delicious. I can't decide which I like best, the yellow or the white."

"It's all made right here in Dr. Anderson's cheese house," stated David. "Along with everything else, he's a Certified Master Cheesemaker and is always bringing samples of cheese to the clinic for everyone to try."

"Well, I can't wait to meet this man of many talents," said Eva, looking around the room.

She noticed an older couple playing checkers at one table, and a middle-aged man sitting at the end of a plush, tan couch reading a book. A woman sat at the other end knitting, appearing quite annoyed that the man was ignoring her. Then her eyes wandered to a place above the fireplace and she gasped. Eva nudged her daughter's arm. "Look at that painting above the mantle."

"I like it," said Karla. "Very charming and rather quaint." The only sound after that was Eva's cup rattling in the saucer.

"Mom? Are you all right?"

Eva didn't answer, her eyes fixated on the painting. Karla noticed the stunned look on her mother's face and carefully took the shaking cup from her hands. Eva blinked, then rubbed her eyes. "Tell me what you see," she said in a voice so soft and low that Karla could barely hear.

"I see a sweet, tranquil scene of a girl and a cow. There are white birches with their autumn yellow leaves and tall pines standing solidly behind them. I love the detail in the birch trees, don't you?"

"And the initials in the right bottom corner?"

"Looks to me like GG with a slash and the numbers two seven...or is that a two and a nine, David?"

He nodded, but his attention was on Dr. Anderson, who had just entered the room. David excused himself and walked toward the food table where the doctor was helping himself to a piece of cheese.

"Oh, David," he said. "I was wondering if you were here. I noticed on the register that we have three new guests from Massachusetts."

"Well, I took you up on your offer and talked my girlfriend and her mother into coming up today. Do you have time to meet them now?"

"Sure do," said Karl.

"They're over by the fireplace admiring the painting," said David, leading the way across the room. "I'm not up on artists and stuff like that, but is that a famous painting?"

"The artist is not well known here," replied Karl. "He was the father of a girl I knew back in Sweden, so it's more of a sentimental thing with me."

"Well, it sure did make a big impression on Karla's mother."

Karl glanced over to the fire place and stood motionless, putting his hand on the back of a chair for support. When David spoke again and received no answer, he turned to see that the doctor was about five paces behind him. His face was white and lifeless, eyes staring in the direction of the fireplace. David walked back thinking the doctor might be ill.

"Are you all right Dr. Anderson?"

Karl heard nothing but the thoughts in his mind. Was this just another illusion? He envisioned her as before, as he had done many times, seeing her sweet smile in the breakfast room, in the orchard or in the haymow that last Midsummer Eve. A deep longing had remained in his heart...and body...for a long time afterwards and it surprised him today that, after almost twenty years, the feeling was still there. It seemed as if today was only yesterday and he was eighteen again.

He blinked and glanced around the room. Everything looked as it should, except for the two women standing in front of the fireplace. He was more certain now than ever that the older woman was his beloved Eva and he dared not take his eyes from her for fear she might not be there when he looked back.

The color of her hair was the same, but shorter than he remembered. Once in a while as she spoke to the younger girl, he saw her profile, but he was still too far away to see her features clearly. She looked thinner. Perhaps that was because of the trim green suit she wore. He noticed her shapely legs and high-heeled shoes. Back in Sweden women had worn skirts far too long to reveal much above their ankles. He smiled to himself thinking she was, indeed, the same woman he'd seen running down the hill a few hours earlier. It hadn't been his imagination after all.

Karl's mouth was dry and his pulse was racing. Breathing deeply, he took a step, but his legs were heavy as lead.

"Dr. Anderson, are you okay?" Karl heard David's voice clearly this time.

"I'm good. In fact, I feel better than I have in twenty years."

"You scared me," said David. "For a minute I thought you were having a stroke."

"Tell me David. What is the name of your girlfriend's mother?"

"Her name is Eva, Eva Gunderson." Again, Karl's legs would not move.

After Eva and Karla finished discussing the painting, Eva wondered where David had gone.

"Over there," said Karla, gesturing behind them. Eva saw David's head briefly, but her eyes went directly to the man he was talking to. Her face froze and for a moment her body felt lifeless, although she was aware that Karla's arm was around her. The charming yellow house, the cows and the painting flooded her mind...and now the unforgotten face she thought she'd never see again. Karl was looking directly at her and he smiled. Karla saw her mother's face brighten, saw her step out of her shoes and run across the room.

Eva felt the soft thick rug beneath her toes as she pushed forward, her eyes on the beaming face of her beloved. Then she was in his arms, locked in his firm, loving embrace. For what it seemed a very long time, neither could let go of the other, until she felt his cheek against her face, his lips finding hers and it was as if the whole room exploded. Then Karl held her at arm's length and they gazed into each other's eyes. She smiled and all the guests clapped and hollered...for what, they didn't know, but they all surmised it was a happy occasion deserving some sort of celebration.

For a moment Karla had watched her mother's strange, erratic behavior with unbelieving eyes, so unlike her usual serious and well-ordered manner. Then Karla slowly followed, stopping to take David's arm as they looked at each other in astonishment, then wonder, applauding robustly because everyone else was doing the same.

Eva turned to Karla and took her hand.

"Karla, I'd like you to meet your father."

Eva took Karl's hand.

"Karl, this is our daughter, Karla."

THE END